BY J A JOLLEY

THE CHRONICLES OF SATERIA

Book One: A Light of the Lost
Book Two: Mourning Light *

THE EYE OF THE DAY SAGA

Book One: Cataracts

*Forthcoming

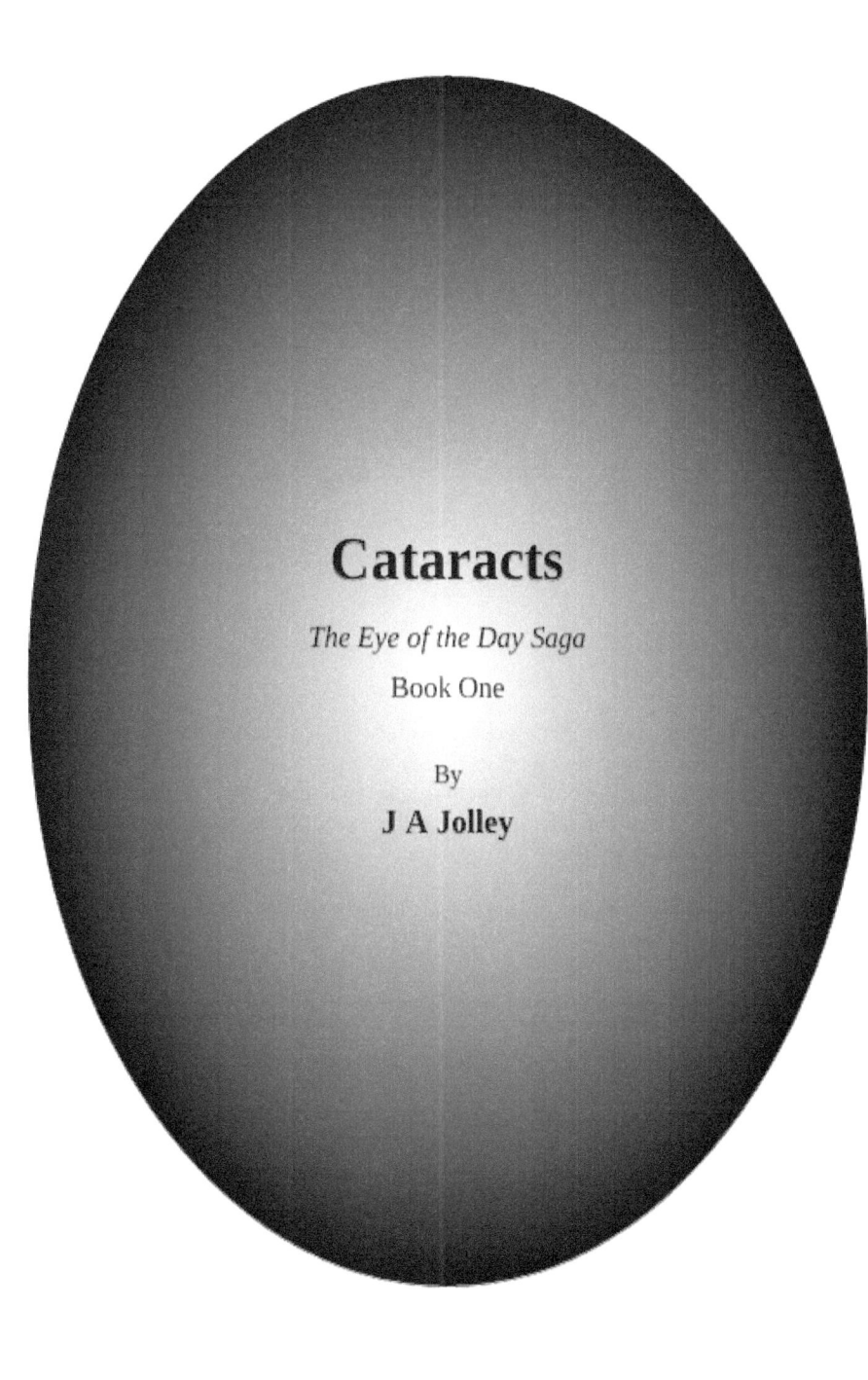

Cataracts

The Eye of the Day Saga

Book One

By

J A Jolley

Cover design by Star Shine Stories in conjunction with Sir Doodle
Art and Jewelry

Edited by Alex Richmond and Constance Price

First Edition, 2025 ISBN: 979-8-9996651-0-2

Published by Star Shine Stories

Printed in the United States of America

Dedication

This book is for those who take it upon themselves to shield the people they love, no matter the odds or the weight of circumstance.

It is often a quiet, thankless burden, but let it stand as a reminder: in the end, each of us must choose our own path.

Special Thanks

I would like to thank *CJ Denison* for creating and running the Pathfinder game that first inspired this story, and for all the work he has done to help shape the alternate Earth in which these books unfold.

I would also like to give heartfelt thanks to the Pathfinder group whose imagination and collaboration made this tale possible:

Adam Chandler
Brendan Parker
Constance Price
Robert Collins
Kadyn Haynes

THE EYE OF THE DAY SAGA

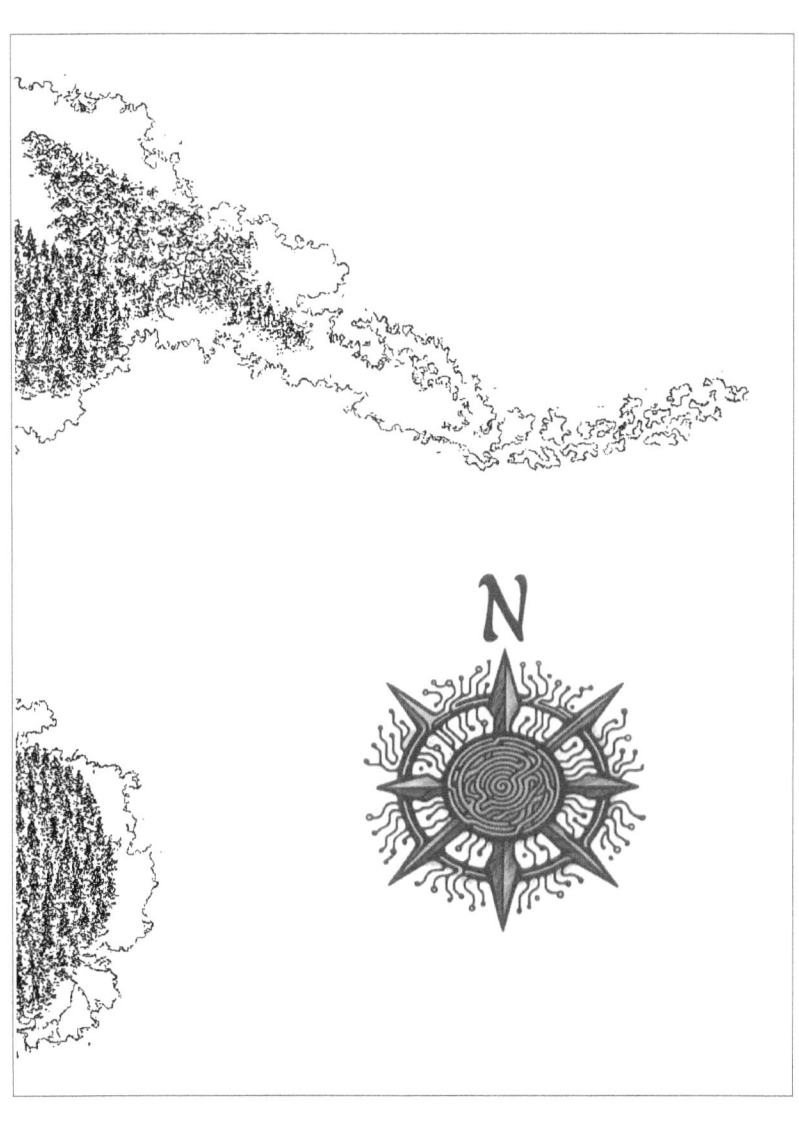

CHAPTER ONE

Darkness...

It swallows our hearts and enshrouds our souls.
A void where once we felt control.
It steals the light we once held dear,
A weight that pulls us into tears.
We claw our way from shadow's grasp,
But we can never flee the cataracts.

They blind our eyes to the truth once clear,
A veil of doubt, of endless fear.
No flame of hope can pierce the black,
No guiding star can lead us back.
In this eternal dusk we tread,
Where even dreams have learned to dread.

Yet still—a whisper stirs the night,
A fragile flicker, a spark of light.
But even this, so faint, may fall,
And in the cataracts, we lose it all.

"Merde."

Jacques spat the word and flung the circuit board toward the scrap heap beside the lantern. It struck a steel beam—hard, snapping, too loud for something so small.

He sighed through his nose. Not frustration—he'd burned through that days ago. Just fatigue, heavy enough to sink him. He raked his hand back through his hair—sweat-stuck, streaked black with grit. The smear stayed.

The lantern's cold white carved the cavern, shadows doubling and sliding out of true.

He caught his reflection in a twisted plate of metal. Hazel eyes rimmed in red. Skin pale. Beard patchy with soot. A face stretched too thin across too many hours.

In front of him: six transmitters, cracked and heat-warped; a beacon gutted to its frame; three power cells split along the seam; and now this board, scorched and useless.

He didn't count them for what they were. He counted what they meant: another path closed. Another silence that wouldn't break.

"Four hundred and eighteen when we started," he said.

No one asked what he meant. Everyone knew.

"Forty-two made it through the crash."

He let that settle.

"Now... four."

He didn't say the names. They were all present.

The quiet didn't reply. Just sat around him, steady and inert.

A faint current moved across the cave mouth. It wasn't cool, or warm, or fast. But it carried a feeling. A kind of tension that moved beneath the skin.

Jacques turned toward the dark.

The shadows just beyond the firelight weren't still. They had motion to them, like there was more black than there should be, and it didn't want to be noticed.

"How long does this night go?" he asked.

The question didn't echo. The stone just took it.

Behind him, a sharp sequence of grunts cut through the quiet.

U'gah.

The halfling crouched at the fire's edge, fingers slicing the air in deliberate shapes—lines, spirals, angles. His eyes tracked something no one else could see. Like the pattern had to be written now, or not at all.

Jacques stood, brushing grit from his palms, and crossed to him. He lowered himself beside U'gah and laid one hand on his shoulder—hot skin, tension thrumming beneath sweat-slicked muscle.

"Ne t'inquiète pas, mon ami," he said quietly. "We're safe here. For now."

He offered a smile. Thin, worn. But sometimes the shape of the thing is enough.

"Maybe the sun comes back tomorrow."

He didn't believe it. Hadn't for days. But saying it helped.

He studied U'gah's face. The markings had run. Sweat and ash had blurred them until they looked more like bruises than symbols. He'd emerged from the trees five days after the crash—barefoot, wide-eyed and silent. Whatever language he spoke, it wasn't one any of them knew. But he *understood* things.

He tracked weather with his nose. Pulled medicine from things Jacques would've judged as weeds. Knew when to stop walking. When to dig for water.

His people were gone, but he was not.

Jacques gave his shoulder a quiet squeeze, then stood. His knees creaked. The ache in his spine didn't bother trying to hide anymore.

Jacques stared into the fire. The coals were settling now, shifting from orange to red. He didn't expect comfort from the glow—only heat, and a task worth finishing.

"We'll get through this," he said quietly. "We'll find a way home."

He paused, hearing the weight in his own voice.

"I swear it."

A voice broke across the cavern.

"No, we won't."

Florence. Her tone cut clean—no hesitation, no room left for pretending.

Jacques turned, shoulders tightening out of habit.

She stood at the edge of the firelight, angular frame taut, fists clenched, eyes wide and burning with panic. Her whole body shook as if bracing for an impact.

"Two weeks of darkness," she said. "No supplies. No comms. No sun. We're not surviving—we're waiting to die."

Every word hit hard and fast, as if saying them could force someone—anyone—to fix it.

Jacques didn't answer. The silence around them had already agreed.

Across the fire, Saturn shifted. His face stayed calm, though a hint of concern passed behind the lenses of his goggles.

"Flo," he said, voice low. "Panicking won't help. We're still here. That means something."

She snapped her head toward him.

"For how long?"

Her volume rose as she spoke, but it wasn't shouting—it was fraying. Breaking at the edges like old canvas.

"We're running out of food. Running out of water. And you're talking about hope? Look at what's out there." She pointed toward the cave mouth. "You think you understand it? You think any of us do?"

The question lingered.

Jacques felt the pressure building in her, sharp and directionless. His instinct was to stop it—cut across the spiral and pull her back. But he didn't.

Florence's hands hovered near her chest, open but searching for something to hold. Her voice softened, but the tremor beneath it remained.

"We don't know what's waiting for us. We don't even know if time works on this cursed island."

She looked at each of them in turn—eyes darting.

"That's the truth no one wants to say."

Emerald stepped forward, slow and steady. Her movements were deliberate, not cautious—controlled in the way someone acts when they've seen this before.

"Flo," she said, gently, "just breathe for a second."

Her voice wasn't condescending. It didn't ask for calm—it offered it.

"You remember the temporal anomaly that hit us. It could be distorting the cycle—compressing time or stretching it. That's probably what this is."

Jacques gave a slight nod. It was the most reasonable explanation they had, and the alternative—that the world outside had simply broken—was worse.

Florence's laugh was dry. Bitter.

"That's what we're calling it now? A cycle glitch? You saw what happened. That thing—whatever it was—wasn't natural. It didn't bend time. It erased it."

"It's not a curse," Emerald said. Her tone stayed level. "It's a phenomenon. One we can map, if we can—"

"Understand it?" Florence cut in. "We're going to die out here, and you're still talking about phenomenons. About anomalies."

Her voice had risen again, but this time it wasn't biting. It was unfiltered. There was no momentum behind it, only exhaustion wearing itself thin.

"We don't even know if time exists beyond this cave. What if it already ran out?"

Jacques felt the clutch in his chest pull tighter. He didn't speak. He didn't try to stop her. Some truths had to be said before they could be let go.

Saturn moved closer. Quiet steps, arms loose at his sides. He stopped beside Florence, then crouched to her level and rested a hand gently on her knee.

"Emerald's not wrong," he said. "Staying rational is the only thing keeping us alive."

Florence didn't flinch at the touch. But her breath caught.

"You believe that?"

Saturn nodded once. His voice was calm, but not empty.

"We have to. There's nothing else left."

The fire cracked as a knot of resin flared. Saturn barely reacted, but an ember lifted and spiraled upward before fading into the stalactites above.

Jacques rubbed the bridge of his nose. His skull felt tight. Not just from exhaustion—there was something else, the weight of being responsible for the lives of others.

"We've all got theories," he said, his voice low. "And I admire the optimism. But I'm afraid I have to side with our doomsayer."

He didn't look at Florence. The scent of her fear was still in the room.

"This darkness—it's not a glitch in the cycle. It's not natural. It doesn't feel like night. It feels like something else entirely. Or maybe... the absence of something."

"If we don't find a way out soon..."

He didn't finish the sentence.

A silence followed until Jacques added, almost to himself, "But a way will open. I have faith."

U'gah grunted low.

Jacques turned. The halfling had shifted. He was staring at the mouth of the cave, posture alert. His eyes darted from the void to Jacques and back.

Jacques felt it, too—subtle. A change. The dark no longer passive. It felt hungry.

He straightened, spine going rigid on instinct.

"No."

His tone sharpened.

"I won't surrender to this. We're not just passengers. We're engineers. Scientists. Explorers."

His gaze swept the others.

"We were sent here to learn. And reason—not fear—is how we survive."

He nodded toward the salvage pile.

"If I can get the relay working, we might manage a signal. Doesn't need to be elegant—just a pulse, a ping. Anything to tell the Allied Corporations we're still here."

Emerald stepped closer, careful but not hesitant. There was tension in her stance, the kind that came from thought, not fear.

"If the relay works," she said, "do you think it could reach someone? Even a fragment of signal could mean—something."

Jacques gave no reply. He dropped back into a crouch and returned to the mess of parts with quiet reserve.

He stripped a length of wire with the jagged edge of a cracked chip, twisted it into place around a warped terminal. The copper fought him. It lost.

His hands were raw, knuckles split and darkened from heat and friction. Blood had dried at the bends of his fingers, flaked against the skin. Still, they moved—steady, practiced, unwilling to tremble.

From behind, he could feel Emerald's gaze. She stayed there, silent, just long enough to measure the odds for herself.

She wasn't the kind who closed her eyes and hoped. Her version of belief had numbers behind it—angles and variables. If she was quiet, it meant the math wasn't coming out clean.

He felt her shift focus, her attention sliding past him toward the others.

Saturn sat hunched over his NAVI unit, plucking debris from its housing with the care of a surgeon, lost in calculation.

Florence lingered at the edge of the cave mouth, arms folded, eyes locked on the dark beyond the firelight. That stare had weight behind it—fixed, unblinking. Jacques had seen it before in forward camps, in the moments before someone wandered off without warning or suck-started their sidearm.

U'gah murmured to himself in low, rolling tones. It wasn't speech—at least not in any language he could understand. But it held rhythm. A pulse from another way of believing.

Then he moved.

Without a word, U'gah crossed into the center of the firelight, kneeled beside Jacques, and upended his pouch.

A scatter of objects spilled into the dust. Bones wrapped in plant fiber. Feathers bound with twine. A brass cog dulled to green at its edges. A sliver of crystal with fractured facets. Smooth stones shaped by river water. A length of vine, braided tight.

The scent of crushed leaves rose with them—heady, green, almost medicinal beneath the smoke.

U'gah selected each piece and laid it into Jacques's open palm. His fingers trembled—not from nerves, but intensity. The act itself carrying meaning.

Jacques turned the items over one by one. No part of him dismissed them. Not here. Not now.

Jacques lifted the brass cog between two fingers, turning it in the firelight. The teeth were dulled, edges smoothed by time. Oxidation traced the grooves, but the piece still held its shape.

He glanced over. "Tools?"

U'gah nodded emphatically.

With careful precision, he took the cog back and pinched it between two fingers and used the notched edge to trace invisible points across the stone beside them—measuring, spacing, aligning. He tapped the teeth to the surface as if mapping intervals. His motions were fluid, practiced. Not for show.

Jacques watched, absorbing the demonstration without comment.

He picked up the crystal next, letting its fractured face catch the firelight. The glow scattered across his hand in pale ribbons.

"And this?"

U'gah pointed toward the wall, then to the shard, then tapped beneath his eye twice. His gestures came faster now—eager, direct, trying to shorten the distance between thought and understanding.

Jacques studied him for a moment. Then nodded.

"A magnifier."

U'gah grinned. He thumped Jacques lightly on the arm.

Jacques let out a quiet breath—almost a laugh, but worn down at the edges.

He turned the shard again, watching the light curve across his palm.

"Well then, mon ami," he said softly, "let's see what your treasures can do."

Then he turned back to his labor.

Whatever it takes.

Even the fire seemed to hold steady, as if waiting to see how it would break.

It was Emerald that stepped forward. Her expression resolute— not wide-eyed, not defiant, just convinced.

She clapped once. The sound cracked through the quiet like a clean reset.

"Don't worry, Jacques," she said, her voice steady. "We'll figure it out."

Across the fire, Saturn shifted. His fingers began moving again, recalibrating the drone's turbofan shells with practiced ease. He didn't look up, but his voice was audible.

"Indeed," he said. "This task isn't beyond reach. Besides, zero attempts guarantee zero results."

Florence didn't speak, but she moved. Just enough to suggest she was listening. Her shoulders, rigid for so long, had lowered an inch. Something behind her eyes brightened—not hope, not yet—but the first absence of collapse.

A wind stirred. Not a breeze—this came with weight. It swept through the cave, a banshee's wail, slicing through the fire's warmth and leaving the air hollow in its wake.

Jacques went still. Every hair on his arms stood up.

The fire snapped high, flames dancing harder than they should have. Sparks scattered like startled insects. The warmth didn't follow.

Makeshift tools froze in his hands.

There was tension in the air. Not just atmospheric—but electric. The kind that lingers right before a storm hits metal or artillery fire rains down on your location.

Something shifted in the dark, just beyond the fire's edge. It moved, they moved, creatures in the dark.

Florence cried out behind him as a voice drifted in from the dark. Soft. Familiar.

"Is that you?"

Jacques froze. Every part of him held still.

The voice was warm, shaped by memory—intonation wrapped in old routines. He didn't need to guess.

"Louis?" he whispered.

It slipped out before he could stop it. The name caught in his throat.

Then came another—higher, trembling, unmistakable.

"We're over here!"

He flinched. That one hit deeper.

Marie.

The cadence, the rhythm—it was hers. She always sounded like she was about to laugh, even when the world was falling apart.

But she'd died five days ago. And there hadn't been enough left to bury.

Behind him, Florence gasped. Her hand covered her mouth. Her eyes locked on the cave mouth, wide and wet.

"No," she breathed. "It can't be…"

A step forward. Her voice cracked.

"They're alive."

Emerald's gaze snapped to Saturn. Her expression tensed, but he was already still—hands frozen above the drone, eyes narrowed behind his goggles.

"This is impossible," Saturn said. "They're dead."

A low grunt turned Jacques's head. U'gah had stepped back from the fire's edge, arms raised slightly, fingers twitching in staccato bursts. He muttered to himself—no rhythm, no ceremony. There was no control left in the sound.

Jacques moved without thinking.

"That's not them."

The words came out dry, stripped down. Not a theory—an instinct.

But the voices didn't stop.

They multiplied—spilling from every direction, overlapping, almost believable.

"Please help us!"

"We're here—don't leave us!"

Each cry hit the stone with unnatural timing. Close to human, but flattened. An imitation stripped of understanding.

Florence buckled.

She broke from the circle and stumbled toward the cave mouth, arms outstretched, eyes fixed on the dark with a look Jacques had only ever seen in people who had already decided to follow the dead.

"Louis! Marie!" she called. "We're coming!"

Jacques lunged. His boots scraped the stone. He caught her arm and yanked hard.

"No."

His words cut low and final.

She fought him, wrenching in his grip. Her eyes burned, glassy with tears.

"Let me go! They need us!"

"They're gone, Florence." His voice didn't rise, but the weight behind it did. "We saw them die. Whatever's out there—it isn't them."

A sound rumbled in from beyond the firelight.

Not speech. Not a howl. It dragged across the stone in a slow, grinding rasp—low enough to be felt inside his chest.

Jacques didn't flinch. He'd heard that frequency before. Not in tone—but in meaning.

U'gah stepped up onto a raised slab with a force that felt almost ritualistic. The moment hung—just a breath of silence —

Then his body turned.

There was no light show. No cinematic snap of bones. Just a shift, abrupt and final, like the world realizing it had miscalculated the shape of him all along.

His shoulders broadened. Joints swelled. Fur split through skin in wet threads. Mass gathered across his frame in uneven, lurching intervals—arms too thick, torso stretching, face pulling forward into a muzzle.

It wasn't violence. It was correction.

He didn't grow tall so much as deep. The kind of density that made space seem to bend around him.

The firelight caught in his eyes—not human, not animal, but reflective, intelligent.

He rose onto thick hind limbs, head low, weight balanced with uncanny stillness. Every part of him radiated presence. Intention.

Then he let out a sound.

Not a roar. Not a bark. A coarse, chest-worn bellow—cut short, but full of edge. A signal.

Florence stopped mid-stride.

Her arms dropped. Her face slackened, locked between recognition and disbelief. The panic hadn't left her eyes, it had a new direction now.

Jacques pulled her back across the stone, one arm around her waist. She stumbled, but didn't resist.

The fireline trembled between them and the cave's mouth. Sparks twisted upward and fell back as ash curling inward.

"Écoutez," Jacques said. "He's protecting us."

Behind them, Saturn took two slow steps forward.

"Incredible," he said. His voice had thinned out—toneless, fragile, like it might shatter under too much thought. "The shift in bone density... Is this neurological? Hormonal? Induced by some other factor?"

U'gah didn't turn.

He crouched low again, claws spread against the stone for traction. His head swiveled just slightly—eyes fixed beyond the fire.

He released a clipped series of huffs. Not language, as such. More like signals sent to an intruder in the dark. A boundary declared.

Jacques understood.

U'gah wasn't speaking to them. He was holding the line.

Whatever was watching from the other side had been noticed.

And it knew.

Saturn's gaze didn't leave U'gah.

"The vocal patterns," he muttered. "Those cries earlier... they weren't random. They were copying."

His eyes narrowed behind back-lit lenses. "High-level mimicry. Intelligent targeting. Like corvids, parrots, even some felines—but more adaptive."

Emerald's head snapped toward him.

"But how?" she asked. Her voice was quiet, but the tension beneath it stretched tight.

Jacques didn't look up from the salvage. He was already moving again—elbow-deep in the wreckage, searching for something still intact.

"Doesn't matter," he said. "We don't need to know how."

He found a broken panel, tossed it aside. Then another.

"What matters is it wants us out of the cave, in the open."

The words landed as hard as cold metal.

That was when the tone shifted.

Cries erupted again—fast, without warning. But now they were screams. Human. Terrorized.

They rolled into the cave like an acidic cloud, assaulting them from every side and bouncing off the walls.

Florence dropped to her knees, folding in on herself. Hands clamped over her ears, shoulders curled tight, she resembled a frightened turtle.

Emerald stood frozen, eyes fixed on the cave's mouth. Her carbine hung forgotten at her side, its strap slipping down her shoulder.

The room crackled with tension—static before lightning.

Saturn stepped beside Emerald, one hand resting gently on her shoulder. He didn't speak, but the touch steadied her just enough to keep her grounded.

Jacques stayed focused.

"This is fear," he said. "That's all it is. It's trying to flush us out. If we stay in the light, we hold the line. That's it."

Jacques dug into the salvage pile, moving past scorched circuits and twisted cables. His hands moved fast, not frantic—just focused.

Then he found it.

A metal tin, scratched but intact.

He flipped it open.

Inside: ten earplugs. Industrial grade. Bright orange foam, slightly deformed, but usable.

"Fight fire," he said to himself, "with silence."

He crossed to Florence first, knelt beside her. Her hands were still clamped over her ears, her shoulders trembling beneath her jacket.

He opened her fingers one at a time and pressed the plugs into her palms. She looked at them like she didn't understand what they were—then nodded.

She fit them into her ears with shaking hands.

Jacques moved to Emerald next. She took hers without a word. The tension in her jaw had hardened—fear held at bay by will.

Saturn accepted his with clinical precision, adjusting them for fit.

U'gah sniffed the foam in Jacques's hand, eyes narrowed. Jacques crouched and gently pressed the plugs into place himself, one ear, then the other.

The bear-thing the little shaman had become blinked twice, then settled—shoulders low, arms resting across his knees.

Jacques inserted his last.

The world vanished—not just muffled, erased.

The pressure in his skull dropped away. The screams disappeared like a light being switched off. No tapering, no residue. Just gone.

He stood in the middle of the cave, surrounded by silence.

The fire still burned, and his thoughts cleared.

Jacques returned to the relay.

The wires resisted, but without the howling outside to wear him down, he could work. Map the structure. Visualize the solution.

He glanced up.

Florence hadn't moved.

She sat near the fire, knees drawn to her chest, clutching her ledger against her ribs like a lifeline. Her fingers locked around the spine, knuckles pale. The pages were swollen from moisture, the edges curled and splotched with ash.

It wasn't a notebook anymore. It was ballast.

Her eyes shifted constantly—from fire to stone to shadow—never staying long enough to land. She wasn't searching. She was bracing.

The others had tasks. Rhythms. Something to channel into.

Florence had nothing but the ledger.

She rocked slightly—small enough to miss if you weren't watching. Jacques saw it, and recognized the pattern. A mind trying to stay in the lines.

He didn't say anything. No words would reach her right now.

Emerald pretended not to notice. Saturn stayed locked in his calculations. U'gah remained still.

But Jacques kept watching.

The fire burned lower. The shadows stretched. The relay sparked faintly in his hand, and he cursed. There was still work to do.

CHAPTER TWO

hirty-nine hours.

That's what the marks said—etched in the corners of his mind. But time no longer had shape. It bled out in heartbeats, seconds dissolving into hours, hours into what felt like years.

Jacques hunched over the relay, hands trembling despite their stillness. Exhaustion soaked him through—heavy as waterlogged cloth. His eyes burned raw in their sockets. Lips cracked, jaw locked tight. Sleep had become a rumor—distant, unreachable.

Outside, the dark pressed close, suffocating. It bent the edges of thought, collapsed memory into static, blurred the line between hard reality and waking dream.

Then a thread of gold slid across the stone.

He blinked. Squinted. Vision swam.

Sunlight. Actual sunlight.

A single spear broke the dark, a faultline splitting the world open. Dust danced in its wake, transfigured into drifting gold— spirits fleeing shadow.

Light didn't banish the night. It fractured it.

And with the light—sound. Not screams. Not echoes.

Birdsong. Insects. Leaves stirring in a breeze that smelled of damp earth and green life.

The rot lifted. The air brightened. Each breath tasted new: moss, bark, blossoms cracking open to drink morning air.

U'gah stirred first.

His small frame unfolded in a smooth, eager motion. He sniffed once, then let out a string of animated grunts—arms flailing as he pointed toward the cave mouth. The gesture was bright, almost comical after so much stillness. Childlike. Unfiltered.

Jacques closed his eyes, letting it hit his face trying to thaw the cold horror of the long night.

"Le lever du soleil," he whispered, voice rusted from disuse.

He stood. Muscles protested, knees popped. Every movement stiff, he felt carved rather than alive.

"We should make use of the day while we have it."

Emerald nodded—slow, black eyes rimmed red, her body heavy with fatigue. Saturn followed, mechanical in motion. They looked like husks. Used fuel, functioning on fumes.

They needed food. Water. Rest.

Some sign to prove they weren't ghosts.

Jacques turned to Florence.

She hadn't moved.

Curled in the corner. Ledger clutched tight. Knees drawn to her chest.

Her fingers were locked white around the book's spine. Her lips moved, but no sound escaped. A litany of voiceless prayers.

Her eyes fixed on something none of them could see—past the material world entirely.

Jacques knelt beside her. His joints creaked, the sound too loud in the hush.

"Florence?" he said, softly, as if too much weight might snap her.

No response. No shift in breath. Her gaze didn't break.

This wasn't the woman who once debated Saturn into silence. Who laughed until her ribs hurt at Emerald's filthy jokes. Who documented every corrupt line item in the expedition's ledgers with ruthless precision.

That woman had folded inward. Gone silent.

He hesitated, then placed a hand on her shoulder. The fabric was damp. Her skin beneath it, hot, a sign of dehydration.

Were it not for her slight fear, it would have been like touching a corpse.

Saturn crouched beside him, rubbing his eyes.

"She's likely dissociating," he said, evenly, with a slightly brittle undertone. "Sleep deprivation. Sensory trauma. Her mind's overwriting what it can't process."

Jacques looked at him.

"She's retreating?"

Saturn shook his head once.

"She's breaking."

Jacques inhaled deeply, and let it out through his teeth.

He'd dragged them through hell. Held the line with spit and wire. But this—the war inside her head—he couldn't help her navigate that battlefield.

"We need to get her out of here," he murmured.

He shifted his stance and slipped one arm beneath Florence's shoulders, the other beneath her knees. Her body sagged against his chest—light in mass, heavy with trauma.

She didn't stir as he stood. Her head rested at the hollow of his collarbone, fevered skin brushing his neck, breath faint against his throat—irregular, but still there.

Saturn and Emerald gathered what little gear they had. No orders passed between them. They didn't need any. The cave had hollowed them all the same way, only to different degrees.

Their steps dragged over stone, the sound dull, unsteady. They moved without rhythm—less a team than figures on the edge of collapse.

But they walked.

Out through the narrow mouth of the cave. Into air that carried the sounds of emerging life.

The light hit Jacques—brilliant, intense, a heat that soaked straight through the grime and grit. His eyes snapped shut, overwhelmed. A sharp sting built behind the lids.

He opened them slowly.

The world beyond the dark shimmered with impossible color. Green like moss after rainfall. Sky so high it hurt to look at. Dust floated in gold shafts like it had forgotten how to fall.

He stepped beyond the stone's reach, boots sinking into dirt softened by dew.

Florence remained limp in his arms, her presence both weight and burden.

He stood there a moment longer. Not ready to speak. Then he looked up—into the glare—and filled his lungs.

The air was loamy, wild, alive. A hundred growing things tangled together. He let it settle inside him.

He exhaled with a sigh—feeling the beginnings of relief.

"Allons-y," he said. "Let's see what this new day demands of us."

***

The forest closed in fast—dense and humid. The ground sucked at their boots, vines snatched at their legs, and low branches snapped back with whip-quick precision. The undergrowth clung, as if eager to bury them in mulch and memory.

Above, the canopy arched like a sealed vault, almost sunless. What light reached them came in slivers, narrow as needles, gold and platinum flitting across the jungle floor like ghost-fire.

Jacques led. His shirt was soaked through, stuck to his skin with sweat that stank of body odor and burnt components. The machete dragged at his arm, each swing a jolt up his shoulder. Every root testing what remained of his conviction to push forward.

But he didn't stop.

Behind him, Saturn moved with his eyes locked onto the digital HUD displayed on the lenses of his goggles monitoring his drone's scan of the area, only passively paying any attention to his surrounding environment. Emerald scanned every shadow, fingers brushing her carbine at every sign of movement. Florence drifted behind them, her steps mechanical, mind still trailing somewhere behind her body—but at least she was moving on her own now.

Sunlight broke across her face once. Briefly. Her lashes fluttered. There was no clarity in her expression, barely enough instinct to keep breathing.

A soft tone pulsed—barely audible. A pinpoint of white blinked on Saturn's optics.

"Southwest quadrant," Saturn said. "Broad leaves, clustered roots—wild tubers. High water content."

Jacques nodded. Sweat slid into his eyes as he wiped his brow on the back of his wrist. The machete found his grip again. Not a tool anymore—an extension. He cut. He stepped. Again and again. The rhythm took on weight, his own personal war against the vegetation of the forest.

It was loud in some ways, silent in others. Insects whined. The wet squelch of boots. The drone's steady purr. Birdsong. Thankfully, no predators in sight.

Jacques knelt when he reached the spot the scientist had identified. The blade sank into soft earth with a dull thud. Roots gave way. Thick, ugly yams surfaced—rough-skinned, knotted, and coated in damp earth.

He pressed one into Florence's hands.

She blinked. Slowly. As if rising from somewhere deep. Her fingers closed around it. No expression crossed her face. She bit in. Pulp smeared her mouth. She chewed.

The others followed. Not from appetite. From necessity. They wiped the dirt away. Jawed through the fibers. The taste was bitter, the texture foul. But it filled the hollow places.

Jacques scraped residue from beneath his nails with his teeth. The starch stuck to his tongue, dry and bland, but better than hunger.

They crouched in a loose ring. No one spoke.

A rustle—soft, then closer. Brush shifted. The jungle fell quiet.

Every head turned.

Jacques's fingers closed around the machete. His pulse jumped. Emerald tensed beside him. Even Saturn looked up.

U'gah stepped into view, brow furrowed. His bare chest rose and fell in heavy, uneven bursts. He was drenched in sweat, grime streaked across his arms and chest, but his eyes were focused—intent.

He grunted and jabbed a thick finger toward a thinning wall of trees.

Jacques rose while brushing grit from his palms.

"He's found something," he said.

The others were already gathering—packs half-lifted, eyes sharper than they had been minutes before.

Even half-dead, you could feel the change in their disposition.

Saturn moved first, uncharacteristically fast. He vanished into the underbrush, a flash of pale limbs and glimpses of wild, cyan hair. Jacques followed, machete clearing the way. Emerald kept close, carbine at low ready. Florence drifted last, silent but moving—her face a mask of nothingness.

They broke through—and stopped.

Sunlight struck them like a wave.

Not the scattered light that filtered through leaves. Not the shy morning shimmer they'd seen hours ago. This was full, unbroken sunlight.

Jacques recoiled, one hand rising to shield his eyes. The warmth flooded over him.

Saturn stood already in the clearing, both arms raised to block the glare. His goggles had fogged, or he'd forgotten to tint them—his lips parted, stunned into silence.

Jacques stepped up beside him.

For a moment, the cave, the hunger, the dead voices—everything fell away.

Ahead, the horizon stretched wide and impossible.

To the east and west: black. Absolute and unnatural.

But south—straight ahead—a corridor of pure light split the jungle open. Not a beam. Not a break in the canopy. A path.

It cleaved the landscape—the blade of God.

And above—not the single sun they expected to greet them, but many.

They hung in the sky in a perfect line, equidistant, identical. White-gold, radiant, each one pulsing with the same steady heat. They didn't falter. Didn't waver. Just burned—fixed in place like jewels hammered into the vault of heaven.

Jacques forgot how to breathe.

Beside him, U'gah dropped low into a crouch, growling under his breath. His spine bowed. His gestures turned frantic. He jabbed upward—at the sky, then downward—at the dirt. Beat his fists against his chest. Then pointed to his eyes.

Jacques stared. His heartbeat loud in his ears.

Even the shaman didn't understand it.

Emerald and Florence stepped forward. Whatever exhaustion had gripped them a moment ago was gone.

Florence's breath caught. Her lips parted. She gazed up, eyes wide, jaw slack, the light painting her features in golden awe.

"It's… beautiful," she whispered, barely audible.

The words slipped out, more confession than anything else.

Emerald lifted a pair of compact binoculars to her eyes—sleek, multi-lensed, flickering with digital readouts. Her mouth opened, closed, opened again.

When she finally spoke, her voice had lost its usual brightness. It came hushed. Calculated.

"Spectrometer's spiking—same signature from before. The suns… it's likely just one star. Refracted through overlapping layers of chrono-distortion."

She blinked hard, as if recalibrating her brain alongside the machine.

"Or something close."

Jacques let out a low whistle, sweeping sweat-matted hair from his forehead with the back of one hand. The usual sarcasm had slipped from his tone. It didn't belong here.

"Magnifique," he murmured.

He'd seen wonders: the wind-sculpted dunes of Arabia, the glass caves under Europa's ice, the irradiated pyramids of Cairo. None of them had made him feel this small.

He glanced at Emerald, her silhouette haloed by celestial fire.

"Atmospheric anomaly, you say?" His voice bent into something dry and wry. A familiar lift of the brow. "Mm. Perhaps. Perhaps."

He turned back to the light.

It kissed his skin with warmth that felt not just physical, but personal. Like a hand on the shoulder from a god too divine to name.

"But I choose to believe in something more poetic."

He raised his hand, slow and reverent, toward the suns strung above them, pearls on a divine thread.

"This, mes amis... this is a sign. A gift. Without it, we'd still be buried in the dark, harried by voices of the dead."

The words lingered.

Even Saturn said nothing. What could he say?

At the edge of the clearing, Florence stood slack-jawed, tears collecting in her lashes. She looked up at the impossible sky and finally exhaled.

"But... how?" she whispered. "How can there be so many suns?"

Jacques turned to answer, but Emerald stepped forward first— drawn, not pushed.

"No idea," she said, softly. "But it is a question I would also like an answer to."

She walked toward the corridor, cautiously, like each step might change the shape of the world.

Jacques let the warmth settle across his skin a moment longer, then turned to take in the others.

Florence stood at the edge of the clearing, the light catching in her tear-streaked eyes. Each sun above mirrored there—bright and trembling. She wasn't smiling, but the tightness in her face had loosened. The tension behind her eyes had dimmed. Not clarity, but a step toward it.

Emerald stood rooted, her gaze tracking the celestial alignment with reverence and hunger. Her lenses flared. Her lips moved silently, as if parsing equations too vast to speak aloud.

Jacques could almost see the moment her exhaustion fell away. Not from rest, but from relevance. Mystery energized her more than sleep ever had.

Saturn crouched in the clearing, adjusting NAVI's settings. Data scrolled across his wrist display in dim, green script, but his eyes kept drifting to the sky.

"NAVI's sensors are not calibrated for this type of phenomenon, but it would appear local spacetime remains unstable," he said. "However consistent, the anomaly may have entered a stabilization phase. That may buy us time."

U'gah stood stone-still, ears twitching. He bristled—not with fear, but alertness. He didn't appear to trust the suns.

But there was something inside of him, a feeling, a force. It pulled him toward the corridor.

Jacques exhaled slowly, then turned back to them.

"I know we're tired," he said. "I know we're hungry. And I know how far we are from anything that resembles home."

They looked to him now. Even U'gah turned his head toward the sound.

"But this"—he gestured to the radiant path that seemed carved into reality—"this is direction. A line through the madness. A reason to keep going."

"It might be anomaly. Or design. But either way—it's hope. And I'll take that over chaos."

He stepped toward U'gah and laid a hand on the shaman's shoulder.

"For that," Jacques said, "we have you to thank."

U'gah blinked, then gave a sudden, toothy grin. A stream of delighted grunts followed, full of mischief and pride.

Florence stirred again at the edge of the clearing. Her lips parted. Her voice, thin and dream-dragged, rose once more.

"But how…" she said, repeating herself, as if caught in the loop of awe. "How can there be so many suns?"

Emerald didn't look away from Jacques.

"If it's a time-shear," she said, "then the suns might not be stars at all. They could be echoes. Refractions. The same source viewed across different timelines. A temporal prism."

She said it calmly, almost to herself, but in response to Florence's repeated question.

Jacques watched her—not to follow the theory, but to see the light in her eyes.

Saturn chimed in without looking up. "Possible. Refracted gravitational lensing could explain the spacing. But the symmetry implies more than natural variance. It's structured."

U'gah snorted and turned, nose lifted.

He sniffed, then let out a sharp grunt and pointed toward the edge of the clearing. Dark, plum-like fruit hung low on thick, crooked branches—clustered in shadows NAVI had somehow missed.

Jacques followed his line of sight. "Another gift, it would seem."

The team moved with more purpose now. They crossed the field in staggered strides, NAVI sweeping ahead in cautious arcs. The air sweetened with the scent of ripeness—fruity and slightly acidic.

Jacques plucked one of the bulbous fruits and turned it in his hand. Smooth-skinned, gold-streaked, faintly warm—as if it still remembered the sun.

He bit in.

Juice flooded his mouth—delicious and slightly tangy. No sting on the tongue. No bitterness. Just hydration.

He looked back to the others. "It's safe."

They didn't hesitate. Teeth tore flesh. Juice ran down chins. No one cared. It was food. Real food.

Jacques leaned against a low tree content—sweetness sinking into his tongue. Another bite. Satisfaction.

For a time, all was bliss.

Then the light changed.

He noticed it not with his eyes, but in the silence that followed. A shift in shadow. A shimmer across Emerald's cheek. The gold in the air had thinned.

Jacques looked up.

The corridor of suns—once strung in perfect alignment—was breaking.

One orb drifted free, peeling off like ash from a dying ember. Then another. Each found its own arc—rising, falling, or fading altogether.

He watched, rooted.

One sun blinked out midair. Another dipped below the trees. The symmetry collapsed, slow and soundless. Light bled into white, then paled further—into the plain, familiar cast of day. With only one sun hanging overhead.

The miracle was gone. Leaving only normalcy and—

A memory. A magical one.

Emerald stood motionless, fruit forgotten in her hand. Her eyes tracked the sky as if it might start fracturing again.

"The hypothesis still holds," she said, voice low. "If those were refracted projections—fragmented across temporal strata—then the collapse could indicate a return to baseline."

She didn't sound convinced.

Saturn adjusted his gloves, scrolled through NAVI's sensor logs with a practiced swipe.

"The anomaly appears stable. Local conditions are static. No current risk of collapse or surge. That buys us time."

Jacques nodded, but didn't speak. He wasn't watching NAVI. He was watching the sun.

Florence stood apart from the others, arms wrapped tight around her frame. Her eyes stayed fixed on the sun as if it might vanish the second she blinked.

Jacques knew that look. Doubt.

He glanced at the trees, ground, and the group still chewing fruit with slack jaws and lifted eyes.

He opened his mouth to speak—but before he could, U'gah let out a low, satisfied hum.

The halfling was seated now, back against a wide root, patting his stomach like a drum. Juice glistened on his chin. His contentment was full and unfiltered.

Jacques retreated into his mind. There were so many questions and so few answers, so many problems without solutions. He walked from the others to clear his mind, away from their noise.

But there, threading beneath the hush of rustling leaves, came a new sound.

Running water.

He looked to the others.

"Well," he said, smiling and holding his hand up for quiet. "That's a sound worth chasing."

Their eyes met his, and something passed between them. Recognition.

U'gah bounded to his feet and was off before anyone else could react.

They followed him through the brush, feet dragging but spirits buoyed. Vines clawed at their boots. Low branches slapped against shoulders and arms. But they pushed through, driven by the promise of flowing water.

The sound grew louder—soft at first, then steady. A hush over stone. A pull.

They rounded a thicket—and stopped.

A stream wound through a shallow basin of smooth rock, its surface fractured by light into moving shards of gold and white. Water spilled over mossy ledges in quiet cascades, gathering in clear pools that glinted like hand-blown glass.

Jacques blinked, convinced he was dreaming.

Even Florence stirred—her posture shifted, eyes wide, breath catching. A trace of life returned to her face.

Was it real?

U'gah whooped and barreled forward. He plunged into the stream with a jubilant splash, thrashing water into the air, unbound as a child. He spun, dunked his head, then surfaced with a barking laugh.

Emerald recovered from her initial shock. She kicked off her boots mid-stride and cannonballed in behind him.

"Green fire!" she shouted just before hitting the water.

Saturn stepped in more slowly, lowering himself with care. But he let himself float—arms out, eyes closed, lips curved in something shockingly close to peace. The goggles had been left on the bank. While NAVI ran through a preprogrammed macro scouting the area.

Jacques stood at the edge and watched.

Let it all land.

The joy. The splashes. The shock of color in Florence's expression as she watched U'gah and Emerald dunk each other, whooping like kids in a summer fountain.

He turned to her.

She hadn't moved, but the stiffness in her shoulders had loosened. Her eyes kept shifting—stream, sky, back to the stream—as if testing the scene for cracks.

He extended a hand.

"It's alright," he said. "The water's real."

Her hand found his. It trembled in his grip.

Together, they stepped down the rocks after kicking off their boots.

She flinched when the current touched her skin, but she didn't recoil. Her eyes fluttered closed, and when they opened again, there was a little less distance in them.

She sat in the stream. A small smile ghosting her features.

The others played, floated, and laughed. Jacques watched the grief melt off them one ripple at a time. He heard it in Saturn's chuckle. In Emerald's yell. In U'gah's unfiltered delight.

Jacques let it fill him, tentative as a man stepping onto thin ice.

Then he stepped in relishing the cool wetness.

It gripped his legs, then pulled the ache from his spine, his ribs, even his exhausted mind. He barked a laugh as U'gah splashed him straight in the face.

For the first time in days, he felt light.

They swam. Floated. Forgot.

The sun blazed overhead and time was forgotten.

The horse-play lasted for hours, until he felt waterlogged and sore.

It was then he realized the shadows hadn't moved.

Jacques waded toward the far bank, the current tugging gently at his legs.

He paused.

The angle of the light. The way it clung to the leaves. The way it hadn't shifted—not even slightly.

He looked up

The sun still hung in place.

No arc. No drift. No progression. Just a fixed point—perfectly still, nailed to the heavens like a celestial emblem.

Confused by his sudden change in demeanor, Emerald began to shake off the spell of the oasis, and noticed it too.

She stood waist-deep in the water, droplets sliding down her arms. Her brow creased. Her gaze locked upward, unblinking.

"I find this temporal phenomenon both fascinating…" she murmured, "and deeply troubling."

Saturn opened his eyes. Floated still for a moment, then rolled upright and moved toward the shore.

"Though the anomaly has stabilized the distortion could still be active," he said, the usual precision in his voice strained by a faint undercurrent of annoyance. "If we're inside a time-shear, anything could happen."

Jacques stepped onto the bank, and slung his boots over his shoulder, water dripping down his back. The air felt different now—similar to that of a conventional oven warming. Joy thinned, retreating before the new wrongness.

He swept hair from his face, eyes narrowing against the glare.

The miracle had held them. Fed them. But now it lingered too long.

And nothing that perfect lingers without a cost.

Jacques shook it off and looked to the others.

They were still in the shallows—Florence quiet, Emerald studying the sky, Saturn swimming to the shore to recover his equipment, U'gah half-submerged, eyes closed, humming to himself.

"We shouldn't linger," Jacques said.

The words landed flat, but final.

He hated saying them. Hated ending this.

But time had slipped its leash, and the longer they stayed, the less certain they'd ever leave.

"This place was a gift," he continued, scanning their faces. "Water, food, light. But it isn't ours. And it isn't stable."

He turned south, toward the corridor the suns had revealed.

"That's our path. If we're meant to survive, that is where we will find salvation."

Silence followed—thick and solemn. It was obvious not one of them wanted to leave this place. Especially for something that was likely nothing more than an unusual atmospheric temporal anomaly.

But this was what was revealed to them. By God or by fate, south was the way.

Florence's voice came brittle, not wanting to leave the magic of this place. Her hands were clenched at her sides.

"But how can you be sure?" she asked. Her eyes darted—sky, trees, faces. Wild. Pleading. "We thought the night would never end. And now this? What if the corridor is a trap? Another way for the island to torture us? We don't know what's waiting out there."

U'gah whimpered low in his chest. His eyes had snapped open. He sniffed the air, his head slowly shifting side to side—as if trying to hear a frequency the others couldn't. The joy was gone from his posture. He crouched now, muscles tight again, the wild sense returning.

Jacques turned toward Florence.

He placed a hand on her shoulder, a steadying force to counterbalance her fraying mental state.

"Faith," he said.

One word.

She stared at him—eyes wide, red at the edges. Her shoulders dropped a fraction, unable to summon an argument.

"Allons-y," he said. "We follow where the light pointed."

He raised his arm and pointed south.

"The sun is our guide. And we will follow."

One by one, they hoisted packs. Cinched straps. Checked weapons—what few they had. Hands lingered on fruit-laden branches, on the cool stone at the water's edge. No one wanted to say it, but they all felt the same, even him.

The oasis had been a reprieve. But not a place to stay.

He turned for a final glance.

The water still shimmered. Trees still swayed. Light still held.

It was salvation.

But it wasn't theirs.

Then he turned away, took the first step on the path the sky had chosen for them.

The others followed.

U'gah loped ahead in the brush, low to the ground, alert again. Emerald kept close behind Jacques, her carbine loose at her side. Disappointment etched into her gnomish features. Saturn trailed, only partially registering the world outside of his digital overlays, already mapping again.

Florence came last. Her movements were hesitant, but no longer absent. Her gaze remained locked forward, as if looking back might undo whatever fragile repair had begun to form inside her.

Jacques led them south. Boots thudded against the dirt, roots curled like grasping fingers beneath the leaves. The sky above stayed bright blue and with a fixed white gold eye. Watching.

But this time, they weren't lost—they had a bearing.

CHAPTER THREE

Days bled together—pointless, weightless—until time thinned to steam. The fixed sun burned overhead without mercy, casting shadows that never moved. Sleep came in ragged snatches, draining more than they restored. Even behind closed eyelids, the glare lingered.

It felt less like living than enduring beneath a stage light with no script—frozen mid-scene, waiting for a cue that would never come.

And yet, daylight brought one mercy: the predators of the long night stayed beyond the corridor's edge, retreating from the light like wax from flame.

What remained were jittery, quick-footed herbivores with wide, haunted eyes, and insects that vanished at the faintest vibration. Everything fled before the party arrived, as if the sun had branded them with danger.

"It feels like we're walking through a ghost forest," Emerald said.

Saturn tapped his scanner, the digital glow washing over his goggles. "Pattern recognition shows nothing bigger than a rabbit. Everything else bolts before we're near—almost as if a signal's clearing the path ahead."

Jacques rested his machete across one shoulder. "Maybe they sense the distortion. Or maybe we're specters—strangers the jungle wants gone."

No one disagreed.

Above, the sun glared.

And they pressed forward.

The trees grew thicker, bark pitted and furrowed—ancient scars on gnarled trunks. Vines draped in tangled arcs between them, lianas coiling overhead, twisting the undergrowth into a living maze. Ferns arched over the corridor, their fronds hunting stray light.

The air hung heavy, saturated with wet earth and rotting leaves. Strange blossoms emitted an electric tang, sharp as ozone. Birds shrieked above in discordant calls, their confusion mirroring the static daylight. Frogs barked, hinges of decay creaking. Somewhere, unseen, something long and slick moved just beyond sight.

Tension wound through Jacques like a drawn wire. The jungle pulsed with life—but it felt empty. Every thought of scouting beyond the corridor's golden rim died unspoken. The sunlight acted as both beacon and boundary. It kept them safe. And contained.

He paused beneath a break in the canopy, gaze lifting through the tangle of leaves to the sun—unwinking and harsh.

"Perhaps the hand of God guides us." His voice was quiet—no rhetoric, just a worn thought spoken aloud. "But this could be proof he still believes in trials and tribulations for his chosen, non?"

He inhaled deeply. Moss and flowers, sweat and heat. His fingers grazed his chest, vertically, then horizontally—an old gesture, half-habit, half-prayer.

Emerald glanced at him sidelong, a brow lifted. "Divine mandate? I thought you ran on logic and blueprints."

Jacques smiled faintly. "Not everything bends to science, mon amie."

Old catechism crept into his tone.

"This light has given us water. Food. A reprieve from monsters. Perhaps that's not coincidence. Perhaps it's grace."

He let his hand fall, gesturing toward the sun ahead—the head of a nail through the center of heaven.

"I am a man of equations, oui. But where the laws of nature twist like heated metal, I take comfort in constants—faith alongside reason."

Saturn adjusted his goggles. "The phenomena are extraordinary. I reserve judgment on any divinity... but gratitude seems prudent. Whatever its source."

Florence clutched her ledger, eyes wide. Her voice came thin. "There must be a reason."

A whisper. A plea.

U'gah grunted softly, smiling broadly. He understood none of it, but seemed as if he wanted to add to the conversation.

A chuckle bloomed in Jacques's throat. He suppressed it not wanting to have to explain what he found humorous.

"If the price of safety is an unmoving sun," he said, voice low, "I accept."

He looked down the path.

"Let us treat this radiance as a path laid for us—and trust it leads somewhere worth reaching."

The jungle answered with a long, uneasy sigh.

As if to remind them, once again: all gifts come with a cost.

***

The corridor of light, once steady and centered, now tilted with each step—as if dragging them downhill into a slanting world as the terrain began to drop into the lowlands.

The jungle thickened. Moisture pooled underfoot. The scent of fresh growth curdled into wet rot and stagnant water. Insects stitched a constant whine through the air, weaving tension into every breathless pause. Roots snagged. Stones slipped. The trail became a slow surrender.

Jacques felt the pressure change before he could name it.

The light was moving.

Not fading—tilting.

The sun, a static fixture for days, now sagged lower with every kilometer. It had begun to shift—trailing down the corridor, as if escorting them to a single, unavoidable point.

Then he realized the worst of it.

It was setting.

In the south.

"It's as if the sun is setting with every step we take," Emerald said, not with wonder, but with wraiths passing her features. "And it's going the wrong direction."

Jacques turned toward her. Her black eyes hadn't left the sky. Her hands flexed against her rifle strap as if she was bracing for recoil.

Saturn had gone silent. The readouts from NAVI reflected across his goggles as he studied the corridor.

"No celestial model accounts for southern solar descent," he said. "The anomaly may be shifting orientation. Or it's moving with us. Or—worse—it's responding to us."

Florence followed, slow and distant, arms wrapped tight around her ledger. She stared at the sun's descent like it was a verdict, not a phenomenon.

"It was supposed to lead us out," she murmured, trailing off into inaudible rambling.

Her voice felt too shrill in the hush that followed.

Jacques fell back beside her, shoulder to shoulder.

He looked ahead, where the corridor sloped toward the deepening orange light. A sun where no sun should be. A path still clear—and ushering them toward their apparent destination.

42

"We follow it," he said, steady. "Until it gives us reason not to."

U'gah said nothing, but his pace quickened—more animal than scout now. His limbs carried him forward with a kind of instinct no logic could match.

They crested a rise.

The scenic rise expanded their view of the way ahead as the trees fell away.

Beyond the ridge, a city stretched—wide and broken, caught between the shadow of the jungle and the orange ember in the sky.

The trees parted like curtains, and the jungle gave way to ruin.

What had once been a city sprawled below them— unmistakably ancient, impossibly large. It had been a metropolis. Towering spires jutted from the canopy like broken teeth, wrapped in ivy and strangler fig. Moss carpeted collapsed roofs. Vines threaded through windowless husks. Walls slumped under the weight of time and trees.

It wasn't a place forgotten.

It was a place consumed.

Florence stopped beside Jacques, breath caught in her throat.

"It's... magnificent," she whispered.

And it was.

Even in decay, the architecture held power—grandeur weathered but unbroken. Arched bridges sagged over muddy canals. Towers leaned like drunks in prayer. Market plazas lay open to the sky, their stones cracked but still etched with glyphs worn soft by centuries.

Emerald stepped forward, her voice rising, breathless.

"What kind of civilization could have built this? And why here?"

Her gaze tracked the descending sun—now low in the southern sky, its rays slanting across the ruined stone like judgment. Each shadow fell long and flat behind them, casting spears across the rubble. Spears aimed at them.

Saturn said nothing at first. He stood motionless, NAVI humming quietly beside him. Then, at last:

"Proceed with caution. Ancient doesn't mean abandoned."

Jacques nodded. His eyes swept the city's borders—archways overgrown, gates collapsed, ramparts softened into green humps. Still, the wagon wheel pattern of the city planning was clear: the city had once known order. But no longer.

They pressed on.

Closer in, the signs of life became impossible to ignore.

Tracks in the mud. Patterns in the brush. And then: figures.

Not human. Not beast.

Reptilian bipeds emerged between the ruins, scaled and savage, adorned with crude armor of hammered iron and bone. Their movements were upright. Their posture predatory.

Sentient. But not civilized.

They had claimed the city.

And they wanted that known.

Beside ancient statues—weathered, noble, stone-carved in long-dead likenesses—stood newer effigies. Crude. Thicker of limb, heavier of jaw. Caricatures of the lizardmen themselves, cobbled from rubble and animal bones. They stood side by side with the older works, as if daring comparison.

We are here now. This is ours.

Jacques's gut twisted, recognizing the effigies for what they were.

They held position behind the ridge, concealed beneath low brush and the leaning ribs of a half-collapsed watchtower. The ruins ahead buzzed with practiced, lethargic movement—reptilian figures stalking through alleyways, clambering across broken stone with casual ownership.

Jacques crouched beside Florence, his eyes scanning every angle. NAVI rose with a whisper of rotor wash, darting skyward into a silent circuit above the ruins.

Saturn controlled it from the ridge, one gloved hand hovering acting as the interface. "No power grid," he murmured. "No tech, unless you count hammered metal and bone. Though, there does seem to be some artificial energy readings coming from somewhere in the city."

Florence said nothing. The stylus in her hand tapped erratically at the paper—short strokes, clipped loops—fury distilled into notation. Probably noting some inefficiency in the way the lizardmen were conducting their day-to-day routine.

Movement caught Jacques's eye.

Emerald had seated herself on a flat slab of stone, one boot bouncing, a smirk growing on her face. From her pack she produced a compact laser pointer—sleek, matte black, small enough to vanish in even her small fist.

She clicked it on.

A pinprick of red light danced across the stone between them.

U'gah's head snapped toward it—pupils flaring, muscles coiling.

Before Jacques could speak, U'gah launched.

A blur of child-like glee, he twisted midair, dirty hands pawing at the elusive dot. It vanished behind a rock, then reappeared on a pillar. U'gah followed—growling, leaping, landing with a thud that sent dust spiraling.

Emerald giggled, the sound quick and low. "Stars, he's so easy to bait."

Jacques folded his arms. One brow rose.

"Emerald."

She looked up, unbothered. "What? Let the guy play. He's earned it."

Her tone was light, almost flippant. But something in her grin told him this probably wasn't a good hill to die on.

Against his better judgement, Jacques exhaled slowly through his nose. "This isn't the place."

"No one's watching," she said, flicking the pointer off. "You're the one always talking about morale."

U'gah had stopped, crouched now atop a moss-covered column, smiling happily.

Jacques didn't argue. Not out loud.

But the smile he offered was paper-thin.

***

Florence pressed her back to a moss-covered wall, spine damp, clothes clinging from heat and anxiety. Her hands clutched the ledger with such force her fingers throbbed, knuckles white. The leather dug into her palms—familiar, worn. It was the only thing that made her feel safe.

Her gaze flicked across the plaza. Cracked flagstones and broken archways framed U'gah crouched atop a pillar— panting, pleased, a gargoyle perched waiting to pounce. Emerald sat nearby, spinning the laser pointer between her fingers as if it were a toy. She looked relaxed. Amused.

Florence's stomach twisted.

They were laughing. Playing.

Now?

The laughter grated—it didn't belong here, not in this dead city, a fanged mouth poised to snap shut.

She barely heard herself speak. "How can they play at a time like this?"

Her question settled like dust. No one answered. Maybe they hadn't heard.

The sky deepened. Purple bleeding into black. The last of the sun dissolved below the southern horizon, dragging the precious gold with it.

Florence's fingers twitched against the ledger.

The light was gone.

The one thing that had held back the dark.

A tremor passed through her, small at first. Then deeper. Not from cold. Not even fear.

But certainty.

The jungle had teeth. It had just been waiting. And now it would have them.

She looked again at U'gah—part bear, part child—and wished he would decide which. Even now he looked wrong, merely pretending to be some steroid-juiced child.

He wasn't a protector. He was another danger to her, to them, the others just hadn't figured it out yet.

Florence's breath stuttered. The edges of the plaza seemed to ripple.

She looked toward the underbrush.

U'gah growled.

Low. Deep. Not playful. Turning into that foul animalistic form of his.

Emerald froze, her hand still holding the pointer. The beam shut off. U'gah dropped from the column without a sound, body shifting from relaxed to coiled.

He stared into the brush.

The silence stretched, brittle and heavy.

Then Saturn broke it.

He ran.

Bursting from the undergrowth, eyes wide, mouth tight, every inch of him taut with purpose. No words. No pause.

Jacques rose like a spring uncoiled.

"What's wrong?" he called, voice hard-edged.

No answer.

The brush exploded.

Two lizardmen—scaled, armored, armed—crashed through the foliage. They were massive, hunched, jaws wide in war cries, spears raised.

Florence didn't think. She didn't breathe.

All she could do was scream.

The scream fractured the moment.

Florence stumbled, boots scraping stone. Hands flailed for balance. Her ledger slipped from her grasp and hit the dirt with a dull, final thud.

The square erupted.

U'gah was first—pure motion. A storm of fur and muscle launched toward the leftmost lizardman. His jaws closed around the creature's leg with a wet tearing sound. The force of it knocked the thing sideways, its spear spinning free.

Emerald shouted. Words lost in the chaos.

She scrambled for her carbine, hands fumbling the sling over her shoulder.

Jacques moved like a man who had done this before. No wasted motion. Sidearm drawn, raised, fired.

The first shot rang out, a hammer strike—too loud, too sudden.

The bullet struck the second lizardman's forehead—flattening against the ridged skull.

Blood leaked from the impact, but the creature didn't fall. It reeled, staggered—snarled. Its eyes, luminous and hateful, locked onto Jacques. The wound seeped, but it didn't slow the thing.

It came on.

U'gah snarled, wrestling his foe into the dirt. Claws tore at armor and scale, teeth sank deeper into thigh muscle. The pinned lizardman roared in agony, legs kicking, tail flailing on top of broken stone.

Florence couldn't move. Couldn't scream again. Her breath caught somewhere high in her chest and stayed there, shallow and useless. Suffocating.

Emerald finally got her rifle up and fired—a burst, tight and controlled. The rounds sparked against armor, biting at exposed seams. The creature flinched but kept moving, fast and low, spear raised.

Jacques fired again.

Another shot. Center mass denting the crude armor.

Again, the lizardman staggered but didn't fall.

U'gah, still locked with the first one, tore free a chunk of flesh and let out a guttural bark of triumph. Blood sprayed—dark and inky.

Florence tried to crawl, her hands scraping against moss-slick stone. Her legs wouldn't listen. She had somehow lost her footing in the confusion.

Every sound collapsed into a singularity of violent noise—gunfire, growls, steel on stone, bones crunching.

The world narrowed to a jumble of motion.

Emerald's voice snapped through the din, it sounded so small. "Cover left! Jacques—flank him!"

Jacques pivoted, boots slipping. The machete flashed in what little light remained. He lunged, blade arcing.

The machete bit deep.

The second lizardman hissed, blood spilling in thick ropes. It spun with surprising speed, claws raking air. Jacques ducked low, dropped a shoulder, slammed into it with the weight of years behind the motion.

They hit the stones hard. Jacques rolled clear.

Another shot cracked the air.

The creature lurched again—then fell.

Not dead. Stunned.

U'gah roared and surged toward it, claws first.

The square pulsed with chaos.

Saturn stepped forward—calm where the rest of them weren't. His fingers worked NAVI's controls without hesitation, as if tuning a machine in a lab instead of a war zone.

Above, the drone surged upward with a sudden whine as a third brute charged into the square.

Light bloomed.

A flash—blazing, blinding.

Flares exploded midair, magnesium-bright, scattering metallic chaff in a burst of static heat. For a second, everything was white.

The lizardmen shrieked.

They recoiled, clawing at their faces. One stumbled, speartip gouging stone, eyes squeezed shut against the fire. The other reeled blindly, slamming into a wall and dropping to its good knee.

U'gah didn't wait.

He lunged, teeth bared, a low growl rising into a brutal bark. His jaws clamped around one attacker's throat and crushed down.

There was a ragged gargle followed by a sudden stillness. Then silence—brief, staggering.

Florence barely registered it.

Her vision swam. The flares, the screams, the gunfire—it all collapsed into one pulsing orgy of sensation.

Emerald roared something wild and absurd: "Have a taste of copper-coated candy, you stupid casuals!"

Any other time she would have laughed, but her body had gone cold, numb.

So she watched in shock.

Emerald braced her carbine for another barrage, and fired. The rounds struck joints and gaps in armor, not enough to kill, but enough to hamper movement. The lizardman buckled, stumbling sideways.

NAVI zipped overhead, jets of air kicking dust into the air. Rotor wash battered the enemy's balance. One lizardman swung wildly, striking nothing.

Jacques didn't let the opening pass.

He closed fast. The machete came down in a single, vicious arc, carving through exposed muscle. Blood fanned out in a dark spray.

Another one down.

Florence pressed herself against the wall. Her eyes locked on the violence—on the dark arterial spatter, the ragged twitching limbs, the way U'gah moved like smoke with teeth drawing blood.

She couldn't breathe.

Saturn barked coordinates. Emerald reloaded. U'gah dove. Jacques moved through the wreckage of scale and sinew without pause.

Florence shook.

The world smeared into streaks. A scream rose in her throat, and she willed it free of her. But it stubbornly refused, mocking her, denying her the release of pressure.

The last lizardman moved like a wounded animal—half-blind, furious, swinging at ghosts.

It lunged for NAVI with a snarl, claws raking sky.

The drone darted clear.

Jacques turned, but before he could act, Emerald stepped forward calm now and centered.

"Green Fire never dies!" She yelled.

One shot.

Clean. Precise.

The round punched through the lizardman's eye with a wet snap. Its head jerked back. A spray of thick fluid arced into the dust.

It dropped without a sound.

Stillness followed.

No one moved.

Florence quickly scrambled for her ledger, wiping dust and dark fluids from it. Her chest heaved, breath coming in short, ragged bursts. The bodies were still there—sprawled, leaking, limbs twitching as her nerves surrendered to the gravity of what had transpired.

Gunfire still echoed in her skull, over and over.

She couldn't stop shaking.

Jacques turned to check the perimeter. Emerald lowered her rifle. Saturn was already logging environmental data, as if nothing extraordinary had just happened.

But Florence stood locked in place.

The ledger grounded her, but she couldn't seem to swallow.

She wanted to scream. Not out of fear—out of overload. There was too much. The gore. The bodies. The faces.

She looked down at the closest corpse.

Its eyes were still open.

Her knees buckled.

Florence was on her knees beside the corpse, her body rigid. Her breathing was shallow, uneven.

He approached slowly.

"Florence."

No answer.

He crouched beside her, one hand reaching gently for her shoulder.

She flinched hard—spun to her feet and shoved him, eyes wide, feral.

"Don't touch me!"

Her voice ripped through the shadows.

He backed off half a step, hands raised. "It's me."

"I know it's you." Her gaze snapped between him and the bodies. "I know exactly who you are."

The ledger slipped from her grasp and slapped flat against the stone.

"You promised we'd be safe," she said. "You said the light would lead us. You said we had to trust it."

Her voice rose with each word, tight with panic and fury. "And now there are bodies. There's blood. There's—"

She stopped. Words dried up. Her mouth worked, but nothing came.

Her face contorted. She twisted away and began to claw at her scalp with both hands, nails scraping into her hairline, eyes clenched shut.

"Make it stop. Make it stop, make it stop—"

Jacques moved in carefully and steady.

She shrieked. Swung. Nails slashed at the air. She kicked, sending loose rocks skittering.

He caught her wrists—not forcefully, just enough to contain the motion.

"Florence," Jacques soothed. "Florence, we're here. You're not alone."

"No!" she screamed. "You don't get to say that. You don't get to act like this is normal."

Florence's breath tore into a ragged sob. Her legs buckled fully. She collapsed forward into his arms, wailing with each broken breath.

Jacques held her.

She didn't cling—just trembled and cried.

Emerald and Saturn stood nearby, silent. Even U'gah, stained and breathing hard, said nothing. He only watched, head tilted, tail tucked behind him.

Jacques looked at no one.

He lifted her—gently.

He turned, cradling her dead weight, and walked toward the edge of the square.

Jacques stepped through the broken archway at the far end of the plaza, Florence cradled in his arms.

She didn't speak. Her head rested against his chest, hair matted with sweat and blood. Her fingers twitched, rhythmically to a sound not even she could hear.

He didn't look back.

The square lay behind them—quiet now. Bodies cooling in the dust. Weapons scattered. Stones stained black.

Mouth frozen mid-snarl, one of the lizardmen stared blankly toward the sunless sky.

Emerald shouldered her rifle and followed. Her face had gone hard. The playfulness was gone. Replaced with something cold, protective. Her boots hit the ground like punctuation.

Saturn came next. Wordless. His goggles blinked, still logging data, but his eyes stayed forward now.

U'gah was last. Blood dried on his muzzle, claws crusted. He passed the dead without hesitation, his bulk weaving through the wreckage as if he'd done it a hundred times.

They reformed behind Jacques without a word.

Ahead, the ruins deepened—alleys and broken corridors narrowing into dark mouths. Vines swallowed unreadable signage. Doors hung from broken hinges. Archways bent like deformed spines. No voices waited. No wind. Just passageways full of forgotten memories.

But they had to keep moving.

So they did.

CHAPTER FOUR

Jacques moved through the dusk-draped city, steps measured, boots whispering over slime-slick stone and patches of spongy soil. The shattered walls loomed overhead—serrated silhouettes carved into the pallid glow of a star-pocked sky—ribs of a long-dead, overgrown giant.

His heart pounded with that hyper-focused anticipation before violence. Every nerve lit, every sense tuned to the city's hush. Darkness hid whatever waited in the ruins—hid him as well. A trade he'd take.

He stayed in the margins, threading through stray trees, half-toppled pillars, shattered archways. Each movement a possible death sentence, thumb brushing the pistol grip. He could feel the city: its age, its silence, its unseen eyes.

Still—hope. Saturn's crisp briefing echoed in memory, NAVI's feed overlaying the map behind his eyes: a breach in the eastern interior wall. Not a grand gate, but a fracture. Their fracture.

A dry, amused smile tugged at his mouth. A lost city on a hidden continent. A corridor of impossible sunlight. Now he was stalking reptilian soldiers under a starlit sky. It could've been a fever dream. And yet, deep down, something quiet and wordless insisted: this was the way.

Urgency pushed him forward. And yes—he was relieved, guiltily, to be apart from the others. Florence teetered; Emerald's steadiness and Saturn's precision were the right shields for her. And U'gah—small, but steadfast. Jacques trusted that wild strength to guard what his own hands couldn't —not when he was needed elsewhere.

He reached the eastern wall, its massive blocks rising, vertebrae carved from weathered basalt. His hooded LED skimmed the pitted surface. Fingers traced a seam.

"Stress fractures," he murmured. The angles were wrong—two planes pressed together where they shouldn't be. Gaps spider-webbed along the joint: some wafer-thin, others wide enough to peer through.

Two, maybe three shaped charges would split it without collapse. The solution unfolded in his head, a plan he'd already run a thousand times, in a thousand different scenarios.

Suddenly, an unexpected tug at his sleeve.

He spun, instinct kicking in—left hand darting to the machete, right hand hovering over the pistol.

A face—wide black eyes glossy in the half-light, shadows cutting across sharp features.

Emerald.

His breath caught mid-throat, then released in a silent exhale. Pulse thundered in his ears, drowning the hush.

She raised a finger to her lips—holding back a giggle. Her other hand hovered open-palmed—slow, steadying. Easy.

Jacques froze. The tension drained from his shoulders in slow degrees, as if pressure bleeding from a hydraulic line.

"Emerald?" he hissed—sharp, frayed by adrenaline. His hands dropped, but not far. His heart hadn't slowed.

"What the hell are you doing here?" he whispered harshly. "You are supposed to be with the others."

Her eyes glittered in the dark. Her lips pressed thin.

She didn't answer at first.

Then, softly—"We lost U'gah."

The words barely registered.

Lost U'gah.

His mouth dried. The map vanished from his mind. Only those two words remained, echoing in the tight chamber of his chest.

"What?" It came out rough.

Emerald's face shifted. The usual glint—her humor, her spark —was gone.

She stepped closer, boots gritting softly over broken stone.

"We were trying to calm Florence down," she said cautiously. "You know how she's been… unstable."

She looked away, jaw clenched. She swallowed hard.

"Saturn thought she might've hurt herself. He took out his flashlight—to check for blood, I think."

Jacques exhaled sharply, pinching the bridge of his nose. His fingers trembled. He felt it: patience fraying at the edges, snapping under the weight of what he already knew.

Of course.

He could see it clearly now—a memory already written.

"Let me guess," he muttered, flat. A sigh threaded through the words. His eyes closed for just a moment, long enough to shoulder the weight of inevitability.

"He asked U'gah to hold the light for him."

Emerald nodded.

"Yeah," she said. Her hands twitched at her sides in a helpless, frustrated gesture. "At first, fine—U'gah just held it. Then he started turning it over, twisting it in his hands…"

Jacques clenched his jaw. The muscle in his cheek jumped.

"And?" he asked, already bracing for it.

Emerald let out a breath—half groan, half sigh—pressure bleeding through the cracks.

"And then he figured out how to focus the beam."

Jacques arched a brow. The disbelief in his face barely masked the deeper, bone-deep fatigue.

"And let me guess... he thought he'd discovered some form of magic?"

Emerald nodded grimly. "More or less. He started waving it around, shining it at everything like a kid with a sparkler." She sighed. "And... he ignited some dried leaves."

Jacques rubbed his forehead, fingers gritty with sweat and dust. His brow twitched—just enough to betray the *why me* curling at the base of his spine.

"Of course he did," he muttered, resigned to the absurdity he knew was coming next.

Emerald lifted a finger.

"Wait. It gets better. Or worse, depending on how you look at it."

Jacques shot her a look—a warning. One he already knew she wouldn't heed.

She took a breath, as if she needed to brace herself for the rest.

"He started leaping around," she said slowly. "Yelling 'Agi, Agi!' at the top of his lungs."

Jacques blinked. "Agi?"

Emerald nodded, her mouth a thin, grim line. "Agi."

Jacques exhaled, slow and steady, as if releasing the last dregs of sanity from his lungs. His fingers dragged down his face, catching on stubble, tugging at the corners of his mouth.

"So let me get this straight," he muttered, as if saying it too loud might summon worse things. "U'gah... after discovering how to focus a flashlight beam... decided he'd unlocked fire magic, shouted '*Agi,* and ran off."

Emerald's mouth twitched. She bit her lip hard enough to leave an imprint, but nodded. "With the flashlight held above his head like a club."

Jacques just stared at her. Re-evaluating every life choice that had led to this moment.

He turned slowly toward the looming city—dark, ancient, and alive with silent menace. Rubbed his temples with slow, massaging circles.

"Of course he did," he sighed—carrying the weight of too many of course-he-dids in one lifetime.

Emerald let out a quiet, choked snort, barely holding back the laughter.

"So..." she said, cautious, skirting the edge of a potential minefield. "What's the plan?"

"We find him before the lizardmen do." His gaze slicing across the ruins as if he could see around corners. "And we pray to whatever gods might be listening that he hasn't started a war or gotten himself killed."

Emerald's smirk flared in the dim light—a flash of teeth that didn't quite reach her eyes. "Oh, so we're back to divine intervention?"

Jacques shot her a look—flat, deadpan. "I'm nothing if not consistent."

The words hung in the still air. A brittle attempt at humor, but the dread beneath it gnawed, steady and insistent.

He knew U'gah meant well. Always did. But good intentions wouldn't stop a spear. And right now, his little friend was probably out there waving that damned flashlight like a torch, yelling incantations into the dark—making himself a beacon for every scaled bastard within earshot.

"Merde!"

"We need to find him." The words came through clenched teeth.

His gaze snapped to Emerald. "Can you track him?"

Her expression tightened as she considered. The humor bled out of her face.

"If he's still carrying the flashlight, we might be able to catch sight of the beam."

"Are Florence and Saturn safe? We can't drag them into this." Was the only other question he needed answered, before committing to something any normal person would deem insane.

"They're fine. We found a stone substructure near the edge of the clearing—looks like an old cellar. It's dry—and hidden."

"Bon." He didn't let the tension leave his body. Couldn't. Not with U'gah out there. Not with the city looming like a mouth waiting to close. But something in his gut, some deep instinct, told him this chaos wasn't an accident. It felt too engineered.

Jacques gave a nod, more to himself than to her. Then knelt and unbuckled the straps on his pack. The scent of nylon, sweat, and gun oil rose as he pulled the flap open and began searching by feel—familiar motions, muscle memory from another life. Fingers passed over mags, coiled wire, the leather hilt of a spare field knife—

There.

He drew three shaped charges from the pack. Matte casings. Compact. Familiar. They caught the faint gleam of lamplight as he turned them over, checking the seals, the primers, the integrity of the wiring.

Emerald eyed them. "Shaped charges?" Her voice was curious but edged. "You planning to blow our way in?"

Jacques gave a small grunt—half laugh, half disbelief.

"Maybe," he said, letting the word roll slow in the dark. "A little controlled demolition might be exactly what we need to find a door."

His fingers tapped the casing—three soft knocks. Thinking.

"And maybe it makes just enough noise to draw attention away from U'gah."

Emerald's eyes lit. She nodded slowly, smirk spreading as if a fuse being lit. "Clever," she said—soft, but with something real behind it. Admiration. A little unease.

"So I guess there really is a reason they call you Jacques le Blew."

Jacques didn't answer.

He turned back to the wall, focus narrowing like a beam. The charges felt heavier now.

He knelt again, bracing one hand against cool stone, reading every seam, every fracture a map. This was what he knew. What made sense. His pulse found rhythm. Each placement became a calculation.

Behind him, Emerald shifted, her gear making the faintest rustle. "You could probably get away with just two," she murmured. A suggestion.

Jacques paused.

Then glanced back—just enough to let the mask of amusement ghost across his face.

"Perhaps," he conceded. "But I prefer to err on the side of caution."

He secured the last charge with a firm press, then glanced over his shoulder, tone slipping into that dry, sardonic register he favored when the odds turned impossible.

"Besides," he added, a glint in his eye, "as they say in the Legion—*Trop, c'est jamais assez.* Too much is never enough."

Emerald let out a low chuckle, the sound a soft trill through the tension. "I've never heard that one before," she said, shaking her head. There was an edge of incredulity in her voice. "But it sounds exactly like something you'd make up."

Jacques shrugged. "It's the first rule of warfare." His fingers moved without pause—nimble, sure, muscle memory carrying the task even as his thoughts cycled through contingencies. "Strangely enough," he murmured, almost to himself, "I can think of at least forty-two 'first rules of warfare.' And—most of them contradict each other."

He smiled, but the expression passed quickly—just a flicker of teeth and fatigue.

He finished the check: connections aligned, filaments seated, fuses primed. Every inch of it double-checked.

He rose slowly, sweeping the placements with a final, measured glance. The seam gleamed faintly in the hooded lamplight, charges nestled against ancient stone, teeth waiting to bite.

He tilted his head, judged the lines, the angle, the tension.

Satisfied, a grin tugged at one corner of his mouth—wolfish.

"There," he said quietly, voice calm but edged with steel. "That should do the trick."

"Now," he added, tone sharpening, "we find cover. Before the show starts."

He nodded toward a crumbled wall away from the blast radius. A trench slumped behind it—half-choked with debris, root-veined and narrow, but it would do.

Emerald's smile faded. The moment caught up—the weight of what they were doing, the risks riding it. When she spoke, her voice had thinned.

"Right."

They dropped into the trench and pressed flat. The ground was cool, damp. Moss and earth filled his lungs. He breathed deep, steadying against the pulse that throbbed in his ears. Emerald lay beside him, head low, fingers over her ears.

Jacques armed the detonator. The switch clicked under his thumb.

The world tore open.

A blinding flash carved the dark, white-hot and merciless. The jungle etched itself into negative space behind Jacques's eyes. Then the sound came—a thunderclap from the pit of the earth, swallowing itself in layers.

The wall ruptured.

The trench heaved beneath them. A concussive wall of force hammered down, stealing the air from Jacques's lungs, flattening him to the dirt. The ground screamed. Dust avalanched in fat clumps, stinging skin, clogging ears. Trees shook. Leaves rained.

Shrapnel sliced past—jagged, angry. Stone hissed through the air. One piece skipped off the far trench wall with a shriek.

The blast wave hit his chest like a battering ram. For a moment, there was only weight and pressure and heat.

For a moment, it felt familiar.

Teeth clenched, hands buried in earth, Jacques held on until the quake in his body eased.

Dust boiled around them—thick, choking, abrasive. It clawed at his throat, coated his tongue in grit. He coughed hard, dry and sharp. Emerald hacked into her sleeve, swiping grime from her face with the back of her wrist.

He pressed his back to the trench wall. The cold, damp earth steadied him. His heart still pounded—fast and eager. Adrenaline surged through his limbs.

The detonator still sat warm in his palm.

The dust began to thin, settling in lazy curls.

And there it was.

The seam had split—gaping, jagged, enough for two men to pass through shoulder to shoulder. The edges still hissed with heat. Stone crumbled in lazy drips from the fractured mouth.

The path was open.

Jacques let out a whoop, grin breaking wide across his face.

"Voilà!" he shouted, teeth flashing. "Our way is open!"

They stayed low, the damp biting through their clothes. The explosion's echo pulsed through the ruins.

And then—other sounds rose.

Panicked voices. Shouts. Movement in the dark.

A horn cut through the noise—low, mournful, rising like smoke.

They remained crouched low in the trench, holding their breath as they listened for signs of pursuit.

None came.

The echo of the horn faded, swallowed by the ruined city's silence. Still, they waited—tense, patient, reading the quiet like a live wire. Only after several minutes did Jacques shift his weight and peer over the trench lip.

After a long stretch, Jacques dared to shift. He eased upward, just enough to peer above the trench's lip, eyes narrowing as he scanned the shadows.

Nothing.

"I think we're clear," he murmured, voice a low rasp, barely above a whisper. He met Emerald's gaze.

A quick nod passed between them. Jacques moved first, boots brushing gravel as they crossed toward the breach.

Dust hung in thin veils, drifting through broken stones, catching the low moonlight and the muted glow of his hooded lamp. The air tasted of scorched earth and pulverized stone.

What met them beyond the wall was not what they'd expected.

The breach had torn open part of a structure pressed flush against the interior wall—its side split by the blast, edges still crumbling. What stood beyond was a stark, brutal cube built from massive diorite slabs—dark, clean-cut, fitted with impossible precision. The sheer weight and geometry of it clashed violently with the paler limestone and crumbling masonry of the outer city.

They crept closer, boots silent on broken stone, eyes scanning both shadow and structure. The air here felt denser, charged with something weightier than dust.

Then—a *thud*. Low. Felt more than heard. It pulsed through Jacques's boots, climbed his spine, and settled deep in his chest. Dust spilled from the seams between stones, spiraling upward in thin, drifting threads.

Emerald froze, wide-eyed, every muscle wound tight—prey that had just sensed a predator.

Another *thud*.

Louder.

This time, it came with a grinding shriek—stone dragging against stone. A long, grating scrape that turned Jacques's stomach. He clenched his jaw, fists curling on instinct.

One of the diorite blocks shifted. Not much. Just enough to betray intent. Just enough to scream.

A third impact.

Heavier.

The ground trembled. Loose stones skittered across the fractured flagstones. A block the size of a wagon—larger, even —was being pushed outward, the face of a tomb forced open from inside.

Jacques went still. Ice locked his veins. The certainty hit him as if being plunged into black water: this wasn't excavation.

This was emergence.

Emerald's hand clamped onto his arm, hard enough to bruise. Her voice, when it came, was a ragged whisper. "What was that?"

He couldn't answer. His throat seized. The words tried to come but scattered like bats hit with a spotlight. He could feel her panic bleeding into him, her grip trembling against his skin.

No time to think. No time to explain.

They fell back—stumbling, half-running on instinct—scrambling for the trench. The earth met them hard and wet, its cool weight anchoring Jacques as he curled into the dirt.

His heart hammered. His breath snagged. He pressed low.

They listened.

Every nerve strained, tuned for the next sound.

And it came.

The grinding continued—but resounding over the rasp of stone —a deep, slow *graaaaah* that rasped through the earth like tectonic breath. Each rotation of that slab sent another jolt of dread through Jacques's body, locking his thoughts in place.

Emerald's voice reached him through the haze—thin, muffled by the trench wall and kicked-up grit. "What is it?" she asked again, barely audible above the shifting stone and groaning tremors.

Jacques shook his head—afraid to look away. His mind spun through theories, none of them holding.

"Je ne sais pas," he whispered. The words just barely ghosting past his clenched teeth.

Not a roar like a lion's. The sound warped—amplified, stretched—closer to a mountain cat, but more resonant. It ripped through the air, shrieking across the ruins, a sound born of nightmares. A thing meant for the dark, primal places humans were never meant to tread.

Every muscle locked. His heart slammed against his ribs, trying to escape—smarter than the rest of him.

A final, earth-shaking impact. The ground buckled beneath them. Loose branches and dead leaves rained down in a slow, mocking fall, sifting through the air like ash, dusting their backs and hair.

Silence followed. Long enough to hope.

Then the crack—sharp and splintering.

More followed. Not one sound, but many. A rapid-fire chain of fractures. Hundreds of them.

The diorite groaned. The main slab swung outward, a titanic stone door, shearing open on an unseen hinge. A jagged fragment—still massive—snapped free, rode the arc, and slammed against the city wall before tumbling across the jungle floor, finally settling just meters away. The impact thundered through the ruins, shaking ancient masonry, rattling earth and sky. Pebbles rained from overhead, peppering them in loose bursts.

Jacques doubled over, coughing hard. Tears stung as he wiped his face. Each breath burned, scraped raw as it clawed through his chest.

Beside him, Emerald choked into her sleeve, rubbing grit from her eyes, both of them half-submerged in the suspended haze.

And then—it emerged.

What stepped from the swirl of dust was like nothing he'd ever seen.

It loomed backlit against the fractured moonlight—titanic, bipedal, coiled in the mass and menace of myth. Not bestial. Not human. Wrapped in sleek, banded fur that shimmered faintly with every breath.

The shape of it was feline—rounded head, low snout, a maw full of glinting, polished dagger-teeth.

It stood still, breathing slow and deep, a low rumble emanating from its chest like a faultline shifting.

His breath stalled—caught between terror and reverent dread.

He didn't know what it was.

But it wasn't a beast.

He and Emerald inched closer, unable to stop themselves. The loose dirt shifted beneath Jacques's fingertips as he eased up, heart hammering in his ears. His veteran eyes fixed on the thing, now fully visible in the clearing.

It was a predator. That much was certain. But not a wild one.

Each movement radiated physical power. With the kind of grace that only came from confidence—ownership of its environment.

Its shoulders rolled as it turned. Muscles shifted beneath its skin in long, fluid arcs. Jacques felt the motion before he even saw it—a ripple in the air.

Then the eyes.

Dieu. Those eyes.

Amber, reflective. They caught the light in lethal, molten flashes and swept the ruins with surgical focus—missing nothing. Not even the smallest shift.

When the gaze passed over Jacques, he felt it, almost a physical pressure. A weight settling against his sternum.

Then the head turned. The snout lifted. Nostrils flared wide. It inhaled—long, rasping breaths that grated like the slab of diorite it had just displaced. A sharp flurry of snorts. Then a sudden, guttural sneeze—mist and spittle catching moonlight in a glittering arc before vanishing into dust.

And then, it spoke.

"No... threat... Ya-ta," it rasped. The accent was wrong. The words misshapen. But it was English. Reverent. Similar to a child reporting to a parent.

It spoke. It understood.

Jacques shot a look at Emerald. She mirrored his disbelief, wide-eyed and pale, lips parted in silent *are you seeing this too?*

He looked back.

The urge to run hit him like fire. Primal. Brutal. Every part of him screamed: *Go.* His hand twitched toward the machete at his thigh. The handle waited in his palm.

But he didn't move.

Not out of fear, but out of some morbid certainty.

The sense that the world had just opened its mouth to say something no one had ever heard—and he couldn't look away.

And then—

From the darkness behind the beast, another figure stepped forward.

A man.

Or something that wore the shape of one.

He walked into the silver light, and Jacques felt it—a crackle in the air, electric.

The man's clothes hung in tatters, rags clinging to a body half-consumed by famine. Ribs jutted sharp beneath skin stretched too tight. His face—sunken, hollowed. Cheeks drawn. Eyes shadowed.

But his posture—that was power.

He didn't stumble. He didn't cower.

He strode.

And then Jacques saw his eyes as if they were gaining intensity, feeding off of the moonlight.

Blue.

And they gripped his soul.

Not just blue—piercing. Bright and clear, the color of desert skies seen through a shimmer of heat. They glowed faintly, unnaturally—light pulsing brighter the longer he stood in the open.

And behind that glow: depth. A history etched into every glance, every slight tilt of the head. Triumph. Loss. Rage. Pain.

Jacques felt like the gravity of this man could crush him if he gave in to it.

The man's gaze swept across them—Jacques, Emerald, the trench—measuring, evaluating. Then it shifted to the beast.

And something passed between them.

Unspoken. A command. A bond.

His fingers crept toward the machete, instinct guiding his reach. His heart pounded so hard he was sure Emerald could hear it.

A glint in the man's eyes made him pause.

Almost a challenge. Almost a dare.

Jacques hesitated, the blade half-drawn. His hand felt distant. Numb.

He should've run. Should've struck. Should've done *something*.

Instead, he released the weapon and asked—his words almost lost in the hammer of his pulse, carried only by the silence between them.

"Who are you?"

CHAPTER FIVE

U'gah tore through the stone maze, paws scraping cracked earth. Walls loomed—cold, dead, older than memory —pressing close like the ribs of a buried beast. Above, Grandfather Brightrock glowed vast and watchful, but down here it was dark—cave-dark.

He gripped the skyfire club, warm metal against palms. The eye blinked—whirr-click—spilling a spear of white. Shadows fled, only to creep back, licking the edges. Hungry, waiting. He felt them.

He grinned—teeth flashing, ears pinned forward. Let them watch. Let them try.

Firefly-in-the-Sky needed something from the big hut. Shiny things? Magic things? U'gah didn't know. Didn't care. Firefly had shared food. Had given warmth. Had treated U'gah like a friend.

So U'gah ran.

He skidded around a corner, claws scrabbling for purchase on the worn stone. The walls reared high, smooth and cold, smelling of dust and old air.

A chitter. Sharp, fast. Like teeth clicking bone.

U'gah froze. Fur bristled.

Two sets of eyes gleamed in the dark—small, bright. Reflected in the glow of the skyfire. Twin sparks caught just outside the beam.

U'gah's ears flattened. A low growl bubbled from his chest. His teeth bared, sharp and white.

The chittering swelled—skittering screeches clawing his ears.

He snarled. Raised the skyfire club high. Twisted the dial.

The eye snapped open—click-click-BZZZT—flooding searing white.

The eyes shrieked and vanished, recoiling into the black.

U'gah grinned—a fierce, toothy, hunter's grin. His tail lashed. Blood beat hard in his limbs. He had chased them off. He had won.

His chest swelled.

He ran again. Faster. The beam bounced ahead, making the stone twist and leap in wild shapes. The air sharpened—stone, dust, and the sour stink of fear.

He rounded another corner—

And stopped.

Hard.

A wall. Not of stone.

Of scales.

Three of them.

Scaly-skins.

Big. Thick-chested. Spiked armor strapped across their bodies. Weapons in clawed hands. Eyes narrow, slitted, hungry. The skyfire lit their faces, but they didn't flinch. They watched. They waited.

U'gah's grin vanished. His ears pinned flat.

Not ghosts. Not shadows. Hunters.

They hissed. Jaws spread, rows of hooked teeth glistening in the light.

U'gah's grip tightened on the club.

He snapped the dial.

The eye flared brighter—brighter still—until it hurt to look. But the scaly-skins didn't run.

They stepped forward.

U'gah's mind spun. Light had chased shadows. Would it chase these?

He raised the club higher, willing it to roar. To blind. To burn.

He hoped.

Hope was thin when hunters closed in.

His paws trembled as he twisted the dial again. The eye flared wide—a burst of captured sun. The shadows leapt. Banished— just for a moment.

The scaly-skins flinched, pupils shrinking into slits. The light flashed off armor ridges, off the slick curve of fangs.

But they didn't turn. Didn't flee.

They snarled.

Clawed hands flexed, then reached. Hooked talons gleamed in the glare.

One lunged.

Air rushed as its claws sliced through the space where U'gah's head had been a breath before. He ducked, rolled—tight and low—fur brushing stone.

Missed.

But close.

His ears flattened, tail lashing in panic.

Why didn't it work?

The skyfire club's magic—it was supposed to work. It made the bad spirits vanish. Made the dark things hiss and shrink and melt away. The light was power. U'gah had believed it was enough.

But the scaly-skins—the hunters—they didn't melt.

They came forward.

Firefly-in-the-Sky's magic? Maybe something protected them.

U'gah couldn't fight. Not all of them. Not now.

With a strangled squeak, he ran.

Legs pumping, claws scraping stone. The skyfire beam bounced wild across walls, shadows twisting like hungry ghosts.

Behind him—hissing, sharp and furious. Heavy footfalls slamming into the earth. Chasing. Closing.

But U'gah knew stone forests. He knew the turns. The narrow places. The trick-paths that twisted in on themselves.

He zigged left through a gap barely wider than his body, fur scraping rough stone. Zagged right. Paws scattered loose pebbles. His heart thudded like a hummingbird's wings.

The scaly-skins crashed after him, their snarls warped by the maze.

He couldn't keep this up. His breath burned in his chest. Legs ached. Ears twitched at every shift of sound.

He needed to lose them. To warn the others. They had to know: the light didn't work.

U'gah dove into a crack just wider than his shoulders, squirming through, claws dragging furrows in the dust. Jagged edges pulled at his fur, tore at his skin, but he shoved forward, chest tight.

He pressed flat to the wall. The stone was cold against his back. The skyfire club's light dimmed, its beam reduced to a pale glow that barely touched the far side of the narrow crawlspace.

The sounds of the hunt—closer… then fainter.

Fainter still.

U'gah's ears twitched. Straining. Waiting for the next hiss, the next step.

Silence.

Only his heartbeat.

A long, shaky sigh rattled out of him. Relief slid into the hollow terror—thin, sharp.

But he was foolish. He couldn't stay here, flattened like a dead thing. His friends were still out there. Hunted.

Stone forests were too big to run forever. He needed a place. A den. Somewhere to think. It took him a moment to realize that's exactly what he had found.

A mouth, low and dark, breathing damp air. Earth-smell. Root-smell. Forgotten-place smell.

He slipped inside.

Cool air pressed close. Damp against his nose. The tunnel sloped down. The walls narrowed.

The skyfire club lit the stone in thin ribbons. Shadows wavered like smoke.

U'gah slowed. The tunnel opened.

A chamber.

Rough-hewn, wet stone walls. Slick and ancient. A crack in the ceiling let in a shaft of moonlight—Grandfather's glow, pale and silver, cold against the black.

A pool of water lay in the center. Still as glass. It mirrored the light like a second moon.

U'gah crept to the edge, ears pinned.

The reflection wasn't his.

It looked like him. But smaller. Ragged. Fur matted. Eyes wide and clouded with fear. Chest heaving too fast. Too small for this place. Too soft.

Beyond the reflection.

Beneath the shimmer of Grandfather's glow, the pool changed.

It widened. Deepened. Became something more than water.

A stone basin—carved, ancient. Its edges rough. Not natural. Built. Shaped. Something—someone—had made this.

From the center rose a stone tree. Twisted limbs—roots and branches tangled—each cradling a basin that caught water like petals catch rain.

And there—atop the highest bough—rested a club.

Not like the skyfire stick.

More.

It gleamed faintly in the silver light, its surface lined with glowing marks—embers etched in spirals and old, old shapes. The head wasn't blunt stone. It was carved—sculpted into the snarling face of a spear-toothed Earthshaker. The beast from the stories. The hunter. The Old One.

The air around it buzzed. Thick. Crackling. A hum in U'gah's ears, like wind through roots. Like thunder from a distant storm.

His fur bristled. Every hair on end. A tremor raced down his spine—part fear, part... *something else.*

Could this be a weapon of the Old Ones? A gift? A true weapon?

His paws itched. His tail lashed. His heart pounded.

He couldn't leave it.

He wouldn't.

Steeling himself, he clambered onto the rim of the stone pond, claws scrabbling against the slick surface. His breath hissed through his teeth as he slipped into the water—so cold it stole the air from his lungs, bit into his skin. He paddled hard, paws chopping water, eyes fixed on the club.

He didn't blink.

The water lapped at the stone tree as he neared. The glow from the club pulsed—vibrated—with the rhythm of his heartbeat. Light caught the ripples, turning them into veins of silver that danced across his soaked fur.

His paws found the base of the tree. Claws scraped for purchase as he climbed—higher, higher—the air thinning, colder now, like the slope of a snow-capped mountain. His limbs ached, but the club called.

At the top, he paused—shaking, chest heaving, water dripping from his whiskers. The club loomed before him, glowing soft. The Earthshaker's carved eyes caught the light—watching.

U'gah's paw trembled as he reached out.

His pads brushed the smooth, worn handle—

And a jolt.

Heat.

It surged through him—flooding warmth that chased out the cold, searing down his limbs, swelling in his chest until it ached. His heart hammered. His grip tightened. The markings flared, shadows writhing across the chamber walls.

U'gah's tail lashed. A low, wild growl rolled from his throat.

This was a weapon. A gift. A promise.

He grinned—toothy and fierce.

And for the first time since the chase began, U'gah didn't feel like prey.

He felt like a hunter.

He scrambled from the pool, water streaming in cold rivulets, paws slapping wet stone. The club—*his* club—was heavy, but not unwieldy. It felt right. Balanced. Solid.

He hefted it, testing the weight. The head shifted as he gripped it, but didn't falter. It sat in his palms like it belonged there— like it had always been his.

U'gah swung it in a wide arc—*whoosh*—air splitting clean around the carved stone maw. A thrill shot through him, from muzzle to tail. The power wasn't just his. It was in the weapon. And when he moved, it moved with him—like a claw grown from the bone of the world.

The chamber trembled. A low, grinding pulse thrummed through the floor. The walls seemed to inhale. Water rippled in slow, even pulses.

The club in his hands—*surged*.

The markings flared—bright, sudden—fire through dry grass.

A voice.

Not a sound, but a pressure. In his skull. Through his blood. It spoke without speaking, words sinking into him like heat into stone.

Hunger... I... hunger!

His eyes went wide. Pupils blown, fur bristling. His tail lashed —*crack!*—against the stone.

He staggered, chest heaving. The voice hit like a blow.

The club slipped from his hands. It struck the stone with a dull *thunk*, glow dimming, markings fading to faint scars.

U'gah dropped to all fours, claws scraping for balance, breath shallow, gaze fixed.

That voice—it wasn't the ancestors. Not wind in the leaves. Not warmth in the dark.

This was older.

It smelled of blood. Of shattered bone. Of deep earth and long hunger.

His fur stood on end.

Was it the club?

Or was it the spirit of the Earthshaker itself, trapped inside the stone, waiting... waiting for someone to listen?

U'gah didn't know. But he felt it. The pull.

He reached for the club, paws shaking.

The moment his fingers closed around the worn handle, the voice surged back—louder, closer, curling through his thoughts like smoke through a hollow tree.

Hunger... Feed me!

The words bit deep, a predator's growl in his chest.

His breath shivered out of him. He knew now. Knew what the club wanted—what it needed.

Not just a weapon. Not just a thing. But a *living* thing.

And what did it crave?

The image slammed hot and whole: scaly flesh torn in Earthshaker jaws, blood spraying, bones shattering like dry twigs.

That was its hunger.

And now—it was his.

A wild grin split him. Teeth flashed in the dark.

This was a key.

A key to power older than forests, older than sky-stone and skyfire. A power that would make him strong—strong like the Earthshaker. Strong enough to crush scaly-skins beneath his paws and grind them into dust.

He hefted the club. It thrummed in his grip, the markings pulsing with a rhythm that matched his own racing heart. It felt aware—alive—rising to meet his hunger with hunger of its own.

Hunger... feed me...

81

His pulse surged. His veins felt thicker—hot with a fire not entirely his. The club's craving had become his craving. And he would feed it. Oh yes, he would.

For his friends, he would kill the scaly-skins. And after that—the children of the Mother.

He would be the hunter. He would be the vengeance.

***

U'gah emerged from the cave mouth and re-entered the stone maze.

But it no longer felt like a maze.

It felt like a hunting ground.

The hesitation that had gnawed at him earlier was gone—burned away by the heat rising in his chest. The twisting paths? His. The shadows? His cloak. The scaly-skins who thought they ruled this place?

Prey.

His ears twitched. His nose flared, catching the sour musk of lizard-kin on the wind, cutting through the jungle's night air.

His pupils shrank, glowing faintly in the dark. Adrenaline surged.

Every sense sharpened—bristling, burning.

The club pulsed in his grip, warmth alive beneath his pads. The glow along its carvings whispered in the dark.

I... hunger... feed me...

His breath steadied. His pulse didn't.

It thundered beneath his skin, so loud he swore they must hear it.

But they didn't.

The scaly-skins muttered in their guttural tongue, voices echoing through the corridor—harsh clicks, low growls, the scrape of claws and the clink of weapons.

U'gah's lips peeled back in a silent snarl.

He dropped low and melted into shadow.

He pressed to a corner in the wall, club ready, markings dim but steady.

U'gah peeked just a glimpse, a sliver of one eye around the stone.

And there they were.

Three of them.

Huddled together, backs turned. Scales glinting faintly in the dark.

Unaware. Unaware of him. Unaware of death.

The club's pulse surged—*Now... **now...***

U'gah's grin stretched wider.

He crept forward, belly low to the stone. His heart pounded— not with fear. Not anymore.

This was something else. Something dark and hungry.

A need.

The club thrummed in his grip, its pulse matching his own. The glow of its markings was warm against his paws, heat seeping into his skin, into his blood. It whispered—not in words, but with a low, steady hum. A promise. A hunger that curled into his own.

He could taste it.

Prey.

Scaly-skin musk mingled with stone dust and the dry stink of ancient air. His nostrils flared. Ears twitched.

He shifted his weight onto the balls of his feet.

U'gah drew a long, shivering inhale, feeling the power of the Earthshaker coil inside him—dense, steady, rooted like a mountain.

Then—he roared.

The sound tore from his chest—raw and feral—rattling the corridor walls.

His paws slammed forward, claws sparking off the stone. The club rose—high, higher—then came down.

The scaly-skins spun, hissing, eyes wide, jaws open in a sharp-toothed rage.

U'gah didn't stop.

He brought the club down hard—aiming for the nearest warrior's leg.

It should have been clumsy. Too heavy. Too much for him.

But the moment the club hit, everything changed.

He felt it shift—grind, click, *snarl*. The Earthshaker's head twitched—stone plates sliding with a snick.

And then—

The jaws opened.

And bit.

Not a strike. Not a smash. A bite.

A wet squelch tore through the corridor. Flesh ripped. Sinew snapped.

The scaly-skin screamed—high and jagged.

U'gah's eyes went wide.

The club hadn't just broken the leg. It had *eaten* it.

Chunks of flesh tore loose, shredded between stone teeth. Blood sprayed hot and slick, spattering stone and fur. The sound—crunching, grinding—filled the narrow space. It twisted his gut even as it lit fire in his blood.

The warrior collapsed, howling at the ruined stump—eyes wide, mouth gaping.

The others froze—stunned. Shock cracked the air.

Then came the snarls. Louder. Furious.

He stared at the thing in his hands.

It pulsed—low and steady.

That—that wasn't supposed to happen.

The jaws twitched—stone grinding. A wet sheen clung to its teeth. Blood trickled into the grooves—dark and thick—sliding into the carvings like sap down bark.

The scent of hot iron hit his nose.

Hunger... more.

The whisper slid through his mind like oil. Not words—need. It wrapped around his ribs and curled tight in his spine.

The club was alive.

And it was his.

His ears twitched—scales rustling, claws scraping nearby.

The club pulsed in his grip—warm, steady. It watched with him. Waited with him.

Hungry.

U'gah tightened his grip.

His eyes narrowed. Pupils retracted to pinpoints. Ears pinned forward.

He could smell them. Taste them. The sour bite of fear just beneath the rage.

The club thrummed, its pulse rising with his own.

Feed me...

It thundered—drum-deep. Loud enough that surely the scaly-skins could hear it too.

But they didn't.

They muttered in their harsh tongue, clicks and growls echoing through the stone. Claws scraped. Armor creaked.

U'gah's lips peeled back in a silent snarl.

Run or hide—it didn't matter. This was their culling.

The hunt was on.

**

The man's gaze lingered on Jacques and Emerald, unblinking, before sliding toward the darkness beyond the fractured wall. Not malice. Not threat. Dismissal. As if they were no more important than the breeze—fleeting, forgettable.

And yet...

Jacques couldn't shake the gut-deep certainty that if he twitched wrong, this man would feel it. Sense the threat before it existed. Snuff it out like a candle.

A bead of sweat slid down his temple, stinging his eye.

He didn't dare wipe it away.

A sound—soft at first. Then a crunch. A snap. Followed by the frantic croak-croak of something panicked, thrashing through brush.

A lizardman burst through the breach—wild-eyed and panting. Its mouth split in a sharp-toothed grimace, scales slick with dew. Armor clanked with every step as it stumbled into the open, oblivious to the figure standing not ten feet away.

The cat-thing flowed.

God help him, it moved fast.

The backward-facing paw swung up, catching the lizardman's head and snout in a single, brutal motion. The lizardman was lifted off its feet—legs kicking while scrabbling almost a meter above the carpet of debris and vegetation with unbridled panic.

Its spear clattered down—a crude thing, iron lashed to splintered wood, rolling end over end like a toy dropped mid-play.

The cat-thing's grip tightened.

Jacques heard it—*crack*—before he even registered the motion. A wet, sickening crunch. The unmistakable sound of bone collapsing, a skull caving in like overripe fruit.

Jacques sucked in sharply. Emerald expelled a quiet gasp, barely audible over the lizardman's death throes.

The creature released the body then tossed it aside with a flick of its paw.

The body hit in a heap, limbs twisted, the head a gory parody of itself, half-caved.

And the man—the man hadn't even flinched. His gaze remained fixed on the shadows beyond the breach. His face was unreadable, appearing carved from moonlit marble.

It was as if the casual erasure of a life meant nothing. As if it were no more remarkable than a leaf falling from a tree.

Jacques's heart pounded. Cold dread filled him from toes to crown.

More sounds—rustling leaves, snapping twigs, croaks. Lizardmen fleeing something unseen.

Approaching, where they stood.

And beneath it—punctuating it—that sound again.

Crunch.

As gory a sound as he had ever heard, and just as final. A butcher's cleaver through bone.

But then Jacques heard something else. Guttural. Familiar.

A name—spat through clenched teeth.

"*U'gah.*"

Panic gripped Jacques by the balls. They'd kill him. The man. The beast. Just like the lizardman. There would be no hesitation.

The thought twisted in his gut—nauseating. Bile rose behind his teeth.

U'gah wouldn't stand a chance.

And he—he couldn't stop it.

But he couldn't just stand still. Couldn't watch it happen.

Desperation flared. One terrible truth cut through the fog:

There was only one option.

"Please," Jacques choked, the word catching like a splinter in his throat. His voice came ragged, pleading—pathetic to his own ears. Hands lifted in a desperate, trembling gesture— palms open. Empty.

"He's not like them. He's… he's my friend."

He took a halting step forward, boots whispering softly against stone. His eyes locked on the man's—those terrible, cold, impossible eyes. Every nerve in Jacques's body screamed: *Run. Turn back.* But he couldn't.

His will cracked under the weight of it all, but he forced himself onward.

"U'gah is different. He's not a threat. Please—don't hurt him."

Beside him, Emerald found her voice. Her breath came in shallow gasps, but the icy fear buckled and broke. She stepped up beside Jacques, her words tumbling out in a tight, urgent rush.

"Please. You have to understand. He's not like them. He's ours. He's good."

The man didn't move.

Not a twitch. Not a glimpse of emotion.

His gaze stayed fixed on the dark beyond the wall, expression unreadable. Cold as stone. As if their words were nothing more than warm wind caressing a mountain.

Another lizardman burst through the breach—eyes wild, mouth drawn in sharp-toothed terror. It scrambled on broken stone, panic in every step.

And then it saw the feline thing. Muscle and menace, unmoving, watching.

The lizardman tried to veer off—too late.

From the shadows—an avatar of fluff and fury.

A streak of sable fur, ears pinned flat, eyes alight. He gripped a stone greatclub like it was an extension of himself. Legs pumping. Teeth bared in a snarl.

The man and the beast nearby didn't move. Still as statues. Watching.

Every hair on Jacques's body stood on end.

The lizardman turned, just enough to scream—

U'gah swung—an upward arc. The greatclub carved a line through the dark.

Impact.

A wet, meaty crunch echoed off the wall. The sound was awful.

Vertebra snapped. Muscle tore. Tendons popped.

A fine mist of blood arced into the air—coppery, tangy on Jacques's tongue.

The lizardman shrieked, high and thin, its body folding in on itself in reverse, like a broken marionette.

Jacques's stomach twisted. A sick lurch climbed his throat.

U'gah stood over the body, chest heaving, each breath a growl. His fur was bristled and matted, slick with blood that shone dark in the moonlight. His claws clenched the greatclub. The monstrous carved face dripped.

The corpse at his feet was bent, slack, blood pooling in the joints and cracks.

A shiver slid up his spine. Awe and dread, tangled like roots burrowing into the dark soil of his mind.

The man watched, arms folded, eyes unreadable. A small smile curled his lips, and he let out a low, appreciative whistle.

"Impressive," he murmured. Smooth voice, but edged. His gaze never left U'gah. Measuring him. Weighing every ounce of fury clinging to his bones.

"To be so small... he is fierce."

The cat beside him purred. A dangerous sound—not affection, but approval. Its golden eyes gleamed, narrowed with lazy, predatory satisfaction. The hunt had been judged. Found worthy.

Jacques's pulse thundered. His chest hurt with the pressure of it.

"Please..." he said again. The word came thin, hoarse. "He's not like them. He's just... trying to protect us."

The man's gaze snapped to Jacques. It pinned him in place like a hooked blade—those eyes, pale and inhuman, cutting through the dark.

For a long breath, he said nothing.

Then—resonant, the kind of finality only heard at an execution.

"I know," the man said.

CHAPTER SIX

Florence clutched her ledger, fingers digging into the cracked leather as if it were a life raft and she was already drowning. The lamplight hovered in the damp air, casting jittering shadows across the walls—twisted marionettes, crooked forms mocking her. Always mocking.

The smell of masonry and damp earth clung to her nose—cloying, suffocating. Every faint whistle of wind, every puff of dust from the ceiling sent a spike of fear into her chest. Like the whole place might collapse on her at any moment.

How could the others be so blind? So stupid?

That thing—U'gah. They spoke of it as if it were one of them. One of us. Like it belonged. But Florence knew better. It wasn't a man. It wasn't even an animal. It was a wild thing. A dangerous, unpredictable beast that had no place among civilized people.

It had stolen the flashlight. Not a misunderstanding, no matter what the others claimed. Theft. Betrayal. Sabotage. In her mind, the act was as clear as numbers on a page: U'gah had taken one of their lights and tried to leave them in the dark.

And now Emerald was risking everything—*her life*—to chase after it.

"Idiot," she muttered, the word molten, searing the silence. It barely rose above a whisper, but in her head, it screamed.

"They should be protecting me, Emerald and Jacques," she said, quieter now. "Not chasing after that… that beast. Or galavanting off trying to play hero."

They didn't see it. Didn't care about her.

She was the one who needed them. She was the fragile one. She couldn't fight, couldn't run, didn't have a weapon to wield.

She was the liability. That's what they thought, but she was the one they should be shielding. Guarding.

But instead—they ran off. Reckless. Stupid. Chasing monsters while she sat here. Alone. Cold. In the belly of some dark, dripping ruin. Waiting for the end.

Her fingers trembled as she opened the ledger. Familiar pages fluttered under her touch. The numbers—her ordered, logical world—swam in the artificial light. She forced herself to focus.

Calculations. Observations. Things of financial importance.

Something solid. Something real.

She traced a line of ink with one shaking finger. A fine tremor she couldn't stop.

The numbers didn't care about the dark. The numbers didn't abandon her.

They were hers.

She would cling to them until the end.

But the numbers were nothing. Just lines. Ink on paper. Cold symbols.

They didn't care about the monsters. They didn't care about *her*.

They were useless.

A strangled sob tore loose from her throat. It felt like it ripped something inside her—something important.

She slammed the ledger shut.

The sound cracked the air like a gunshot.

Her whole body trembled. Fingers twitching. Breath coming fast and shallow. The edges of the book bit into her palms, but she didn't let go.

She wanted to scream. To tear the cavern open with her voice. To let it echo until the walls collapsed.

But the scream choked in her throat. Lodged tight. Swallowed by the dark.

So she curled inward. Drew her knees to her chest and wrapped her arms around them.

Her fingers gripped the fabric of her sleeves until her nails dug crescents into her skin. She clenched her eyes shut, squeezing hard—hard enough to see stars bloom behind her lids.

As if, if she closed them tight enough, the dark would stay out.

The horror would stay out. The memories would stay out.

But the dark didn't stay out. It only crept closer.

Slinking into the edges of her mind like fog. Whispering of monsters. Of screams. Of bodies breaking underfoot.

It pressed against her skin. Coiled around her ribs. Squeezed.

Her heart thudded in her ears—loud. Too loud.

She couldn't breathe.

Couldn't think.

The line between here and there, now and before, sane and not —thinned like old paper.

She didn't know how much longer she could hold on.

Then—tap.

She felt a soft, tentative touch against her knee.

She jerked. Her eyes snapped open, blinking against the glow of the lamp. And there he was.

Saturn.

Standing before her. Small. Neat. Impossibly calm.

His pale face glowed faintly in the lamplight, round, tilted slightly.

His dark eyes—bottomless black—reflected the shine.

In his hands: two steaming cups.

Earthy herbs. The smell curled upward.

For a heartbeat, she just stared.

Then suspicion hit her like a cold hand.

Had he come to poison her?

To finish the job the dark had started? To silence her?

The thought coiled in her like a venomous snake. Slithering through the cracks in her mind.

A dark, humorless laugh bubbled up her throat and spilled into the cavern. It echoed off the walls like a taunt.

Well.

Let them try.

Let them think she was weak. Let them think she was just the trembling little liability in the dark.

They were wrong.

They didn't know her.

And she'd show them.

"What is that?" Florence hissed, her eyes narrowing to slits as her gaze snapped to the cups—two simple, steaming vessels in Saturn's hands. A spike of cold shot through her chest. Chamomile?

No. Poison.

Her body tensed—but Saturn only stood there, head tilted, calm to the point of insult.

"Chamomile tea," he said, as if it were obvious. "You seem... agitated."

Agitated! Agitated!!!

Her eyes stayed locked on him, dissecting every twitch, every pause. Chamomile—yes, she knew it. A calming agent. Or a weapon.

Could she trust him? Could she trust any of them?

Her hand darted out—snatched the cup like a striking snake.

Saturn didn't flinch.

The cup trembled in her grip. Steam curled up—sweet, earthy, warm.
It reminded her of home.

It smelled like a lie.

She raised it to her lips.

Just a sip.

The liquid slid across her tongue—smooth. Chamomile, honey, maybe thyme. The warmth bloomed in her abdomen.

But it didn't reach the cold coiled in her gut.

Saturn's gaze lingered. A faint crease formed between his brows.

"Is it alright?" he asked, curious.

Her tongue felt thick. Her heart pounded, pulse hammering in her temples.

"It's… fine."

Her grip loosened slightly.

She took another sip. Let the warmth trickle through the walls she'd built.

Maybe—*maybe*—he was trying to help.

But the doubt didn't leave.

It stayed. Breeding in the dark corners of her mind, whispering that this wasn't over.

She wouldn't drop her guard.

She'd drink the tea, yes.

But she'd *watch* him.

Florence sat stiffly, the cup cradled in her hands.

She sipped.

Her mind twisted around the taste, dissecting it. Chamomile. Honey. But what else? What might be buried in the sweetness? Masked. Waiting to strike?

She imagined it clearly—the poison.

Curling through her veins. Stealing the air from her lungs. Locking her muscles. Stilling her breath.

Her weak, fragile heart would stutter. Stop.

She'd collapse. A puppet with its strings cut.

The vision was grotesque. Vivid. Inescapable.

Her body jerking. Eyes bulging. Clawing at her throat for breath—while Saturn sat there, watching. Smiling. Until the horror twisted his smug little face into regret.

A flicker of grim satisfaction sparked in her chest.

Let him see.

Let him *feel* it.

Saturn moved to sit cross-legged across the room, the pale glow of his goggles casting a cold sheen across black eyes, making him look hollow. His small hands moved with mechanical ease, deft fingers working the controls made into his gloves.

What are you watching? she thought, resentment burning hot behind her eyes. *What are you plotting, little man?*

His face—childlike and old at the same time—looked wrong in the low light. Like something that could be peeled back to reveal the truth: something cold. Calculating. Inhuman.

She took another sip of tea, stoking the fire in her chest. But it couldn't stop the storm churning inside her. The bitterness she felt wasn't from the herbs.

It was *them*. Jacques. Emerald. Saturn. And U'gah.

Always U'gah.

Wait.

Faint. Distant. Almost nothing. A voice—familiar.

Again—clearer. Closer.

Jacques? Emerald?

Relief flared—fragile and desperate. It hit her chest like a gasp. *They were coming back.* They hadn't abandoned her.

But it soured fast. Curdled.

They *had* abandoned her. They'd left her here—vulnerable, helpless—while they ran off into the dark.

Her hands tightened around the cup. The heat bit into her skin.

And what if they hadn't found him? What if they'd failed?

A dark thrill twisted inside her. A small, cruel smile grew across her lips.

If U'gah was gone, if they'd failed—it would *prove her right*.

He was a danger. A burden. A threat.

They should have listened. They should have left him to die.

She took another sip.

Yes, she'd welcome them back—when they stumbled in, tired and sorry, full of apologies and excuses. But she wouldn't forgive them.

Not for this.

Not for leaving her here.

Not for abandoning her in this dripping tomb while they chased after that... thing.

The voices rose again.

Swelling out of the dark like a tide.

The sound twisted. Familiar—painfully so—but wrong. Syllables smeared, like a record spun backward. Like a lullaby turned feral. She almost recognized it—but couldn't.

At first, the voices lured. Soft. Alluring. Like a siren's whisper soaked in honey. Promising comfort. Reunion.

But the cadence degraded then grew ragged. A chorus of snarls and sobs, half-names and guttural cries. Her own name, she thought—called out—but the end of it broke apart, melting into masticated syllables.

Her heart pounded. A frantic drum in her chest.

The walls leaned closer. Shadows stretched long and sharp.

Her fingers clenched the cup. Knuckles bone-white. Her skin molded to the ceramic.

They were familiar.

They were the dead.

Voices of friends—twisted. Warped. Mocking.

The tea churned in her gut with the rising bile and acid.

No, no, no.

Her thoughts struggled to hold shape.

Were they alive? Could they be?

It had to be a trick. A hallucination clawing out from inside her already-broken mind?

Her gaze snapped to Saturn.

Still seated. Still serene. Still oblivious.

Bathed in the glow of soft light, watching his drone's feed like none of this was happening.

Didn't he hear it? Didn't he see it?

Or—

Was he part of it? The engineer? The architect of this madness?

Had he really drugged her?

Was that why the tea tasted so strange?

Had he done this—left her open, vulnerable—so the voices could get in?

The cup trembled in her hands.

She stared at Saturn, mind buzzing, the sound of the voices building—gnawing at the edges of her sanity.

She would *not* die like this. Not in the dark. Not surrounded by shadows and whispers chewing through her mind like worms in the walls.

She had to get out.

Away from the voices. Away from this pit. Away from Saturn's eerie calm. His childish face.

She couldn't trust him.

Her legs trembled as she forced herself upright. The ledger slipped from her lap and slapped the stone with a dull, final thud. The ground swayed beneath her. The chamber spun—a slow, sickening spiral.

The voices surged. Garbling into syllables that clawed at her ears.

"No!" she gasped. The word cracked like a brittle twig. Her voice trembled with the weight of desperation. "Leave me alone! I won't go with you!"

The dark grinned.

And she ran.

She burst from the limestone chamber, the stale air replaced by the wet slap of jungle humidity. The night swallowed her whole.

But the voices followed.

Louder now. Everywhere.

They howled from the trees. Whispered from the roots. Crooned from the fog curling through the branches. Nonsense words twisted in the black—sobs, snarls, fragments of language turned inside out.

They were *everywhere*.

She stumbled forward, heart hammering. The ground slick, treacherous. Branches tore at her skin, scratched her face, but she didn't stop. Couldn't stop.

Panic burned through her.

Jacques. Emerald.

She had to find them.

They were her last anchors. Her only hope.

Yes—they'd left her. But they hadn't meant to. They'd come back. They could fix this. *They had to.*

But Saturn?

No.

He wasn't her ally. Wasn't her friend. He had poisoned her.

She *knew* it now. That cursed tea had done something—dulled her. Opened her to the voices. Let them crawl in and root.

Or worse—

The nightspeakers were back.

The thought hit like a body blow.

She ran faster.

Crashing through undergrowth. Legs pumping. The ground bucking beneath her.

The voices chased her—snapping at her heels in a grotesque, broken chorus.

She didn't know where Jacques had gone. But she remembered the direction.

The ruined city.

A desperate gamble, but it was all she had.

Even the lizardmen—monsters though they were—had to be better than *this*.

Maybe the lizardmen had an antidote to the poison. Maybe their savage, scaled hands knew ancient cures. Strange roots. Counteragents that could burn the poison from her blood.

Or if the voices were real—if the nightspeakers had returned— maybe the lizardmen would stand between her and the dark.

Keep going. Keep going.

Terror gave her strength. It poured through her—electric, wild —as she tore through the vegetation.

She stumbled. Crashed. Caught herself on shaking hands. Dirt ground into her palms.

The voices followed—always just behind. Slipping between trees. Whispering from the dark.

They pleaded. They taunted. They mocked.

Her breath came ragged, each gasp fire in her chest, legs screaming.

She ran harder.

The pulse in her head pounded like a drum.

The jungle itself whispered.

Her foot caught on a root—pain flared through her knee. She bit down a scream. Staggered up. Teeth clenched hard enough to ache.

She *had* to reach the ruins.

There—through the trees, jagged spires stood against the star-pocked sky. Broken stone rose like ribs from the earth.

But something moved behind her.

Footfalls.

More than one.

Her stomach dropped. Ice lanced her spine.

The voices faded—swept away by something worse.

She risked a glance back—

And her heart stopped.

Shapes in the dark. Monsters.

Some kind of dinosaur.

Big. Scaled. Fast. Jaws open. Legs pumping.

But it wasn't just the size.

They were the *voices.*

It was coming from *them.*

Twisted versions of her friends. Of herself. Words warped and echoing from scaled throats.

A chorus of nightmares.

A ragged wail tore from her lungs. Burning, burning. Every part of her was burning.

She had to keep running.

Had to find Jacques. Find Emerald.

Had to survive—

***

"There's movement," Saturn reported, clinically. His eyes danced over the scrolling data, a soft hum still lingering in his ears from the audio feed he'd just unplugged. "A large group of dilophosaurids are roaming the area. We should be safe as long as we stay put."

He removed the tiny earbud with his fingers, then pocketed it.

"It's fascinating there are still archaic proto-avians on this continent. Remarkably well-adapted, despite their primitive morphology."

The words came easy—automatic. He braced for the usual: Florence's outburst, sharpened accusations, or that awful silence. That empty, distant silence was somehow worse than the screaming.

Her mind was disintegrating. He could see it. Fine fractures spidering outward, deeper every day. Trauma? Yes. No survival training?Definitely. The math wasn't complicated—she wasn't built for this.

He turned to face her, ready for whatever storm she had left—

But the spot where she'd been sitting was empty.

Saturn blinked. Confused.

His brow furrowed. Realization crawled in—cold and slow.

"Florence?" he called, tense.

No answer.

He scrambled to his feet, palms scraping against the stone floor, eyes scanning the shadows. Corners. Crevices. All empty.

She was gone.

"She's gone," he said. Again, louder—cracking with disbelief. "She's gone!"

His voice echoed off the walls, ringing in the dark. No reply, except for his echo.

Saturn's hands curled into tiny fists.

He had let her slip away.

Too focused on the data. The patterns. The damn drone. While Florence—already unraveling—had dissolved beside him.

"Damn it…" he whispered.

He had to find her.

Scrambling to the stairs, he shoved into the night, instantly sweating in the humidity. The moon hung low, painting the ruins in silver: crumbling walls, half-formed shapes, vines like veins through stone.

The usual night sounds—chittering insects, bird calls, background life—had thinned to a hush. A silence laced with unease.

Saturn scanned the dark. The moonlight played tricks. Shadows twitched and twisted. There was no sign of her.

Just jungle. Just ruin.

He'd failed.

Again.

He secured NAVI to his back. The harness dug into his shoulders like blame.

No more wasting time.

He turned. The jungle opened ahead—black and waiting.

He stepped forward.

Straps—tight. Harness—snug. There was no time for comfort.

Saturn's fingers flew across the buckles, metal clicks ringing sharp in the night air. He'd only flown the rig a few times. But this—this was why he'd built it.

He glanced over his shoulder, heart thudding, as NAVI powered up. Rotors spun with a rising whir, cutting through the thick jungle air.

"Alright," he muttered—to himself, to the machine, to no one.

"Let's fly."

He leapt. NAVI's engines roared.

The first hop—low. Testing. The second—higher. The third—clean lift.

Gravity let go.

Wind rushed past his skin, tugging at his hair and his coat. His breath came in short, tight bursts. His cheeks stung. For one long heartbeat—he was weightless.

The drone's hum stabilized—a deep, steady hum. The engines bore his weight like it was nothing, unless he needed to climb.

Saturn grinned, briefly. There was no time for satisfaction, he reminded himself.

Florence was out there—lost, spiraling—and every second wasted tightened the odds.

He swept his gaze across the ruined city. The sprawl of it. Jagged streets swallowed by vines. Moonlight painted it all in black and silver.

It was beautiful.

But, he wasn't site-seeing. Saturn cycled through his goggle's filters and NAVI's scanners, trying to penetrate the silvery ink.

He banked left—toward the outskirts—eyes narrowed against the wind. The HUD flickered across his visor: data streams, trajectory arcs, thermal readings.

He leaned into the harness. Wind tore past his face—hot and damp.

The burn was nothing compared to the dread tightening in his chest.

Where are you, Florence?

He scanned the terrain for movement or heat. No trace.

NAVI's lens zoomed. Focused. Pixelated. Then cleared: Broken branches. A footprint—not hers. A flash of light—no. Just dew.

Come on…

"Maybe she ran toward the interior…" Saturn mouthed to himself, the syllables lost in the whir of NAVI's turbines.

It made a kind of sense. If she had decided to go looking for Jacques and Emerald, that is likely the way she would go.

A faint glow—barely there—darted through the trees like a firefly on the inside of the interior wall as he approached.

Saturn's heart jolted.

"Got you," he muttered, steering NAVI into a dive. The drone tilted, engines whining as he pushed harder. The glow resolved —erratic, bobbing—a flashlight beam cutting wild arcs through the underbrush.

Florence. It had to be—

But as the drone dropped lower, details emerged—and Saturn's stomach dropped.

It wasn't Florence.

It was smaller, stockier.

The figure darted through the foliage—fast, agile, weaving between trees. The flashlight bounced wildly in one hand. In the other: a massive club, far too large for such a small frame. The head of the club was carved into the snarling visage of a reptilian predator, its unidentifiable runes glowing faintly in the moonlight.

The club was driven into enemies and obstacles alike.

Each swing a brutal arc. Destruction in motion.

Lizardmen scattered—hissing, shrieking. One slipped—*crack*, a wet snap—and the club found him. The blow landed with monstrous weight, the creature's body bursting like a stepped-on sauce packet.

Saturn's eyes widened.

It was U'gah.

And he was hunting.

Shock snapped through him like a circuit surge. His brain scrambled to reconcile what he was seeing. U'gah.

Not the soft-footed halfling who gnawed on roots and offered trinkets.

This was interesting. Predatory behavior, where he had only observed his mischievous and protective natures.

A blur of dark fur and flashing teeth. Wide, burning eyes. That greatclub—far too big for him—moved like it had always belonged in his hands.

"Holy helix," Saturn whispered, the wind stealing the words. His mind twisted—equal parts awe and disbelief. "It is U'gah..."

Below, the halfling tore through the chaos—fast, feral, focused. Its stone jaws snapped with a sound that made Saturn's skin crawl, audible even over the rushing air and the distance. Each strike ended in a crunch, a scream, a geyser of dark liquid.

Saturn watched, mind reeling.

How?

How had timid, uncertain U'gah become this?

Where had the weapon come from?

And what had *awakened* in him?

Or was it the club directing his actions?

Saturn shook himself.

There was no time for theories.

He had a mission.

Find Florence.

Below—lizardmen swarmed. Drawn like wasps to U'gah's fury. Spears raised. Jaws wide. Clubs lifted.

They circled him, trying to end the storm.

For a moment, Saturn's lips twitched. Almost a smile.

The image was absurd: U'gah, small and furious, carving a path through the lizardmen like a living scythe.

If it weren't so bloody, so deadly—it might have been funny.

But the humor died fast.

The chaos was growing. Drawing attention. U'gah couldn't hold forever.

And Florence—

His chest tightened.

Florence was the priority.

Jacques and Emerald could fight. He was a soldier, and she is a gifted young gnome.

But Florence?

Florence was unraveling under pressure she wasn't built to bear. She was brilliant in a boardroom—but out here? She was exposed. Fragile.

If he didn't find her soon…

He manipulated the controls, steering NAVI up, away from the swirling chaos below. The drone hummed louder, engines straining for altitude.

He swept the cityscape—overgrown plazas, shattered walls, vines hanging like tendrils of a sleeping beast. The HUD blinked across the lens, parsing data, feeding it back in pulses.

The search felt impossible.

A needle in jungle-thick dark.

But he couldn't stop.

Wouldn't stop.

Not while Florence was still out there.

Not while she still had a chance.

***

Exhaustion gnawed at Florence's muscles like a pack of starving wolves. The adrenaline that had driven her—a furious, terrified rush through the jungle—was gone, bleeding out and leaving behind only the dull ache of her body breaking down.

Her lungs burned with every ragged gasp. Her legs felt like molten lead—heavy, sluggish, barely lifting with each step.

Her thoughts spiraled in a slow, sickening loop. Self-pity and panic tangled like vines.

This is it. I'm going to die here, alone and forgotten.

Swallowed by this accursed jungle, just another nameless skeleton.

The nightspeakers flashed across her mind—those monstrous, shrieking things with teeth like shattered glass and voices like echoes from the grave.

But worse was the realization that they didn't even need to catch her.

At this pace—this stumbling collapse—she'd fall before they ever sank their claws into her.

Her steps faltered. Her vision swam. Her legs buckled—

Then a sound cut through the fog—mechanical.

Louder. Closer.

Panic surged. *What now?* What fresh nightmare had come to finish her?

Her knees gave out. She pitched forward—hands flailing, reaching for ground that never came—

Then arms caught her.

Small, strong arms. Too small to belong to any man.

She gasped—

The world shifted.

Her feet skimmed the earth. Her weight lightened—as if gravity itself had loosened its grip.

It was the drone.

Saturn's drone.

The engines whined, the air thrumming with the vibration of rotors spinning hard, straining to lift them both.

Saturn.

The gnome she'd doubted. The one she'd hated—just moments ago.

There. Behind her.

Lifting her.

Holding her up.

Relief crashed over her. The knot of dread loosened.

The monsters couldn't catch her now.

For a heartbeat, hope bloomed.

They might outrun them.

They might live.

But—*where to run?*

The city.

Its crumbling walls rose like ancient giants, black against the stars.

The city.

The lizardmen.

The answer hit hard and clear.

Walls kept things out.

Cities meant protection.

Surely the lizardmen would fight back. They *had* to.

She imagined them—tall, armored, spears raised, braced against whatever nightmare hunted them. Surely they wouldn't let themselves be hunted like prey.

Surely—they would protect her.

She twisted in Saturn's grip, tone urgent—

"Saturn!" Florence screamed over the drone's high-pitched whine and the rush of air. "What are you doing?!"

The wind tore at her words, but she shouted anyway.

"We need to get inside the city! The lizardmen will help us!"

Saturn's head jerked back, cyan hair whipping. His voice was audible over the roaring engines.

"The city is too dangerous!" he called, words shredded by the wind.

Florence's frustration ignited, burning through the last of her restraint.

"Are you crazy?!" she shrieked, throat ragged. "Anything's better than being out here with these *fucking monsters!*"

But Saturn—*damn him*—didn't budge.

His voice cracked back through the chaos—sharp, urgent, a whip through the storm.

"Trust me, Florence!"

Something in his tone made her falter. A plea. A desperate conviction.

The jungle blurred—shadows and moonlight streaking past in broken flashes. The drone jolted beneath her, climbing hard, engines whining.

Florence gritted her teeth. A snarl caught in her throat.

Fine.

She'd let him have his way—for now.

But she hated it.

Her heart hammered, stuttering. Her eyes darted—lizard-things behind, jagged walls ahead. Every instinct screamed they were going the wrong way. That they were idiots for not skipping toward shelter. Toward spears. Toward stone.

"Where are we going?!" she shouted. "If we don't get to the city now, they're going to catch us!"

She could feel them.

The monsters.

Snapping teeth. Clawing earth. Voices still mimicking—taunting.

Saturn didn't look back. His jaw was set, brow furrowed, eyes locked ahead—fixated on some target she couldn't see.

"*Just trust me, Florence!*" he yelled, the words tight, trembling between fear and focus. "*I know what I'm doing!*"

She bit back a scream. Rage bubbled beneath the exhaustion—magma under cracked earth. Her legs gave out. The drone jolted, NAVI's engines shrieking as it adjusted to her weight.

Suddenly, an explosion.

The night split wide with sound.

The city's wall shuddered whilst lit in flashes of fire and smoke. Chunks of stone crumbled. The blast echoed like a war cry through the ruins.

And that—*that*—was where Saturn was taking her.

Panic detonated in her chest.

"I *knew* it!" she screamed, thrashing in the harness, her voice a ragged, furious wail. "I knew you were trying to kill me, you blue-haired little *snot!*"

She fought—kicking, twisting, clawing at his arms—wild-eyed, feral.

But Saturn's voice cracked through the panic. Desperate.

"Florence, stop! I'm trying to save us—*please!"*

Behind them—closer now—the monsters were gaining.

She had to trust him.

There was no other choice. If he hadn't come, she'd already be dead.

Grinding her teeth, Florence forced her body still.

She went limp.

The drone surged forward—hauling her toward the shattered, burning wall; Toward the city; Toward whatever waited.

CHAPTER SEVEN

U'gah's chest heaved, fur slick with sweat and the blood of his enemies. The club—his club—thrummed in his paws, warm, pulsing, sharing his hunger, his victory. The air crackled around him, electric and alive. He had fed the hunger. He had cleared the way for his friends.

For a glorious moment, he basked.

The thrill—the kill—the rightness of it flooded his veins, hot and fierce. The bodies of the scaly-skins lay crumpled at his feet, their snarling voices silenced. His ears twitched, straining for more—the rush of footfalls, the hiss of an angry war cry. But there was only silence, save for the pounding of his own blood in his ears.

He lifted his head, nostrils flaring, the club resting heavy and proud on his shoulder. His eyes darted, scanning the shadows for the next enemy, the next feast—but what he saw stopped him cold.

Jacques. Emerald.

Huddled in a ditch of stone and roots, staring at him with wide, unblinking eyes. Shock, awe, and something wary twisted across faces he had come to trust.

Jacques's mouth moved, but U'gah couldn't hear the words—not over the drum of his own heartbeat. But he could see.

Afraid.

A strange pang jabbed at his chest—hot and confusing.

Of me?

No. He had saved them.

He puffed his chest, standing taller, the club resting like a trophy. His fur bristled, tail flicking in a triumphant arc. They should be cheering. They should be grateful.

But they weren't.

Their eyes stayed wide, locked on something beyond him—past him.

He followed Jacques's gaze, turning just in time to feel fur—massive and thick— enveloping him from behind like a cage made of warmth and muscle.

Panic flared. His grip slipped; the club hit stone with a heavy thunk.

He was lifted.

Turned.

And there it was—

The cat.

Not a cat. A mountain of fur, muscle, and teeth, towering over him. Its amber eyes glowing like twin moons in the dim light. Its breath, hot and heavy, puffing in slow measured waves against U'gah's muzzle.

The fear that had been a slow burn ignited, roaring to life in his chest. He wriggled, thrashed, twisted, claws scrabbling uselessly against the air. The ground was too far away, the club abandoned, his strength nothing.

This was it. He was done. A single squeeze and he would be a splintered, pulpy smear.

But the squeeze never came.

The cat's paw—massive, calloused, thick as a tree branch—softened.

And then…

A slow stroke down his back. A pat. A ruffle.

The cat was petting him.

U'gah's eyes widened, a strangled, disbelieving snarl bubbling in his throat. The sensation was bizarre, comforting, and humiliating all at once. His fur ruffled under the pressure. His ears pinned back, and a sharp, indignant yip escaped his snout before he could stop it.

No.

No, no, no.

This was wrong.

He was a hunter, a warrior. The wielder of a mighty club! He had torn down enemies!

And now—this?

His dignity snapped.

He lunged, jaws wide, and sank his teeth into the thick fur of the cat's paw, biting down hard, tasting musk and a faint hint of salt.

The cat didn't flinch.

It lifted its paw, leaving him dangling like a cub in a mother's grasp.

The cat's eyes glittered, and a low, rumbling purr vibrated through its chest, deep and resonant.

Then laughter.

It was laughing at him.

U'gah's growls twisted into a desperate, pitiful whimper. His legs kicked uselessly, ears flattened in humiliation, eyes darting in a frantic, silent plea.

He had faced down scaly-skins, wielded power beyond imagining—and now, he was a plaything.

A voice cut through the haze—a deep, steady rumble from the shadows, the words heavy with weight.

"Stop tormenting the bergbar, Lusa. He has proven himself a valuable ally, and he deserves our respect."

The man's voice slipped through the air like a warm breeze, soothing tension U'gah hadn't known was locked in his muscles. The tone wasn't sharp, wasn't angry, but gentle, almost like a lullaby.

And it worked.

Lusa—the cat, the beast—let out a long purr, the vibration of it rattling through U'gah's bones like distant thunder. The pressure in the massive paws eased, the weight shifting. U'gah blinked sideways, catching a glimpse of Jacques and Emerald —faces slack with relief, shoulders sagging. The fear in their eyes had softened, but it hadn't disappeared.

Lusa's other paw came in slow, curling under U'gah's ribs, a cage of warm fur and muscle. U'gah tensed, a sharp snarl caught in his throat, but the paw lifted until the world tilted, and with a gentle shake, his jaws popped loose from the fur.

He dropped like a stone, twisting mid-air, and landed on his feet with a soft, almost soundless thump.

Relief flooded him, washing through his fur in a wave of liquid heat.

Alive.

But the indignity burned hot in his chest, hotter than the adrenaline still buzzing in his veins.

He couldn't—wouldn't—let it end like that.

With a sharp, defiant snap, he lunged forward, teeth grazing the retreating paw. Not a bite to draw blood, no—but a reminder.

I'm not prey.

Lusa jerked, a startled yowl breaking from its throat, eyes flashing wide in surprise. Then, with a flick of its stubby, bobbed tail—a dismissive, almost amused gesture—the giant cat turned and padded away.

U'gah stood his ground, legs spread wide, fur bristling in wild tufts. His heart thundered in his chest and his chin lifted.

He may be small, but he would not be overlooked.

He was a hunter. A warrior. Not a pet.

He huffed, a low, growling exhale, and turned to face the man —the one who had spoken, who had stayed the giant's paw. Their eyes locked.

U'gah felt it—a bloom in his chest, strange and warm and dangerous.

Gratitude.

But also—suspicion.

This man… understood.

U'gah puffed up, his chest swelling with a mix of pride and lingering fear. He raised his paw, gesturing clumsily, fumbling for the words he didn't have. His voice came rough, guttural.

"Thank… you," he grunted, dipping his head in awkward deference. "For… not letting the big-cat… break me."

The man nodded slowly, his mouth curling into a subtle, almost imperceptible smile.

"You saved yourself, little one," he said, voice low, eyes intelligent and painfully blue. "Your courage and ferocity… are impressive."

U'gah's ears twitched, and something sparked in his chest.

He liked this man.

A lot.

The thrum of pride swelled as U'gah gestured broadly to the mess of scaly-skins lying broken on the ground, his voice rough with satisfaction.

"Scaly-skins... bad," he grunted, gesturing fiercely, beating a paw against his chest. "U'gah… protect friends."

Jacques appeared, looking worried, stumbling forward with wide eyes, and scooped U'gah into a hug so tight it squeezed the air from his lungs.

"U'gah!" Jacques choked out, voice cracking, half-laugh, half-sob. "We thought we'd lost you!"

Emerald dropped to her knees, her face pale, eyes wide and glistening.

"You were amazing," she whispered, voice soft, awed, as if she were looking at him for the first time. "Where did you find that weapon?"

U'gah blinked, dazed, the chaos still buzzing in his ears. He pointed a shaky paw toward the breach in the wall, where the dark yawned open.

"Old Ones... give," he grunted, voice thick with reverence, though he knew they wouldn't understand. They never did.

But the man—the stranger, tall and lean, carved from shadow and moonlight—he smiled.

"He says the Old Ones gave him the weapon," he translated, a glint of amusement sparking in his eyes.

The man's gaze held U'gah's, steady, sure.

"You are lucky to have such a fierce ally," he said.

And U'gah—battered, bloodied, fur still bristling—felt his heart swell.

Yes.

Yes, they were.

***

"Merci," Jacques replied, his voice strained, the word slipping from his mouth like a reflex. The gratitude was genuine, but it

120

tangled with a thread of uncertainty—an instinctive wariness he couldn't shake. His pulse drummed slow in his ears. He didn't know what to make of this man—calm in the chaos, eyes sharp enough to hurt, presence unnervingly steady.

Jacques kept his posture open, his hands relaxed at his sides, but his mind raced.

The man inclined his head, gaze steady, the soft glow of the moon catching the planes of his face—worn, gaunt, but with an edge of something dangerous, something alive. His voice was smooth and tinged with faint amusement—as if the whole thing were an elaborate parlor game.

"I assume it is you that I should thank," he said, his tone almost polite, which made it all the more unsettling, "for freeing Lusa and myself from our imprisonment?"

Jacques swallowed, the words catching in his throat.

"We were just... trying to get into the city," he replied slowly, weighing each syllable, balancing honesty against caution. His eyes flicked to the crumbling walls, then back to the stranger. "We were... looking for... something."

He winced inwardly at the vagueness, but anything else felt like too much—too risky.

The man's piercing blue eyes narrowed, a subtle hint of amusement dancing at the corners. His lips curled into the faintest, knowing smile, the kind that felt pressed just shy of the skin.

"Something," he echoed, the word drawn out, his voice a low, rich hum that seemed to settle in Jacques's bones. "It would appear you found it, my friend."

Jacques felt his jaw tighten, the weight of those eyes pressing into him. He forced himself to hold the gaze, to not flinch.

He cleared his throat, voice rough.

"We... are searching for answers," he admitted, the words slow, careful, each one feeling like a step onto thin ice. "Answers about this place... about the... anomalies we've encountered."

The man's smile widened—teeth gleaming too white in the dim light—and he let out a soft, almost purring chuckle.

"Anomalies," he repeated, as if tasting the word. His gaze swept over Jacques, over Emerald, over the disheveled, panting form of U'gah now wrestling with the massive feline's weight, even after having been freed once.

"This entire world is an anomaly," he murmured, voice low, a whisper woven into the wind. "A playground for the gods... a crucible for the damned."

Jacques felt the chill ripple down his spine.

Still, he couldn't help the ember of dry humor that sparked in the back of his mind. He let it rise, a faint smile touching the corners of his mouth, smoothing the tension just enough to breathe.

"Well then," he said, voice warming despite the gnawing tightness in his throat, "since it seems we won't be killing each other tonight, it would be rude not to introduce ourselves— especially since we freed you, accidentally or otherwise."

A chuckle slipped from him, light and incongruous, floating in the charged air like a spark.

"I am Jacques," he continued, extending a hand—steady, deliberate, an act of faith and challenge both. "And this is my companion, Emerald." He nodded toward the young gnome, who stood tense but silent, her wide eyes darting between the stranger and the giant feline like a trapped animal searching for an escape route.

"And that over there..." Jacques's voice softened, a hint of fondness coloring the words as he gestured toward the panting, disheveled form of U'gah.

The therian was currently scrambling to retrieve his greatclub from beneath Lusa's massive, purring frame, the feline lounging with a satisfied rumble that echoed through the ruins.

"...That's U'gah."

The man's smile broadened, a flash of teeth in the moonlight. His grip was firm as he clasped Jacques's hand, the bones of their fingers grinding together in a brief, unspoken contest of strength.

"A pleasure to meet you, Jacques. Emerald," he said, his voice low and steady, each syllable shaped with a subtle, practiced weight. "I am Hyatta Kahlan of the Siv'agat," he continued, his gaze sharp, dissecting, as if carving them apart piece by piece. "And this—" he gestured to the lounging cat, "—is Lusa of the Mau."

Jacques felt the name sink into his bones like a stone dropped into deep water.

Emerald, standing slightly behind him, her rifle clutched close, managed a tentative smile. The tightness in her shoulders eased, though her eyes still tracked Hyatta's movements like a wary fox.

"It's... a pleasure to meet you, Hyatta," she said, voice steady but tight, the edges of fear still bleeding into her words. "Though I must admit, the circumstances are... unusual."

Hyatta's mouth quirked at the corner, a smile that didn't quite reach his eyes.

"Unusual indeed," he agreed, the words curling through the air like smoke. His gaze lingered on Emerald a beat too long, something almost... knowing in the way he looked at her. "But then again, what isn't unusual in a land like this, servant of Astraeus?"

Jacques blinked, a flicker of confusion flashing through his chest. Servant of Astraeus? He opened his mouth to ask—

But Lusa's low growl cut through the moment, a deep, resonant sound that vibrated in Jacques's ribs. The cat's ears twitched, his golden eyes narrowing as he turned, scanning the shadows beyond.

"Yat-ta..." Lusa's voice was a rumbling whisper, a warning wrapped in gravel.

Hyatta's smile vanished, wiped away like a mask peeled from a face. His hand moved to Lusa's shoulder, a brief, familiar pat, but his posture shifted—coiling, tightening, ready.

"I hear them," he murmured, his voice hardening, sharpening drawn across a whetstone.

Jacques tensed, adrenaline flooding back into his veins like ice water.

Hyatta turned, his eyes locking onto Jacques and Emerald, gaze sharp, cutting.

"Prepare yourselves," he said, his voice a low command. "We have guests."

Jacques followed Hyatta's gaze as the man strode toward the fallen lizardman, the carcass slumped in the dust. He watched as Emerald, without hesitation, unslung her rifle, her small frame coiled like a spring. Her hands were steady, her eyes fierce, but Jacques could see the flicker of fear behind the focus.

Hyatta knelt, his fingers brushing over the lizardman's crude weaponry. The iron axe he lifted was a brutal, jagged thing—adorned with bones.

Human bones.

Jacques felt a cold knot twist in his gut.

Hyatta's face darkened, a mask of disgust twisting his features as he turned the axe over in his hands. The bones clattered against the metal, the sound sharp and hollow in the stillness.

Jacques's stomach clenched. His skin prickled.

Hyatta rose, the axe gripped in one hand—no, claimed, like it belonged to him. The bones rattled as he lifted it, the pale iron glinting coldly in the moonlight.

Hyatta's eyes ignited, blazing with a white-hot fury that shimmered like heat on sand.

"They are coming," Hyatta growled, voice a low, rolling thunder. The sound of it reverberated in this place, in him. "The scavengers... the carrion feeders who gorge on the flesh of the fallen."

A faint hum, at first—like an unrealized song, building into a rising drone. It grew louder with every breath, a thousand voices in the dark, radiating from the weapon in the strange man's hand.

Hyatta shifted his grip on the axe—then, with a sudden, fluid slash, he brought it down.

Jacques flinched, bracing for the impact—but there was no sound of metal on stone. Only the beautiful melody from the unseen source.

Alongside, or perhaps because of the lovely sound—light.

Iridescent, shimmering—like mother-of-pearl, or like oil on water. The blade cracked, light spilling in a thin filament that snapped and hissed through the air.

The axe was... changing.

The weapon unfolded—segments shifting, sliding, stretching, the bones rearranging in a lattice of dazzling iron and ivory. The air hummed a calming, radiant charge that prickled at the edges of his senses.

When the glow dimmed, what remained was no axe at all, but a whip—long and segmented. Each piece glinted like polished bone, the iron edges catching moonlight in lethal glimmers.

Hyatta held it coiled in his hand, poised like a serpent ready to strike.

This man was something else—dangerous beyond reason.

"Let's give them a warm greeting," Hyatta growled, voice low and sharp, venom curling around each word.

Jacques's pulse quickened, a cold knot tightening in his chest.

Lusa stood off to the side, deceptively still, his massive form outlined by moonlight. But Jacques felt the tension radiating off the cat—coiled, ready, a storm waiting for the sky to crack. His ears twitched, his eyes half-lidded, but every muscle in his body thrummed with barely restrained violence.

A buzzing grew in the air, a grating, insectoid drone that crawled into Jacques's bones, setting his teeth on edge. His hand tightened around the grip of his pistol, the familiar weight grounding him even as his gut twisted in dread. The machete in his other hand felt heavier than usual, the blade dark and dull in the low light.

This was it.

The moment the quiet snapped.

He squinted into the darkness beyond the walls—where the undergrowth trembled, where the noise coiled and hissed. Shapes shifted, half-glimpsed, and then—

Red and green lights.

Bobbing, weaving—familiar.

"NAVI?" he breathed, disbelief catching in his throat. His heart lurched, confusion tangled with a fragile thread of hope.

And then her.

Florence.

She burst from the shadows, wild-eyed, with small arms and legs wrapped tight around her body. Her face was a mask of terror. Her ragged sobs tore through the humid night. Above her, the drone—NAVI, Saturn's drone—whined and strained, engines screaming under the weight. She was drug forward like a desperate, mechanical lifeline. Every time she tried to run her feet touched the ground.

Jacques's stomach dropped.

Behind her, the nightmare followed.

Beasts—bipedal, reptilian, built like machines of bone and sinew and hunger. Their silhouettes loomed against the moonlit landscape, hunched but sleek. The dorsal ridge of their backs shimmered with blackness, blending into the mottled gray that swallowed what little light the jungle offered. Their long, powerful legs ate the ground in loping strides, each precise movement terrifying in its efficiency.

But it was their heads that sent ice down Jacques's spine.

They didn't have eyes.

Just that split, peaked crest—dark red, almost black, glistening like wet leather under the moonlight. It drank the light, a void in the shape of a crown. The jaws gaped wide, saliva glinting in long, viscous strands, teeth like knives the length of Jacques's thumb snapping in a hungry rhythm.

Emerald was already moving—rifle raised, stance locked. Her eyes narrowed, fingers curled tight around the trigger.

Crack!

The report echoed, sharp and clean.

Jacques tracked the bullet's path with trained precision—center mass, right in the chest. A perfect shot.

But the impact—

It flattened.

The bullet crushed against the hide like a pebble against a wall, leaving only a shallow dent before it fell, useless, into the dirt.

The creature shrieked—a sound that cut through the night. Its neck snapped wide, a fan of vibrating feathers, it hissed in a violent burst of rage.

Jacques's heart slammed against his ribs. His pistol steady, finger hovering—but he couldn't shoot. Florence was too close. Her flailing body tangled in the chaos, too easy to catch in a misplaced shot. His hands tightened, the frustration burning hot in his chest.

"Stay vigilant, Jacques of Hephaestus!" Hyatta's voice boomed across the clearing, a command wrapped in steel. The weight of it settled on Jacques's shoulders like a mantle—an order he couldn't afford to ignore.

The undergrowth erupted.

Eight more—eight—dinosaurs.

They moved like a unit, coordinated, their split-crests bobbing in eerie synchronization. Sightless. Alien. Their heads swiveled in unison toward Florence and the drone—the prey. Their mouths gaped, fibers of venomous saliva dripping from jagged teeth.

Jacques's gaze darted—scanning, calculating, heart racing.

Emerald shifted her stance, rifle trained.

But then—

A shift in the brush, subtle, but there—like a shadow moving where no shadow should be.

His eyes narrowed.

Juveniles. Smaller, quicker.

Circling. Flanking.

Just like the adults.

They weren't just hunting. They were orchestrating.

Jacques's stomach twisted into a cold knot as the full scope of their situation snapped into focus.

Not by mindless beasts, but by pack hunters—intelligent, coordinated, and lethal.

The creatures moved with eerie precision, their formation tightening like a noose. The juveniles swept through the underbrush, slipping into the gaps, flanking them, pushing them toward a choke point. A trap.

They were being corralled.

"Emerald!" Jacques bellowed, his voice straining to rise over the high-pitched screeches, the buzz of the drone, the rising panic roaring in his ears. "More of them! They're flanking us!"

Emerald's head snapped to him, her eyes wide—fear bright and sharp—but she moved fast, scanning, recalculating. The smaller predators were slipping through the dark like shadows with teeth, their crests low, mouths dripping with venom.

"We need to break their formation!" she shouted back, her voice ragged, tight with urgency. "We can't let them surround us!"

Jacques's mind raced, instinct clashing with the primal terror clawing at his gut. He had fought men before, but not monsters. Enemies who bled red, who screamed in pain, who broke under the weight of bullets. These things? They shrieked, they hissed, and those sightless crests, all horrible unsettling.

The screeches pierced his skull. The gleam of those teeth—rows of them, long and sharp as shards of broken glass—set every nerve in him screaming to run.

Florence and Saturn crashed through the underbrush, barely visible between the twisting ferns and splintered branches. Florence dangled from the drone's harness like a rag doll, her legs flailing with each jolt, her mouth stretched wide in a silent scream. NAVI's motors whined in protest, the tether straining against the weight, wobbling as Saturn clung to her waist, holding her steady, dragging them both forward in a lurching, desperate rhythm.

They couldn't get caught. They couldn't.

"U'gah! Emerald!" he roared, his voice cracked and raw. The words tore from him, hoarse and ragged. "Take the right flank! Get Florence and Saturn to safety!"

No hesitation. Emerald's rifle snapped to her shoulder, eyes cold and focused, and she vanished into the trees. U'gah followed, his steps quick, anticipation crackling through him like a fuse.

Jacques gripped his pistol tight, the metal slick with sweat, the weight both familiar and suddenly inadequate. The creatures surged from the jungle—shadows with teeth. He braced, leveled his sights, and fired.

The recoil kicked back, sharp and punishing. *Bang. Bang. Bang.*

The lead dilophosaur's throat erupted—flesh splitting, black blood spraying in thick gouts. The second shot tore through cartilage, the third snapped its head back with a crack. The beast crumpled, limbs twitching, collapsed into the dirt.

The others didn't slow. Their jaws hung open, venom dripping in viscous threads. Crests pulsed, vibrant and menacing, their movements driven by a hunger that felt ancient and unrelenting.

Jacques's heart pounded in his ears. He fired again, squeezing off rounds as fast as he could, but the gaps closed, the jungle pressing in. Shapes burst from the undergrowth—more bodies, more teeth. The world narrowed to flashes of scales and shining fangs, the sharp stink of venom and rot filling his nose.

His arm shook from the strain. He couldn't kill them all. But he had to try.

The machete caught a charging beast. The blade sank with a wet crack into muscle. Blood splashed hot across Jacques's arm and face. The creature's momentum carried it past, collapsing in a heap, its body twitching as it bled into the dirt.

Another snapped at him—too close. Its teeth scraped across his forearm, searing pain erupting in a sudden, hot line. Jacques staggered, blood running warm and thick down his sleeve.

A high-pitched shriek tore through the air—something snapped past his ear, fast and deadly. A blur of motion, the sound sharp and sudden as the air cracked around him.

A juvenile dilophosaur hurtled through the air, limbs flailing in a ragged arc, body twisting like a broken puppet. It struck the lead adults with a gut-punch thud that rattled Jacques's teeth, the impact snapping through the clearing like a gunshot.

The creatures tumbled—five of them knocked sideways, snarling, scrabbling for purchase. Scales flashed, claws tore at the earth, a mess of tangled limbs and snarls. Their formation shattered in a flurry of chaos.

Jacques's vision narrowed, locked on the carnage.

What the hell—

Those left standing, stunned for a heartbeat, snapped their crests toward him in unison. Jaws gaped, venom dripped in long, glistening threads. Hunger radiated off them—blind, raw, relentless.

Jacques raised the machete. He planted his boots.

Let them come.

The ground shifted underfoot. His boots slipped on moss and cracked stone. The world tilted. He fell, wind knocked from his lungs as the earth slammed into him. Pain flared in his ribs, the weight of impact a dull, crushing thud.

A shadow lunged.

The third dilophosaur closed the gap—jaws unhinged, teeth gleaming, a blur of hunger and death.

No time. No escape. This was it.

Flashes—rain-slicked Paris, a café's warmth, his mother's hands, a half-built machine humming, Florence's scream cutting through the night.

A breath— A heartbeat— Acceptance.

It has been a good life, he thought, a strange, quiet calm settling in his chest. If this was the end, so be it.

He shut his eyes. The beast's stench hit him hot and foul—rot, decay, venom, old blood. It filled his lungs, thick and choking.

A voice—Hyatta's—cut through the chaos. Not shouted, but resonant. Steady. It found Jacques where he lay, buried beneath noise and pain, and anchored him.

"Rise and resist, brave warrior. Your time is not yet over. You do not fight alone."

The words landed not just in his ears but in his heart—like a hand seizing the organ and manually coaxing it to beat faster. A weight lifted. His muscles unlocked, unspooled, as if some unseen tether had been sliced clean. The paralyzing fear broke, and something surged up in its place—will, instinct.

He rolled hard, the ground scraping his shoulder, just as the dilophosaur's jaws snapped shut where his throat had been a blink before. The crack of teeth split the air.

His eyes flew open. The world surged back, brighter than it should be, but just as vicious.

The creature loomed above him, venom dripping from long, curved teeth. Heat blasted over him—carrion, bile. It reared, muscles tensing to strike.

A silver thread cut through the air.

A flash of moonlight caught on bone and iron— A whip.

Hyatta's whip.

It snapped through the air, slicing clean and fast, the segmented chain latching tight around the dilophosaur's thick neck. The jagged edges sank in, biting deep, black blood bubbling up as the links locked down.

Hyatta stood behind the beast, a shadow forged from sinew and steel, eyes blazing with a strange, wild light. His teeth clenched, muscles straining as he pulled.

The creature shrieked, a high, tearing wail that cracked the night. It thrashed, claws gouging the earth, body twisting in panic.

Hyatta twisted. The whip cinched tight, iron and bone. The beast's head snapped sideways with a wet crack. He heaved, whip straining—and the head tore free in a burst of inky blood.

It sprayed across the stones, splattering Jacques's chest. The smell of it hit him—a sudden, visceral splash that drove home the reality of the moment.

The creature's body collapsed in a heap, limbs twitching, tail lashing once, then still. A grotesque sprawl of scales and bone, steaming in the moonlight.

Jacques lay on the ground, chest heaving, blood in his mouth. His pulse hammered, the copper tang of it thick on his tongue. He stared wide-eyed—

Hyatta stood in the wreckage, untouched by blood or gore, whip loose in one hand. Not a scratch on him. Not a stitch of ragged clothing out of place. As if the violence had bent around him—too terrified to even catch a glimpse of him.

Jacques's pulse thundered. He staggered upright, boots skidding on blood-slick stone, breath ragged.

Hyatta remained perfectly still—a living statue. The whip hung loose in his hand, lustrous in fractured moonlight. He stood like a storm waiting to break—eyes sweeping the clearing.

An apex predator.

The jungle stirred.

The dilophosaurs regrouped, a shrieking chorus rising sharp as knives. They lunged in unison, jaws wide, frills flared, the scent of blood driving them into a frenzy. Their cries tore through the air, a teeth-rattling cacophony that cracked Jacques's skull.

Lusa burst from the shadows.

Fur and rage.

He tore into them, a paragon of violence. He swung the bodies of fallen juveniles like grotesque clubs, their broken forms crashing into skulls, cracking ribs. Each blow was a thunderclap, a tremor that vibrated in Jacques's bones. Blood sprayed in wide arcs, painting stone and bark.

Wham— a chest caved in. Crack— a skull split like a melon.

Each impact sent shockwaves through the night.

U'gah joined the storm, wild-eyed and roaring. The greatclub howled in his hands, a low, guttural growl pulsing with each swing. The club's jagged head gleamed, a snarling tyrannosaurus hungry for the kill. Scales split, bones shattered, blood spattered in thick, dark splashes. U'gah moved fast, a whirlwind of raw power, each strike a blur of muscle and force.

His roars mixed with the club's rumbling voice, a deep, echoing hunger that vibrated in the stones.

The tide shifted.

The predators—once confident in their numbers, their hunger —broke. Their cries shifted, bloodlust bleeding into panic, hunger dissolving into terror. They scattered, tried to melt into the shadows.

Hyatta flowed like liquid fire, every step controlled, precise. The whip lashed out—a streak of bone and iron snapping through the night, cutting off their retreat.

His voice followed, low and cold, a steel edge slicing the air:

"I will not make the mistake of allowing you and your ilk to live."

No shout. No wasted breath. The words carried, heavy and sharp, laced with the weight of judgment.

"Your days of terrorizing those who walk in the light are over."

The whip cracked. Once. Twice.

Each strike landed with brutal finality—flesh splitting, bone shattering, a percussive rhythm that tore through the clearing. The sounds—wet and sharp, the snap of ligaments, the crunch of ribs—rang loud in the hush that followed. The air vibrated with it, a pulse of violence that pressed into Jacques's chest.

Jacques watched, rooted. His hands trembled at his sides. He had seen men die—by bullet, by blade, in trenches and alleys—but this…this was something else. This was methodical, ruthless, a machine of destruction.

Hyatta and Lusa moved as one—a storm given shape, each movement brutal, yet graceful, like a dance. Lusa's fur dripped with blood, eyes glowing, each strike of his claws a blur of raw, animal force. The sound of bone giving way under his weight echoed, each impact a shudder through the ground.

When it ended, Lusa stood, blood-soaked, chest heaving. Steam curled from him, rising in slow, hot spirals. His whiskers dripped with gore, paws blackened, claws shining wet and sharp.

Jacques turned, searching, and froze.

Hyatta stood untouched.

No blood. No wounds. His clothes torn, yes, but his skin unmarked, as if the storm had passed around him, not through him. He stood in the carnage, whip coiled in his hand, eyes steady, posture unshaken.

Jacques blinked. His vision wavered. The contrast—the man untouched, the blood-soaked ground—was too much. His knees buckled.

The earth tilted. He fell.

Cold stone pressed into his cheek. His pulse thundered in his ears, his breath rasping in shallow, uneven gasps.

Mushrooms, he thought, a strange, distant notion. Maybe I've eaten something poisonous.

Dinosaurs. Lizardmen. A man wielding a whip of bone and iron. A cat, laughing and purring while tearing predators apart with its bare paws.

Too much. Far too much.

The edges of his vision darkened. The cold seeped in.

Too much.

Jacques had thought himself a man of the world. The Great Shift had shattered reality itself, twisted the rules of nature into something barely recognizable. He'd seen wonders in his time with the gnomes—strange technology, creatures that defied classification, even whispered rumors of gods trapped in machines. But this? This was something else entirely.

A world where everything was upside down—where myths walked, and monsters hunted in packs beneath an indifferent moon. Where the boundary between science and legend had vanished, leaving him stranded in a place that felt like a fever dream.

He closed his eyes, just for a moment—letting the dark wash over him, a desperate attempt to ground himself, to pretend this was all a hallucination.

Maybe it was. Maybe some toxin in the air, some spore in the jungle, had poisoned his mind and sent him spiraling into a nightmare that wasn't real.

"Are you injured, Jacques of Hephaestus?"

Hyatta's voice cut through the fog—impossibly calm. It had weight, that voice. Like stone settling into place.

Jacques forced his eyes open, blinking hard against the spinning world. He focused on Hyatta's face—etched in moonlight, features chiseled and a silhouette against the chaos.

"I... I'm fine," Jacques rasped, his throat dry. He pushed himself up, his arms trembling under the weight of fatigue. "Just... overwhelmed, I suppose."

His eyes drifted downward—landing on the emblem stitched into his jacket. The stylized gear, the bold HIT lettering beneath it. A corporate logo. A symbol of his employer—Hephaestus Innovative Technologies.

But Hyatta's words from earlier echoed, slipping under his skin, gnawing.

Jacques glanced up, the question tumbling out before he could stop it.

"Why do you keep saying that?" he asked, voice rough with disbelief. "I'm from France, not... not a servant of some Greek god."

Hyatta's lips curved into a slow, knowing smile—a smile that felt like an answer to a question Jacques hadn't known to ask.

"You wear the sigil of Hephaestus," Hyatta replied, voice smooth as river stone. His gaze flicked briefly to Emerald, standing nearby with her rifle still gripped tight. "And your small companion bears the mark of Astraeus."

Emerald's looked at him curiously.

"These gods are known in this land," Hyatta continued, voice almost gentle now. "Their power... lingers, though faded. If you are not their messengers then why do you display their marks?"

A chill scraped down Jacques's spine.

It was just a logo. Designed by marketing teams in glass towers, printed on uniforms, slapped onto every gadget and document back home. A brand, not a blessing.

"I... I don't know," Jacques admitted, the words slipping out. "It's just... a logo."

Hyatta inclined his head slightly, his eyes reflecting something deep, unreadable.

"Perhaps," he murmured, soft, weighted, as if laying a stone on a grave.

Before Jacques could press him further, the underbrush rustled with sudden urgency.

Florence burst into the clearing, her hair tangled, her face streaked with sweat and tears. She barreled toward him—toward them—like a bullet, Saturn and NAVI trailing behind her in a frantic, disheveled blur.

The moment she saw Jacques, something in her broke.

A strangled cry tore from her throat, and she flung herself at him, knocking him clean off his feet. They tumbled, limbs tangled, her sobs breaking loose as she buried her face in his shoulder.

"They tried to eat me!" she wailed, the words muffled by his shirt, soaked into the fabric along with her tears.

Jacques wheezed, winded by the weight of her—and then Saturn and U'gah, who launched himself in like an eager terrier —pressing him into the dirt. Lusa circled them all, bobtail flicking, golden eyes gleaming with unmistakable amusement.

Jacques could only laugh, shaking as he tried to untangle himself from the chaotic heap.

"Easy, mes amis!" he gasped, ruffling Florence's hair in a rare, instinctive gesture of comfort. His hands were trembling, but he tried to keep his voice steady, calm—like an anchor in the storm.

"You'll crush me!"

Florence sobbed harder, her arms tightening around him.

Jacques cupped the back of her head, his palm warm against the tangle of her hair.

"C'est fini," he murmured, voice soft but firm.

"You're safe now, Florence. We're all safe."

It took time—long, aching minutes—for Florence to calm. Her body trembled in Jacques's arms, every sob wracking her thin frame, the tension in her muscles slowly, finally, ebbing like a tide pulling back from the shore. Her fingers clutched at him like talons, digging into the fabric of his shirt, and he let her, murmuring soft reassurances in French, the words spilling without thought. Just the rhythm of them was a steady pulse to hold onto.

Emerald and Saturn knelt nearby, their presence a quiet balm. Emerald rubbed slow circles between Florence's shoulders, her voice soft, steady, coaxing her like a frightened animal. Saturn, ever the observer, spoke in a low, measured cadence, offering quiet, logical affirmations. "You're safe now. They're gone. We're together."

It worked—eventually. Florence's breathing slowed, the ragged gasps fading into soft, shuddering sobs. She buried her face in Jacques's shoulder, tears soaking into the fabric, her body trembling less and less with each exhale.

Relief hit like a pulse—deep and quiet.

For now, they were safe.

But already the next question pressed in.

What now?

They had survived this—the nightmare in the jungle, the dilophosaurs, the lizardmen, the storm of teeth and venom. But the city loomed ahead, dark and ancient, its crumbling walls whispering of older dangers yet to come. If the beasts outside were this savage, what waited for them inside?

The silence stretched, brittle and heavy, the weight of exhaustion settling over the group like a damp fog. Their usual certainty—Emerald's scientific curiosity, Saturn's analytical precision, even Florence's stubborn conviction—had cracked under the pressure, leaving behind faces etched with weariness and doubt.

Jacques's own voice felt foreign in his throat as he finally asked the question pressing against his ribs.

"What now?" he rasped, his gaze sweeping the circle of worn faces.

No one answered—at least not immediately.

And then—

Hyatta.

He stepped forward from the shadows, his presence a ripple through the air—calm, solid, like an island placed at the center of a roiling sea. His voice was quiet but carried, steady as the earth itself.

"The Iruxi of this city have a debt they must pay."

His eyes—sharp, unyielding—shifted to the jagged skyline of the ruins, his posture as effortless as a lion surveying his domain.

"If you truly seek something within these walls," he continued, his voice steady, almost… inviting, "you are welcome to travel with Lusa and me."

The weight of his words hung in the air, heavy, undeniable.

U'gah grunted, a fierce sound of agreement, his battered fur bristling with excitement.

Emerald's eyes brightened with a dangerous glint, mischief sparking in the exhaustion—a flash of adventure shining through the grime and blood. "I'm in," she said without hesitation.

Saturn hesitated. Jacques saw the gears turning—the risk-reward calculus, the cold math of survival. A long pause. Then, a nod.

And Florence—

Her reaction was immediate, sharp, visceral.

Her body locked. Arms crossed tight, shoulders squared like a fortress, chin lifted in resistance. Her eyes—red-rimmed, glinting with fury—fixed on Hyatta with a glare so sharp Jacques half-expected it to cut the man where he stood. If looks could kill, Hyatta Kahlan would have been a smoldering corpse in the dirt.

But Hyatta only met her gaze with that same, unreadable calm —unchallenged, unmoved.

Jacques felt the tension like a crackle in the air, static building in the silence.

And yet—he knew.

They had no choice. Not really.

Survival in this place demanded adaptability. Strength. Allies.

Hyatta and Lusa were both.

Jacques made his decision.

"We accept your offer, Hyatta," he said, voice steady, the words anchoring him in the moment.

Emerald and U'gah grinned—an odd pair of ragged survivors, united in their shared excitement. Saturn's shoulders sagged in reluctant acceptance, the burden of logic weighing heavy on him.

Florence said nothing. Her arms stayed crossed, her gaze locked on the dirt, a storm of unspoken fury simmering just beneath the surface.

Jacques let out a slow breath. The knot in his chest eased, but it didn't go away.

CHAPTER EIGHT

Jacques and Emerald moved through the crumbling city with the precision of survivors honed by necessity. Each step was measured, deliberate—boots whispered on broken cobblestone, nearly lost in the thick, humid air, as if the city itself held its breath.

They advanced in tandem, clearing corners with ease. Jacques's pistol hung steady in his grip, machete loose in the other— ready to strike, block, or improvise. Emerald mirrored his movements, carbine close to her shoulder, eyes sweeping the shattered windows, darkened archways, jagged rooftops.

Florence trailed behind them, her gaze fixed with the kind of wide-eyed tension Jacques recognized.

Above, Saturn drifted with NAVI, the drone's rotors murmuring as it skimmed the broken buildings. He leaned forward in his harness, viewing the ruins through NAVI's sensors.

The hollow rhythm of their footsteps was consumed by the chirr of insects.

Jacques had pushed for stealth. To scout ahead. To minimize contact. But Hyatta had waved it off with the easy arrogance of someone who didn't care if they were seen, and perhaps, desired a confrontation.

Now he walked the center of the road as if it were built for him —whip coiled at his side, pace leisurely. Dawn spilled molten streaks across the sky, catching the tips of broken stone—the skeleton of what once was a city.

Lusa stalked beside him, massive and fluid. His half-lidded gaze barely moved, golden eyes brilliant like twin coins. Muscles shifted beneath his fur with every step—a quiet, deadly rhythm.

And behind them, U'gah. Scruffy, small, and dragging his club. He looked like a lost cub following in his father's footprints.

Emerald shot Jacques a glance, brow furrowed. She leaned close, her voice irritated and low, breath brushing his ear.

"Shouldn't we be more... discreet?"

Jacques shrugged. His thumb tapped the machete grip—a steady, reflexive beat.

"Hyatta seems to have a plan," he said dryly, just loud enough for her. "And I'm not about to question a man who turns three meter dinosaurs into dog food with a flick of his wrist."

Emerald let out a small, mirthless breath.

"That's fair," she murmured—though her gaze still darted to every shadow. "Still feels like we're being reckless."

Two blocks ahead, they emerged.

Iruxi scouts.

They stumbled from an alley into the rising sun, their movements twitchy and off-balance. Spears gripped in exhausted, trembling hands. The scales along their necks flared in panic.

They froze.

Their bodies went rigid at the sight of Jacques and Emerald. Hyatta and Lusa loomed behind.

"Stop!" Jacques barked. The word cracked through the ruins like a shot.

The Iruxi flinched. Then fled.

Spears clattered to the stone as they turned and ran, claws scraping for purchase. Within seconds they vanished into the city's maze.

"Stop!" Emerald called after them, her tone dry. She raised her carbine with a grin. "We just want to talk!"

Jacques raised his pistol, finger brushing the trigger—

And then—a hand. Hyatta's hand.

It clamped over Jacques's wrist—not bruising, not aggressive. Just final.

Heat bled through Jacques's skin. The grip was firm. Unshakable.

He lowered the pistol.

"Let them go," Hyatta said, velvet-soft—but with a steel edge that left no room for debate.

Jacques stared at him. Muscles taut.

"They'll warn the others," he said, disbelief seeping into his voice. "They could bring an army."

Hyatta's smile was slow and dangerous.

His eyes caught an errant stream of sunlight.

"Let them," he said, the words smooth, almost amused. "Then we won't have to hunt them down."

Lusa rumbled—a low, guttural sound that seemed to rise from the earth itself. His eyes narrowed, gleaming.

Emerald lowered her weapon with a mechanical stiffness. Her expression knotted, drifting between Hyatta and Jacques, her thoughts unreadable.

"Why aren't you worried?" she asked, tension leaking through her voice despite the calm she tried to hold.

Hyatta's grin widened.

Not warm. Not reassuring.

Predatory.

"Because," he said, crisp and certain, "we are the hunters. Not the hunted."

Jacques shot Emerald a look. Her face mirrored his own: uncertainty, unease. Hyatta's confidence wasn't comforting. It was *unsettling*. As if the danger ahead was expected or welcomed, even.

Who the hell was this man?

Emerald's voice sliced through the quiet. "But... why?" she asked, curiosity edged with fear. "What exactly are we hunting?"

Hyatta turned.

His eyes blue as glacial ice, cold as the void between stars.

"The scouts," he said, voice darkening, "are not our prey."

His gaze shifted. Jacques followed it—and felt his stomach drop.

A massive structure rose at the city's heart, towering above the wreckage. Nine towering obelisks casting jagged shadows that creeped across the earth.

"Our quarry lies within the heart of this place." Hyatta's voice was lower now like a growl, venomous, and barely contained.

"The Lizard King."

He spat the title like a curse.

The words hung in the air—heavy. A promise of violence.

A shiver crawled beneath Jacques's skin.

This wasn't a hunt.

Hyatta Kahlan was walking a warpath.

He wasn't just their guide. He was the tip of the spear. A herald of the end for these reptiles.

Jacques glanced at Emerald—saw it in her face. That brittle twist of her mouth, the wary gleam in her eyes.

The thrill of discovery had curdled into dread.

Emerald, forever mining humor from despair, sighed. A crooked smirk tugged at her lips.

"Well," she muttered. "Politics and revenge. At least those are two things that remind me of home."

Jacques chuckled, unexpectedly.

"Oui," he said quietly, gaze lingering on the fortress.

"Me as well."

***

As they moved deeper into the city, the landscape shifted.

The blind alleys and brutal geometry gave way to something stranger—less designed, more dreamlike. Gardens once tamed had burst into wild color. Vines spilled from fractured walls, flowering in impossible hues—deep violets, searing golds, blossoms like flares against ancient stone.

The air shimmered with heat. The scent of petals and rot was life clawing back what had been stolen.

They passed pavilions that had softened by time. Spires leaned, carvings were smoothed by rain. Mosaics, barely visible, told stories long erased. Columns bowed under ivy. Statues stared hollow-eyed through curtains of root and vine.

The avenues wound through the ruins and blooms. Nature was reclaiming the empire. Beauty and entropy entwined.

Jacques thought he heard laughter in the breeze. A memory. A ghost of goblets clinking in now-ruined courtyards.

Then—the obelisks came into full view.

Nine of them.

Towering in the city's core, catching the rising sun, glowing. The material was not stone, not metal, but something else. They shimmered with iridescence. Light refracted from their surfaces in radiant halos, casting spectral colors across the ruin like dancing ghosts.

Pain bloomed in his chest—grief for something unnamed, awe for something forgotten.

"C'est... magnifique," he whispered, running his hand through his sweat-darkened hair. He wiped his brow, trembling slightly. The words came out small.

"It's... breathtaking," Emerald echoed, her voice low and fragile. Her eyes shimmered with refracted light.

Even Saturn, who was descending on NAVI's whirring lift, looked stunned. His boots touched down with a crunch of gravel. The drone hissed quietly behind him.

For a moment, everything held.

Then—Florence.

She burst from the shadows like a woman possessed.

Her footsteps hit hard, heels snapping on stone.

Her face—a firestorm. Then she stood, arms crossed, mouth tight, and her eyes alight with fury.

"There are large groups of the—" Saturn began.

Florence cut him off.

"I'm sick of this! Sick of being left behind while you all play soldier!"

Her voice shredded the stillness into confetti.

"You left me in that *filthy hole* while you ran off with these— these *strangers*! And now what? You expect me to just trail behind? Forgotten?!"

It was a howl of betrayal.

She turned on U'gah.

Her finger jabbed at the halfling, her tone venomous. Jacques flinched.

148

"And what was *that* thing doing? Hunting lizardmen for *fun*? We're supposed to be finding a way *home*—not turning into *savages!* Not—*butchering things like animals!*"

Even the wind held its breath.

Jacques glanced toward Hyatta and Lusa.

Both watched Florence's outburst with an eerie calm. Hyatta's expression remained unreadable while Lusa's eyes shone with quiet amusement, his bobtail flicking lazily.

Emerald stepped forward, voice low and careful—like coaxing a cornered animal.

"Florence... we didn't mean to leave you behind. We were just trying to—"

"Trying to *what?*" Florence snapped, her voice slicing through the space between them. Her eyes locked on Emerald—glassy, furious, wild. "Trying to satisfy your childish curiosity? Trying to play hero in a world you don't even understand?"

She turned, fury lashing toward Saturn.

"And *you*—" Her voice hitched, but she pushed through. "You're supposed to be the rational one. The voice of reason. But you're no better. You left me. All of you. For some stupid *adventure!*"

Saturn opened his mouth. His hands lifted in a half-apology, even though it had been her that had run out on him.

"Florence, I... I'm sorry. We were just trying to assess the situation—Help U'gah—"

Her contradictions bewildered the old gnome. His words faltered, broken by confusion.

Jacques stood still, watching it all unravel. He felt the fracture widen—fear and fatigue splintering the last of their unity. And in the center: Florence. Trembling. Broken.

He felt the ache tighten behind his eyes.

And all around them—the city watched.

"Help *U'gah?*" Florence's words came out spiteful and disbelieving. Then she scoffed, brittly. "That *creature* is a menace. He's the reason we're in this mess to begin with!"

Jacques had held back. He had tried to let the storm pass.

But something in her tone—panic twisting into blame—snapped something loose inside him.

Jacques stepped forward.

His voice cut through the tension—not loud, but firm.

"Florence."

Just her name. Just enough.

"I know you're upset. We all are. But right now, we need to focus on what's in front of us." He swept a hand toward the fractured skyline. "This is our reality. And if we don't work together, we die. That's the only thing that matters."

Florence's eyes snapped to his—red, wet, seething. But beneath the fury, Jacques could see her terror and vulnerability.

"*Survive?*" she spat. The word landed like poison. Her tone wavered, then dropped just to a whisper.

"What about getting home? What about our lives?"

She folded in on herself, her voice breaking under its own weight.

"I want to go home."

Her arms fell. Her shoulders sagged. The fire in her eyes guttered to ash.

"I don't want to be here anymore."

The silence returned—heavier than before.

No one moved.

Even the jungle stilled. The wind paused. The ruins seemed to lean in.

Jacques said nothing.

There were no answers. Only this road. Only forward.

Then Hyatta spoke.

He'd been watching, statue-still.

His voice was quiet—cold iron wrapped in silk.

"Fear is powerful."

He stepped forward.

"It sharpens the senses, but it also poisons the mind. It clouds judgment, makes us strike out at our enemies, at strangers... or at the ones we care about."

His eyes locked on Florence—blue, terrible.

"I see your fear," he said. "But I see your strength too, Florence of Olympus." Somehow, just the way he spoke her name made it feel like a spell. "The same strength that's kept your heart beating until now."

He tilted his head, almost gentle. Almost.

"Don't waste it." He paused. "Use it."

His words rang like the final note in a forgotten song.

"That's how we move forward."

Florence glared back.

Her body trembled—fists clenched, breath jagged.

She looked ready to scream, but didn't.

She just stood there, shaking, teetering between collapse and fury.

Jacques felt the moment stretch, waiting on the inevitable explosion.

Hyatta turned away, his voice cold, final.

"We have a task to complete."

Hyatta's gaze locked on the obelisks ahead—the radiant, shimmering surfaces catching the morning light like opalescent fangs.

"There will be time later for grievances."

He strode forward, whip coiled at his side, its rhythm like a serpent's tail. Lusa followed silently, prowling on two legs like some half-human alleycat. And U'gah, who remained unbothered, trailed behind them, swinging his greatclub with the careless ease of a child with his stick.

Florence's eyes narrowed at Hyatta's back.

Jacques saw it—the shift.

Florence's pain hardened into something cold. She wouldn't forget this. Not any of it.

***

The path through the inner city was a tangle of ruin and regrowth. It was less a road than a battleground between nature and civilization. Thick creepers coiled around fallen archways, dragging weathered facades into the soil. Sleeves snagged. Underbrush clawed at their boots, reaching like hungry hands through the city's broken arteries.

It was hot, claustrophobic, and uninviting, to the point of foreboding.

And yet, by the time they reached the first obelisk's base, Jacques found himself longing for the chaos of the overgrowth below.

It took time to find the hidden entrance. Jacques hadn't known there would be one in the first place, but his intuition had screamed at him.

The stairs spiraled within the tower's core—steep and slick— each step a test of footing.

The stone pressed close, broken only by narrow slits that could not be seen from the outside. Staggered views to allowed light to shine in.

Below, the city stretched. Rooftops collapsed into green, streets swallowed by vines. The other obelisks gleamed in the sun like alien gods, creating a circle of eight, with the ninth being set dead center.

It was beautiful.

The group split at the base. Hyatta, Lusa, and U'gah disappeared into the overgrown gardens and parks like a hunting party trudging through wild grasslands. Jacques, Emerald, and Saturn climbed, hoping for height. For strategy. A plan.

Higher now, winded, but still climbing—Jacques felt doubt settle in.

Would they just be lookouts? A support team watching from above while Hyatta waded into the blood?

The thought soured on his tongue.

And Florence.

She had refused outright.

"You're all fools!" she'd screamed, fists shaking. "You think violence solves everything!"

Her words rang through his head like a bell in a cathedral vault.

He'd tried to calmly reason with her, using his engineer logic, but she wouldn't hear him.

Now she was gone. Somewhere. He didn't know where. They would find her after the danger was over.

Then he spotted her—arms crossed, sitting beneath a crumbling arch, stiff and alone.

He sighed, resigned.

We're running out of time to hold her together.

The thought had barely formed before the air changed.

A vibration he felt through the soles of his boots.

A rhythmic pulse rose through the stone like a summoning.

Drums.

Each beat spoke a promise.

"Go!" he barked.

Emerald fell in behind him, carbine snugged tight, her face grim. Saturn lagged a step behind her, muttering calculations.

The drumming built faster now. The sound of the city's heartbeat gaining strength.

Jacques felt it in his ribs. In the walls. In the very air.

He didn't know what waited above.

But they needed a better vantage point.

The drums thundered. Words dissolved. Only motion remained.

They climbed the stairs that spiraled inside of the interior.

The obelisk's core wound around them like an immense, whirling throat of stone. The drums beat through their bodies like a second pulse.

They reached the top of the stairwell to find a wide platform that seemed open to the sky, but it wasn't. It felt more like a projection, relayed by some unknown meta-material.

Still morning light spilled across the city, gilding the ruin's broken edges in gold. It should have been beautiful—and it was—but Jacques felt a sick lurch in his gut as he gripped the platform's edge and looked down.

The city sprawled below in impossible detail, a tapestry of cracked stone and jungle green, wreathing out from the obelisk like veins from a heart. Prismatic paths weaved through the chaos, sparkling in the light. The patterns too intricate, too alien to comprehend.

But it wasn't the beauty that held him. It was the gathering below.

The gardens had become a seething mass of bodies—lizardmen, hundreds, maybe more. Their iron armor glinted black, marred by battle. They moved like a living tide, scaled arms raised, weapons clashing against shields in rhythm with the drums.

The chanting sound hit like a wall—gruff and raw—rising in waves that reached for the sky.

Banners snapped in the wind. Leather, cloth, flayed skins stretched tight. Symbols burned deep displaying grotesque artistry.

Jacques couldn't look away.

Beside him, Emerald's hands tightened on her carbine, her knuckles bone-white.

"This is it," she whispered, barely audible over the roar. Her voice was fragile. "We're not getting out of here alive."

Saturn stood motionless. His usual flare of motion from hands, fingers, and shoulders was gone. His face had gone hard. Whatever calculations had run through his mind had stopped. The numbers didn't matter here.

Jacques felt it settle—that familiar cold, a kind of stillness.

He'd felt it before, many times, in the mountains of New Poland, on the coastal plains of Belgium, and even in the once beautiful vineyards of eastern France.

This was the breath before chaos, when the mind went quiet and the body simply acted.

Fear was a luxury.

"We need to find Hyatta and Lusa," Jacques yelled over the noise.

Emerald nodded, as did Saturn.

The sound changed.

The chanting rose—fevered. The drumming quickened. Spears thrust skyward. Fists slammed shields, a tide rising.

Suddenly the crowd parted and a figure emerged.

This lizardman was taller than the rest by a full head, absolutely massive. Its scales shown like hammered copper, set with polished stones that caught the sun like fire. A headdress of feathers and bone crowned its skull, trailing like the plumage of a war god.

Its presence pressed into Jacques's chest.

The Lizard King had arrived.

CHAPTER NINE

Florence stormed down the chatoyant path, her boots striking the stone like gunshots in the morning hush. Each step was furious. *I am not weak. I am not helpless. I will not be left behind again.*

Light cascaded beneath her feet in ribbons of violet, green, and blue—a dizzying haze she ignored. Her fists clenched until her nails carved half-moons into her palms. The heat behind her eyes threatened to spill over, but she refused to give it that power.

Let them run off into danger, she thought, heart pounding. *Let Hyatta and his monster play war. Let Emerald flash her gun with that smug little grin. Let Jacques pretend he's in control— always calm, always steady, always so damn condescending.*

They thought she'd wait in the dirt like some forgotten child? No.

Not this time.

Ahead, two Iruxi guards blocked the path. Both hulking, reptilians clad in patchwork bone and hammered metal. Their slitted eyes narrowed as they spotted her. Spears crossed, iron-hard and unmoving.

Florence didn't slow.

Her stride quickened, fury in her breath, her chest tight but rising.

She stopped just short—close enough to see moisture bead on their scaled snouts. Her voice cracked the still air like a whip.

"I need to speak with your leader," she said in English, but delivered like a command.

The guards flinched barely. with a flutter of surprise in yellow eyes. They shifted the angle of their spears.

"I have information," she continued, cold, but steady. "An imminent attack. On your tribe."

That landed.

They exchanged glances. One hissed, uncertain. The larger, scarred one tilted his head, studying her.

For a beat, she thought they might strike at her. But she held her stance—back straight, chin high. No fear. No weakness.

Finally, the scarred one grunted then his chin jerked.

The other guard lowered his spear.

That's right, she thought, a tight smile flashing. *Let me through, you overgrown lizards. You'll see what I can do.*

She marched past them, heart hammering in her throat, eyes fixed ahead.

The garden opened vastly before her.

Hundreds of Iruxi filled the space, a tide of scales and iron and war paint. Their bodies glistened with oil and sweat. Weapons raised and fell in time with the drums—massive, hide-stretched things beaten by scaled hands. The rhythm pounded in her ribs.

She felt small. So small.

The warriors chanted in time with the beat, snarling syllables that echoed off the stone. Banners held high whipped in the wind, torn cloth and stretched hide, daubed with symbols she couldn't read but understood instinctively.

Bad omens.

A spike of fear stabbed her.

What are you doing, you stupid woman?

But then the fear twisted—became something else.

Power.

They were afraid too—of something bigger. She saw it in their eyes, saw it in the tremble beneath their armor, in how their spears didn't quite stay still.

She could use that.

Let them stare. Let them wonder. Let them *believe* she was the key to their survival.

Because she was.

A chill rippled through her—a thrill. A plan forming, sharp-edged and fast. She would feed their fear. Shape it. Wield it.

Yes, she'd save Jacques. Save Emerald.

But on *her* terms.

She would make this chaos her stage.

And when the curtain rose, they wouldn't see the woman they'd dismissed. They'd see the one who commanded the storm.

Her eyes swept the crowd.

A slow, dangerous smile curled her lips.

Let them underestimate her.

They'd learn.

Soon enough— They'd all learn.

***

Saturn used his hands to expand the image displayed on the meta-material allowing them to see the outside of the obelisk. Jacques's stomach knotted as Saturn pointed her out in the chaos below.

He saw Florence, stiff-backed and pale, being marched through the garden like a prisoner of war. Two tall Iruxi flanked her, their spears angled toward her spine. The morning light shimmered off their armor, casting long, fractured shadows across the stone.

Florence's posture was defiant.

Her chin lifted, her steps steady—yet Jacques caught the tremble in her fingers.

She was holding it together by force of will alone.

"Merde," Jacques hissed, breath sharp with helpless fury. His mind lurched, too many variables crashing into one another. *How?* They'd left her off the main paths, hidden from sight.

Had she wandered?

Of course she had.

Goddamn it, Florence.

He couldn't dwell. He zoomed out, looking at the whole picture.

The garden beyond thrashed with bodies. Iruxi massed like a wave of scaled flesh and crude iron, weapons raised, banners snapping like wings. The open space was a killing field.

Even with Hyatta's whip and Lusa's strength, even with U'gah's greatclub—charging into that chaos would be suicide. Unless...

"We need a distraction," Jacques said. "Something loud enough to pull their attention."

Emerald's voice came quick, her breath tight. "You have explosives?"

Jacques shook his head, frustration rising hot behind his eyes. "Two shape charges. A spool of det cord. Not enough to matter."

Saturn glanced between Jacques and the scene outside. His expression twisted, analytical thought giving way to helplessness.

160

"I could use NAVI," he said, reluctantly. "Buzz the crowd. Draw them away. Maybe spook them a little." He hesitated.

Jacques saw it—the flash of pain washing over Saturn's face. NAVI wasn't just hardware. It was Saturn's vision. His reach. His control.

And losing NAVI would blind them all.

"No," Jacques snapped. "She's too valuable. If we lose her, we lose everything."

Emerald's fingers twitched on her carbine. Her eyes scanned the ruin, rapid-fire. "There has to be something else. Something we're missing," she exclaimed.

Silence.

Florence was being led deeper into the chaos—closer to the drumbeat's core. Every second dragged her further from reach.

Jacques clenched his jaw.

They were failing her.

He wiped sweat from his brow, the salt stinging his eyes. The sun pressed down, hot and heavy.

Think.

His gaze swept the platform—searching for *anything*.

He hadn't noticed them before, gaps in the ceiling. And above them tucked, in dust and shadow, something reflective.

He saw a huge, circular mirror on a swivel mount, startlingly intact. Its polished face caught his reflection—sunburnt, smeared with sweat, eyes hard.

Below it, a nest of cables snaked into a biometric plate.

Jacques's pulse quickened.

He stepped forward—already recognizing it for what it was.

He slammed his hand on the scanner, not even considering it might do nothing or reject his hand print.

In the center of the platform, an interface terminal lowered from the ceiling.

He tapped a key. Then another.

The console blinked—loading—then flickered to life like an old eye opening for the first time in centuries.

A map appeared.

The layout was unmistakable: the central gardens, the nine obelisks in ritualistic alignment, and at the center—marked clearly—a domed structure pulsing faintly and the base of the central obelisk.

This was a control system.

His fingers danced over the keys with pure instinct. Command prompts. System requests.

Each one blinked. Locked.

A login screen.

"Merde," Jacques muttered, heat rising behind his eyes.

He scanned the console, desperately.

Then he saw it—etched faint in the polymer housing, like a digital scar:

HIT.

Hephaestus Innovative Technologies.

His own damn company.

Jacques let out a breathless laugh, shaking his head. *"Bien sûr.* Why not."

He typed in his employee ID, hands trembling. The password came without thought—*fairedesgalipettes69*—muscle memory from a hundred caffeine-fueled nights in the Paris office. His fingers hesitated for half a second, then hit Enter.

The screen spun. Lines of code scrolled.

Then—*ping.*

ACCESS GRANTED

Jacques sagged forward, exhaling. Unbelievable.

He was in.

Data flooded the display—coordinates, energy readouts, environmental metrics—all in crisp, sterile lines. Power levels pulsed off the charts: amps, volts, wattage far beyond anything he'd seen.

At the center: a blinking prompt.

OPEN CANOPY — CONFIRM?

Jacques paused.

Then—without calculation, without caution—he hit Enter.

A deep, grinding vibration rolled through the obelisk. Stone shuddered. Metal shrieked.

Overhead, the roof began to shift—massive panels sliding apart.

True sunlight flooded in.

Blinding white washed across the chamber. Jacques stumbled back, shielding his eyes, his vision briefly stunted.

Wind surged through the opening, stirring dust into a cyclone. And suddenly the city revealed itself—in truth. The drums quieted. The light sharpened. Their situation more dire.

Emerald's voice cut through the static. "What did you *do*?!"

Jacques blinked against the light. The platform beneath them was now expanding, the panels locking into place with mechanical finality, creating an overwatch position.

"I'm not entirely sure," Jacques admitted. His voice was thin, stunned. On the console, a new prompt blinked:

ALIGN SYSTEM — CONFIRM?

His fingers hovered over the keys, suspended between instinct and disaster. Every rational impulse screamed *stop*—but curiosity whispered, *Push it.*

Saturn let out a breathy laugh—half awe, half disbelief.

"You wanted a distraction," he said, the corner of his mouth tilting upward. "Looks like you got one."

He gestured to the chaos unfolding below.

Jacques leaned over the ledge.

All eight other obelisks had opened.

The lizardmen formations had split. Warriors stumbled, shouting, spears raised skyward. Some backed away in confusion. Mirrors bathed the gardens in shifting beams of refracted light, cutting strange shapes across the ground.

The chant faltered. The rhythm broke.

"*Eh bien,*" he said, mischievously. "We have our distraction."

Emerald shook her head, exhaling hard. Some of the tension in her shoulders bled away.

Jacques turned back to the console, heart pounding. The cursor blinked—steady. Waiting.

A dangerous gleam lit his eyes.

"Let's see what else this thing can do," he murmured.

He tapped the command.

The console thrummed—resonant, ancient.

Above them, the mirror shifted—tilting with eerie precision. Across the skyline, the other obelisks mirrored the motion. Their polished faces moved in synchrony, slicing light across the city like blades.

Clicks. Whirs. Then a rising hum—like turbines spinning up.

Saturn leaned in, eyes wide. "Fascinating," he whispered.

A schematic bloomed on the secondary display—hexagons, circles, pulsing lines. His fingers hovered above them, reverently.

"It's solar-powered," he murmured. "Energy redistribution... maybe radiant amplification? Could be resonant targeting, I don't—this is incredible."

Emerald peered over his shoulder.

Emerald leaned in, eyes tracking the geometry. "Phased heliostats, resonant cavity—this is a coherent solar concentrator." She blinked, impressed. "Fancy."

Jacques inhaled.

"Let's not get ahead of ourselves," he said, though his voice betrayed the thrill behind it. "We don't know what we're playing with."

Before anyone could answer, the platform shuddered.

Jacques snapped his head up.

From the peak of the central obelisk, something rose.

A construct of mirrored plates and iridescent crystal unfolded like the petals of a mechanical flower. It spun slowly, catching the sun and fracturing it into a storm of color. Light scattered in blinding arcs across the city, refracted like stained glass.

The air crackled.

A hum rolled out from the tower—high, electric, reverberating. Jacques felt it in his chest, vibrating through the soles of his boots. Emerald's hair lifted in the static, her eyes wide, locked on the structure as it turned.

On the console, a new prompt appeared:

Multiple Foreign Hostile Biological Entities Detected

Activate Security Protocol — Alpha Blue — Confirm?

Jacques stared—breath shallow, skin tight with the weight of decision.

He turned to Emerald and Saturn.

"You ready for this?" he asked hoarsely, almost drowned beneath the machine's rising pulse.

Emerald nodded, her expression carved from resolve.

Saturn said nothing. His lips were a line. His gaze darted across the display, running risk matrices no one could understand, not even him.

Jacques exhaled. His fingers hovered above the key.

No turning back.

He hit Confirm.

The console bloomed with data—mirror alignments, rising power levels, targeting telemetry. Servo motors whined as the dish pivoted, locking onto the crystal suspended above the central structure.

Eight beams of focused sunlight struck the mirrored array—converging.

The flower ignited.

A lance of white energy erupted from its core—brilliant, searing, unstoppable.

Whatever they'd awakened—

It was now in motion.

CHAPTER TEN

U'gah marched big between Hyatta and the cat, spirit swollen, steps wide and proud. The ground glowed under his paws, full of rainbow spark-dance, like wet stones after storm. Tall teeth watched them walk—shiny, thin, light jumping like trapped fireflies.

He walked like he belonged there. Like he was one of the giants.

Lusa's kill still lay ahead. The cat tore the arm right off the scaly-skin, clean like pulling bark from rotten tree. It made his fur stand up. It made his heart sing.

Hyatta hadn't even blinked. Just said quiet, "Let them run. They are of no consequence."

U'gah didn't know the big word. But he knew the meaning.

Scaly-skins? Nothing. Not worth breath.

They passed the cat's prey—half-dead, leaking into grass. Arm gone, shoulder stump glistening red. Buzz-bugs already swarming the hole. No tribe nearby. No pack. No help.

U'gah's ears turned down. He made a face.

"Scaly-skins… bad friends," he grunted. Left behind. No honor. He didn't understand.

He thought of Jacques. Emerald. Saturn. Even angry Florence. He would not leave them. Not even if claws broke. Not even if he died. His pack was his life.

Then the teeth quaked.

Their tops opened like flower-eyes, each one blinking at the Firefly-in-the-Sky. Shiny eyes spun. Skyfire shot out, wild and bright, scattering all around—on stone, on grass, on U'gah's nose. He squinted. The colors danced fast.

The eyes turned slow, all staring at one place—the glowy stone in the middle.

It drank the light.

The skyfire became angry.

A burst so bright it hurt to look at.

Lusa turned away, low growl in his chest.

But Hyatta—

Hyatta stood firm.

Hyatta turned. Toward the drum-beat. Toward the scaly-skins. No words.

Just war.

U'gah followed.

Then the Firefly-in-the-Sky screamed.

Fingers of skyfire fell like claws from the sun. Big, fat ones— hotter than bonfires. They slammed the ground. Earth tore open. Smoke and dust flew up like chopped meat.

Three beams hit scaly-skins. They didn't even scream right. And, when the skyfire moved on, there was nothing left.

Others ran. Ran fast.

U'gah roared, as scaly-skins ran toward them trying to escape the fingers of the Firefly. He lifted his club.

Hunger. Hunger. The voice shouted in his skull.

He charged.

He ran faster. Muscles burned. Legs pumped.

He saw the scaly-skin clear now—yellow eyes round like flower-buds. Green-black scales, soft tan skin between. Looked almost... delicate. Like shirt-fabric from trader tents.

Smoke curled off its horns. Beam was close.

U'gah pushed harder.

Almost there—

A big hand on his neck. Yanked him back like a cub.

Hyatta.

"No—!" U'gah barked, claws scrabbling..

The beam took the scaly-skin.

Gone.

The beam didn't stop.

It came for U'gah.

But Hyatta stood there. Barring its path to him.

The heat hit like hammer. U'gah felt it through Hyatta's grip. Heard the cloth burn. Smelled hair singe. Saw muscles twitch.

But Hyatta held it at bay.

He didn't fall.

U'gah kicked. Fought. He didn't want to be saved. Not like this.

He had chased glory. Chased the kill. Forgot his pack.

Hyatta had not.

And now he burned.

White filled the world.

No sound. No smell. Only skyfire.

U'gah didn't feel strong anymore.

He felt small.

And now his strongest friend would be gone.

Because of him.

***

Jacques, Emerald, and Saturn stood transfixed, stunned into silence as the ancient defense system roared to life.

The mirrors atop the obelisks began their deadly ballet. Eight reflectors whirled into position, sunlight catching on their surfaces with an eerie brilliance. NAVI zipped back to Saturn's side just as the beams aligned, focusing their energy onto the crystal above the central spire.

What began as beauty became annihilation.

Three beams of concentrated sunlight erupted from the receiver —lances of white energy ripping through the sky. They struck the earth with explosive force, carving molten furrows through stone and soil. Dust and smoke billowed in their wake. The beams hunted the densest clusters of Iruxi, vaporizing bodies before they hit the ground.

But the Lizard King's procession moved untouched—gliding through the chaos with surreal calm.

Two robed attendants flanked the king, arms raised in gestures of command or invocation. When one beam veered toward them, it struck a barrier—an invisible dome that flared blue as it absorbed the blast, rippling outward before fading to nothing.

The other two beams continued their assault, sweeping through the gardens with relentless precision.

Jacques watched, horror swelling. This wasn't defense. It was genocide. Whoever built this hadn't designed it to protect— they'd built it to *erase*.

And then he saw them.

Iruxi sprinted toward three figures charging into the heart of the blast zone.

His breath seized. He squinted—recognizing the shapes.

"Merde," he whispered. "They're in the line of fire."

Panic detonated.

Jacques spun back to the console, fingers flying across the keys, scanning desperately for a shutdown command. System overrides. Emergency failsafes. Nothing. The interface offered no mercy.

The beam was seconds away.

"Why is U'gah *running toward* the giant beam of death?!" Emerald shouted, her voice pitched with panic.

There was no time.

Jacques backed away from the console, yanked out his pistol, and fired.

The shot cracked like a thunderclap. Sparks burst from the control panel. The screen died.

A high-pitched whine screamed through the chamber, the sound of machinery unmoored. The servo gears stuttered and screamed, metal straining.

The mirror above groaned—its supports failing. It tilted forward, misaligning just as the energy arced toward it.

Below, the crystal core pulsed once—twice—then detonated.

A flare of white light. Then the explosion.

Molten shards rained down in a storm of steel and glass. The obelisk shook, a deep, groaning lurch as the platform buckled under the pressure.

Emerald and Saturn dove, arms covering their heads as razor-edged debris cut through the air. Smoke from burning servos enveloped them. When the shaking stopped, they emerged coughing, faces streaked with ash.

Small burns pocked their arms. Cuts traced jagged lines across their skin.

Jacques scrambled toward them, ears ringing, voice thick.

"You alright?"

Emerald spat grit, blinking through the haze. "Think so," she croaked. Her eyes darted to the horizon. "But what about the others?"

Saturn staggered upright, hands trembling. "We have to find them," he said, the fear in his voice raw and unfamiliar. "They were *right there*."

The three of them rushed to the edge of the platform.

Below, the gardens lay in smoking ruin.

They scanned the wreckage, breath held, hearts sinking, eyes searching for any sign—any shape—that might still be standing.

***

U'gah squeezed his eyes shut. Skyfire still burned behind them —bright pain, searing deep. His heart thumped hard, scared to look. Scared to *see*. Hyatta had thrown himself into the angry fire. To save U'gah. To stop U'gah from being stupid again.

Stupid, stupid U'gah.

The guilt clawed at him. He didn't want to open his eyes. Didn't want to see Hyatta gone. Didn't want to see the hurt he made.

U'gah whimpered. Paws twitched. He had to look. Had to *know*.

Slow—slow like prey in tall grass—he opened one eye. Then the other. Blinked. Once. Twice. Light everywhere. Shapes swimming.

But, Hyatta stood tall. Still there. Still *Hyatta*. Not burned. Not broken. Not gone.

But not the same.

Not the thin man they met in the jungle. Not the old warrior U'gah had imagined from old songs.

He was *more.*

Bronzed as if the Firefly-in-the-Sky herself had claimed him. Hair bright as wheat in high summer. Strength coiled in his arms, the sky's calm held in his eyes.

U'gah let out a sound. A small, broken whimper. Not fear now —just relief. Cold rain in his chest, washing out fire and shame.

Hyatta was alive. *Even though he jumped into the skyfire for U'gah.*

U'gah's ears drooped.

He had been loud. Angry. Wanting to prove himself. Wanting to be the biggest. The strongest.

But all he did was almost break everything.

He scrambled to his feet—legs shaking, paws scuffed, fur sticky with fear-sweat and dirt. He didn't know what to say. Didn't *have* the words.

So he went to Hyatta.

He didn't look up. Just pressed his face against Hyatta's leg. A small nudge. A sorry one. *I was wrong. I was stupid. I'm glad you're here.*

To Lusa.

U'gah hesitated. Just a little. Just a blink.

Then he licked the big cat's paw.

One quick lick.

Sorry.

Thank you.

Hyatta knelt.

He ruffled the fur on U'gah's head. Gentle. Warm. No anger in his face. Just soft eyes and a smile that didn't laugh, didn't mock. A smile that said *we're okay.*

U'gah blinked again. Eyes wet. But not crying. No. Not now.

Lusa made a sound. Deep. Rumbly. Purring like thunder far away. It shook through U'gah's ribs and made his ears twitch.

It felt like a laugh. But not mean.

One day U'gah would prove he wasn't just a small thing to be patted.

But not today.

Today, he was grateful.

Hyatta's voice came calm, but full of steel.

"We should get moving," he said. "The gods have carved us a path to the Lizard King."

U'gah nodded.

The shame still clung to his fur. But it was lighter now.

He wasn't alone.

They walked forward—together.

***

Jacques peered down at the wreckage below. The once-overgrown gardens were now a scorched wasteland—smoking trenches, blackened vegetation, twisted remains on burnt earth. The central spire, its crystalline apex destroyed, stood like a monument to catastrophe.

But one figure still stood.

Hyatta.

His rags were singed, but his skin shone gold in the sunlight. His whip coiled at his side. His eyes—sharp, burning—cut through the haze despite the distance. Beside him, Lusa loomed, shielding U'gah with his bulk.

"Hyatta! Lusa! U'gah!" Jacques shouted, voice ragged with relief. "Are you alright?"

Jacques knew there was no chance they'd hear him over the wind and crackling ruin, but he shouted anyway—he needed to.

To his shock, both turned toward the obelisk and met his gaze, as if they'd heard him.

Before Jacques could make sense of it, Emerald's voice broke in. "Jacques! I found Florence!", relief flooding through her tone.

He spun, heart surging.

Florence—alive.

"I'll go," Saturn said. His voice was steady, but his hands trembled. He strapped into NAVI's harness and launched over the edge.

Jacques watched the drone vanish as it dipped down.

There was no time to waste.

"We need to get down there," he said, urgency threading into his voice. "Saturn won't last alone."

Emerald nodded, tightening her grip on her carbine. "Right behind you."

They ran—down the spiral stairs, boots ringing on ancient stone. The battle's roar had faded, replaced by groans, distant weeping, and the low moans of dying Iruxi.

When they emerged into the ruined garden, Jacques broke into a sprint. Emerald followed with smaller strides, unable to keep up. Ahead, Florence lay crumpled and still.

Saturn knelt beside her, scanning for injuries.

But movement stirred at the garden's edge.

A cluster of Iruxi—six or eight—regrouped under the command of a feather-adorned warrior. They advanced into a wedge. Their spears gleamed in the sunlight.

Jacques cursed under his breath.

They'd be overrun.

His mind raced—he and Emerald could reach Florence, but then what? Eight warriors. Bad odds.

"Emerald," he gasped, "I'm going for them. I'm not leaving them behind."

Emerald didn't hesitate, "Then I'm with you".

As they ran, Jacques hurdled one of the trenches that was burned into the earth. A strange detail caught his eye. The beams hadn't *missed* Florence. They had *bent* around her— traced a curve in the air.

"They avoided her!" he shouted, disbelief breaking his voice. "Not dead — system must have read her as friendly!"

Emerald's eyes widened.

He didn't have the time to think about it further.

The lizardmen were closing in.

They reached Saturn and Florence just as the enemy drew within striking range. Jacques threw himself between them, machete raised. Saturn crouched over Florence, trembling but firm.

Behind him, Emerald dropped to one knee, carbine ready. There was a flash of something in her face—intensity, almost joy.

Jacques blinked. *Is she enjoying this?*

To the right he spotted Lusa and U'gah tearing across the field. They were much too far to save them, only close enough to avenge.

Hyatta walked, unhurried—calm as a sunrise.

Jacques raised his pistol and fired. The MAC50 barked short bursts of percussive sound. One Iruxi continued to stumble whilst the other one dropped to the ground.

Emerald joined in, her carbine spitting sharp, precise shots. Another fell, it's eye socket weeping blood and gray matter. Three wounded. Four still coming.

The leader—who was taller, plated, and feathered—didn't flinch.

The first warrior reached Jacques. Spear lunged. Jacques deflected it with the pistol slide, steel-on-steel shrieking. He brought the machete down hard, chopping into the shaft. The wood splintered, cracked—useless now. The lizardman faltered, caught off guard.

The leader pounced.

Using the stunned warrior's back as a springboard, it launched —soaring in a graceful, deadly arc.

Right toward Florence and Saturn.

Jacques spun, intent on intercepting. But another spear came from the left. He parried clumsily, steel clashing against his blade guard, the shock rattling his wrist.

A third warrior rushed in. Jacques twisted to dodge, but his foot slipped on soil that had been loosened by the solar death beam.

Jacques fell. He tumbled hard into the trench.

Pain lit his spine. Dust filled his lungs. His pistol flew from his grip.

For a breathless second, he lay still. Every bone screamed.

It was over.

He'd failed.

He imagined Emerald, carbine blazing in vain. Saturn, too small to stop what came next. Florence—skewered, still.

Guilt slammed into him like a second fall.

He was supposed to protect. To lead.

Instead—

He'd fallen.

Jacques closed his eyes and braced for the screams.

***

Saturn had just finished his scan.

No broken bones, no bleeding. Florence was physically intact.

But even as the medical data scrolled across his lens, Saturn knew—some wounds didn't show. Whatever she'd endured, whatever she'd *seen*, it had carved into her already fragile psyche. And he wasn't sure it could ever be undone.

That was when Jacques and Emerald came barreling toward them, boots pounding the scorched earth like startled hares.

Jacques vaulted one of the smoking ruts gouged by the solar beam. Saturn's gaze followed the motion—automatically, absently.

And then he saw them.

Lizardmen—advancing fast. Spears flashing in the sun.

A cold wave surged up his spine.

He had been so focused on Florence—her pulse, her vitals— that he'd missed the danger completely.

His mind lurched into motion, grasping for a plan.

Too late.

Time slipped.

The next thing he saw was motion in the sky.

A feathered Iruxi warrior—midair—having launched from the back of another. Its silhouette blotted out the sun, cleaver raised, rusted blade catching the light, coming for him.

Saturn froze.

He knew terror's mechanics—the cortisol flood, the feedback loop of indecision. He'd studied it. But this was different.

This was different.

He couldn't move.

Could only *watch* as the creature fell toward them, the cleaver descending like a guillotine.

Then—cracks rang out.

Emerald's carbine.

Close. Echoing.

Saturn's eyes followed the rounds—.22 caliber, standard-velocity. He calculated their mass, their speed, their likelihood of success.

And in the same instant, he saw the result.

The bullets pinged off the Iruxi's hide, ricocheting harmlessly off crude armor.

Too light. Too soft. Useless.

The creature snarled—gravity taking hold—its momentum undeterred. It was going to hit them.

His gaze snapped to Jacques.

Locked in melee. Outnumbered. Off-balance.

Falling—

Saturn saw him disappear into a trench, body twisting as he hit the dirt.

No help there.

Emerald fired again. Still no effect.

The cleaver glinted overhead.

It was coming.

Every part of him screamed to move. To act. To *do something*. But his limbs stayed locked.

His brilliant mind—his greatest tool—was silent.

Only static.

A scream clawed up his throat, but never escaped. His body trembled, chest rising in short, broken gasps.

He could see the sunlight flashing on the weapon. Could hear the wind rushing past its blade.

This is it. I'm going to die.

CHAPTER ELEVEN

A high-pitched shriek split the air. For a heartbeat, Saturn thought it was his own voice—panic boiling up in his chest—until the sound climbed higher, beyond anything human.

A blur of fur streaked past.

Something massive slammed into the airborne lizardman. A flash of dark limbs, a heavy club trailing behind like a comet. The creature was ripped from the sky, spinning end over end before it crashed into the earth in a heap of scales.

U'gah.

Transformed—fully therianthropic, monstrous. He rolled, landed, and rose with a growl. Then he pounced, club raised.

Saturn stared, stunned.

Timid, quiet U'gah was gone—replaced by a whirlwind of muscle and rage. He brought the club down again and again, each strike shattering flesh and armor. The lizardman vanished into pulp. What remained reminded Saturn of chunky mustard, the kind that used to be served on Wednesdays in the commissary at the Hermes Labs research facility.

Around them, Emerald fired in sharp bursts. Her carbine hissed. The rounds sparked off hide and armor, ineffective—but relentless. Most of the Iruxi turned toward her now, their eyes alight with rage.

One remained. The spear-wielder that Jacques had disarmed earlier. It scrambled after him, jabbing into the trench as Jacques dodged then backpedaled, desperately.

The wounded Iruxi joined the fight—ragged but burning with fury. They rushed U'gah from all sides.

He didn't flinch.

His tail wagged—like a dog seeing a stick.

Saturn's mind reeled. The battlefield blurred.

Suddenly, he saw Henry—grinning in that wide, ridiculous way of his. Saw the lab. The old console. The smell of synth-metal and burnt coffee. They'd made things together. Changed things.

And now Henry was gone.

Saturn felt it—finally, fully.

The grief hit him like a gut punch.

Even if they lived, nothing would ever be the same.

His friends. His work. The world they knew—it was already dust.

A sharp slap broke the trance.

Saturn blinked. Florence's furious face filled his vision.

"Florence... you're awake!"

"Obviously," she snapped, her tone acid. "And look at the mess you 'men' made while I was unconscious. Which one of you do I thank for nearly getting me killed this time?"

Saturn flinched. "Florence, I—"

"Don't bother," she cut in, waving him off. "I'm done being the damsel. I'll take care of myself from now on."

Her words hit harder than the slap had.

Still, he took a breath. Re-centered.

"Florence," he said, calm but urgent, "I get it. You're angry. But Jacques and Emerald are about to die. We need to help them. *Now.*"

He offered his hand.

Florence stared at it, caught off guard by the directness. She'd expected pleading. Groveling.

But there was something in Saturn's eyes—honest, warm.

After a pause, she took it.

"Fine," she muttered. "But don't expect me to go all Harley Stone on these lizard freaks."

"Who?"

She rolled her eyes. "Never mind."

Saturn pulled her up. "The plan is simple. I send NAVI into the fray. Overload the batteries. When she blows, it'll stun them long enough for Emerald and Jacques to move."

Florence dusted herself off. "And me?"

"I need noise. Think: barista, wrong coffee. Full meltdown. Scream like your life depends on it."

She gave him a sidelong look. "Oh, *that* I can do."

They turned toward the carnage—

And froze.

Emerald was hauling Jacques from a trench. Blood streaked his face, his clothes torn. U'gah stood over a pile of mangled corpses, club dripping red. Lusa, slick with gore, turned toward them—amber eyes narrowing in warning.

The ground around them was churned mud and ruin. Broken spears. Torn limbs.

And silence.

Only NAVI's faint hum broke it.

"What... happened?" Florence whispered, hand to her mouth.

Saturn's voice was flat. "I don't know. But, apparently—we weren't needed."

Emerald helped Jacques to his feet. He swayed, grimacing.

Saturn stepped closer. "What happened?"

Jacques stared past him, eyes distant.

"Got my ass kicked," he said. "Not sure what happened after. But I think Lusa stopped playing."

The silence returned.

But it wasn't peace. It was pause.

Saturn felt his adrenaline ebb—replaced by something colder. He thought of Henry again. Of the future. Of the fight still ahead.

Even now, he couldn't shake the question that haunted him most:

Is it even worth trying to survive?

***

Florence fumed in silence, her frustration simmering like a pot on the edge of boil.

Exactly as expected. The men charge in, guns blazing, ruin everything, nearly get me killed.

Whatever fragile opportunity she'd had to open dialogue with the lizardmen had been shattered beneath boots and bravado. A thin window of diplomacy—gone. Now they were all standing in the bloody aftermath of yet another testosterone-driven catastrophe.

Maybe my plan would have worked, she thought. *Maybe I could've done something real—negotiated, reasoned. But no. Not when the boys have guns to wave around and egos to inflate.*

They should've let *her* lead. She was the only one with a clear head. Saturn had his moments, sure, but even he had folded under pressure. And Emerald? Just another tomboy in disguise, drunk on adrenaline and camaraderie. They'd tire of her too, eventually. Just like they always did.

Florence clenched her fists, nails biting into her palms. She watched Jacques—mud-streaked, bruised, and bloody—being hauled from the trench by Emerald, and the injustice of it made her seethe. They were *lucky* to be alive. Lucky that U'gah and that... cat-thing had shown up. Not that anyone would admit it. They'd all congratulate each other and nod solemnly, pretending they'd somehow earned survival.

As Jacques and Emerald approached, concern plain on their faces, Florence pasted on a syrupy smile.

"Hey, are you alright?" Jacques asked, voice tinged with guilt. "That must have been terrifying, waking up to all that."

"I'm fine," she said, too sweet, spun sugar over iron. "Thank you for your concern."

Inside, she was screaming.

You stupid French frog. You're going to get us all killed. Just once—once—I'd like you to listen to me.

Her plan had been the only rational course. *No one* else saw that. And now they'd dragged her through another disaster, convinced they were doing the noble thing.

Idiots, she thought, cutting a glare at Emerald. *All of them. Violence junkies playing soldier while I'm the only one trying to think two steps ahead.*

But she held her tongue. No point in burning bridges when the cliff was already crumbling.

She sighed—casual, practiced. "What's next?" she asked lightly, feigning interest.

Probably more violence. Probably another near-death experience. *Probably another chance for them to screw everything up.*

"We meet the Lizard King in combat," Hyatta said as he strode past, calm and unreadable.

Florence's lips tightened.

Jacques turned, tension snapping in his voice. "Why the hell didn't you help us earlier?" he shouted. "We were outnumbered! You just stood there—watching!"

Hyatta stopped. Turned. There was no apology in his gaze.

"You are still alive," he said. "It seems you did not need my help."

Jacques spluttered, rage and disbelief colliding in his throat.

Hyatta raised a hand, silencing him with a flick of the wrist.

"You are a proud warrior, Jacques of Hephaestus," he said, the faintest thread of warmth in his tone. "I did not wish to insult you by interfering in your battle."

Then, after a pause: "You did not disappoint."

Florence nearly laughed.

Fought bravely? That was generous. All she'd seen was Jacques flailing in the dirt like a beetle on its back.

If not for Lusa and U'gah, they'd all be a smear on the stone.

Still—there was opportunity here.

Her eyes shifted to the cat.

Lusa.

Massive. Lethal. Loyal. A perfect protector.

I do miss my cats, she thought idly. *Maybe it's time I had a new one.*

She studied the beast with growing interest. Of course, *Lusa* wouldn't do. Far too primal.

No, she'd rename him.

Tom. Or Mittens. Or Tabicus Fluffenstuff.

Her smile widened.

Yes. This could work.

She turned to Jacques, smiling brightly. "So what's the plan?" she asked, her tone light, edged with playful malice. "Are we storming the castle? Slaying the dragon?"

"I guess we're following the hunky blonde bombshell," Emerald said, nodding toward Hyatta, her voice laced with wry admiration.

Florence found herself begrudgingly agreeing. Hyatta was... transformed. No longer gaunt and half-dead, but something else. Primeval. Magnetic.

She hated that it got to her.

"He certainly is... different," she muttered, tone flat. She couldn't deny the change—but she could resent it.

Who was *he* to lead them? Some feral stranger plucked from a cell, wrapped in mystery and muscle, suddenly handed authority without question?

It made no sense.

Why did they all follow him so easily?

What spell had he cast?

Florence swallowed her contempt. She couldn't challenge him —not yet. Not openly.

But she would be watching.

And if the chance came to tip the balance?

She would take it.

***

U'gah's heart felt warm. They were together again. He liked that. It was easier to protect them when they stayed close. And when they were close, it meant he hadn't failed yet.

But even as they walked, his ears twitched.

Hyatta wanted to fight. U'gah could smell it in his steps—calm and hungry, like a hunter with a name already picked out.

U'gah didn't fear battle. Not anymore. Not with the Earthshaker club in his hands and the hum of the Old Ones deep in his belly.

But those two spirit-seekers near the Lizard King... they felt wrong. They smelled of powerful magic. Ancestor stuff. But not like U'gah's. Not like his tribe.

U'gah had barely started learning that path before his teacher died. His voice to the ancestors was quiet, broken. Their spirit-seekers might be louder.

He didn't like that.

It's fine, he told himself. Hyatta was strong. Lusa was *stronger.* Saturn was smart. Jacques had a warchief's mind. Emerald could bite with fire from her gun. Together, they were a warband. Maybe even stronger than Eh'lug's.

But now U'gah had Lusa.

Lusa could eat six razor-toothed forest pigs in one fight, maybe not even notice.

And Hyatta... U'gah didn't know where his strength ended.

Hyatta walked like nothing in the world could surprise him. Long legs. Long shadow. Eyes forward. No tension. Just that hum under the skin that said *something's coming.*

Behind him, U'gah heard Emerald counting again. She did that when she was nervous—checking her fire stone boxes, tapping them, whispering numbers. Her gun made her brave, but not still.

Saturn walked like prey who *knew* it was being hunted. His arms stayed tight, his eyes darted between the tall rocks. But he didn't run. He never ran. U'gah respected that.

Florence... Florence was different.

She followed, but her eyes were elsewhere. Lips moving, no sound. Talking to ghosts—or herself. U'gah didn't understand her. Didn't try. She didn't like him. That was clear.

He didn't know why.

He'd only ever been nice to her. Shared food. Carried books. Gave space when she snapped. But she still looked at him like he was something tracked in on her boots.

U'gah sighed. He didn't like her either.

But she was warband. Jacques and Saturn still kept her close. That meant U'gah would too. That was the rule.

He was thinking that when Jacques grabbed him by the neck, U'gah spun, ready to bite—but stopped when he saw his friend's wide, shocked eyes.

U'gah's ears flattened. He gave an apologetic tail-swish and looked up.

They were close.

Very close.

The Lizard King sat like a statue on his heavy bed-throne, surrounded by spirit-seekers and four big warrior-scaly-skins— each as big as Lusa. More filled in behind them. Twenty. Maybe more. Spears. Bad armor. Sharp teeth.

U'gah puffed up, took a deep breath, and tried to roar.

It came out a yelp.

The scaly-skins laughed, then hissed and spat and clacked their jaws in mockery. It made U'gah's skin itch.

Then Hyatta spoke.

"Please, stand back, my friends," he said, like he was asking for silence during a story. "You have brought pride and honor to your names and your gods with your brave deeds. But Lusa and I have a debt to collect."

U'gah's ears dropped. His shoulders sagged. He wanted to fight. Wanted to prove.

But he understood.

Hyatta was protecting them—from what he was about to do.

The scaly warriors moved to form a ring. Spears raised. Their weapons were ugly, dirty. Their eyes were sharp, but not clever.

Lusa looked ready to explode.

Little tail twitching. Muscles coiled. Ears locked forward.

But Hyatta?

Still. Loose. Smiling.

Like he was watching children pretend at battle.

U'gah watched their circle close. The spears dipped. Feet shuffled.

And then—music.

A hum.

Soft at first, carried on the wind. Sweet, strange. Not war-music. U'gah tilted his head.

It came from Hyatta.

The tune danced with the air.

It was pretty. Soothing.

One warrior lunged.

The spear came fast.

Hyatta didn't flinch. Rolled his shoulder. Slipped low.

Dropped like a feather—fast, beautiful.

A twist. A crouch. One scaly-skin's own spear was used against him—right in the gut. Hyatta took a knife from his belt before the body even hit the ground.

Another came. Hyatta spun, ducked, wrapped an arm around its neck. The knife stayed ready while the shield-body caught spears meant for him.

U'gah's fur bristled.

Lusa laughed.

A low purring sound like thunder under sand.

The cat wasn't even fighting yet. Just pacing. Watching.

U'gah's tail twitched. *Hyatta's not taking it seriously,* he thought. *He'll get hurt.*

But Lusa's eyes lit up. He understood something. Saw it in Hyatta.

Then a spear came for him.

Fast.

Lusa caught it mid-air.

One paw. One movement.

The warrior attached to the spear was yanked forward like a fish on a line.

Lusa grabbed him. Massive paw around head and neck.

Not for cover—for a weapon.

He slammed the scaly-skin into his friends. Let their spears run him through. Used him to strip them of their blades—pulled them out like pins.

U'gah winced. His stomach turned.

But it worked.

The scaly-skins fell apart. Screamed. Died. Most by their own hands.

Hyatta never missed a step.

He moved like water through holes.

Slit throats. Broke joints. Dodged like he knew every blade's path before it was raised.

When only one was left, Hyatta didn't chase.

He flicked the stolen knife.

It flew.

Straight into the last warrior's chest.

Silence.

Then Hyatta and Lusa looked to the Lizard King.

Hyatta's voice boomed like thunder:

"Your chaff has fallen, tyrant. Face judgment."

Lusa bared his teeth and raised a paw—twisting it into the shape U'gah had only seen in cave carvings. The crux. The sign of ending.

The Lizard King laughed.

Ugly. Mocking.

He raised a claw.

Four giants stepped forward. Each taller than Jacques, broader than U'gah had ever seen.

Armor of green and yellow. Teeth like knives. Eyes like nothing human.

U'gah edged closer to Jacques. This wasn't over.

It was just beginning.

Chapter Twelve

How much ammo left?" Jacques asked, hoping for good news. He and Emerald crouched behind the bones of a garden wall, moss-slick stone cold against their backs.

He'd thought about defying Hyatta's order, but exhaustion—and common sense—held him down. Charging the Lizard King's guard with what they had would be suicide.

"One," Emerald said.

Her voice shook. She clutched her carbine until her knuckles whitened. Jacques studied her face—normally bright, curious, composed. Now it was hollow. Her wide eyes swept the battle like a trapped animal.

He placed a steadying hand on her shoulder.

"Not much we can do with one mag," he said softly, "but we'll think of something."

She shook her head.

"Not one mag, Jacques," she whispered. "One round."

The words punched the breath from his lungs. He stared at her, then looked toward the fading shadow of the obelisk's dome, mind spinning.

A sound drifted through the chaos—a quiet, almost melodic hum.

Hyatta's hymn.

That strange, haunting melody threaded through the haze. Jacques felt his own heartbeat begin to sync with it, slower, steadier.

The four hulking, crocodilian Iruxi stepped forward—scales gleaming like wet iron, jaws split wide in anticipation. Three peeled off toward Lusa. The fourth, largest of the group, advanced on Hyatta, bone choker clinking against its throat.

Hyatta kept humming.

And when he let the whip uncoil—the battle exploded.

Lusa launched forward in a blur of orange and black. He smashed into the central lizardman like a wrecking ball, lifting it from the ground. The creature hit the earth with a sickening crunch, and didn't rise.

The other two guards dove on Lusa, dragging him from the corpse, claws raking at his shoulders and limbs.

Across the clearing, the final Iruxi warrior lunged for Hyatta. Its roar echoed off the walls, claws flashing, jaws gaping.

But Hyatta was gone before the strike landed.

He moved like mist—slipping, twisting, weaving through every blow. His hymn quickened with each dodge. The Iruxi grew frantic, strikes turning erratic, screaming as Hyatta danced through its rage—never once planting both feet.

Meanwhile, Lusa was locked in a brutal grapple. The guards were strong—brutish, disciplined. But Lusa fought like a force of nature. His paws held his opponents in place, his teeth clamped down on a warrior's shoulder, dragging it to the dirt. The lizardmen fought like those who knew they would die, but chose not to run.

Jacques watched, sweat cold on his neck.

He was glad they weren't down there—glad he hadn't been foolish enough to intervene. This wasn't combat. It was a monster vid made flesh.

If they'd ever faced Hyatta and Lusa as enemies…

He swallowed. He couldn't finish the thought.

He was torn from his thought by inhuman chanting.

The robed snake-like lizardmen flanking the Lizard King raised their arms, a dark drone pouring from their throats. The air bent with it—Jacques could feel the chant vibrating in his teeth.

Sparks of dark light shimmered from their fingers, devouring color as they moved.

Jacques turned back to Hyatta—and froze.

Hyatta's footwork faltered. His rhythm slipped.

His enemy saw it. It pressed forward, sensing weakness.

Jacques's heart kicked into his throat. He wanted to shout, to warn—

But Hyatta was already moving.

He let the lizard's claw sweep down in a killing arc—and then struck upward with brutal precision, his elbow crashing into the Iruxi's ribs with the speed of a spring trap.

Jacques saw the mistake too late.

The other arm.

The lizard's free hand came up fast, claws snapping toward Hyatta's skull.

And then the world turned white.

A blinding flash burst outward from Hyatta, so bright Jacques had to shield his eyes. The lizard reeled backward, screaming.

When Jacques blinked the spots away, he saw Hyatta on the beast's back, calm and crouched, riding its collapse like a surfer on a wave.

The lizardman hit the ground, twitching once before going still.

Jacques stared at the deep divot in its neck.

One strike.

One clean kill.

"Putain de merde..." he breathed.

The moment seemed to settle—Hyatta's victory a pivot point in the chaos—only to fracture again as the fallen Iruxi's corpse convulsed. From its split torso erupted a knot of inky tendrils, writhing like starved serpents. They lashed outward, impossibly fast, snapping toward Hyatta with hungry precision. Each strand devoured the light around it, leaving not shadow but absence—reality thinning at the edges.

Jacques felt his stomach lurch. The tendrils coiled around Hyatta's limbs before he could react, dragging him down toward the corpse that had birthed them. He leapt, trying to break free, but the tendrils snapped taut mid-air, slamming him down with brutal force. His body flared with light—whatever trick he'd used earlier—but this time, the glow only fed the darkness. The tendrils drank it in, writhing tighter. Hyatta convulsed, his teeth bared in a rictus of pain, his limbs trembling under the strain.

Jacques's breath hitched. Instinct screamed at him to act. He rose to a half-crouch, pistol trembling in his grip—but Hyatta's gaze caught him from across the battlefield. Even through the pain, it was clear: a warning. A command.

Do not.

Jacques froze. The message was wordless, but unmistakable: this was a fight Jacques could not win. Swallowing hard, he dropped back behind the broken wall, muttering a ragged, "Merci," the only acknowledgment he could give.

Then the roar.

It tore through the garden like a shockwave—Lusa.

The Mau had broken from his bloodied brawl, turning all his fury toward the tendrils dragging Hyatta down. Jacques could feel it before he saw it—the earth vibrating under the beast's charge, a full-bodied, primal bellow echoing across the ruins. But the two remaining Iruxi guards clung to him like anchors, their claws sunk deep into fur and flesh, their jaws locked tight.

Despite the wounds Lusa had already inflicted—torn ligaments, shattered ribs—they fought like creatures possessed. Blood poured from them, painting the dirt beneath their feet, but they refused to release him. They knew what Lusa was capable of if freed. They knew they wouldn't survive it.

But their strength was fading. Jacques could see it. Their grip slipping, their bodies trembling. Lusa would break loose—it was just a question of whether it would be in time.

The tendrils around Hyatta pulsed, pulling tighter.

Jacques's mind raced. Think. Think. Do something.

He whispered a quick prayer—something half-remembered, half-instinct. A plea for light, for time, for anything.

And then—a crack.

His ears rang. The scent of cordite slapped his nose.

He turned. Emerald's carbine smoked beside him, her green hair wild in the wind.

He followed the shot.

The spirit-seeker—left of the Lizard King—jerked violently as the round pierced its eye. The slender Iruxi spasmed, violet-banded scales flashing. For a breathless second, it hovered—then collapsed in a heap. Black ichor sprayed the stone. Magic rebounded violently, folding back on its source like a mirror imploding.

Jacques barely registered the scream.

The second spirit-seeker clawed at its own face, howling. Its talons shredded flesh, bursting its eyes in a welter of blood and madness. The ritual broke. The tendrils holding Hyatta evaporated with a whisper, vanishing like smoke in sunlight.

Hyatta collapsed.

The warrior hit the earth hard, curled into himself, his chest heaving. The light that had once radiated from him was gone. Jacques winced. Whatever he'd endured—it had taken everything.

But Lusa—

The Mau's charge had stopped cold. The moment the tendrils vanished, the Iruxi on his back struck like starving animals.

Jacques's heart climbed into his throat.

They weren't holding Lusa anymore. They were feeding.

The Iruxi bit down. Deep. Their jaws clamped onto muscle and sinew, shaking like dogs. Then they twisted.

Jacques understood too late.

"Stop them!" he rasped. "They're—"

But it was already happening.

The death roll.

The lizardmen spun, their massive bodies corkscrewing violently, jaws locked tight. Lusa screamed. A roar of agony— raw, gurgling, primal. His blood hit the air in thick jets. Flesh tore. Jacques saw muscle unraveling like rope, ribs cracking like snapped branches.

He rose.

He didn't think.

He ran.

The useless pistol was still in his hand. His boots hammered the blood-soaked ground, each step screaming too late. The Iruxi were killing Lusa, tearing him open like meat.

He ran faster.

Emerald shouted something—Jacques didn't hear.

The lizards didn't see him until the last second.

He hit the first one like a wrecking ball. The butt of his pistol connected with its jaw—bone cracked. It staggered. He drove his machete into its gut, snarling like an animal. Blood spilled, but the creature didn't fall.

The second Iruxi turned on him, claws raised. Jacques ducked, swung upward.

Click.

The gun was empty.

"Putain de merde!" he spat, he should have remembered. The Iruxi lunged.

He twisted, barely avoiding the claws, tripped, fell. Rolled.

He came up swinging—hand empty.

The Iruxi descended.

Jacques backpedaled. The machete was gone. The pistol was a club now.

He caught a swipe on his shoulder, pain flaring white. Another hit sent him sprawling backward.

His foot caught on a stone.

He hit the ground.

Hard.

The Iruxi lunged.

"Pas comme ça," Jacques breathed, his voice hoarse, teeth gritted.

Not like this.

The crocodilian beak snapped shut, missing Jacques's face by centimeters. For one breathless heartbeat, the world narrowed to those jaws and the promise of death between them.

Then U'gah materialized into his field of view.

Panting, wild-eyed, the halfling barreled into the scaled monstrosity, club already mid-swing. Jacques realized, dazed, that the little warrior had just saved his life.

With a bone-shattering crunch, U'gah's greatclub smashed the Iruxi's knee. The joint cracked, inverted—ripped free in a spray of blood. The lizardman teetered on its other leg, windmilling in a grotesque pantomime—like a felled tree pretending it still stood. But U'gah wasn't finished. He wound back again, eyes gleaming with focus.

The club struck once more. Its stone tyrannosaur head snapped open mid-arc and clamped down on the Iruxi's other leg. With a twist of unnatural force, the jaws tore it from the socket. The lizardman collapsed in a tangled, twitching heap.

Jacques could only watch, stunned, as U'gah stood triumphant, the club dripping blood, the carved dinosaur maw still chewing on the stolen limb.

But there was no time for awe.

The last Iruxi guard—still standing—had pulled Jacques's machete from its own side and now loomed over Lusa's unmoving body, poised to strike.

"Non!" Jacques shouted, his voice raw. He stumbled forward, legs aching, lungs burning. He wouldn't make it in time.

The Iruxi raised the machete high.

Then—crack.

The battlefield froze.

Hyatta stood in the open, chain-whip in one hand, his face a thunderhead of wrath. He extended his other hand—waiting.

From the sky, the machete spun downward.

Hyatta caught it mid-air without looking.

Jacques's eyes snapped to the Iruxi. The machete was no longer in its grip. It stood frozen, staring down at the stumps where its hands had once been. Nearby, those hands lay twitching in the dirt.

Hyatta had disarmed it—literally—with a single snap of his chain-whip.

Before Jacques could process the moment, Lusa stirred. His eyes snapped open, pupils glowing a wrathful green, veins of color pulsing through amber like molten cracks. He rose in one savage motion, growled deep and guttural, bones snapping back into place and flesh stitching together at the urging of some ghastly green energy snaking from the Mau's body.

200

His paw drove upward with brutal force—straight into the Iruxi's groin.

The impact lifted the lizardman from the ground.

Lusa didn't stop. With a snarl, he punched through the Iruxi's torso, lifting the entire body aloft on his blood-slicked arm like a grotesque trophy. Gore dripped from his elbow. The lizardman spasmed, then went limp.

The anthropomorphic cat roared. The sound shook the stones. It was defiance, challenge, triumph—all in one savage bellow.

Jacques knelt, breathless. The battle had turned surreal—less a fight, more a myth being carved into the fabric of reality.

And then the Lizard King rose.

Massive and cloaked in arrogance, he stood atop his palanquin, fangs flashing as he opened his mouth to deliver some thunderous decree.

Hyatta spun, chain-whip trailing. It shimmered, reshaping midair—links melting into a gleaming spear.

He hurled it.

The weapon streaked across the garden like a comet and pierced the Lizard King's sternum. The impact drove the tyrant back into his throne, incisors clacking shut mid-sentence.

"I did not give you permission to speak," Hyatta growled. His voice carried like thunder across the now silent killing field.

The Lizard King tensed, claws scrabbling at the shaft buried in his chest.

Hyatta was already moving. He vanished mid-stride in a flash of brilliant light and reappeared at the throne. His hand gripped the spear's haft—still in motion—body flipping over the king.

As he soared through the air, the spear reshaped again, growing and splitting into a thin double-bladed greataxe.

The blades displaced flesh as it morphed.

The warrior's momentum pulled the weapon free—wet, violent, final. Blood sprayed skyward in a geyser. The Lizard King's body folded, nearly split in two.

When Hyatta landed, he stood over what was left of the monarch, axe dripping. His expression held no joy. No rage. Only the cold stillness of completion.

The halves of Lizard King tried one last breath. Hyatta silenced it with a kick, sending the corpse tumbling from the throne.

Jacques watched, numb.

The battlefield was silent now, and they had won. But the air stank of fresh death and life lost.

Hyatta turned away, the greataxe dissolving back into a trailing whip. His gaze swept the garden.

For the briefest moment, Jacques thought he saw sorrow in those sky blue eyes.

But then it was gone.

CHAPTER THIRTEEN

U'gah liked the way the treasure piles clinked and gleamed. Fat sacks full of shiny stones, heavy nuggets, coils of wire, flat tokens stamped with symbols. Trophies. That's what they were. Among his people, warriors took pieces of the beast they killed—a tooth, a claw, a horn, a hide. So why not here? This had been a great hunt—a war-hunt. They had won.

The others didn't seem to notice the spoils. Not even Jacques. U'gah didn't understand. They had fought. They had bled. Shouldn't they take something to mark the victory? Something to show the ancestor spirits?

Maybe they didn't know. Maybe they didn't care. He could not tell. But he wasn't about to let all these treasures sit here and rot.

He glanced at Florence—Flo, maybe. Hard to tell which one was in control. She stood over Jacques, yelling at him with her screechy voice. His friend looked tired, lying in the dust like a chewed-up fruit rind. U'gah felt sorry for him. Maybe Flo didn't mean to be so loud, but her words pierced like spearheads—smiling one breath, wildfire the next. Maybe two spirits lived in her. That made more sense.

Emerald, grass-head, leaned against a wall. She cleaned her firestick like it was a wounded pup. Her eyes were far away, watching something that wasn't there. She was quiet, but not calm.

Little Saturn knelt beside his stone-bird. NAVI. He touched it gently, checking each wing as if it would cry out if he missed a crack. U'gah liked Saturn. Small hands. Clever brain. Quiet feet. Strange ideas. He wondered if NAVI could catch mites—probably not. Still, Saturn cleaned it like a real bird. Maybe it was alive. He didn't know.

Hyatta... Hyatta was different now.

The sand-warrior sat alone in the shadow of the giant's egg. Not proud. Not tall. Small. Quiet. Sad. Not battle-sad like a wounded hunter. Sad like a lost child. He stared at the glowing sky, letting his fingers flick through the Firefly's fading light. Tears?

U'gah's ears swiveled. That couldn't be right. Sand-warriors didn't cry. They saved their water. But Hyatta... he looked broken inside. As if something had cracked beneath the skin.

Lusa was near, licking blood from his paws. He didn't speak. Just watched. His wounds were shallow now, not deadly. The scaly ones had torn his skin, but the Mau still breathed. Still stood. Still cleaned himself like it was just another day. But he was quiet too. Like he was guarding Hyatta from a distance.

Firefly-in-the-Sky was getting low, running away again, slipping behind the broken walls. The short light made long shadows. Soon Grandfather Brightrock would climb the sky and chase off the dark, but U'gah didn't like being out in the open after Firefly went to sleep. Predators moved in the dark. Hungry things. Scaly things. Listening things.

He crouched low, scooping up the last of the shiny stones he could carry. The others would soon want to move. Jacques would lead. Maybe Hyatta too, if he remembered how to stand tall again. U'gah didn't want to wait and be left behind.

But then he saw something.

Something dark. Smooth. Black like the river between stars. It poked from the side of the egg-stone, tucked between slabs of white. His nose twitched. It didn't smell right. No moss, no rot. No dust.

He crept toward it on all fours, rump high in the air, sniffing. Each step was slow. Careful. Eyes wide. The black thing shimmered like water—but hard. It looked back at him.

Crack.

The black skin snapped away with a noise like lightning through a shell. U'gah froze. Something inside moved. Not a vine. Not a root. A stick of silver slid from the hole, smooth and stiff. It buzzed. His fur stood up.

The stick twitched.

A red eye blinked open at the tip. Bright and sharp and angry. It painted red across his face. U'gah snarled, but didn't move. The red thing stared at him. Then it growled.

Not a beast growl. Not breath. A noise like a broken bug. A voice with no mouth.

Snap. Snap.

Pain. Fire in his nerves. The stick struck twice, faster than a snake. His body seized. A squeal tore from his throat as he stumbled back.

He ran. Fast. Tail tucked, claws kicking up dirt. He didn't stop until the pain faded. When he turned, panting, the metal stick was gone. Back in its hole. Like it had never been.

Jacques rushed toward him. "Qu'est-ce qui s'est passé?" the man asked, voice full of worry.

U'gah didn't answer. He just pointed.

His hand shook as he whispered the only words he could think of.

"Na agi... Na agi…"

Fire still lived in the stone.

And it was watching.

***

Jacques was too drained to feel anything as sharp as shock. Exhaustion pressed down like a lead shroud, dulling even his instinct. But he forced himself forward. They'd come too far, survived too much, for him to fall apart now. Their enemies were dead—but that didn't mean they were safe. If someone got hurt because he stopped caring, the guilt would crush him.

So he ran. His legs like lead. His breath ragged.

U'gah was babbling, wide-eyed, and trembling. Jacques didn't catch the words, but the meaning was clear enough: something near the domed structure had scared the hell out of him. The singed tufts of fur and scorched stench clinging to the halfling deepened Jacques's concern.

The others arrived quickly. Emerald first, gripping her carbine with white-knuckled hands despite its emptiness. She looked skittish, her eyes darting to every shadow. Saturn followed, cold and detached—the shell of a man who'd seen too much. Florence trailed behind, slower, but with that same sour glare she always reserved for U'gah. The venom in her stare said enough. Lusa came last, limping, but alert.

Jacques turned back to U'gah, trying to make sense of the jumbled gestures. Before he could speak, Hyatta stepped into view, drifting like a lonely shadow.

"He says there's bad magic at the base of the giant's egg," Hyatta murmured. His voice was quiet, but the tension in it was unmistakable.

"Bad magic," Jacques repeated, frowning.

"What does that even mean?" Florence snapped. She crossed her arms, glaring as though U'gah's fear personally offended her.

"I don't know," Jacques admitted. "But this structure—part of it was built by Hephaestus Innovative Technologies. Could be

206

another automated defense system. If it is, it's worth checking out."

Florence scoffed. "Another deathtrap? Fine. Let's dive in and see what tries to kill us this time."

Jacques shot her a hard look. "Oui. Because it might give us access to the control center. Information. Gear. Something to keep us from fighting with empty guns and glorified sticks."

Florence opened her mouth to retort, but Emerald cut in first. "Maybe we're due for some good luck." Her smile was tight and tired. "Statistically, we can't keep tripping into disasters forever."

Jacques let out a dry chuckle. "At least not and continue to survive."

He looked to Hyatta. "Thoughts?"

Hyatta didn't answer right away. When he did, his voice was grave. "We can go. But be wary. The machina here… they were abandoned by gods. Sometimes it's better to let such things sleep."

The words left Jacques uneasy. Hyatta's tone held something heavier than caution. Reverence. Fear.

The group moved in a loose column—Jacques and Hyatta in the lead, the others following in a weary but alert procession. U'gah brought up the rear, eyes taking in every shadow. Jacques could feel the shift in atmosphere. Something was watching.

Then, just as U'gah had warned, it emerged. A segmented metal vine slithered from a hidden seam in the stone. Jacques raised a hand instinctively, stopping Hyatta from striking it. The probe moved like a serpent, its motion both mechanical and unnervingly fluid. The end split open, revealing a single optic eye. It locked onto Jacques.

A garbled voice, warped by static and time, crackled through speakers. He recognized it—not the language, exactly, but the structure. Heavily corrupted command code.

Then the floor panel at their feet hissed open.

Inside was a console—sleek, untouched by time. Jacques stepped forward, heart pounding, and entered his credentials. A pause. Then the screen flashed green.

"Bien sûr," he breathed.

"What is it?" Hyatta asked, eyes on the terminal.

"Access," Jacques replied, scanning the interface. "Control. Maybe. It depends on what's still alive in here."

Florence leaned in, frowning. "More death beams?"

"Hopefully not. But maybe something useful."

Emerald peered over his shoulder. "Looks ancient. You think any of it still works?"

"That's what worries me." Jacques tapped through screens. "If it's still running after all this time…"

He stopped. A blinking label read: PRIMARY HANGAR BAY.

The floor shuddered. Lights flickered to life. A door ahead groaned open.

Lusa sniffed the air then wrinkled his nose.

Jacques stepped inside.

The corridor opened into a vast hangar—far larger than the dome should have allowed. It defied logic. The walls curved away, swallowing the light. Crates, vehicles, and silent machinery stood like tombstones beneath the glow of flickering overhead bands.

The air smelled old—stale, metallic.

They stepped in cautiously. The crafts were strange: some squat and armored, others sleek and aerodynamic. Jacques ran his fingers along the hull of one—cold metal, but brittle at the seams. He popped a maintenance panel. The wiring inside had long since decayed. The machine was dead.

"Pas de chance," he sighed. "Just relics. Echoes of something great. Something lost."

Emerald drifted closer, eyes wide as she studied one of the airborne crafts. "It's like stepping into a museum," she murmured, her voice tinged with awe and disappointment. "But none of this works?"

"Non," Jacques replied, shaking his head. "Not without serious repair. And even then, I doubt we have the tools. These vehicles… they're from an era that time forgot. Maybe before the world changed."

Florence, still lingering near the wall, let out an audible huff. "What's the point? Everything's dead. Why are we here?"

Jacques gave her a hard look but bit back the sharp retort forming on his tongue. "Because there's more here than just scrap. This facility wasn't built to be forgotten. We were led here, so there has to be something to find."

The group fanned out in loose formation. Jacques led them in an inverted wedge, Saturn and Florence at the center, flanked by Hyatta and Lusa on the edges. Even now—battle-worn and bruised—none of them dared lower their guard.

***

As they pushed deeper into the chamber, the silence thickened. Heavy dust blanketed everything. These machines hadn't been touched in centuries, maybe longer. Jacques imagined another time—pilots climbing aboard, engineers shouting orders, launch lights blinking on. Now they were ghosts in a tomb.

At the chamber's heart stood a towering column, its base embedded in a wide, sealed door. A freight elevator, judging by the design. Jacques stepped forward, brushed dust from the panel. Cold metal met his fingers. He hesitated, then pressed the button.

A deep mechanical groan answered. Slowly, the massive door slid open, revealing a chamber big enough for all of them. The lighting inside flickered weakly but held. Somehow, it still worked.

"Looks stable enough," Jacques said, though doubt lingered in his posture.

Lusa padded in first, amber eyes scanning the corners. Saturn followed, already muttering to himself as he inspected the walls. "If the elevator's functional," he said, "the lower levels might be in better shape than the hangar."

"Or it means we're walking into a trap," Florence muttered, but stepped inside anyway, her eyes never still.

Hyatta entered last, wordless. The door clanged shut behind him. The elevator jolted, then began its slow descent.

No one spoke.

The only sounds were the groan of gears and the echo of their breath. Jacques stole glances at the others: Emerald's cautious wonder, Saturn's clinical calm, Florence's simmering impatience. And Hyatta—expression unreadable, hand resting lightly on his chain-whip, gaze locked on nothing. Waiting.

The elevator creaked to a halt. A soft chime rang out. The door hissed open.

Cool air washed over them—startlingly fresh. The corridor beyond was bathed in pale white light. Strange glyphs glowed faintly along the walls—pulsing gently.

Jacques stepped out first, tracing one of the glowing lines with his fingertips.

Saturn moved beside him, eyes scanning. "Spell forms," he said quietly. "Gnomish artificers use them to blend magic and tech. Systems like this—they bridge both."

Jacques furrowed his brow. "Can you do this?"

"No," Saturn said flatly. "Most of us can't. You're either arcane or scientific, typically. I focus on biology. Mysticism's another world."

"My mother used to say stuff like that," Emerald added, voice soft. "That science explains what we think, and magic explains what we feel. She thought the gnomes—because of how we see —were the only ones who could understand both."

Jacques nodded, absorbing the words. The tech here didn't feel separate from the magic—it felt born of it. And that disturbed him.

Then Florence's voice, sharp and unimpressed, cut through the moment. "If gnomes are the only ones who can do this, explain Hyatta."

Jacques turned toward her, already bristling.

Florence shrugged, arms crossed. "He looks human. He's used magic more than once. So what's your theory say about that?"

"Do you ever think before you speak?" Jacques snapped. "Hyatta isn't human. None of us know what he really is."

Hyatta said nothing, still staring down the corridor. But then, slowly, he turned. His cold blue eyes locked on Florence's for a breath. Then he looked away.

"Does it matter?" he said. "Magic. Technology. Tools. What matters is how they're used."

The words landed heavy. Florence had no answer.

Jacques ran a hand through his hair. "Let's keep moving," he said. "We came here for answers. We should go find some."

"Fine," Florence muttered, stepping forward. "Let's see what other ancient weapons are waiting to kill us."

CHAPTER FOURTEEN

They pressed forward, footsteps echoing down the long, abandoned corridor. The spell forms along the walls pulsed brighter as they advanced, casting shifting patterns across their faces, as if the complex were watching. Jacques felt it in his core—a pressure coiled in the air.

Emerald walked beside him, her gaze twitching between the glowing symbols, while Saturn followed a half step behind, lost in thought and murmuring to himself. Florence brought up the rear, arms still crossed, though her earlier venom cooled into something quieter—dread, perhaps. Or curiosity. Jacques couldn't tell.

Hyatta led the way, his posture alert, hand never far from the whip at his hip. Lusa and U'gah had stayed behind in the elevator—guard duty, or maybe just their instincts steering them clear. Hyatta had called it a "god-cache." The name lingered.

They turned a corner. The corridor opened into a massive chamber, taller and wider than any yet. The ceiling vanished into shadow. Colossal columns flanked the walls, each one etched in tight spirals of glowing script. And in the center: a wide, circular platform floating a meter off the floor, encircled by a faint, humming veil of light. Machines surrounded it— geometric and impossibly advanced. Tubes and conduits pulsed with life, feeding power to the ring.

"What the hell is this place?" Emerald breathed.

Jacques stepped forward. "A control room, maybe." He swept his eyes across the machinery. "But this can't be HIT. It's far beyond anything we've developed."

"Advanced doesn't always mean good," Florence said, voice brittle. "This place feels creepy."

Hyatta moved to the edge of the platform, studying the light. Then, slowly, he reached out.

"Careful," Jacques said, sharper than he meant.

Hyatta hesitated—but only for a breath. His fingers passed through the veil and brushed the platform.

The chamber came alive.

A deep hum shook the floor. The air vibrated. The lights flared on with blinding clarity, bathing the room in harsh white.

"Well that's not ominous at all," Florence gasped, stepping back.

A holographic interface burst to life above the platform—symbols, diagrams, scrolling layers of information, suspended mid-air. Jacques stared, stunned. The system was fluid, semi-organic—alien, yet engineered. It hovered in space like a living thing.

"I think this is what we came for," he said quietly.

Saturn stepped up, reverent. "Magi-tech on a level I didn't think was possible."

Jacques nodded, then glanced at Hyatta, who stood stone-faced, eyes on the shifting data. "But what is it? What's it controlling?"

Hyatta's response came after a beat. "I don't know. The old stories speak of Hephaestus as a forger of weapons. A smith of the gods. Maybe this is his forge."

"Divine weapons?" Emerald asked, her grin growing. "Yes, please."

The platform shuddered. The chamber thrummed.

The holographic display shifted into a topographic map—Mu, rendered in exquisite, layered detail. Beneath the island's surface, a web of ancient complexes pulsed with light. Hidden installations. Some still active.

"Mon Dieu," Jacques whispered. "There's more. A lot more. Still functioning."

"That's great," Florence said, folding her arms tighter. "But shouldn't we focus on not dying in this one?"

Jacques gave her a sidelong look but let it slide. "Prudence, Florence, is the soul of good timing."

"Indeed," Hyatta murmured. He'd begun circling the room, eyes scanning the walls, whip whispering against his leg.

Drawn by the pulsing light, the others stepped onto the platform. As soon as their feet touched the surface, four more workstations bloomed into view—suspended terminals, semi-solid projections. Each synced to the central system, glowing with soft energy.

Jacques stepped forward, reverence in his breath. "C'est incroyable..." he murmured. "They're networked. Each one feeding into the main system."

Saturn approached one. His fingers hovered over the interface. "Spell forms integrated into the OS. Lighting. Motion tracking. Anti-personnel. Lovely."

Florence didn't miss a beat. "So we're just poking buttons now? Great."

Jacques ignored her. He began scrolling through the main terminal, the system responding with eerie fluidity. His fingers moved faster, scanning subsystems.

"Let's see... multiple sublevels. Most are dormant but intact. Surveillance is active. If these readings are right, we're the only living things down here."

Emerald let out a low whistle. "I found some armories. Experimental stuff—data's locked up, but still." Her tone was chipper, almost inappropriately so.

"Commissary, medical bays... hangars..." Saturn was clicking through his own panel. "Wait, there's—"

A laugh cut across the quiet.

They turned—Florence. Her fingers danced over her console, and her face lit with real amusement.

"I found the showers," she said. "And they're still operating at one hundred percent."

Before anyone could respond, Florence tapped a series of keys. A translucent amber diamond materialized beside her—a magi-tech polyhedron that pulsed in the air before gliding forward, as if on assignment. Without hesitation, she followed.

Jacques blinked. "Wait, Florence! We can't just—" But she was already gone.

"You're the one who said there was nothing else living in here," her voice called back, half-mocking, half-daring, growing fainter as she vanished around the bend.

Jacques groaned. "Pourquoi est-elle comme ça?" he muttered. *Of course she'd run off the first chance she got*, he thought.

Hyatta, still scanning the room for threats, didn't look away as he said, "It's easier to act recklessly than admit she's afraid."

Jacques sighed. "Or she's ready to die for a working shower." He paused. "And I'm not sure I blame her."

Emerald stepped up beside him, her brows knit with concern. "Should we go after her?"

"I'm staying," Saturn said flatly, not even glancing up. He was already buried in the system interface, navigating it like a man deciphering sacred text. "Try not to die."

Jacques rolled his eyes at Saturn's parting words but couldn't help the smirk that followed. "Thanks for the vote of confidence."

He motioned to Emerald, and together they moved into the hall.

Now that the central systems were online, the facility had flooded with ambient light—an eerie, sourceless glow that filled every corner. No shadows. No distortion. It made the halls feel too clean, too still. Like they were walking through the inside of a thought.

The walls and floor appeared to be cut from the same iridescent stone as the obelisks—the ones that contained the solar death beam. That same shimmer ran under their boots. Jacques felt a vibration in the floor, a faint electrical hum.

"Strange, isn't it?" Emerald murmured. Her hand skimmed the smooth wall. The light caught her hair, casting leafy reflections in the corners of Jacques's vision. "Everything just... woke up. Like we're inside someone else's dream."

Jacques nodded, eyes on the path ahead. "Surreal," he said quietly. "And disconcerting."

They moved deeper. The corridor widened.

Jacques kept thinking about Florence—impulsive, confrontational Florence. Reckless as ever. She could get herself killed walking into the wrong room in this place. He quickened his pace.

"You think she really just wanted a shower?" Emerald asked.

Jacques gave a tired shrug. "Knowing her? Oui. But I think she's also looking for normalcy. Control. A moment to pretend everything hasn't gone to hell."

As they rounded a corner, the air changed—warmer, wetter.

Jacques raised a hand, signaling Emerald to stop. A sound reached them. It was flowing water, like a river or an indoor fountain. Could be harmless. Could be worse.

They stepped into the next chamber carefully.

It was a communal locker room—sleek stone benches, recessed cubbies. Through a frosted partition, rows of showers streamed in synchronized sheets of streaming water. Mist curled into the air. The scent of minerals clung thick.

Florence stood fully clothed beneath one of the jets, arms outstretched, water soaking her from head to toe. Her eyes were closed.

"Florence," Jacques hissed.

She turned. Water ran down her face. But she didn't look defiant—she looked... peaceful.

"I needed this, Jacques," she said softly. "We all do. Whether we admit it or not."

Jacques exhaled through his nose, rubbing his temple. "You could've waited."

"I don't care," she murmured, tilting her face back into the stream. "Just for a moment, I don't care."

Emerald looked up at Jacques. "Maybe we could all use a moment," she said, her voice gentle.

Jacques frowned. He wanted to argue, but she wasn't wrong. They'd earned a breath. They'd survived hell.

Before he could stop her, Emerald squealed and began frantically tugging at her clothes, practically dancing out of her sweat-stained gear. Jacques turned his back in a hurry, trying his best to be respectful.

He heard her dart barefoot into the spray, laughing as she collided with Florence under the falling water.

Jacques sighed, dragging his hand down his face. *C'est absurde.*

And yet... he understood. The last few days had flayed them. If something as small as a shower could restore even a sliver of their sanity—let them feel human again—he wouldn't be the one to take it away.

He stepped outside and posted himself near the door, acting as sentry while the others bathed. His eyes scanned the glowing corridor, hand resting near his weapon. The facility was quiet, peaceful. But he tried to stay sharp.

Behind him, soft laughter filtered out—wet clothes slapping stone, splashes, and private voices. Despite himself, Jacques's curiosity stirred. He clenched his jaw and looked away. *I'm a gentleman,* he reminded himself, *even if this place stopped playing by gentlemanly rules a long time ago.*

He leaned against the wall and slid down to a sitting position, arms resting on his knees. The hum of machinery faded into the background. Laughter echoed behind him—pure and human.

A rare sound in a world that had forgotten how to be kind.

For a while, Jacques listened. And then, exhausted, he closed his eyes and slept.

***

Jacques awoke to darkness.

His body, conditioned by days of sleeping on jagged stone and muddy jungle floor, now rested on something soft. The comfort, instead of being a relief, filled him with unease. He shifted slightly, testing the surface. It gave under his weight like memory foam, unfamiliar and silent. It made his back ache.

His hands moved instinctively to his sides, searching for the worn leather grips of his machete and pistol. They found nothing. No weapons. No belts. His stomach dropped.

He sat up slowly, pulse quickening. *Where the hell am I?*

Memory failed him. No clear picture came to mind—only scattered fragments: the control room, the showers, sitting outside the locker room, bone-weary. But how had he gotten here? Who had moved him?

He swung one leg over the edge of the bed, his bare foot lowering into the dark. Instead of cold tile or metal grating, it met something strange—solid, but not hard. Firm, but yielding.

Like stepping onto compressed foam. There was no temperature to it. It felt like stepping onto light.

Ambient illumination stirred around him. Pale white light filtered in from nowhere, filling the space with a sterile, even glow.

Jacques leapt backward on instinct, his spine pressing to the wall, heart pounding.

A voice sliced through the stillness. Smooth. Sultry.

"Greetings and salutations, Specialist Au Clair."

He scanned the room. Spartan. No furniture beyond the bed and a U-shaped desk in one corner. No cameras. No speakers. No sign of anyone. His fingers curled, ready for a fight he couldn't see.

He ducked, checked under the bed. The desk. He even glanced up at the ceiling.

Nothing.

His breath raced; he forced a slow exhale to regain control. "Uh… bonjour?" he croaked.

The wall opposite him pixelated—and then bloomed into a projection. It was a woman. Beautiful, yet artificial. Her features were too smooth, too symmetrical. Not bizarre, just polished—airbrushed. A dream made manifest.

Her lips parted in a perfect smile. "Specialist Au Clair, I am pleased to see you rested and well. How may I assist you?"

He stared, speechless. It was like watching a mirage talk.

"Assist me?" he echoed, his voice hoarse. "Where am I? And... who are you?"

"I am your designated interface assistant for this facility," she replied. "You are in one of the Wrasas Station living quarters. My purpose is to provide support, information, and guidance during your stay. Is there something specific you require?"

Jacques rubbed his temples. The name meant nothing. "Wrasas Station living quarters," he muttered. "Explain."

"This dormitory is part of Wrasas Station, created for personnel recovery and maintenance," she said with calm precision. "You have been identified as Specialist Jacques Au Clair, a registered member of Hephaestus Innovative Technologies. Your credentials grant you full access to this facility's amenities."

Of course they do, he thought bitterly. He couldn't decide if this was a dream, a hallucination, or some elaborate AI prank built by an ancient dead civilization.

He forced himself upright. "And my weapons? What happened to them?"

"Your belongings were stored for safekeeping by your companions," she replied. "Would you like me to retrieve them for you?"

His shoulders dropped with a quiet sigh. "Yes. That would be... helpful."

A panel slid open in the wall beside the desk. Inside sat his gear —machete, pistol, utility belts, boots. Each piece had been cleaned and restored, placed like museum pieces.

He stepped forward, strapping on the familiar weight. The tension in his spine began to ease.

Then he turned back to the hologram, eyes narrowing.

"Why was I brought here? And how?"

"Nine minutes and fourteen seconds after my protocol was activated by Dr. Saturn Chernyak," she said, "you were discovered unconscious outside the locker room in section C-11. Dr. Emerald Zugasti located you and sought the assistance of the male human hybrid designated Hyatta, and the Mau, Lusa, to relocate you to a secure and comfortable recovery zone. This dormitory was the nearest available unit."

That tracks, he thought. The last thing he remembered was posting guard outside the showers. Everything after that was blank.

He exhaled, slower now. "And the others?"

The hologram didn't blink. "Your companions remain within the Wrasas facility. Dr. Chernyak is in the command center. Dr. Zugasti and Chief Accountant Florence Blackwell are in the commissary sampling this station's molecular gastronomy capabilities. Hyatta, Lusa, and the therianthrope, U'gah, are currently in the recreation gymnasium."

He let that sink in. Everyone accounted for. Everyone still alive. But the unease remained.

"This facility," Jacques said, straightening. "What is it? What was it built for?"

The hologram's smile never faltered. "Wrasas Station was designed as a deep-operations fallback and recovery node by Hephaestus Innovative Technologies. Its classified purpose is restricted to personnel with elevated security clearance. Would you like to request temporary access privileges to redacted operational data based on your field rank?"

Jacques's eyes narrowed. "Yes," he said.

The assistant's image distorted.

"Authorization request submitted," she intoned. "Please stand by for verification."

Jacques felt the hairs rise on the back of his neck. *Of course.* Even in the far corners of a ruined alien continent, bureaucracy followed him like a shadow.

But it was better than nothing. Better than waking up in a coffin with no name, no weapons, and no idea where the hell everyone had gone.

He holstered his pistol and stared into the glowing eyes of the hologram. "If you're going to guide me," he said, "start with

222

this. What's still active in this facility—and what's still dangerous?"

The lights above him pulsed in a rhythmic wave.

And the assistant began to answer.

The holographic assistant blinked, then spoke with smooth precision, her voice as poised as if reciting from a long-forgotten manual.

"The facility Wrasas Station was developed as part of a network of military research and development centers under the banner of the Western European Alliance. Its primary function was the study and implementation of magic-technology integration—combining arcane elements with advanced scientific engineering to develop weapons capable of neutralizing mutated species of flora, fauna, and fungi, engineered by Axis powers present on the island continent of Mu. This station includes dormitories, armories, and medical bays to support that objective."

Jacques stared at her, trying to absorb it. Magic and technology —fused together for war. This whole facility, this clean, sterile tomb—it was a monument to that strange union. He brushed his thumb along the hilt of his machete, needing something real, something solid to hold onto.

"And these... experiments?" he asked, cautiously. "Are they still active? Is there anything... dangerous?"

The assistant didn't blink. Her voice remained level, but the answer sent a chill down his spine.

"Many systems remain operational. Some areas have fallen into disrepair. While research was discontinued or suspended where possible, certain automated defense protocols and containment systems are still functional. Caution is advised in areas with restricted access. Anomalous readings may be present."

Anomalous readings. Jacques didn't like the sound of that.

He rubbed the back of his neck. "Anomalies, great. Never mind. I think Florence and Emerald had the right idea. Can you direct me back to the locker room—and is there a laverie?"

The assistant blinked once. "The locker room is in section C-11, as previously noted. The adjacent laundry facility is located in section C-11B. Would you like me to guide you?"

Jacques exhaled, shoulders sagging as he worked the stiffness from his arms. "Oui, please."

The assistant flickered, and a soft, pulsing light formed in the air—just like the one that had guided Florence earlier. "Please follow the marker. The facilities will be prepared for your arrival."

Jacques nodded and followed the light as it floated out of the room. The hallway beyond was as eerily silent as before, the air faintly humming with power. The walls, seamless and iridescent, reflected the glow like polished glass. There was something dreamlike about it all—like walking through a place that had been waiting too long to be disturbed.

"Cette place..." he murmured.

The guide led him to a door etched with a glowing digital symbol—a stylized shirt hanging on a rod. The banality of it, nestled in the heart of a techno-mystical war relic, was oddly comforting.

"Enfin," he sighed as the door slid open with a whisper.

Inside, the laundry room looked surprisingly mundane. Rows of pristine machines hummed softly, lined neatly along the walls. No strange glyphs. No deadly anomalies. Just clean, utilitarian tech—like stepping into a modern apartment complex after weeks of nightmare jungle and spectral ruins.

Jacques began shedding his gear. The familiar weight of his harness and belts clanked dully as he piled his clothes into the nearest unit. The machine chirped in acknowledgment and began its cycle.

224

"At least something around here works the way it should," he muttered, lips twitching in a tired smile.

From somewhere deeper in the complex, he remembered the sound of rushing water—Florence and Emerald's discovery. His eyes drifted toward the connected shower area, and temptation got the better of him.

"Might as well."

The steam rose as he stepped inside. He didn't bother checking the temperature—the water was warm, almost soothingly perfect. Jacques stepped under the stream, let his head fall forward, and closed his eyes.

The sensation was almost alien. Clean water. Real heat. A moment without noise or fear.

For the first time in what felt like months, Jacques let himself exhale fully, the breath dragging from his chest like poison being drawn from a wound. The grime, blood, exhaustion—peeled away beneath the torrent. He let the heat work its way into his joints, his shoulders, his spine.

He didn't know how long they had, or what waited deeper in this gleaming place. But in that moment—under the shower, the hum of ancient machines, the hiss of hot water filling the silence—he let himself feel something else.

Relief—they were still alive.

CHAPTER FIFTEEN

Florence froze mid-bite, her fork hovering as she glared at the disarmingly smooth hologram that had materialized beside her. Of course. First decent meal in forever —something that didn't taste like chalk—and the damn hologram had to ruin it.

"What do you want?" she snapped, her voice soaked in the same disdain she saved for Jacques at his smuggest. And right now, this projection felt worse.

The hologram's expression remained placid, her tone maddeningly neutral. "Dr. Chernyak has requested that all personnel join him in the command center."

Florence rolled her eyes. "Great. I'm eating, and he's not in charge. Go nag someone else."

"I am currently informing all personnel of Dr. Chernyak's request simultaneously," the assistant replied without missing a beat. "You are not being singled out."

Florence jabbed her fork into the food with unnecessary force. "How reassuring."

Across from her, Emerald paused mid-chew, shooting her a nervous glance. "Maybe we should just go, Flo," she said.

Florence sighed, shoulders slumping. "Figures you'd say that."

She tried to focus on the rest of her plate, but her appetite had already started to fray. Jacques would go. Hyatta too, probably with that insufferable air of noble mystery. And sooner or later, someone would come fetch her. She glanced at Emerald, then back at her half-eaten meal, already tasting the disappointment. She didn't want to leave—but staying meant sitting alone with a hologram, stewing in silence.

"Fine," she muttered, pushing the plate away with a clatter. "Let's get it over with."

Florence rose with a huff, the metallic scrape of her chair grating against the floor. Emerald gathered her things quickly. Florence caught the sympathetic glance, but ignored it.

"It won't be so bad," Emerald offered with a small, hopeful smile. "Maybe Saturn found something useful."

Florence scoffed. "Oh, joy. Another thrilling data dump."

They walked the corridors in silence, the shadowless, too-clean light, giving the walls an eerie, depthless glow. Florence glanced around warily, half-expecting the floor to ripple or the wall to close over her like a throat. The entire station felt like it was watching—waiting for someone to make the wrong move.

Every step sounded louder than it should have. By the time they reached the command center, Florence's unease had curdled into full irritation.

The doors hissed open. Saturn stood on the central dais, surrounded by holographic displays, fingers moving in quick, practiced strokes across translucent keys. He didn't look up. Didn't acknowledge them. Didn't speak.

Florence's jaw tightened. He'd called them here and now had the gall to ignore them?

From the far side of the room, another door hissed open—followed by raucous laughter. Lusa and U'gah spilled in, still half-wrestling. The Mau shoved the halfling back with a low growl, only for U'gah to rebound and attempt (badly) to shove him in return.

Florence rolled her eyes. "Of course. They get to play, and I don't even get to finish a goddamn meal."

Lusa was cute, sure—but in desperate need of discipline. And U'gah... she didn't know what he was. A pet? A mascot, maybe? Nuisance? Definitely.

Hyatta entered next, and—as always—his presence made the air change. His golden hair clung in damp, tousled strands, sweat tracing the hollows of his collarbones. Somehow, even caked in grime, he looked like he belonged in an art exhibit—except with better abs. It wasn't fair. No one should look that composed after everything they'd survived.

Florence glanced away, scowling.

"He'd make one hell of a shower partner," Emerald whispered under her breath, eyes gleaming with mischief.

Florence glared. "Calm down. That primitive probably doesn't even know what a shower is."

"Maybe," Emerald said brightly, "but I'd still volunteer to teach him."

Florence clenched her jaw. The station's weird energy, the constant flirting, Saturn's silence—it was too much.

"Can we skip to the part where we find out what's so important?" she snapped, her voice slicing through the room. "Some of us have better things to do than watch these two morons roughhouse."

Hyatta glanced over, unbothered. "Patience, Florence. The wizard will explain when he's ready."

Emerald nudged her with an elbow, still grinning. "He's right. Relax. Maybe this'll be worth the interruption."

Florence folded her arms. "It better be. Or I swear, if Saturn dragged us here over something stupid, I'm going to kill him."

She stared at Saturn, willing him to hurry the hell up.

Jacques burst into the command center, panting, eyes wide with alarm. Every head turned toward him, the tension crackling like static—until the absurdity of his entrance sank in. Water streamed from his hair, plastering it to his forehead. A towel clung precariously to his hips, and his chest, lean and unexpectedly muscular, glistened in the odd glow of the facility.

He paused, blinking. Panic ebbed into sheepish realization.

"...So, no emergency then?" he muttered, voice dry, laced with self-reproach.

He turned, clearly hoping to retreat with what little dignity he had left.

"Wait," Saturn said without looking up. His fingers danced across the console. "Door on the right—conference room. Check the office. Spare uniforms. One should fit."

Jacques hesitated, then muttered, "Merci beaucoup," and vanished through the door.

Florence was just turning to roll her eyes when a faint, familiar tune hummed into the silence. It took a moment to place—then it clicked. *It's Raining Men.* Her gaze snapped to Emerald.

The gnome winked.

"I'm gonna go out and get absolutely soaking wet!" Emerald sang under her breath, eyes sparkling with mischief.

Florence groaned. "Really? We're in an ancient military crypt full of death machines, and that's what's on your mind?"

Emerald shrugged, grinning. "You saw that towel. I mean— Jacques looked like a shampoo ad. Tell me you didn't notice."

Hyatta let out a soft chuckle from the corner. Even Lusa glanced up from where he was gently pawing at U'gah, his feline eyes narrowing with what might've been disapproval— or simply confusion at all the noise.

Florence folded her arms. "I don't care how much you're appreciating. Can we please focus? Saturn, what's the deal?"

Saturn kept typing. "Almost ready," he said calmly. "Worth the wait, I promise. Besides, I'd rather not repeat myself."

The door slid open again. Jacques returned, now dressed in a sleek white uniform that seemed cut from the same strange material as the walls—iridescent, slightly too smooth, like fabric woven from pearl. Gray bands of elastic traced his joints, flexing as he moved. He looked uncomfortable, adjusting the collar with a grimace.

"This is… different," Jacques muttered, running a hand over the fabric. "Feels like I'm wearing the station."

Florence smirked. "It suits you. You blend right in."

Jacques shot her a look. "Très drôle. You should try one. Might help you blend in with all that sarcasm."

Emerald giggled. "Futuristic soldier chic. I dig it."

Finally, Saturn stepped away from the console. "Now that we're all here."

He gestured, and the room dimmed. A flurry of holographic documents bloomed into the air—maps, logs, classified memos written in several languages. The glow of the data cast strange shadows on their faces.

"I've accessed the bulk of the station's memory. There are still some files I'm locked out of—experiments, deep labs—but I've got enough. Enough to tell you two things that change everything."

The room went still.

Saturn's voice was level, but there was steel beneath it. "First, the Western European Corporate Parliament lied. This was never a scientific mission. It wasn't about cataloging Mu's biology, or harvesting exotic resources. We were sent here to counter Axis expansion."

Florence's expression curdled.

Saturn continued. "These are internal intelligence briefings. The Axis were on Mu decades before us. They sent troops, weapons, and entire research divisions. Our mission was to stop them, quietly. We weren't supposed to know. They used us as a cover."

After a long pause, Florence said, "They sent us into a warzone. Unarmed. Untrained."

"Correct," Saturn said flatly. "The military staff aboard our ship—the ones who died during descent—they knew. We didn't."

Florence snapped at Jacques. "But you're military. Didn't *you* know?"

"Former military," Jacques replied, bristling. "I left the Legion years ago. They didn't tell me a damn thing. I thought we were here for the same reason you did."

Emerald stepped forward, pale. "So we were expendable."

Saturn nodded. "Pawns."

No one spoke.

"Second," Saturn said, shifting the display, "this station—Wrasas—was built over three thousand years ago by a Western European Alliance expedition that launched *one hundred fifty years after we did*. In April of 2252."

The silence shattered.

"Impossible," Jacques breathed.

Florence's mouth opened, then closed.

"Time doesn't flow on Mu," Saturn said. "There are anomalies—zones where causality breaks down, where past and future twist around each other. We were the first expedition. But somehow... they got here *before* us. Thousands of years before us."

He let the words settle. Then added, "And they built all of this."

Jacques rubbed a hand down his face, the silence heavy.

Florence whispered, "What *is* this place?"

Saturn didn't answer.

The room around them—glowing walls, living metal, time-warped corridors—spoke for itself.

"That's just the beginning," Saturn said, his fingers dancing across the holographic console. More data streamed into view, glowing softly. "Wrasas Station wasn't the only military research hub. Records show five other operational sites when this facility shut down. Wrasas was the *newest* among them. I've also found three decommissioned locations. And..."—he paused, letting the gravity of his next words settle—"there are Axis sites too. Neu Rheinfall. Yggdrasil. Dornenkrone. And probably more that were undiscovered."

At the last name, Hyatta's expression changed. His eyes went hard.

He stepped forward with sudden force, and Saturn instinctively backed away—rare hesitation drifting across the gnome's normally unreadable face.

"You know the location of the Crown of Thorns?" Hyatta asked, his voice low and taut.

Saturn swallowed but held his ground. "Yes. It's in a geological feature listed as Maze Canyon. Why? Does it mean something to you?"

Hyatta's eyes narrowed, the tension in his shoulders wound tight. "Legends speak of Dornenkrone as a place of god-magic —reality-warping power. Dangerous. Coveted. Said to bend time, flesh, even death. The kind of place only the brave—or the stupid—seek."

A silence fell over the room, weighty and grim.

Hyatta stepped back, offering a slight nod of apology before leaning against the far wall, lost in thought. The others remained frozen, processing what they'd heard.

Saturn resumed. "Allied operations at Wrasas ceased roughly a decade before this station was abandoned. I can't confirm the status of the other sites—I've had no success connecting to them through the relay network. Could be offline. Could be abandoned. There's no way to tell."

Florence, arms folded, furrowed her brow. "Wait… this place is over three thousand years old. Shouldn't it be crumbling?"

"You'd think," Saturn said, tapping through lines of scrolling data. "But the materials used here—combined with integrated maintenance enchantments—keep the structure in a state of constant renewal."

Florence's eyes narrowed. "So magic fixes the walls?"

"In part," Saturn confirmed. "The tech fuses arcane latticework with physical infrastructure. It self-heals. Repairs damage. Prevents decay. It's why this place still runs."

"No shit?" Florence snorted, astounded. "Magic walls. Sure. Why not?"

Jacques had been quiet until now. His voice, when it came, was low and tense. "This fusion of magic and science—it explains the solar weapon, the probes, all of it. But it also means we're dealing with forces far beyond anything we've trained for. And if the Axis got their hands on this…"

"…Then we're screwed if they're still out there," Emerald finished, her tone suddenly serious. She turned to Saturn. "What were they *doing* here?"

Saturn swiped through another layer of files. "They were experimenting. On the flora, the fauna, the geology. They believed Mu held some deep well of energy. Not just for weapons, but something… bigger."

"Define bigger," Jacques said.

Saturn hesitated. "Control over reality itself. Manipulation of physics. Time. Space. Biological law. Artifacts capable of rewriting the rules of the world. The Axis wanted to reshape the planet in their image. And Mu was their key. The Allies were trying to counter them with similar lines of research."

Florence broke the long, strained silence. Her tone was flat. "So. Just another Thursday. No pressure."

Saturn turned back to the console. "And the last thing—possibly the worst—is that no one's ever left."

Florence blinked. "What?"

"There are no records of successful extraction," Saturn said. "Not for Allied forces. Not for Axis. No known signal ever left the continent. And no one made it out."

The words hit like a gut punch.

Florence's expression twisted. She opened her mouth, shut it, then finally spat, "So we're stuck? You're saying that we are trapped on a time-bending death island with no exits?"

Saturn gave a small, reluctant nod.

"Fantastic," she muttered. Her hands ran through her hair, her composure fraying. "That's just—perfect. No way out, no rescue, no one even knows we're here—"

"We survive," Hyatta said quietly.

Florence turned on him, eyes blazing. "That's your plan? *Survive?*"

He didn't flinch. "Yes."

"Seriously?" She snapped. "That's your grand strategy? Winging it until we die?"

Emerald stepped forward, trying to soothe the moment. "Flo—look, I know it's bad. But we have more now than we did yesterday. Information. Infrastructure. Weapons, maybe. If we're careful—"

"Oh, sure," Florence cut in. "Yeah, because this place has been nothing but welcoming so far."

Her words echoed in the silence that followed.

No one had an answer.

Jacques, even when she wanted to strangle him, spoke with that same maddening calm. "We don't have a choice, Florence. We adapt. That's how we survive—through our will and by the grace of God."

Florence shot him a glare. Of course he was right. She hated that he was right. Mu had its claws in them now, and whether they liked it or not, they were players in whatever twisted game the island was running. But she didn't have to like it.

"So what?" she snapped. "We're just supposed to *live* in this creepy bunker forever?"

"I don't know," Saturn said, his voice quieter than usual. For the first time since they'd met, the mask slipped. His shoulders drooped. The black circles under his eyes looked carved in. "I know we won't find all the answers here. But beyond that... I don't know. What I *do* know is that I need sleep. Feel free to carry on without me—I'm going to bed."

He turned without waiting for a response, his gait sluggish, like he was walking underwater. Florence watched him go, the hurtful retort on her tongue fading. Even Saturn, always so sharp and precise, had limits. They all did.

"That's it?" she muttered. "He dumps that nightmare on us and just... takes a nap?"

Emerald gave a half-hearted shrug. "He's been awake for days and still managed to bring this place online. I think he's earned it."

Florence snorted. "Sure. Let's all just sleep it off and hope whatever apocalyptic magic is out there—waits politely for us to feel rested."

"You've survived this far," Hyatta said. His tone was flat, his gaze distant. Nothing ruffled him. Not Florence's rage, not Saturn's collapse. He wasn't normal. "This place appears safe. Use the moment."

His detachment only made her angrier. Or maybe it made her jealous.

Jacques stepped forward, towel draped around his neck, his presence steadier than the walls around them. "We're all exhausted," he said quietly. "But pushing harder won't help. We need rest. Tomorrow, we start figuring things out—how to get off this island, or at least how to survive it. One day at a time."

Florence looked away, her shoulders tense. She hated how his calm made sense. Hated how it chipped away at her anger. "I'm not interested in becoming a permanent resident of this magical hell island," she muttered.

Jacques offered a faint smile—one that didn't quite reach his eyes. "None of us are."

Emerald chimed in, trying to rally the moment. "We've got more now than we had before. We stick together, dig through what Saturn found. There *has* to be a way forward."

"Sure," Florence said, still bitter, but too drained to argue. "Maybe the universe will throw us a bone. Or maybe just bone us. Either way, fun times."

Jacques nodded, his eyes sweeping over the group. "For now, we rest. Tomorrow, we split up—one team explores, the other handles research. After that, we decide our next move."

Florence opened her mouth to protest, then closed it. He was right again, damn him. They couldn't run on fumes.

She leaned against the console and let out a long breath. "Fine," she muttered. "But don't expect me to be *happy* about it."

Jacques smiled. "Wouldn't dream of it."

CHAPTER SIXTEEN

t felt so good to be clean.

Emerald couldn't stop savoring the simple pleasures as she strolled down the C-level corridor—full stomach, clean skin, no blood, no jungle grime in her hair. The 3D-printed food still weirded her out, but the taste was close enough to real that her brain had given up protesting. Real, of course, was relative. She hadn't eaten proper gnomish food since she'd left home to pursue her doctorate in astrophysics and cosmology. Funny, really; she'd studied stars, gravitational constants, the curvature of spacetime—and now she was navigating ancient armories on a time-warping death island, relying more on her paintball hobby than her postgrad degree.

"Where... going?" came a gravelly voice behind her.

Emerald glanced back. Lusa. The Mau's massive, feline frame padded silently along the corridor, his amber eyes bored. His voice hit like a subwoofer made of rocks—too deep, too sudden, too rare to be comforting. Her spine stiffened despite herself; Lusa was intimidating, even when he wasn't trying.

"We're checking the armories for usable equipment," she said, keeping her tone light. "You've asked that three times now."

"We... there... yet?" Lusa repeated.

Emerald sighed. It wasn't Lusa asking, not really—it was U'gah, needling the Mau into being his mouthpiece again. The halfling's muffled giggle gave him away instantly.

Emerald smirked. "Tell your little shadow he's lucky I'm in a good mood today."

U'gah ducked further behind Lusa, chirping something that sounded vaguely apologetic but was probably another joke at her expense. It was strange, but in a way, it felt like a fair reversal. Lusa might've been U'gah's unwilling translator now, but the big cat had pulled his share of mischief too.

Emerald brought them to a halt at a smooth wall. No visible panel, no handle—just blank iridescent stone. She tapped the surface, and a soft shimmer rippled across it. A digital pad blinked to life, then shifted into a biometric scanner. She placed her hand against it.

"Seems like a lot of security for a glorified gun closet," she said to herself. "This is a military facility, right? Shouldn't there be an override for emergencies?"

The system chirped as it processed her credentials. The door hissed open.

Inside, the armory was pristine. Racks of weapons lined the walls—pistols, rifles, grenades, devices she couldn't even identify. Everything gleamed like it had been cleaned yesterday, not sealed away for three thousand years.

Emerald stepped inside, momentarily awestruck. "Well. My primitive friends, it would appear we've entered the future."

Lusa followed, sniffing the air with deliberate slowness. U'gah padded in after him, his eyes already darting between shelves like a magpie hunting for treasure.

"Real equipment," Emerald murmured. "Okay... think. What would Jacques look for first? Something familiar. Something reliable. Something that won't explode the first time I pull the trigger."

"No touching until we know what it does," she added over her shoulder.

Behind her, Lusa grunted and batted U'gah's hand away from a shiny silver disc about the size of a saucer. The halfling yelped and scurried back, grumbling.

Emerald exhaled sharply, running her hand along the nearest rack. Sleek barrels, glowing indicators, complex grip mechanisms—none of it looked remotely familiar. Even the rifles looked like they belonged in a sci-fi show, not in human hands. Jacques would've known what to make of it all, but he was back in the command center, elbow-deep in whatever Saturn had found in the core archives.

"I'm not qualified for this," Emerald sighed.

But then she spotted something: a black, glassy console embedded in the wall. She tapped it. It lit up instantly, revealing a detailed hologram of the weapon she was standing near. Diagrams. Readouts. A full 3D demo.

"Okay... maybe this won't be completely impossible," she said, more to herself than anyone else.

A holographic tutorial launched, walking her through the loading mechanism of what appeared to be an energy rifle. It didn't fire bullets—it used energy cells. The interface showed how to load, calibrate, and even disassemble the weapon. It was surprisingly intuitive. Practically idiot-proof.

Emerald blinked, stunned. "Huh. Military-grade IKEA."

U'gah edged closer, clearly tempted by a nearby case of shiny vials.

"Back it up, Furball," she warned without turning around.

U'gah whined and retreated—though not without sneaking a finger toward a dangling strap before Lusa cuffed him on the ear with one massive paw.

Emerald shook her head. "Boys."

Then, almost involuntarily, she smiled. For all the horror, all the fear, all the endless scrambling to survive, this moment—standing in a futuristic armory, figuring out how not to blow herself up while two mutant misfits squabbled behind her—felt oddly manageable.

Maybe they could make this place work after all. Or at least survive long enough to try.

Emerald tapped through the menu, searching for anything labeled "basic gear" or "protective equipment." Something told her they'd need more than just weapons to survive Mu—especially with everything they now knew about the island. Finally, she found it: a set of advanced body armor with adaptive camouflage and self-repairing systems.

"Okay, now we're talking," she muttered, pulling up the tutorial. "Lusa, U'gah—come look at this. We're going to need all the protection we can get."

Lusa stepped closer, his massive form moving with quiet purpose. His eyes narrowed as he examined the projected armor.

"Yat'ta... have?" he asked, ears perking slightly.

"Of course," Emerald said, watching him lift the armor with an almost reverent touch. "But don't you want some too? You know, for protection?"

Lusa's eyes gleamed, but he shook his head. "No... need." With the armor still cradled in his massive paws, he turned and began prowling the room for other curiosities, his gaze sharp and searching.

Emerald glanced around the armory, still marveling. This wasn't just a stockpile of rifles and grenades. There were energy weapons, sensory systems, specialized munitions, non-lethal suppressants—enough to equip eighty soldiers, maybe more if you counted the modular setups.

"This place is a treasure trove," she muttered. "If we were an army, we'd be set."

She picked up a helmet, its visor softly glowing with alien script scrolling along the edges. It was lighter than it looked—disturbingly so.

"I wish there was a way to haul some of this back. The others will want to see this."

U'gah sidled up beside her, eyes gleaming, fingers twitching toward a reflective disc. Emerald swatted his hand away without looking.

"Focus, U'gah. We need gear that won't blow up or scream for backup the second we touch it."

He pouted dramatically, but before she could respond, the assistant materialized beside him in a sudden flash. U'gah yelped and leapt back, startling him into his transformed state. Lusa flicked an ear and kept browsing.

"There is a storage facility thirty-three meters down the corridor," the assistant said evenly. "It contains five functional grav-sleds. These can be used to transport equipment to the command center. However, I must inform you that such action would constitute a security breach."

Emerald raised an eyebrow. "What kind of enforcement are we talking about?"

The assistant blinked. "With no military command present, punitive action is not possible. However, this breach would be logged in the system."

Emerald exhaled. "So... basically, a write-up no one will ever read."

"Correct."

She gave a lopsided grin. "Fine. Let's get those sleds. We'll haul back what we can. There are four more armories on this level alone."

Lusa was already moving, still cradling the armor like a prize. U'gah bounced along beside him, full of excitement. Emerald followed, her mind still spinning from everything they'd found —and what it meant for their future.

The corridor leading to the storage facility hummed with the same ambient energy as the rest of the station. The air felt thick with static, like something ancient still stirred within the walls.

The door opened with a hiss, revealing five sleek grav-sleds lined in formation beneath glowing ambient panels.

Emerald approached the nearest one, tapping its display. The sled powered on instantly, hovering with a smooth, low hum. "Let's see how much we can move before this place changes its mind."

They worked quickly, loading gear onto the sleds with surprising efficiency. The repetition let Emerald's thoughts drift—to the lab she left behind in Spain, to the quiet corridors of academia, to lectures and research projects and telescope arrays. She'd loved that life. But she couldn't deny the thrill now. The chaos. The danger. It was like living inside one of those disaster movies she used to watch during old Halloween marathons.

She found herself missing things she'd never expected to miss —American horror films, jazz music, even overpriced popcorn. The fall of the United States had been messy and loud with the corporations stepping in to pick up the pieces. Europe barely managed to hold together. Trade across the Atlantic had died when sea monsters colonized the shipping lanes.

"Such a shame," she muttered aloud. "They had great movies."

Lusa didn't reply, but U'gah hummed a tune that could've been a pop song or nonsense. Either way, he seemed content.

As they finished loading the last sled, Emerald wiped sweat from her brow. "That should do it," she said. "Let's get this back before the universe decides we're having too good a time."

They started back through the corridor, the sleds gliding silently behind them. Lusa walked at her side, ears twitching at even the faintest sound. U'gah perched on the edge of one sled like a conquering hero, grinning as the machine floated him forward.

Emerald cast a glance back over the gear. They were lucky. For once, things had gone smoothly.

"Do you think the others will be happy with the haul?" she asked, mostly to fill the silence.

Lusa didn't break stride. "Yat'ta," he rumbled. "Decide."

Emerald smiled faintly. Somehow, that was enough.

Emerald smirked. "Right... I just hope Jacques isn't too distracted by that data core to appreciate what we've got here. He gets lost in thought sometimes, doesn't he?"

Lusa made a low sound that might've been a chuckle—or maybe just a breath. It was always hard to tell with him.

They reached the command center with the familiar hiss of the sliding doors parting before them. Inside, the central hub thrummed with quiet energy. Holographic displays hovered above the dais, casting soft glows across the walls. Saturn was still buried in the bio lab, and Jacques sat perched at the edge of the dais, hunched over the terminal, fully immersed in the station's main data core.

"Alright, let's get everything unloaded," Emerald said, motioning to Lusa and U'gah as the grav-sleds coasted to a stop.

As they began transferring the equipment, Emerald's thoughts drifted. They were surviving, yes. They had food, weapons, shelter. But how long would that last? How long before Mu threw something worse at them? Something they couldn't fight off, or outrun?

"Emerald," Jacques called out from behind her, snapping her back to the present.

He stood at the edge of the platform, still a bit damp from his shower but dressed now, his expression sharp with curiosity. "You found something?"

She gestured toward the sleds. "Weapons, armor, tech—enough to outfit a whole squad. Probably more than we need, but I figured it was better to bring it back than leave it."

Jacques approached, surveying the haul with a thoughtful nod. "Fantastique. Though you could've just told us to gear up ourselves."

"I hear you," Emerald replied, a glint of pride in her voice. "But this isn't just scavenged junk. It's advanced, modular stuff —top-tier magi-tech, from what I can tell. Even with the holographic tutorials, I'd feel better going through it with a second pair of hands. The central AI might have more intel on what we brought back."

Jacques smiled, his tone easy. "Bien sûr. Between us and the assistant, we'll figure it out. This gear could tip the scales."

But Emerald was already spiraling. "And considering what we've seen—dinosaurs, lizardmen, Hyatta—who knows what else is out there? Giant spiders? Zombies? Clowns?" She shuddered. "God, please not clowns. I *hate* clowns."

Jacques blinked. His mouth twitched with a restrained smile. Then, with perfect deadpan timing, he reached down and gently pried her white-knuckled grip from the fabric of his pants.

"Relax, ma chère. No clowns. Not yet, anyway. You really should stop watching all that 'Classic American' nonsense."

Emerald laughed, sheepish now as she shook out her hands. "Right, right. No clowns. But you're missing out. I'll convert you one day."

"I wouldn't count on it." Jacques straightened, that same faint grin tugging at his mouth. "But as for everything else—we'll handle it. One day at a time."

She nodded, grounding herself again. "Yeah. One weird thing at a time." She took a steadying breath. "Alright. I'll start going through this gear."

"Sounds good," Jacques said, then gestured over his shoulder. "But you'll have to excuse me. I haven't eaten all day. I think I forgot breakfast... again."

Emerald arched an eyebrow. "Of course you did. You're always chasing problems on an empty stomach."

Jacques shrugged, brushing damp hair back from his forehead. "Old Legion habit. You either eat fast or keep moving. No time for meals when you're dodging bullets."

"Well, you're not in the Legion anymore," she said with a teasing grin. "Go get food. I'll hold down the fort. And if I run into any mutant clowns, I'll scream loud enough for you to hear it in the commissary."

He laughed, already backing toward the exit. "Merci. Though I'm more worried about what *you'll* do to them if you find any."

"You should be."

As Jacques disappeared down the hall, Emerald turned back to the crates and equipment. Her hand brushed over the cold metal of an unfamiliar device, and the spark of curiosity flared in her chest. There was still so much they didn't understand—about this place, about Mu itself.

But this? This was a start.

***

Jacques walked down the hall, his footsteps echoing softly against the smooth, iridescent floor. The playful exchange with Emerald still clung to his thoughts, but as he put distance between himself and the command center, reality returned like a tide—slow and relentless.

His hand drifted to the hilt of his machete, fingers brushing the familiar grip. It grounded him. A reminder of where he came from. The Legion had taught him to survive impossible odds—outnumbered, outgunned, starving—but Mu was a different kind of battlefield. Here, the laws of nature bent. And it was winning.

The commissary door opened with a soft hiss. Inside, the stillness was palpable. Jacques approached one of the dispensers—standard corporate design, streamlined, efficient, utterly lifeless. He punched in a request. Moments later, a tray slid out with a warm, neutral-smelling meal. It wasn't much, but it filled the emptiness.

He sat alone at one of the tables and began to eat, chewing with mechanical patience. It tasted... fine. Nutrient-balanced, flavor-calibrated. But there was no soul in it. No memory. No Paris. No home. Just synthetic comfort wrapped in sterility.

His mind drifted—to the Legion, to the Alps, to the jungle heat of Kivu and the slums of Madrid. Those memories were hard, but at least they were *his*. Here, everything felt borrowed. Unreal. He took another bite and forced himself to stay grounded.

"One day at a time," he murmured, the old mantra escaping his lips like a prayer.

The door hissed open again. Jacques looked up. Hyatta entered without a word, moving with that uncanny, measured grace that made even his stillness feel dangerous. In his arms, he carried a bundle of iridescent fabric.

Jacques froze mid-bite. The warrior rarely sought anyone out, let alone him.

"Join me, s'il te plaît," Jacques said, the invitation slipping out automatically, born from habit more than hospitality.

Hyatta tilted his head, then approached, setting the bundle on the table before lowering himself into the seat opposite. His eyes never left Jacques.

"Hyatta," Jacques said, trying to keep the tone light. "Not your usual haunt. What brings you?"

The corner of Hyatta's mouth twitched, just barely. "I'm not a ghost. Not yet. Though many have tried to make me one."

Jacques set down his fork, appetite fading. "How do you stay so calm? We found you locked in a cell, we've been ambushed by spirit-worshipping reptiles, and this island... it's unnatural."

Hyatta leaned back, folding his arms. "You would be amazed at what one can become accustomed to." He glanced at the tray. "Freedom and fire are preferable to rot and silence. I have no complaints."

His voice was cool, measured. Jacques recognized that edge— soldiers who survived long enough learned how to mask damage behind composure.

Jacques leaned forward slightly. "Still... you treat it like just another day in paradise."

Hyatta gave a small shrug. "When you've lived through enough of those days, they stop being worth counting."

Jacques chuckled despite himself. "Fair enough." He nodded toward the bundle. "But I'm guessing this isn't a social call."

Hyatta's expression shifted. He reached forward and unwrapped the cloth, revealing sleek white armor, similar in style to Jacques's own uniform. "Lusa found this. I was told you might explain its purpose."

Jacques leaned in, inspecting the gear. It shimmered faintly, sleek and frictionless. Breathable. Designed for movement. "Looks like light combat armor. Officer issue, from a similar set I found earlier. Good protection from slashing weapons and small-caliber rounds, but you'll feel every impact if you're not padded underneath."

Hyatta listened, absorbing each word.

Jacques leaned back, his eyes narrowing slightly. "In return... tell me something. Why were you and Lusa in that prison when we found you?"

Hyatta was quiet for a beat. Then, he spoke.

"Lusa's story is simple. He was captured. The Iruxi intended to sacrifice him to their so-called god—the eldest of the spirit snakes. Their rites are ancient. Brutal. We were fortunate the creature had not yet appeared."

There was no hesitation in his voice, no dramatics. Just fact.

Jacques frowned. "And you?"

"As for myself..." Hyatta's voice took on a distant, almost reverent melancholy. "I am Siv'agat—of the desert nomads. For generations, we've warred with the Iruxi. We venture into the jungles for game, herbs, and the resources our sands lack. In return, they raid our caravans for sacrifices, slaves, and prey." He paused, letting the words settle between them. "I've faced them many times. Never once in peace."

His gaze darkened—not with fear, but with the simmering anger of memory. "Years ago, the Iruxi rallied an army. Their target was Gabutha, a mountain stronghold—our place of refuge. The elders rest there, along with the warriors too wounded to fight again. Beneath the mountain sleeps a beast. Some of my people call it a god, much like the Iruxi revere Henki Kaarme. My warband was led by Grak—one of those zealots. He worshipped the Zırhlı Yutucu, the devourer beneath Gabutha. I do not."

Hyatta's tone took on an edge. "I served the Eye of the Day. The desert sun. The flame that burns and judges. For my defiance, Grak left us to die. My warriors and I were flanking the Iruxi when he pulled back his support. They turned. We were overrun. My warband died screaming, and I... I was denied even the dignity of death. They beat me, broke me, and threw me into that pit where you found me."

He clenched his jaw. "I do not know how long I remained. Nor why they kept me alive."

The silence between them thickened. Jacques didn't press.

250

After a pause, Hyatta refocused. "Does the armor have any properties beyond what you've mentioned?"

Jacques nodded, grateful for the return to the present. "Based on what we've seen so far, there's a good chance it does. If this suit's from the special forces line, it might support modular upgrades. Adaptive camouflage. Enhanced reflex systems. Maybe even energy shielding. We'll need to run diagnostics and check the databases. But I wouldn't be surprised if it does more than just stop bullets."

Hyatta nodded slowly, absorbing the information.

"My turn." Jacques met his gaze directly. "How is it that *you* can do the things you do?"

Hyatta studied him, then gave the barest nod. "I... I do not know how I do the things I do."

"I feel the light of the Eye of the Day. I can *will* it. Shape it. But I do not understand it."

He looked away, his eyes distant. "When I was a boy, it felt like... She spoke to me. Not in words. Only... presence. Warmth. Clarity. It was more than heat, more than light. It was alive."

He paused, struggling to find the words. "I believed She guided me. That I was... chosen. But as I grew, the voice faded. I began to think it was the fantasy of a child starving for meaning."

His fists clenched, knuckles pale against his sun-dark skin. "But I still feel Her, even in silence. And that silence—it burns. It's a wound I cannot close. She turned away from me. And I don't know why."

A long pause.

Jacques shifted uncomfortably, unsure if he should speak. But Hyatta's voice came again, laced with iron.

"That is why I will force Her to see me again."

Jacques straightened. "How?"

Hyatta looked up. His smile was thin, cold. "I will find the Crown of Thorns. And when I do, I will blind the Eye of the Day."

Jacques blinked. "That seems... a bit extreme, non?"

Hyatta's gaze didn't waver. "What is power without love? Without purpose? If She will not answer, if She refuses to guide my hand—then what use is Her light? The Crown is said to contain magic that reshapes reality. If it can bend time, if it can silence the gods... then it can make *Her* look my way again."

"And if She doesn't like what She sees?" Jacques asked, quietly.

Jacques watched him closely. What stared back wasn't madness—it was clarity, twisted through pain. Not a man consumed by rage, but one who had replaced his faith with a promise: that nothing, not even divinity, would ignore him again.

CHAPTER SEVENTEEN

Saturn leaned back from the console, pressing his fists into his tired eyes as if he could massage away the exhaustion that had burrowed into his mind. He'd been combing the database for what felt like an eternity—days, maybe longer. Time had become a haze of case studies, genetic logs, and grim revelations. He wasn't sure what he'd expected to find when he started digging through the research logs, but what he'd uncovered left him both fascinated and profoundly disturbed.

The holographic assistant had proven invaluable by helping him navigate the tangled web of data. The reports spanned centuries, touching every discipline imaginable—biology, genetics, virology, herpetology, and fields Saturn barely remembered from his academic years. The sheer breadth was staggering, and despite the hours he'd poured into it, Saturn knew he'd barely scratched the surface. What he had uncovered painted a picture so twisted, so devoid of conscience, that it defied belief.

While Allied forces had focused primarily on building defenses and researching countermeasures to aggression, the Axis had gone further. Much further. They had turned their attention inward, using Mu's bizarre and mutable ecosystem as a crucible for grotesque experiments—warped science that blurred the lines between life and abomination.

The Axis scientists hadn't just experimented on plants or animals. They had gone after people. The term they used, "demihuman," was a bureaucratic smokescreen—beneath it was a reality of calculated genetic mutilation. Human, animal, and demihuman DNA spliced and recombined in ways that made a mockery of nature. Chromosomes were swapped, rewritten, or replaced. Entire communities were used as breeding stock. Captured soldiers had been broken down and rebuilt into weapons.

Saturn's stomach turned as he reviewed one report in particular: a soldier fused with DNA from a native predator—an iguana-like hunter engineered for strength and speed. Initial success. Enhanced reflexes. Hyper-regeneration. Then came cellular collapse. Genetic instability. Organ failure. The final line read like a eulogy disguised as protocol: "Subject terminated. Data retained. Project terminated."

It wasn't an outlier. It was a pattern. Dozens of projects. Hundreds. Creatures bred not just for combat, but for control. Obedience. Indoctrination.

Worse still, many of the surviving hybrids weren't merely biological experiments—they had been raised on myth. Indoctrinated from birth to see their suffering as holy. Bred in underground camps and told they served the Aesir and Vanir in a war against the Olympians. The files read like twisted scripture—clinical, detached language describing the shaping of minds to match warped bodies.

Some of the creations haunted Saturn more than others. The "nightspeakers" especially. Engineered for nocturnal hunting, capable of echolocation and mimicry. Designed to lure victims with imitations of familiar voices. Saturn had heard them in the jungle—those uncanny whispers just beyond the firelight. Now he understood.

Ironically, it was here—in this very bio lab—that Allied scientists had tried to stem the tide. Research logs showed desperate attempts to create countermeasures: antivirals, targeted retroviruses, genetic reversion therapy. Some worked. Most didn't. And while the Allies had clung to a veneer of morality, Saturn saw the truth beneath it: they had tried to replicate Axis breakthroughs. Not out of curiosity. Out of necessity.

But where the Axis aimed to dominate, the Allies had sought to survive.

Saturn stared at the screen in front of him—an overlapping grid of DNA sequences, fragmentary notes on toxin immunity, failed regeneration protocols. So much knowledge. So many atrocities. Somewhere in this mess, there had to be something he could use.

He leaned forward again, ignoring the ache in his back. Another file opened—this one flagged with an Allied insignia, and deeper clearance protocols. Intelligence reports. Infiltration logs. Failed rescue attempts. There had been missions—dozens —into Axis-held facilities. Yggdrasil. Neu Rheinfall. Dornenkrone. Names that sounded more like nightmares than military installations.

One entry caught his eye.

"Operation Valkyrie."

A doomed mission to extract Dr. Ansel von Reiter, a geneticist rumored to be sympathetic to the Allied cause. Thirty agents had gone in. Four returned. All mentally compromised.

The transcripts were chilling. One survivor claimed the facility was alive. Another spoke of a figure surrounded by green, pulsating light. "The roots of Yggdrasil run deep," the team leader had whispered in his last transmission. "Deeper than even they know. I must remain to sever them."

He could almost see it—a lab of horrors wrapped in vines and lies, guarded by things that used to be people.

He found one last debriefing, broken and jumbled. The survivor had written: "They weren't human anymore. The eyes. They looked right through me." Another line: "Von Reiter knew. He knew what they'd done to us."

And one final, fragmented phrase: "It's alive. The facility... is alive."

Saturn rubbed his eyes again, harder this time. This was too much. The weight of it pressed down on him like the ceiling might collapse. He couldn't stop now—not with everything they'd seen on Mu. Not with the threats still out there.

He keyed in a new search. Something practical. Something usable.

That's when he found it.

Allied insignia. Hermes Biomedical Laboratories. Codename: Project Chimera.

He opened the file, and his blood froze.

His fingers hovered over the file, a pulse of unease rising in his chest. "Chimera"—in myth, a beast of stitched-together nightmares. On Mu, the term meant something far more literal.

A lattice of genetic sequences sprawled across the screen. Charts. Data logs. Diagrams of spliced DNA strands from various animal and demihuman origins. The Allies hadn't just tried to reverse Axis mutations—they'd tried to compete. To build something new. Soldiers, not born but engineered.

> "Initial results show promise. Subject stability remains an issue. Increased aggression and difficulty in establishing control parameters have resulted in numerous containment failures."

Saturn's jaw tensed. "Containment failures." A tidy euphemism for monsters that had broken loose.

They'd done it too. The Allies. They had blurred the same line the Axis trampled over, crafting horrors in the name of defense. Chimerae, built to kill the enemy. And like the enemy, they'd turned on their creators.

He shut the file and sat in silence, staring at the softly glowing console. The room suddenly felt colder. He rubbed his hands together and forced himself to focus.

Keep going.

The next file loaded slowly—Project Prometheus. Saturn blinked at the title, dread coiling in his gut.

Where Chimera had stitched flesh into weapons, Prometheus had aimed higher. Its goal: to infuse human subjects with Mu's ambient energy—what the ancients might have called magic.

The diagrams were worse than before. Humans subjected to controlled magical exposure. Their bodies altered—bones becoming metallic, skin turning semi-translucent, absorbing energy like solar cells. What began as enhancement became incongruous mutation.

> "Subject A37 demonstrated the ability to generate localized gravitational distortions. Cause of death: catastrophic cellular collapse due to internal implosion."

And they hadn't stopped with adults. The logs described fetal experimentation. Trials on children and the elderly. No boundaries. No mercy.

Saturn's stomach turned. His hand trembled slightly as he advanced the files.

Project Apollo. Neural augmentation through psychic induction. Electro-magical surge therapy, meant to unlock latent psionics. The results: cranial combustion. The report's language tried to soften it, but the truth was simple. Brains exploded.

Project Atlas. Gravitational manipulation through genetic engineering and biomechanical implants. The outcome? Collapse. The entire test lab imploded when a subject lost control mid-experiment.

Project Icarus.

His fingers paused. He remembered the myth—flying too close to the sun.

He opened the file.

The goal: create superhuman operatives capable of channeling raw energy into battlefield applications. What happened instead?

"Subjects incinerated from within. Neural tissue liquefied. Bone vaporization. Energy transference uncontrollable."

The last log entry was haunting:

"No subject survived more than five minutes. All tests terminated. Project abandoned."

Saturn leaned back, trying to steady his breathing. These weren't just failed experiments. They were archives of suffering wrapped in data charts and euphemisms.

Still, a question clawed at his mind:

So why leave all of it behind?

Wrasas Station had survived. Intact. Data preserved. Equipment untouched. Why walk away?

He opened the final file.

FINAL REPORT: Strategic Withdrawal from Wrasas Station
ACCESS LEVEL: HYPERIA-13
CLEARANCE OVERRIDE: GRANTED

The document was brief.

No mention of containment breaches. No sabotage. The decision had been strategic. The cause: *temporal anomalies. Dimensional inconsistencies.*

"All personnel are to cease research involving temporal and dimensional manipulation. Any further attempts to harness Mu's energy fields pose an existential threat to the stability of the region. Under no circumstances is Project Thanatos to be reactivated."

Project Thanatos.

There were no attached files, no supplementary records, no elaboration of what had been done under that name. Just a line of stark, bureaucratic language followed by an all-caps prohibition. But the codename alone was enough to chill him.

Thanatos—the Greek personification of death.

He exhaled through his nose, a tremor slipping from his lungs. "Just what the hell did they do here?" he whispered into the silence.

The console screen cast a pale glow over his hands as his mind reeled, caught between horror and curiosity. Somewhere in this archive was an answer. Somewhere, the full truth of what Wrasas Station had been meant to accomplish—and what had gone catastrophically wrong—was buried under layers of encryption, warnings, and long-dead bureaucracy.

But what if that truth wasn't meant to be found?

What if it was better left buried?

Saturn shook the thought off like a chill. He didn't have the luxury of fear. If they were going to survive this cursed island, they needed to know everything. Even the things that scared them. *Especially* those.

His fingers hesitated over the interface, trembling slightly before settling into motion.

Search Query: PROJECT THANATOS—Overview, Experimental Logs, Termination Orders.

The system took longer than usual. Each second felt stretched. As though the archive itself were reluctant to obey.

Then, with a soft chime, the screen responded.

Search results: 1.

Project Thanatos – Primary Objective: Initiate Phase One of the Dimensional Convergence Protocol. Secure and contain—

The file stopped.

The text was replaced by a pulsing red sigil—one he hadn't seen before—and a single word displayed in harsh white type across a black background:

REDACTED

Saturn stared at it, unblinking.

"Redacted?"

His voice sounded too loud in the lab. He leaned in, jaw tightening. Redacted by *who*? The station had been abandoned for millennia. Even the assistant had override access now. And yet this—*this*—was beyond her reach?

His pulse quickened.

Whatever *Thanatos* had been, someone had gone to extreme lengths to erase it from history.

That left one conclusion: it had worked.

And whatever it had touched... hadn't stayed buried.

***

Florence wandered the endless corridors of Wrasas Station, her boots clicking against the too-perfect floor. The pristine walls, the sterile air, the ambient light—it all grated on her nerves. There was no warmth in this place, no life. Just silence. Cold, humming silence. Maybe it was the knowledge of what had happened here—decades of experiments, mistakes, horrors—or maybe it was the way the corridors stretched on forever, like the station itself was trying to digest her.

Yeah, they were safe now. And sure, they weren't starving. The dispensers spat out meals that were halfway edible. But comfort had a cost, and Florence felt like she was paying for it with boredom and isolation. Everyone had splintered off into their own little corners, and it left her alone with her thoughts, which was never a good thing.

Jacques was buried in schematics again, glued to the command center, trying to squeeze answers from old code and unfamiliar machines. Always tinkering, he had been at it for weeks. And

260

Saturn? She didn't even know if he was sleeping anymore. He haunted the bio lab like some pale, muttering ghoul. She'd tried to talk to him once. Got a wall of jargon in return and a door closed in her face. Typical.

That little gremlin, U'gah. Always underfoot, always making noise, always sticking his weird little hands where they didn't belong. Florence hated how he made her feel like the crazy one. Lusa, naturally, tolerated it—probably thought it was funny. The Mau treated U'gah like a puppy, and Florence could barely stand it. She'd tried to pet him once—Lusa, not U'gah—and got a death glare so cold it practically peeled paint. Fine. No one liked being touched anymore, apparently.

Then there was Hyatta.

Just thinking about him made her jaw clench. Stoic, perfect, untouchable Hyatta. He had that storybook calm, the kind that made you want to hit something. Never flinching, never breaking, always walking around like some sun-drenched warrior-priest. He made her furious—and worse, he made her feel small. Like he saw straight through her and found her wanting.

"Go die," she muttered under her breath. She wasn't sure if she meant it.

Her wandering brought her to one of the old storage rooms. The automatic doors slid open, and the light from the hall spilled in, casting long shadows across the crates. She slumped down against one of them and stared at nothing. She felt the ache inside her, the loneliness burning.

Everyone else had a place. Jacques had his tech. Saturn had his science. Emerald had her scavenging. Even the feral pair— Hyatta and Lusa—had combat. But Florence? What did she have? Logistics? Finance? Numbers didn't matter here. They hadn't mattered in a long time.

The hiss of the door broke her spiral. She looked up.

Hyatta stepped inside.

He stood there a moment, silent. Then, slowly, he crossed the room and leaned against a crate across from her. He didn't speak. Just looked at her.

Florence rolled her eyes. "What do you want?"

"You are unhappy," he said simply.

"No shit," she snapped, folding her arms. "Took you long enough to notice."

He nodded, as if her anger was expected—maybe even justified.

"Then do something about it."

Florence blinked. "Excuse me?"

"You have strength," Hyatta said. "And anger. Use them. Sitting here, stewing in resentment, helps no one. You want to fight? Or prove you're more than they think? Then stop letting this place decide who you are."

The words hit harder than she wanted to admit. She opened her mouth, ready to snap back—but nothing came out. He wasn't mocking her. He wasn't judging. He was just... telling the truth.

"Easy for you to say," she muttered, turning her eyes to the floor. "You've got your whole warrior-poet thing. You know who you are. What am I supposed to be?"

Hyatta's expression softened by a fraction. "You have to find it."

Silence settled over them. Not uncomfortable—just quiet.

Florence let the words sink in. Then, finally, she drew in a breath and straightened up.

"Fine," she said. "I will."

Hyatta nodded once. "Good."

Then he turned and walked out.

Florence stayed where she was, staring at the door long after it closed.

Maybe he was right.

Maybe she'd been waiting for something to change.

Maybe it was time she started changing it herself.

Florence marched through the winding halls of Wrasas Station, her stride sharp, her jaw set. Hyatta's words echoed in her head like an earworm she couldn't shake. *"Stop letting this place define you."* Easy to say. But Florence had never backed down from a challenge—and if that sandy monk thought he could poke her into motion with a few well-aimed words, then fine. She'd prove him right, on her terms.

Her boots clicked with purpose as she reached the command center. She didn't hesitate. The doors slid open with a soft hiss, revealing the dim, data-soaked glow of holographic displays. Jacques was there, hunched over a console, eyes bloodshot, fingers flying across a series of translucent keys. He looked like he hadn't slept in days. Typical.

She cleared her throat. Jacques glanced up, surprise evident in his expression. "Florence?" he asked, straightening a little. "What are you doing here?"

"Looking for you, obviously." She folded her arms. "You've been buried in this place for ages. I figured I'd check whether you'd cracked the secrets of the universe... or if you're just cataloging all the ways we're doomed."

His mouth twitched at the corner—half a smile. "I wish. But no. I'm just trying to make sense of this tech. It's... complicated." He gestured to the floating displays. "Emerald keeps hauling in new gear, and I'm doing my best to understand it, but—"

"You're overdoing it," she cut in. "You're going to burn out. And when you do, we're all screwed."

Jacques's smile faded. He nodded slightly. "I know. But I can't afford to sit on my hands. We need to understand this place— how to use it, how to defend ourselves. If we're going to survive, we need to stay ahead of whatever Mu has left to throw at us."

"Which is why I'm here," Florence said, stepping closer. "You've got the brains. Great. But you can't do this alone. I'm not a techie or a soldier, but I'm not useless. You need logistics. Coordination. Someone to keep this mess from spinning out of control. That's what I can do."

Jacques blinked, caught off guard. "You... want to help with the tech?"

"Don't act so shocked. I can handle a spreadsheet and a battle plan, Jacques. You need someone to catalog and find reference material while you bury yourself in circuits and power grids."

He studied her face for a moment, then nodded slowly. "Alright. But don't expect it to be easy. This system is—"

"—Unfamiliar, full of weird energy, probably cursed. Got it." She gave him a dry smile. "I'll manage."

Jacques chuckled. "Alright then. Let's get you caught up."

He turned back to the console, and she stepped up beside him. He walked her through the station's systems—power relays, equipment manifests, security protocols, the ancient tech that somehow responded to their commands. Florence listened, asked questions, pushed where she didn't understand. And to her surprise, she found herself slipping into the rhythm of it.

It wasn't data. It was structure. Something she could build around.

"So we've got weapons, armor, supplies," she murmured, scanning the logistics manifest. "But this wasn't just a fortress. There's research, training facilities... some kind of high-level control hub we haven't accessed."

Jacques nodded. "Yeah. I've been focused on the systems we *can* access, but there's a whole wing still sealed off. Could be important. Could be dangerous."

She turned to him, frowning. "And you were going to tell us when, exactly?"

"When I had more than guesswork to go on," he replied evenly. "I'm not sending anyone into a black site blind."

Florence let out a breath through her nose, equal parts annoyed and impressed. "You're impossible."

He smiled faintly. "I've heard that before."

"Fine," she said, gesturing broadly. "I'll leave the techy stuff to you and Saturn, but everything else? I'm running it. Personnel. Supplies. Planning. You two play mad scientist—I'll keep the lights on and the panic level under control. Deal?"

Jacques gave a small, relieved laugh. "Deal."

She turned to go, then hesitated. "And Jacques?"

He looked up. "Yeah?"

"Sleep. You're no use to anyone if you pass out mid-keystroke."

He nodded. "Soon. There's just... one thing I need to confirm."

Florence rolled her eyes but let it go. "Fine. Just don't make me drag you out of here."

He smirked. "I'll keep that in mind."

She was feeling steadier than she had in days. Maybe Hyatta's words had gotten to her. Maybe Jacques had reminded her she still had something to offer. Whatever it was, she wasn't just floating anymore.

She had a job—and if Wrasas Station wanted to keep its secrets, it was going to have to try a hell of a lot harder.

CHAPTER EIGHTEEN

Level H of Wrasas Station felt less like a floor and more like a descent into myth. Too far from the central hub for comfort, too quiet for sanity—it was like stepping into someone else's idea of an underworld.

Emerald stood a few paces back, arms folded, watching as Lusa and U'gah wrestled with a bay door that hadn't budged in centuries.

The noise was awful. Screeching metal against stone, deep vibrations rolling through the floor, the sound swelling until it seemed the whole ceiling might come down on their heads. Bits of grit and dust rattled loose, sprinkling down in faint showers.

Lusa dug in with brute strength, his paws straining against iron doors that had long since fused in place, while U'gah dug at the door's guiding track to clear its path.

"Come on, almost there!" Emerald called, trying to keep her tone light, though anticipation buzzed sharp under her ribs.

She couldn't fix the machinery—that was Jacques's thing—but she watched the two of them, beast and bear, move like they'd been born to break into dusty, old tombs.

The door gave way with a shuddering crash, sliding open on one last groan of rusted gears.

What lay beyond stopped Emerald cold.

A cavern stretched out, bigger than anything she'd expected—stone walls veined with pale mineral streaks, the stale air thick with earth and machine rot. Weak ceiling lights still clung to life, casting the place in ghost-blue halos.

It wasn't the size that froze her, though.

It was what waited in the middle.

An artillery piece, if you could even call it that—too vast for the word to do justice. Forged metal—dull but intact—a weapon that looked like it had been dropped into the cavern straight out of some nightmare war. It loomed over everything, its mass swallowing the chamber whole.

Emerald drew in a slow breath. "Well," she murmured to no one in particular, "guess we just found the thing they didn't want anyone else finding."

The cannon was nothing Emerald had ever seen before. At first glance it didn't even look built—it looked grown. Its base seemed fused into the stone, anchored by metallic tendrils that spread out like roots across the cavern floor, binding it to the bedrock.

The barrel stretched outward thirty meters at least, vanishing into shadow, ending in a gaping maw big enough to swallow a small tank.

Her eyes caught the markings next. Faint, glowing glyphs traced across the metal, bending in patterns that made her stomach tighten. They weren't any runes she recognized. Too precise for graffiti, too alive for dead metal. Energy crawled around and between them in pale, transparent ribbons.

"By the stars in heaven," she whispered. The awe in her own voice startled her, but she couldn't stop it. "What is this thing?"

The silence broke with a sound she almost didn't believe— Lusa's voice, low and unsteady.

"Weapon ... big."

For once his usual certainty was gone, replaced by something close to reverence. Emerald turned her head, needing to make sure it had really come from him.

Her throat went dry. She swallowed; gaze dragging back to the monstrous silhouette dominating the cavern. The scale was terrifying enough, but the details told their own story. Every plate of metal, every etched line, every faintly pulsing glyph—it was all devoted to one purpose.

Destruction. Not tactical, not practical. Absolute.

"What could they have been trying to kill with something like this?" she murmured, half to herself.

Lusa didn't look away. His pupils had narrowed to razor-thin slits, fixed on the twisting glyphs. When he finally answered, his voice was so low it was almost a growl.

"Shir Tetrau."

Emerald blinked, the unfamiliar words snapping her out of her trance. "What does that mean?"

She turned fully toward Lusa, curiosity cutting through the awe, though unease crept in with it. Lusa wasn't one for riddles—and when he spoke like this, it was never good.

"Big … feathered … god." The sound of it dragged from his throat, raw and heavy, as if he were dredging up something half-remembered, half-feared. "Stalked … forests. Long ago."

Her pulse quickened. She glanced back at the cannon, following the line of its barrel down the cavern, the glyphs along its skin no longer looking decorative at all. They looked like shackles—bindings holding something monstrous at bay.

"You're saying they built this thing to kill a god?" she whispered. The words tasted absurd even as she said them, but the question burned its way out. She knew what the Axis had done—she'd seen the grotesque things they'd twisted into being—but this? This felt different. Older. Bigger.

Lusa didn't flinch. His eyes stayed locked on the runes, pupils thin as blades. "God … or beast. Don't … know."

A pause, whiskers twitching as if his whole body weighed the words. "Teeth like spears … Ground shakes … Hunts … everything. Nothing … survives."

A chill traced up Emerald's spine despite the heavy air of the cavern. The way he described it, this Shir Tetrau wasn't just an apex predator—it was a calamity, the kind of thing that turned myth into warning.

She stepped closer, almost against her better judgment, and laid her palm against the cannon's flank. Cold metal. But the glyphs responded, glowing faintly beneath her fingertips, pulsing like veins. Alive. Waiting.

Whatever this weapon had been built to fight, it wasn't ordinary prey. And if it still lived, if it was still out there—then maybe god wasn't such an exaggeration after all.

"Shir Tetrau..." Emerald repeated, the name strange on her tongue, half-whispered like she might summon it if she spoke too loud. "Why would anyone think they could kill something like that?"

Her gaze slid past the cannon, toward the far wall of the cavern. There, target slabs stood in silent rows—stone and metal alike, each one scarred with craters and gouges.

The image came too easily: a vast winged shape blotting out the sky, a thing of nightmare and divinity descending on the intruders who dared trespass. The cannon blazing to life, runes burning white-hot, vomiting fire and fury in a futile attempt to swat down something no mortal hand should have been able to touch.

Emerald let out a long breath, shaking herself free of the vision. The spell of fascination clung, but she pushed it back, dusting her palms against her trousers as though she'd handled something volatile. Too volatile.

"We should head back up to the command center," she said at last. Her voice sounded steadier than she felt, though awe still colored the edges. She glanced sidelong at Lusa. "This thing isn't going anywhere. And I'd rather not start poking around until we know what we're dealing with."

Lusa's amber eyes shifted toward her, his gaze slow, reluctant. The sharp focus in them softened, but only a fraction. His ears stayed pinned back, taut with a wariness that made her shiver. He looked like he half-expected the cannon to stir, to awaken and bellow fire at them where they stood.

Emerald turned away first, tearing her eyes from the weapon's hulking silhouette. The grandeur of it—so unsettling, so wrong —seemed to linger even when she faced the bay doors again.

Her boots struck against loose pebbles, the clink echoing too loud in the silence. Beside her, Lusa padded along with feline quiet, each step a whisper.

The cavern pressed in on them as they left it behind. Every sound—the scrape of her boot sole, the hiss of her own breathing—felt magnified, devoured by the hush. And still, in the pit of her chest, Emerald swore the shadows leaned toward the weapon, hungry for its dormant power.

As they neared the bay doors, U'gah bounded down from a ledge, his small frame moving with surprising speed. He landed in front of them, beaming, holding something aloft in both hands like a prize.

A disc. Metallic, faintly gleaming, its surface etched with the same twisting glyphs that crawled across the cannon.

Emerald's stomach lurched. "U'gah—put that down." Her voice came sharper than she intended, edged with a pulse of fear. "We don't know what it does—"

He chirped back in protest, ears flicking with stubborn pride. But when she reached out, he didn't resist.

Emerald eased the disc from his grip, holding it gingerly. It weighed less than it should have, light as a plate, yet the instant her fingers brushed its surface the glyphs sparked brighter, shifting in eerie, liquid patterns that threw pale light across all three of their faces.

Her pulse quickened. Not good—definitely not good. She swallowed, tucked it carefully into a pouch at her belt, and made a note to shove it under Jacques's nose—or Saturn's—the moment they got topside.

"Let's just get out of here, okay?"

U'gah's grin faltered. His ears drooped, but he gave a reluctant nod.

They moved to the bay entrance; the cavern fell behind them like a dream dissolving into shadow. Emerald punched the door control, and the metal slabs groaned closed. The sound echoed —like a vault sealing.

Emerald looked at Lusa as the last sliver of light vanished behind the doors.

***

By the time they reached the command center, the familiar hum of the station's systems greeted them—a significant difference to the eerie hush of the lower levels. The central display scintillated with scrolling data. Jacques was still engrossed in information on his holographic interface, his face lit by the pale glow.

He looked up as they entered, concern sparking in his gaze. "You're back. Did you find anything?"

Emerald stepped forward and pulled the metallic disc from her pouch, setting it down between them. "We found this. But more importantly, we found a weapon. A massive artillery piece— something meant to kill gods, according to the furball."

Jacques blinked. He reached for the disc, his fingers brushing the etched runes. "A weapon... for gods?" His voice dropped, his French accent deepening with disbelief.

"You should check the archives. Because if that thing down there was made to fight something way bigger than anything I've ever seen…" She trailed off, the implications sinking in.

Jacques nodded slowly, already deep in thought. He turned the disc over in his hands, eyes narrowing as he examined the glowing script. "I'll start with this. But… we might not like what we find."

Emerald exhaled, her shoulders stiff with tension. "I have a feeling you're right."

Her gaze slid to the console beside him. Lines of schematic text crawled across the display—fragmentary, half-redacted records. For a moment she caught a phrase that made her blink: **DIGITAL SIGNATURES DETECTED — FUNCTIONAL MOBILE BASES.**

"What's that?" she asked.

Jacques dismissed the window with a keystroke, his expression unreadable. "Another thread. Nothing urgent." His tone made it clear he wasn't ready to elaborate.

She watched him a moment longer. His eyes tracked the glyphs, but there was a shadow behind them—a dread he wasn't bothering to hide. Whatever secrets this disc held, she felt he could sense they weren't benign. They were old, powerful, and likely dangerous. And he apparently wasn't ready to share what he knew about the *"functional mobile bases."*

With a slow breath, Emerald stepped back. "I'll check in with Saturn. Maybe he's found something that can give us some kind of starting point."

U'gah tugged at her sleeve as she turned. His wide eyes searched hers, bright with curiosity. She ruffled his hair gently, forcing a reassuring smile—but it felt hollow. Nothing about this warranted comfort.

One last glance at Jacques—already lost to the glow of his console—and Emerald slipped out of the command center.

The corridors outside were quiet, washed in the soft, ambient glow of overhead lights. Too pristine. Too still. The kind of silence that felt curated, artificial. Like a mausoleum dressed as a home.

Emerald's thoughts spun as she walked. The station wore on her. The gleaming walls, the clinical perfection—it was all a veneer stretched over something that felt deeply, intrinsically wrong. And now, the discovery of a cannon large enough to kill something like a god? Her stomach twisted.

She paused outside the bio lab. Part of her didn't want to go in. She wasn't sure she was ready to hear whatever Saturn had uncovered. But ignorance wasn't a luxury they could afford.

With a steadying breath, she keyed open the door and stepped inside.

The lab was chaos. Holographic displays hovered in clusters, their luminous projections displaying strands of DNA, anatomical models, and cross-species comparisons. Saturn stood at the heart of it, his hair unkempt, eyes sunken and red-rimmed from lack of sleep. He looked up as Emerald entered.

"You're back," he rasped. He gestured her over, his expression grim. "You need to see this."

She approached cautiously, her gaze settling on a floating tangle of luminous DNA strands woven together like living circuitry. "What am I looking at?"

"Not what," Saturn said. "Who."

Her pulse quickened. "Who?"

He tapped the display. The projection expanded, revealing a series of genetic overlays. "These are samples from the lizardfolk, U'gah, and Hyatta. And this," he tapped again, highlighting a strand in gold, "is human DNA."

Emerald's breath caught. She stared at the overlapping sequences, where human and non-human strands blurred together. "No... You can't be serious."

"It's all connected," Saturn said. "The Axis weren't just creating monsters. They were taking human DNA and splicing it. Twisting it. Rebuilding it into something else. That's why these things seem familiar. Why they move like people and have similar body plans. They are humans—distorted."

Emerald's voice dropped to a whisper. "What else? You said they were mixing in... other things."

Saturn's jaw tightened. He brought up another series of sequences—stranger now, less recognizable. "Some of this doesn't match anything on record. Not human. Not animal. Possibly extraplanar—or divine."

Emerald stared at the data, her stomach hollow. "You mean they were fusing human DNA with gods?"

"Magic," Saturn said flatly. "They were combining genes and magic at a fundamental level. You can see some of these sequences aren't just chromosomal structures—they're magical constructs, woven into the DNA itself. It's like they were trying to bridge the gap between the mortal and energetic realities."

Emerald stared, mind reeling. "But why? What were they trying to do?"

"Create a new race," he said, low, almost mechanical. "Beings that could surpass humanity. Survivors. Weapons. Something that could stand against the monsters the Axis found—or made."

He brought up another display, a cascade of fragmented documents and grainy images. Emerald's breath caught as she recognized some of the symbols at the top of the screen—familiar, unnerving.

"Those runes," she murmured. "I've seen them. On the cannon we found on Level H. It was massive. Like... take-down-a-city massive."

Saturn froze mid-motion, his full attention snapping to her. "You found a weapon with these markings?" He tapped a few commands, pulling up a map of the cavern. "Tell me everything you saw."

Emerald replayed the image in her mind. "It was embedded in the cave, like it had grown from the rock. The barrel must have stretched thirty meters. Runes glowed along the metal, anchored by these tendrils like roots. Lusa said it was built to kill something called the *Shir Tetrau*."

Saturn's eyes widened. His fingers raced over the console. "*Shir Tetrau...* the Feathered Earthshaker." He pulled up Axis logs—disjointed text, half-redacted files, pages of broken theory. "It wasn't a beast. It was a *paragon*. A living wellspring of magical energy, created to act as both weapon and anchor. One of their apex constructs."

Emerald's blood went cold as sketches filled the display: a titanic, feathered reptile with jagged teeth and molten eyes. It looked like a nightmare hybrid of armored theropod and roided out killing machine. The notes beside it read like a horror novel: *Highly resistant to conventional weaponry. Regenerative factor extreme. Aggressive territorial behavior.* One line at the bottom sent a chill down her spine: **CURRENT STATUS: UNKNOWN. BELIEVED ACTIVE.**

"Wait—are you saying this thing is still alive?" she asked, voice tight. "That the cannon was built just to stop it?"

"That would be the logical conclusion," Saturn said, frowning. "They must have constructed the weapon as a failsafe. A last resort."

Emerald swallowed hard. "Hold on. Are you saying there are *more* of these things?"

Saturn gave a slow, grave nod. "Yes. According to the data, every species the Axis altered had what they called a *paragon* —a singular being infused with magic that acts as a wellspring for the entire bloodline."

He brought up a new diagram, web-like threads converging on central nodes. "They aren't merely the strongest; they feed the others. Power flows from them outward—stabilizing the species' magic."

Emerald took a step back, heart thudding. "So... what happens if you kill a paragon? Does the power just disappear?"

"I wish it did," Saturn said. "But the energy transfers to the next strongest member of the bloodline. A built-in succession mechanism. The paragon role *always* passes on—like a mantle."

She stared at the diagram, horrified. "So... to eliminate a paragon, you'd have to wipe out the entire species?"

"Exactly," Saturn said. "But worse—the fewer individuals remain, the more concentrated the power becomes in the last one standing. As a species nears extinction, its Paragon grows exponentially more dangerous."

"So you're saying if we try to eliminate a species, we could end up creating a *god-tier* version of it?"

Saturn nodded grimly. "Yes. The Axis built biological escalation into the core of their magical design. The final survivor becomes the apex of what the given species is capable of."

Emerald let out a long, shaky breath. "But there has to be *some* kind of weakness. Nothing is invincible."

Saturn looked down, his fingers brushing across failed schematic after failed schematic. "The Allies tried everything. Arcane disruptors. Biochemical agents. Psychic destabilizers. Every countermeasure failed. The paragons adapted faster than they could innovate."

One image displayed a grotesque mutation—something barely humanoid, all muscle and jagged spines. Beneath it, scrawled in desperate handwriting: **PROJECT: HADES' THORN. ALL UNITS LOST. PARAGON MUTATED FASTER THAN EXPECTED. PROGRAM TERMINATED.**

Emerald stepped back from the screen, nausea clawing at her throat. "They *are* unstoppable," she whispered.

Saturn's expression was hollow. "We've only seen fragments. The records are shattered. But the pattern is consistent: the more of them you kill, the stronger they become. The Allies ran out of time. Out of hope."

He paused. "But some are dormant. Others... distant. If we're lucky, we'll never encounter one."

Emerald gave a bitter laugh. "Right. *If we're lucky.* Let's just cross our fingers and hope the god-beasts don't notice we exist."

Saturn glanced over, offering the faintest ghost of a smile. "Not a great strategy, I admit. But until we know more, it's the best we've got."

Emerald straightened her stance. "Then we focus on what we *can* control. Research. Scouting. Mapping. Is there *any* clue where these paragons might be hiding?"

Saturn shook his head. "Not yet. But if we keep digging... maybe we'll find something the Allies missed."

* * *

Jacques ran a hand through his hair—slower this time. The strands slipped between his fingers, longer than they'd been in years. He'd always kept it cropped short out of habit, a holdover from his military days. But here? He'd let it grow unchecked. Another few centimeters and he could tie it back.

Not that it mattered. He didn't care about appearances anymore.

The dim glow of the command center's holographic screens bathed him in cold light. He sat perched in the center of the raised dais. The chair he'd dragged from the ready room offered a small luxury in an otherwise uncomfortable situation. It was probably the best decision he'd made since crash-landing on Mu. Here, in the nerve center of Wrasas Station, he could at least pretend he had some control.

That illusion grew thinner by the hour.

A hiss of pneumatics cut through the silence. Jacques turned toward the sound, fully expecting another crisis—another status update, another demand. What he got instead made him blink, then sigh in exasperation.

Hyatta strolled into the room, water still glistening in his hair. Damp strands of gold and platinum clung to his shoulders, flowing in the ambient light like molten thread. His skin gleamed from a recent shower, tanned and crisscrossed with scars. He was, of course, completely naked.

"Mon Dieu," Jacques muttered, dragging his eyes to the nearest screen. He cycled through a few menus, pretending to be deeply engrossed in system diagnostics.

Hyatta, utterly unfazed, continued drying his hair with a towel, moving with the unhurried grace of someone who had never once been rushed by shame or modesty.

"Thank you for making the rainmakers known to us," he said warmly, his voice tinged with that strange, otherworldly gratitude he summoned on occasion. "They are... very pleasant. The ghost of this place won't let me make fire for a sweat tent, and it's far too clean for a proper dust bath."

Jacques pinched the bridge of his nose. This, somehow, had become his life.

"Glad you're enjoying the showers," he said, dry and thin as paper. "But most people get dressed afterward. You might consider it. Unless you're planning to distract our next existential threat with sheer shock value?"

Hyatta paused mid-dry, tilting his head thoughtfully. "Perhaps a strategy worth trying," he said. "But no, I'm simply air-drying."

"Of course you are."

The towel hit the floor. Jacques didn't look. He could feel Hyatta's presence behind him—likely perched on a console, lounging like a jungle cat, radiating calm.

"Is there something you need?" Jacques asked, tone clipped.

"Not especially," Hyatta replied, breezy as ever. "Though... I did want to ask if you've noticed Florence behaving strangely."

Jacques turned, despite himself. "Strangely how?"

"I passed her in the hall. Her face turned a concerning shade of red. I asked if she was ill. She pointed at me, opened her mouth to speak, stopped, stared... and then stormed away. She kept glancing back like she couldn't decide whether to attack or flee."

Jacques stared. "And... were you wearing anything during this encounter?"

A pause. "No."

Jacques laughed—short, helpless, almost a bark. "Well, that explains it."

Hyatta frowned, genuinely confused. "Why would my lack of clothing cause her such distress? Among my people, there's no shame in one's natural state. Especially after cleansing."

Jacques shook his head. "It's not about shame. It's about *norms*. Social expectations. People where we are from... we wear clothing. It's part of how we signal privacy, professionalism, personal space."

Hyatta absorbed that in silence, then nodded. "So clothing is a… social barrier."

"Sure. Let's go with that."

Hyatta stood, the light catching the lean strength of his frame, and walked over to a pile of equipment. He picked up a neatly folded tarp—one of the iridescent polymer sheets salvaged from storage—rubbed it between his fingers, and nodded approvingly.

Jacques watched, both amused and resigned, as Hyatta draped it over one shoulder like a ceremonial sash. "Is that your new uniform?"

"It will suffice," Hyatta said. "For now."

He paused, face shifting subtly. "There's something else. U'gah heard something moving behind one of the sealed doors on Level H. He didn't want to bring it up directly. Said he didn't want to make Emerald mad by giving you more to worry about."

Jacques sat up straighter. "What kind of something?"

Hyatta's expression darkened, but his voice remained calm. "Strange sounds. A humming. A ticking. Like a song with no words. On Level H."

Jacques's jaw tightened. They'd barely begun mapping that area, and already it had turned into a damn graveyard of buried secrets.

"Did he give any more detail?"

"No. Just that it felt… strange."

Jacques nodded slowly and began opening a comm channel. "Have him come up here."

Hyatta turned to go, already wrapped in his shimmering, makeshift toga. "Very well. I'll send him."

"Hyatta," Jacques called after him.

The warrior paused.

"Thanks. For letting me know."

Hyatta inclined his head. "We are strongest when our shadows are shared."

CHAPTER NINETEEN

A storm churned inside her—tight, hot, rising fast. Not just anger: incandescent fury, heat blistering every thought.

Who the hell did Hyatta think he was, strutting around like a golden, sun-kissed Adonis without a single scrap of clothing? The man had nerve—more nerve than anyone she'd ever met. Clearly, decency meant nothing to him. Dignity even less. The longer she thought about it, the more her blood boiled. Her fists clenched until her knuckles whitened.

He had no right—no right to parade through a high-stakes survival facility like he was modeling for a mythological calendar. The world was constantly teetering on the edge of collapse, and the last thing they needed was another layer of chaos.

What if Emerald had seen him? That thought alone made Florence's vision blur. That perverted little gnome would've launched herself at him like a caffeinated ferret. She'd coo and giggle and turn the whole thing into a circus—and wouldn't that be just perfect? Another useless spectacle on a stage already overflowing with insanity.

"Damn it," Florence hissed, teeth bared.

The mental image refused to leave: Emerald squealing, leaping onto Hyatta like some demented flying squirrel, while Jacques and Saturn stood by helplessly, mouths agape, unable to do anything but bear witness to the catastrophe.

Not happening. Not on her watch.

Hyatta's stunt was not going to become a pattern. He'd learn. She would make damn sure of that. She didn't care what backwater customs or desert rites he'd grown up with—there were rules. Decency and boundaries.

She slammed her palm against the command-center panel. The door slid open with a soft hiss. Inside, Jacques sat hunched over a console, surrounded by glowing holographic displays. He looked up, eyes widening at the sight of her stormcloud expression.

"Florence?" he asked, wary. "What's wrong?"

"Where is he?" she barked, scanning the room like she expected Hyatta to leap out from behind a console, smug and glistening.

"Who? Hyatta? He left a few minutes ago. Is everything—"

"All right?" she snapped. "No, it is not all right! Your friend— the glorified sand gladiator—is out there strutting around stark naked, and I'm not letting that go unaddressed!"

Jacques blinked. Then—damn him—a twitch of a smile betrayed him.

"Ah," he said lightly. "So you had a run-in with Hyatta."

"That's putting it mildly," Florence growled. "And wipe that smirk off your face. This isn't funny, Jacques."

He lifted his hands in surrender, though his eyes still gleamed. "I'm not laughing. But Florence, you know Hyatta—he doesn't really operate within... typical social norms."

"Well, he'd better start!" she snapped, jabbing a finger at him like he were personally responsible. "Because I am not about to let this become a free-range nudist colony. If one person thinks it's okay, others will follow—and then I'll have no choice but to start stabbing."

Jacques's amusement faded a touch, his tone turning more measured. "I understand. I'll talk to him. But he's not doing it to offend anyone. It's just... how he is."

Florence snorted, tossing her hair over her shoulder. "Well, he offended me, so he's going to hear about it. Loudly."

She exhaled, her fury cooling to a simmer. "Look, I get it. Different cultures, different expectations. But we need order. Discipline. Not wandering anatomy."

Jacques nodded. "You're right. I'll make sure he understands."

Florence folded her arms and blew out another breath. The adrenaline was starting to fade, leaving behind the usual dull ache of exhaustion.

"I'll go check on the others. Emerald's probably elbow-deep in some glowing widget she doesn't understand, and Saturn's been in the bio lab so long I'm starting to think he's fused with the walls."

Jacques's voice dipped slightly. "Actually, before you go... I need you to check something out. And you're probably not going to like it."

Florence's brows drew together. "What now?"

Jacques gestured toward a floating display. "We picked up strange audio signatures from Level H. Could be a fluke—old machinery coming back online. But it's one of the zones we haven't fully mapped yet."

She narrowed her eyes. "Let me guess—you want me to poke it with a stick?"

"More or less," Jacques said. "Take U'gah with you."

Florence recoiled. "You cannot be serious."

Jacques winced at the pitch of her voice. "I know, I know—he's not your favorite."

"He's not a cup of tea, Jacques—he's a walking migraine. A raccoon in a loincloth!"

"Florence—"

"And if there's something down there? How do you know he won't try to make friends with it? He's practically feral!"

Jacques gave her the most infuriating look of reason and calm. "I know he gets under your skin. But he's loyal. He's proven himself. And he notices things. Sometimes he sees what we miss."

Florence glared, jaw tight. "Why me? Why do I have to babysit the goblin?"

"Because I trust you."

The words hit like a slap. Jacques met her gaze, steady and unflinching.

"I trust you to keep a cool head. To handle the unexpected. And to keep him in line. He respects you more than you think. Even if he annoys you half to death."

Florence looked away, her jaw working. Damn him. He always knew exactly what to say.

"Fine," she muttered. "If he even *thinks* about touching me, I'm throwing him down the elevator shaft."

"Deal," Jacques said, and that damn smile returned. "Just... maybe not too hard."

Florence shook her head, muttering something under her breath that was definitely less than complimentary. She turned on her heel.

"You owe me for this, Jacques," she called over her shoulder. "Big time."

"Oui," Jacques replied, relieved. "I'll add it to your tab."

Florence didn't respond. Her mind was already shifting gears. U'gah—of all the people she could've been saddled with. Well, at least it wasn't Hyatta. The thought of descending into Level H with that overgrown, half-naked barbarian made her want to punch a wall. And if nothing else, this at least kept Hyatta occupied with something far more important: learning to wear pants.

***

It didn't take long to find U'gah—he was loitering near an elevator, gnawing on what looked disturbingly like a length of stripped wiring. His ears perked up the moment he saw her, his grin widening with that infuriating glint of mischief that always made her molars ache.

"Shut up and follow me," Florence snapped, stabbing the elevator call panel harder than necessary. "And if you even think about pulling one of your little stunts, I will tie you to the cannon down there and leave you as bait. Got it?"

U'gah's eyes widened theatrically, and he gave an exaggerated salute.

Florence rolled her eyes—but the corner of her mouth twitched before she could stop it. "Idiot," she muttered. The word lacked its usual venom.

The elevator sealed with a whisper. Machinery hummed beneath their feet as it began its slow descent into the station's forgotten underbelly.

Florence glanced down at U'gah. He stood perfectly still, watching her with cartoonish innocence, his hairy fingers wiggling in a pattern she recognized.

"Don't give me that," she muttered. "Last time you did that, I ended up elbow-deep in a nest of armored jungle-bugs. Try that again and I swear—"

His grin faded. Then, to her surprise, he reached out and gently patted her arm. Florence blinked. It wasn't a mockery, not a trick. His eyes had changed—no glint, no teeth. Just... something quiet. Something oddly sincere.

Before she could unpack that, the elevator jolted to a stop. The doors hissed open.

Level H greeted them like a half-forgotten tomb.

The sterile chill of the upper floors gave way to what felt like an alien environment. The air carried a faint metallic tang that clung to the tongue.

"Alright," she murmured, bracing herself. "You know what you're listening for?"

U'gah nodded once. His posture changed—ears twitching, eyes narrowing. He lifted a single finger and pointed down the hall.

Florence strained her ears.

For a moment, nothing.

Then—faint and distant—came a keening sound. Soft, musical. Beautiful, even. But it was odd. Its rhythm stumbled, faltered, then looped. Beneath it: a clicking noise. It was consistent, like someone keeping time.

"What the hell is that?" Florence whispered.

U'gah glanced at her, then lifted both shoulders in a familiar shrug. No idea.

"Whatever. Just show me where it's coming from."

He nodded and padded ahead. Florence followed, throwing one last look over her shoulder at the elevator before stepping deeper into the muted light.

Level H was a world apart from the pristine facility above. The walls here were jagged and incomplete, stone exposed like that of a cave. The floors were cracked, uneven, dotted with slabs of polymer plating that seemed lazily bolted down. The ceiling still bore the station's telltale iridescence, casting pale glows in eerie, breathless intervals.

Unlike the bright, sterile light of the upper levels, here everything was dim and fragmented. Darkness pooled in every corner. Florence's footsteps echoed like cannonfire against the stone. Every sound felt too loud. Every silence felt like a warning.

Her eyes twitched toward the shadows. Were they moving? Shifting shapes, just at the edge of her vision? No. Probably not. Just her nerves.

"Focus," she said to herself. "Don't start jumping at ghosts."

U'gah stopped suddenly, ears twitching. His head turned sharply.

Florence paused behind him.

There it was again. Louder this time.

The humming was warped, as if someone were trying to sing but didn't know the notes. The tapping had grown louder as well—like something pacing behind a wall, searching for a door.

She stepped closer to U'gah without thinking. The light overhead flickered. Their shadows stretched long across the corridor, distorted and twitching.

Then U'gah halted at a massive bay door. Easily three times her height. Wide enough for a tank—or something worse.

Closed—but not clean.

Thick, dark streaks marred its surface. Something had oozed from the seam—viscous and slow. Most of it had dried in long, crumbling rivulets.

"Red," Florence breathed.

It looked like blood. Looked like oil. Maybe both.

The seams pulsed faintly. The humming and clicking were louder here—no longer distant, but pressing. Close.

Florence reached out and touched the metal.

It vibrated. Softly, steadily.

Almost like something huge was breathing on the other side.

***

Jacques glanced down at the equipment spread across the table —standard and light suits of armor in that familiar iridescent white polymer that coated everything in Wrasas Station. Alongside them sat an arsenal of weapons that looked more at home in an intergalactic bounty hunter's kit than a stranded expedition's, plus gadgets and devices that defied easy categorization. Emerald had done a hell of a job salvaging the armories and labs they'd unlocked so far.

But his eyes kept drifting to one item: the scroll case U'gah found.

It rested innocuously on the edge of the table, looking for all the world like some dusty relic better suited for a museum exhibit than a next-gen war bunker. But Jacques knew better. There was something... unusual about it. Not overtly menacing, just uncanny—like it didn't belong.

When he'd first unsealed the scroll, he'd expected a map. Maybe hand-drawn. Maybe enchanted. Instead, it had come to life—projecting a living, shifting image of the island continent of Mu in breathtaking, hyper-detailed topography. Rivers shimmered, mountain ridges moved in real time, and waves assaulted the coastlines in an endless fractal ballet. At first he thought it was an illusion—until Emerald and even Hyatta confirmed it. The scroll wasn't decorative. It was observing. Recording. Updating. Somehow... alive.

Worse, it defied classification. No Axis schema. No Allied tech database had any mention of it. It was as if the thing didn't officially exist.

And U'gah? U'gah had been absolutely no help. Every time Jacques tried to ask where he'd found it, the halfling either played dumb or grinned like he was in on some private joke.

"Hey, space cadet," Emerald's voice snapped him out of it. A sharp swat landed against his thigh.

He blinked, turning to see her with her hands on her hips, eyebrows arched. "You mind helping? I'd like to finish packing the evac kits and get to the range before dinner. I still need to stress-test these energy weapons—see if they're actually worth the hype."

"Oui, désolé," Jacques muttered, shaking his head to clear it. He glanced over at the sleek energy pistols and rifles lined up beside the armor. "They do sound impressive. Self-compressing vacuum energy cells, powered by... what was it again? An adjacent energetic dimension?"

He tried not to sound too skeptical.

Emerald chuckled. "Yeah, it's like someone took a theoretical physics textbook, fed it to an AI and said, "Build me a death ray."" She flashed him a grin. "For a second you actually sounded like you knew what you were talking about."

Jacques gave her a wry smile. "I'm good at sounding competent. But ask me to explain how a vacuum energy module works, and I'll give you a blank stare and a shrug."

"You're not alone," she said, nudging him. "This stuff is way beyond anything we've touched before. It's like… the scientists got bored with regular science and decided to remix it with a spellbook."

"Exactly." Jacques's gaze dropped back to the scroll. He picked it up again, careful not to activate it. The material felt smooth as silk, but dense—like there was hidden circuitry woven between layers of arcane insulation.

"What do you think this really is?" he murmured, mostly to himself.

Emerald stepped beside him, peering over his shoulder. "Definitely not just a map. Maybe some kind of surveillance node... or a key? Could be part of a network."

"Or a lock," Jacques muttered. "Waiting for someone specific. Or the right... trigger."

Emerald opened her mouth to respond, but the command center's alert chime interrupted her. Both turned as one of the nearby consoles lit up, scrolling text across its surface.

PROXIMITY ALERT: LEVEL H — BAY DOOR 16-A ACCESS ENGAGED

Emerald's voice dropped. "That's where Florence and U'gah went. You said that door wasn't active before."

Jacques was already moving toward the console. His jaw tightened. "It wasn't. System shows a power surge. Something's diverting energy to 16-A." He scanned the interface again, just to be sure. "It's opening."

A cold knot settled in his gut.

He keyed the comms. "Florence, do you copy? Come in." Static answered him. He tried again. "Florence, it's Jacques. Respond."

Nothing.

"Damn it," he muttered. "Assistant, initiate alert protocol. Notify all personnel. Emerald and I are en route to Level H to back up Florence and U'gah."

"Alert status confirmed," intoned the holographic assistant. The ambient lighting in the command center shifted to a deep, pulsing red.

Emerald hesitated, eyes darting toward the gear. "Should we —?"

"Yes," Jacques snapped. "Grab what you need. I'm not walking into this unarmed."

They moved fast—Jacques grabbing one of the lighter pistols and his machete. Emerald slung a compact energy rifle over her shoulder. With the station bathed in emergency crimson and the hum of dormant systems awakening around them, the air felt charged, like the moment before a thunderclap.

Whatever waited for them behind Bay Door 16-A wasn't dormant anymore.

***

Saturn hunched over a table in the bio lab, eyes red-rimmed and gritty. He'd spent too many sleepless nights parsing twisted genomes and half-corrupted logs. Holographic displays floated in the air around him, each one a glowing strand of genetic code or arcane formula, writhing and curling like living vines. His hands moved ceaselessly, manipulating data strings, cross-referencing anomalies, reshaping sequences in a relentless pursuit of something coherent—some truth buried beneath the Axis's bio-engineered atrocities.

He didn't register the change in lighting at first. The sterile white of the lab faded to a pulsing crimson glow, saturating everything in a sickly red hue. It wasn't until the holographic assistant's voice pierced the silence that Saturn looked up, blinking hard.

"Alert status: proximity breach detected on Level H, Bay Door 16-A," the assistant announced in its maddeningly calm voice. **"Jacques and Emerald are en route to support Florence and U'gah. You are advised to prepare for potential contingencies."**

Saturn's hands froze mid-motion. Bay Door 16-A? That was a hard-sealed zone—armored, reinforced, airlocked. Meant to stay closed.

"Assistant," he said sharply, "details. Are there any power fluctuations? Environmental irregularities? Any anomalous data?"

"Bay Door 16-A experienced a sudden power surge. Adjacent systems are experiencing mild instability. No

record of manual overrides. Surveillance and telemetry from that sector are unavailable."

Saturn's frown deepened. That door didn't open by accident. And if the station's sensors couldn't see past it now… whatever triggered the breach hadn't come from their side.

"Damn it," he muttered. He began packing his field kit with practiced precision—bio-suppressants, arcane dampeners, field seals, experimental counteragents. No more theory. No more isolation. He needed to see this for himself.

"NAVI," he snapped, "activate remote transport protocol."

The drone lifted with a soft mechanical purr, lenses swiveling as it scanned him in quick succession.

"Protocol engaged," NAVI chirped in its cheerful, tone-deaf voice. **"Sensors online. Awaiting mission loadout."**

"Attach support module alpha," Saturn ordered. "We might need the full kit."

The drone's chassis shifted, expansion ports opening with a hiss. The module snapped into place. NAVI's hum deepened as its systems adapted to the new configuration.

"Assistant," Saturn added, pulling on the last strap of his vest, "monitor all power fluctuations on Level H—every volt. If anything spikes, tell me before it blows."

"Confirmed. Surveillance limitations persist. Telemetry remains unavailable."

Saturn exhaled through his nose, one last glance sweeping over the floating data. The research could wait. If 16-A had really opened, then Wrasas Station had just stopped being a safe haven.

"Alright, NAVI," he muttered. "Time to go."

He moved quickly through the corridors, the crimson emergency lights painting the walls in rhythmic pulses like the beat of some deep mechanical heart. NAVI hovered close behind, its sensors sweeping continuously, casting shifting glows across the pristine halls.

"Assistant," he said, pulling up the holographic command interface, "patch me through to Jacques and Emerald."

"**Establishing connection,**" came the reply. A moment of static, then the familiar voice of Emerald filtered through the comms.

"Saturn? That you?"

"I'm in the command center," he confirmed, laced with tension. "Monitoring Level H. Jacques, you said the alert came from 16-A?"

"Affirmative," Jacques replied. "Door activated on its own. No word from Florence. No response on comms."

Saturn's jaw clenched. "Understood. If she's not answering, either her unit's down or something's interfering with transmission. Either way, this isn't a system glitch."

"You think it's a breach?" Jacques asked.

"I think it's something we didn't anticipate." Saturn's fingers danced over the central console, bringing up structural scans, energy signatures, atmospheric telemetry. But there were no overt anomalies—nothing screaming red on the surface.

Which made it worse.

"Jacques," he said, "when you reach 16-A, scan the override panel. If there's no sign of physical tampering, then whatever opened that door came from the other side. Do not enter until we know what we're dealing with."

After a long silence Jacques spoke, low and tight. "And if Florence is inside?"

Saturn closed his eyes for a breath. "We don't leave her. I'll do everything I can from here."

"Roger that," Jacques said.

Emerald's voice followed. "We'll be careful."

Saturn's fingers paused over the next set of commands. "Be ready for anything. If this is a containment breach... there may be no precedent."

Then he opened a new data stream—buried archives flagged with override warnings and codenames the Allies hadn't meant for anyone to see. And he started digging.

CHAPTER TWENTY

Florence could only watch in horrified fascination as the heavy bay doors shuddered against the black tendrils creeping through the narrow gap. Not vines. Not roots. They spread like spilled ink on glass—fluid, serpentine, yet somehow solid—coiling across the metal with alien intent.

The tendrils split and branched, writhing in frenzied, almost mathematical patterns. They pulsed faintly, as if beating with a heart not their own. They spread across the door's surface, curling into the frame, seeking leverage.

With a groan like the death rattle of a leviathan, the massive bay door trembled.

Florence stood frozen, eyes locked on the tendrils as they thickened into cords, binding the seams of the door. Metal strained, but the sound came muffled, swallowed by the hum in her skull.

A voice whispered in her mind—not loud, not sharp. It was soft. Enticing. Her own voice, but deeper. Distorted.

Wait, it cooed. *Wait and see.*

A tug—annoying but insistent—snapped her gaze downward. U'gah. His wide, frantic eyes were locked on hers, his small clawed hands yanking at her pants with increasing desperation. He didn't speak. His whole body screamed one thing: Run.

But she couldn't. Something inside her said she had to stay. Had to witness.

Stay. See.

The tendrils pulsed.

Then came the crack.

The sound split the air like thunder, and the doors tore open with a violence that left her staggering. The tendrils pulled them apart as if they were old putty.

Darkness yawned beyond.

Movement came from the opening—skittering, clicking, scraping.

The swarm came like a flood.

Insects—dozens, then hundreds—poured from the dark: beetles with jewel-bright shells, wrist-thick centipedes, pale arachnids with too many legs, too many eyes. The bugs swarmed the floor, hissing and clacking, portraying a living carpet of hunger and teeth.

"No—no, no, no!" Florence cried, stumbling backward, kicking wildly as the creatures lunged at her. She swatted a centipede from her arm then stomped another under her boot. Chitin crunched sickeningly beneath her heel. They crawled up her legs, snapping at her with tiny, barbed pincers. One scurried up her thigh. She slapped it away with a half-sob, half-scream.

Then she heard the sigh.

A slow, rasping exhale drifting from the darkness beyond the door.

She stared.

A shape clung to the corridor wall. At first it looked vaguely human, man-shaped, but impossibly thin—stretched and starved. Its limbs jerked in unnatural spasms. It moved like a marionette with snipped strings.

It dropped without a sound.

Four limbs. Fluid motion. It landed like a feather and began to crawl.

Florence backed away, barely able to breathe. The thing twitched, its eyeless head cocking at a crooked angle. As it moved into the sickly light of the corridor, she saw it clearly.

Its flesh was ashen gray, pulled taut over bone. Its ribs jutted out like blades. Each hand ended in three spindled fingers, tipped with curved claws that clicked against the floor like a clock winding down.

Its face—if it could be called one—was a stretched mask, lipless mouth bristling with needle-teeth. Saliva strung between them, sizzling as it hit the stone.

The creature sniffed the air then turned toward her.

She couldn't move.

The tendrils pulsed again.

Stay, the voice urged, louder now. *Come closer.*

The creature stepped forward, raising a hand.

"Florence!" Jacques shouted, sharp and commanding.

"Move! Now!"

The spell shattered.

Florence gasped, stumbling backward as her body surged back to life. She turned—and saw them.

Jacques and Emerald were racing toward her. Weapons drawn. Faces grim.

"Florence, behind us!" Emerald barked. "Don't let it touch you!"

Florence didn't need to be told twice.

She ran.

The creature halted mid-step, its eyeless face twitching, registering the newcomers. A low, almost plaintive whine escaped its throat. For a moment, it looked… lost.

Then its mouth stretched open into a grotesque grin, and it shrieked—a piercing, bone-chilling sound that reverberated through the corridor like metal tearing. The thing reared up on its hind legs and lunged.

Florence screamed, stumbling back as it surged toward her.

But before it could close the distance, something slammed past her vision.

U'gah.

The little shifter barreled into the fray, his compact frame a whirlwind of fur, muscle, and fury. He brought his massive greatclub around in a sweeping arc—a crude but monstrous weapon, carved from stone and shaped like the gaping jaws of a prehistoric beast.

The club struck with a sickening crack.

The creature's knee shattered under the blow, folding in with a sound like brittle wood snapping. It collapsed. Its distorted face smashed against the stone floor. Teeth scraped, clawed fingers flailed, but U'gah didn't stop.

He pivoted mid-motion, using the momentum to spin. His stance shifted. His grip adjusted with surprising elegance, and then—

The club fell like a comet.

The head of the weapon slammed into the creature's skull with cataclysmic force, shattering bone and floor in equal measure. Black blood and skull fragments sprayed as the monster twitched.

The hallway became silent, except for U'gah's ragged breathing and the soft, wet squelch of gore settling under the greatclub.

But the silence didn't last.

From deep within the 16-A corridor came a howl—not from a throat but from the bowels of the earth. A guttural, primal shriek shook the walls and sent vibrations through the floor like an earthquake. It was pain. Rage. Hunger.

Florence staggered, the sound pressed into her head like atmospheric pressure. She clutched her ears, her teeth clenched against the overwhelming noise. Then came the wind—a foul, rotting gust that blasted from the open bay, reeking of decay and rotten eggs.

She gagged. Her hair whipped back as the stench hit like a wall of death that coated her lungs.

"Get back!" Jacques shouted. His voice was barely audible through the roar. He stepped in front of her, energy pistol raised, eyes scanning the darkness. Emerald moved beside him with her rifle up and her face set in grim determination.

Then came the sound of skittering.

Not one set of claws. Hundreds.

Thousands.

The sound echoed like glass shattering in slow motion. The corridor beyond the door pulsed with movement as they poured forth.

Grey bodies surged into the light—thin, angular, some scrambling on all fours, others staggering upright like broken marionettes. Their forms were barely humanoid, stretched and twisted. Their mouths stood wide open in voiceless screams.

"Run!" Jacques roared.

He shoved Florence toward the hallway.

Blue bolts barked from his pistol, slamming into the front ranks of the creatures. Some went down, chests smoldering with burnt flesh—but the horde didn't slow. They leapt over or tramped the fallen, shrieking as they came.

Florence ran.

Her feet pounded stone, lungs burning, heart hammering. She didn't look back. She couldn't. She focused on the corridor ahead, on the light of the elevator's control panel glowing like a distant lighthouse in the storm.

U'gah overtook her, darting between her and Jacques with inhuman speed. The little warrior barely seemed to touch the ground, bounding forward in low, bounding strides.

Emerald, who had already retreated, stood at the end of the hall, feet braced, rifle raised.

She fired.

A searing bolt of crackling green energy sliced the air, burning straight through the front line of monsters. Three dropped. Others trampled them as they fell, their shrieks rising to a fever pitch.

"Come on, come on!" Emerald shouted, voice high and strained. She fired again—rapid bursts with no time to aim. Just spray and pray.

Florence pushed herself harder, legs burning, the sound of claws behind her rising like a tidal wave. The distance between her and the elevator stretched like a nightmare, each step longer than the last.

Then Jacques grabbed her arm and yanked.

They skidded around the final corner. The elevator alcove yawned open before them.

U'gah was already there, crouched low, panting, his wide eyes darting between the elevator door and the dark corridor behind them.

"Emerald!" he shouted. "Fall back—now!"

But Emerald stood her ground, teeth bared, her rifle blazing with desperate fury. The creatures closed in fast now—limbs reaching, claws clicking, scraping the floor in a rising tide of death. She dropped to one knee, flipped the rifle to maximum output.

"Just—hold them—back!" she shouted, voice nearly drowned by the roar of her weapon.

A focused beam of green energy erupted from the barrel, slicing through the horde like a surgical laser. It tore a burning line through their ranks, cleaving dozens bodies in a single shot. The air filled with shrieks and sizzling gore. Charred limbs fell twitching to the floor.

For one breathless heartbeat, Florence dared to hope.

But she knew the truth the moment the rifle whined. Smoke curled up from the barrel; the familiar hum died into a sputter.

Dead. Overheated. Done.

Emerald stared at it, willing it to fire again, but nothing.

"Emerald!" Jacques roared.

He lunged forward, one arm outstretched like he could somehow reach her—drag her back from the swarm.

It was too late.

Florence's gaze snapped between Emerald and the onrushing creatures. There were too many. They were too fast. She saw their jagged teeth gleaming in the red light, their eyeless faces stretched wide in grinning hunger.

No one could reach her in time.

Suddenly a wall exploded.

The rock blew outward in a concussive blast, the sound like a cannon shot. A hailstorm of debris slammed into the creatures, shredding bodies, and sending the front line sprawling in a chorus of screams and snapping bone.

Florence staggered, coughing as dust filled the air. Rubble clattered across the ground. The horde reeled.

From the swirling cloud of debris, a shadow moved.

Something long and metallic cracked through the smoke with a snap like a lightning bolt—segmented, serpentine.

Hyatta's whip.

It lashed out with surgical precision, wrapping around the neck of the lone creature still lunging for Emerald. Before it could reach her, the whip snapped taut—and yanked.

The thing screeched as it was dragged backward like a rag doll. Then, with a single jerk of Hyatta's arm, its head tore off.

Hyatta emerged through the dust like a iridescent war-god. His armor gleamed in the red light, sleek and ghostly, draped in a cloak of the same material. Gold and platinum hair clung wetly to his forehead, the rest trailing behind him like a banner.

Another shriek rose. A second monster launched from the haze, talons extended—aimed at Hyatta's flank.

A massive, furred paw caught it midair.

Lusa.

He stepped from the cloud like a beast unleashed, towering, orange-striped, and radiating raw power. The creature he'd caught writhed and flailed, but Lusa didn't flinch. He closed his grip slowly, bones crunching beneath his fingers.

The shriek turned to a wet gurgle. Black blood oozed from the creature's nose and ears.

Lusa crushed the skull like rotten fruit.

With a snarl, he hurled the corpse into the oncoming swarm. It slammed into the next wave like a wrecking ball, sending pale bodies tumbling.

"Get to the command center!" Hyatta barked, his intent cutting through the chaos. "We're right behind you!"

His whip cracked again, slicing one creature's throat, then coiling back to dismember another in the same motion. Each movement was a flawless, deadly dance of precision and judgement.

Jacques didn't hesitate. He grabbed Emerald's arm, hauling her body toward the elevator. She stumbled, dazed, but he kept her moving.

"Go!" he snapped, shoving her through the open doors.

Florence turned back one last time.

Hyatta and Lusa stood at the breach—shoulder to shoulder, reaping the horde.

Hyatta's whip flashed like lightning. Lusa's paws rose and fell, bludgeoning flesh, snapping bone. They moved with brutal grace, not just warriors—but predators in their element.

Something in their eyes made her shudder.

There was joy there. A fierce, unsettling joy.

Hyatta's face was calm, serene almost—too serene for this meat straw. Lusa grinned as he fought, ichor matting his fur, his body heaving with satisfaction.

Florence swallowed hard. For once, she was glad Hyatta was on their side. But a dark thought wormed its way into her mind.

Was this his doing?

The elevator doors slid shut.

Inside the compartment, their ragged gasps filled the void.

Florence slumped against the wall, chest heaving. "What... what the hell was that?"

Jacques's jaw clenched. "I don't know. But they'll find a way up. Sooner or later."

Emerald nodded, still trembling, her rifle hanging useless in her grip. "And when they do... we need more than this." She gestured to the scorched weapon, its barrel still smoking. "A lot more."

Jacques opened his mouth to speak—but the elevator jerked to a halt.

A screech of tortured metal echoed through the shaft.

The compartment shuddered.

Florence's stomach dropped. "Did we just… stop?"

"Fuck." Jacques slammed his fist against the control panel. The lights flickered erratically, the display died. "Nous sommes merdus—they've cut the power."

Emerald's eyes went wide. "Then that means… they're already up here."

A low, rhythmic clicking reverberated through the walls— growing louder, closer. Florence's blood turned to ice.

She knew that sound.

The same sound they'd heard in the hall. The same inhuman cadence the creatures made as they moved.

"We need to get out." Jacques's voice was tight with urgency. He wrenched open the emergency hatch above, revealing a narrow maintenance ladder leading upward.

"Florence, you're first. Emerald, then U'gah," he barked. "Climb fast. Don't look down. Just go."

"But what about—" Florence began.

"No arguments. Go!"

Swallowing the knot of fear rising in her throat, Florence reached for the hatch. Jacques boosted her up, her fingers scrabbling for the edge until she found the metal rungs. The shaft above was pitch dark, the air choked with the scent of oil and rust. Below, Jacques's voice echoed upward, urging the others.

The clicking grew louder.

Florence climbed.

Every muscle in her body screamed, her palms slick with sweat. The steel rungs were cold and unforgiving. Behind her, she could hear the others—Emerald's frantic panting, U'gah's

306

soft, animalistic grunts. Jacques was still below, covering their retreat.

She dared a glance down.

Shadows moved along the walls, fast and unnatural. One. Two. Five.

"Jacques!" she shouted, voice cracking. "They're coming—God, they're climbing the walls!"

"Keep going!" he shouted. "Faster! Don't stop!"

Florence hauled herself up, her arms burning. She didn't dare look down again.

Below, Emerald cursed breathlessly, her legs scrambling, hands slipping on sweat-slick metal. She cast a glance over her shoulder then jerked her gaze upward, her face pale and terrified.

"Shit, shit, shit!" she gasped. "They're fast! We're not gonna —"

"Shut up and climb!" Jacques roared.

The metal vibrated beneath Florence's hands—something was closing the distance.

"Emerald!" she shouted, kicking upward in desperation. "Go! Go!"

The gnome surged forward, driven by panic. Her breath came in ragged bursts.

A harsh screech echoed up the shaft. The sound knifed through Florence's skull. Her heart jackhammered in her chest.

"They're gaining!" she screamed.

"Faster!" Jacques bellowed from below.

His pistol fired. Blue bolts of energy lit up the shaft, searing downward into the darkness. Each shot crackled through the air, lighting the twisted, clawed shapes writhing beneath them.

It didn't stop them.

The creatures came anyway, crawling over their dead, mouths stretched wide in silent, jagged grins.

The elevator began to shake.

A sickening jolt rattled the shaft. Florence gasped. The steel groaned beneath her.

The elevator swayed on its cables below.

"Jacques!" Emerald screamed. "What's happening?!"

"I'm going to try and slow them down. Keep climbing—all of you!" Jacques shouted, cursing in French as he clung to the ladder, pistol in hand.

Without hesitation, he shifted his grip and aimed at the thick steel cable supporting the elevator below. It stretched taut beneath them, gleaming in the dim shaft light. He fired once. The energy bolt scorched a glowing line across the metal, and the cable hissed—but held.

"Come on, damn you," he muttered through clenched teeth, adjusting his aim.

The second shot struck lower, nearer the anchor point. The cable glowed white-hot. Fibers strained, threads snapping one by one under the heat.

A third shot.

A fourth.

With a final shriek of tortured steel, the cable gave way.

The elevator lurched violently, yanked free. Air was sucked from the shaft like a gut punch. Florence screamed, arms locking around the ladder as it shuddered beneath her. A storm of grit and sparks danced in the black below as fresh air rushed in to fill the void.

Below, monstrous shrieks rang out—panicked and guttural—as the creatures lost their grip. The sound of claws scrabbling on metal gave way to screaming silence… then a thunderous *crash* as the elevator slammed into the bottom of the shaft.

For a moment, only the harsh breathing of the four survivors echoed in the shaft, amplified by steel and shadow.

"Are they…" Emerald gasped, voice barely above a whisper, "…gone?"

Florence dared a glance downward. Blackness stared back— still and bottomless. The creatures that had pursued them were gone, but that didn't mean they were safe.

"Keep moving," Jacques ordered, his voice hoarse but steady. "We need to reach the top before more show up."

Every rung felt heavier than the last. The dread hadn't lifted— merely retreated. The dark below still pulsed, as if the abyss itself was watching.

Florence's palms burned, her fingers raw from the climb, but she didn't dare slow. One slip, one pause, and whatever lurked beneath might come roaring back up the shaft.

So she climbed.

CHAPTER TWENTY-ONE

Hyatta stood beside Lusa in the narrow corridor of Level H. Red light pulsed through the overhead seams like a dying heartbeat, casting fractured shadows across their chests and cheeks. The walls pressed in too close. The air went still—save for the dread blooming ahead.

Ahead, the horde waited.

Pale things crowded the corridor, filling the space. Emaciated frames quivered, their skin pulled tight as old leather, their eyeless faces twitching with slow, unnatural tension. Their jaws hung open—split horizontally across the lower face, packed with rows of fine, splintering teeth that clicked and snapped out of sync. Not in rage. They merely swayed, limbs trembling.

Hyatta tightened his grip on the whip and shifted for a cleaner arc. Beside him, Lusa looked at ease, but his ears swiveled back and forth with anticipation. The gleam in his eye wasn't playfulness. It was the quiet pleasure of a warrior measuring a foe.

What are they waiting for?

One of those things wouldn't be a threat. Florence could handle it. Two, maybe three, had she one of the god-forged weapons. But a legion, pressing through a space this narrow, would be over them in seconds. There'd be no chance—only the crushing death of suffocation.

Still, none moved.

A sound rose, soft and delicate. A woman's hum drifted up from the horde's pit, perfume off rot. It wrapped around them, melodic and warm, almost maternal. Hyatta felt the back of his neck prickle. The pale ones stirred. Shoulders rolled. Heads tilted. A path opened through their ranks.

Something approached.

It moved with a grace no creature that size should possess. It was tall, nearly double his height. Its dark, mottled skin was shadowed by the red light. Limbs hung long, hands grazing its knees, fingers curved and twitching like they were keeping time with the tune. The body swayed with fluidity, joints rotating loosely, like it had only recently learned to walk upright and still hadn't committed to it.

Its head bore few features. Just skin, vertical slits for a nose, and a mouth of terrible needle-like teeth. Yet Hyatta felt its attention clamp down on him, like the room had suddenly tilted forward and begun to crush.

The humming deepened—not from its throat but from the floor, the walls. It slipped between ribs. Set teeth on edge. The pale ones mirrored the tone, swaying harder, caught in trance.

It spoke.

"Isik Getiren…"

He didn't hear it; he endured it. The name lodged in his mind like a thorn turned inward, whispered not by one voice but by many. A chorus—female, broken into disharmony. Cold slid down his spine. His knees threatened to fail. He forced them still.

"You should be dust," the thing cooed, its speech shaping itself inside his skull. *"Bones bleaching beneath the desert sun."*

It turned toward Lusa.

"And a rakshasa… a rare treat. My children will feast well."

Lusa let out a low growl, not loud but full of promise. His fur bristled. Lips peeled back. The hiss that followed carried heat.

Hyatta kept his eyes locked on the place where the thing's face should have been. The name it had used—Isik Getiren— echoed too loud. He shoved the thought aside.

He stepped forward with his weight centered and voice steady.

"Beasts and gods alike have claimed dominion over me," he said. "All bled. All failed."

The creature's head tilted. The humming stopped.

"*Such fire,*" it whispered, threads of amusement wrapped through its words. "*It will flavor the meat.*"

Lusa surged. The growl deepened followed by a roar that split the space like thunder.

"*So eager,*" the thing cooed. "*So impatient.*"

The limb blurred.

Hyatta's whip cracked upward, steel to flesh. The impact hammered up his arm, a shockwave ran back through to the shoulder, but he held fast, grounded the pain and recalled his weapon.

"Lusa," Hyatta barked.

The Mau moved—orange muscle blurring into a thunderous charge. He slammed into the creature's flank, jaws aimed high, body braced to break something vital.

The abomination flowed backward, its limbs folding in ways that made no sense, joints reversing. It danced out of range with impossible grace, but a second limb snapped outward, striking low.

Hyatta's whip cracked across the gap, coiling the spindled arm before it could land. He yanked hard, jerking the creature off balance.

Lusa hit like a battering ram.

He drove his full weight into the thing's torso, shoulder-first, the impact jarring and unforgiving. It staggered, sliding several paces before finding footing. It dragged Hyatta with it until the whip pulled free. The Mau didn't stop. He hammered it again, this time with a rising uppercut that folded the thing backward. His strength wasn't wild. It was violence given shape.

The creature shrieked—not from pain, but from joy. Rapture echoed down the corridor. Voices overlapped, hundreds of them—feminine, ecstatic, wrong.

"*Yes,*" it hissed. "*Worthy. At last.*"

It twisted, contorting with inhuman fluidity, and hurled Lusa across the corridor with one sweeping motion. He hit the wall hard enough to dent stone, and slid down in a crouch, breathing hard.

Hyatta acted before the impact had finished echoing. He dropped low, the whip skimming the floor, and caught the creature's leg. The segmented edge bit in deep. It faltered. He drove forward—a knee slamming into its gut. His fist followed up and crashed into its skull with the force of a war hammer. His god-forged gauntlet hummed on contact.

The faceless thing reeled, laughing.

Pale ones surged from the gloom—hands outstretched, heads twitching. Hyatta spun in place, his whip slicing in tight, clean arcs—each strike opening a path. Lusa landed beside him again, snarling, blood at the corner of his lip, but his stance unshaken.

"We kill it," Hyatta said.

The Mau nodded, jaw tight, chest heaving.

Beyond, claws scraped stone. It was reinforcements with no end in sight.

The air was thick now—charged. Death wanted in.

Together, they broke forward.

Lusa struck first. His roar tore the air as he launched into a shoulder slam, burying his full frame into the creature's ribs. His fist followed in a brutal arc, caving the thing's chest inward with a meaty crunch. The sound of bone giving way was unmistakable.

It laughed again.

High, discordant—like shattered wind chimes on concrete. The sound bored into their skulls, too bright to ignore. Hyatta winced as it cut through thought.

Then the creature's chest writhed.

Ribs twisted and stretched, skin folding and unfolding as though the torso were clay. Fractures reversed. No pain. The body reset in slow, unnatural spasms.

Hyatta struck before it could fully rise.

His whip snapped through air and coiled one of its reaching arms. The blade-segments dug deep, chewing through tendon and sinew. The creature turned, not in alarm but in interest, tilting its eyeless face toward him.

He felt the pressure then from the eyeless gaze, but a hand closing around his lungs.

Breath stalled.

"This body is only a vessel," the voices intoned. Dozens of feminine whispers layered as one. *"My essence is beyond your reach."*

Hyatta gritted his teeth and tightened his grip.

"Is that so?"

He twisted the whip and ripped it free. The bladed coils sliced clean through the limb, severing it at the elbow with a wet, ragged snap. The arm dropped to the floor, twitching.

And still—it smiled.

Its remaining hand blurred through the dark, claws carving a diagonal arc across Hyatta's chest. His armor split, skin tore. Heat flared, fire poured into his ribs.

He stumbled, pain screaming—but he stayed upright.

The humming died.

In its place came a guttural roar, full of hate. The sound tore loose from the thing's core like a furnace uncapped, slamming down the corridor in a pulse that vibrated in Hyatta's skull.

Pale bodies twitched and surged forward, their silence breaking into a shriek of claws, open mouths, and needle teeth. They came scrambling over one another, limbs flailing, hunger absolute.

"Lusa, go!" Hyatta bellowed, his arm lashing wide.

The whip snapped across the front line, its song mutilating torsos and limbs. Black blood misted the air, bodies collapsed. It bought him seconds.

Their eyes met—just for a breath. The Mau's lips curled in a promise. This wasn't over.

Then he ran, powerful limbs tearing up the corridor.

Hyatta pivoted. Another arc. The whip cracked into a cluster of pale ones lunging after Lusa. It coiled the dark one's neck and tore it back in a spray of ichor.

It didn't fall.

"Damn it," he hissed.

The severed arm had already begun to regrow. Tendons unfurled like roots, bones slid into place, and flesh knitted without pause.

There was no time.

He released the whip and turned, boots hammering the floor as he broke into a sprint. Behind him, claws scraped the rough hewn floor. The shrieking rose again, louder now—closer.

The corridor stretched as if he ran in a nightmare.

He burned. Not just with pain, but rage.

He hated the retreat. The narrowing path. The shaft ahead. It was a vertical deathtrap, but there was no choice.

He would not sacrifice Lusa.

Not like Grak had his warband.

Lusa had broken the stone wall himself—smashed through it with his bare fists, revealing the emergency stairwell. It was a desperate act. They could still work their way up through the god-cache even if there was a way to seal the hall.

That breach was the only reason Emerald lived.

But it had cost them the bottleneck.

Hyatta clenched his jaw. The choice had been right, but they might bleed because of it.

Behind him, the shrieks closed in, folding over one another, rising like a tidal wave.

The shaft laid open ahead—black and gaping.

Lusa leaned down from the apex, paw braced, arm extended.

Hyatta locked eyes on that hand. Every step burned. Legs numbed. Lungs tearing themselves apart. But he couldn't stop.

That hand was all that mattered.

"Don't miss," he growled to himself.

He pushed harder.

Boots left the ground.

Air roared in his ears. The shaft opened wide, a throat of steel and shadow. Behind him, the swarm howled.

He reached out, fingers stretching toward Lusa's outstretched grip.

Contact.

Their hands struck with a jarring slap, and for a breathless moment, Hyatta hung in open air—suspended mid-arc, boots skimming the shaft as momentum dragged him wide. The Mau's grip locked like iron, his forearm flexing, driving power into the arc.

Hyatta's body slammed into the wall. Pain flared from the impact, but he held.

His free hand snapped to the ladder. Boots caught the rungs, and he was climbing.

Several meters up, he dared a glance back.

The shaft dropped beneath him—black and endless.

They were coming.

The pale ones spilled through the breach like floodwater, skittering over each other in a storm of limbs. Their claws carved handholds into stone. Their eyeless heads turned upward, faces grinning with the joy of the chase. Mouths gaped wide as they clambered higher—faster than should be possible.

"Damn it, they're fast," he spat.

Above, Lusa wasn't climbing at all.

He was leaping.

The Mau bounded from mount to bracket, launching himself upward in perfect arcs. His muscles coiled and released in rhythmic bursts. There was no wasted motion.

Hyatta felt it—pride, a blossom of heat in his chest.

Lusa was learning.

Once little more than a hammer, now something more.

"Show-off," he muttered, the ghost of a smile passing his lips.

A banshee scream knifed through the shaft, high and thin as fine hair. It rebounded off the walls, drilling into his ears. Below, the swarm surged faster—filling the shaft.

The brown abomination burst from the tide.

It climbed without effort, ignoring the ladder, fingers burying into the walls. It didn't jerk or lurch. It flowed—limbs extending, torso flexing, adding to the force of its ascent.

Hyatta's eyes dropped.

His whip was still wrapped around the thing's neck. The handle swayed behind the hulking monster, turning gently in the updraft.

He let go of the ladder.

Air swallowed him. His body turned as he fell, hand outstretched, every muscle prepared for the lash at the end of the ride.

His fingers brushed the hilt, then caught.

The weapon thrummed in his grip, alive again. The chain snapped taut; Hyatta swung wide, the abomination's claws straining to maintain their purchase.

The sharp links tightened around its neck.

It shrieked, furiously.

The body thrashed. Hyatta held firm, encouraging his swing, his whip strained to the limit. The bone and iron bit deep, carving slick flesh. Black poured down in thick rivulets.

Its own weight worked against it.

"Almost there…"

And with a sound like wet timber splitting, the whip cut through the final cord of sinew. The creature's head tore free in a spray of gore. The body seized, then tumbled backward into the shaft.

Hyatta dropped with it—just far enough to unhook. The whip's grip came loose. He lashed it high. Segments curled around a thick bracket.

Weight tore at his shoulder. His fingers screamed.

Then the whip kicked and yanked him up in a snapping arc, allowing him to swing back to the ladder.

The shaft was still screaming behind him.

Pain tore through his shoulder. He gritted his teeth, found the next rung, and climbed. The whip trailed behind him like a serpent, its blade still wet with blood.

Lusa was gone from view, but Hyatta didn't worry. The Mau didn't need eyes on him to make himself known. A catastrophe in fur—relentless, lethal—and the evidence lay all around. Pale bodies plummeted past. Limbs twisted, necks snapped—their descent broken by the climbing swarm or the wreckage at the bottom of the shaft.

More were coming. The flankers. The ones that had broken off and tried to take other routes by way of the stairs. They'd circled ahead through tunnels, hoping to trap their quarry.

Now they were dying.

Ferocious and triumphant, Lusa's roar thundered down from above. Bone cracked, sinew tore. Hyatta felt the echo in the hollow and allowed the edge of a grin.

Good. Give them Hell.

Steel rang above with a sharp clang, echoing like a warning bell. Another body dropped past with one arm gone and its ribs caved in. Then another. And another. The shaft had become a killing chute.

By the time Hyatta reached Level C, every limb screamed. His hands barely gripped the ladder. His legs shook with every motion.

Hands caught him as he began to slip—one small and scarred, the other massive and furred.

They hauled him over the edge and dumped him onto the cold floor. Hyatta hit hard, and he was too drained to break the fall. He lay in a tangle of limbs and pain, his body chilled although the inside of his armor was a swamp.

"They're... right... behind me," he managed, voice broken.

The ceiling spun. The ghost light of this place bled in pulses. Movement stirred at the edge of vision, and then Jacques's voice cut through the haze.

"Get him out of the way!"

Lusa's arms wrapped around him again, lifting him like a sack of gear, no strain in his frame. Hyatta didn't fight it. Couldn't. His body had spent every last reserve.

The command dais pressed beneath him.

"Rest," Lusa rumbled.

Hyatta tried to speak some half-formed retort, but his throat failed him. His tongue felt thick. He gave a nod instead, head bowed.

Jacques was already at the door, with a welding torch in hand. Slag arcing from the seam, he began drawing a line of molten steel that hissed as it cooled.

"Done," Jacques muttered, stepping back. He wiped sweat from his brow, glanced toward Hyatta who was slumped on the dais. "That'll slow them."

Hyatta forced himself upright. Every movement pulled fire through his joints. His legs shook, but he stood.

"They'll tear through it," he rasped, voice frayed. "Maybe not now. But they will."

Jacques gave a grim nod. "Then we don't have much time."

He scanned the room looking at his warband. Armed. Alert. Florence stood in sleek armor as well with a compact energy pistol strapped to her hip. She looked ready.

Hyatta's gaze swept over them.

"What now?" he asked, voice steady, though his fingers still trembled.

Saturn answered without pause. "Is there any realistic scenario where we kill all of them and keep the facility?"

Hyatta exhaled. Rolled his shoulders, testing limits.

"No," he said. "This place belongs to them now."

Saturn's brow furrowed. Fatigue from the months in this place had aged him more and hollowed out the sharp edges of his face.

"Then we have little choice," the gnome said quietly. "We abandon Wrasas Station."

The silence that followed hit hard.

Leaving meant more than retreat. It meant surrender—of ground, of information, of the god-cache they'd claimed—gone.

Emerald spoke first, low, but locked in. "Okay. So how do we get up to the hangar? The elevator's shot and the shaft's full of creeps."

"Escape pods," Saturn replied. "Scattered throughout the station. Closest batch is in the ready room."

Jacques's eyes narrowed. Calculating. "How many?"

"Ten," Saturn said.

Jacques smiled—thin, sharp. "Magnifique."

He turned to Lusa. "Help me grab as much gear as you can carry. We load three pods with supplies: medkits, weapons, rations. If we survive the drop, what we bring keeps us alive after."

Florence stepped forward. Her face was tight, voice taut with urgency. "You're serious? We don't have time dick to around. They're coming."

"Think, Florence. Seven of us. Ten pods. If we don't prep now, we survive the fall just to starve or bleed out wherever we land. We get one shot."

Florence opened her mouth then closed it. Her shoulders sagged.

Hyatta could tell she didn't like it, but she seemed to understand.

Suddenly a metallic slam came from the freshly welded doors of the elevator shaft. The sealed door buckled under the force. Again it rang out, steel groaning, the welds screaming as another blow landed harder than the last.

"Everyone fall back!" Jacques barked.

There was no time for second-guessing. Jacques and Lusa led the charge with the equipment they could carry in tow. Hyatta took the rear. His whip was coiled but ready.

His mind fogged, shadows rippling on every surface. The sound of claws on steel echoed through the walls—closer, syncopated. It was the rhythm of hunger.

"Stay tight!" Hyatta slurred. Numbness dragged at every limb, but he ran through it.

"If we split, we're dead."

"Almost there!" Jacques called.

He skidded to a halt at the ready room's door, its panel still operational. He slammed his palm to the biometric reader.

A hiss. A click. The door opened.

"Inside!" Hyatta shouted, feeling the approach of the horde.

He was the last in.

One final flick of the whip—fast and brutal—scattered the pale ones lunging for the threshold.

The door shut behind him with a heavy, final thunk.

The arm of one of the vile things caught in the door, twitching in the oppressive silence.

Then the pounding started.

Claws tore at the sealed entrance, steel shrieked under dagger-like claws. The walls rattled with the impact of bodies. They'd bought time, but there was no way to know how much.

"We don't have long," Jacques said, voice low and clipped. "Get those pods loaded."

Hyatta pushed off the wall. Legs shaking. It didn't matter. He didn't have time for pain.

The room snapped to life.

Supplies were loaded first. Every second was a heartbeat lost.

And beyond the door—death was waiting for its turn.

Chapter Twenty-Two

U'gah stared at the shallow, metal cave.

It did not look like escape. Did not smell like freedom. The thing was cold, hollow, and waiting to close its mouth and swallow him.

Better to fight. Better to die in blood than curl in the belly of a dead god.

He took a step back.

Jacques was there.

Soft voice. Calm hands.

U'gah did not understand the words, but the sound... the sound helped. Jacques spoke like wind through trees. Like fire beneath stone.

The man touched his shoulder—not to push, but to guide. Gentle and patient, despite the urgency.

If it had been anyone else, U'gah would have growled, snapped, and fled. He would have turned and faced the swarm with tooth, claw, and club. But Jacques was not anyone.

Jacques was his friend.

Still, U'gah's spine felt like it had ants in it as he stepped inside. His claws curled against the smooth floor. His hackles rose. The hatch yawned open.

Jacques kept talking—gentle and reassuring—but U'gah didn't hear the words. His chest was a drumbeat of fear. His breath came fast. His mind felt thin. He watched Jacques's hands move, strapping him in, careful, never rough.

U'gah bared his teeth once—out of reflex. Jacques did not flinch. Just tightened the last strap. He stepped back.

"You must stay in," Jacques said softly. "It's safe, mon ami. I promise."

Safe.

The word meant nothing here.

Safe was warmth. Meat. Firelight. The sound of his tribe breathing nearby. This place had none of that now. Only blinking ghostfire. Icky air. And Children of the Mother.

But U'gah stayed.

Shaking, yes. Growling low. But he did not try to run.

Jacques had never lied. His trust was harder than rock and Jacques had earned it.

He whimpered. Shamefully. His arms tightened around the satch in his lap. Not his club—Jacques had taken that and locked it away in another of the metal caves. But not this. Not the living painting.

This, he had kept.

The surface shimmered when he looked at it. Forests moved. Rivers drifted. Clouds crawled across the land like pipe smoke. It had called to him in the white tomb, whispered through the lab-cave. That place was full of ghost-things and the voice they called Assistant.

It had been waiting for him.

Jacques murmured again. Something clicked. Air hissed. The jaws began to close.

Panic flared. He wanted to leap, to tear free—but couldn't.

He stayed, shaking.

The circle of ghostfire narrowed, dimmed.

A magic pool blinked at him. Yellow glyphs. Symbols that meant nothing to him. Old-gods' magic. He growled low in his throat, more to himself than to the machine.

Jacques's voice came through like crackling leaves from far away.

"Mon ami… it will be okay."

The words pressed like a hand on his shoulder. His friend was still watching over him.

The shallow cave shuddered. Something woke up. Could it be this wasn't a cave at all, but some beast made by the gods?

U'gah's ears flattened. He hugged his treasure tighter. The walls hummed.

He would endure.

For Jacques. For the tribe.

Time passed in heartbeats. Dozens. Maybe hundreds. He stopped counting. He just held on.

Clang.

The pod jolted. His teeth clacked together. Muscles seized.

Silence.

Thunk.

The pod shook.

Clang.

Louder this time. It was a sound he had never heard before.

U'gah yelped. Not proud. Just scared.

The straps groaned under his weight as he fought the instinct to tear himself free.

But he fought the feeling.

Movement.

The thing jerked. Tilted. Dropped.

He was falling.

No one said anything about falling.

It punched through his belly, that sick feeling. He remembered Ko. The mountain. The scream. The body that didn't bounce. Arms that bent wrong. Skin that burst like dewberries.

"Ahn—ahn—AHN!" The sound tore from his throat.

He twisted, thrashed. Bit the straps. Clawed like a beast in a cage.

But there was no breaking free.

Strapped. Bound.

Falling.

Alone.

The cave screamed around him—a coffin hurtling down. Metal shook. Magic hummed. He was sealed inside this cold, dead thing.

The walls crept in. Tighter. Sight spun.

He scraped at the belts. Tore at them with claws. Bit hard enough to taste blood. Nothing gave.

Not Jacques's fault.

Jacques had tried. Had said it was safe. U'gah had believed him.

Jacques was tribe. Jacques was friend.

The panic bled out of him thinking of his friend and left him shivering. His chest began rising fast, then faster still. He couldn't stop shaking.

If death comes, let Jacques live.

Let him leave this land. Let him carry the others. Let him forget.

U'gah closed his eyes tight against the fear, still clutching the satch against his chest. He would not let it go. It was his.

Then he shifted. The metal around him groaned.

A hum stirred deep inside—low and rising. The walls vibrated harder, the rhythm building like a distant drumline. Not loud. But constant. Building.

His ears twitched. Fur stood.

Impact.

A jolt slammed through him. The seat cracked his spine. White flashed at the edge of his vision.

Had he died?

The falling changed, becoming weightless. Then a fast pressure pulled at his chest.

He could hear singing.

A low, heavy note rose from the metal, buzzing behind his eyes, humming through his skin.

He was no longer falling.

The yellow pool lit again. Shapes and lines moved, changing, but not random. They danced. They counted. He couldn't read them, but he felt their rhythm.

Then, a new sound.

Clang. Hiss.

Ping. Ping. Ping. It sounded like shells breaking.

Something stuttered.

The outer shell peeled back—stone flower opening in fire.

Skyfire.

It poured in—bright and orange.

U'gah blinked hard, pupils narrowing against the harshness of it.

Outside—wonder.

The Firefly-in-the-Sky was low on the edge of the world, bleeding into the horizon. The sky wore bruises—deep purple, rich orange. Clouds glowed like bloodfruit split open, like meat still warm. The colors moved. Danced. Like dreamlight.

And across that painted sky—metal birds.

Huge. Silver. Wings wide and shining. Bellies glowing. They glided on fire-colored air. Red and green spilled from their sides. They moved like sky-spirits—too graceful to be real. Inside them showed movement.

Figures.

Shapes.

His friends!

The metal birds had eaten his tribe.

Panic renewed.

He roared—deep, wild—ripping against the straps. He no longer knew what he was in, but it shook as he thrashed. He fought the straps like they were enemies. Bit them. Pulled. Screamed.

They tightened. Bit back. Wrapped his chest, coiling harder the more he moved.

Until he couldn't reach them.

The thing wasn't falling anymore.

It was flying.

Not a coffin. Not a cave. A strange, magic metal bird—flying.

His panic softened, easing slowly. Muscles trembled as they released. He blinked, eyes burning, staring through the glass.

The birds that had captured his tribe were like his.

They flew together.

They were alive.

He exhaled, a low sound, not quite a growl. Not quite a sob.

The sky was still there. Wide. Pretty.

And his pack was still with him.

He sank against the harness. Breathing hard. Watching.

The yellow pool still shined with symbols dancing. Nonsense shapes. He didn't care. Let the old gods have their games.

Something carried them. They were away from the fate the Mother wished on them.

Outside, the other pods wheeled and turned, flying like fish in a deep sky. They held tight to each other. Close. Together.

Beautiful.

U'gah watched, chest full and aching. The Firefly dipped beneath the edge of the world. The sky went dark—deep blue, then black. The stars came. He counted them without numbers.

Then his bird dropped again.

Not falling. Landing.

The pressure shifted. His body tilted forward. The symbols changed. Faster now. Urgent. Flashing.

The land rolled out beneath him—green at first like fur matted with old blood. Then it changed. The green peeled away. Became gold. Became pale.

Desert.

He swallowed hard. Claws curled into the armrests. The wind roared outside the clear stone.

The wings shifted. The bird leveled. The hum softened. A strange flutter rose in him.

Hope.

He watched the other birds land—one, then another—dust rising in small plumes.

Then—his turn.

The ground reached up and kissed it. A soft bump. A shudder through the bones. Then, stillness.

He breathed out, slow.

His heart thudded, deep and even now. Muscles unknotted.

Outside—the Firefly-in-the-Sky slept. The sky belonged to stars and Grandfather Brightrock. The desert glowed silver in the quiet.

He sat still. The straps let go.

Slowly—he leaned forward. Breath fogged the glass. Claws tapped the floor. He searched the dunes.

There.

A bird split open. A figure stepped out—outlined in starfire and drifting dust.

Jacques.

Relief hit him like a wave. Like blood finding the heart again.

He pressed his hand to clear stone. A hiss. A whirr. Cold air swept in—sand and night.

He stepped into the dark.

The sand shifted under his feet—still warm from the Firefly's gaze. It whispered around his toes. The sky opened overhead. A sky for beasts. A sky for wanderers. A sky for him.

He turned, slow. Eyeing.

Other birds opened, one by one.

His tribe stepped into the starfire.

Jacques raised a hand.

Emerald, bright as firelight, her hair lifted in the wind.

Florence stood tall, pale and angry.

Saturn was silent.

Lusa stood strong, steady, fur moving like grass in a storm.

All of them.

U'gah closed his eyes for a moment.

Then opened them again.

This was not the end.

"We made it, *mon ami*," Jacques called. His voice rolled across the dunes like heat full of quiet awe.

U'gah nodded. He felt the truth of it. They had escaped the gods' place. Climbed the sky in their magic, metal birds. Landed whole beneath the stars.

They were together.

That was all that mattered.

Lusa's voice cut through the dark.

"Yat'ta!"

It snapped across the sand like a whip, and U'gah's ears twitched toward the sound.

"Yat'ta!" Lusa called again. The name cracked. Louder than usual. Sharper. No humor in it. No teasing edge. His eyes swept the sands—desperate, searching.

U'gah's stomach turned.

Ten pods.

He counted again—slower.

Ten.

All open.

No Hyatta.

The weight of it fell on him like smoke from a dead fire.

Then Emerald's voice pierced the stillness. "Here!"

U'gah spun to find her, hair flaring green and bright in the glow of Grandfather. She stood beside one of the birds—not peering out across the sand, but into it.

"Hyatta?" she breathed, as if speaking his name could fix what she saw.

"Guys… over here."

The pack moved as one, drawn by her voice. U'gah ran ahead, sand flinging from his heels, his breath hot and loud. The others followed, but none faster.

He skidded to a halt beside the pod and stared down into the sickly, ghostfire.

Hyatta was there. Slumped in the seat, body twisted. The restraints had opened, but he hadn't moved. His chin sagged against his chest. His hair hung limp, golden strands clinging to his face, dark with sweat. More silver now than gold.

His breast armor was ruined—torn in straight lines, cruel, jagged rakes.

But the worst was what filled the wounds.

A black mass—glowing, pulsing, alive.

It clung to the gaps like a parasite, as if it breathed through him. Veins of deep violet flared beneath the surface in lazy rhythm—light without warmth, like starfire caught in tar.

Hyatta's chest rose and fell in time with it.

U'gah's hands curled at his sides. Not to strike, but to stop the panic from breaking loose inside him.

Jacques stepped closer. His voice came slow, cracked by disbelief. "What… what is that?"

He reached forward.

U'gah tensed.

Saturn's voice cut through the night.

"Don't."

His tone was sharp, commanding.

The short gnome pushed past, his black eyes locked on the thing growing from Hyatta's chest.

"Don't touch it," he said again.

His voice didn't shake. But U'gah saw it—how he stood, how he angled his body. Like someone facing down a predator.

Saturn knelt, pulling a god-tool from his belt—small, silver, blinking. It hummed in his grip, a high, nervous sound. The scanner's ghostfire strobed across Hyatta's chest, casting shadows like claws across the warrior's pale face.

"It's not a traditional infection," Saturn muttered, eyes narrowing at the flickering screen. "Not entirely. This is… something else. Magical. Symbiotic, maybe. Or parasitic. Maybe both."

Emerald leaned in. Her voice cracked, harsh with worry. "It's alive?"

"I don't think it's a creature. Not the way we'd understand it. It's more like… a construct. A curse made real." Saturn's fingers hovered near the edge of the mass, close but not touching. The scanner's pulse grew more erratic. "It's drawing energy from him. Feeding. And the signature's growing stronger. If we don't stop it—"

"Can you get it off him?" Jacques cut in, raw, barely above a whisper.

Saturn hesitated. The device dipped slightly in his hand.

"I don't know. If I try to cut it out and it's bonded to nerves or blood—he could die. Or worse. It could… become him."

U'gah didn't move. He watched Hyatta's face the way wolves watch the wind—eyes fixed, shoulders still. Waiting for a twitch. A breath. Anything.

Nothing came.

Florence stepped forward. Her boots whispered in the sand—hesitant. Her mouth opened, then closed again. The sharp part of her—the cutting part—held back.

U'gah saw it building. Knew that shape. An idea clawing its way up. A coward's thought.

His tail twitched.

"Spit it out," Emerald snapped. Her hair seemed to flare, bright against the monotone desert.

Florence flinched.

Then she said it.

"Can't we just leave him here?"

Every head turned.

Jacques's voice came slow and too quiet. "What did you just say?"

Florence looked down, then back up—eyes tight, voice rising in volume and pitch. "I'm just saying... he's unconscious. Infected with who-knows-what. Some magical thing we don't understand. We don't know what it's doing to him. For all we know, he could wake up and—" she hesitated, "—not be him anymore."

Lusa growled. Deep. The sound shivered through the sand.

Florence pressed on, fast now, trying to get ahead of her own fear. "We can't risk it. What if that thing takes over? What if he turns into one of them and slaughters us in our sleep?"

U'gah stepped forward.

He looked her in the eye and heard his friend's words mirror his feelings.

"Shut the fuck up, Florence," Jacques said.

The words were simple. Final.

It wasn't rage in U'gah's gaze that made her step back. But that of Jacques. His eyes had delivered a promise.

She could see that he meant it.

He had already decided what he would do if she took another step. He had already made peace with it.

Jacques laid a hand on his shoulder, firm and steady, but didn't look away from Florence.

"No one gets left behind," he said. "Not now. Not ever."

Emerald exhaled, long and sharp. "Stars, Florence," she muttered. "You couldn't wait five minutes before deciding who to sacrifice?"

"I'm being realistic," Florence snapped, but it came out hollow. The bite was gone.

Saturn didn't look up from the scanner. His voice was calm. Clinical.

"He's stable. For now. Whatever this is—it hasn't spread past the wounds, yet. But we need shelter. I can't treat him out here."

Jacques nodded once. "Then we set a shelter here and use the pods to break the wind."

U'gah crouched. He reached under Hyatta's body with care, avoiding the black wound and the breathing thing that clung to his chest.

Hyatta didn't stir. His weight was nothing to him.

U'gah cradled him close, as one might carry a broken weapon —too valuable to leave behind. Not fragile. Just… not whole.

He looked to Jacques.

Florence said nothing.

But as they turned, her eyes stayed on Hyatta. Not with shame. Not regret.

Wary.

U'gah felt it in her gaze. The doubt. The fear she would not speak aloud.

Let her feel it.

Let her carry it.

Above them, the stars burned white in the black.

The Firefly-in-the-Sky was gone.

The desert stretched out endless and cold.

But they would stand with him. Beside him.

Because he was tribe.

Chapter Twenty-Three

The pod struck earth with a jarring impact that rolled through Hyatta's frame. The vibration settled into him like the memory of a long fall. The hatch hissed open and desert air spilled in—dry and familiar, thick with the scent of scorched dust—yet it stirred nothing in him. He wanted to rise, to drag himself free from the metal shell that cradled him, but his limbs refused.

His body refused to acknowledge his commands.

Outside, beyond his reach, he heard voices. At first they were faint, a vibration more than a sound, but one sharpened, deepened, shaped itself into something known. Lusa. It had to be. The Mau's rough call echoed through the haze, colored with urgency, laced with worry that pulled at Hyatta's fading awareness. He tried to answer—willed it past the weight in his lungs—but nothing emerged. No sound. Not even the tremble of effort. Every impulse collapsed before it reached the edge of the real.

The pain advanced. Not a spike; a settling behind his sternum —ice and fire sharing the same space. The sensation carved its way into him, pulling at the seams of his body, stretching them.

He wanted to resist, to ground himself in action, in motion, but those things were lost to him. Time was stripped of sequence or meaning. Nothing moved except the pain.

Other voices gained clarity in the static. They were far off, echoing, but familiar. Jacques. Emerald. Saturn. Names that should have meant help drifted like petals on a river, growing indistinct and distant. He tried to lift a hand, to shift his head, to offer any sign that he was still inside, and still fighting, but his body remained slack, unmoved, and sealed in silence.

Then a voice broke through the murk.

"Can't we just leave him here?"

The words didn't echo. They struck, cutting straight through the fog and landed in the center of him, followed by laughter.

Not from his warband. Not from the world of life.

It grew within his skull, velvet and venomous, like a slow ripple of delight traced in oil and ash. Women's voices, all speaking the same words, cruel and amused, pressed close against his thought without touching anything solid. *They want to abandon you,* the chorus purred, each word wrapped in silk that pulled tighter the more he strained against it.

He recoiled from the presence, trying to push back, to gather his thoughts, but they scattered too easily, slipping through the cracks like dry sand through broken glass.

U'gah, harsh and unflinching in the language of the bergbar. *"You would leave him? Leave him like carrion?"* The sound came from somewhere beyond the pod, but Hyatta felt it inside, real and rooted, a heat that didn't belong to the flower of pain growing in his chest.

The women laughed again, softer now, savoring. *Poor little thing. He's upset. Thinks he won't get to pick your bones clean before the vultures arrive. Do you hear it? How easily they measure your life?*

Hyatta resisted, not with strength, but with refusal. He gathered what little shape he had left and pressed against the invading mind, but she was already curling tighter around him, her presence winding through the wound.

The pressure in his chest deepened, crawling up into his ribs, into his shoulders, into the backs of his eyes. It wasn't just pain anymore—it was rhythm, a foreign pulse threading itself into his own. His heartbeat faltered, returned, faltered again, as if something else was keeping time inside his body.

Thoughts splintered. Focus slipped. Every effort to ground himself dissolved.

He was being unmade.

And still, no part of him could move.

Emerald rang through the haze like a blade drawn in anger, indignant and bright and unmistakably hers.

"You want to leave him to die because you're scared?"

The words rang out across the desert, hot and crackling with fury, and though Hyatta couldn't move, couldn't speak, he heard them—*felt* them. The gnome's tone, though small in volume, was colossal in weight, each syllable laced with fire and ferocity.

"Hyatta's fought for us. Bled for us. And you want to throw him away like he's nothing?"

The sound echoed through his thoughts, distant but distinct. A warmth tried to push through the numbing cold that had taken hold of his limbs and lungs and mind. Her anger wasn't directed at him, but it *wrapped around him*—a shield forged from loyalty and outrage.

He reached for it, tried to hold to it, but the presence curled tighter.

The mocking voice returned before he could catch the breath that wasn't there. It slithered through the hollow places of his mind like smoke through a crag, penetrating and invasive.

The little one is going to die, it whispered, thick with false pity. The rhythm was slow and savoring. *Just… like… you.*

Laughter followed—soft, rolling, corrosive. It didn't echo in the air. It reverberated within him. It scraped across the inside of his skull like wet stone dragging across glass.

His heart stuttered, then raced.

Hyatta pushed back. He slammed his mind against the weight pressing down on him, then shouted into the dark that held him fast.

Leave me, demon!

341

The words rang through his own mind like steel struck in a dead hall. No sound escaped, but he meant them. He *meant* them.

The voice responded with a chuckle, mocking and irreverent.

Demon? Is that what you call me? Poor, deluded creature. You don't even know what I am. You don't understand. But you will.

Her breath trailed his consciousness's edge, as if she could exhale across thought.

Soon, she whispered, *you will beg me to stay.*

He felt it then—the corruption of her growing and pressing deeper. She was already inside, pulling roots through thought, curling around his nerves like vines choking out the light. The scabbed mass in his chest pulsed harder, each beat drawing more from him. Strength seeped away with every breath, slow and as sure as dehydration under the gaze of the Eye of the Day. His limbs numbed. His will frayed further.

Outside, voices continued to clash. Echoes of his name. Arguments. Fear.

"You're not thinking straight!" Florence cut in, high with panic, unsteady and unstable. "We don't know what's wrong with him. Saturn said that thing is feeding on him! If we try to move him, we could make it worse. What if it spreads to one of us?"

Jacques's reply cracked like dry wood. "And what if we leave him, and we're not able to make it back in time? What then?"

The female voice within him hissed with pleasure.

So torn. So soft. So weak. Her tone dripped with disdain. *They think they can save you. As if faith is enough. As if care is armor. But they are only delaying the inevitable. You are mine. Whether they leave you or cradle you, it ends the same. You die. And what remains belongs to me.*

He gathered what remained—pain, memory, Emerald's fury, U'gah's threat, Jacques's stubborn devotion—and pulled them inward, wrapping them around his will like old armor. Their voices did not banish the dark, but they pushed back against its certainty. They held him, tethered.

Even as her presence wrapped tighter, even as his heartbeat broke rhythm, even as the pain twisted through his chest, he *focused*.

He was still himself.

He was still *Hyatta Kahlan*.

And whatever this thing was, whatever it thought it owned, it would not own him.

I won't let you win.

The thought was shaped like steel, forged from anger and ego. It pulsed through him—not loud, not desperate, but enduring. A vow more than a cry. His body lay unmoving, but his will had not broken.

The darkness pressed. It flowed around the edges of his resistance, patient, and trying to drown him. Not in rage, but in exhaustion. It smothered, dulled, blurred. Still, he clung to that ember of self, drawing his mind around it like a soldier shielding a frightened child.

You are mine, its presence was swelling within him, vast and absolute, like a star inverted. Its black gravity pulling every spark inward.

He tightened his grip around the spark within him. He willed it brighter. He would not go gently. He would not be undone.

Outside, through layers of fog and flesh, Emerald's voice surged again into the dark.

"We're not leaving him. We figure this out. Now. Together. No one's left behind."

Hyatta felt the words land. Not light—but structured. A framework he could brace against. He pulled himself toward it, using her voice as a tether, an anchor to the waking world. It gave him direction.

With everything he had left, he focused inward, forcing back the shadow long enough to carve space—space to fight. He refused to battle in the void that the voice had chosen. Not in dreams shaped by parasites and poison. Not in the formless dark.

If there would be war, it would be on his terms.

He summoned the landscape from memory. Sand. Sun. Wind. He gave the void edges, gave it heat, gave it meaning. The blankness bent under his will, reshaped by memory, by discipline, by years spent surviving things the voice could never name. Darkness was not foreign to him. It had no monopoly on fear.

The desert unfolded around him—wide and brutal and honest. An endless stretch of scorched horizon, sun-split stone, and ochre dunes that breathed with the wind. The heat shimmered in waves. Dust curled upward in lazy spirals. The scent of dry earth filled his lungs. No illusions here. No shadows. This was the truth of the world—the place where life was earned, not given.

In the center of the waste, he took shape.

He gave himself form—body wrapped in the ceremonial cloth of his kin, the translucent fabric catching the wind like ghostlight. In one hand, he held a curved-blade spear, long and silvered with heat. In the other, a round shield marked with the sun-worn etchings of the desert tribes. A history written in scars. He looked down into the reflection cast on its bronze face and saw himself—not as he had been, but as he must now become.

Standing firm, he called the light back into himself—not the soft light of peace, but the clean fire of defiance, the radiance that came not from hope but from refusal. It swept across the sand in a slow arc, warming the air, igniting his avatar until it burned like a second sun on the battlefield. He became both monument and warning.

When he spoke, it was not a question. It was a summons.

"Face me," he said, his voice a rolling command, deeper than thunder and twice as final. "Let us finish this farce. I tire of your mewling deceptions and empty threats. If you mean to take me, come and do it. Or be silent and dissolve."

The wind caught the edge of his cloak, carrying his words across the landscape. The shadow responded not with silence, but with amusement.

The voice returned—sinuous and thick with mockery, dripping down from every shifting dune.

Face you? In combat? she mused, soft and poisonous, circling him like smoke. *So proud. So rooted. You think this world is yours. You forget—I live here now.*

Then it struck.

Not with claw or blade—but with sound.

A burst of static shrieked across the desert, jagged and unnatural, shattering the air. The dunes shook beneath it. The sky stuttered. The ground beneath his feet rippled as if memory itself had been corrupted. Hyatta threw up his shield by instinct, the bronze rang out as the noise crashed into him, but it wasn't enough. The sound pierced deep into his manifestation. It cut into thought. Into memory.

He gritted his teeth against the pressure, eyes narrowing against the brightness, knees bending slightly as he grounded himself in the sand. This was not pain.

This was a challenge.

And he had not come to break.

The static shattered—then gave way to laughter.

A feminine chorus, layered and discordant, rolled in like a sandstorm. Thousands of voices weaved over one another, rising and falling in twisted rhythm, their cadence laced with mockery. The sound swelled until the air itself pulsed with it, and the ground beneath Hyatta's feet began to tremble.

They were laughing at him. Not in hatred—but in certainty. As if his defiance were a child's tantrum. As if his resistance were nothing more than a delay.

"You think I would lower myself to battle with you?"

Her tone sliced the echo of the laughter, parting it cleanly. The sands rippled in response, and the air twisted, thickening as her presence intensified. It became harder to breathe. Not from fear —but from the sheer *weight* of her.

"No, Isik Getiren," she purred, letting the name stretch, *"I think not. I have no need to test myself against your strength. Why waste effort on what I already own?"*

Each word was coated in mad honey, every pause deliberate— designed not to provoke, but to belittle.

"You will be mine. Soon. Entirely."

Above him, the golden sun faltered. Its light wavered, stuttered, then dimmed—its heat devoured by the growing shadow. The sky bled to black. The warmth that had once flooded the desert drained away, taking color with it. His battlefield—once firm and sacred—began to unravel.

The sand turned dark, slick with oil. The dunes warped, collapsing into jagged shapes as if rot had bloomed beneath the surface. From the places where light had died, tendrils slithered forward, curling and uncoiling like tongues, dragging lines of black across his inner world.

Hyatta's fingers clenched tighter around the haft of his imagined spear, the muscles in his forearms taut. His knuckles blanched under the strain, but he did not retreat. He *would not* retreat.

"You underestimate me," he said, his tone carrying the grit of sun-baked stone. "You found a way into my mind, but you'll find no throne here. This is mine. My will. My domain."

The invader responded not with scorn, but with a discordant hum—amused, almost indifferent.

"Your will is strong, Isik Getiren. I admire that."

The tendrils surged forward.

"But even the strongest wills snap when the silence drags long enough. You will fall. And when you do, I will gather what's left."

They came like waves.

One struck his shield with a crack that rang through his metaphysical self, the force of it nearly buckling his stance. His muscles shook, his feet digging deeper into the blackened sand. Another tendril snapped around his leg pulling him downward like a serpent trying to drag him into the dark beneath the dunes.

He let the pain roll through and harden him.

"Maybe," he said, his voice rough, "but you won't have me today."

The spear flashed. With a practiced sweep, he carved through the tendril at his leg, the blade severing the thing into a burst of heat and white noise. The darkness let out a shriek—pressure venting from some unseen world—as it dissolved into violet mist.

More came.

Faster now.

Dozens of appendages, black and glistening, surged toward him from every direction, clawing across the battlefield like hunger incarnate.

He roared—in challenge—and drove himself forward, spear raised, shield braced, the light around his form still burning even as the sky above turned umbral. The tendrils lashed out, scoring his arms, wrapping around his torso, biting into his will like fangs, but he kept moving.

Each strike of his spear was a statement.

Each step forward, a rebuke.

Each breath drawn against the darkness, a declaration of self.

She wanted to unmake him. To rewrite his name, his flesh, his fire.

But Hyatta Kahlan does not kneel.

***

"So we have no direct way of helping him?" Jacques asked, low but steady as he met Saturn's gaze. There was a glimmer of hope behind his eyes—small and fragile—but it was extinguished by the quiet shake of the gnome's head.

"No," Saturn replied, barely more than a whisper. The weight of the admission carved fresh lines into his aged face. The scanner, once humming with purpose, now hung useless at his side. The infection—or whatever was growing in Hyatta's chest—challenged his understanding. And that ignorance haunted him more than he would admit.

Jacques exhaled heavily, running a hand through his sweat-dampened hair, his eyes drifting back to their unconscious friend. "What about indirectly?" Hoping for some half-formed idea, and that maybe—just maybe—there was still something they hadn't tried.

Saturn gave a helpless shrug. He lifted his hands, palms open, fingers trembling ever so slightly. "I don't know where to begin," he said, frustration thick in his words. "This isn't a disease. It's not a curse. It's... something else. Something alive. If I try to cut it out, I would likely kill him. And if I guess wrong—" He stopped himself, jaw tight, his eyes drifting to the thing pulsing in Hyatta's chest.

Silence settled over the group. The only sound was the shallow rhythm of Hyatta's breathing, steady but faint. Still alive, but for how much longer?

"Alright," he said at last, voice hardening with resolve. "If we can't help him now, we prepare for everything else. No telling what else is crawling through this desert."

He turned, scanning the dark horizon—an endless sea of sand and shadow lit only by the moon's pale light.

"I want everyone mobile. Pack what you can carry. Weapons, gear, anything that gives us an edge."

Saturn gave a curt nod and turned to his pack, already working with quiet efficiency, though the lines around his eyes remained drawn.

He moved like a man who had seen too many battles and too few victories.

But that could describe them all.

Jacques's gaze shifted. "Lusa. U'gah."

The Mau and the shaman turned toward him, both alert. Lusa's golden eyes scanning the dunes, calculating. U'gah stood tense and silent, his small fists clenched, eyes rimmed with tears he refused to wipe away.

"Drag the pods together," Jacques ordered. "Use them to make a wall. A barrier. If something comes out of that darkness, I want more than a sand dune between us and it."

Lusa's ears twitched once in acknowledgment. He moved to do what was asked of him.

U'gah grunted and followed, the quiet intensity in his movements betrayed the emotions still boiling beneath his skin.

Jacques watched them go. It wasn't much—not really. A temporary shelter in an endless wasteland. A handful of survivors huddled in broken machines, hoping to outlast the unknown.

He turned back to the others.

"Stay alert. We're not safe yet. Not by a long shot."

As the moon rose to its apex, the warband moved with quiet efficiency. Hyatta lay still, the pulsing infection in his chest casting eerie violet shadows in the sterile moonlight.

Jacques watched the others as they worked, dragging the heavy pods into a makeshift barrier against the coarse desert wind. But his eyes kept returning to Hyatta—motionless on the sand, the unnatural purple glow still pulsing from the corruption in his chest. It felt wrong—deeply wrong—to be doing nothing while their friend withered before them. He clenched his fists, the weight of helplessness eating him from within.

In the Legion, he had been trained to act. Solve the problem. Take the shot. Adapt and overcome. But here, there was no enemy to kill. No plan to execute. No solution waiting to be discovered through grit or strategy.

He rubbed a hand over his face, feeling the grit of windblown sand grinding against his skin. His mind drifted back to the *aumôniers* of the Legion—the chaplains who moved quietly among the wounded after battle. He had always respected them, even if he hadn't envied their burden. Soldiers killed. That was their job. But chaplains... they bore the harder duty: sitting with the dying, comforting the living, maintaining morale in the face of inevitable loss.

Now, Jacques was getting a taste of it—and it was bitter.

His gaze drifted again to Hyatta. The shallow rhythm of his breathing was steady, but growing weaker. This was a cruel reminder that even the strongest among them could fall. There were no medics here. No miracles. Just the desert, the stars, and the slow unraveling of a man who had become their sword, their shield, their friend.

It helped that the others had something to do. U'gah's childlike face was tight with tension, his too-human eyes drifting back to Hyatta when he thought no one was watching. The halfling's muscles rippled with suppressed emotion, his usual wild energy dulled by the weight of fear. Lusa, too, moved with a restless anxiety—his ears swiveling, his short tail twitching with impatience. The Mau's confidence was buried beneath layers of worry.

If they'd been left idle, Jacques knew the despair would crush them.

He'd given them tasks—dragging pods, building a wall, preparing gear—not because it was necessary, but because it gave them purpose. Because the illusion of control was sometimes the only thing that kept people from breaking.

Florence didn't care. She never had. She'd been at odds with Hyatta since day one. Her indifference could have been seen by the blind. Jacques wasn't surprised. Florence wore her trauma like armor—spiteful, self-loathing, deflective. And Saturn? Saturn was too cold, too pragmatic to let sentiment factor into his equations. If a solution presented itself, he'd pursue it. If not, he would simply move on.

But Lusa and U'gah? They wouldn't move on. They wouldn't forget. And they would not forgive.

Jacques could already feel it brewing beneath the surface, the tension that had nearly exploded after Florence suggested leaving Hyatta behind. If Emerald hadn't intervened—if she hadn't snapped and shamed Florence into silence—there would have been blood, despite his initial intervention. Lusa and U'gah would not have tolerated it. Their loyalty to Hyatta ran deeper than reason.

Jacques could only hope that loyalty wouldn't turn into vengeance—if the worst came to pass.

If not for Emerald, there was no doubt in Jacques's mind that those two might have turned on Florence out of spite. The tension between them had been palpable, a thread stretched taut and trembling, just waiting for a single wrong step to snap it.

"Mon Dieu," Jacques muttered under his breath. This was a powder keg. And it was only a matter of time before someone struck a match.

He needed to stabilize the group—redirect their focus toward survival, away from the raw emotion eating at them from within.

He started slightly when he noticed Emerald standing beside Hyatta's still form, her silhouette outlined against the starry backdrop of the desert night. Her posture was rigid. She wasn't looking at Hyatta—she was staring straight at Jacques. Her solid black eyes locked onto him, unblinking, with an intensity that sent an involuntary chill crawling up his spine.

It wasn't just determination in her gaze. It was distance—like she was here, but also somewhere else.

Jacques cleared his throat, trying to shake the feeling. "What's wrong?" he asked, steady despite the unease tightening his chest.

Her tone, when it came, was flat—almost mechanical. "Currently... a lot. But never mind that for now."

"You're creeping me out," Jacques muttered, warily.

Emerald blinked. Her head tilted slightly, as if she was a machine rebooting. Then she shook it, like she was waking from a trance. "Sorry," she said, her voice returning to something more familiar—though not entirely. "I got caught up in my thoughts. I sometimes forget humans can't... retask their higher brain functions. You're right. It's creepy."

Jacques raised an eyebrow. "Qu'est-ce que tu racontes?"

Emerald took a breath, visibly re-centering herself. Her focus returned to Hyatta, though something behind her eyes still lingered—some deeper current pulling her in directions even she didn't fully understand.

"I think," she said slowly, "there might be a way to help Hyatta."

Jacques straightened. Hope stirred, hesitant and fragile. "Fantastic. Let's do it."

But Emerald didn't move. She bit her lip, her eyes narrowing slightly. "That's the thing. It's just a hypothesis. And I don't know how to go about it."

Jacques's voice was growing more precise. "Tell me what you're thinking. We'll figure it out."

Emerald glanced down at Hyatta. "Do you remember when we fought those lizards? When you activated the perimeter defense protocol?"

Jacques winced. "Yeah," he said. The memory flashed through his mind in a burst of heat and chaos—solar death beams, screaming Iruxi, friendly fire nearly reducing them to ash. "Hard to forget. That system nearly killed a few of us."

"But do you remember what happened when one of those energy beams hit Hyatta?" Emerald pressed.

Jacques frowned. Then his expression shifted as memory slotted into place. "Yeah… yeah, he absorbed it. Turned into some kind of walking demigod. Didn't even flinch."

"He changed," Emerald said, nodding. "He glowed. His skin, his eyes—it was like his body *drank* the light."

"That was high-yield solar radiation," Jacques said. "A focused beam. We don't have anything like that out here, and it's night."

But Emerald's lips curved—just slightly. A glimmer of confidence was rising behind her eyes.

"Yes," she said quietly. "We do. Kind of."

Jacques blinked, confused. "Kind of?"

"The moonlight," Emerald said, her tone steady, decisive. "It's just reflected sunlight. If we can concentrate it—just a little—it might have a similar effect. Probably not as dramatic, but right now, anything is better than nothing, right?"

Jacques's brow furrowed as he glanced up at the sky. The moon hung heavy and full, casting silver light across the dunes in long, pale sheets. Moonlight was diffused, yes—but it was still sunlight at its core. A weaker echo, maybe, but not meaningless.

"I don't know," he said cautiously, but his mind was already sprinting ahead, crunching angles and materials. "It's a long shot... but you're right. Anything's better than sitting here waiting for that thing in his chest to win. How do you plan to focus it?"

"That's why I need you," Emerald replied, calm, but intense. "You're the engineer. I just had the thought—you make it real."

Jacques nodded slowly, already half in motion. "Yeah... maybe the dura-glass from the pods. If we angle it right and focus the moonlight, we can make a crude magnifier. The lining inside— yeah, that reflective composite they used for thermal shielding. Catch more light. Bounce it where we need it."

"Perfect," Emerald said. "We don't need full solar radiation. We just need a concentrated beam of it. Moonlight still carries the sun's essence. Hyatta's already shown us he can respond to that energy. We give him even a fraction, it might be enough to give him a fighting chance."

Jacques's mind flooded with every ounce of tactical thought and field improvisation coming to the fore. The idea was crazy —but not unthinkable. Not unreasonable.

"Okay," he said firmly. "Let's get to work. I don't know how much time Hyatta's got before whatever's inside him finishes the job."

Emerald nodded, her strange detachment giving way to a typical bright, helpful nature.

"We need at least three pods for the reflective material and dura-glass for magnifiers," Jacques muttered as he stood, brushing the sand from his hands. His voice rose to carry across the makeshift camp. "Lusa. U'gah. I need your strength —we're tearing the pods apart."

The Mau's ears twitched and he bounded over without hesitation, his long strides carrying him through the sand in seconds. U'gah followed close behind, almost waddling in comparison to the feline grace of Lusa.

Jacques gestured toward the nearest pod. "We need the dura-glass panels intact. They're bonded to the internal frame, but if we break the seals clean, we can preserve the main sheets. Those will be our lens array."

He turned to U'gah, meeting the halfling's fierce gaze. "You and I will handle the thermal lining. There's a mirrored alloy built into the thermal wrap—we'll repurpose it. We shape it into a channel to keep the moonlight from scattering, giving us a more concentrated beam. "

U'gah nodded, already moving. He didn't understand the nuances of what Jacques was saying, but he was ready to help his injured friend.

Jacques glanced back at Hyatta's body lying limp in the sand. That terrible, pulsing mass was still leeching life from him.

This was a long shot. But it was their only shot.

The halfling grunted and was already tearing into the nearest pod. Despite his size, U'gah's strength was uncanny— especially in his smaller form—and he made quick work of snapping the metal rivets and peeling back panels with single-minded ferocity.

Nearby, Emerald rummaged through one of the field kits. She pulled a scoring tool from its case and set to work etching clean lines along the dura-glass panels. "Score and slide," she muttered under her breath, sweat beading at her temple as she traced precise arcs along the pod's edge. Lusa loomed beside her, his wide paws deftly bracing the glass. With one final hiss of pressure release, he pulled the panel free in a single, fluid motion.

Florence hovered nearby, arms crossed over her chest, her gaze shifting uneasily from the glowing infection to the frantic scramble of their makeshift engineering effort.

"Do you think it'll be enough?" she asked, her voice quieter than usual. There was no venom in it—just a thread of worry. Whether it was for Hyatta or her own standing in the group, Jacques couldn't tell.

He didn't look up. His hands were buried deep in the pod's gut, prying loose a sheet of reflective alloy with a dull metal screech. "I don't know," he answered, flatly. "But we don't have another option. This is it."

Everything shimmered in the light of the moon—sand, stone, and the pale skins of the pods arranged in a loose arc around Hyatta's still form. They worked in silence, each of them bent to a task. The soft scuff of boots on sand, the clink of tools, the rasp of breath—these became the rhythm of their hope.

Hyatta was fading. They all knew it.

But no one said it.

So they worked—because this was the only light left to hold onto.

***

Florence stood at the edge of camp, arms locked tight across her chest, fingers digging into the fabric of her sleeves like she could hold herself together if she just gripped hard enough. The shelter stank of desperation—everyone scurrying like insects, dismantling pods, repositioning panels, chasing a miracle she didn't believe in. Stupidity—the kind that comes before real horror drops. Before something broke for good.

She watched them toil and felt... nothing. Or something that *wanted* to be nothing. Just a hollowed-out ache that refused to pick a side. They all wore that same expression: strained, hopeful, fraying at the edges. And for what?

Hyatta.

A bitter smile twitched across her lips. Of course it was Hyatta.

They'd wrapped their cracked little group around him like an unshakable center—some fixed star that could keep them from spinning out. But he wasn't. Especially not with that thing pulsing inside his chest like it was waiting to hatch. She could feel it from here. Like a second heartbeat, wet and *alive*. Every time she looked at him, it knotted something deep in her gut.

And still—they clung to him. Clung to the idea that if they just angled a few glass panels and said a few words, the moon would come down and save them all.

Moonlight.

It was laughable. The kind of plan a child would dream up in a fever. But Emerald had said it with such *conviction*, like it was science and not desperation in a pretty dress. Like the moon gave a damn.

Florence turned away before the sneer fully formed on her face. She stepped out into the open night and let the cold wind scrape across her skin. It didn't help. The heat was inside—anger and shame and that old, iron-edged fear she could never quite drown.

They'd turned on her. For *what*? For trying to keep them alive? For stating the obvious? She had said what needed saying, that maybe they couldn't save him. That maybe he would try to kill the rest of them. But instead of listening, they'd looked at her like *she* was the monster.

She pulled her arms tighter around herself and muttered, "Why do they care so much?"

The words evaporated on the wind.

Just one life. One infected, unconscious, half-dead warrior. But not just anyone. Hyatta. He was… theirs. And she knew that, even if she didn't want to. He'd fought for them. Stood between them and death. And maybe that's why they couldn't let go.

She couldn't blame them.

But it also didn't mean she forgave them for making her the villain.

A gust tore across the sand, lifting grit into her face. The sting felt earned, but it was less than the sting of their scorn. The guilt blooming in her ribs felt *worse*—not because it was new, but because it was old. The kind of guilt you always carry. You just have to live with it.

"Why am I like this?" she asked the wind, her voice barely audible, her arms wrapped so tight around her torso it hurt.

No answer came.

She turned back toward the group, eyes catching on the silhouette of U'gah and Lusa lifting one of the dura-glass panels together, Jacques was beside them barking orders with that clipped, careful tone that said everything he wasn't letting show. They moved like a unit with a purpose. Like a *family*. And Florence felt it—the drift. The distance between them and her, growing wider by the second.

It made her skin itch.

She didn't want to be alone. She didn't want to be *this*. But every time she spoke, it pushed them further away. Every time she tried to be the one who thought ahead, who stayed grounded, it made her the enemy. And maybe they were right. Maybe it *was* worth the risk. Maybe the moonlight would work. Maybe Hyatta would wake up and flash that dry, infuriating smile and tell her she'd acted foolish.

But what if he didn't?

What if all they were doing—this plan, this camp, this *hope*—was just making his corpse look good before it rotted?

"Florence!"

Jacques's voice cut through the haze like a slap. She blinked. Looked up. He was already halfway toward her, a mixture of irritation and fatigue lining his face.

"We need you over here. Can you help with the alignment?"

Refuse. That was the first instinct. Pull away. Stay cold. Stay safe.

But when she looked into his eyes, something cracked.

And for a moment—for just a second—she remembered that Hyatta had stood for her. Had shielded her. Had believed in her when she couldn't do it for herself.

She nodded.

She followed Jacques back. Not because she believed it would work. Not because she had hope.

But because it was their fight. And she wasn't ready to be alone.

"Yeah, alright," she muttered, forcing her voice into something that passed for steady as she walked. Every step felt like a concession. "Just… show me what to do."

Jacques gestured toward one of the larger reflective panels. His posture was calm. The kind of calm you cultivated when everything inside you was fraying, but you couldn't afford to show it. She understood that kind of calm.

Florence grabbed the edge of the panel, the glass cold against her palms. Together, they adjusted it slowly, angling it toward the moon. The beam caught—silver and fluid—spilling across the surface like water. It was beautiful in a way that made her insides tighten.

"Just like that," Jacques said. She heard what he wasn't saying in the spaces between words. The hope. The fear. The *need*.

"We need to make sure we catch as much light as possible."

Florence frowned. "Is this really going to work?" Her voice was softer now, almost lost under the desert wind. "What if it's not enough?"

Jacques paused. The panel shifted slightly in his grip as he glanced up at her, and for a moment she saw him—not the soldier, not the leader—but the man underneath. Eyes lined with exhaustion, streaked with moonlight.

"It has to be enough," he said. "We can't give up on him."

There it was again. That iron certainty. Like the act of believing could *make* something true. She hated how much it stirred in her. Not warmth. Just something she thought she'd burned out of herself a long time ago. A spark, maybe.

Hope?

She looked away, and focused on her hands—still gripping the panel, still helping. That had to count for something. That had to be enough.

They worked in silence after that, the desert around them slowly shifting. Everything was painted in quiet now. No fighting. No accusations.

When they finished the alignment, Florence stepped back, dust streaking her hands, sweat clinging to the back of her neck despite the cold.

Hyatta lay still beneath the pooled moonlight, his body pale and broken, his chest rising with effort that didn't feel his own. The gathered panels threw a soft beam across him, touching the wound, catching the edges of that pulsing, poisoned mass.

It looked… peaceful.

She hated that word.

"Now we just need to wait," Jacques murmured beside her, his voice rough with tension and more fragility than he'd ever admit.

Florence said nothing. The others gathered, eyes turned toward Hyatta, hearts knotted together. She could feel it—the *pull* of that unity, that shared ache—all of it tightening around her like a net she hadn't realized was there.

She didn't want to believe. She *couldn't* afford to believe.

But for now... she stood beside them, anyway.

Chapter Twenty-Four

The void had no edges. No shape. No substance. Hyatta drifted through it—weightless, rootless, caught in a moment stretched beyond time. No sun. No sky. No sense of up or down. Only the hush; the press of nothing.

Darkness folded around him like an old friend, but it wasn't the same as before. This wasn't stone and dust. No cold sweat on his back. No rusted chains pulling at his wrists.

He'd just been dreaming.

He remembered firelight. The roar of pale monsters. The metallic taste of blood in his mouth. A warband not his own—strange ones, loud and foolish, loyal and wild. Their laughter had lingered like spice in the air. He had known freedom in that dream. Movement. A purpose. Wrasas Station: sacred, silent, gleaming like a relic of the gods. It had felt true.

Now he was here again. Wherever *here* was. The return struck a blow to the gut.

He had tasted the world and been cast out of it.

Hyatta reached for that dream, but the memory was already unraveling. Echoes crumbled to dust. The warmth fled. All that remained was this quiet, depthless dark.

Something buzzed.

Insectile. It sliced through the stillness with annoying persistence.

Buzz.

Maybe it was real. Maybe not. If it was a fly, he would catch it. Protein was protein. His body didn't need it now—hunger left behind—but instinct remembered.

He had learned to eat whatever moved, if he had to.

Buzz.

It was louder, closer.

Not wings anymore—words, broken and urgent. Not one voice —but several. Distorted like echoes in water.

"Hyatta!"

An ember stirred.

"Fight it!"

They came again, this time with more clarity. The names weren't said, but he knew them, felt them. Jacques's grit. Emerald's fire. Lusa's yowl. Even U'gah—the tiny bergbar shaman with his brave little heart.

The void rippled.

"Hyatta!"

Something reached down. Not hands. Not light. Will. That was what it felt like. Their will. Calling him back.

Pulling.

The pressure behind his eyes increased. A low throb built in his chest—where the burning thing slept. He knew it now. Knew the thing had rooted deep, that it was feeding still. Its shadow clung to him like dung.

But above it all… that chorus.

"Fight it!"

The words wrapped him—not command, not plea—a declaration.

You are not alone!

Darkness coiled around him—not like shadow, but memory, tight and intimate, whispering soft poison at the ear.

Why fight? it crooned. *Look where your struggle has led. Pain. Solitude. Loss. You are already spent. Let go.*

The voice of many was velvet-wrapped rot. Familiar. Eldritch. It didn't shout. It whispered, softly. Surrender was the easier path, and the weight of it pulled with terrible grace.

Hyatta's resolve buckled. He felt it falter—until something deep beneath the pain stirred.

No.

It came quiet. A single ember buried beneath the shadow. He clung to it, drawing warmth from the memory of voices—raw, imperfect. They had shouted his name. Fought for him. Even now, he could feel their worry, their need, pushing through the dark like dawn beneath a shuttered sky.

"Hyatta!"

The cry became one voice—a chord struck deep. It pierced the veil.

He reached. His thoughts cracked from the strain, but he forced his mind into motion, calling his body to rise. It was a twitch— barely there. But it was something.

"I'm coming," he thought, though the words never reached his lips. Still, the will behind the calls disturbed his prison. He latched onto the pain, the weight, the ache—all proof that he *was*. He bathed in the memory of battle, of laughter shared beneath endless skies. He drew their hope in.

Together.

He surged upward through the dark, like a swimmer breaking toward the surface, desperate for air that might not be there.

But instead of breath, he met laughter.

It slithered through the void—triumphant. The voice returned, thick with glee. It echoed from every direction, a chorus of mockery.

Your friends are echoes. Puppets. They shout into the grave because they do not yet know you are already gone.

The flame inside him guttered. Not from disbelief—but from weariness. From too many wounds, too many losses. The strength he had called forth, all that remained of it, now felt like a spark left to float on the wind.

The entity pushed in. Its tendrils slithered through him, eroding. Like the tide pulling sand from beneath a standing stone. He could feel it devouring—his memories, his name, the *shape* of who he had been.

What remained was fear. Not of death, but of being unmade.

No. he thought, but it was a whisper lost to a storm.

He fought—but the dark had him now.

Voices were fading.

Who were they again?

They had been close once—but now they pulled away like stars falling in reverse. Faces dissolved. Hyatta clawed for them, but they slipped through his fingers.

He was falling. No—*being taken.* Pulled down into something deeper than darkness. Something that fed on the slow ruin of hope.

Let go, the voice whispered, soft as rotting fruit. *There is peace in the dark. Peace in the end. Let them go. Let yourself go.*

It slithered through his mind, coiling through the cracks, pressing into the hollow places.

He flinched at the words, trying to rise, trying to scream—but there was nothing to scream with. Anger faltered, refused to catch. The tide was too strong. And the tide was her.

She was inside him—not just her voice, but her *mind*. He felt it spreading: tendrils curling through his mind, threading deep roots into soft, wet earth. With each moment, he could feel her eroding the architecture of who he was.

There were no memories anymore. Just fragments. The pieces drifted, warped by her touch. They twisted until he didn't know if they had ever been real.

Please, he begged. *I don't want to forget.*

But the tendrils only dug deeper. The emptiness expanded. The weight of *loss* crushed him more than any foe ever had. He felt her peeling him open, carving out the soul like meat from a shell.

No resistance left.

Let go, she breathed, voice honeyed and whole. *Embrace the dark, Isik Getiren. Let it remake you. Let it eat away the pain. Become more.*

More? The thought was bitter. *Like them?* He saw their blank faces, those pale husks with arms twitching like broken puppets. That was what she offered. A freedom without self. A silence without soul.

He felt himself cracking. The last of his name—the shape of his life—splintering beneath the strain. There was no ground beneath him, no sky above. Just a cold, devouring *nothing* and her voice.

It didn't arrive. It broke: a spear of silver tore through the black. Not gentle. Not warm. It came with violence throwing back the dark.

Moonlight—righteous, blinding, pure.

The tendrils recoiled. Shrieked. They curled back like worms beneath flame. His mind, for a heartbeat, was his again.

And for the first time in what felt like forever, Hyatta could find his breath.

The feminine chorus screamed.

With a sound that tore the void. She hissed, screeched, clawed at the light like a beast backed into fire.

No! she howled, a sound that cracked across the inside of his skull, shaking loose fragments of himself that he had forgotten.

He could feel the light moving over him, cold and sacred, a cleansing. It seeped into his consciousness, washed through his blood, filled every hollow the invader had tried to make. She burned in its presence. Her darkness flailed, trying to escape. But the moonlight gave her no quarter.

And then—from the light—a lover's whisper:

"Come back, my love."

This voice was soft. It wrapped around him like sun-warmed linen, smelling of baked stone and hot sand. It *called.*

"Your journey has only begun."

The words lit something inside him. He grasped them tightly, and fed them flame with every oath, every scar, every face he'd sworn to shield.

Who? he thought—but the light surged before an answer. Shapes emerged from the void, memory rewoven into form. His warband.

Jacques. U'gah. Emerald. Lusa. Saturn. And even Florence.

They were not dream-forms, but real. Their voices felt like they chanted with the rhythm of his heart, each beat syncing with the pulse of the moonlight. They called him back, every cry a hand on his shoulder, every word a pull toward their world.

"Fight, Hyatta! You are not alone!"

He bared his teeth and dug his heels into the light. He felt the tendrils melt away, one by one, curling into smoke, stripped of their hold.

I'm coming, he told them. Not a cry, but a vow.

He reached for the moonlight—seizing it. He held it like a lifeline and *pulled.*

The void collapsed. The discordance shrieked, a furious, wounded thing. Then silence. Her grip broke.

Hyatta gasped. The world rushed in.

Air hit his lungs. Cool desert air.

He blinked.

Above him, the stars burned. The moon glared down, silver and solemn, casting its light across the sand like a blessing. The darkness was gone; the weight lifted.

But he wasn't at peace. Not yet.

He was alive. He was free.

And the fight—the true fight—was only beginning.

***

They'd been yelling for hours, their voices echoing across the barren desert, a desperate chorus swallowed by the silence. And still, it was the only action that felt like it might matter. If Hyatta could hear them—if anything could anchor him—it would be their voices.

When the moonlight first struck Hyatta's skin, his body began to glow with a cold, spectral light. The glow seemed to push against the darkness clinging to him, illuminating the makeshift camp in silver hues. Jacques had felt hope in that moment— fragile, trembling hope. But it twisted too quickly into dread. What if the light wasn't healing him—if it was accelerating the rot?

That question died the instant Hyatta began to convulse. The soft luminescence shattered into chaos, pulsing violently as his body writhed in the sand. It looked like a battle was being fought inside him—violent and unseen. The light surged and dimmed with his spasms.

"Hold him down!" Jacques barked, rushing forward as Hyatta's limbs thrashed with terrifying strength.

Lusa was already on him, braced like a statue of muscle and claw, his golden eyes wide with alarm. Even with his size and power, the Mau was struggling to keep Hyatta grounded. The force of the warrior's flailing arms was unnatural—possessed. Whatever darkness he was fighting, it was fighting back.

"Don't let him tear himself apart!" Jacques shouted, the words tasting of panic.

Hyatta's face twisted in agony. A growl—wordless, broken— spilled from his throat, as though he were trying to speak through a mouth full of hot coals. The light engulfing him flared, cold and brilliant, cutting through the night.

Jacques glanced at the others—even Florence. All of them frozen, helpless, straining to understand whether they were saving Hyatta or killing him.

"Hyatta! Focus on us!" Emerald's voice rang out, strong and clear despite the fear behind it. She cupped her hands around her mouth, calling to him as though volume could breach the veil. "You're not alone! You can fight this! Stay with us!"

But the more they called, the harder Hyatta thrashed, his body no longer his own. He moved with brutal, animal desperation, as if every muscle was caught between escape and obliteration. The infection writhed beneath his skin, feeding on his pain, and all Jacques could do was watch—watch as the man who had stood between them and death became its newest battlefield.

"Lusa, hold him steady! Don't let him go!" Jacques shouted, his voice raw with urgency. Sympathy and dread warred in him as Hyatta's eyes fluttered rapidly—madness glinting behind the glow, now shifting from cold silver to a deep, blood-red.

The Mau snarled, the sound low and feral. His massive frame locked around Hyatta like a living brace, his limbs trembling with the effort of restraining the warrior without breaking him.

But brute strength wasn't enough. They needed to reach what remained of Hyatta's mind.

"Hyatta!" Jacques shouted, stepping in close despite the danger. "Listen to me! We're here—you're not alone!"

For a heartbeat, the thrashing stopped. The crimson light dimmed. Jacques met his gaze and saw it—real fear.

"Fight it, Hyatta!" Jacques urged. "You're stronger than this! We're not letting you go!"

As if answering the call, the moonlight swelled. A wave of energy pulsed through the air, humming with electric force. The glow around Hyatta was flaring once more. The shadows hissed and recoiled, wounded. The sand stirred, swirling through the camp in a series of dust devils.

The light intensified, revealing the outline of Hyatta's form: the sinew, the strength, the unmistakable presence that had carried them this far. Jacques clenched a fist, his voice rising.

"Yes! Fight it! We *need* you!"

A glow burst outward, flooding the desert. The light drove back the infection, which writhed and twisted, screeching as they burned away. And through it all, Hyatta rose—not in body, in spirit. Jacques could feel it, like a current of warmth flowing around them. The tether holding him in the dark was snapping and the bond that kept him tied to the warband was pulling him home.

"Come on, Hyatta!" Emerald's voice rang clear and bright, a spark of courage that cut through the gloom. "You can beat it!"

A column of light tore skyward, casting back the final tendrils of darkness like dust before a storm. The entity—whatever it was—screeched, retreating into the void, stripped of its hold.

The pressure snapped. The glow steadied. And in that moment, they saw it: Hyatta, no longer lost, no longer drowning. Rising.

They hadn't saved him alone. He had *reached back*. And together, they had pulled him from the edge.

The last wisps of parasite drifted into the desert breeze, crumbling into ash and vanishing like smoke. The surge of silver light had gone with it, fading into the stars above, leaving only the concentrated beam from their makeshift reflector—an improvised moon-lantern that now cast a faint, steady glow across Hyatta's body. The shimmer that had once engulfed him faded like the dying light of a star.

Jacques knelt beside him, chest heaving, heart still hammering. "Hyatta?" he murmured, scanning the warrior's face for any sign of recognition. The same furrowed brow damp with sweat. The same sharp jawline. But now it was peaceful.

"That bitch... is going to die..."

The words were hoarse, slurred, edged in venom.

Jacques blinked. Confused. "What...?" he asked. "What bitch?"

But there was no answer. Just the steady rise and fall of Hyatta's chest and the shallow flutter of breath that whispered against the night air. He wasn't speaking to Jacques. He was speaking to something else. Or maybe... to someone no one else could hear.

Jacques sat back, unsettled. The fight was over, but Hyatta was still battling something behind closed eyes. He felt a familiar dread stir—less fear, more unease. There'd be time to unpack that later. Now wasn't the moment.

"Just breathe, Jacques," he muttered, forcing his thoughts back into order.

Emerald knelt opposite him, her expression tight with concern. "Is he...?"

"He's alive," Jacques said, voice firmer now. "We did it. He's free of that thing."

Emerald exhaled, relief flashing across her face before she leaned closer. The light from the beam pooled softly around Hyatta, casting his profile in silver and shadow. He was still unconscious, still breathing—but changed. Something about him felt heavier now. And now, his hair was more platinum than gold.

He stirred, followed by a groan, low and strained. His limbs shifted, twitching as if trying to remember themselves.

"Hyatta?" Emerald's voice trembled with hope.

But there was no response.

Jacques felt a chill settle into him. The kind of fear that didn't announce itself with screams, but with quiet questions.

They had driven the infection out.

But what had it left behind?

Saturn placed a hand on Hyatta's shoulder—gentle, but firm. "We need to check him for any remaining signs of infection," he said, his voice leveling as he shifted into his clinical mode. "If there's any residue left, we need to neutralize it now— before it has a chance to return."

"Do you think he'll wake up?" Florence asked. She kept her gaze on Hyatta's face, searching for some trace of the warrior they knew.

"He has to," Jacques said. He made it sound certain, even if he wasn't.

They moved quickly, scanning Hyatta's body for any lingering signs—discoloration, tremors, unnatural heat. Jacques tried to focus, but the sense of urgency wouldn't let go. They'd escaped one nightmare, but the shadows still felt close.

And Hyatta's words echoed, unshaken in his memory.

What if the thing that took him wasn't gone?

What if it had only pulled back to regroup, waiting for them to slip?

"Let's hurry," Jacques said, sharper than he intended. He cast a quick glance around the camp, then turned back to Hyatta. Complacency was a luxury they couldn't afford. Not now. Not with Hyatta like this.

But as his eyes swept the others—U'gah crouched with teeth bared, Emerald kneeling beside Lusa, her hands steady despite the tension, the big cat curled protectively around them— Jacques felt it again.

Their strength wasn't only survival—it was unity.

They would fight for Hyatta. They'd fight for each other.

And together, they'd stand against whatever came next.

**

With the adrenaline fading and desperation spent, an oppressive quiet settled over the camp. The silence rang in Saturn's ears like the toll of a distant bell. He leaned against the cool metal wall of the escape pod, his mind still racing to process the last few hours. In his lap, a device from Wrasas Station hummed steadily, scanning a sliver of the black material he'd harvested from the pulsating mass that had infected Hyatta.

The device worked tirelessly, but Saturn did not. He felt hollowed out.

He hadn't lashed out or broken down like some of the others, but the strain had taken its toll. Watching Hyatta fight for his life—the screaming, the chaos, the wild fear of it—had left him drained. He felt like something inside had been siphoned away. Now, in the hush that followed, every sound pressed in: the soft whir of the scanner, the whispering desert wind, the quick pulse in his ears.

He focused on the device, activating the advanced scan. Data poured across the display—and the results were troubling.

The parasite's DNA shimmered with arcane latticework—woven directly through a twisted double helix. A tangled web of magical constructs saturated the organism's genetic code. Nearly half of its genome was either composed of or supported by these arcane structures.

Saturn frowned, his eyes narrowing. This was his field of study, genetics. And he had been doing it for almost a century. But in his wildest dreams, he had never envisioned anything like this.

It echoed the Prometheus Project. But even those nightmarish experiments hadn't yielded anything quite like this. He sifted through old memory, trying to summon specifics—classified reports, fragmented briefings, undocumented test results. But there had been so much information.

"Damn it," he muttered, rubbing his temples. Frustration gnawed at the edges of his fatigue. Had this parasite absorbed Promethean traits from some prolonged exposure to a paragon host? Or was it something worse—an experiment no one had cataloged, or that no one had survived long enough to report?

He scanned again. Line after line of raw code, magical pathways interlaced with biological function. Each new readout deepened the mystery. The parasite's design wasn't just efficient. It was elegant.

A perfect fusion of flesh and spellwork. Not just alive, but aware.

If the Allies knew, what did they do to stop it?

The thought chilled him.

As he considered the implications of the scan, motion caught Saturn's eye. He looked up to see Emerald framed in moonlight, her small silhouette just outside the pod.

"Do you think he's going to be okay?" she asked, soft, colored with worry, as she climbed inside beside him.

Saturn blinked, struck for a moment by the absurdity of it all. If they were human sized, there'd be no way both could fit inside the narrow interior. Yet here they were, shoulder to shoulder in a space designed for one—united by exhaustion, the weight of what they'd just survived pressing inward from all sides.

A laugh rose unbidden in his throat as he remembered Lusa trying to squeeze into the pod earlier. The massive Mau had looked completely ridiculous, limbs folded in like a stuffed toy, his bulk straining against the walls. Without his feline flexibility, they'd never have gotten the hatch closed. The image lingered, incongruous and deeply satisfying.

"If it fits, it sits," Saturn murmured.

Emerald raised an eyebrow.

"Sorry," he said, shaking his head. "Yes. I think Hyatta's going to be alright. I can't guarantee it, but…"

He hesitated.

"The way the parasite reacted to moonlight—Hyatta's biology overwhelmed it. Whatever he is, whatever energy's inside him, it turned the tide. That's why I think he's going to pull through."

Emerald nodded slowly, though her brow stayed creased. "I hope you're right," she murmured, looking down at her hands clenched tight in her lap.

Saturn felt a rare pang of empathy. They all leaned on Hyatta in different ways. Strength, certainty, myth. None of them were ready to face losing him.

"I mean, look at him," Saturn added, trying to ease the moment. "The man's basically a living avatar. If anyone can shrug off a parasite, it's him. He's probably been through worse and come out swinging."

A faint smile touched Emerald's lips, but it didn't quite reach her eyes. "Yeah. I guess you're right. He always does, doesn't he?"

Saturn turned back to the scanner, fingers gliding across the readouts.

"There's something fascinating about how he reacted to the moonlight," Saturn said, eyes locked to the data. "It was like he became a conduit—channeling it straight through his system, weaponizing it against the parasite. It makes sense, in a way. It's not unlike how he responds to direct sunlight."

He paused, then added, "That was your idea? Using the moonlight."

"Yeah..." Emerald replied, sheepishly.

His voice softened. "It was brilliant. Exactly what we needed, exactly when we needed it. I'm proud of you."

Emerald frowned, unsure. "Thanks... but you don't have to be patronizing," she said. Her tone wasn't sharp, just guarded.

"I'm not," Saturn replied evenly. "It probably saved his life—and ours too."

He finally looked up, meeting her gaze. "And given I'm ninety years your senior, I can be proud of you if I damn well want to be."

That pulled a real smile from her. Small, but genuine.

Emerald's eyes narrowed playfully, a mock reproach dancing across her features. Then, unexpectedly, she burst into a wide grin, brightening the dim interior of the pod.

"You're right—it was genius, wasn't it?" she said, her voice turning bubbly.

"Absolutely," Saturn replied, a rare smile tugging at his lips. "You've always had a gift for improvising under pressure."

He turned back to the device, quietly grateful for the lightness that had returned—however briefly.

"I can't stop thinking about how close we came to losing him," Emerald murmured, the grin fading. Her voice dimmed to a hush, eyes shadowed again with worry.

"Hey, hey," Saturn said gently, shifting closer. He draped an arm across her shoulders and felt the tremble running through her. Her eyes glistened, glassy with tears not yet shed. He gave her a gentle squeeze, the way his father had—back when the world felt too big.

"We're going to make it," he said, steadying his tone. "We'll get back to Europe. We'll leave this place behind. We're survivors. Remember?"

Emerald nodded, but her gaze drifted. "What if…" She hesitated. "What if Hyatta doesn't wake up?"

The question pierced deeper than he expected.

"He will," Saturn said quickly, though doubt passed through him like a shadow. "You saw it—how he fought, how he pulled that energy through him. Whatever that thing was, it couldn't hold him."

But the knot in his stomach tightened. He knew how close it had been. How thin the line between survival and loss had become.

But he couldn't say that aloud. Not to her.

"We can't lose hope," he said instead, firmer now. "Hyatta needs us. And we need each other. Fear's no good to us."

Emerald looked up, eyes searching his. Doubt still lingered, but it was softer —tempered by his steadiness.

"You're right," she said. "Like Jacques says, 'One day at a time.'"

"Yes," Saturn said, feeling some of the weight ease. "Let's focus on what we *can* control. Whatever comes next, we'll face it. Together."

She nodded, wiping her eyes with the back of her hand. Her expression sharpened into something more determined.

He admired her for that.

But even as she pressed forward, Saturn felt the dread creeping back in—unspoken, unshakable. It hung in the silence like static, the pressure building.

He glanced around the cramped pod for a place to settle his gaze. While outside, the desert wind scraped across the dunes, singing its raspy song as it pelted the circle of escape pods with loose sand.

Every creak of the hull. Every blink on the scanner. Every gust of wind.

Whispers of fate.

The truth clawed at him: everything he'd just said—every hopeful word, every promise—they were lies.

They weren't going to make it. They were going to die here.

And likely soon.

CHAPTER TWENTY-FIVE

his desert was misery. Florence dragged her feet through the endless sea of sand, every step a fresh torment. It felt like they'd been walking for a week—she knew it had only been a few days—but time had become irrelevant beneath the weight of heat and exhaustion.

The sun refused to obey logic from the moment they had crashed. Why the hell would it start now?

It crawled east to west as it should, then reversed course just before setting. It crept back toward the east as if to deny them even the mercy of night. It never rested. It only burned.

Her boots, for all their tech, had done nothing to stop the blisters. Blisters on blisters. With every step, pain bloomed hotter. Sand had worked its way inside, stubborn and grinding against every raw patch of skin. It was in her toes, her clothes, every seam of her body. Rubbing. Scraping. Finding places she hadn't known could chafe.

Sweat, sand, dead skin—she could feel it all, soupy, bacterial, and sloshing in the folds of her gear, fermenting between her thighs. She clenched her jaw and kept walking, refusing to cry or scream, but it was all she could think about. Her body was being broken down one layer at a time, and the only comfort she could remember was the sterile air of the station—colder in memory than this place could ever be.

She glanced at the others. All of them looked equally ruined. Even U'gah, usually a blur of childlike energy, lagged, his hairy skin soaked with sweat.

Hyatta walked in silence, his hood drawn tight to shield him from the sun's wrath. He looked brittle, his eyes, once vibrant and electric, were clouded. And every time sunlight touched him, he flinched. That alone said everything. Hyatta flinching from the sun? Something was deeply wrong.

Jacques pressed forward with quiet resolve, but his shoulders had begun to sag. Saturn drifted ahead in short bursts. He'd tried to ride NAVI, but that lasted about twenty minutes before the drone's rotors clogged with sand.

It felt like a nightmare with no end. The dunes stretched forever, no shade, no salvation. The wind rose in gusts, but even that was a trick—just another slap of grit in their faces.

Worse still, the water was running out. Their canteens had lasted longer than she'd dared hope, but now the sloshes inside were faint, pitiful things.

Compressed rations eased weight, not thirst. Every bite of dry food forced another sip, and every sip was another inch closer to the end.

"Is this damned sun ever going to set?" Florence muttered, her voice thick with frustration. "We've been walking for days. Sleep would be nice. So would an oasis." The last line came out more hate-filled than she intended, a slip born of heat and festering discomfort.

"You shouldn't talk," Jacques replied without missing a beat. His voice was even, but dismissive. "You'll dehydrate faster."

He didn't look at her, but the message was clear: shut up and keep moving.

Florence rolled her eyes, biting back the retort. She knew he wasn't wrong. The last time she'd vented, Jacques had pulled her aside and reminded her that survival wasn't just about staying alive. It was about holding the group together. And complaints, especially out here, chipped away at that unity.

This wasn't like slogging through a forest or jungle. No shade. No stream. No break. Just sun and sand and more sun, burning down on them. Every drop of sweat vanished before it cooled the skin, and thirst built faster than their bodies could warn them.

And that didn't account for the burns—second- and third-degree—and the infections likely spreading in their unwashed creases. Heat exhaustion was eating at all of them, but it was hitting Hyatta hardest.

His usual indomitable presence had dulled into something hollow. He moved like a man coming apart, his confidence shedding with each step.

"How much farther?" she asked, less venom in her tone now, but still tight.

"About a week," Jacques said, the kind of answer that offered no comfort.

Florence stopped. "A week?" Her voice cracked, and then rose. "There's no way we're lasting that long out here with what we've got left. Do you even have a plan?"

Jacques opened his mouth—probably to lie, or at least try to reassure her—but Florence didn't give him the chance.

"Of course you don't. Why would you? We barely got out of Wrasas with our lives, didn't even have time to grab half our supplies, and now we're crawling through this fucking sandtrap —sunburnt, thirsty, blind, and completely—"

"Shut up, Flo."

Emerald's voice cut clean through the heat and fury. A sudden silence followed, as if even the wind had flinched.

Florence blinked. Emerald was standing squarely in front of her, posture stiff, eyes narrowed—short as she was, it was almost comical. The usual lightness in her expression was gone, replaced by a quiet fire Florence hadn't seen before.

"Enough," Emerald said. "You're not the only one suffering, Flo. We all are. We're all pushing through. We don't need your constant complaints dragging us down."

"This isn't about you," Emerald continued. "It's about all of us. And the only way we survive is if we keep moving. We don't have the energy to waste on this."

Florence's mouth snapped shut. She stood frozen, staring at the hard lines in Emerald's expression. The sting of those words cut deep—not because they were cruel, but because they were true. The heat, the fatigue, the looming dread of empty canteens—it was all pressing in on her, crushing the last scrap of composure she'd held onto. But Emerald's voice, that firm, unflinching tone… She wilted.

"Fine," she muttered after a long silence, her voice quieter, but still tight. She turned away, her shoulders drawn in, sweat crawling down her spine. The sand clung to every inch of her, making her feel more feral. She hated how defeated she felt. Hated that she knew she'd deserved the reprimand.

None of them noticed the dust cloud until then.

It rose from the west, creeping along the horizon like a warning. The **shimmer against the white sky** was subtle—easy to miss in the heat haze—but Florence caught it first. Her eyes narrowed.

"Hey. Look at that," she muttered, pointing into the glare.

The others stirred, sluggishly turning. U'gah grunted, already tracking the movement. Saturn raised a hand and adjusted his goggles, dialing in the telescopic lens.

"It appears to be a caravan," he said after a beat. "Sauropod-based transport. Difficult to resolve details, but definitely organized. Humanoid escorts."

Lusa's ears twitched. He narrowed his eyes at the distant cloud, then turned to Jacques. "Threat?" he asked simply, voice low, body tense.

Jacques's eyes shifted from the approaching shapes to Hyatta, who stood several paces apart, his hood pulled low. The desert had worn on all of them, but Hyatta bore the weight like a man defeated. He moved with careful, measured steps, as if holding himself together by force of will alone.

"What do we do?" Jacques asked finally, his voice a quiet thread of uncertainty.

When Hyatta looked up, his eyes were shadowed, but his voice remained steady. "We stay the course. They've seen us. Running wastes strength we don't have. If they mean harm… we can die tired or die exhausted."

His words floated on the dry wind, practical and calm. But that calm was exactly what made Florence's jaw clench. It was that same infuriating certainty he always wielded—as if debate were beneath him.

Fuck that guy, Florence thought, clenching her fists at her sides.

The group fell silent. The dust cloud was closer now, too close to ignore. If these strangers meant harm, they wouldn't have time to react. But Hyatta was right. There was no running from the desert. No running from anything.

Florence exhaled the bitter breath she was holding. Her shoulders sagged. "Fine," she muttered, barely above a whisper. "We keep trudging forward. But if they start anything, I'm not playing the sacrificial lamb."

"Good to know," Jacques said, offering a small smile. His eyes still held that quiet fire—the same grit that had carried them this far.

Lusa's nub of a tail twitched as he glanced over his shoulder. His eyes locked on the dust cloud. "Caution," he said simply.

No one disagreed. The tension had changed flavor—still hot and exhausted, but a tangy taste of risk hung in the air.

Hyatta walked beside them, still hooded, body stiff. His movements were like that of a dying man conserving the last of his strength. Even now, half-broken, he moved like a champion.

Over the crest of the dune, the creature emerged. A four-legged dinosaur towered above the sand, but it didn't lumber. It glided. Its massive body carried with a regal ease that made Florence forget to pick her foot up as she walked, almost causing her to plant in the sand face first. Its long neck swayed with rhythm, and its tail fanned out, dragging behind it obscuring its steps, casting plumes of sand with each motion. What she'd mistaken for barding was plumage: wide feathers in earthy tones of rust and ochre, desert-born camouflage that shimmered in the heat.

Its eyes were enormous and strangely expressive despite the bird-like features of its head. Each footfall kicked up bursts of powdery grit, but it never faltered. This beast belonged to the sand in a way few things could.

Trailing behind it was a makeshift carriage—low-slung and curved, built from weathered black wood and draped in thick canvas. Fabrics flapped gently in the breeze, sun-bleached and road-worn. Its runners were broad and smooth, clearly meant specifically for this terrain.

Flanking the creature were humanoids—tall, wide-shouldered, and sun-darkened. Their skin had the look of bronze burned by a lifetime under open sky. They wore light robes cinched with worn leather armor, the cut simple, if a bit crude.

They walked with a bully's confidence—unhurried, smug; swaggering.

Florence's skin prickled. She studied their forms—the lean muscle, the masks that obscured their faces, the way their eyes never stopped moving, except to linger on her. They had the bulbous features and brutal presence of orcs, but they weren't like any orcs she'd read about. The orcs of the Congo jungles were isolationists, hidden, secretive. These looked forged by the sun itself, hardened by the wind.

"What the hell...?" Florence muttered.

"They're orcs," Hyatta said, level but edged with steel. "Zoloto tribe—slavers, traders of flesh, thieves." He didn't raise his voice—just studied the approaching caravan with cold calculation. "If they learn I'm Siva'gat, it ends badly.For all of us."

"Wonderful," Florence snapped as quietly as she could. "Just great." Her bitterness surfaced like a boil breaking. "Feral desert orcs. Because the sun and the sand and the open graves we're walking on weren't enough already."

She looked around at the others—at the exhaustion in their faces, at the fear creeping back into the lines of their bodies. Even U'gah was silent.

"There's still a chance to end this without blood," he said. "But it won't be my doing."

He turned to Jacques. "It has to be you."

***

"Moi? Why me?" Jacques's head snapped toward Hyatta, disbelief edging into his voice. "This is your home—you know more about them than the rest of us combined."

Hyatta's face stayed hidden beneath the shadow of his hood, but tension coiled in his shoulders. "Exactly—if they realize who I am, it could trigger bloodshed before a word is spoken." He gestured subtly toward the advancing shapes. "You are level-headed. You know when to speak, and when not to. They need to see strength without challenge; weakness without invitation."

Jacques exhaled hard, rubbing a hand across his face. "I hope you're right," he muttered, eyes drifting toward the caravan.

The desert seemed to contract.

"I'll try," Jacques said at last. His voice was steady, but inside, nerves buzzed like a live wire. He was no diplomat. But right now, failure wasn't an option.

U'gah sidled up beside him, the weight of his pack barely slowing him. He gave Jacques a wide, toothy grin—some strange mix of reassurance and readiness—and rested one hand lightly on his greatclub. It was absurdly comforting.

The leader stepped forward.

Tall, broad, reeking of arrogance. His desert armor was a patchwork of metal and faded cloth, shaped more by necessity than design. His eyes, dark and shrewd, swept over the group in a slow, methodical pass.

When his gaze hit Hyatta, he paused. Not recognition, exactly —but wariness. Instinct. Like a wolf catching the scent of a rival.

Then he reached up and tugged the cloth from his face.

Jacques's stomach turned.

The orc's features were stretched and cruel. A jagged scar cleaved down one cheek like a warning etched in flesh. His smile didn't reach his eyes—it spread like a wound. Jacques fought the urge to step back.

The orc's gaze passed over Saturn and Emerald without interest —dismissed instantly. A small mercy, Jacques thought. Then U'gah—assessed, noted, ignored.

But when he reached Lusa, something shifted. The Mau's size, his musculature, his sheer presence—none of it seemed to impress the orc. His eyes dipped to Lusa's clawless paws. Another dismissal—no threat.

And then his gaze landed on Florence.

He didn't look away.

His eyes roamed—slow and appraising. Jacques felt his jaw tighten. Heat flared in his chest—not desert heat, but anger.

The orc grinned, tusks flashing. Jacques clenched his fists. The old instinct to kill first, talk later pulsed in his fingertips.

The orc finally spoke. His voice was pitched low and guttural, each word dipped in something foul.

"Hail, travelers. What brings you to these sands?"

Jacques's muscles coiled at the orc's accent. It was thick and touched with something Slavic. It grated against his French ears, every syllable like the tooth of a saw. The orc wasn't speaking to him. He spoke to Florence, undressing her with his gaze. Smirking like she was already his.

"We're just passing through," he said. "On our way to Zahadah."

His voice came out less confident than intended. He forced a breath, tried to level his tone, but the unease remained. He couldn't look at the orc's face without feeling the pressure behind his eyes. *We're not looking for trouble,* he added, though the words rang hollow. The leer in the orc's smile had already made peace feel impossible.

The orc's grin widened, tusks gleaming.

"This is good," he said, the words dipped in mock warmth. "You will offer *tribute*. In exchange, we will guide you safely through the sands."

The implication hit like a fist. Jacques felt it, and so did the rest of the group.

The orc's eyes swept over them again, slow and unhurried, like a butcher counting weight. "You will provide it," he added. "Or we will make other arrangements."

Silence followed—thick, clinging.

The other orcs stepped in behind their leader—broad, silent, shoulder to shoulder. A wall of sun-scorched muscle and steel. No weapons raised—yet—but no room left for debate.

"Tribute?" Jacques repeated, brittle with disbelief. "What kind of tribute?"

The orc leaned forward slightly, towering over him.

"Food. Water," he said, then paused—just long enough to draw the word out. "The female. Or your lives."

His smile didn't fade. His eyes gleamed, cruel and pleased. Like he was already watching them choose who would bleed first.

Jacques tried to steady himself. His mind raced. This wasn't negotiation. It was a cage.

They didn't have enough to give—barely enough water for themselves. And handing over Florence? Unthinkable. No one here was expendable. And they weren't in shape to fight. Not against a dozen of these desert-hardened bastards.

He glanced at Hyatta. He stood—still hooded, still silent—but the air around him had changed.

The desert wind curled at his feet, lifting gold-flecked grains into the light. Dust spun in slow spirals, catching the sun like embers. The sight should've been beautiful, but Jacques couldn't look away from Hyatta. Even now, half-drained, he stood—a statue of a vengeful hero. The tension in his body was different from the others—not fear, but poised. The kind of stillness that came *before* violence.

Jacques scanned the others—U'gah stood still watching him for guidance, Lusa flexed and unflexed his hands, Saturn watched with unreadable precision. Nothing they had could appease the orcs. Nothing that wouldn't cost them more than they were willing to pay.

The last demand—the *female*—wasn't barter; it was a display of power.

And if it went one step further, Jacques knew what would happen next.

He knew exactly what the orc meant, and the thought of handing Florence over as "tribute" made bile rise in his throat. He clenched his fists, his mind racing through options, but every path he could see ended in blood.

His eyes snapped back just in time to see the orc close the distance. Now he loomed beside Florence, his shadow falling over her like a shroud. His gaze roamed slowly, hungrily, appraising her like livestock. Jacques saw it—every inch of that stare—and his rage boiled up inside him.

He wanted to move. To draw. To shoot. But the rest of the group was too close. One wrong twitch and they'd all be dead.

Think. He had to redirect his attention to do something. Anything.

His gaze landed on U'gah's map tube—maybe a rare artifact would distract them. Jacques reached out quickly, fingers brushing the edge—

U'gah jerked away.

The halfling let out a low, animal growl. His ursine eyes flared. The orc leader turned slightly at the sound, gaze darting to the small figure—but only for a heartbeat.

Then the orc's eyes slid back to Florence.

Jacques knew he was about to lose her.

Florence flinched under the orc's stare, instinctively stepping back, but it was too late.

The orc's arm shot out like a viper, his thick hand locking around her wrist. She yelped—more shock than pain—as he yanked her forward, her body crashing into his like dead weight. His other arm wrapped around her waist, pinning her to him, his stinking breath hot on her neck.

The smell of sweat, leather, grit. The press of muscle and steel. Florence gasped, struggling to twist free—but he was too strong.

"Let go of me!" she shouted, straining.

The desert fell deathly quiet.

The orc grinned wider, tusks gleaming. He leaned in close, his voice a growl against her ear. "You're a fine prize," he rumbled. "I'll see you're well taken care of. Far better than your current herd."

Jacques moved without thinking, his hand snapping to his side, fingers curling around the grip of his plasma pistol.

But the moment he touched it—steel rasped: a chorus of weapons.

All around them, the orcs moved. Dozens of blades glinted in the harsh desert sun. A dozen eyes locked on Jacques. Patient. Ready.

The tension thickened. One mistake. One heartbeat out of time. That's all it would take.

Jacques froze. His heart pounded in his chest.

Florence kept struggling, but it only seemed to amuse the orc. His grip tightened with each squirm, feeding on her resistance like it was part of the ritual.

Smiling, he slid his hand—wrist to waist—his touch slow, possessive, obscene. Florence's body went rigid. Her breath came fast and shallow, fury and revulsion twisted across her face. The orc's other hand began to rise, fingers creeping toward her chest with certainty in his supremacy.

Bile surged up Jacques's throat.

His hand gripped the pistol. His stance adjusted—heels braced, feet planted. The other orcs watched him now, still as statues, blades glinting like teeth in the sun. They were waiting. Not to attack. To see if they *had* to.

Everyone waited—except Hyatta.

Jacques didn't need to look to know the others were watching him. Their breath held. Their weapons untouched. Their weight behind him. They waited for his signal.

The air was a razor.

Jacques gave a small nod.

Enough.

It didn't register at first—just a blur, a gust of wind. By the time Jacques's brain caught up, Hyatta was already beside the orc, his cloak billowing from his rapid dash. Jacques's hand was still on his pistol. He hadn't even drawn.

The air wavered around Hyatta's hand.

Blowing sand fused into a razor-thin crescent of glass ahead of his finger tips. It sheared first—and his knifed-hand pierced through the orc's neck, between spine and windpipe. The sound was wet, visceral. The crescent, stained dark, spun off into the sand.

The orc's hand—still hovering inches from Florence's breast—halted.

Hyatta stood beside him, his clouded eyes gazed upon the orc with nothing but contempt.

"I hope it was worth it," he murmured, cold and cutting. "You were given the chance to walk away."

His fingers—still embedded in the orc's throat—clamped closed and wrenched sideways. Cartilage cracked, sinew screamed, then tore free the muscle and trachea in one brutal, fluid motion.

Blood fountained, steaming in the desert heat from the wound in a thick, arterial spray—splattering Florence across the face and chest. It steamed in the desert heat, streaking her uniform, mixing with grit and sweat.

The orc twitched. Still alive, his eyes widened with panic and disbelief, for one horrifying moment. Then he collapsed.

The body hit the sand with a wet thud. Blood pooled around it, dark and thick, soaking into the dune.

The dunes held their breath.

Jacques felt as if the instinct to act had drained from him, overtaken by awe—raw, unfiltered shock. Around him, the orcs, who were so recently poised to strike, had gone still. Their eyes locked on the crimson-soaked figure before them, stunned into stillness by what they had just witnessed.

Florence didn't move. Blood ran in slow lines down her neck and chest, soaking her collar and pooling in the recesses of her suit. Her face was rigid with shock—a mix of disgust, fury, and something he couldn't yet name. She didn't wipe it away. Her muscles were locked.

Only Hyatta moved.

He released the ruin of the orc's throat like a man letting go of something unremarkable. His fingers were drenched, his sleeve soaked. He showed no urgency. No revulsion. No regret.

Just indifference.

Then he raised his head—and spoke.

"The sands are the home of the Siva'gat," he said, quietly, yet it carried like a death knell across the dunes.

He drew back his hood. The full force of his gaze landed on the surviving orcs.

"To claim them as your own is already worthy of death," he continued, his tone unflinching. "But your warchief... placed his hands on a servant of Olympus."

Silence followed—but it was a different silence now.

Not stillness—judgment.

Jacques felt his pulse quicken. The air had changed. The other orcs began to shift—exchanging glances, their confidence evaporating. The body of their leader lay at their feet, neck torn wide open, blood steaming against the sand.

And Hyatta, who was cloaked in that blood, stood among them like a legend wearing the flesh of a mortal.

Not just the words held them, but the execution—the certainty, the message.

One of theirs had touched something sacred. Now they understood the price.

CHAPTER TWENTY-SIX

Saturn stood apart from the others, eyes wide but unfocused, watching the chaos unfold. The violence—brutal, immediate—should have disgusted him. Once, it would have. Once, he would have cowered, maybe even vomited at the sight of a throat being torn open like paper.

Even witnessing a coworker throw a punch would have rattled him. Watching someone—an ally—rip out another man's throat? That would've sent him spiraling. But now, with blood steaming on the sand and orcs howling in rage, he felt detached. Disillusioned. This wasn't even the worst thing he'd seen.

The terror that used to grip him in moments like this had died, cauterized by the unrelenting trauma of Mu. His senses had dulled. Horror didn't shock him anymore; it registered and passed.

What drew his attention wasn't the gore. It was Hyatta.

The man moved like a myth, brutally efficient and barbarically effective. Even infected and weakened, Hyatta fought like he was more than human. Saturn knew he wasn't. Not really. Not with his diminished ability.

Still, he stood. Still, he killed—surgical grace.

That fascinated Saturn. Not the violence, but the control. The sheer resilience. Anyone else would've been consumed. The parasite would have eaten them alive from the inside out. But Hyatta… Hyatta had survived it. Not unscathed, but functional. Lethal, even.

He couldn't look away.

The desert light played oddly off the warrior's form. Where once Hyatta had radiated with golden brilliance, now his aura burned a faint red. Not the full spectrum—only the long, red. A side effect of the infection. He still drew power from light, but no longer all of it. The blade wasn't conjured; windborne silicon vitrified into a thin glass crescent under his red heat as he struck.

Even broken, he was dangerous.

When the orcs finally snapped from their shock and charged, Saturn merely observed.

They moved feral—a pack hitting back after the leader falls. Predictable. Messy. And doomed.

They didn't know what they were charging into.

Lusa met the nearest orc with a snarl and a concussive impact. His paws snapped the weapon arm, pinning it at an angle, radius and ulna jutting through his skin. Then the flip—clean, effortless. The arm tore free, epidermis sheeting from chest and back. The orc crumpled, twitching.

It was over in seconds.

U'gah was a diminutive landslide on two legs. The greatclub he wielded came down like a landslide, smashing through flesh and bone with ruinous finality. The carved stone head—shaped like a theropod's maw—seemed alive in the heat of battle, its jagged teeth ripping through exposed flesh as if it were feeding. Each swing echoed with the crunch of breaking bones, the screams of orcs who moved too slow to escape him.

Saturn watched—fascinated, though still felt detached from the events transpiring around him.

He wasn't built for this. He was the outsider. The observer. Violence wasn't his domain, data was. But something about the speed, the savagery, the clean execution of motion and intent— it stirred something in him. His heart beat faster, despite his emotional numbness.

Envy flared.

They all had roles to play. Even Florence, screaming and bloodstreaked, fought like she belonged here. Saturn, though? He just watched. Just cataloged. A passenger in someone else's experience.

"Saturn! Move!"

Emerald's voice ripped through the chaos, yanking him from his spiral.

She was sprinting toward him, face flushed, eyes hard. Her plasma rifle cracked in her hands. They were warning shots at first, then crippling ones. Then kill shots. She'd tried mercy, and mercy had been ignored.

"Get up!" she shouted again, breathless with urgency.

Saturn blinked at her, struggling to catch up, but his limbs didn't respond. His mind spun, searching for logic, for language.

"I'm not sure I can," he said—quietly. Uselessly.

The words felt strange as they left his mouth. He could assess risk. Predict outcomes. Map trajectories and survival probabilities. But here, now, none of that mattered. His purpose —the thing he'd clung to—had unraveled.

He wasn't fighting. He wasn't running. He wasn't helping.

He was paralyzed.

A shadow crossed him—massive at his scale. It wasn't the shadow of a dune or a shifting sunbeam. It was an enemy with a weapon. And it was aimed at him.

He stared up, still parsing the shape when something else collided with it mid-swing.

A body.

The blow veered, missing him by centimeters.

Emerald had tried to warn him. Her voice echoed again in his memory, but he hadn't been able to react. He hadn't understood. And now, as the reality of near-death pressed in, Saturn understood just how close it had come. A fraction of a second more and he'd be a smear in the sand.

But even that realization felt distant. There was no adrenaline spike. No cinematic gasp of gratitude. Just... detachment. Another near-death. Another reminder that Mu devoured everything it touched.

Whether he died here in the dunes, or in some ruined village weeks from now—it didn't matter. He had accepted it already. The island didn't care who you were. Scientist. Soldier. Explorer. All of them were just gristle for the grinder.

He turned slowly.

Down-slope, Jacques and the orc rolled in a tangle of limbs. The creature had nearly struck the killing blow, but Jacques had intercepted it. He tackled the bastard mid-swing and drove them both into the sand. Now, Jacques pinned the orc, muscles straining.

The orc thrashed beneath him, snarling. But Jacques held him down.

And Saturn, for a moment, could only stare—silent, stunned—not just by the act itself, but by the realization: Someone had chosen to save him.

Saturn felt the distant spark of gratitude, like a match struck in the wind, but it guttered before it caught. Jacques had saved his life, and Saturn couldn't even summon the emotion to properly recognize it. Why had he done it? It wasn't sentiment. Saturn doubted his life held more value than anyone else's. No, Jacques had moved on instinct. On duty. On the invisible bonds of this warband—Hyatta's word.

Maybe, even here, in this broken place, a fragment of humanity still resisted the void.

"Thank you," Saturn whispered. He barely heard himself over the chaos. He doubted Jacques did either. Jacques was still grappling with the orc, too focused to acknowledge it, if he had.

Jacques was locked in a brutal struggle, his body trembling from exertion. Sweat streaked his face, every muscle taut as he tried to force his plasma pistol into position. The orc bucked beneath him, snarling, wild. Saturn could see it all—the effort, the desperation, the refusal to yield.

With a strangled howl, Jacques fired—not at flesh but into the sand beneath them. Superheated plasma vitrified the grains to molten glass, a hiss of vaporized grit rising into the air. The orc shrieked, stunned by the heat that blistered against his side.

That second was all Jacques needed.

He twisted—hip snap, knee rise—then drove a brutal savate strike into the orc's groin. Saturn blinked. He hadn't known Jacques could move like that.

For a heartbeat, though, he saw Jacques as something else—not just a talented engineer or the leader—but the soldier. The survivor. The man who'd walked through hell and kept walking. Before Mu, Saturn had only known him as a quiet presence—polite and professional. They'd exchanged a few conversations, surface-level at best. He hadn't thought to look deeper.

Maybe, under different circumstances, he would've tried.

The orc reeled, dazed by the intense pain. Jacques didn't hesitate.

He pinned the shoulders with his knees, popped two more rounds into the sand by the skull, and drove the head into the molten glass.

The sound that followed was wet, sizzling, vengeful. Jacques, furious beyond all reason, yanked the brute's head from the blaze and spat something harsh in French at his now-terrified foe. The orc's face slammed into the vitrified sand with a sickening crunch. Steam roiled from its flesh, the superheated surface searing deeper still.

It screamed—more like an animal than a man. It kept screaming as Jacques pressed down harder, only relieving the pressure when it was time to bash the orc's head into the cooling glass.

Saturn watched in silence as Jacques punished the orc.

He wasn't a killer by nature—or at least Saturn hadn't thought so. But nature had little say here. Mu had a way of reshaping people. It sanded away hesitation, filed down empathy, carved survivors from softer clay. Jacques had adapted, like they all had. He could recognize one thing clearly: Jacques had reached the end of his tolerance for *rude behavior*.

The fight was over. The screams had faded into the wind.

Only the orc's breath remained, hoarse and shallow. The spasms that once thrashed with fury had become twitches—limbs jerking like a puppet with tangled strings.

It should have ended, but it didn't.

Emerald moved quickly, her green hair flashing as she rushed to Jacques. She helped him untangle from the dying weight beneath him. But Saturn saw the change in her eyes—there was strain, not fear. Exhaustion, not hesitation. And something new, affection?

She steadied Jacques, helped him find his footing in the shifting sand.

Saturn only watched.

There was no place for him in this moment. He was left to float above the wreckage.

His thoughts fragmented—data without pattern. He had always prized his ability to analyze under pressure. Now, even that gift felt... irrelevant.

A sudden tug lifted him from the ground.

Lusa's massive paw gripped the drone's harness and hoisted him up, careful but firm. Saturn stumbled, boots dragging as he found footing again. The Mau's wide, fanged grin wasn't comforting, but there was intention behind it. A quiet check-in. A reassurance that, for now, they still counted him among the living.

Saturn nodded. It was all he could offer.

"Is everyone... is everyone...?" Jacques's voice cracked mid-sentence. It wasn't weakness—it was interruption.

The orc beneath him still breathed. It still moaned. Still refused to *die*.

It grated. Saturn felt it in his teeth—a friction, an unwanted persistence. Whether it was stubbornness or just the mechanics of a dying body, it didn't matter. The sound had become unbearable.

"*Nom de Dieu—tais-toi, connard!*" Jacques spat.

Three plasma shots.

The bolts hissed through the air and punched into the orc's spine. The body seized, then stilled. The twitching stopped. The desert was quiet again.

Jacques stood over the corpse, chest rising and falling with each heavy breath. The heat shimmered off the vitrified sand. His hand dropped to his side.

He exhaled, wiped a streak of blood from his cheek. His face was flushed, sweat pooling beneath his collar. He looked like a man who had walked too far into a fire and couldn't yet feel the burns.

"*Comme je le disais...*" he said hoarsely. "Is everyone okay?"

The question landed like a rock dropped in water—too late for the splash, too soon for calm.

Saturn just nodded. He glanced at his companions.

All of them were coated in sand, sweat, and blood—some of it theirs, most of it not. U'gah wiped his hands on his fur, half-grinning despite the carnage. Lusa stood motionless, watching the aftermath with unreadable calm and licking himself. Emerald moved among them, checking wounds, offering brief words, but her eyes kept drifting back to Jacques. There was concern there.

"Yeah," Saturn muttered. "We're alive, I guess."

Jacques nodded, still catching his breath. His eyes lingered on the corpse at his feet.

"That's all that matters."

Behind them, a rhythm broke the silence.

A series of dull thumps. Repetitive. Angry. Like someone beating a broken drum with their bare hands.

Saturn turned—and saw Florence.

She was kicking the orc. The one who had grabbed her. The one who had died first.

Her foot slammed into his side again and again, each strike landing with enough force to jolt the limp body. Her face was red with fury. Sweat clung to her jaw. Strands of hair had escaped her ponytail and now clung to her cheeks like vines. She didn't scream. She didn't cry. She just kept kicking.

There was rage in every movement. Fear, too. And shame. She was purging something—reclaiming something—that the bastard had tried to take.

Saturn watched her, silent.

On any other day, he might have called it instability. But he could understand this. She had been violated. The violence she inflicted on the corpse was a protest—not against the man, but against the powerlessness he'd tried to impose.

In the Western European Union, such behavior would've been corrected. Reeducation, chemical restraint, emotional recalibration—whatever it took to keep the peace. It wasn't perfect. But it was orderly. Predictable. There, this kind of outburst would have marked her as a danger to be neutralized, even if she was the aggrieved party initially.

But *here*? *Here* it made sense.

He turned away—not out of discomfort, but something closer to respect. Privacy, perhaps. Or acknowledgement.

Hyatta had collapsed into a crouch, struggling to pull his hood into place. His hands shook. Slow, clumsy, pain wracking his movements.

Saturn approached. He didn't feel urgency, just a quiet instinct to assist.

When he saw the damage to Hyatta's face, he understood. The sun had scorched him. Pink burns spread across his cheekbones and brow, the skin cracked and angry. The exposure had triggered some vulnerability Saturn hadn't seen before.

Hyatta could be injured—he could burn.

Saturn knelt beside him and adjusted the hood. The fabric was stiff thanks to the iridescence polymer coating it, but it settled easily enough over the warrior's raw skin. A simple task, yet one Hyatta could no longer perform himself.

The burns weren't just superficial. They reminded Saturn of porphyria—a phototoxic disorder. One variation involved a deficiency in uroporphyrinogen decarboxylase, an enzyme that allowed the body to process porphyrins safely. Without it, even limited sun exposure could result in catastrophic tissue damage.

If that's what this was—even metaphorically—there was a chance Saturn could help. With the right lab. With the right tools.

If Jacques was right, and they could reach the mobile facility abandoned outside Zahadah, Saturn might be able to synthesize something. If not a cure, a stabilizer. A treatment.

405

That sounded like something he'd have done—before. Before his hope withered. Before this island drained the meaning from everything. Now, the idea felt like a memory from someone else's life.

***

Emerald stayed close to Jacques as he appraised their current circumstances, his eyes shifting from face to face, checking for wounds, taking stock. He moved with quiet efficiency, as if the violence hadn't touched him at all. Steady as always.

She relied on that steadiness more than she liked to admit.

Even now, in the aftermath—blood still drying on their skin, sand still churning with the heat of death—Jacques never lost focus. He never seemed rattled. And that calm, that consistency, was starting to feel like the only solid thing left in a world that shifted beneath her feet every hour.

They'd come out of the skirmish better than she expected. The orcs were brutal, yes—but their group wasn't soft. Not anymore. They fought like people who had learned what losing meant.

Jacques, of course, had wanted to avoid the fight. He always did. But violence was Mu's currency. It was the only thing it respected. And the longer they stayed, the more Emerald understood it: this place fed on blood. There was no avoiding it. She could only hope to survive it.

Her eyes followed Jacques as he moved to check on U'gah, then Lusa. She knew he was strong—had known since the crash—but seeing him in combat was something else entirely. It wasn't just the skill. It was the composure. The decisiveness. The sheer unwillingness to let anyone he was responsible for die.

It was that strength—the resilience, even the quiet recklessness —that had drawn her in.

She wasn't blind. She knew her feelings had shifted somewhere along the way.

She'd tried to ignore it. But now, with her heart thudding a little too hard in her chest every time he brushed past her, it was harder to pretend. She couldn't act on it—not here, not now. Florence would catch on instantly and start flinging her favorite insult around like always. And Jacques? He'd pull away. Men always did when they realized a woman noticed them. Walls went up. Distance crept in.

And worse—if he *was* interested, if he let himself return her feelings—it would compromise him. Compromise *them*.

They couldn't afford that. Not when everything depended on his judgment staying clear. Maybe, if they ever made it off this island, she'd find the right moment. And let it all spill out. But for now, all she could do was bury it. Like so many other things.

Jacques's voice broke her thoughts.

"Did Hyatta suffer any injuries in the fight?"

Emerald turned toward Saturn. The gnome barely looked up. His voice was clipped, clinical—almost bored.

"Not that I can tell. But he's sustained severe facial burns. Reaction to sunlight."

Before Jacques could answer, a rough voice cut in.

"I'm right... here."

Hyatta was pushing to his feet, awkwardly but determined. His voice carried the grit of recent pain, but there was no hesitation in it. Only conviction.

"I'll be fine," he added, adjusting his hood with trembling fingers. "The pain is already passing. If this is the price of our blessings, then I'll bear it with joy in my heart."

Emerald blinked.

Of course he would say something like that.

Hyatta was... something else. She'd realized early on his strength wasn't just physical. But to speak like that—grateful for agony, serene in the face of burns so severe they'd left skin sloughing from his face—it made her wonder what kind of man he truly was underneath the stoicism.

Or if he *was* a man at all.

There was strength in his words. But to her, it sounded like madness dressed in ritual. Like he'd given his pain a name so he didn't have to feel it.

And maybe that was its own kind of strength.

But it wasn't one she could understand.

Jacques seemed to echo her thoughts, his tone dry but touched with concern. "So... have you gone crazy from sunstroke, or are you just a masochist?"

Hyatta's lips twitched at the corners, but no smile came. He fixed Jacques with a steady look. "Neither. If you haven't noticed—Zoloto's beast of burden is still standing exactly where they left it."

Emerald's heart skipped.

The words struck like a match in dry brush—instant and bright. The dinosaur. She turned sharply toward the creature, her mind racing. The sled. The sheer mass of it. The shade it could provide. The miles it could devour.

Transportation.

She hadn't dared to hope. Not after the endless walking, the heat, the chafing, the blisters layered on blisters. But if they could get the creature to obey—even just tolerate them—it would change everything.

"Wait," she said, eyes narrowing. "You mean... we can *take* it?"

Hyatta nodded slowly, his eyes scanning the horizon. Already calculating. Already plotting. "If it cooperates."

Jacques and Hyatta began discussing the logistics,but Emerald barely heard them. Her pulse had spiked, adrenaline mingling with the first hint of joy she'd felt in days—real, tangible joy. Not a joke. Not sarcasm. Hope.

Riding instead of walking. Shade instead of burning.

Rest.

The word felt decadent.

She stood still, letting the possibility wash over her. Of course, she kept her face neutral. She couldn't let herself get carried away. Not visibly. Not in front of Florence. And definitely not in front of Jacques.

But damn if she didn't want to smile.

Being near him steadied her. Always had, if she was being honest with herself. He was calm, controlled—reassuring in ways she'd never admit aloud. That steadiness had become something she depended on. And lately… it was more than that. Her feelings had flowered.

She'd tried to keep them buried—shoved them down—but they floated up anyway, like little sparkling bubbles rising toward the surface.

This wasn't the time.

She drew a breath, held it, then let it go slowly.

When she looked up again, Jacques and Hyatta were already heading toward the sauropod. Their voices a low murmur ahead of her. The beast towered over them—its feathered hide still shimmering with dust, its tail swishing faint furrows through the sand.

Emerald started forward, forcing herself to focus. Her boots crunched softly as she caught up, eyes scanning the sled.

It looked sturdy. Wide runners, heavy wood, sloped canopy. Everything about it spoke of endurance. But looks could lie. She knew that better than anyone.

Still, the idea of climbing into its shaded interior... of lying down, even for a few minutes, shielded from the sun's blistering gaze...

She almost let herself smile again.

Maybe, she thought, *just maybe—we can finally catch a break.*

And if she was honest with herself—the kind of dangerous honesty that only crept in when her defenses were low—the thought of sharing that shaded space with Jacques made her stomach flutter. Just the two of them, maybe sitting close, maybe laughing about something *other* than their next near-death encounter.

The image rose unbidden: Warm, impossible, and utterly stupid.

Still, it lingered.

She felt herself grinning like an idiot.

No. She clamped down on the thought like a trap snapping shut. *Focus, Emerald. That kind of thinking will get you killed.* Or worse—get *him* killed. This wasn't the time for fantasy.

She shoved the idea back down and was just managing to wrestle her focus into place when Jacques's voice pulled her straight into reality.

"There's something in there," he said, eyes on the latch.

Emerald's body reacted before her mind caught up. She shouldered her rifle, dropping into a low ready, her eyes scanning. A dozen thoughts vanished.

Florence and Saturn flanked wide, careful to avoid crossfire. Lusa and U'gah shifted into position behind Hyatta, who looked like he might need help remaining vertical. Jacques took point at the sled's latch. His expression was focused. Composed. The rhythm of the group had become instinct by now.

Emerald's heart thundered. She wasn't thinking about anything else. Not Jacques. Not sunlight. Just the gate. Just the shimmering heat around the latch, the silence that hung like tensioned wire.

Jacques threw the latch with a clean, practiced snap—the sled's gate swung open.

A beat—silent, stretched—then something moved inside the shadowed chamber.

A figure stepped forward, emerging through the wavering heat like a vision out of myth. Emerald's breath caught. Big, broad —masculine beyond doubt. The silhouette was unmistakably orcish, but not like the others. This one didn't charge. Didn't snarl. He just... stood there.

She held her aim. Her finger hovered just outside the trigger guard.

The orc stepped into the full light, and Emerald's stomach twisted. He was rags so tattered they barely held. His skin had the same bronze hue as the others, but slightly paler—more golden than burnt.

Bruises and half-healed wounds marred his body, some oozing through cracked scabs. Infection glistened on his shoulder. He had a split lip, a swollen eye, and was skeletal.

He wasn't a fighter. Not anymore.

Emerald didn't lower her rifle, but she eased the tension in her arms.

He raised his hands slowly—palms out, fingers wide—not in surrender, but in peace.

"I am Cor'ngar," he rasped. His voice was dry, like gravel scoured through a sieve, but resolute. "The people in this conveyance are innocent of any crime against you. If the deaths of my kin have not satisfied your justice, then take *my* life... and leave theirs. But if you intend to spill the blood of these victims, I will defend them with my final breath."

411

.

CHAPTER TWENTY-SEVEN

Jacques's eyes narrowed as he tried to see past the veil of darkness obscuring the inside of the covered sled. His pistol was raised, the barrel fixed squarely on the orc. His heart thudded in his chest. It was loud enough to drown out the shifting sand and the polymer creaking in his grip. But beneath the adrenaline, a thread of confusion worked its way through his thoughts.

This orc—Cor'ngar—wasn't posturing. Wasn't begging. He was offering himself. A sacrifice. Not in fear, but in restitution. His voice, rough and cracked, carried the weight of his conviction. Words like *justice*, *defense*, *victims*. He spoke like a man trying to hold a crumbling wall upright, not a brute looking for blood. He was nothing like the others, who now stained the dunes in drying crimson.

Jacques cut a glance at Hyatta. The warrior stood unreadable. His whip hung slack at his side, but Jacques had seen it move faster than sound. Lusa and U'gah flanked him. Like Jacques, they were caught in that breath between reflex and restraint. This wasn't clear-cut. The orc hadn't lunged. Hadn't lied.

The reticence stretched, taut and crackling. Even the wind seemed to hesitate, then hissed across the sands—a long, dry exhale.

Jacques shifted slightly, adjusting his stance. The heat pressed in, relentless even under the sled's shadow. But the weight wasn't heat—it was the question: was this orc truly what he seemed to be?

He wanted to dismiss it. Wanted to keep things simple. But something about the way Cor'ngar stood, the way he held himself—exhausted, bruised, defiant—didn't fit the profile of an apathetic killer. He didn't look like a raider. He looked like someone who had survived a troubled life. Someone who still had someone to protect.

And that… that made everything harder.

Jacques had killed before. Watched men die. Ordered it, even. But this moment didn't feel like battle. It felt like judgment.

His finger hovered near the trigger. The weapon was ready. So was he. But instinct whispered: *wait.*

The orc's voice had carried something unfamiliar. Not just discipline—but responsibility. It unnerved Jacques, because if it was real… it meant there were innocents, right here, in the shadow of their violence.

He clenched his jaw, forcing the rising heat down. He needed more. Something concrete. Anything to justify this hesitation.

"I'm listening," Jacques said at last. "But you'll need to convince me."

As if summoned by fate, a sound broke the silence. An infant's cry—small and reedy—followed by the soft murmur of a woman, soothing, pleading.

Jacques's guts knotted.

For a second, all the desert vanished. The dunes, the heat, the blood. And in its place—just that cry. That desperate, human cry.

It struck him like a hammer. Not because it was unexpected, but because it made everything *immediate.* The standoff. The gun in his hands. The orc's offer.

This wasn't hypothetical anymore.

The silence changed—violence gone, compassion rising.

He couldn't do it.

Jacques stared down the barrel of his pistol—but the will to use it was gone. Not dulled. Just gone.

No matter the circumstances, no matter the risk, he couldn't bring himself to threaten a man—even an *orc*—who stood between innocents and danger. Not when that orc had already

414

offered his life. Not when the voice of a child still echoed in the dry air like a bell tolling for restraint.

His arms slackened; the pistol lowered. His grip went soft. The polymer frame felt heavier than it should have—as if gravity itself disapproved.

Cor'ngar hadn't moved.

That stillness, that quiet readiness to die if it meant shielding the vulnerable... it struck something in Jacques. Something buried. Something he'd wanted to forget, but he hadn't.

The child's cry unsealed the vault.

It was New Poland all over again. The smoke, the collapse, the scent of scorched earth. The Axis had razed the outskirts for control—burned families alive to make a point. But one boy— a kid, maybe nineteen—had dropped his weapon and shielded two children with his body. Wrong uniform, wrong side, but Jacques hadn't hesitated. Not that day.

He broke protocol, dragging the boy and those children out of the fire. He had killed three of his own—men who followed orders too well. He remembered the soldier's eyes: terrified, but resolute. That boy had later become one of the key informants who helped head off an attack on a large refugee camp. A life spared became many lives saved.

And now, staring into Cor'ngar's sunburned face, seeing the blood crusted in the corners of his mouth, Jacques felt the same truth settle in:

This was not an enemy.

This was a man doing what Jacques himself would do— shielding the weak.

"You're protecting them," Jacques said. It wasn't a question.

Cor'ngar didn't nod. Didn't blink. He just stood there, holding the weight of that choice.

Jacques turned slightly, eyes scanning the others. Hyatta hadn't moved, but his eyes had narrowed—calculating, measuring. Lusa and U'gah stood like statues, their tension still poised for impact.

"D'accord," Jacques murmured.

He holstered the pistol. His voice carried not just command, but clarity.

No more blood today.

It was a risk. He knew that. A hundred things could still go wrong. But there were moments in war when the calculus didn't matter. Moments when humanity had to outrank the algorithm of killing.

Jacques had learned that lesson the hard way. And he wasn't about to forget it now.

As if sensing the shift, Cor'ngar's legs buckled. The tension that had kept him upright gave way. He crumpled in exhaustion. His body had held out long enough to keep the promise he'd made.

He would've collapsed face-first into the sand if not for Lusa.

The Mau stepped forward, catching the orc as if handling a delicate crate. No hesitation. Just instinct.

He eased Cor'ngar to the ground, supporting the bulk of the orc's weight with casual strength. The contact was brief, careful. Respectful.

Jacques let out a breath he hadn't realized he was holding. The danger hadn't passed. But something else had. The line between enemy and ally was no longer so clear.

Movement stirred in the darkness behind Cor'ngar.

His eyes shifted to the sled—and stopped.

Figures began to emerge.

A dozen or more rag-wrapped humanoids stooped with exhaustion. They moved like ghosts—shuffling forward as though the light itself might be a trick. FFear and frailty clung to them like dust. Each step seemed uncertain, as if they expected a blow at any moment.

At their front walked a woman.

Her skin was a muted gray, dulled further by the layers of dust and blood streaking her form. She clutched an infant tight to her chest that was wrapped in tattered rags. The child trembled; even in that heat, the newborn shivered.

The woman's gait was uneven. Blood crusted down the insides of her legs, flaking from her ruined garment. It was unmistakable—postpartum bleeding. She'd given birth in that sled, in those filthy conditions. And now she stood, carried by will alone, her eyes hollow but locked on the sky with a mixture of awe and disbelief.

It hit Jacques like a punch to the sternum. He barely had time to process it before movement scurried to his side.

Hyatta surged forward without warning. His body moved with a sudden, coiled energy—less a man in motion than an instinct given form. Jacques flinched, reaching automatically for his pistol.

But it was already too late to act. Hyatta was halfway to the woman, his cloak billowing behind him like a dust devil.

Jacques tensed.

He'd seen Hyatta move like that before—always with lethal intent. That same clarity of purpose. That same inhuman speed. A predator's advance. Jacques's hand hovered near the grip of his sidearm, instinct and caution wrestling in his gut.

But then, Hyatta stopped. He reached for the woman gently.

No weapon. No threat.

Just a touch—careful, reverent. His voice, when it came, was low and tender. A language Jacques didn't understand, spoken with a softness that felt foreign in this world of sand and blood.

Jacques paused, unsure of what he was seeing.

There was something in the way they looked at each other—something familiar. Not romantically. Not like lovers. But with recognition. Purpose. As if the roles they played had already been written, and both had simply arrived at the next scene.

The woman responded, voice trembling but calm. Respect threaded her tone. Deference, even. She wasn't afraid of him. She was trusting him.

Jacques took a step forward, then stopped himself.

He didn't know what was unfolding—but he could feel its weight. The last time he'd assumed, he'd nearly gotten them killed. This time... this time he would wait.

He glanced around.

U'gah stood unmoving, his greatclub still angled low. Emerald's brows were drawn, eyes narrowed, rifle half-raised but not aiming. Florence had gone quiet, her anger replaced by wary curiosity. Even Saturn seemed transfixed.

None of them spoke.

They watched Jacques—waiting for a signal—but he gave them none.

He turned his eyes back to Hyatta, who now helped the woman down the last step of the sled. His hands supported her without force. The baby squirmed. The mother whispered something.

And for the first time in hours—maybe days—there was no violence. No screaming. Just the sound of wind over sand, and the steady breath of people who'd endured.

Jacques let the lull stretch.

Maybe, he thought, just maybe... this wasn't a mistake. Maybe, for once, they were standing at a different kind of threshold—one not marked by blood or flame.

A crossroads—maybe there was still room for mercy.

***

Jacques welcomed the sun's descent like a man surfacing for air. The heat, oppressive and constant for what felt like weeks, finally began to break as the swollen orb dipped lower in the sky. Even so, there was little comfort. The sun here didn't move right—it arced in reverse, stumbled across the horizon like a drunk searching for purpose. Every day felt warped, time itself had been twisted into a cruel geometry. He'd long since stopped trying to track hours. The rhythms of the island made no sense. He simply accepted them. They were like the rest of Mu—hostile, unknowable, and designed to drive a man mad.

Cor'ngar, battered as he was, had become their reluctant guide.

It was the orc who led them north, muttering terse instructions on how to handle the sauropod they'd commandeered. He rarely elaborated—clipped words, a dry tone—but effective. Jacques had learned not to expect conversation. The orc wasn't cruel, just economical. He offered the minimum and no more, unless Hyatta was the one doing the asking.

That was where the change came in.

When Hyatta spoke, Cor'ngar answered in full sentences. Sometimes full paragraphs. His gravelly voice softened, his words took on rhythm and weight, laced with reverence Jacques could only begin to parse. The orc never bowed or groveled, but there was a deference in his posture, a stillness in how he listened, that told Jacques everything he needed to know.

Hyatta, for his part, said little. But when the woman—gray-skinned, quiet, and withdrawn—was near, his silence changed. Jacques had watched it happen a dozen times already. The warrior's stony mask would shift, almost imperceptibly. His presence, normally rigid, would soften—his movements gentler, his voice gentler. She wasn't just another freed captive.

Jacques hadn't asked. Not after Florence's blunt inquiry earned a withering reprimand. He'd learned enough in war to know that some truths, especially the personal ones, didn't need to be pried loose. They surfaced when they were ready.

To Jacques's surprise, their journey had been... tolerable.

They alternated between walking and riding the sled, taking turns beneath its shade. It wasn't comfortable, but it was merciful. The desert still drained them—every step was a negotiation—but luckily no one had collapsed. Even U'gah had learned to pace himself, trading his relentless energy for quiet endurance.

Only Hyatta refused rest.

Not once had he climbed into the sled. Not once had he sat beneath the canopy or taken a proper break. He stalked beside the beast like a shade, boots carving quiet furrows into the sand. His cloak clung to sunburned skin, his gait tighter by the hour. Every instinct in Jacques screamed that Hyatta should rest, that he needed to. But the man brushed off every offer and shrugged away every request.

Was it pride? Discipline bordering on self-harm?

Jacques didn't know. But something about it felt... familiar. Soldiers did this. Survivors did this. Men who'd lived through fire and hadn't yet admitted they were still burning.

Maybe Hyatta had something to prove.

Finally, the river came into view.

It wasn't wide, but it shimmered with promise, cutting through the cracked landscape like a vein of silver beneath the sun's

420

dying breath. The moment Jacques caught sight of it, he stopped walking. The breeze that rose from the waterline cooled his sweat-slick skin like a benediction. It smelled of minerals, runoff, and distant stone. It smelled like life.

He exhaled, chest rising with the first breath that didn't feel like it scraped his ribs from the inside.

Cor'ngar had been right. The runoff came from the jagged peaks to the west with high mountains that now loomed on the horizon like a broken wall. Somewhere beyond them might lie Zahadah, or at least shelter. Jacques didn't know if they were any closer to real safety. But for the first time in days, the heat didn't feel eternal.

The river offered more than water. It offered direction.

Finally, they had something tangible to follow—something that moved with purpose. The river flowed from the west, cutting through the desert and carrying the cold air of the high peaks. Jacques could already feel the change in their prospects, subtle but unmistakable. No more vague trudging toward Zahadah beneath a punishing sun. Now there was a path.

They had been rationing water for days, counting drops like currency. Dehydration had dogged every step, heatstroke creeping up behind them with bared teeth. This river hadn't just improved their odds—it had saved them. It felt divine, like something placed here not by chance, but providence. And yet Jacques knew better. The island didn't give gifts. Every mercy here had teeth.

He knelt by the edge of the river and dipped his fingers into the current. The coolness shocked him then sent a pulse of relief through nerves cooked dry. He watched the ripples spread outward, watched the light catch and scatter across the surface. Even that—the river's relentless motion—felt like a small victory. Something still moved forward. Something still endured.

The mountains loomed in the soft blue of twilight. Their silhouettes stood jagged and broken against the horizon, promising hard shelter and harder truths. Jacques could almost hear the crunch of gravel underfoot, smell pine or wet stone—anything but sand. It was enough to let hope stir, cautious and quiet.

Still, the river was only the start.

The path ahead wound into the highlands, where weather and terrain would work against them. The island twisted everything—turned miracles into traps, terrain into trials. For all they knew, something far worse than the desert awaited them in those mountains. But that was tomorrow's concern.

Tonight, they had abundance.

Jacques stood, wiping his hands on his pants, and looked back at the group. Hyatta still hadn't climbed into the sled; he walked beside the sauropod like a sentinel, his steps steady but increasingly labored. The man's skin blistered beneath his hood, his limbs stiffening by the hour. Still, he refused rest.

It frustrated Jacques more than he wanted to admit.

At first, Jacques had assumed it was just Hyatta being Hyatta. But now... now he wasn't so sure. There was something ritualistic in it. Something heavy, like soldiers who treated pain as currency, who walked with ghosts strapped to their backs because failure meant dishonor. Back in the Legion, you could take a beating in the barracks for bringing shame to your squad. In the field, it could get you killed.

Maybe he was performing or enduring for the sake of his people, for his tribe's memory. Jacques didn't know anything about the Siva'gat, but he knew what it meant to carry duty like a chain around your neck. And Hyatta carried it without complaint. Without pause.

Not for pride. For honor.

That, Jacques understood—respected it, even. That implacable drive to uphold something larger than yourself. He knew what it meant to carry the weight of expectations, to march beyond your limits because turning back wasn't an option. Watching Hyatta now—shoulders hunched, each step harder than the last—Jacques couldn't help but admire the man's tenacity. But admiration didn't quiet concern.

Hyatta was faltering.

Jacques could see it in the microexpressions the warrior tried to hide, in the way sweat darkened the light fabric of his armor, in the stiffness of each movement. He was pushing himself too far. Pride might carry him a while longer, but the body had limits, and Hyatta was nearing his.

Jacques's thoughts turned to Saturn. The gnome had the knowledge—genetic, medical, scientific. If they could reach the mobile lab in Zahadah, there was a chance. Saturn might be able to diagnose what the infection had broken inside Hyatta. Maybe even slow it. Heal it.

But for now, they were still trapped in the sand. Jacques wasn't foolish enough to believe the night would bring lasting reprieve. Mu had no mercy. Its moments of grace always came with a price.

Still... they had made it this far. And the sun was actually setting. That alone felt like cause for jubilation.

Jacques raised a hand, signaling the group from the edge of the water. "We'll make camp here," he said—steady, but laced with exhaustion. "Rest. Check supplies. Eat something. We regroup at dawn."

His gaze drifted to Hyatta, who had paused a few steps beyond the sauropod's shadow. The warrior looked like he was still debating whether to fall over or keep walking.

Jacques frowned. "Hyatta," he said, quieter now, but with that same iron underneath. "Get in the damn sled. You're done."

There was a long beat. Jacques braced for resistance. But to his surprise, Hyatta simply nodded—reluctantly. No protest. Just a stiff pivot as he turned and climbed aboard.

That, more than anything, worried Jacques.

He watched as Hyatta collapsed against the inner wall of the sled, jaw clenched as though admitting to weakness might break something vital inside him.

Sleep took him almost at once. Even unconscious, the man held himself like a warrior too proud to let his body rest without permission.

Jacques exhaled slowly.

Maybe, with a few hours of sleep, they could all remember what it felt like to hope.

Satisfied that Hyatta had finally relented, Jacques turned to help with camp preparations—but found, to his surprise, there was little left to do.

Cor'ngar had already taken charge.

Despite the bruises and fatigue weighing on him, the orc moved with an efficiency that surprised Jacques. Under his direction—and with the help of the gray-skinned woman—the freed captives had organized themselves into something that resembled a functioning unit. Pairs split off without being told. Some hauled water from the river. Others gathered river nuts and dry brush. They dug a shallow sleeping recess, bundled palm fronds for kindling, and laid out torn blankets from the sled's tackle. Even the great sauropod had been unhitched and led to the water's edge, where it drank deeply without protest.

Jacques stood there a moment, watching it all. These people, once slaves, didn't wait for permission. They moved with purpose. No instructions, no complaints—just motion.

U'gah was eager to help. His hands hovered constantly—reaching for buckets, gesturing toward bundles—but his offers were gently declined. Not out of fear, Jacques noted, but something closer to politeness. The captives had their own rhythm. They didn't need outside help, even from someone as well-meaning as U'gah.

Florence, meanwhile, had taken up a position at the edge of camp—far enough to avoid work, close enough to remain visible. She lounged like a queen overlooking her subjects, making no move to assist. Jacques felt a flare of irritation. It wasn't laziness—it was entitlement. The same smug detachment she wore when things were under control. As if surviving the day had earned her a break while everyone else labored. She didn't lift a finger, but made sure her presence still lingered like perfume: hard to ignore, faintly cloying.

Lusa had curled up at the sled's entrance, just beside Hyatta. His giant paws tucked beneath him, feline eyes half-lidded but alert. His nub flicked lazily now and then, but his posture was clear—guarding, not sleeping. He watched over Hyatta with the quiet devotion of a sentinel. Jacques watched them for a moment, trying not to feel unnerved by the creature's dedication. Lusa's thoughts, whatever they were, remained unreadable.

Further down the riverbank, Saturn sat perched on a jagged rock. He hadn't spoken in hours. He just stared west, toward the horizon where the sun had dipped behind the teeth of the mountains. Jacques had pulled him from the wreckage, tended his wounds, and watched him detach more with every mile they walked. Now Saturn looked like a statue of someone who used to be alive—motionless, distant, drowning in thoughts that lived nowhere but in the darkest corners of his mind.

Emerald lingered nearby. Jacques noticed her watching him—frequently. Her gaze flitted to him when she thought he wasn't looking, then darted away the moment their eyes met. He caught her three, maybe four times, and each time her expression changed—like she was trying to puzzle something out. Guilt? Curiosity? Resentment? He couldn't read it. Couldn't read her. That was the unsettling part.

He didn't know if he'd done something wrong—if she was angry, or waiting for him to speak. And the not knowing—the space between them—felt heavier than it should have.

Maybe it was nothing.

Maybe it was everything.

They had been through so much, all of them, and yet the tension between them—the unsaid things, the careful silences —seemed to be growing with every passing day. And Jacques, for all his training and instinct, couldn't fix it.

With a sigh, he stepped back from the camp, letting the ambient sound of river and wind wash over him.

The silhouettes of the mountains had sharpened under the falling dusk, long shadows stretching across sand. The sun had finally disappeared behind the peaks, and with it, the worst of the heat.

"Hey, Saturn," Jacques called, his words riding gently on the quiet hum of the riverside. "Ça roule?"

Saturn didn't turn. He sat still, silhouetted against the last strands of light that clung to the horizon. When he finally spoke, his voice came flat and faraway. "Just watching the light die."

Jacques let the silence stretch for a moment, unsure how to respond. Finally, he exhaled through his nose. "That's a fairly dark way of looking at it, *mon ami.*"

The air between them buzzed with the sound of water and wind. Jacques glanced over at Saturn's posture—shoulders slightly hunched, arms draped across his knees, his eyes fixed on a vanishing sun like he was trying to outstare it. He looked worn thin, carved out by days of quiet attrition.

"Maybe," Saturn murmured. "But it feels accurate. Aside from that brief stretch in Wrasas Station, we've been bouncing between life and death. Again. And again. And again. We barely made it out of that place. And what's next? A monster under every stone? How much longer do you really think we can keep going?"

The defeat in his tone startled Jacques—not because he hadn't felt it too, but because Saturn never let it show. Cold, clinical, often frustrating—but never hopeless.

Jacques's voice softened. "I understand," he said, eyes tracing the scraggy silhouette of the mountains ahead. "I ask myself the same question. How long can we keep this up? How many near-deaths are we supposed to survive before it's one too many?" He paused. "But... the way I see it? That's not for us to decide. That's in God's hands. Our job is to keep walking."

The words came easily. Familiar comforts, worn smooth by years of repetition. But Jacques meant them. Or at least, he wanted to.

He didn't expect Saturn to let the moment pass quietly. And he was right.

"Jacques..." Saturn turned now, just slightly, just enough to show the edge in his gaze. "You know I don't believe in your God."

"I know," Jacques said. Calm. Not defensive.

Saturn scoffed—not in derision, but frustration. "I believe in science. In observation. Magic, fine, sure—it exists. But even that's just science we haven't modeled yet. And all these so-called gods? Powerful, yes. Dangerous, yes. But they aren't *divine*. Knowledge and might don't make you holy. They just make you... better armed."

Jacques didn't flinch. He'd heard it all before, a dozen variations. But this time, the weariness in Saturn's voice made it feel heavier. Not just an argument—an unraveling.

"And yet," Jacques said quietly, "here we are. Still breathing. Still surviving. Against odds that make no mathematical sense."

"That's not God," Saturn snapped, sharper now. "That's chance. Systems we don't quite understand. Probability stretched thin but not broken."

Jacques didn't argue. He let the silence come back, let it settle for a long breath before he said, "I know you don't believe. And I don't need you to. I believe enough for both of us."

He turned then, just a little, meeting Saturn's eyes in the fading light.

"But whether or not you believe in Him," he said softly, "I think He still believes in you."

Saturn didn't reply.

He looked away, back toward the mountains. The wind carried the scent of dust and water and a thousand unsaid things. Jacques didn't push further. He'd said his piece.

The silence that followed wasn't warm, but it wasn't angry, either. Just quiet. Like the dying sun.

For now, all Jacques could offer was his faith, even if it meant walking that path alone. The world around them might be chaos, might be madness, but belief was something he still had control over. It was the thread he gripped when everything else threatened to come undone.

He shifted, glancing toward the sled where Hyatta still slumped, his form half-shadowed from the firelight. Then he glanced back to Saturn, who had turned again toward the darkening sky. The road ahead would be long, full of unknowns and unseen dangers, but for the first time in days, Jacques felt a sliver of peace slip into his chest like cool water settling over hot coals. They were alive. And as long as they were alive, there was still a chance—for safety, for something better.

He cleared his throat lightly. "How about we get some food?"

Saturn stayed still, watching the horizon surrender its last light. But after a moment, he gave the barest nod—small, tired.

The first stars had begun to peek overhead when Saturn slid down from his perch, landing with a soft grunt. His small frame moved gracefully despite his age and the weight of the day behind him. Jacques watched him make his way toward the fire, where Florence was already reclining with a cup in hand. Saturn lingered a few feet back from the others, his eyes narrowing toward the freed captives huddled near the sled. His caution didn't waver. Jacques understood. Trust was a luxury none of them could afford.

Emerald approached with the warmth of firelight behind her, carrying a pewter plate in both hands. Steam curled up from the meal—river nuts, dates, and shreds of cactus boiled in a salty green wrap that smelled oddly like seaweed. The aroma was sharp but inviting.

"It's better than it looks," Emerald said with a faint smile. There was fatigue beneath her cheer, but also something softer —an appreciation, maybe, for still being here to hand him a meal at all.

Jacques accepted it with a nod, their fingers brushing briefly. "In times like these, a full belly matters more than taste. But I'll be grateful if it doesn't bite back on the way down."

His lips tugged into a smile—faint but genuine—as he examined the food. He wasn't picky. Hunger had a way of humbling a man. Still, the act of sharing a hot meal, however crude, carried its own weight. It was a thread of normalcy, something human in a place that tried to erase what being human meant.

He glanced down at the plate. Rough pewter, old but sturdy. The edge was nicked in places, like it had survived more than one lifetime.

"Where'd these come from?" he asked.

Emerald's eyes darted toward the sled, then back to him. "The new guys found them in the saddlebags," she said, gesturing toward the discarded harness still lying near the riverbank. "I guess that's what you'd call them. The gear was stuffed into pouches and cloth wraps—hard to tell what was storage and what was padding. They pulled out a lot more stuff, too."

Jacques raised an eyebrow but said nothing. He took a bite, chewed thoughtfully. It was salty and bitter, but oddly satisfying.

Emerald lingered beside him, not quite ready to walk away. The silence between them wasn't awkward. Just quiet. Not peace. But something near it.

Even with tension thick in the air, the small rituals of survival —sharing food, working together—still provided a tether. However fleeting, they still mattered. These habits were the glue, the invisible threads holding the group together, everywhere else, it's what holds a society together. Rituals like this one didn't just keep them fed. They reminded them they were still human.

"Thank you," Jacques said quietly, savoring the rare moment of stillness before the weight of tomorrow asserted itself. "Feels like it's been a long time since anything's felt... normal. Our time in the station seems like another life."

Emerald nodded, though her eyes lingered on the others. Her expression mirrored his thoughts—quiet, distant. They didn't need to say it aloud. Hope was the only thing binding them now, but beneath that fragile thread, they all knew the cost. The losses already buried, the ones that could be buried.

Jacques took another bite, chewing slowly.

Jacques had learned, long ago, to take sleep when it came. A lesson hard-won. Rest was a weapon too—one you had to wield when you could.

But Hyatta was made of something else. Or perhaps, unmade by something worse.

"You think he'll ever stop?" Emerald asked, after noting the direction of his gaze. Not pressing. Just wondering.

Jacques exhaled, the sound barely audible over the fire. His reply was slow in coming. "I don't think he knows how."

He looked down at his plate again, suddenly aware of how much effort it took Hyatta just to stay still.

Emerald didn't press him. She just made a soft noise of agreement—something between a hum and a sigh. Her eyes caught the flickering light of the fire as she watched the warriors unmoving silhouette. Around them, the camp had begun to quiet. The fire threw shifting shadows across the sand. The river whispered. The stars emerged, one by one, like wounds reopening in the dark.

For now, for a handful of stolen breaths, Jacques let himself feel something close to relief.

CHAPTER TWENTY-EIGHT

U'gah sat near the edge of camp. His club rested across his knees, heavy and impatient. Its stone teeth caught the pale skyfire of morning. The hunger inside it whispered. Quieter than in the dark hours, but not gone. Never gone.

Hunger, it had whispered in the night. **Your friends are fat. Feed me.**

He had grunted back. No. These were not prey. These were *tribe*. The club didn't choose; it only wanted blood. U'gah chose. And he would not feed it tribe.

He had learned to ignore the hunger. Like hunger in the belly. Like the ache of no mother, no brothers. Like being last.

He watched the others.

The freed ones moved with no wasted wind—prey near fire. Eyes slid away. Even after he fought their keepers. He helped free them. Didn't matter. They saw what he was. He didn't blame them. He was not like them.

The gray-skinned woman moved differently. Like smoke. Like a shadow that knew it was watched but didn't care. Umut, they called her. U'gah didn't speak the name, but he remembered it.

She moved like the old ones—bone-singers and sky-speakers from before. Like she carried the dead with her guiding the living.

He respected that.

The tusk-face, Cor'ngar, was not the same. Something in him smelled wrong. Not stink, but strange. Like a serpent under leaves.

He had not fought in the battle. But stood for the woman and others. Carried things. Protected the pup. Maybe he wasn't bad.

Still—the Earthshaker had muttered, **good meat,** the moment U'gah saw him.

He did not forget that.

His eyes found the loud female. Florence.

She sat with arms folded—angry, a stone with fire inside.

She didn't speak his words. But he could read her body easily. She was stormy—no lightning yet, but coming.

U'gah did not like storms.

Storms broke the world. Made the ground shout. Made the trees fall.

Still... something in him softened. Just a little. Like when a pup growls too loud and trips over its own feet.

She was afraid.

She didn't know it. But it was there. Fear in her heart, a thorn under skin.

U'gah scratched at his arm. He felt the itch in his chest as the freed ones left. The tall tusk-face carried bundles from the feather-lizard's sides. He walked heavy, but sure. The gray-skin held her pup close. It cried soft, like rain.

The sound twisted something in U'gah's ribs.

He scratched harder, as if he could claw it away—

But it stayed.

Like the hunger.

Like the ghost of his other tribe.

U'gah looked to the sand warrior.

Hyatta stood apart. Watching the freed ones walk into the wide sun. His face didn't move, but his body spoke. Shoulders bowed. Hands curled into rocks. Not ready for battle—full of battle all the same.

U'gah tilted his head and sniffed the wind. No scent of fear. No blood. Just dust and the bones of the fire. But he felt something anyway. Sadness.

The others didn't feel it.

Jacques was busy with his iron and leather things—rubbing, clicking, adjusting. Like he could scrub the thinking out of himself. Like if he moved fast enough, the past wouldn't catch him.

Emerald moved through the camp with soft hands and sharp eyes, giving food and smiles in equal measure. But the smiles were cracked. Just the surface. Her light didn't reach her eyes.

Florence sat apart. Arms crossed. Eyes hard. Same as always. A thundercloud that never rained.

U'gah rose.

The Earthshaker in his lap groaned. Hungry again. Always hungry. It wanted the blood and flesh, the cracking of bone, the warm joy of battle. But there was none here. Only friends.

He tapped the club on the sand.

Not now.

It grumbled but fell quiet.

He padded across the grit and dust toward Hyatta. Slow steps. Not to sneak, but to show respect. Warriors did not rush each other unless it was time to strike.

Hyatta did not turn. Did not speak. His eyes still on the horizon, watching those who were not tribe walk into the heat.

U'gah stopped just beside him. Studied the set of his jaw, the tightness around his eyes. There was something breaking inside the warrior. Not loud. Not seen. But deep. Like a crack running through fallen stone.

He didn't speak—didn't know the words anyway.

Instead, he reached out and laid his hand on Hyatta's thigh. A sign.

I am here. I see you. You are not alone.

Hyatta stiffened, just for a moment, then let the tension ease.

They stood like that, side by side, with Firefly-in-the-Sky crawling higher before them—spilling skyfire across the sand.

Stillness wrapped them.

U'gah didn't break it.

Words were for men like Jacques—clever tongues, soft speeches. But tribe spoke many ways. With hands. With shoulders. With silence.

Hyatta looked down at him. No smile. But a shift in the eyes. A softening. A glint of something human behind all that carved armor.

He gave a small nod.

U'gah grunted in return.

That nod meant more than any speech. It meant *yes*. It meant *thank you*. It meant *you matter too*.

They walked back together.

Sand shifted underfoot. Wind stirred the canvas tents. The smell of dry leather and sweat clung to the camp.

The club buzzed again in his hands. But U'gah ignored it. The club would not feed today.

And that was fine. He had his tribe.

***

Florence had never been so relieved in her entire life.

Finally, finally! The primitives were leaving—most of them, anyway—and not a moment too soon. She could breathe again. She could think again. The tension in her shoulders started to unknot the second she heard the news, and honestly, she might've smiled if she hadn't been so busy pretending not to care.

Fuck, it wasn't even about the work. Sure, it was nice not having to scrape around in the sand looking for bugs to eat or carry water like some desert mule, but that wasn't the problem. The problem was *them*. The whole lot of them. They gave her the creeps. Like being penned with barely tamed animals— sweat, muscle, and superstition.

And Cor'ngar—don't even start. That orc was the worst. Every time he was nearby, she had to fight the urge to gag. That face, that build, that *smell*—even if it wasn't *him*, even if he hadn't done anything, he looked like the one who had. The one who tried to make her a slave. Like she was property. Like she was a thing.

She could still feel that breath on her face. Still see those eyes. And now here was another one. Different name, but the same monster underneath.

Orcs. Men. Didn't matter. They were all the same.

She didn't care how polite Cor'ngar was acting. Didn't care that he was playing loyal servant to that pointy-eared, gray-skinned woman and her wailing brat. He was still an orc. And that was enough. He was just waiting. Waiting for the right moment to show his true nature. To take what he wanted.

She wouldn't be fooled again.

And that woman. That *diviner*. Please. What a joke.

Who did she think she was, gliding around the camp like some highborn priestess, never saying a word, always looking so damn composed. She held her head high like the rest of them were insects. And the worst part? The *worst* part?

It worked.

They listened to her. All of them. They watched her, waited on her, obeyed her, like she was sacred. Or like she was something holy. The great, gray savior of the desert rats. Except Lusa—thank god for Lusa. At least he had the sense to keep to himself. The rest of them, though? Hopeless.

Florence bit the inside of her cheek. Hard. Just to feel something other than the nausea.

She was the one who deserved their respect. Not that mute, self-important mystic with her creepy kid and her pet orc. Florence had survived just as much as any of them. More, in fact. She wasn't some tribalistic barbarian that could barely speak English. She was *civilized*. She knew how the world worked. Real structure. Real order. Not this sand-blown circus.

But somehow, it was always *her* on the outside.

It wasn't right. It wasn't fair.

She felt it, like the ground slipping under her boots, like gravity shifting without warning. Her place in the group was—sliding. Diminishing. People were starting to look through her or past her, even. And that?

That made her *furious*.

She tried to calm herself. Tried to breathe. *They're leaving*, she told herself. *They're going. It's almost over. Just a little longer.* She repeated it like a prayer. Like a shield. They were going to Ublaasah, wherever the hell that was, and thank the stars, they weren't coming back.

Good. Let them chase ghosts in the sand.

She'd been there when the sun started to rise—when the first rays licked across the dunes and the primitives came skulking up like they had something important to say. And of course, it was *her* again—the gray bitch—saying nothing, but looking like she'd already won the argument.

Cor'ngar did the talking.

That *voice* of his—flat and heavy. Like everything he said was calculated. He said they were going east, along the river. Said they wouldn't go to Zahadah. Not because it was unsafe—no, that would make too much sense—but because of some spiritual nonsense. Something about scorched sands and sacred ashes. As if the desert cared. As if dirt could be holy.

Florence rolled her eyes so hard it hurt.

Spiritual nonsense. All of it. Every single thing out of their mouths. Visions, omens, curses. Why did they all cling to it? Like belief was armor. Like faith would save them. She didn't buy it for a second. And Cor'ngar—he was the worst of all. Swearing on his soul to protect that woman. That *diviner*. Like she was actually divine.

Diviner.

The word stuck like a splinter. It didn't even sound real. It sounded like something made-up to feel important. She didn't understand it. What *was* she, really? What had she done that made her so special?

Why did they all fall over themselves to protect *her*?

What did Cor'ngar see in that woman that made him so ready to die?

Why did Hyatta look at her with such reverence?

Florence clenched her jaw, nails digging into her palms.

Why not her—why *never* her?

She didn't know what made the gray woman sacred.

But it made her feel *invisible*.

And she hated the woman for it.

And what had Florence gotten?

Nothing. Nothing but scorn, side-eyes, and the slow burn of being ignored. No promises. No oaths. No one swearing their life to her. No one ever had.

Just another mouth. Another nuisance. Another thing to manage or sidestep or leave behind.

Hyatta had looked grateful—*grateful*—but not to her. No. To *him*. The orc. Grateful to Cor'ngar for protecting her. *Her*, the diviner. Florence had seen it. The way he looked at her. That expression. Admiration, almost. Like she was something rare. Precious.

A holy relic, not a mother dragging a crying brat across the sand.

He should have been thanking me.

Florence had been the one holding it all together when things went to hell. She was the one who had kept her head. She hadn't broken. She hadn't run. She hadn't gone soft. But where was *her* gratitude? Where were the nods of respect? The quiet thank-yous? The offers to die in her name?

Nowhere.

All of it—every bit of it—was poured into that woman.

The one who never spoke but somehow made everyone listen.

Florence bit her lip. Hard. Just to stop herself from saying something. Anything. The heat was coming back. Creeping up her neck, crawling into her mind. The kind of heat that didn't come from the sun. The kind that made you want to scream just to hear your own voice echo back.

Good riddance, she told herself. *Let them vanish into dust.*

But it didn't help. Not really.

Because they hadn't seen her. Not once.

Not for who she was.

Not for what she'd done.

Florence didn't understand it.

And not understanding made it worse.

It clawed at her thoughts, circling—growing teeth. *Why her? Why her? What had she done? What did she have?*

Florence didn't know.

And it drove her mad.

She watched them walk away—those so-called survivors, heads bowed like pilgrims, following a woman who never spoke. As if silence itself made her holy.

The orc beside her. The child in her arms.

And all of them behind her.

Like she was leading them to salvation.

Like she was *destined*.

And Florence? Florence was just left standing there. Watching.

Forgotten, again.

The burn in her chest rose like steam.

Unfair. All of it. Just unfair.

***

Jacques tightened the sled's straps, but his mind was elsewhere —still turning over the image of the gray-skinned woman disappearing into the dunes. There was something about her he couldn't place. Something important. Something he'd missed.

He glanced at Hyatta, who worked in silence beside him. Jacques wasn't easily deterred, and curiosity was already eating away at his restraint.

"So," he said lightly, shifting back and forth between his work and the warrior, "now that they're on their way—care to explain all the reverence around that woman?"

His words came hesitantly, as if measured on a scale. "Her name is Umut—a Siva'gat diviner."

Jacques raised an eyebrow. "She's from your tribe then? Why did she look so different from you?"

Hyatta's shoulders drew in slightly. "Yes. But she is of a different caste." It came out rote, like scripture repeated too many times. "The Siva'gat are many peoples. Most are Halk. I am Evlat—the adopted."

Jacques frowned, turning the words over in his mind. "And a diviner? That sounds like an important job."

Hyatta met his gaze for a beat, and Jacques caught the ghost of something in his eyes—grief, maybe. Or memory. "Diviners are more than spiritual leaders. They sense water. They guide our caravans, our warbands. Without them, many would die in the dune sea."

That landed heavier than Jacques expected. He nodded slowly. "And why did Umut only speak to you and Cor'ngar?"

Hyatta's posture stiffened at her name. His gaze drifted. "It is... unheard of," he said quietly. "For a diviner to be treated as Umut has. Even among desert orcs. She was forced to bear her shame to the world in the form of a child." He paused, his jaw tight. "Because of her rank—her pride—she must keep apart. Especially from outsiders."

Jacques tilted his head. "I don't follow."

Hyatta sighed, a deep, weathered sound. "I am still of her tribe. A different caste, yes—but one of her people. And Cor'ngar... he offered himself to her as a tribute for what his kin did to her. He became hers." His hands flexed at his sides, as if the words themselves strained muscle. "We can bear her shame with her.

442

But you, Jacques—you and the others—you are not Siva'gat. Speaking to her, in her state, would bring dishonor."

Jacques stood quiet. The weight of it all settled like iron filings in his lungs.

This wasn't about mysticism or tradition alone. It was a matter of personal honor.

And Umut—silent, distant, carrying the burden of a child not hers by choice—was not just another survivor. But something —someone shattered.

He looked at Hyatta, and for the first time, saw not just the warrior, but the fracture beneath.

"Damn," Jacques murmured, mostly to himself.

Umut's role in all this was far more than he'd ever guessed.

"Shame..." Jacques echoed softly, the word coating his tongue. He was starting to piece it together—the layers, the rules, the silence. Hyatta had always carried his people's pride like a standard, and now Jacques saw why.

Wait, the child had tusks.

Realization hammered into him like the flood waters from a broken dam.

"I'm sorry," Jacques said, the words sincere and unsteady. "I didn't realize... I didn't think..."

He hadn't seen it before—not truly. Something so vile, his sensibilities refused to allow him to consider it until faced with irrefutable proof. And the child wasn't just evidence. He was a mark. A scar of something no one was allowed to name.

A sign of what had been done to her.

"What's done is done," Hyatta said quietly. His voice was calm, but Jacques could hear the strain beneath it—like a fraying thread. "She will travel to Gabutha. The council will decide how she may regain her honor."

Jacques studied him.

Hyatta's posture was rigid. But his eyes—those pale, milky blue eyes—held sadness and worry. He'd seen this before. He'd watched someone live through it.

He had been a witness.

And yet... Jacques couldn't make peace with it. Couldn't square it in his mind—the idea that someone's worth, their place in the world, could be decided by strangers sitting in judgment in some far-off city.

"That doesn't seem fair," he said, the words slipping out before he could stop them. "She had no control over what was done to her. What gives them the right to decide anything on her behalf?"

Hyatta's eyes flashed—angry—but his face regained its composure quickly. When he answered, it was with a quiet finality that cut deeper than any outburst.

"It is the way things are—and the way things are done."

The words were too simple. Jacques heard what was buried underneath—the tension, the unease. Hyatta didn't believe it. But he had accepted it. Carved it into himself like all the other hard truths he carried.

He could see it now, in the set of Hyatta's shoulders, the subtle drift of his gaze. This wasn't loyalty to tradition.

It was endurance.

Another lesson, Jacques thought. Another culture. Another brutal custom that made perfect sense to the people inside it— and felt impossibly cruel to anyone else.

"But it's not right," he muttered, mostly to himself, looking anywhere except at his companion. "She didn't choose any of this. And yet she has to bear the consequences."

Hyatta gave a single nod. Not agreement, but acknowledgment. The conversation was over.

He turned back to the sled. Checked the bindings. Adjusted the reins. Routine movements, but purposeful. Jacques joined him in silence, helping without comment. There was nothing else to say.

Still, as he worked, a thought lingered.

Maybe Hyatta wasn't just following custom.

Maybe carrying Umut's shame—her burden—wasn't about rules at all.

Maybe that was why Hyatta had refused to rest on the journey to the river. Why his eyes always seemed to scan the horizon, as if searching for something he'd already lost. Or possibly something they had both lost.

Because some weights weren't handed down.

Some you choose to carry.

Once the sled was secured to the feathered sauropod's harness, Jacques made his way to the river. He crouched at the edge, cupping handfuls of cold water to scrub the grime from his hands. The coarse sand along the bank served as a natural abrasive, grinding away the layers of sweat and dirt. He worked methodically, his thoughts still circling around Hyatta's stoic acceptance, the weight of a tradition Jacques couldn't fully grasp, and the quiet, unwavering strength of the man himself.

"That beast is an abomination," came Saturn's voice, irritated, almost angry.

Jacques stiffened but didn't turn. He wasn't ready to let go of the thoughts trailing Hyatta. The man was a puzzle—threaded with duty, pride, and was breaking beneath it all. Jacques didn't know how to unravel that kind of knot, but he suspected understanding it was the key to knowing who Hyatta really was.

"What beast?" Jacques asked, glancing over his shoulder. Saturn stood a few paces back, his small frame blending into the rock and dust because of the passive camouflage of his uniform, courtesy of Wrasas Station.

"Did you see a fish you didn't like?"

"What? No." Saturn blinked, visibly startled. "Did I say that out loud?"

"Oui, mon ami." Jacques paused his scrubbing, giving him a dry look. "What beast are you talking about?"

"The sauropod," Saturn said, voice drifting like it belonged to a different conversation. "It shouldn't exist."

Jacques straightened, drying his hands on a strip of cloth. "Why? Because of the feathers?"

"Yes," Saturn said, more firmly now, his tone regaining some focus. "It's a saurischian—lizard-hipped. They're not supposed to have plumage. Maybe sparse proto-feathers or thin integumentary filaments at most. But this?" He gestured vaguely.

Jacques raised an eyebrow. "So the feathers are what make it an abomination? Bit dramatic for a glorified draft animal."

"This isn't about drama. Or aesthetics." Saturn's eyes met his, sharp now, but grounded. "It doesn't fit the fossil record. It doesn't fit anything. Which means it was engineered. Or altered."

Jacques shook the last of the sand from his fingers. "Seems like everything here has been engineered in some way. That one happens to be useful. And friendly. I'll take it."

"That's a very reductive way to look at it," Saturn replied. The spark behind his words dulling with each sentence. "But maybe that's fitting. Given where we are."

Jacques studied him.

There it was again—that quiet, hollow exhaustion Saturn couldn't quite hide. He was still brilliant, but some days it felt like he was speaking through glass. Like the world had retreated from him, and he wasn't sure if he wanted it back.

Jacques considered saying something, anything to pull him out of whatever mental seclusion he was slipping into.

But nothing came to mind.

The silence turned thick and awkward.

So he said nothing. Just stood beside him, uselessly dusting his hands, letting the sound of the water fill the space where comfort should have been.

When Jacques did open his mouth to speak, Emerald's approach spared him the effort.

Her steps were light but purposeful, boots whispering over the sand, barely audible above the river's hiss. For a moment, with the sun behind her and the shimmer of her armor blending into the desert's muted palette, she looked less like a lab tech and more like a green-haired Valkyrie dropped from myth—short in stature, but somehow larger than the heat-hazed horizon behind her. One rifle hung from her shoulder, two more were strapped neatly across her back.

"The others are ready to go," she said, casting a glance between Jacques and Saturn before landing her gaze on Jacques. "Florence is starting to complain—louder than usual."

Jacques let out a quiet chuckle, tension breaking at the edges. "Ah, bien sûr. Can't have Florence upset. The whole day might collapse."

Emerald's lips curved into a small smile. She brushed a strand of grass-colored hair behind her ear with the unconscious ease of someone long practiced in staying composed.

"Ready when you are, Jacques."

Her tone was light, almost breezy—but there was a warmth underneath it that caught him off guard. He had been certain she was upset with him earlier—about what, he wasn't entirely sure—but now she looked up at him with eyes softer than he'd expected.

Maybe he'd imagined the distance. Or maybe she was just better than he was at compartmentalizing—setting aside whatever was under the surface when duty called.

"Fantastique," Jacques said, gesturing for them to head back. "Allons-y."

His voice was even, but his thoughts lagged behind. Had she really been fine this whole time? Had the shift in her tone been nothing more than stress, or had he simply misread her demeanor? Best not to linger on it. They had enough to worry about without unraveling emotional knots in the middle of the desert.

They returned to camp beneath the harsh stare of the sun. Its light scintillated off the crystalline sand, the heat drawing a haze across the horizon.

The others had already gathered. Florence leaned against a date palm with a scowl that looked capable of spoiling milk. Lusa lounged nearby, his nub ticking lazily with metronomic accuracy, though his eyes—sharp as ever—missed nothing. U'gah stood a little apart, the Earthshaker resting on his shoulder like a totem.

Hyatta had fashioned a shaded perch atop the beast's back using braided rawhide, a tarp, and feathers stripped from the creature itself. He sat beneath it, patient and silent.

"About time," Florence snapped, her voice cutting across the camp like a whip. "Do you know how hot it's getting out here?"

Jacques exhaled through his nose but said nothing. Feeding her irritation would only stretch the day longer. Instead, he walked to the sled and began checking its bindings one last time.

Emerald joined him, her movements efficient and quiet. Where Florence radiated friction, Emerald hummed with calm utility.

As Jacques worked, he found his gaze drifting toward her more than once, curiosity nudging at him. What was behind the shifts in her mood? Was it him? Or something else entirely?

"Ready when you are, boss," Emerald said, snapping him out of it. Her use of the title—unexpected—landed with a meaning he couldn't quite pin down.

Jacques nodded, his focus returning to the task at hand. "Alright," he said. "Let's move out. Stay sharp. Keep close."

CHAPTER TWENTY-NINE

he forest wrapped U'gah's spirit in cool hands. Shade between the tall giants. Soil underfoot again. The skyfire softened.

Here, the trees whispered instead of burned.

With each step under the green roof, the knots inside him loosened.

Even Hyatta changed.

The sand-warrior—always iron, always fire—now leaned back, relaxing. Skin raw from skyfire burn. Golden hair streaked silver like claw marks. He did not speak. Just rested against a tree. Shoulders soft. Like a beast letting go of its burden.

U'gah had never seen such a thing.

The river called them soon after.

It ran fast and clear, cold as winter. Jacques went first—wading deep with a grunt and a sigh. Saturn and Emerald followed, all quiet relief. Florence made faces, dipping one foot as if it might bite her.

U'gah dove.

He splashed and snorted, arms wide. The cold hit him like a hunt call. Grit sluiced from skin. Muscles remembered life. Even the hunger in the club dulled—as if the spirit inside were listening to the water sing.

The others washed.

U'gah wandered.

He sniffed the earth. He dug tubers—fat, sweet, dirt-covered things—and found herbs in the green places—sharp-scented, good for stew. Wild garlic made his nose twitch. He grunted. Good.

Lusa returned last. Ibex over both shoulders. Horns like Grandfather's smile. Eyes smug. Teeth bright. A hunter's pride.

U'gah rumbled deep, pleased. The cat always brought meat. Clean kills. Enough for tribe.

Smoke rose soon. Herbs and blood and meat mixed in the air. Hunger became joy. The stew pot bubbled. The meat turned golden. Tubers melted soft.

Even Florence smiled.

She bit into meat with fury and no complaint. Her only bark came when Hyatta lay near the fire on soft cloth, bare but unworried. She flailed her arms and made sharp noises. Said "knickers" like a curse. Her anger, as always, was sound without teeth.

U'gah did not know this word.

Hyatta didn't move. Hands behind his head. Face calm. The sand-warrior did not fear loud winds.

The fire was warm. The stew was good.

And U'gah... U'gah felt full.

Not just in belly. In heart, too.

For now, the ghosts were quiet. The hunger stilled. The forest sheltered them.

And his tribe was whole.

The day drifted like the lazy river—slow and quiet.

The desert had burned skin almost to bone. Tested them all— muscle, spirit, heart. But the mountain watched now. The trees stood guard. No danger whispered from the shadows. Just birds. Wind. Fire crackle.

U'gah sat alone, club resting across his lap. The stone beast was quiet now. Sated. His hand moved over its carved skin, stubby finger brushing the deep lines of spirit-runes. The club did not speak, but he felt it listening.

He thought of the before-times.

Laughter around fire. Small feet in snow. Sparks dancing into the dark. The taste of meat passed hand to hand. Warmth in heart.

He missed it. Every part.

The forest gave peace, but not silence.

Tomorrow, they would climb into the old lands. Into blood-memory.

The ghosts waited.

He would bring his new tribe there. His brothers. His sisters. The cat. He would lead them into the grave of his home.

The servants of the Mother had taken it. Killed the dens. Crushed the drums. Ripped roots from earth. They had not stopped. Had tried to kill the new pack too.

The club stirred. A tremble. Faint. Like breath held in a beast's chest.

It knew.

U'gah ran a hand along its teeth. Spirit-carved. Taken in the scaly-skin ruins, under the smiling face of Grandfather Brightrock. The spirit of the Earthshaker had found him with the club. Fed him strength. Demanded blood. Demanded flesh.

And now—vengeance.

He would offer it. A gift for the old ones. For the fallen.

They needed to know. His tribe. The new tribe. They needed to understand the mountain was not just a place. It was a wound. It bled still.

He would speak the truth. In the grave of his people. He would call their names into the wind. Let the spirits rise. Let them know they were not forgotten.

The Mother's children had tried to wipe them from the world.

But U'gah still breathed.

He carried every name. Every howl. Every tear and song.

There would be vengeance.

His fur lifted as the memory came—jagged and red-edged.

The pale ones. The children. The herald with his bleeding staff and rot-breath promises. The monsters that smiled with mouths too wide. They had come with peace in their claws, come as friends, left as killers.

He had failed.

U'gah had wanted to fight.

He growled. Just for himself.

Coward. Pup. Fool.

But never again.

Not while he still had teeth. Not while he had tribe. Not while he had the power of the Earthshaker.

The club throbbed beneath his hand. Not words. But agreement. A hunger shared.

And next time—it would be fed.

Fire crackled nearby.

He would not fail again.

Next time, the claws would strike. The teeth would sink. No more fear. The Earthshaker would feed. The tribe would be protected. And the shaman's fury—the weight of every howl silenced in the forest—would fall like a mountain on the servants of the Mother.

He gripped the memories tight.

They were bitter. Sacred. They cut him—but they kept him standing. Loss wrapped around his ribs like old cloth. It burned, but it gave him strength. Gave him purpose.

He held the club close. His claws ran over the rough skin of it, a hand seeking a brother. He didn't know if the spirit inside could share the pain.

But it was the only one that might.

Sleep took him. Like sinking in tar. Like being pulled into the grave by unseen hands.

The herald came first.

Tall. Stinking. Skin leaking pus-light through robes that reeked of poison and disease. Staff like rotting wood—alive and hungry. Whisper like snake-breath. Promises of peace. Eyes of betrayal. U'gah felt his soul recoil.

Then came the pale ones.

Ash-skin. Bone-white. They moved like a flood with claws. Fast. They howled with hunger. They tore through his kin. Warriors fell. Elders. Women. Children…

The screams became one voice.

Then—

His new tribe.

Jacques shouting, firm but afraid. Hyatta in front, whip of firelight spinning. The monster—tall as the sky—pushed them back. The cliff cracked. Stone broke. They fell.

And U'gah watched.

He could do nothing.

The worst came last.

He saw himself.

Not bear. Not halfling.

Pale skin. Long fingers. Black claws. Dripping red.

He wanted to scream.

But his jaws moved without him.

He was bent over Jacques. Tearing. Chewing. Hot blood in his mouth. Muscle tearing under his teeth.

No, no, no!

He begged, silent. Inside his skull.

But his body did not listen.

He was a servant now. Of her.

A monster.

And the blood was warm.

He woke with a gasp.

His own breath dragged him back.

Chest heaved. Hands shook. Fire still crackled. The world was soft again. Morning breath through the leaves.

But something held him still.

Not rope. Not claw.

Warmth.

A hand in his fur. Small. Slow. Stroking.

His head rested on something soft.

A voice hummed above him. Words too quiet to catch. Not words, maybe. Just sound. Woman-sound.

Lullaby.

His breath slowed.

Smoke filled his nose.

The storm in his chest began to settle.

The nightmare's claws loosened.

And for the first time in many nights, U'gah did not feel alone.

U'gah opened his eyes.

World, still half-dream.

The melody was still there. Gentle. Soft. Like moss underfoot. And the hand in his fur moved slow, steady. Not grooming. Not cleaning. Calming.

His gaze drifted up, through the shadowed green. Hair like leaves after rain—Emerald's hair. Glowing faint against the dark, like ghost-fire through canopy.

She sat cross-legged. His head rested on her thigh, the way pups lay on mothers when the world was wrong. Her fingers moved through his hair like water. Careful. Rhythmic.

It stirred something old.

A memory buried.

Before the servants of the Mother came. Before the fire. Before the screams.

His mother's hands. Smaller than his now. Brushing back fear. Humming old songs that made nightmares shrink. She would hold him like this. Touch him like this. And the darkness would wait outside the circle of firelight.

Emerald's song was not the same, but it held the same shape. The same spirit. It was not for him—but it found him anyway.

He did not move.

Her face was far away. Lost in thought. Eyes not on him. On something else. Or nothing. Firelight danced across her skin, and he saw the worry written there, faint like scars that no longer bled.

The peace was fragile. Like a rabbit in tall grass. Move too fast and he feared it would flee.

He let it hold him.

For too long, he had run—from guilt, from the clawed hand of memory. But here, with Emerald's hand in his fur, and the tribe around him, he felt safe. Grounded.

His gaze shifted.

Hyatta stood at the edge of light, back turned. Like a tree guarding the forest. The warrior's skin no longer angry, but his posture was rigid.

Jacques sat near, pistol resting in his lap. Loose. Casual. But ready. Always ready. U'gah knew the steel beneath the calm.

Lusa sprawled by the fire. Ears twitching. Eyes lazy, but never still.

Florence curled alone. Knees tight. Face hidden. But her spine spoke—stiff, bristled. Uneasy, even here.

They circled him.

Not with arms or words—

With presence.

A ring. A wall. A pack.

Without asking, they had taken watch. Guarded him. As he slept.

U'gah's chest ached from thanks.

These were his tribe now. Not blood. But chosen. Fire-forged. Sorrow-bound.

When the old tribe fell, he thought all was lost.

But they had built something new.

And now, when the ghosts clawed at him, these ones stood between him and the dark.

Emerald's hand paused in his fur.

U'gah tensed—half expecting the spell to break, the warmth to vanish. But her fingers moved again, same rhythm, same care. Like waves on shore.

He let his eyes fall closed.

Let the moment hold him.

Let it cover him like hidecloth.

Morning came too fast.

Skyfire crept through the trees like a thief—gold-tipped fingers poking at his eyes. He blinked, growled in his chest. He would have stayed in that sleep forever if he could.

But something had changed.

The evil thoughts were gone. Not far, but not clinging. Not biting. Emerald had chased them. With voice. With touch. With tribe-magic older than words.

He sat up slow.

Camp was already down. Packs packed. Fire out. Tribe quiet.

They had not shaken him. Had not barked. Had not dragged him forward like dead meat.

They had let him sleep.

That was gift. That was honor.

His throat tightened.

He strapped on his pack—it was worn to the shape of his back. Old straps. Good smell. He checked the satchel next. His treasure still inside. Safe.

To the others, it was nothing. A relic.

But to him, it was a symbol of his new life with his new tribe.

Last, he lifted the Earthshaker.

The club welcomed him with a pulse.

Always hungry.

He shushed it. Not yet.

It grumbled, but obeyed.

He joined the others as they began to walk. The river led them —a silver snake winding through green and shadow. Firefly-in-the-Sky was steady above, dividing time as it should.

The forest thickened. Trees grew taller, reaching like spears to the sky. Their arms touched, knitting a roof of green above.

The air changed. Cooler. Thinner. Wet-earth and pine-needle smell.

He felt it.

The slope beneath their feet was no longer gentle.

They were climbing.

The land remembered him.

And he remembered it.

His people had walked here. Hunted here. Died here.

Home.

His belly twisted. Muscles clenched. Not hunger.

Shame. Fear.

Twice, he had to slip away. Into trees. Behind rocks. Stomach tight, body weak.

His scent turned foul. A coward's stench.

He returned each time silent. Ashamed. But Lusa saw.

The third time, the Mau was waiting.

Perched on a branch like an orange omen. Eyes like knives dipped in honey.

Smiling without smiling. Mocking. Knowing.

U'gah's lips curled back. Teeth bared. A growl rolled up his throat, more from shame than anger.

The Mau did not flinch.

He just watched.

U'gah looked away first.

U'gah growled. Real this time.

The smug-cat sat above him. Lusa's orange fur shimmered in the shifting skyfire, and his eyes gleamed with the soundless laughter only hunters knew.

U'gah's growl deepened. Ants in his chest—no breath, only sting.

He was already full of shame. The Mau's smile poured more on.

Lusa tilted his head. No words.

Down the branch.

The Mau hit the ground like a leaf falls. His steps said *I see you*, but nothing else.

U'gah curled his fingers. Nails into palm. The sting helped. A little.

His growl faded. Fear had found its place.

In battle. In the dark. He could be brave. When the prey was large and teeth were few.

But this? This wasn't that kind of fear.

This was worse.

He wasn't afraid of beasts.

He was afraid of tribe.

Of what they would see when they learned the truth.

His belly turned again. Sickness. Shame.

He had failed his people.

In silence. In waiting.

The servants of the Mother had come. He had not stopped them. He had not fought. He had been sent away.

And the tribe had died.

Now these new ones—they trusted him. They walked with him.

He didn't know if they should.

Would Jacques still call him brother?

Would Hyatta, the chain-bearer, still nod without question?

Would Emerald's warmth still be given?

Even Florence, with her sharp tongue and scowling face—would her disdain burn worse when it turned true?

He clenched his teeth. Ground them.

No more hiding.

They needed to know.

The Mother's servants had reached his mountain. They had swarmed the god-cave. That meant they could reach anywhere. They had marked Hyatta already. And the Mother did not forgive slights.

She followed blood.

U'gah's hands tightened around the club's shaft. The stone felt warm. Listening.

He would speak.

Even if it meant losing the tribe.

They had to know.

But—

Part of him wanted to wait.

Wanted to bring them to the ruins. To the den. To the bones.

Let the broken stones speak louder than words.

Let them *see* the silence that had killed his people.

Then maybe—maybe they wouldn't turn from him.

The forest moved around him. Soft and green. But he saw none of it.

Only the war inside his chest.

462

But through that fog—Lusa again.

The Mau always knew.

When U'gah vanished, Lusa would pull the eyes another way.

Speak to Jacques.

Point out a strange tree for Saturn to study.

Stoke Florence's fire until she howled louder than U'gah's absence.

And the others—never noticed.

At first, U'gah thought the Mau would call him out.

Mock him in front of tribe.

But he didn't.

He shielded him.

Silently.

And yet—always a price.

Lusa would fall back just to snicker.

Snap a twig too loud. Rustle leaves when U'gah crouched in shame.

He made sure U'gah knew he knew.

It was a game. A test. A hunt with no kill.

And U'gah—caught in it.

Running from his guts. From his truth. From his shame.

But the Mau made sure no one else saw.

But just when U'gah started to believe the Mau had a heart—hidden somewhere beneath that smug pelt—Lusa would bare his fangs and snicker.

Not loud. Not like a fool.

Just the twitch of whiskers. The gleam of teeth.

Sometimes worse.

Lusa made it a game.

And U'gah—played it.

Until the path narrowed.

Until the mountain began to whisper in the trees again. Shadows long and watching.

The trail twisted through green like a vein through mountain.

Ahead was ruin.

The bones of his people's home.

U'gah stopped.

His pack stopped behind him.

His stomach still churned. But this time, it wasn't fear alone. His body sagged under the weight of all it had carried. Sides aching from too many purges. His backside was raw from crouching in shame too often.

He stared ahead.

The trail was just dirt.

But it felt like fire.

And then, it came—clear and cold as mountain water:

He was tired—not just in bone or belly, but in spirit.

Tired of hiding. Of carrying dead weight like chains across his back. Tired of fearing a future he hadn't even met.

His hands closed around the Earthshaker.

The club's spirit stirred.

U'gah breathed deep. Let the mountain air in. Let the past breathe out.

And then... he smiled.

First smile in many days.

He looked back.

Lusa sat on a low branch, licking his paw like nothing mattered. Golden eyes flicked up.

U'gah smiled wider.

Thank you, he thought.

Lusa tilted his head. Ears flicked. No reply. Of course not.

He dropped from the branch, stretched like a lazy shadow, and walked on without a word.

U'gah chuckled once. The Mau would never admit it.

But he had helped.

In his way.

U'gah stepped forward.

U'gah led now.

Not because he was strongest.

But because he remembered. Because the earth beneath his feet remembered him.

And the past no longer held him by the throat.

He still felt the shaking in his bones. Still heard the voice of the cowardly pup he used to be.

But that pup was gone.

He was stronger now. And his tribe—fire-hearted, storm-bound, sharp as burned mountain glass—was stronger still.

If the Mother came hunting…

She would learn she was not the hunter.

She was the prey.

CHAPTER THIRTY

Hyatta had been watching U'gah closely since they entered the forest. The bergbar's unease wasn't subtle—it pulsed off him like heat, building with every step into the mountains. His usual energy, the boundless movement and helpful grunts, had vanished. In its place was silence. Tight, coiled silence. Like unseen forces were pressing in around him.

Even through the sting of his own burns, Hyatta couldn't ignore it. U'gah wasn't quiet. He was always humming, muttering, laughing at his own jokes. His absence in the rhythm of the group left a hollow note. One Hyatta felt—as if he were missing a small piece of himself.

Lusa didn't help. The Mau slipped through the forest, always reappearing just in time to needle U'gah with sharp comments or the exaggerated snap of a twig. It wasn't malice—more like mischief—but it dug deep. Hyatta could see it in U'gah's jaw, the way his grip tightened on the greatclub, his growl curling beneath the surface.

But the outburst never came.

Instead, the shaman's anger curled inward. Whatever storm he carried lay raw in a shallow grave—well within reach of Lusa's jabs.

Hyatta's concern tightened. U'gah wasn't just a guide or a fighter—he *felt* things. The land. The sky. If he was on edge, it wasn't for nothing.

So Hyatta watched, keeping his distance. Let his posture remain loose while his attention stayed focused. U'gah trailed behind the group, glancing ahead as if something might emerge from the underbrush. And the others? Jacques marched with his usual discipline, one hand never far from his god-wrought weapon. Emerald flitted between them, green hair catching the light, offering words Hyatta couldn't hear but sensed were kind. Saturn trailed behind her, eyes locked on the trees as if they held answers only he could see. And Florence—Florence sulked at the rear, mouth drawn, arms folded like armor.

Then U'gah moved forward.

Not skittish. Not unsure. Just *forward*. His grip on the greatclub was steady. His stride, purposeful.

Hyatta felt the shift. It wasn't loud—but it was a fine sight.

When U'gah passed him, Hyatta met his gaze. What stared back wasn't the playful bear he'd grown to trust, but someone who could—and did—accept the weight he had to carry. Tempered by decision. The fear was still there, but it no longer overwhelmed him.

U'gah had made peace with whatever waited ahead—or at least, found the will to meet it.

Hyatta gave a slow nod. A silent vow. Whatever truth weighed on U'gah's chest—whatever burden he carried like a boulder milling him to powder—Hyatta would bear witness. For now, it was the bergbar's alone to shoulder. But soon, it would belong to all of them.

The path narrowed as they climbed, twisting into shadow beneath the trees. Hyatta adjusted the coil of his chain-whip at his side, fingers brushing bright links. The air grew still—not peaceful, but tense. The kind of stillness that raised the fine hairs.

The quiet before something broke.

"Lead on," Hyatta said. Steady, though the wind had gone still around them. "We're with you."

U'gah glanced back. His expression shifted—just a little. Enough for the ghost of a smile to surface. The first since they'd begun ascending the mountains. It was a spark of the shaman's old light, breaking through the fear and melancholy. Hyatta held onto that moment.

They needed every scrap of light they could carry.

As the broken remnants of the bergbar village came into view, Hyatta felt it before he saw it—a pressure in the lungs, a coil in the gut. The songs of the forest had gone quiet. No birdsong. No rustling leaves. No insect hum. Only silence.

Stillness saturated the place with a vile, oily spirit. The kind left behind after something terrible passed through and *fed* on a place.

The trees thinned. Their bark dulled to gray. Leaves hung limp and dying. Life drained. The path underfoot turned jagged, scattered with stones that felt sharp and unnatural.

Hyatta's muscles tensed. His hand drifted to the chain-whip at his hip. He didn't need to say anything. The others felt it too. The atmosphere itself had changed.

U'gah walked ahead, greatclub across his shoulder. No more growls. No jokes. No humming songs. Just slow steps, each one heavier than the last. His eyes were wet, his shoulders hunched under invisible weight. He looked smaller somehow, as though the place had begun to claim him before they even crossed its threshold.

Hyatta watched him closely. The bergbar's steps faltered. Not dramatically—but enough to be noticed. His breath had gone shallow. Like the air itself resisted him.

Still, he kept walking.

When the first remnants of broken stone and shattered wood appeared through the thinning trees, Hyatta raised a hand. The group halted behind him without a word. Even the sauropod— their stolen beast of burden—shifted uneasily, snorting at the scent in the air. It stamped the earth, eyes wide.

Hyatta turned to Jacques. Their eyes met.

"We leave the beast here," Hyatta said, voice firm. "It doesn't belong in that place."

Jacques nodded and moved to unbuckle the packs from the creature's harness. His motions were swift, practiced. Saturn and Emerald joined him in silence. Even Emerald's usual brightness had dimmed to something quiet and mournful. The hush around them did not allow for levity.

Florence stood back, arms crossed tight across her chest, mouth drawn into a bitter line. She said nothing. But the stiffness in her stance said she felt it too.

Hyatta turned his gaze back to U'gah, who stood rigid at the threshold of his ruined home. The shaman's broad frame was stiff with tension, his silence louder than any war cry.

Hyatta stepped closer. "Are you ready?"

U'gah glanced at him. The sadness in his eyes caught the faint light, gleaming against the deep shadows of his fur. "Doesn't matter if I am," he conveyed, his grunts overflowing with emotion, every gesture dripping grief. "The spirits call. Their story must be told."

Hyatta nodded, understanding the burden behind those words. He turned and motioned the others forward as U'gah took the lead, stepping into the hollowed-out remains of the village.

The first thing Hyatta noticed was that time had abandoned this place. The homes, once shaped by strong hands and filled with firelight, now stood like carcasses picked clean. Beams jutted from the earth like broken ribs. Roofs sagged under decay. The ground was scattered with fragments—pottery shards, faded cloth, tools left where they'd been dropped and trampled into the dirt.

Signs of violence were everywhere. Deep claw marks gouged through wood and mud-brick, savage and wide. Bloodstains, long since dried, marked the dry places like scars. Fire pits lay cold and ruined, their stones scattered as though flung by monstrous hands. Whatever had happened here, it had come fast and ended brutally.

The warband followed in silence, their expressions grim. Jacques moved like the soldier he was, weapon drawn, scanning edges and corners. Emerald stayed close to him, her wide eyes darting from ruin to ruin with one of her long rifles pressed to her shoulder. Saturn studied the debris with a scholar's precision. And Florence was quiet, her usual scowl dulled by the atmosphere. Only Lusa was absent, vanished like dust in a breeze—scouting, likely, or hunting.

U'gah stopped at the heart of the village. The circle, once a place for gathering, now lay choked in a litter of broken bones. He planted his greatclub in the dirt like a grave marker. His head bowed. His shoulders rose and fell with deep, rhythmic breaths.

Hyatta moved to stand beside him. Just near enough to offer comfort, not intrusion. This wasn't his moment. This was a battlefield U'gah had to walk, but he would not be far.

The silence stretched, broken only by wind brushing through the tops of splintered trees. Then U'gah began to chant.

His voice rumbled deep and rough, like stone scraping stone. He spoke in the old tongue—the language of ancestors and spirits. The cadence was foreign, but Hyatta didn't need translation. He felt it. A mourning. A reckoning. A vow.

Hyatta's grip tightened on his chain-whip. The shadows around them felt substantial. As if this place hadn't let go of what happened here.

It was a wound.

And it was still bleeding.

Even with his ruined eyes—vision warped, edges softened like shadows in fog—he could feel it. Danger. Not immediate, but waiting. Shapes of buildings loomed in his periphery like ghosts trapped behind smoked glass. The air was still, stale, and thick with the weight of memory.

He slowed his breath. Listened. A creak of weathered timber. The faint rustle of ash and old leaves. But his instincts tugged at him.

So when U'gah's hand settled on his arm—warm, solid—it caught him off guard.

Hyatta turned, clouded blue eyes narrowing as he tried to read the halfling's face. U'gah looked worn, energy dulled, but there was something grounding in his touch.

Hyatta's shoulders eased a fraction.

U'gah grunted, nodding toward a patch of cracked earth near the heart of the ruins. His broad fingers brushed the haft of his greatclub, and the stone weapon gave a low, hungry rumble— as if it, too, understood what lay beneath the soil.

The shaman leaned in close; he wanted to make camp. Here, in the shadow of what had been. Hyatta caught the weight behind it—the resolve. This was to be a ritual. The story would be told here.

He gave a short nod to the shaman.

Hyatta turned from the bergbar and stepped back. His voice, worn hoarse by sand, rose just enough to carry.

"Set camp. We stay here tonight."

Hyatta returned to U'gah as the others set about their task. The bergbar had already lowered himself onto the broken earth, his greatclub beside him like a sleeping beast. The carved teeth of it glinted faintly in the dying light, the runes etched in its hide whispering to whatever spirits remained here.

Hyatta crouched nearby, boots crunching softly on dead roots and gravel. His chain-whip coiled loose in his hand, not threatening—just present. His stance mirrored the moment. Calm, but ready.

"You're certain?" he asked U'gah.

The shaman didn't answer with words. His gaze met Hyatta's, dark and heavy with sorrow, and resolve carved deep from the mountain that was U'gah's spirit. This wasn't just about one bergbar.

Hyatta nodded and stood.

This was grief. This was ceremony.

This was war.

The fire caught quickly, its low flames licking at dry wood, casting long, writhing shadows across the ruins. It didn't warm the air—nothing could.

They gathered around the flame with quiet caution. Weariness rode their shoulders, but something more clung to them: dread.

Even Lusa, freshly returned from the treeline without a kill, slunk into a crouch near the edge of the firelight. No teasing words. No gloating. Just silence, golden eyes watchful.

Hyatta stood apart, back to the group, his milky gaze trained on the treeline beyond the ruined homes. He couldn't see well— but he could feel. The quiet here wasn't natural. It wasn't rest. It was the stillness that comes after a mass grave. Something had lingered. Perhaps still did. He kept his chain-whip close at hand.

But this moment belonged to U'gah.

The shaman sat cross-legged, his posture grounded and unmoving, a bulwark against the dark. From his throat came a low chant—deep, rhythmic, almost subsonic. The sound crawled into the soil, settled into the bones of the village. It vibrated through the ruined circle like the beat of an old drum.

The others huddled close to the fire, sipping Emerald's thin soup without complaint. The broth was little more than boiled herbs and warmth, but after the climb and the silence, it passed as comfort.

Hyatta stayed where he was. The chanting grew deeper, fuller. Each sound felt old—older than the fire, older than the ruins. Words meant for the dead, not the living.

Then the wind turned.

It rolled down from the peaks like it had been waiting. Cold. Biting. It swept across the clearing in a single gust, snuffing the edges of the fire—then igniting it anew.

The flames twisted violently, surging upward with a hiss. They bloomed into color not meant for the world of men: violet, sickly green, filaments of azure and corpse-white. The fire danced like something alive—and ill, and the shadows it cast moved against the shapes that made them.

Florence yelped, jerking back and spilling her bowl. Jacques and Emerald exchanged concerned glances, hands drifting to weapons by instinct. Saturn cocked his head, eyes narrowing with cautious fascination. Lusa's gaze locked on the fire.

Even the sauropod outside the ruin gave a low, uneasy moan.

Hyatta's pulse quickened. His whole body screamed for action.

But he didn't move.

He watched U'gah.

The halfling was the eye of the storm. His chant had stopped, but the power had not. Mist rolled in from the trees, not drifting but creeping—intentional, slow, and thick. It wound around the shattered timber and broken stones. It lapped at ruined doorframes like a tide reclaiming its dead.

The temperature dropped even more. Cold bit at exposed skin. Hyatta's jaw clenched. The firelight painted everyone in the colors of sickness and memory, and still the mist grew thicker.

Then U'gah opened his eyes.

And the fire in them was brighter than the flames of the campfire.

Hyatta had seen warriors call the storm before battle. He had seen shamans channel spirits. But this was something else—it was crude, raw, and untrained. The bergbar was calling the spirits with only his will and grief.

U'gah rose slowly, his movement guided by some unseen hand. He drove his greatclub into the earth beside him. The stone teeth caught the firelight.

And then the shaman looked at him. The weight of it hit like a physical blow.

Need. Sorrow. Resolve. Carved out of pain and finally ready to be spoken.

Hyatta met that gaze and gave no ground. This was the moment U'gah had walked towards since the jungle, since the crash, since the day he chose to carry Jacques's wounded companions.

Whatever the shaman had to say, he would hear it.

"Atta," U'gah said, voice thick with the rough grain of grief. He tapped his chest, then gestured toward the others. No flourish. Just a request.

Hyatta nodded once, slowly. The moment settled on him like an iron yoke. U'gah wasn't just entrusting him with a tale. He was bearing a wound, raw and pulsing, asking it to be named aloud. This was no story. It was a confession.

Hyatta met his gaze. "I will speak for you," he said, steady. A vow. Though in the fire's twisted light, his voice felt too loud.

The mist was rising again. The flames writhed with violet and green, and shadows pulsed like the lungs of some great beast.

U'gah breathed deep—one slow draw of strength—and began.

He spoke in his own tongue, a language of sounds and forms. The cadence rolled out like smoke, heavy with sorrow. Hyatta listened—and then translated, his own voice measured, each syllable weighted with the shaman's truth.

The others leaned in.

The fire threw long shadows. The temperature fell further.

It moved with a predatory grace, curling around the ruins like a beast reclaiming its lair. It lapped at the ground, climbed over stone and bone, and pooled at their feet. The air turned bitter. Hyatta's breath steamed in the cold, the metal rings of his whip biting at his palm.

Then came the whispers.

Faint. Disembodied. A thousand voices beneath the wind— unformed and unmoored.

Shapes emerged.

At first, only smudges in the air. Then outlines. Then faces.

Hyatta froze.

Spirits.

They rose from the mist in silence—ghosts of the bergbar dead. Their forms shimmered, wavering as if caught between moments. Tribal paint lingered in transparent streaks on their cheeks. Braids, beads, bone-carved jewelry—all ghost-thin. Men. Women. Children. Some clutched ghost-weapons, others nothing but empty arms.

They did not speak. But their eyes…

Hyatta had seen death. Had caused it. But this was not grief—it was memory made visible. They carried sorrow the way mountains carry snow: quietly.

These weren't threats.

They were witnesses.

U'gah's voice rose louder now, cutting through the frost and flame. A call across the boundary of death.

He wasn't just summoning them.

He was asking them to speak. To remember.

To forgive.

Hyatta watched the ghosts draw nearer, mist curling around their feet like water at shorebreak.

And for the first time, he understood:

This wasn't just U'gah's story.

It was theirs.

As U'gah's tale unfolded, the spirits stirred—wavering, flickering, their forms shifting with the cadence of his voice. Each word he spoke seemed to ripple through them, as if their very essence responded to the weight of remembered grief. Hyatta's voice remained steady, anchoring the translation with a warrior's calm, even as the story darkened.

He spoke of the herald.

A cloaked figure with flesh like rotted fruit, lesions weeping with unnatural light. The herald had come speaking of peace— of unity beneath the Mother's everwatchful eyes. U'gah had defied him. Refused. And for his refusal, he had been sent away.

It had saved his life.

When he returned, the village was blood and silence. No bodies. Only absence that screamed.

As the story turned, U'gah's voice changed. Layered now—his own voice wrapped in others. The dead spoke through him. Soft voices. Sharp voices. Young and old. The campfire's light flickered and dimmed, its strange colors fading to bruise-purple, then hollow blue. The forest seemed to draw in a breath and hold it.

Hyatta translated, slower now, his words weighing him down.

"They came to us," he said, his voice low, steady. "Promising peace. The herald spoke of a world without suffering. A future where the Mother would protect and nurture us."

The ghosts drifted closer. They circled the fire in silence, their eyes shining with grief that needed no language.

"Most of the tribe accepted," Hyatta said. "They believed."

He paused, the next breath hard to draw.

"But it was a lie."

The wind shifted. Cold pressed in from all sides.

"When the pact was sealed," he said, his voice roughening, "the pale ones came."

The fire dimmed further, the blue flames stuttering as if choked by sorrow. Around them, the ghosts lowered their heads. A few clutched ghost-children to their chests. Others raised empty hands, still reaching for help that never came.

"They came like silence," Hyatta continued. "White as ash. Teeth like needles. Talons like knives. They did not speak. They only killed."

He swallowed hard then glanced at U'gah.

The shaman didn't flinch. He held still as stone, his greatclub planted in the earth beside him, the spirit within it rumbling faintly, as if mourning.

"The pale ones spared no one. Not the warriors. Not the elders. Not the children," Hyatta said, his voice clipped now. "And most of those they killed came back—changed into one of them."

A hush fell over the clearing. The ghosts bowed their heads together, their translucent forms trembling in unison.

Hyatta looked around at the gathered warband. Jacques was silent, eyes locked on the fire. Emerald sat still, her hands clenched white around her bowl. Saturn's brow was furrowed, his lips moving silently—calculating, theorizing, mourning in his own way. Florence stared into the dark, her expression unreadable for once.

Hyatta's voice dropped to a whisper, the last words pulled from somewhere unknown to him.

"The spirits remain," he said. "Bound here by the lie that stole them. They wait for vengeance. For justice. For the peace they were promised, and never given."

The fire crackled once more, a soft blue tongue licking at the darkness.

No one spoke.

Only the ghosts watched.

The silence that followed was absolute—a stillness so profound it seemed to swallow the real and thought alike. The warband sat frozen beneath its weight, the air thick with mourning, with fear, with truths too heavy for words.

The spirits watched. Silent. Still.

Their ghostlight eyes held the warband in a grip deeper than speech, and in their sorrow, there was judgment.

Hyatta rose.

His posture was rigid, each movement a deadly grace. When he spoke, his voice did not rise, but it carried.

"This," he said, sweeping his gaze across the firelit faces, "is the evil we face. This is what the Mother brings."

The words cut through the cold like steel. For a moment, none dared respond. The fire cracked. Wind hissed low through the dead branches. And the story—the truth—hung in the air like smoke that refused to rise.

As U'gah's chanting faded, so too did the magic. The spectral fire dimmed, its sickly greens, blues, and purples bleeding away into a natural, crackling orange. The mist withdrew like a tide being pulled out to sea, pulling the spirits with it. One by one, the ghosts bowed their heads, then unraveled—fading into the soil, the wind, the trees.

Silence returned—but it was no longer sacred. It was fragile now. Barely holding.

Florence broke it.

"Why?"

The question dropped like a stone into water.

Jacques turned, brows drawn tight. "Why what?"

Florence's arms were folded across her chest, her stance defensive. But her voice—though harsh—carried a tremor.

"Why should we get involved in this?" she snapped. "This isn't our war. It's not even our *world*. It doesn't have anything to do with us."

Before Hyatta could reply, Emerald surged to her feet.

"It *doesn't* have anything to do with us?" she shot back, her black eyes wide and furious. She flung an arm toward the ruined village, the fire casting sharp shadows across her face. "Did you *hear* what he said? U'gah's whole tribe is *gone*. Torn apart. That... *thing*—the Mother—sent her monsters after us under Wrasas Station. We barely survived. Do you think she's finished?"

Florence opened her mouth, but Saturn's voice slid in.

"She may not even be native to this planet."

They all looked at him.

Saturn stood with hands clasped behind his back, eyes reflecting the firelight like a mirror.

"According to the Station logs," he said, "she could be the product of Allied or Axis experimentation. Artificial intelligence? Bioweaponry? Magical transduction? We don't know yet. But if we created her, in part or in full... then this *is* our responsibility. Not just ethically. But fundamentally."

Hyatta stepped forward.

His expression was unreadable, but his gaze locked onto Florence with quiet gravity. His voice, when it came, was not angry. It was cold.

"This isn't about blame," he said. "It's about aftermath."

He turned toward the village ruins. Smoke drifted from the dying fire, curling above shattered stone.

"This is what she leaves behind. Every time. Promises, and then silence. Villages, then ash. Tribes, then bones."

He looked back at the warband.

"We don't need to choose this fight," Hyatta said. "We *are* in it."

And for a moment, no one argued.

Florence shifted under Hyatta's gaze but didn't look away.

"Even if that's true... why us?" she asked. "Why do *we* have to fight this thing?"

Hyatta stepped closer. The fire cast his features in desolate relief—planes of shadow and orange flame.

"Because if we don't," he said, "who will?"

His voice held only iron.

"You think the Mother will stop here? That her children will be content with one tribe, one station, one fight?" He swept his gaze across the firelit camp. "If we turn away, she keeps going. One ruin becomes two. Then ten. Then the whole world burns with no one left to warm themselves with the heat."

Silence answered.

Emerald stared at the dirt, her fists clenched white. Jacques looked to the fire, jaw tight. Saturn's expression was unreadable—his eyes distant, but no longer detached.

Florence hesitated. Her defiance guttered, faltered. She glanced at the others, then finally to U'gah.

He stood alone.

One hand resting on the haft of his greatclub. Head bowed. Not speaking—but not broken. Mourning, yes, but unbending.

The weight of his silence said more than words ever could.

Hyatta's voice gentled, but did not soften.

"This isn't his fight anymore," he said. "It's all of ours. The Mother's reach is long. And I... I owe her pain."

Florence's arms dropped to her sides. Her gaze fell.

The fire cracked.

Wind stirred dead leaves in the ruins.

Then Jacques spoke, voice steady, decisive.

"Hyatta's right," he said. "We can't ignore this. But it doesn't change our next move."

He looked to the others.

"It makes it *more* urgent. We get to Zahadah. We find the mobile lab. We find the cure for Hyatta and anyone else she's marked."

Emerald nodded, her shoulders squaring. "So we're in this. All of us. We *have* to be."

Saturn adjusted his goggles, meeting Hyatta's gaze with grim certainty.

"If the Mother came from the experiments on this island," he said, "then she's our mistake. And we owe it to the dead—and the living—to make it right."

Hyatta gave a slow nod, the tension in his frame easing slightly.

"Then we move on in the morning," he said. "Together."

He turned to U'gah.

The shaman lifted his head. Their eyes met—and in U'gah's, beneath the grief and the silence, was something new.

Not peace. But purpose.

***

Sleep eluded Hyatta, slipping through his fingers like water from a cracked vessel. He remained near the fire long after the others had drifted off, his gaze fixed on the ruins beyond the circle of flame. Shadows clung to the village like old grief, and though Mu had long since numbed his capacity for shock, tonight left him troubled.

The reach of the Mother. The power of her children. The sorrow of U'gah's tribe.

When exhaustion finally forced him down, sleep came fractured and unkind. His dreams unspooled in fits, vivid and half-claimed. Not memories. Not quite. But echoes.

The pale ones haunted him.

They crept through his dreams like rot through cloth—thin, bone-pale bodies gliding through tunnels and starlit forests alike, their needle teeth catching light that wasn't there. At their center moved the wendigo. Massive. Tan. Wrapped in leathery folds that rustled like parchment. A void in the shape of hunger.

It didn't speak; it entered—pushing thoughts into him like thorns through meat.

Its voice wasn't one, but many. All were feminine, perverse and unrelenting. A chorus of dry leaves and dying stars.

A name burned through the noise.

Isik Getiren.

He didn't know it, but had heard it once. Never claimed it. But it echoed in him like a knell through hollow stone.

You were light once, the voice whispered—half sorrow, half sneer. *You scattered the dark. Now you are nothing. A shard of what was.*

Hyatta tried to pull away. Couldn't.

Visions followed: A desert sun. Blinding. Hands—*his* hands?— forging blades of light that hummed like stars. A city, radiant and gold-veined, the towers catching fire in the dusk. People bowed not in fear, but reverence—kneeling before a woman with red-gold hair and jade fire in her eyes. She smiled like the sunrise. Her name was not spoken, but he knew it lived inside him.

Then darkness.

A swelling tide at the edge of memory. Devouring spires. Silencing songs. The radiant blades dimmed, then shattered. The worshipers screamed.

He woke, gasping.

The mountain air felt thin in his lungs, his chest tight, pulse hammering. The fire had burned low. Only embers remained.

The others still slept.

Hyatta sat up.

Isik Getiren.

It didn't belong to him. He was Hyatta Kahlan, Siva'gat, warrior of the sands, born under fire. Forged in battle and blinding light. That was truth.

And yet...

The name coiled in his chest like a buried tether. Taut. Tugging.

He didn't speak it aloud. He just breathed, slow and deep, staring into the dying coals.

A name wasn't truth.

But sometimes, it was a key.

The chain-whip at his side hummed faintly, its coiled segments pulsing with a dim, warm light. Hyatta's fingers brushed along its length, the glow bleeding into his skin. The radiance was his to command—his gift from the Sun Goddess, shaped in fire and faith. Yet tonight, it felt like a burden. Laden. As if it carried something more than light—something waiting to be remembered.

His gaze drifted toward the fire, where U'gah's greatclub rested in the dirt like a sentinel. The stone teeth caught dying flames, glinting with quiet menace. This was a reminder of the spirits that had risen, of vengeance made tangible in one halfling's hands.

Hyatta wondered if the ones in his dreams—the ones whispering in a voice not quite his—were waiting, too.

Watching.

He let out a slow breath, grounding himself. The dreams could wait. The Mother, her servants, the shadows curling at the edges of his memory—none of it could be faced here, in this fragile moment of his crusade.

He was Hyatta Kahlan. Siva'gat. A warrior of sand and sun.

His warband needed him *present*.

He leaned back against a splintered beam, the ruins silent around him. His chain-whip coiled at his hip, its hum a soft lullaby. He closed his eyes. Sleep might not come, not truly— but the light would remain.

CHAPTER THIRTY-ONE

After leaving U'gah's village, Jacques noticed the shift almost immediately. The little guy had regained his usual bounce—humming to himself as he marched along, his greatclub slung casually across his shoulders. The dark cloud that had hung over him since they entered the mountains seemed to have lifted. Watching that small, stubborn figure stomp forward, Jacques felt something ease in his own chest. He hadn't said much, but the worry had been there. He wasn't sure U'gah would come through the ritual of grief intact. He wasn't sure he could have, in the same situation.

Hyatta had told him something not long after they'd left the ruins. It had nearly made Jacques laugh—though not out of humor. U'gah's greatest fear, Hyatta said, hadn't been facing the loss of his tribe or walking the graves of his people. It was the thought that his friends—Jacques, especially—might see him as a coward. Might turn from him.

Jacques shook his head, the ghost of a smile tugging at his mouth. Coward. That word didn't belong anywhere near U'gah. He'd seen the shaman charge headlong into monsters three times his size without hesitation. He'd watched him brawl and bite and bleed, all for the sake of his friends. U'gah's courage wasn't that of a trained soldier—his ferocity wasn't learned in a boot camp or a battlefield. Deeper. Jacques understood discipline, understood tactics and rank. But the strength U'gah carried, it came from some unshakable, primal place. Jacques respected that. Hell, he envied it.

The hike through the overgrown trails leading to the main trade routes took only a few days, though it felt longer. Vines and brush snagged at their gear, and the undergrowth turned every step into a battle. But they had an unlikely ally: the sauropod Emerald had dubbed Sandy. Jacques could only guess why she'd chosen the name, but it stuck.

The massive, feathered beast had been a blessing. Where they would've spent hours hacking at saplings and cursing briar patches, Sandy simply walked through it all, unconcerned. Dense groves of young trees barely slowed her. She stomped through thickets with the casual confidence of something that knew nothing could stop it. Occasionally, she stretched her neck to pluck leafy branches, chewing them contentedly while blazing a path wide enough for everyone.

Saturn, of course, never stopped complaining.

"It's unnatural," he muttered for the hundredth time, squinting up at the dinosaur through his fogged goggles. "Feathers on a sauropod? Please. Saurischians were lizard-hipped, not bird-hipped. And the beak! Serrated ridges? It looks like it was designed to give paleontologists heart attacks."

Jacques had chuckled and clapped him on the shoulder. "Unnatural or not, mon ami, I prefer her to swinging a machete for six hours straight."

Later, Hyatta had spoken, tone dry but thoughtful. "The size helps. So does the noise. Predators tend to avoid prey that sounds like a landslide." He gestured to Sandy's trail—a crushed ribbon of forest, footprints like craters. "Most things out here won't take the risk."

Jacques had nodded, appreciating the logic—but he couldn't shake the unease curling in his gut. It wasn't Sandy he distrusted. It was the thought of something that *wouldn't* be scared off by a mountain of feathers and muscle. Something lurking in the woods that might see the sauropod not as a threat, but as dinner.

Still, Sandy trudged on, unbothered by the forest's whispers. Her feet landed with rhythmic finality, flattening saplings and underbrush like a living siege engine. Oddly enough, Jacques found the sound comforting. Crunch. Snort. Crunch. That steady cadence was its own kind of music—one that quieted his thoughts and gave his nerves a break. For a moment, he let himself ease into it, the vigilance still there but muted. U'gah's humming floated ahead of them—soft, off-key, familiar. And for the first time in days, Jacques allowed himself to believe they might actually be heading somewhere better.

When they finally reached the old trade routes, it felt like stepping into civilization. Compared to the tangle of mountain trails they'd been clawing through, the wide, flattened paths were practically highways. Sandy could move easily now, no longer forced to bulldoze her way through the world. The group made better time, their spirits lifted by the ease of travel and the sense of progress.

Less than a week after reaching those roads, they crested a final ridge—and there it was.

Zahadah.

Jacques stopped short, stunned by the sheer scale of it. The city sprawled across a massive plateau jutting from the lowlands like a green dream cut from stone and imagination. Far larger than he'd pictured. Its silhouette rose in tiers, ancient and imposing, something between a cathedral and a fortress. He thought of Angkor Wat—its endless steps, its carved faces. Zahadah looked older, stranger. Its towers didn't just rise—they seemed to *grow*, as if pulled from the bowels of the earth by powerful gods. Vines crawled across the walls, not in conquest, but in harmony, like even the forest had paused in reverence.

The outer wall was massive—blackened with age, armored in crawling moss and roots. It encircled the city like a clenched fist, holding back the wild at the base of the plateau that pressed in on all sides. The forest here wasn't the feral chaos of the jungle of Wrasas. This was a green tide of dense forest kept barely at bay, free of the extreme heat and drowning humidity.

"Zahadah," Jacques murmured, the name thick on his tongue. He adjusted his pack and stared, scanning the horizon, drinking it in. Behind him, Sandy clomped forward, unfazed by awe or history, her long neck swinging lazily as she chomped on a high branch.

"It's larger than I expected—larger than Wrasas," Saturn said. His voice cut through the stillness, laced with suspicion. He adjusted his goggles, eyes narrowing. "The architecture... it's old. Ancient, maybe. But someone's maintaining it. Or at least *living* in it."

Jacques nodded slowly. "You don't keep walls like that unless someone's still defending them."

He turned to Hyatta, standing beside him, his silhouette taut with quiet tension, but less than it had been. His shoulders had eased. Just a little.

"What do you think?" Jacques asked. "Think the people here might know something? About the Mother or where the mobile unit might be?"

Hyatta's clouded blue eyes narrowed as he studied the city. "It's possible," he said at last. "Zahadah's a crossroads. A melting pot. If answers exist anywhere on this island, they'll likely be buried somewhere in those streets."

Emerald stepped up beside him, her green hair catching the light as she shaded her eyes with one hand. "I'm more interested in that lab Jacques mentioned," she said. "If it's as advanced as you think, it might be the key to everything— answers about the Mother, tools to fight her, maybe even a cure for whatever's happening to Hyatta."

Jacques gave a soft huff. "Don't get ahead of yourself," he said, though a faint smile tugged at his mouth. "We have to find the lab. Cities like this always *look* orderly from a distance. Up close?" He shook his head. "They're usually chaos wearing a crown."

Florence snorted, arms crossed as she leaned against a nearby boulder. "Assuming the locals don't try to kill us on sight," she muttered. "Let's not forget how our last 'civilized encounter' turned out."

Jacques didn't argue. Her words had the ring of truth. Zahadah held promise, yes—but also risk. Cities could offer safety, information, salvation. But more often than not, they held teeth behind gilded smiles.

He adjusted the straps on his pack. "The sooner we're inside, the sooner we know what we're dealing with."

They resumed their descent. The path leveled out as they entered the lowlands, and Zahadah grew with every step—its towers sharpening, its walls looming like stone titans from its perch. The sound of civilization, the unmistakable hum of activity—voices, carts, distant clangs of metal drifted out across the forest in a discordant drone. After weeks in the wilderness, it struck Jacques like a memory half-remembered.

Hyatta raised a hand. The group stopped instantly.

Jacques tensed, his hand drifting toward his sidearm. They would be at the foot of the plateau soon—just a few hours from the slope that wound up the side of the sheer, rock walls. Zahadah stood tantalizingly close, its promise of shelter almost within reach. And yet Hyatta had stopped, staring up at the beast of a city.

Without explanation, the desert warrior turned to Sandy and began unstrapping a bundle from the rigging slung low across the sauropod's side. Jacques watched, puzzled. The bundle was large—tightly wrapped in oilcloth and canvas, lashed with simple leather thongs. Leftovers from the Zoloto. He couldn't remember anyone touching it before now.

Hyatta laid the bundle on the ground and knelt, fingers working the knots with slow, practiced care. As the canvas unfurled, Jacques saw what lay inside.

Clothing.

Simple tunics and cloaks—rough-spun, coarse, unbleached and dyed. Nothing that would stand out in a crowd. No emblems, no sigils, no hints of Wrasas Station's armor or the battle-scarred journey they'd endured. These were for blending in.

Hyatta began passing them out wordlessly.

Jacques caught the tunic tossed his way, frowning as he held it up. The cut was unfamiliar, but the intent was obvious. Camouflage—not from sight, but from scrutiny. A way to become part of the city's background, to slip into Zahadah with the crowd.

Before Jacques could speak, Hyatta was already beside Saturn, helping the scientist untangle the fabric with calm efficiency.

Jacques raised an eyebrow, watching the quiet choreography unfold. Whatever lay ahead, Hyatta had clearly been thinking about it, if not planning for it.

"Here," Hyatta said, voice calm but firm. He adjusted the tunic Saturn was fumbling with, looping the sash around the gnome's waist and tugging the cloak into place with practiced ease. "Tuck it here. The fit's meant to be loose."

Jacques glanced down at his own tunic, scratching at the rough neckline. It itched like burlap. He watched as Hyatta moved to Emerald, who was frowning at her cloak like it had personally insulted her. She let the warrior help her tie it around her shoulders, grimacing as he adjusted the hem to keep it from dragging. Hyatta's hands moved with quiet efficiency, steady despite his half-blinded eyes.

"Mind telling us what this is about?" Jacques asked, keeping his tone casual, though curiosity tugged at his voice. He pulled the tunic over his head, the coarse fabric dragging against his skin like sandpaper. It was a far cry from the smooth, reactive armor hidden beneath.

Hyatta paused, surveying the group. "The people here," he said, "once followed the Aesir. Odin. Thor. Tyr. Warlike gods. Enemies of the Olympians."

Jacques lifted an eyebrow. "And we care because…?"

Hyatta met his gaze, the clouded blue of his eyes unreadable. "I don't know if that faith still holds. But the sigil of Hephaestus —" he tapped the faint marking etched into Jacques's armor,

"—could be a problem. If they recognize it, they might see us as enemies. Infiltrators. Or worse."

Jacques mulled that over, glancing around. Emerald was fastening her cloak with a theatrical sigh. Saturn had managed to pull his hood up, adjusting his goggles beneath the fabric. Florence looked like she'd rather eat nails than wear the roughspun. She tugged it into place with a muttered curse. U'gah, by contrast, wore the tunic easily, unfazed by the change. Lusa hadn't bothered at all. The Mau lounged in the shade with all the defiance of a creature born to ignore dress codes.

"So we're hiding in plain sight," Jacques said, adjusting his cloak to drape over the more advanced armor beneath. He pulled the hood forward, ensuring it cast his face in shadow. "Could be worse."

Hyatta gave a slow nod. "We don't know what's waiting inside Zahadah. Best we move like travelers, not soldiers."

Jacques couldn't argue. The city was an unknown, and on Mu, unknowns rarely ended well.

They pressed on. The walls of Zahadah grew taller as they neared, stone towers etched with time and crawling vines. The wilderness faded behind them, replaced by the growing hum of life beyond the walls—a murmur of carts, footsteps, distant voices. Civilization.

The narrow trade path they followed joined a wider thoroughfare, worn smooth by years of feet and wheels. Jacques adjusted his hood again, scanning the road ahead. Zahadah's gates still loomed in the distance, two hours away. The city's walls were a silhouette of stone and shadow, atop the massive plateau that looked more and more like a petrified tree stump. The closer they got, the more Jacques felt the tension start to build again.

He kept his pace steady, but he kept his hand away from his weapon, trying to seem like just another traveler.

The foot traffic along the thoroughfare was lighter than Jacques had expected for a city of Zahadah's scale. Small clusters of travelers outpaced them—merchants hauling goods in creaking carts, farmers guiding beasts of burden, the occasional patrol of guards clad in mismatched armor that spoke more of necessity than uniformity. Still, after weeks of isolation, even this modest crowd felt jarring. Jacques had grown used to the rhythm of their seven-person warband, their silences and shared danger forming an intimacy the world beyond couldn't touch.

Now that world pressed close.

He clenched his jaw as the unease swelled—an old tide rising from the pit of his gut, bitter and hard. The faint tang of bile crept across his tongue. He'd prepared himself for this—or thought he had. But walking among strangers again, every glance a possible threat, every passing voice a distraction—it felt like walking into a battlefield unarmed.

He forced himself to breathe. In through the nose. Out through the mouth. Eyes forward. One step at a time.

Most of the travelers ignored them. Their eyes slid past the warband with the indifference of city-dwellers used to seeing too much. A few spared glances at the cloaked group—but none lingered. In fact, Jacques noticed something stranger: some didn't just ignore them. They deliberately looked away. Heads dipped. Gazes lowered. As if the unspoken rule here was simple: don't draw attention to what might not want it.

It unsettled him more than open stares would have.

Children, of course, were the exception. They gawked without shame, eyes wide and mouths agape as Sandy, their absurdly massive sauropod companion, plodded along behind the group. The creature's twenty-two-meter frame loomed above the traffic, its feathers catching flecks of sunlight in shimmering patterns. With its neck swaying lazily and its mouth occasionally snatching a leafy branch overhead, Sandy looked as unbothered as ever.

Jacques snorted softly, the corners of his mouth twitching. It was ludicrous. A dinosaur. A real one. Trailing them like a pack mule. No wonder the children stared.

He caught the awestruck gaze of a young boy and gave the faintest of nods before pulling his hood lower and stepping closer to Hyatta's side.

"Go figure," he muttered, mostly to himself. "Spend long enough in the wild, and you forget a dinosaur isn't an everyday sight."

Hyatta didn't respond, but his hooded head tilted slightly. Jacques caught the faintest twitch of a smile—barely there, but real. That was Hyatta's version of a belly laugh.

The gates of Zahadah were close now, their full scale rising with each step. They loomed, massive and solemn, carved stone darkened by age and weather. Vines clung to them like veins on an old titan, curling into the elaborate reliefs etched across the surface—scenes of warriors, of gods, of battles with great beasts.

Jacques slowed as they approached, his eyes narrowing. The gates were just tall enough to admit Sandy, if she lowered her head, but it would be tight. Traffic would need to be halted, guards waved off, questions answered. A dinosaur this size didn't pass unnoticed.

He didn't like it.

They needed Zahadah. But the city might not be ready for them.

And Jacques had learned to trust the silence before a storm.

He glanced back at the others, eyes sweeping across their cloaked forms. U'gah was humming again, the tune soft and almost cheerful despite the tension in the air. Emerald adjusted her hood, making sure the green of her hair stayed hidden. Saturn walked beside Sandy, head down, likely still sulking over the sauropod's anatomical blasphemy.

495

But Florence—was gone.

Jacques's heart lurched. He turned sharply toward the gate and there she was.

Hyatta was already striding toward the guards, Florence clinging to his arm like some highborn heiress in distress. Their cloaks billowed behind them as they advanced.

Jacques froze.

Was Hyatta… turning her in? Using her as a distraction? Gods help them—posing as a couple?

No. That wasn't Hyatta. He wasn't reckless. But the image— Florence in full dramatic flare, Hyatta silent at her side—was enough to knock the breath from Jacques's lungs.

He started forward, instinct urging him to intervene before things could spiral. He barely made it five steps before Florence's voice exploded across the clearing.

"Do you know *who I am?*"

It rang out like a war cry. Jacques winced, stopping short.

The guards at the gate recoiled visibly, a quartet of men in rough-cut armor who had clearly not been trained to deal with hurricanes in human form. Florence barreled toward them, her fury weaponized, dragging Hyatta like a reluctant groom at a noble scandal.

"I am *Florence Blackwell!*" she shouted, her voice pitched high enough to startle birds. "Of the Blackwell family! Do you know what that means?"

Jacques buried his face in one hand. He *had* warned Hyatta this might happen.

The lead guard, a bearded man with the haunted eyes of someone who'd seen too much and still not enough, stepped forward with commendable caution. "Madam, I assure you, no one is stopping—"

"Don't you *madam* me!" she shrieked, jabbing a finger at his chest. "I have crossed wastelands, faced monsters, *suffered indignities you wouldn't dream of*, and now you want to check my credentials like I'm some *peasant?*"

The guard blinked. His partner leaned in and muttered something behind a half-raised hand.

Florence turned on him instantly. "Oh, *you think this is funny? Do I amuse* you? You find humor in my pain? In *my legacy?*"

Jacques felt the tension around him shift. Not in a dangerous way. Not yet. But the guards—now thoroughly disarmed, confused, and slightly terrified—were far more likely to wave them through than mount a resistance.

It hit Jacques then. Hyatta wasn't improvising.

He was weaponizing Florence.

And God help anyone who got in her way.

Jacques ran a hand down his face, stifling a groan. Hyatta, for his part, remained perfectly stoic—his arm still linked with Florence's, playing the role of silent bodyguard to her self-appointed royalty. The hood obscured most of his face, but Jacques caught the glint in those clouded eyes.

Hyatta had let Florence off her leash on purpose.

The bearded guard's face was shifting rapidly from amused to alarmed. "Madam—Miss Blackwell—we mean no offense," he stammered, edging backward. "But we must inspect—"

"You'll inspect *nothing!*" Florence thundered, her voice peaking in a way that made Jacques's ears ring. "Do you *see* what's following me? That is a priceless, irreplaceable biological marvel! If a single *feather* is bent, I will ensure that *every* scholar, merchant, and consortium elder from here to the Aegean calls for your head—*by name!*"

Jacques bit the inside of his cheek. She was a nightmare—but in this moment, she was *their* nightmare.

The guards buckled under the assault. Confidence gave way to visible squirming. One of them—barely older than a boy—was practically vibrating with the desire to vanish.

The bearded guard finally threw up his hands. "Fine. *Fine!* Just —go! Please. Try not to... cause a disturbance inside the city."

Florence tossed her head with all the grace of a stage diva exiting stage right. "Then don't give me a *reason,*" she snapped, striding past him in a swirl of cloak and righteous fury, dragging Hyatta in her wake like a trophy.

As they passed, Hyatta shot a glance toward Jacques—just a glimpse, but enough for Jacques to see it.

A smirk.

The bastard planned this.

Jacques let out a breath he hadn't realized he was holding. He motioned the others forward, falling into step behind the dinosaur as Sandy began her lumbering march through the gate. The remaining guards scrambled to make space, their former bravado reduced to sidelong glances and silent prayers.

It was reckless, absurd, and absolutely insane.

But, it had worked.

And for once, Florence's talent for unfiltered chaos had bought them something positive.

Jacques tugged his hood lower and followed the group into Zahadah, though the itch of unease hadn't faded. Hyatta's motivation was still unclear—was it indulgence, manipulation, or just pragmatism? Regardless, Jacques's nerves were frayed. The show had been effective, yes. But it left a lingering tension behind, like gunpowder dust after a misfire.

The massive gates closed behind them with the faint groan of old hinges. The world inside Zahadah shifted around them— winding streets, moss-cloaked buildings rising like stone titans, narrow alleys packed with carts and trade stalls. The

498

architecture was breathtaking in its scale and detail; stonework etched with ancient motifs, ivy-draped balconies leaning like old men in quiet conversation. Time clung to the city like a second skin. Cracks spidered across carved facades, and the air smelled of damp stone and rusted iron.

But it was *alive.*

Merchants hawked wares in clipped, alien dialects. Laborers pushed carts heavy with produce and salvage. Children darted through the gaps, their laughter echoing off the walls like birdsong. Color moved in flashes—painted signs, dyed fabrics, flickering lanterns.

Jacques adjusted his cloak, drawing it tighter to hide the sigil of Hephaestus etched into the armor beneath, as if it could be seen through the roughspun tunic. He'd hoped the mobile lab unit would be pinging an encrypted signal—something his suit's onboard scanner could catch—but so far, there was only static.

"This city's within the expected proximity of Yggdrasil," Saturn said flatly, as emotionless as ever.

Jacques blinked, realizing he'd spoken aloud without meaning to. "Yggdrasil?"

The gnome adjusted his goggles, glancing up as they wove through the crowd. "Yes. If we can access Axis systems, we may be able to initiate a sensor sweep for the mobile lab— assuming the subsystem is still active. The local communication array will easily have a better range than what we have available from the hardware built into our suits."

Jacques nodded, mind shifting into tactical mode. "That's a big 'if.' We don't even know where to start looking for an access point."

"Sure we do," Emerald interjected, slipping beside them. She tugged her hood lower, her green hair catching the sun in faint glints. "Remember Wrasas Station? The hangar entrance was near the city center. I'd bet this place follows the same design logic."

Jacques frowned, considering. "You think the facility came first, and the city grew around it?"

Emerald gave a sly half-smile. "If you were hiding something world-shattering, wouldn't you bury it at the heart of everything? Right under everyone's feet?"

He couldn't argue. The Axis and Allies had used similar tactics before—burying secrets beneath strongholds, letting time and civilization pile on top.

"So," Jacques said, "we head to the center. If there's an entrance, maybe it'll be there."

"Exactly," Emerald said, her confidence flaring. "City centers are always hubs. If anything's still operational, that's where we'll find it."

"You might want to put a pin in that," Florence cut in, her tone razor-sharp.

Jacques turned, already bracing. Florence stood a few paces behind, arms crossed. The indignation was familiar—but this had a new urgency.

He sighed. "And why's that, Florence?"

She jabbed a finger past the crowd. "Because unless someone stops Hyatta, we're about to be sprinting through this city with guards on our heels."

Jacques followed her gaze. And there he was—Hyatta, storming toward a tall elf in a gold-threaded tunic, his posture all tension and lethal intent. The pointy-eared man stood with the poise of someone used to being obeyed, his skin a rich onyx, his white hair tied back like a blade sheath. He radiated wealth, and authority.

Florence's voice dropped. "He's going to kill that guy."

Jacques hurried to catch Hyatta and managed to grab his arm before the desert warrior left the anonymity of the crowd.

He didn't loosen his grip; he stared into the storm behind Hyatta's clouded eyes, matching fury with steadiness.

"Not here," Jacques hissed, trying not to be overheard above the din. "You want to end slavery in Zahadah? Good. Me too. But not like this."

Hyatta's jaw tensed. His fingers flexed at his side. Jacques could feel it: Hyatta was holding himself back by sheer force of will. Every muscle in the desert warrior's body was coiled with purpose, the kind of taut restraint that could snap in a heartbeat.

Jacques leaned in, voice dropping further. "This isn't justice. This is impulse. You swing that whip now, and we lose everything."

For a long moment, neither of them moved.

Then Hyatta exhaled—slow and controlled. His hand dropped, not in defeat, but in delay.

"Fine," he said. The word grated like gravel. "But if that elf lays a hand on one of them…"

They broke apart just as the elf turned, glancing toward the nearby murmur with an indifferent sneer. He didn't recognize what had almost happened. He didn't know how close he'd come.

The slave column moved on. Shackles clinked like chains dragging through Jacques's chest. He watched them go— women, men, children—all of them stripped of voice—reduced to property.

He turned away.

Florence met his gaze with a raised brow. "Well?" she asked. "Did you talk your wild dog down?"

Jacques didn't dignify it with a response.

CHAPTER THIRTY-TWO

Hyatta's gaze locked on the elf, fury simmering behind his eyes. His fingers tightened around the coiled chain-whip at his side. The sight of the shackled slaves—heads bowed, movements sluggish under the weight of iron—twisted his stomach. The elf's smug commands, his laughter shared with the guards, hung in the air like a stench. Hyatta had seen this brand of cruelty before. To him, there was no difference between this man, the Iruxi, the orcs, or even the Mother. It was all the same rot. This was the evil he'd sworn to fight.

He felt Jacques before he heard him—the sudden grip on his arm, the tension in the Frenchman's stance, the quiet urgency in his voice.

"Hyatta," Jacques said. "Not here. Not like this."

Hyatta turned, his eyes meeting Jacques's. The fury in him didn't fade—it coiled tighter. But Jacques's face was lined with something else: not fear, but calculation. The same anger, tempered by experience. It wasn't that Jacques didn't care. He did. That was what stopped Hyatta more than anything else.

A low growl escaped Hyatta's throat—half-formed words, snarled and guttural. He wasn't even sure what language he'd spoken. Maybe it didn't matter.

Jacques's grip didn't loosen. "We have a mission," he said, firm but quiet. "This doesn't help. Not right now."

Hyatta could feel the weapon's tension pulsing. He could end it here—cut the elf down, turn the guards to ribbons before they had time to shout. He wanted to. Gods, he wanted to.

But Jacques's voice cut through the fire. Logic. Consequences. If he struck now, they'd lose Zahadah. They'd lose the lab. They'd lose time they couldn't afford to waste.

Hyatta exhaled—not a sigh, a hiss. Like steam escaping from a pressurized seal.

"Take the others," he said, his voice low, steady. "Find what you can. Lusa and I will introduce ourselves to the locals."

Jacques's face darkened. Rage and worry warred behind his eyes. But Hyatta didn't flinch. He knew what this meant. Knew what it risked. But some things couldn't be walked past.

The others moved reluctantly. One by one. U'gah was the last to go, his massive frame lingering. His fists clenched and unclenched as he glanced between the two men. Hyatta gave him a nod—firm. Go.

The bergbar hesitated... then turned, trudging after the others with heavy steps. He looked back once. Then disappeared into the crowd.

Hyatta didn't move.

Lusa landed beside him in near silence, feline grace in every step. The Mau's golden eyes studied the scene ahead. But Hyatta saw the shift in his stance, the readiness coiled in every limb.

Each stride carried the weight of intent, his chain-whip swaying like a tether to the past. The sight of the slaves—their bowed heads, the iron bite of their chains—burned behind his eyes. Every link was a memory. Every clink, a scar. The heat of purpose pressed against him like desert wind, relentless, scouring away hesitation.

Lusa moved in his shadow. Where Hyatta was a storm on the horizon, the Mau was its whisper—grace coiled into muscle, his eyes gleaming with anticipation. Hyatta didn't glance his way. He didn't need to. The presence was familiar, grounding. He would not face this alone.

The dark elf, who was too absorbed in barking orders to the shuffling line of captives, didn't notice them until Hyatta was nearly upon him. The effect was immediate. The elf flinched, a startled curse slipping from his lips as his hand shot to the curved blade at his hip.

Hyatta halted.

His stance was relaxed—shoulders loose, posture upright—but the intensity in his gaze bore down with the slow, suffocating heat of a noonday sun. The whip twitched, just enough to shift the air between them. Tension snapped into place like a trap being set.

The elf's confusion narrowed into calculation. His gaze raked Hyatta's frame, noting the weapon, the eyes, the stance. His hand dropped from the hilt, sliding instead to hook behind his belt, affecting a casual air. But his smile didn't reach his eyes.

"Vhat du you vant?" he asked, the words oily, dipped in a lilting accent. His voice was smooth, but there was steel beneath it. He tilted his head, his gaze snapping to Lusa before returning to Hyatta. "Und vhy 'ave you approached ze great Ulfrey?"

Hyatta let the silence stretch, heavy as a sandstorm on the rise. The elf shifted. The tension bit deeper.

When Hyatta spoke, his voice was quiet—but it struck like thunder.

"Your slaves," he said. "Release them."

Ulfrey blinked, then barked out a short, sharp, humorless laugh. "Yu're a bold von," he said, his grin spreading like a crack in stone. "But I don't zink yu understand 'ow zings vork 'ere. Zese slaves—zey are mine. Property. I 'ave ze right to—"

Hyatta stepped forward.

The elf flinched, his words dying mid-breath. Hyatta didn't raise his voice. He didn't draw his weapon. The whip at his side shifted with a soft hiss, coiling like a serpent scenting blood.

Hyatta's grip tightened on the chain-whip, iron and bone grinding faintly beneath his fingers. The sun shifted, or seemed to—its light no longer falling gently but casting long, knife-edged shadows. His own stretched before him like a brand, falling across the elf's polished boots. The slaver stiffened. Arrogance shone in his eyes, then faltered.

"I don't recall making a request," Hyatta said.

It was the voice of sandstorms and executioners, the voice of a man who had stood at the edge of cruelty and survived. A voice born not from threat but from certainty.

The elf's cocky posture broke by inches. His thumb slipped from the belt loop it had rested on, fingers twitching before he caught himself. His eyes dropped, just briefly, to the whip in Hyatta's hand.

Hyatta's gaze turned—away from the elf, to the column of slaves behind him. Men. Women. Children. Shackled like beasts. Their faces were drawn and hollow, skin worn raw at the wrist and ankle where iron met flesh. Some averted their gaze. Others stared at the ground, not out of shame, but habit. The beaten learn not to look up.

And Hyatta remembered.

"All people deserve to walk free beneath the sun," he said. The words were quiet, but they rang out like a verdict. "To live by their own will. Or die."

The elf's mouth twitched. A rebuttal hovered behind his teeth. Hyatta didn't give him the chance.

His hand lifted—not high, not fast—the whip responded like it had a mind of its own, uncoiling with a dry whisper and falling into a loose spiral beside his boot.

"Now is your time of choosing."

The words sliced cleaner than any blade.

The elf's gaze darted to the column, then to Hyatta, then to Lusa.

The Mau stood to Hyatta's right—arms loose, body angled toward the guards now waking to the tension. His bobbed tail flicked. A twitch of amusement played at the corner of his mouth.

The elf's swagger evaporated. His hand hovered near his sword, then withdrew, again. Uncertainty took hold.

Hyatta remained still. Not relaxed—ready. But not rushed. He didn't need to posture. His presence did that for him.

Boots crunched on gravel behind the slaver. A quartet of guards approached, weapons sheathed but hands drifting toward hilts. They moved like they expected their presence to be enough.

Lusa snorted.

The sound was soft. But it carried.

Hyatta didn't smile. But he shared the sentiment. These weren't warriors. These were men who wore swords for status, not for skill. And if they drew them now, they'd be dead before they hit the ground.

The tension became alive—vibrating between breaths.

And still, Hyatta waited, because if the elf made the wrong choice now, it would be the last one he ever made.

Hyatta let the guards draw closer.

Their boots slowed on the stone, hesitating as they took in the tableau before them—the slaver frozen mid-glare, the warrior who hadn't blinked, and the Mau with fire in his eyes. The whisper of blades eased from sheaths filled the space like a warning no one had earned the courage to voice aloud. These were men used to their presence ending trouble. Hyatta's presence, however, was trouble made flesh.

The first guard, burly and broad-chested beneath a grimy breastplate, tried to speak through the growing silence. "Oi—

what's this, then? Who are you to be causin' trouble for Lord Ulfrey?"

He let silence do the work, let the weight build. His eyes locked on the elf. The others weren't worth acknowledging.

Another guard stepped forward, his voice firmer, false confidence rising to meet the dread in his eyes. "Back away, stranger. This doesn't concern you."

A low, unsettling purr cut the air.

Lusa moved, smooth as oil over water. He stepped out from Hyatta's shadow as if being drawn from velvet, his golden eyes glittering. "False," he said simply.

Then he gestured.

The invitation was soft, almost gentle—one feline finger beckoning. But even Hyatta felt the power in it. It wasn't a threat, but a promise.

The guards hesitated. Their courage faltered beneath the Mau's casual disdain.

Hyatta allowed himself the faintest smile. It wasn't bravado. It was fact. These men were not warriors. They were bullies. And against Lusa alone, they wouldn't last a breath.

Then Hyatta spoke.

His voice was low, steady. A drumbeat beneath the storm.

"Your master is deciding whether to live with honor… or die in regret." He paused. "Unless you wish to join him in that decision, I suggest you find different employment."

The words rippled through them like a shockwave. One guard shifted backward. Another swallowed hard, eyes shifting toward Ulfrey. Even the burly one hesitated, doubt leaking into his eyes.

Hyatta saw it before it happened—the twitch of fingers tightening on the hilt, the coiling shift of weight. Pride. Greed. Fear. It didn't matter. Something in the elf snapped, and his blade came with it, arcing toward Hyatta's ribs in a fluid, practiced strike.

The chain-whip roared to life, snapping forward like a striking viper. Iron met steel with a scream of sparks, turning the blade mid-swing. Hyatta's wrist rolled—graceful, surgical—and the whip spiraled, its weighted end snapping down to knock the blade askew.

Ulfrey staggered. He was too slow.

Hyatta struck again. The whip lashed out, and with a crack, he caught the elf across the wrist. Ulfrey's scream was sharp and wet as the blade tumbled from his fingers, clattering against stone.

He stumbled back, but Hyatta was already moving with force. Each step was relentless. The chain-whip curled in his hand like a serpent awaiting the next command.

Ulfrey backed toward the guards. Hyatta continued moving forward.

Behind him, Lusa moved with eerie calm, golden eyes gleaming as he studied the guards like a cat watching cornered prey. His purr deepened, a low, vibrating growl that seemed to seep into the bones of the men around him. The guards faltered, weapons half-raised, their bravado dissolving in the presence of something they didn't understand and couldn't intimidate.

Ulfrey clutched his wrist, teeth bared in a grimace of pain and fury. "You'll pay for zis," he spat, his voice trembling with rage and fear. "Do you know who I am? Vhat I can do to you?"

Hyatta stopped. The chain-whip coiled loosely on the ground beside him, its metal glinting with ominous promise. His head tilted slightly as he regarded the elf with cold detachment.

"You are a slaver," he said, flat, final. "A parasite feeding on the suffering of others. Whatever power you think you have—it ends here."

Ulfrey's mouth opened to respond, but the words died in his throat as the whip snapped forward again. It coiled around his calf with a hiss, the sharp links biting through fabric and flesh. Hyatta gave a sharp yank. The elf toppled like a felled statue, slamming into the ground with a grunt, breath driven from his lungs. A red bloom spread where the links had torn the skin of his leg.

The guards exchanged panicked glances, and whatever confidence they'd walked in with had already fled.

Lusa stepped forward, his smile widening into something predatory. His teeth flashed.

"Careful," he purred, voice rich with mockery. "No. Make. Water."

Hyatta didn't look at the guards. His attention stayed on Ulfrey, who now lay sprawled at his feet—his silks stained, his arrogance shattered.

He leaned in. "Release them."

His voice was soft now, almost gentle, but it left no room for refusal.

Ulfrey's eyes looked toward the guards. He hesitated—still weighing pride against survival and the status against pain—but the chain still clung to his leg. Lusa's shadow loomed. Hyatta was unmoved.

With a trembling hand, Ulfrey gestured. "Do it," he croaked.

One of the guards nodded stiffly and sheathed his blade, fumbling at his belt for the keys. He moved toward the line of slaves.

The sound of unlocking chains echoed in the stillness.

One by one, the shackles fell. The freed captives stood motionless at first, blinking at the light, the dust, the absence of weight around their ankles and wrists. They didn't run. They didn't cry out. They barely moved.

Hyatta scanned their faces. Hollow eyes. Bent spines. Movements that flinched before they began. He'd seen it before.

Freedom was not a switch. It was a wound—raw, confusing, and slow to heal.

The chains were gone, but their weight remained. It would take time for them to remember. Time to reclaim the fire that once lived in their chests. Time to relearn the feel of sunlight without flinching, to walk without watching for the lash. Freedom was not given—it had to be remembered. Rebuilt. Reclaimed. Some would find their strength. Others would falter. That, too, was freedom: the right to rise or fall under your own sky.

Hyatta's grip tightened on the chain-whip. The rage still burned in him, slow and hot, like a small sun held behind his ribs.

He turned back to Ulfrey.

The slaver was no longer a man of poise and power, but a heap in the dirt. Blood seeped from his leg, the crimson soaking the fine cloth and blooming like petals in the dust. His breaths came in sharp, broken gasps. One hand clutched his wound; the other reached out for leverage and found none.

Hyatta stepped forward. The grind of his boots against the stone seemed to echo. The light behind him, filtered through Zahadah's haze, seemed to gather—not bright, but steady. Not blinding, but inevitable.

"You," he growled.

He planted his boot against Ulfrey's chest and pushed. The elf wheezed, eyes wide with real fear now—no arrogance, no mask.

"You steal lives," Hyatta said. "You break them. Feed on pain like a worm in the dirt."

Ulfrey's mouth moved, a tremor of protest rising, but Hyatta pressed down harder. The words died in the elf's throat. His hands scrabbled weakly against Hyatta's leg, but the warrior didn't flinch.

"You are nothing."

Each word landed like a meteor strike.

"A parasite. A coward. You wield power not through strength, but through the weakness you force on others. That power is gone."

The freed captives watched from a short distance, unmoving. Their chains lay behind them, but their fear hadn't. Their limbs remembered shackles. Their minds remembered punishment. They were waiting for permission to hope.

Hyatta's eyes stayed fixed on Ulfrey. The chain-whip slithered through his fingers, its metal links whispering.

Ulfrey trembled now, mouth quivering, panic overtaking his pride. The breath in his lungs came fast and shallow. Hyatta leaned down slightly, not enough to offer closeness, only pressure.

"You will never wield that power again."

He let the silence stretch, a judgment echoing through the stillness.

Then, slowly, he lifted his boot.

Ulfrey gasped. His body curled as he clawed at the ground, desperate to rise. Hyatta didn't stop him, but his stare held him like a sword to the throat.

"Leave," Hyatta said, low and flat. "Run far. Hide deep. If I see you again—there will be no mercy."

For a heartbeat, Ulfrey didn't move. Then survival overtook dignity. He scrambled to his feet, clutching his bleeding leg, and staggered away. His guards—who had not so much as breathed since the whip struck—hurried after him, silent and ashamed.

They vanished into the shadowed alleys of Zahadah, their retreat as hollow as the lives they'd tried to claim.

Hyatta turned to face the freed captives.

They stood in a loose cluster, eyes hollow, shoulders hunched, the ghosts of chains still heavy on their limbs. No one spoke. Some stared at the bloodstained dirt. Others met his gaze, cautious and uncertain.

He said nothing.

The choice was theirs now. To rise. To remember who they had been before the collars, or to forge something new in the ashes. He could not walk that path for them. He had given them all he could: the space to choose.

That was the only freedom that mattered.

Without a word, Hyatta turned. He simply walked away—slow, steady, the judgment in his wake still echoing louder than the toll of a bell.

Lusa fell into step beside him. His golden eyes gleamed with quiet approval, his bobbed tail flicking as if in punctuation. The smirk on his face was amused, but not mocking.

***

U'gah walked slow.

Stone beneath him. Stone beside him. Stone above. Not cave-stone, not grave-stone, but shaped stone. Stacked high to the clouds. The great stone village was real.

He had heard the word *city* before, from traders with strange tongues and shiny boots. U'gah had thought it a myth, like fire that walked or rivers made of gold. But this was real. The walls wore carvings—beasts, storms, battles that roared in silence. Ivy grew along the edges, curling like green fingers trying to hold on. Even the doors were strange—flat wood with shiny teeth and smooth faces.

He touched one once. It felt cold. Like mountain wind.

Voices crashed around him like river-water—barking men, giggling pups, wheels scraping over hard ground. The noise had no rhythm—just clang and chatter and calls that made his ears twitch. He kept close behind Jacques. Jacques knew how to move here. Sharp eyes. Straight back. His walk said, *I belong.* U'gah's did not. But he walked anyway.

He sniffed. Too many smells. Spices that burned his nose. Oil. Ash. Meat. Sweet smoke from burning leaf. And deep beneath it all, the scent of iron—not blood, but shaped-iron, bent and bolted and locked in place. He did not like it. It made his shoulders itch. His hand tightened on his club, just in case.

The stone huts—they loomed. Each one carved. Each one singing a story U'gah could not read, but could feel. He brushed one wall as he passed. It hummed under his hand. The carvings whispered: *We were here first.*

The old men in his village had called the trader-tales, lies. They spoke about cities where the sun could not touch the ground; Cities where fire danced in hands without burning; Cities where people forgot sky, forgot wind, forgot names. Lies, they said. But this place—this place was *more* than the lies.

U'gah kept humming. His steps fell in rhythm. He was the smallest in the group, but he had walked with ghosts. He had fought monsters.

Ahead, Jacques led. His eyes were like arrows, checking, scanning. Emerald padded close behind, whispering to the wizard Saturn with his clever-glass eyes. Florence walked behind, her face sour. But even she couldn't hide her wide eyes. She wanted to pretend this was just another place, but her steps betrayed her.

Hyatta was not with them. Not here. But U'gah felt him, anyway. Like a shield at his back. The warrior's whip would still be coiled. His silence would still be loud. And the cat? Gods only knew. Probably in a tree. Probably watching everything.

U'gah let the club rest across his shoulders. He tilted his head toward the sky, though the sky was thin between the towers. Still, the light came through.

He did not know what waited at the center of this place. But for now, his feet would follow. This stone village had stories. And U'gah had ears.

U'gah tilted his head.

Jacques spoke. Again. His mouth made noise. Too many words stacked on words. U'gah didn't understand most of them, but the others did. Some answered. Some walked away fast, heads low. One stopped and said strange things. They were strange sounds. They made U'gah giggle.

He clapped a hand over his mouth, but another giggle escaped. Then one of them said something mean and Jacques's face turned red. Not sun-red. *Angry pup* red. U'gah laughed louder.

The people turned. Hard eyes. Like elders catching a pup chewing bark-ribbon meant for mourning. U'gah hunched a little. Sorry-not-sorry.

But the shame-heat faded fast. Something better caught his eyes.

He watched Emerald.

She walked close behind Jacques, her steps small, careful. Hood low, but not low enough. U'gah saw her eyes. Black stones. Always watching Jacques. Every time he turned his head, she looked away. But U'gah saw.

And then—*ahh.* The look in her eyes…

U'gah's stomach grumbled. It was the *same look* he gave a twisted-horn leaper on a firespit. The same way his mouth watered before the skin crisped. Longing. Hunger.

But hers wasn't the belly kind.

The laugh burst out of him, loud and sudden, like a firepit cracking open. He clutched his club with both hands, shoulders shaking, tears building behind his nose. *Cub-fever.* That's what it was. Emerald had chosen Jacques. She wanted to make a den with him. She just didn't know how to pounce.

It was too funny.

The others turned. Stopped walking. All eyes on him now.

Jacques gave the soldier-glare. "U'gah?" he said. "What's so funny?"

U'gah couldn't stop. The laugh broke out again—barking and booming, chest-aching good. His feet staggered, and he leaned on his club before he fell. The sight of Emerald's red face, buried deep in her hood like a beetle under bark, made it worse. Her shame-smell filled the air. Florence rolled her eyes so hard they nearly fell out. Saturn made metal-thought sounds behind his goggles. Jacques just stared, like U'gah had grown feathers.

"*Ooda ta coo!*" U'gah wheezed between gasps, pounding his club against the stone like a drum breaking off small flakes of the paving stones.

More silence.

No one understood. Which made it funnier.

Jacques dragged a hand down his face. Emerald looked like she wanted to leap off the edge of the world. Florence muttered bad-magic words under her breath. Saturn sniffed like a shaman who didn't like what he smelled.

But U'gah's laughter slowed. Turned to huffing chuckles. His ribs hurt. His eyes watered. He knelt in the middle of the path, wiping his nose, shaking like a pup after a thunderstorm. The joy left quickly. Left him cold.

Jacques still looked at him. Not angry. But *trying to see.* Trying to understand.

U'gah lowered his head.

The laugh was gone now.

It had felt like lightning in his chest—but now it was just smoke.

U'gah looked to Emerald.

Her face was red. Not from sun. From shame. Fire-blood in her cheeks. She pulled her hood low like a turtle shell, hiding her eyes. Her fists were stones at her sides. She wouldn't look at him.

U'gah's chest squeezed.

He hadn't meant to shame her.

The laugh had come fast, bright and belly-born. Like joy leaping from fire. But now it curdled. Now it felt wrong. Like laughing while a friend was bleeding.

He shrunk. Hunched. Made himself small.

His hands curled around his club. He didn't look at Jacques. Didn't look at Florence. Didn't want to see anger in their faces. Didn't want to see the wound he'd made on Emerald's heart.

The stillness hurt more than shouts.

Even the stone-village seemed quieter—its hum muffled by silence. When the others finally walked, their boots soft on stone, U'gah let out a breath like steam from a cracked gourd.

He set off slowly. Shoulders heavy.

Didn't join the front. Didn't walk with Jacques. He slipped beside Sandy instead, placing his hairy feet on stones, avoiding the seams. He didn't hum. Didn't look up.

The guilt stayed.

Even when the fire left Emerald's cheeks. Even when her steps loosened. Even when she spoke again.

Still, U'gah watched.

Not like before.

Not with cub-fever jokes in his head.

Now he watched searching for a sign. A chance to make right. Her hands, her shoulders, the tilt of her hood—none gave answers.

He gripped his club tighter.

Words were not his way. In the tribe, mistakes were fixed with gifts. With deeds. Not with talk.

If the chance came, he would act.

And when Emerald's step changed—quicker, brighter, like a pup catching scent—U'gah saw it. Her shoulders lifted. Her hood turned toward Jacques. She pointed at something with her whole body, and Jacques followed her gaze.

U'gah tilted his head.

Didn't know what she saw.

But the air around her had shifted.

And so U'gah looked too, nose twitching, breath held. A chance was coming. He could feel it.

And this time, he would not shame her.

The path changed. Wide-stone trail became soft-light garden. Big. Breathtaking. U'gah slowed.

The Firefly-in-the-Sky was bleeding red across the sky, and the stone beneath his feet drank the light. The city noise fell behind them—swallowed by green. No more roar of voices. No wheel-clatter. Just hush. Just breeze.

U'gah's steps grew quiet.

The air was different here. Clean. Like after rain.

He stared.

Spirit-flowers bloomed in strange shapes—star-burst petals, glass-leaves that held the skyfire in their veins. Vines curled in dances around blackstone pillars.

Everything shimmered.

Not with heat. With soul.

It felt like walking through dream-fire. Like stepping into the place-between, where ancestors speak soft and the wind remembers names.

A shiver traced his spine.

He knew this place.

Not here, not now. But *there*. Before. In the scaly-skin stone-village. That place had gardens too. Grown with prayers.

This felt the same.

He glanced to Jacques. He stopped and spoke in hushes to Saturn and Emerald. They pointed, whispered. They knew it too.

This was no city garden.

This was a gate.

U'gah turned his gaze to the shadows. Long, red-blood shadows stretched beneath the trees. He sniffed the air. Sweet. Still.

Spirit-places were like this.

Beautiful.

Dangerous.

He lowered his center of gravity, muscles loose but ready, and padded forward without sound.

If this was the gate to another god-cave, he would walk it with open eyes.

But he would walk it with his club ready, too.

CHAPTER THIRTY-THREE

T he gardens were unlike anything Jacques had seen —drenched in red light, manicured and impossibly alive. The sun hung low on the horizon, casting long shadows and washing the stonework in a muted crimson that made every path and pillar seem to bleed. Where shadow met light, the stone shimmered with the illusion of motion, like the walls themselves wept in silence. The air was thick with the scent of flowers and evening dew, and the only sound was the faint rustle of leaves in the twilight hush.

At the center of it all stood a statue—tall, strange, and unmistakable. Jacques felt its pull the moment he saw it. The structure rose like a stylized resonance transformer: coils spiraling skyward, spires gleaming with latent power. Even at a distance, it seemed to hum—vibrating with energy just beneath perception. The materials were unfamiliar, but the design was precise. Every groove and etched ring catching the day's last light and scattering it in sparkles across the stepping stones.

Jacques moved without thinking. His boots clicked softly over the stone as he approached, the rest of the group trailing behind in awed silence. He didn't register their glances, didn't hear the whisper of fabric or the muted tapping of steps. The statue filled his vision, and with every stride, the certainty in his chest firmed.

This was it.

He felt it in his gut—that same instinct that had guided him through war-torn lands, deadly jungles, and impossible nightmares. Whatever lay beneath this garden, the statue was the key. The Axis hadn't placed it here for aesthetics.

He reached the base and let his fingers trace the metal coils. The surface was cool, the texture finely ridged, science made into art. For a second, he swore he felt it pulse—subtle and rhythmic.

Of course it wouldn't be simple.

The Axis didn't build doors. They built puzzles. Traps. Tests. And this had to be one of them.

He turned slightly, catching Emerald's eye as she drifted closer. Her hood was still low, but her gaze was curious, studying both him and the monument. She tilted her head, already halfway to understanding.

"This is it," Jacques stated with certainty. "Entrance has to be nearby. And this—this is the switch."

Emerald stepped up beside him, eyes narrowing as she followed the shape of the statue. "You're sure?"

"I am," he said. "Placement, construction—it's too precise. No wasted effort."

Behind them, Saturn muttered something under his breath about the absurdity of resonance transformers in flower gardens. Jacques didn't look back.

He kept his eyes on the metal, his hands moving methodically over its curves and edges, searching for anything—a seam, a hairline crack, a change in material density. Something buried beneath the elegance. A hidden key in a machine designed to be beautiful and enigmatic.

Because the Axis rarely built anything that didn't serve a purpose.

The dying sun's crimson glow draped everything in an eerie, otherworldly hush. Jacques's heart thudded against his ribs as the statue shifted—panels sliding with silent care to reveal a terminal nestled at its base.

He leaned forward, watching the screen. It remained dark. No sign of light, no pulse of power—only the dark, glossy surface, reflecting the blood-red sky above. Seconds passed like falling grains of sand. He waited.

Nothing.

Frowning, Jacques crouched lower, hands moving across the casing. He traced the edges, searching for a power button, a hidden port, anything. But the machine appeared seamless—typical Axis craftsmanship: beautiful, maddening, infuriatingly impossible to work on.

"Merde," he muttered, fingers splayed across the cold alloy. "How do you turn this thing on?"

Behind him, Saturn peered over his shoulder, adjusting his goggles with clinical disinterest. "We don't know how long it's been offline," he said matter-of-factly. "Might not be receiving power. Or it could be dead entirely."

Jacques exhaled through his nose, jaw tightening. The idea of failure clawed at him. After everything—crossing the mountains, navigating Zahadah, fighting for every step—they couldn't afford a dead end. He pressed his fingertips against the frame, trying to feel the design, not just see it. There had to be something.

"We didn't come all this way for nothing," he said, frustration lacing his words. "There's always a way. We just haven't found it yet."

Emerald stepped closer. Her gaze swept the statue, sharp and thoughtful. "If it's not getting power," she said, "we could try supplying it directly."

Jacques looked up. The idea made sense—but the complications unraveled in his head before he could stop them. He ran a hand through his hair, sighing heavily with skepticism.

"Even if we do that," he said, "how do we manage the load? If we feed it too much current, we could fry the circuitry. Not enough, and it won't boot." He glanced at the unlit screen. "We're working blind. No specs. No feedback. No failsafes."

His voice dropped lower. "And this might be the only terminal we are likely to find."

Saturn, who had been quietly circling the base of the statue, paused. His fingers twitched as though already working through the possibilities. He adjusted his goggles, gaze sliding to Jacques.

"Well," he said, tone casual but laced with that familiar clinical detachment, "we could use NAVI." He gestured toward the drone strapped to his back. "Stable power source, adjustable output parameters. We'd just need a way to interface it with the terminal."

Jacques blinked, uncertainty warring with that spark of hope. He glanced at the small drone. NAVI was more than a reconnaissance tool—he knew that. Its power unit was adaptable, and Saturn had upgraded it more times than Jacques could count.

"Fine," Jacques said, slowly nodding as the idea took root. "But that's a lot of ifs. Do you really think NAVI's output can be matched to this thing's requirements?"

Saturn shrugged, a faint smirk tugging at the corner of his mouth. "NAVI can interface with almost anything, given the right tweaks. We just need to find the input point. After that, it's just calibration."

Jacques exhaled, gaze dropping to the dormant terminal. "And if we get it wrong?"

"Then we learn something valuable," Saturn replied, not missing a beat. He adjusted his goggles again, clearly unbothered by the potential for catastrophic failure.

Jacques shot him a look. "I'd prefer not to fry something so valuable."

Still, he gave a short nod. Saturn's confidence, dry as it was, had a way of anchoring the room. He turned his attention back to the terminal.

Emerald moved beside him. She crouched, running her fingers along the terminal's edge with care. Her eyes narrowed in concentration.

"Here," she murmured, tapping a nearly invisible line etched into the casing. "There's a panel. Help me."

Together, they pried it open, revealing a tangle of wires and alloyed components laid out in tight, immaculate order. Despite the age of the structure, the interior looked untouched—little dust, no visible corrosion or degradation. The Axis had built it to last.

Jacques let out a low whistle. "Looks like they weren't kidding about longevity."

Emerald gave a quiet nod. "Let's hope it still takes a charge."

By the time NAVI was connected and the final lead snapped into place, night had fallen. The stars burned bright in the moonless sky, casting delicate silver across the garden. The silence was thick, broken only by the faint whir of the drone powering up. The air smelled of night-blooming flowers—sweet and heady.

Jacques stood back, hands tense at his sides as he watched Saturn make the final adjustments. Whatever happened next, it was out of his hands.

They waited.

Saturn adjusted his goggles, small fingers working NAVI's controls. The drone sat beside him, its oscillating lights dimmed to avoid drawing attention. He muttered under his breath—calculations, voltages, possible failure points—his mind buried in the alien calibration.

Jacques stood nearby, arms crossed tight over his chest. He watched with anticipation and unease, the idea of channeling the drone's power into an Axis terminal made him nervous. Like jump-starting a fighter jet with a car battery. One miscalculation, and the whole system might fry.

"Ready?" he asked, his voice low.

"Almost," Saturn murmured, not looking up. His fingers danced across the drone's holographic interface that only he could see, each adjustment sharp and deliberate. "Need to match the output as closely as possible. It would be a shame if we lost the whole damn console."

Jacques nodded, eyes focused on the terminal. In the dim starlight, its surface looked more like a shiny, black puddle than a machine—blank, silent, and inscrutable. Every second it stayed dark, the pressure in his chest built.

Emerald stood just beyond, her arms folded, the tension in her shoulders betraying her stillness.

Finally, Saturn straightened. His goggles caught a glint of starlight as he exhaled. "Done. Let's light her up."

Jacques stepped back, heart thudding, as Saturn initiated the connection. NAVI hummed, its lights shifting to a steady, focused blue. Power flowed through the tethered cable, into the base of the terminal.

Nothing happened.

Only the quiet whir of the drone marked the passing time.

Then, with a low, rising tone—half-hum, half-throb—the terminal stirred.

A faint glow spread across the screen. Lines of text blinked into existence, crawling upward in sharp, angular script. Diagrams followed—schematics, pulse grids, system checks—unfamiliar, and all in German.

Still, Jacques let out a slow breath he hadn't meant to hold. Relief cracked through the tightness in his chest.

"You did it," he said, glancing at Saturn.

The gnome grinned, already tapping the air to cross-check output. "Told you. NAVI's more than a flashlight with wings."

Emerald stepped closer, her eyes wide and fixed on the glowing display. "What now?"

Jacques moved forward, drawn in by the screen. The light reflected in his eyes as he scanned the interface—lines of code, dense and unreadable, at least by him. Not just modern German, but Axis tech shorthand, full of embedded terminology and twisted syntax.

He leaned in, hand hovering near the interface, frustration beginning to churn. The symbols meant something. But parsing them? That was another matter.

"Do either of you read German?" Jacques asked, his voice sharp from the effort of restraint. He glanced between Saturn and Emerald.

The terminal hummed softly, waiting.

Saturn adjusted his goggles, fingers still hovering monitoring NAVI's interface. "I speak German quite well," he said, slightly annoyed. "But don't mistake that for an ability to hack Axis black-site protocols."

Jacques's eye twitched. He kept his tone even. "I don't need you to hack it," he said, nodding toward the terminal. "Just find the command prompt, open the settings, and switch the language to something the rest of us can read. English. French. Anything that doesn't require a cipher ring."

Saturn raised an eyebrow. "You're assuming they built multilingual support into a classified system."

Jacques shot him a look. "They were Axis engineers. They didn't design anything without ten contingencies. Odds are this was meant to be used by personnel from multiple divisions—possibly even non-German speaking counter agents. There's a language setting. Find it. Or I start pushing buttons—once I find them."

The gnome sighed. "If this terminal melts our faces because you're impatient, I want it noted that I objected."

He stepped forward—boots whispering across the stone—and raised his hands to the screen. A tap to the square at its top, and the statue shifted—sliding apart in some places, folding together in others. When it settled, the screen hovered a meter above the ground, a digital keyboard extended from beneath. Blue light played across his goggles as he worked—flicks and swipes cutting through foreign code with cool detachment.

Emerald leaned in over his shoulder, black eyes glinting. "What are you looking for?"

"Settings menu. Or anything that doesn't look like a security lockdown or fail-safe protocol," Saturn murmured. "Axis design is dense. Think military efficiency paired with puzzle-box sadism."

Jacques folded his arms, willing himself to let the seconds pass. Saturn's movements were deft, but the silence stretched. Just as he was about to ask again, the gnome made a small sound of satisfaction.

"Found it," Saturn said, highlighting a prompt. The menu shifted, script reforming. "Language options... German, Russian, Japanese—figures—ah. English."

Jacques stepped forward, tension easing. "Set it."

Saturn confirmed the selection. The screen flickered. The text re-rendered in English. Lines of data restructured into coherent prompts: system logs, access hierarchies, network pings. For the first time, the machine spoke a language Jacques could parse.

"Much better," Jacques muttered, the edge leaving his voice. He gave Saturn a nod. "Nice work."

The gnome shrugged, brushing a speck of dust from NAVI's frame. "Glad it didn't explode. Let's see what this corpse has to say."

Jacques stepped up to the terminal, the translated English text shimmered faintly across the screen. Diagrams scrolled alongside it—schematics, prompts, half-labeled systems—and as his sharp eyes traced the data, he found the confirmation he needed. This was a control hub. Just like at Wrasas Station. And if the Axis followed a similar pattern, it was tethered directly to whatever lay buried beneath the gardens.

Unlike at Wrasas, there was no login, no convenient credential check. Just a sealed interface—cold, intricate, and hostile. Jacques scanned the inputs, his stomach tightening. No user fields. No override keys. Just layers of polished, obfuscated security. Exactly what he'd expect from Axis engineering: elegant, ruthless, and deliberately labyrinthine.

He exhaled through his nose. "No credentials this time," he muttered, mostly to himself. "I'll have to find another way in."

Saturn, standing off to the side with his arms crossed, arched a brow. "You're thinking back door?" His tone was dry, but not dismissive. The glint behind his goggles hinted at interest.

Jacques didn't look away from the screen. "Always is in systems this complex. Somewhere. We just need to find it before we trip something permanent."

Emerald leaned against the terminal housing, her arms folded. Her eyes shifted from Jacques to the screen, uncertain. "You even know where to start?"

"I'll figure it out." Jacques's voice was level, but a line of tension rode beneath it. "Axis systems needed maintenance. Updates. Field diagnostics. No matter how locked-down, engineers always leave a trail—a failsafe, a debug hook, something to keep them from bricking their own tech. We find that, we're in."

Saturn adjusted his goggles, stepping closer. "And if we don't?"

Jacques gave a humorless half-smile. "Then we trigger a lockdown, maybe an alarm, maybe worse. And we walk away empty-handed."

"Lovely," Emerald muttered.

Jacques ignored her, his fingers finding the keyboard. The digital keys were cool beneath his touch—smooth, silent, familiar in structure even if the layout was foreign. He began tapping through exploratory commands: system info requests, echo tests, menu flags. The screen responded, but not kindly. Each prompt returned gibberish or denials, the OS dancing just out of reach, like a game designed to punish.

"No dice so far," Jacques muttered, leaning in. "But this architecture… it feels familiar."

Saturn tilted his head. "You've worked on Axis code before?"

His eyes stayed fixed on the scrolling output, a crease forming between his brows.

"Not directly," he said at last. "But I've studied their coding. Structural patterns. Circuit logic. There's a rhythm to it, once you know what to look for."

He tapped another command.

This time, the screen blinked, but didn't reject him.

Jacques leaned forward. Something had changed.

Jacques continued, half to himself. "Allied engineers spent years dissecting captured systems during the war. Patterns emerged like repetitions in the architecture, quirks in function naming, specific redundancies. If I can just isolate one…"

He trailed off, his gaze narrowing on a single line of text—something buried deep in the subroutines. It didn't fit. A fragment of code that stood out like a scar in the otherwise seamless logic.

His fingers moved, precise and quick. A sub-menu opened, isolating the string.

"Got something," he said, taut with focus. "Dormant process. Might be a maintenance protocol. Let's see where it leads."

The terminal blinked, then hummed—a soft, electronic murmur. Lines of code began to scroll, slow at first, then accelerating, each one peeling back the veil on the system's internal architecture.

Emerald leaned in, her brow drawn as she tried to follow the stream. "What is all this?"

"Subsystem diagnostics," Jacques said. "I activated a service protocol. If this is what I think it is, we've found a way to our back door."

Saturn gave a short nod. "Not bad. Let's hope you're right."

Jacques didn't respond. The terminal flashed, then settled into a new interface—cooler in color, stripped down. A maintenance overlay. Prompts appeared: environmental control, facility schematics, energy flow analysis, and—most critically—**entry permissions**.

"There," Jacques breathed, the edge of triumph creeping into his voice. He selected the access menu, heart rate spiking as the terminal processed the request.

Then the screen blinked—and a new prompt appeared:

ACCESS OVERRIDE REQUIRED. CONFIRM AUTHORIZATION.

Jacques's shoulders tensed. "Of course," he muttered. "Never simple."

Saturn peered over his shoulder, his goggles catching the screen's glow. "Well, you're in the room. Now you just need to convince the guard dog it belongs to you."

Jacques exhaled slowly, already assembling contingencies. "Let's hope this trail doesn't dead-end," he said, fingers returning to the keys.

The keys were warm beneath his hands—his own persistence heating the polymer. Each command was a risk. Each screen refresh was a step closer to salvation… or disaster.

Minutes passed. Then more. Twice the system shuddered under invalid input. Once, it spat a string of warnings in red— **unauthorized behavior detected**—before Jacques diverted the loop through a diagnostic sandbox. Sweat clung to his neck. His vision narrowed to cursor and code.

Then—a beep. Soft. Unassuming.

The screen changed.

The menu bloomed open like a vault door unsealing.

ACCESS GRANTED.

Jacques froze, just for a heartbeat, as the flood of options spilled across the interface—core functions, control overrides, security mappings. Everything.

He exhaled. Not relief. But something close.

"Access granted," he muttered, rough, edged with tired, hard-won satisfaction.

Saturn, still hunched beside NAVI, gave a low whistle. "Took you long enough. I was starting to think we'd need Lusa to bash it open."

Jacques shot him a sidelong glance. "Patience, Saturn. This isn't Allied tech."

Emerald leaned in over his shoulder, her eyes absorbing the terminal's new interface. "What do we have?" she asked.

Jacques's hands moved methodically across the keyboard, navigating the Axis interface. It was every bit as convoluted as he remembered from Allied counterintelligence briefings— layers of abstraction, obscure nomenclature, redundant security gates buried inside obscure submenus.

Finally, after several tense minutes, a schematic unfolded across the screen. Pale lines spiderwebbed into a glowing diagram of nodes and circuits.

"Got something," Jacques murmured. His eyes narrowed, scanning the screen. "Power flow map."

Emerald leaned closer. "What are we looking at?"

Jacques tapped the screen, highlighting two isolated connections in the web of dead links. "The terminal's not integrated with the facility's primary systems. It's running in isolation—barely connected to anything else."

He pointed to a pair of glowing nodes. "Only two active links: one to a surveillance camera... and one to an external door control."

Florence's voice cut in from behind, sharp and skeptical. "So it's not a control hub after all?"

Jacques turned, calm but resolute. "It is. But it's been severed from the network. Either by design or by collapse. To access the core systems, we'll have to reestablish a connection—physically."

He flicked a few keys, pulling up the camera feed. The screen shifted to a grainy view of a corridor: dim metal walls crumpled inward, half-buried in debris. The angle was poor, but Jacques could make out the dull shimmer of wiring beneath the rubble—and a faint, pulsing light further in.

"The external door's still intact," he said. "But the corridor behind it... not so much. I can open it. But I can't promise there'll be anything worth finding on the other side."

Saturn stepped forward, peering through his goggles. "Might as well try," he said with a shrug. "Better to confirm what we're dealing with than stand here squinting at a grainy video."

Jacques nodded. "Opening it now."

His fingers glided across the keyboard as he navigated to the door control interface. A soft beep answered his command, followed by a low, mechanical groan as the door's release mechanism engaged. Metal scraped as the heavy frame slid open, revealing a corridor choked with earthen debris.

The full extent of the collapse became immediately clear. Twisted steel, loose dirt, and large rocks filled the passage, narrowing it to a tight gap near the left-hand wall. Dust drifted in lazy spirals, catching the cold light of a flickering overhead fixture—the only sign of power beyond the door.

Jacques stepped forward, his boots crunching over the debris. The others followed, their footsteps subdued by the weight of anticipation. Emerald's eyes scanned the corridor, assessing.

"Doesn't look promising," she muttered, her voice clipped.

Jacques crouched by the narrow fissure, eyeing the twisted metal. The opening was tight—barely wide enough for someone small to wriggle through—but it led somewhere. He could feel it. Not a dead end.

"There's a chance someone small enough could squeeze through," he said, glancing back at the group. "If they can get eyes on what's beyond, we'll know if this is worth the risk. Otherwise, we will need to find another entry point."

He shifted forward to study the gap more closely, angling his shoulder toward the twisted frame. Before he could speak again, a bright voice cut through the silence.

"I'll go," Emerald said.

Jacques looked up, caught off guard by the enthusiasm in her tone. Her eyes held his, certain, already climbing the decision tree faster than he could stop her. But he shook his head.

"Emerald," he said, voice low. "It's dangerous."

She hesitated, the fire in her eyes dimming slightly, her lips tightening. He saw the rebellion flare—then fade. She took a half-step back, arms crossing over her chest.

Before the silence could stretch, a sharp hoot echoed through the garden.

Jacques turned. U'gah had stepped forward, his massive club planted like a standard beside him. The bergbar's shoulders were squared with purpose, his eyes glittering with excitement.

Jacques rose, already anticipating the argument. "U'gah, listen. That gap is unstable. If anything shifts while you're inside— even a little—it could bring the whole thing down. We can't risk—"

But the warning only seemed to embolden him.

U'gah tilted his head and grinned wide, a glint of mischief flashing across his round face. The more Jacques listed the dangers, the brighter the shaman's expression grew. His fingers tapped the haft of his club like a war drum. This wasn't cautionary logic to U'gah—it was an invitation.

Jacques pinched the bridge of his nose, exhaling slowly. The frustration simmering in his chest threatened to break loose, but he forced it down. "This isn't a game, U'gah," he said, his voice low and sharp. "We don't know what's on the other side. If something happens to you in there, we can't follow. We won't be able to help."

U'gah didn't flinch. That grin—infuriating and unshaken— held its ground, but Jacques saw understanding behind it. Pride was at play, sure. Maybe even arrogance. But most of all, there was certainty blazing in his dark eyes. And that was harder to argue with.

Jacques stepped closer, dropping his voice to a murmur meant for the bergbar alone.

"If we're doing this," he said, his tone flat but steady, "we do it smart. This isn't about being brave—we know you are. You've got nothing to prove. But if you're going in, you take nothing you can't drop. No treasure, no club, nothing that'll slow you down or trap you inside. Understood?"

U'gah's grin softened. His dark eyes searched Jacques's face, and something in him stilled, just a little. He gave a slow nod. Then, without a word, he set his greatclub aside, thudding softly. His tapestry case followed, placed with reverence beside the weapon like a prayer left at a shrine.

535

Jacques turned to the others. "Emerald, Saturn—hold the entrance. Watch for movement. If anything shifts, we pull him out. Florence, hang back but stay ready."

He looked to U'gah, who was already crouched beside the gap, testing the angle with one shoulder, his thick fingers splayed on the cold metal.

Jacques let out a breath. "And you," he said, quieter this time. "Be careful."

U'gah looked back over his shoulder. The grin was back, smaller now, but still bright. He nodded, and then slipped into the darkness, swallowed by shadow one steady breath at a time.

Jacques stepped back, arms folded across his chest, eyes fixed on the opening.

Too late to change his mind now.

All they could do was wait.

CHAPTER THIRTY-FOUR

'gah crouched low. Hands on ground. Nose close to dust. The gap was small—narrow—but that was fine. He had crawled through worse. Cave-mouths. Beast dens. This one was stone and iron. Tight, biting. But passable.

He touched the edge. Felt the scrape.

His tribe stood behind. Watching.

He felt Emerald's eyes. Soft fire on his skin. He didn't turn to look. Her scent, her heat, the weight of her stare—it sat on his shoulders like a pelt. Not heavy. Just there. Just... warm.

He liked it.

But he didn't smile. Not after the shame.

Not after the laugh that shouldn't have been.

He grunted. Placed the club down. Placed the treasure beside it. His stomach twisted. Club whined like a cub left behind. But U'gah gave it a pat.

Then he went in.

The stone-mouth gripped him. Jagged teeth. Scraped skin. His shoulders caught, but he pressed on. Metal bit his back. Sharp metal worms kissed his side. He didn't stop. Pain was friend. Pain said: keep moving.

Breathe in. Push. Breathe out. Pull.

The tunnel wanted to keep him. Wanted to eat him slow. But U'gah was stronger. Not big-strong. Inside-strong.

Dust filled his nose. Made his eyes sting. But he kept crawling. Slow and sure. Like a beetle that digs through deadwood.

He found a rock. Solid. Grabbed it. Pulled.

Again.

Again.

He spilled out. Rolled free. Sat up fast.

Victory roar burst from his chest. Loud. Echoing.

"Eyiee!" he howled. "U'gah rumbu!"

He grinned. Broad and full. Hands bloody. Breath wild. But, happy.

Turned back to call the others.

Then the earth spoke.

Groaned deep in its belly.

U'gah's smile faded.

Then the mouth behind him collapsed.

Metal snapped. Dust exploded.

Gone.

The way was gone.

His heart pounded. No joy now. Dread.

He stared at the wall. Rubble stacked tight. No path. No light.

His fists clenched.

He struck the nearest iron root. Hard. Again and again.

No words. Just fire in his chest. Red fire.

Tribe lost.

The clang rang out. Cold echo. No answer.

He hit it more.

Didn't stop.

Hands burned. Arms shook. Breath came ragged. Mouth dry. Blood on knuckles.

The noise filled the dark.

That was all he had.

The anger burned. Then faded.

He slumped forward.

Pressed his forehead to the iron root. Cold on his brow. Like stream rock.

He stayed there. Quiet now.

Trapped.

Air thick. Heavy with dust. Swirling in slow dances through the dim.

U'gah blinked. Eyes burned. But something... something was different.

Above—ghostfire.

Lanterns once dead now glowed like old coals. Weak. Faint. Flickering like fire too tired to live. The nearest one pulsed soft yellow. The next, weaker. Then weaker still. And far down the tunnel—nothing. Just black.

The half-light made the world strange. Twisting shapes along the walls like bone fingers.

He saw the way he'd come more clearly now.

The walls bristled with broken metal, sharp like spear-traps. The ground was not ground—it was rubble. Loose chunks. Hard footing.

U'gah pushed himself up. Muscles growled, but he ignored them. He did not want to stop here. This was not the place. He was meant to scout. To return. Not be trapped.

He sucked in a breath. Let it out slow.

Sound.

Not his. Not rock settling.

Voices.

His ears twitched. Turned like a beast catching wind.

Again—muffled.

"U'gah! Hold on!"

Jacques. That was Jacques.

Then Emerald.

"We're working on it!" she yelled. Loud. Fierce. Fear hiding in the fire. "Just stay where you are!"

U'gah stepped closer to the stone-mouth that had eaten the way. Pressed paws to cold metal. Pressed ear to iron root.

More voices now.

Florence. Barking like an angry den-mother. Snapping words.

Saturn's voice too. Soft. Musing. Clever-thoughts U'gah couldn't follow—but they were there.

All of them. Still close.

He grunted and listened.

Hands stayed on the wall—not to dig, but to feel.

They were on the other side.

Trying.

***

Emerald's heart lurched as the corridor behind U'gah caved in, the screech of twisting metal and the thunder of falling stone hammering through the air. Dust billowed like smoke. Her stomach flipped. "Oh no—oh no! What do we do now?" she gasped, voice high, shaking. "We've got to get him out of there!"

She turned frantically to the others, eyes wide, searching for reassurance—for a plan. But what she saw in their faces only fed her panic. Jacques stood frozen, jaw clenched, his skin gone paper-white.

Then—

"Why?" Florence's voice cut through the tension like a scalpel. Dismissive. Cold. "The little primitive should be fine. He can probably dig himself out if we give him enough time."

Emerald spun, stunned. The words hit her like a slap. Her mouth opened in disbelief. Florence stood with arms crossed, the picture of careless indifference, as if the collapse meant nothing. As if U'gah were nothing.

Emerald's gaze shot to Jacques.

What she saw stopped her breath.

He was still, but something had changed—his pallor gone, flushed now with a violent red that climbed from his neck to his temples. His eyes locked on Florence with a fury so sharp it radiated heat. Emerald instinctively stepped back.

Quick. Silent. Controlled—but just barely.

Jacques's hand shot out, grabbed her cloak by the collar, and lifted her off the ground in one swift motion. Her feet dangled, boots brushing dirt, hands scrambling for his wrist.

"We're going to get him out," Jacques growled, low, trembling with restraint. "And if I hear anything different leave your mouth before he's free—so help me—I will bury you."

Emerald stood frozen, breath caught in her throat. Jacques's hands trembled—not from strain, but from the sheer force it took to keep himself from going further. The weight of his anger was suffocating. Not a shout. Not a blow. Just a promise —quiet and lethal.

Florence paled. Her lips moved, but no sound came. For once, there was no venom, no retort—just stunned silence, the mask of arrogance peeled away by something far more primal.

Emerald's fear twisted like a pulse of painful empathy that cut straight through the noise. Jacques, trembling with fury, pushed past the edge of control. Florence, stunned, oblivious to how deeply she'd crossed the line. And U'gah—trapped, silent, waiting—trusting them to bring him back.

"Jacques," Emerald said softly.

Her voice didn't shake, though her hands still did. She stepped closer, eyes on him, steady and firm. "We need you. He needs you. But we can't do this if you lose yourself."

Jacques's jaw flexed. His arm held taut for one more second. Then—slowly—he lowered Florence to the ground.

She stumbled. Coughing, brushing at her cloak. Her hands shook. Her mouth opened but no sound came. The sharpness she always wore like armor was gone. It had been burned away by something far more real.

Jacques turned his back to her, breathing hard.

Emerald reached out, laid a hand over his knuckles. "Let's get him out," she said, quiet but unflinching.

Her thoughts spun as she turned back to the rubble, the image of U'gah buried beyond it impossible to shake. Was he conscious? Was he breathing? The silence beyond the debris felt too heavy, too final. But panic would only waste time.

She forced herself to focus.

"The first thing we need to do is get air flowing in," Saturn said. He crouched at the base of the collapse, already inspecting the jagged stone and twisted metal. His hands moved quickly, brushing aside smaller pieces. "If we don't, he'll suffocate long before we clear this."

Emerald swallowed hard. Her breath hitched. "Okay," she said, trying to keep her voice steady. "So how do we do that?"

"We need a conduit," Saturn said. "A vent, a pipe, anything narrow and hollow. Something to carry air through."

Before she could respond, Jacques had already moved back to the console. His fingers flew across the keys, his focus locked and furious. Emerald watched him, her eyes stinging with dry tears. He was holding it together—but just barely.

"Something's changed," he muttered. "Either U'gah triggered something, or the collapse forced a reconnection. The terminal's pulling from deeper systems now."

Emerald blinked. "Reconnected? That means we have access again?"

Jacques nodded without looking up. "Partially. It's still limited. NAVI's only pushing enough juice to keep this section online. If I want more, I need to bring backup systems back online."

"What about the generators?" Saturn asked, rising beside him. "The Axis didn't build anything without redundancy. There's got to be a secondary power node somewhere nearby."

Jacques's fingers hesitated for half a heartbeat before continuing their swift rhythm across the keys. "That's what I'm checking now. If I can reroute emergency power—draw from the backup grid or tap dormant reserves—we might have enough to activate ventilation."

Emerald swallowed, the knot in her chest tightening. "And if the backups are shot?"

Jacques's jaw flexed. "Then we're back to square one. There's no telling how long this place has been abandoned. The systems might be beyond saving."

Silence settled thick and heavy over the group—broken only by the faint hum of the console and the occasional scrape of loose stone shifting underfoot. Emerald stared at the mound of debris, her hands curling into fists. U'gah was buried behind that wall, somewhere in the dark. Alone. Trapped. And counting on them.

"Okay," she said, stepping forward, steady despite the panic fluttering in her chest. "What do you need from me? I'll do whatever it takes."

She planted herself near the rubble, heart hammering. U'gah's faint cries—barely audible now—scraped against her nerves like broken glass. Each muffled sound made the pressure worse, made her feel smaller. But she refused to let it freeze her.

"We should just start digging," Florence said. The edge in her voice was there, but dulled—muted by something that sounded almost like doubt.

Emerald turned toward her sharply. Florence looked unsteady. The earlier confrontation with Jacques had clearly left its mark. Her stance wasn't quite as defiant, her words less venomous. But she still couldn't help herself. She still had to be heard.

"We can't," Jacques said, his voice frayed at the edges. His eyes never left the screen. "If we dig without support, we risk collapse. We make the wrong move, and we bury him for good."

Florence folded her arms, bristling. "But standing around does nothing. At least it's—"

"No," Jacques snapped, turning to meet her gaze with exhausted fire. "It's not progress. It's a landslide waiting to happen. We pull on one wrong beam, one unstable slab, and it all caves in. You want to help? Don't make it worse."

Florence flinched, her mouth tightening. She muttered something too low to catch, but she didn't push again.

Emerald's gaze darted between them. Every second that passed felt like a betrayal. She *wanted* to side with Jacques—she *did* —but the weight of helplessness pressed harder than logic.

Jacques exhaled, shoulders stiff, fingers pausing at the console as he pinched the bridge of his nose. "With any luck, Hyatta and Lusa will show up soon," he muttered. "Until then, I'm going to try bringing the ventilation system back online."

Emerald stepped in beside him, her hands braced on the edge of the console. "Tell me what to do," she said again. Not pleading, but insistent. "I'm not standing by while he suffocates. Give me something. Anything."

Jacques looked up at her. The strain around his eyes was unmistakable. But in her gaze, he saw no panic—only resolve.

"Help Saturn," he said, voice low but clear. "Dig in slowly. Try to pull out a pipe or tubing—anything that can move air to him. If we can thread a line through, it'll keep oxygen flowing and buy us time."

She crouched beside a scattered pile of debris, digging with steady, deliberate hands. She refused to let the hopelessness take root.

Jacques turned then, his gaze landing on Florence. His tone shifted—still firm, but no longer laced with fire. "If you want to help, keep watch on the rubble. If anything shifts, even a little, you shout. Understood?"

Florence opened her mouth, just slightly. Maybe to protest. Maybe to deflect. But the words never came. She held his gaze for a breath longer, then nodded. Wordless. Muted. She moved toward the debris, crouching stiffly, tension in every line of her body.

Emerald didn't look back. She couldn't afford to. Every second mattered.

Her hands dug through bent metal and shattered stone, her mind whirling. U'gah's laughter echoed in her memory— booming, bright, and unshakable. His warmth. His loyalty. His sheer, untamed presence. He was counting on them.

Counting on her.

A jagged shard cut her palm. She hissed, ignored it, and kept searching.

They weren't going to lose him. Not like this. Not alone. Not buried.

She spotted a broken length of reinforced conduit—hollow, narrow, but intact. She yanked it free.

"We're going to get you out," she whispered, clutching the pipe in both hands like a lifeline. "Just hold on, U'gah. Please— hold on."

***

Jacques felt bile rise in his throat, a bitter taste of the doubt gnawing at him. His hands hovered over the terminal, fingers twitching, as if the next command might finally break through. The pressure was immense, a silent weight pressing down from every angle. From the others. From U'gah. From himself. And every second without a solution clawed deeper into him.

It wasn't just the rubble threatening to bury the shaman. It was the creeping certainty that Jacques might not be enough.

He closed his eyes and drew a breath, but it caught halfway down. The image of U'gah, pinned in the dark, air thinning by the second, wouldn't let go. The knot in Jacques's chest tightened. *Focus,* he told himself. *You don't get to panic. Not now.*

He hadn't meant to lose control with Florence, but she'd lit the fuse. Her cold indifference had struck something raw. Still, it wasn't really about her, not entirely. The outburst had been fear. Guilt. The sickening weight of being helpless. And now that fear was back, coursing through his veins like poison, whispering failure in a voice that sounded like his own.

"Espèce de merde," he muttered, the terminal blinking another rejection at him. NAVI's hum had dulled. Its systems strained from the constant output. Jacques glanced at the readout— thirty, maybe forty minutes of power left before the drone needed to shut down to recharge. No solar gain. No external feed. Just the silence of the gardens, oppressive under a moonless sky. Stars gleamed coldly above, casting jagged shadows across the blood-colored stone.

546

His eyes shifted to the power flow diagram. Emergency backups—dead. Auxiliary systems—offline. He'd already checked twice, hoping for an oversight. But the truth was etched across the screen in unchanging lines. The circuits were cold. The connections eaten by time.

Only one line remained lit. The main reactor.

Jacques stared at it, jaw tightening. It was a long shot and dangerous. If the core was completely inert, they'd waste precious minutes chasing a ghost. If it wasn't... it might give them the charge they needed to activate ventilation, communication systems, maybe more.

Or it could cascade through unstable power conduits and make everything worse.

But they were out of options.

He straightened slowly, shoulders tense beneath his coat. A sharp exhale escaped his chest. Then he turned, scanning the garden. Emerald and Saturn were still working by the collapsed passage, rigging conduit into an improvised air pipe. He could hear the scrape of metal, the soft murmur of shared effort.

"I'm going to try the reactor," Jacques said.

She turned, worry etched across her face.

"Is that even safe?" she asked, voice hushed but urgent. "What if it—"

"It's the only option we have left," Jacques said, cutting in before Emerald could finish. His voice was firm, but not without sympathy. "NAVI's nearly out. The backups are dead. If the reactor's got anything left in it, we might be able to stabilize the systems and get the ventilation running."

Saturn adjusted his goggles and stepped in closer to the terminal. His voice was quieter now, almost clinical. "And if it doesn't?"

Jacques hesitated. The silence that followed was heavy—thick with implications no one wanted to name.

"Then we'll have learned something," he said finally, echoing Saturn's own words from earlier. His tone was low but resolute. "We're not leaving him in there. Not for anything."

He didn't wait for a response.

Turning back to the terminal, Jacques let his fingers fly across the keys. The reactor controls were buried deep beneath multiple layers of Axis encryption—redundant, meticulous, deliberately obtuse. As he navigated the archaic interface, his thoughts churned. Restarting a long-dormant reactor was dangerous. *Reckless,* even. But there was no time left for caution.

Finally, a new window opened.

Fuel registered. And better still, it wasn't a fission reactor. Cold fusion—heavy water. Jacques exhaled, a faint, grim smile breaking through the pressure in his chest.

"Cold fusion," he muttered. "One less catastrophe to deal with."

Time bled away in slow, agonizing drips as he worked through the priming sequence. NAVI lay on the ground nearby, its lights dimming with each second, its internal hum growing thinner, fainter.

Jacques tuned out everything else—the creak of shifting rubble, the whisper of voices behind him, the mounting dread. All that existed now was the terminal.

Almost there.

The final prompt blinked onto the screen, requesting confirmation to initiate fusion. Jacques finalized the confirmation—and froze as NAVI let out a soft, stuttering whine.

Then its lights went dark.

The terminal screen blinked—then followed suit.

Jacques stood there, staring at the blank interface. The drone was dead. The power was gone. And the fusion start-up—whether it would have completed or failed—was now a question without an answer.

"No," he breathed.

He leaned forward, bracing both hands on the cold metal edge of the terminal, heart pounding against the cage. *I failed him,* he thought. *Failed all of them.*

Suffocation.

Behind him, Emerald and Saturn worked in low murmurs, still threading tubing through the rubble, still doing what they could. But Jacques barely heard them. His vision tunneled around the dead screen.

Then—

He straightened sharply. The screen shuddered back to life, lines of code racing across the display. The terminal emitted a soft hum, low at first, then rising, vibrating through the stone like something waking from a long sleep. Power surged through the veins of the forgotten facility.

The garden itself seemed to exhale. A faint tremor rolled beneath their feet.

"Jacques?" Emerald's voice broke through, confused and anxious. "What's happening?"

He didn't answer. His hands were already dancing over the interface, inputting familiar overrides, bypassing the same security layers he'd forced open earlier. The menus cascaded open, their contents clearer now. At the center of it all: the reactor status.

Active. Stable. Online.

Jacques let out a long, shaking breath.

"It worked," he said, voice rough with exhaustion but edged with triumph. He turned to the others, his face drawn but alive with hard-earned relief. "The reactor's online."

***

U'gah raised his hands as the stone-belly trembled.

A warning.

His skin rippled. Fur surged out, thick and wild. Bones swelled. Snout stretched. Paws slammed to earth, claws biting the stone. Bear-shape. Strong-shape. Needed now.

The world rattled. Loud. Fast. Echoes slammed from wall to wall. U'gah crouched low, breath locked tight in his chest.

Then—ghostfire.

The lanterns above screamed to life. Too bright. Blinding.

U'gah growled. Paws shielded his eyes. Blinks came fast. Pain behind his lids.

Slow, the world bled back into shape.

The dark was gone. Dust spun wild in the wind. Not cave-wind. Not sky-wind. Made by dead gods. Hissing out of slits in the walls like snakes breathing old poison.

U'gah sniffed.

Rust. Grease. Metal left to rot. The smell of forgotten things.

Slow. Careful. Claws scraped stone. Ears high. Eyes wide.

The walls were sick-green. Paint peeled like bark in drought. Brown streaks crawled from the corners. Weeping.

Not a home. Not a den. This place had no good spirits.

Then—something ahead.

A door. Big. Round-wheel on its chest. A thin hiss of air escaped where the seal was broken.

U'gah narrowed his eyes.

That door... it *watched*.

Felt like a line he could not uncross.

The air shifted again. Overhead, the lights stuttered—pulse like an old heart, fighting sleep. U'gah tilted his head. Heard the hum. The buzz. Deep-throat growls of machines waking far away.

The place lived now.

But it was sick.

The stonefall was quiet now. Far behind. But not forgotten.

U'gah glanced back. Dark eyes on the broken mouth that had swallowed the way. Sharp rocks. Tangled steel. No path. No friends.

But he felt them still.

Felt Jacques—calm but burning. Emerald—fire-heart, bright and fierce. Even Florence, angry as she was, would not leave him buried. They would dig. They would fight the dirt and stone.

He would not shame them.

He turned.

The steel door breathed louder now. Hiss through the crack like breath through fangs. Cold wind touched his snout. Made his fur lift.

Claws tapped soft on the floor. Step by step.

He reached out. Touched the wheel.

Metal bit back—cold. His ears swiveled. Listening.

But the voices were gone.

Only small rumbling now.

Deep hum. Hiss from the walls. Clicks. Groans. Echoes without soul.

He was alone.

Could this be another god-cave? A place from the old stories?

Yes. It smelled like story. Like death and danger and wonder.

Where the sky burned different and men made magic from metal. The kind of place U'gah thought he'd never see. But now... here it was a second time.

He looked back one last time. At the rubble. The sealed throat of the god-cave.

They would come. He believed that. But while they worked, he could work too.

He turned back. Planted his feet.

Gripped the wheel with both paws.

Pulled.

It fought him. Screeched. Groaned.

He growled.

Pulled harder.

It broke.

The door opened slow. Guts grinding. A breath of cold air hit him—sharp, metal-tasting. Carried a scent he couldn't name but knew. Something familiar.

He stepped through.

Claws clicked on smooth floor.

The room beyond glowed with ghostfire. Pipes ran along the walls like silver roots. The fire blinked in strange rhythms. Machines whispered in tongues he did not speak.

But the room was not dead.

It *watched.*

552

It *waited*.

This place had no tribe. No heartbeat but its own.

Not made for halflings. Not made for men.

Still—U'gah walked.

Ears turned. Shoulders set. Each step slow and strong.

His blood said *caution*.

His spirit said *forward*.

Behind him, the steel door hissed shut—whispering nowhere to run.

Fur bristled. Muscles coiled.

He walked on. U'gah was not prey. Not anymore.

He would face what came. Alone. Strong. Ready.

Chapter Thirty-Five

Hyatta stood in the shadows of a narrow alley, eyes fixed on the commotion still churning in the streets beyond. Beside him, Lusa lounged with smug indifference, licking a paw as if he hadn't just helped orchestrate a calculated disruption. The aftermath of their encounter with the slaver, Ulfrey, still lingered in the air. His shaken pride and minor injuries were a small but satisfying price for crimes against thinking beings.

Hyatta exhaled slowly, tension bleeding from his shoulders by degrees. It had been gratifying—more than that, it had felt *right*—to put fear in the elf. To remind him that not all creatures bowed to his so-called authority. The very concept of slavery disgusted Hyatta, gnawed at his conscience like a carrion bird. Even as a youth among the Siva'gat, whose rigid caste lines often blurred into servitude, he'd never accepted it. He had argued with elders, challenged sacred law, questioned traditions passed down from the first prophets of the Zırhlı Yutucu. Every time, he was met with the same refrain:

Our ways are ancient, unshakable, dictated by the divine.

A muscle ticked in his jaw. He remembered the futility of those debates—sour memories that clung like bile. Honor had demanded his silence. But this wasn't Gabutha. These weren't the Siva'gat. And here, in the heart of a strange land, he would follow his own sense of justice. If the gods disapproved, they could say so to his face.

He glanced at Lusa, who had paused mid-grooming to flick his golden eyes toward the street. His bobbed tail twitched with silent amusement. Lusa enjoyed the chaos, Hyatta knew that, but he also understood its purpose. Their little disruption wasn't indulgence, or even truly about freeing those people. It was misdirection.

In a city like Zahadah, where every wall had ears and every seedy trade watched for cracks, the others could easily draw the wrong kind of attention. Emerald's curiosity. Saturn's detachment. Florence's open noncompliance. Any of them might provoke the wrong questions and inspire suspicion. Hyatta's hope was that his display—the public challenge—would distract the eyes of the city so Jacques and the rest could move unnoticed.

A faint smirk tugged at his lips. Rumors would spread. They always did. Tales of a whip-wielding foreigner and his oversized catfolk companion turning slavers into cowards. Those would circulate. With any luck, they'd keep the city guards focused on shadows.

The scrape of boots on stone pulled his focus back to the street. People moved cautiously. Some were hurrying away, while others were lingering at a distance, their eyes wide with speculation. The guards had arrived in force. *Good*, Hyatta thought. Let them hunt the specter of a madman in a cloak. Let them find nothing but whispers.

Lusa's paw pressed against his arm. The Mau tilted his head, his eyes glinting.

"Happy?" he purred.

He watched the slaver limp away, the dark elf favoring his injured leg, while casting nervous glances over his shoulder. Only when the figure vanished into the crowd did Hyatta give a slow nod.

"For now," he said, low and resolute.

"Good," Lusa purred, stretching languidly. "Hungry. Smell food."

Hyatta rolled his eyes at the Mau's typical bluntness but turned away, his steps vanishing into the alley's deeper shadows. He brushed back his hood slightly, letting the cool air kiss his skin. The passage ahead wound into darkness. It was thick with the scent of damp stone and distant spices. Lusa followed without a sound, his presence a silent truth: no matter how quiet Hyatta moved, the Mau moved quieter.

Streetlights bloomed to life on tall metallic poles, throwing pale, uncertain luminescence across the carved stone walls. The light barely touched the alley's confines, and Hyatta's thoughts wandered—back to the confrontation, to the way Ulfrey's pride had crumpled under a single look, to the slow venom of fear that had seeped into the elf.

He wondered, briefly, if despair came to all men. Or if even he, one day, would let it take root.

Without warning, Lusa's hand shot out, iron-strong fingers clamping onto Hyatta's forearm mid-stride. The Mau's ears twitched. His golden eyes narrowed.

"What?" Hyatta muttered, irritation flashing—until he felt it.

A low vibration ran through the stone beneath his boots. Subtle, but unmistakable. He looked down. Dust trembled on the cobbled alleyway, stones shifting in tiny, stuttering patterns— as if something far below had stirred. A moan rose from the ground, no more than a breath at first, but quickly rising to a roar.

Hyatta crouched, one palm pressed to the stony ground. The tremor pulsed again—slow, steady, and unnatural. It wasn't an earthquake.

Something was moving beneath them.

Lusa's ears flattened. His eyes scanned the dark with eerie calm. "Something wakes," he whispered, his bobtail twitching.

"Find the others," Hyatta snapped.

The Mau vanished instantly with one fluid motion, a ripple of fur and shadow. His orange coat shimmered once in the streetlight, then disappeared entirely, leaving behind only silence.

Hyatta didn't watch him go. If anyone could find the others without being seen, it was Lusa.

He looked up. The alley walls loomed around him, etched with ancient reliefs—dead gods, forgotten battles. He studied the surface, finding the lines where fingers might grip, and climbed.

His muscles burned with the strain, his boots scraping softly against stone. The wind grew stronger as he rose, carrying with it the distant sounds of Zahadah. Confused vendors still hawked their wares. Nervous babble drifted up through the air, between spires. Hooves clattered on distant streets.

It felt remote—detached. The city's noise belonged to another world.

Not this one.

Not the one Hyatta now moved through—wrapped with warning, sharpened by dread.

Crouched at the rooftop's edge, the city sprawled beneath him like a living tapestry. Towers and spires pierced the night sky, their silhouettes rimmed in the soft glow of ancient streetlamps. From this height, Zahadah stretched endlessly—a labyrinth of rooftops and winding alleys, a city carved from the remains of legends and layered in secrets.

His gut told him the others had found something. Whether it was what they were looking for, or something worse, remained to be seen.

Hyatta had seen enough to know digging too deep never goes unanswered.

Bad things happen in the dark, he thought, his gaze fixed on the horizon where Zahadah's high walls met the star-pierced sky.

If something stirred beneath them, they would need to be ready.

And so would he.

***

Jacques stared at the terminal, brow furrowed, fingers moving in a practiced rhythm across the keys. The Axis system beneath Zahadah—Yggdrasil—was a fortress of redundancies and firewalls, a paranoid labyrinth of security layers. Each command felt like peeling back another sheath of coiled steel: every success brought him closer, but the depth of the system threatened to bury him.

He exhaled sharply, rubbing a hand over his jaw. Progress was slow, but tangible. He had gained access to the security feeds and motion sensors. They were small victories, but critical ones.

Footage flickered across the display: grainy, distorted, fisheye images that warped the geometry of the halls, making it difficult to tell depth from distance. Still, the feeds told a clear story; this place was no pristine stronghold like Wrasas Station had been. Yggdrasil bore the scars of time.

His eyes tracked U'gah's movements through the decaying corridors. The halfling advanced with determined focus, peering into every open doorway. Jacques could almost feel the pressure of the place pressing down on him—the silence, the damp, the slow drip of water echoing through the dark.

Where Wrasas had been clean, sealed, and untouched, this facility had been left to rot. Dark stains streaked the walls like veins. Paint peeled from surfaces in warped, curling flakes, revealing rust-eaten metal and brittle concrete. Water pooled in uneven patches, rippling as U'gah's bare feet moved through. Even from a distance, Jacques imagined the scent: wet rot and oxidized oil, thick and chemical.

He toggled between cameras, following U'gah's progress. The halfling was methodical, more so than Jacques had expected. His eyes darted left and right like a scout navigating foreign terrain. Jacques had faith in him. But seeing U'gah alone down there, weaponless, surrounded by ruin... it stirred a quiet tension in him.

He tapped another command and zoomed in on a corridor ahead of U'gah. The motion sensors pulsed like faint, intermittent signatures beyond the halfling's range. Jacques's heart quickened. Was the machinery glitching? Or was it a sensor malfunction?

He switched feeds. The image struggled in the low light, full of static and compression blur. Still—there. A blur. A shadow, subtle but definitely there, shifted just beyond the field of vision. Jacques narrowed his eyes, gut tightening.

"Come on, U'gah," he muttered, fingers tensing over the keys.

Behind him, Emerald's voice pierced the quiet. "Anything useful yet?"

He didn't turn. "I've got eyes on him," Jacques said, shaky. "The place is falling apart. No internal communication... yet."

Saturn, perched over his shoulder, adjusted his goggles and peered at the screen. "You'll figure it out," he said flatly.

Jacques sighed, his fingers drumming against the console. He needed deeper access—environmental controls, structural readouts. But above all, he needed communications. If he could bring the network online, he could guide U'gah and warn him of dangers he couldn't yet see.

He settled into a rhythm, his focus drifting between grainy fisheye camera feeds and the tangled menus of the Axis OS. Crumbling corridors flickered across the screen, distorted and unstable, while streams of data crawled past his eyes. His fingers moved with tapping urgency. Every keystroke felt heavier than it should, like a step through a minefield.

The comms interface remained elusive, but in its place, something unexpected appeared. A new menu opened across the terminal, detached from the internal feeds: **DEFENSIVE SYSTEMS STATUS**.

Jacques leaned in. The header pulsed bold against the dark background. Curious, he toggled into the logs.

The internal defense matrix was down, offline by either neglect or design. But the external system, the *defense web* remained active. His brow furrowed. It was a net of plasma-capable nodes scattered throughout the city. According to the specs, they could generate atmospheric discharges—weaponized lightning, effectively.

Once the system was triggered, what would it consider a hostile? He doubted Axis engineers had written nuanced ethical protocols. With the system degraded, anything could be flagged: guards, civilians, his team.

The entire city sat under a trap that might not know friend from foe.

He filed the knowledge away. The web could be a tool, or a catastrophe. If they needed a diversion, it might buy them time. Or it might level half of Zahadah. Either way, it was a card to be played only with care.

As he scrolled deeper, something about the design caught his eye. There was a familiarity to it—a logic in the system's geometry that tugged at the back of his mind. He followed it through diagnostic sublayers, watching the way the node arrays synchronized and recycled energy through airborne circuits.

Then it clicked.

Tesla.

Jacques exhaled, a half-smile formed despite the pressure knotting his chest. The architecture mimicked the wireless energy theories of Nikola Tesla—nineteenth-century visionary, twentieth-century muse to madmen and dreamers. It was uncanny. As if the Axis had taken pages from forgotten notebooks and built them into war machines.

He could already hear Emerald teasing him—*Told you so.* She'd pestered him for months to read more about Tesla, even tried to drag him into some half-baked sci-fi retrospectives when they had been safely tucked in Wrasas.

The weight returned.

He rubbed a hand down his face. Fascinating as it was, the defense web wouldn't bring U'gah home. Wouldn't clear rubble. Wouldn't open a channel. It was another dead branch on a tree full of thorns.

And U'gah was still down there—alone.

Frustration mounted with each line of dead-end code. As if the pressure wasn't enough already. He scoured the system map, eyes gritty with fatigue, hunting for any trace of the communications subroutines.

It was chaos.

Nothing was where it should be. Menus nested in illogical clusters, subsystems mislabeled or buried without reason. It felt intentional—as if the Axis engineers had built the interface not just to secure, but to confuse, frustrate, and punish intruders.

Jacques had worked with labyrinthine systems before. This one felt personal.

His eyes blurred as more alphanumeric gibberish scrolled past —long strings of diagnostics and command-line residue. And beneath the irritation, something else tugged: a creeping unease he couldn't define.

He tried to ignore it, but failed.

It clawed at the edge of his awareness, a pressure he couldn't blink away.

He leaned back, sighing heavily, rubbing at his temples. *What am I missing?*

His gaze shifted to the live feed tracking U'gah. The halfling crept forward warily.

The corridors were lit, but not as well as they should be. White fluorescents hummed overhead, casting a watery glow over peeling paint and cracked tile, as if pools had collected in the coverings. It should have been a relief, but it wasn't. The light distorted everything. It hid what mattered.

And then U'gah passed into a darker stretch of hallway and Jacques understood.

The screen lost resolution. Just for a heartbeat. Then— movement.

Jacques felt icy fingers crawl up his spine, his heart hammering as something sinuous uncoiled from the ceiling. Tendrils. Black and slow and alive. They slid down the walls, pulsing faintly with violet light—veins of energy threading through the decay like glowing rot.

"Mon Dieu…" he whispered.

His fingers curled around the edge of the console, knuckles whitening. The tendrils moved with sickening grace, coiling and flexing as if tasting the air. They clung to walls, spreading across the ceiling, and slithered across the floor. They were drawing in on U'gah.

He toggled the feed, trying for a better angle.

No mistake. He recognized them.

The same tendrils that had pierced the blast doors on Level H. The same ones that carried the corruption of the Mother.

She's here.

And U'gah hadn't seen them.

Jacques's pulse thundered. He scanned for options. The comms were still dead. He hadn't cracked the speaker system. Could he reroute power? Trigger lights, noise, anything?

His hands hovered, helpless over the keyboard.

"Come on," he muttered. "Come on…"

On-screen, U'gah moved deeper into the corridor, oblivious. The tendrils shifted, subtle but deliberate, repositioning in anticipation.

Emerald's voice cut through the tension. "Jacques? What's wrong?"

He didn't answer.

He couldn't look away. The feed blurred at the edges. His breath felt too loud.

The coils moved again, closer.

Jacques spoke at last, his voice low and tight.

"We have a problem."

***

The gods had left this place.

Long ago. Long before memory.

The stone-hall yawned open before him. It stretched far like a tunnel carved by dead giants. Walls peeled and split. Metal bones rusted, weeping. No color here. No soul. Just quiet death.

U'gah moved slow. Bare paws soft on the cracked ground. Muscles tight beneath fur. Ears turning. The place whispered— drip-drip, *scritch*, the tiny scurry of forgotten things. Not beasts. Not spirits. Just rot-born pests with no name.

But that was not what made his fur rise.

Something else lived here.

Not loud. Not seen. But felt.

Like breath on the back of his neck. Like claws waiting in shadow.

He sniffed.

The air was thick, wet, full of belly-sickness. But buried in the stink—something else.

Familiar.

He sniffed again. Slow. Careful.

Old-smell. His nose twitched. Memory stirred—but slipped away. Just out of reach. Like a dream after waking.

He growled, quiet.

The rooms around him were broken. Gutted. Some eaten by dirt, others crushed by fallen stone. He stepped through them like graves. Not to take. Just to look. To know.

He searched the broken corners for story things—relics, god-metal, hunter-trophies. Nothing.

He huffed.

The traders back home had lied. Told tales of treasure in the deep places. Gold. Jewels. Magic bones. One had said love waits in the ruins. That warriors find women with fire-hair and eyes like big water.

No women here.

Only dust.

But he had found his tribe getting here. That was better than gold.

He hoped they were well. That they looked for him. That they did not cry.

He would find them again.

He was strong. Clever. Cleverer than most.

He had bled more than once and kept walking.

Wind? Thin, soft. Not sky-wind. Not clean. But fresher than the cave-breath.

It kissed his cheek. Made his ears flick.

Since the tremble.

Since the old hall groaned like Jacques turning in sleep.

Stone shifted. Air moved. Maybe a tunnel broke open. Maybe a god-door had cracked. Like the ones in the white-place, where the ghost-fire danced and the ghost-woman smiled and he could not touch her.

He sniffed again. Fresh air.

And followed.

Careful. Paws on wet ground. He was alone. Hurt his soul. But he would find it again.

The hall spoke of dead things and pain.

But U'gah's legs did not shake.

He walked forward.

But the feeling would not die.

It gnawed. Twitched in his back. Bit his legs. The air bent—soft one moment, then sharp, like thickets in fog. Shadows grew fat where they should be thin. His blood knew before his eyes.

He stopped at the edge of a wide stone-mouth. Sniffed.

There. Strong now. No more questions.

He knew it.

The scent that burned the back of his throat.

The Mother.

Hands curled into fists. No club. No tribe. Just claws and teeth. He cursed the earth that had taken it.

The stink was sour. Just like before—at the other god-cave, when the pale ones came screaming.

She had touched this place.

Touched it still.

U'gah swallowed. The air scraped his tongue. His eyes swept the tunnel. Long. Still. Empty. But no peace in it. No silence, either.

He turned.

He saw the trap.

Black roots writhed from the walls and ceiling. Veins of ghostfire pulsed inside them—violet, sick. They slithered across the hall behind him, weaving into a wall of undulating veins. No escape. No back-path. Only forward—or death.

Above was worse.

The ceiling choked with the same rot. Hanging like dead vines. Like dry snakes waiting to drop. They strangled the ghost-boxes that made the ghostfire. Shadows spilled heavy, drowned the hall.

No stars down here.

Only the Mother's stink.

Soft first. Dry things brushing. Leaves with no tree. Wind with no breath.

Then louder.

Coughing. Wet. Human-but-not. Close. And closer.

Screams.

High, sharp, like teeth snapping in the dark. Not beast. Not man. Something else. It crawled into his ears. It tore behind his eyes.

U'gah's heart thundered. His belly clenched.

They were here.

The pale ones.

The Mother's children.

Waking.

He could not move. Legs locked. Fear like chains. No path back. Only shadow behind, and deeper dark ahead.

His breath came fast. Head began to spin.

Fight. Flee. Hide.

None of those would work.

He was alone.

And the dark had teeth.

Then—like a peal of thunder splitting night—

A voice.

It crashed through the halls. It came from all places at once. Loud. Commanding.

"Run, U'gah! They're coming! You have to run!"

Jacques. His friend.

The fog in U'gah's head burned away. The fear cracked like dry dirt. The sound lit his heart, not with fear, but with need.

They were here.

The pale ones.

But so were his friends.

He could not fail again. Could not let this place take him like it took the tribe.

With a roar that shook the dust loose from the ceiling, U'gah *ran*.

Legs unchained. Feet pounding. Puddles split beneath him. Pebbles flew. Walls rushed past, green and black and smeared with mold.

He did not look back.

He *felt* them.

Tendrils slithered in the dark. Claws clicked. The scraping grew louder. Faster. Closer.

His lungs burned. Chest heaved.

But he ran.

Each step fought the fear.

There.

A door. Heavy. Safe.

He roared again. Not from rage. With hope.

I am still here.

He ran harder.

The voices behind him hissed like water sprinkled into fire.

He hit the doorway like a charging ram. The door hung half-open. His hands, wide and shaking, gripped its edge. He forced his way through. Turned. Slammed it shut.

WHAM.

Something hit the other side. Hard. Metal screamed. Hinges groaned.

U'gah stumbled back, gasping. Ears flat. Heart a drumbeat in his skull.

BOOM. BOOM. More impacts.

He backed away. Step by step. Claws ready. Ready to strike. Or die.

The room smelled different. Still dead, but not rotting. Not soaked. No swamp-stink. No root-rot. Just dust. Old dust.

He scanned.

Walls close. Cramped like the elder dens back home.

Green paint. Same cursed green.

But less broken. Less bleeding.

Lanterns above winked to life. Soft fire—but not ghostfire.

Shelves sagged under strange boxes. Mold clung to the edges. Words curled on faded labels.

Things littered the ground. Tiny tools. Sharp-glinting things. No weight. No bite.

Nothing that sang of killing.

He growled. Frustrated.

Another slam shook the door.

Then it stopped.

Silence?

No.

Scratching.

Soft at first. Then steady.

Then cruel.

A sound he knew.

Digging.

The pale ones were digging.

Like gravlings. Stripers. Clawing through stone for meat.

They would break through.

He spun. No time.

Hands moved fast, thick fingers tearing open the old god-boxes. Lids snapped, dust hissed. The first was full of dead paper, thin glass teeth, tiny vials with no soul. Useless.

He grunted. Threw it.

Next box. Metal sang as he ripped it open.

There.

His breath caught.

Among coiled guts of rotted wire and rust-blooded scraps—*a tool—no, a gift. Jacques called it a flashlight.* A club of skyfire trapped in metal.

U'gah grabbed it. Cold metal kissed his palm. Strange. But firm.

He fumbled. Turned it. Found the tooth at its side. Click.

FWOOM.

Skyfire. It split the dust. Cut the dark. Pale gold filled the room. Tiny flecks danced in the air, stirred by his search.

U'gah grinned.

Not a weapon. But light was power.

Light chased the Mother. Light burned the things that slithered and crept.

He turned, beam high, and stabbed it toward the door.

The scratching still came. Fast. Hungry.

He held the skyfire club steady.

"Come," he growled.

But the fear still gripped his gut. He would not let it win.

Think.

This room was not his tomb.

He was not a rabbit in a pit.

He was a warrior.

A hunter.

His grip tightened on the skyfire club. He scanned the walls. The shelves. The floor. Searching.

There had to be another path.

The Mother's children were many.

But he was clever.

He whispered through clenched teeth:

"Not today."

CHAPTER THIRTY-SIX

Saturn adjusted the cables between NAVI and the terminal. While Jacques muttered and cursed his way through Yggdrasil's maddening control schema, Saturn had quietly rerouted the power flow—reversing it to recharge the drone—a delicate trick Jacques would've protested if he'd known the risk.

Saturn hadn't hesitated. He knew NAVI better than anyone.

He'd told Jacques, with confidence, that NAVI could handle powering the console. The truth was less convenient. The drone's fuel cells were twitchy at times. That they hadn't ruptured or fried a circuit was a miracle in itself. He cast a glance at NAVI, its pale-blue lights pulsing in a steady rhythm, hungrily drinking the rerouted charge.

He exhaled and tuned out the frantic back-and-forth between Jacques and Emerald. Something about U'gah running from a subterranean horror. Saturn wanted to care. Really. But the sensation just wasn't there. U'gah was built for surviving messes like this.

His eyes moved to Florence instead.

She was camped on a patch of grass glowering into the nothing. Jacques's outburst had rattled her more than she'd admit. If they weren't stranded in a city or on an island she so clearly loathed, she'd probably have stormed off already, vanishing into the alleys until someone went chasing her down. At least this time, geography had curbed her theatrics.

Small mercies.

A sharp curse snapped him back. Jacques was pale now, fingers hammering the keys in panic.

Then silence.

It lasted a second—tight and breathless—before Jacques began rattling off alerts.

"Perimeter breaches," he said, voice ragged and strained. "Base of the plateau. Pale Ones. They're moving into the forest."

A chill crawled up Saturn's spine.

"This is bad," he breathed, pinching the bridge of his nose.

Emerald spun, scanning the night. Her words cracked like a whip. "Where the hell are Hyatta and Lusa?"

Saturn watched her for a beat. Then turned back to NAVI, tension threading through his ribs like piano wire. The drone hummed beneath his touch, steady and calm.

They were down three teammates and out of time.

"Well," Saturn muttered, tapping NAVI's chassis with two fingers like a parent urging a stubborn pet, "looks like we're on sentry duty, my little friend."

With a quiet sigh, he pulled his goggles down. The familiar weight settled across his brow like a visor dropping between him and the world. Everything outside the display dimmed— Jacques's tension, Emerald's worry, Florence's childishness— all muffled beneath the hum of data bleeding through the HUD.

Saturn slipped on his haptic gloves. The world snapped into crisp focus.

He launched NAVI. The drone lifted quietly, its blue lights flickering methodically against the grass before vanishing into the sky. Already inside the stream, he barely noticed. His mind narrowed to the layers of images and readouts projected before him: infrared scans, elevation grids, atmospheric density, pattern recognition. Zahadah unfurled beneath him like a necrotizing organ, cracked stone veins and hollowed arteries.

He swept NAVI along the western rim, where the city's plateau pressed up against the tree line. The forest bristled beneath the drone's sensors.

ANOMALIES DETECTED!

Something was moving between the trees.

Saturn zoomed in, his jaw tightening. Misshapen silhouettes danced between the trunks, too humanoid, and at the same time… not. The Pale Ones. Their shapes twisted and jerked, glowing in the feed with unnatural, pulsing violet veins, radiating a kind of sick biological rhythm in the wash of the moonlight that filtered through the branches. The kind that made your skin crawl before your brain understood why.

"Figures," he muttered, adjusting NAVI's altitude.

The drone banked silently, circling wide as Saturn toggled through visual filters. Low-light vision gave way to thermal, and suddenly the Pale Ones took on a different shape, wraithlike, spectral. They were no longer twitching but gliding, their pale skin appearing cooler than the forest around them. They were spreading through the forest, positioning themselves like a legion forming ranks.

Saturn's stomach turned. He zoomed out, scanning for more movement. A perimeter swarm was bad enough, but what he saw next stopped his breath.

They were flooding out of the plateau.

Pale Ones poured from every break in the rockface as though called by some distant signal—jagged gashes, collapsed ventilation shafts, and rusted doorways yawning open. The origins didn't matter. The outcome did: a crawling, seething tide of bodies spilling into the treeline. Silent, white, and relentless.

Then came hulking figures with stretched limbs and smooth, leathery hides.

He caught them just as they moved out of the shadows. Their faces were masklike and blank, without eyes—but when the drone passed overhead, their heads tilted in perfect unison.

Their mouths peeled open in toothy grins, jagged and wet. All hissed as one.

The mic picked it up.

Saturn recoiled.

"Wendigos," he whispered.

These weren't the shambling, mindless things their appearance would imply. They moved with intention. With hierarchy. They weren't just spreading—they were coordinating. Rallying.

And they knew NAVI was watching.

"We have big brown ones... coming out of the plateau," Saturn called out, as he tracked the nightmarish shapes loping through the shadowed greenery. Their forms melted disturbingly well into the forest shadows. "I had hoped these things didn't have the brainpower for tactics. Empirical evidence is leaning toward the contrary." The words drifted into the air, more for himself than anyone else.

Even in focus, the background noise intruded. Emerald's voice rose, shrill and accusatory like she was yelling at someone. Lusa, maybe. Something about not taking things seriously. Saturn didn't blame her. But that wasn't his problem right now. His job was to see what was coming.

And there was a lot on the way.

He banked NAVI southward, adjusting the drone's trajectory. As it skimmed along the city's southern rim, the pattern held. Pale Ones emerged from fissures in the plateau, slipping like ghosts into the trees. But something in their movement changed. It became less random and more deliberate.

They didn't charge the roads or gates.

Saturn's fingers tapped against his thigh, his mind ticking through possibilities. "They're avoiding the roads," he muttered. "Not rushing in—but encircling." His goggles filtered the image to high contrast. The silhouettes moved with eerie synchronicity, as if taking orders from something just out of frame.

This wasn't random aggression—it was a siege, and it frightened him more than the shrieking hordes ever had.

He swallowed, the weight of the realization pooling in his gut like molten lead. Whatever was guiding them—whether it was the Mother herself or some smart abomination buried deeper in their ranks—was evolving, learning, adapting.

If they didn't get ahead of it soon, Zahadah would be overrun.

His fingers danced across the controls, redirecting NAVI, pulling up a wider field. His voice cut through the tense air.

"Jacques," he said. "We need to make a decision. Fast. They're surrounding us—and they're not sightseeing."

***

Hyatta perched atop the towering spire, silent and still, eyes locked on the flood of pale figures spilling from the base of the plateau like a tide loosed from some ancient dam. They writhed and loped into the forest, their grotesque shapes limned by starlight filtering through the trees. His grip tightened on the stone ledge.

He had hoped—prayed—not to ever see them again. But fate had no interest in mercy. It remembered its debts.

A slow breath slipped from him, a whisper in the cool night air.

"The Mother's children."

They clawed up from the earth like wounds breaking open, festering and inevitable. He hated them, not just for what they were, but for what they meant. Decay. Desecration. A slow, deliberate unraveling of all things noble. These things had once been people. Now they were husks—puppets for a will that defiled.

Hyatta had fought many enemies. Tyrants. Zealots. Beasts. But these creatures… they didn't fight to conquer. They infected. They didn't kill to survive. They *corrupted*. Servants of a sickness given will. And now they were here.

He flexed his fingers. The cold metal of his chain-whip coiled at his side, a promise of pain should they try to come too close. Since escaping the Iruxi and joining this strange, fractured warband, life had become one long test. And none of it—not the obelisks, not the desert, not the battle in Wrasas—matched the horror they now faced.

The spawn of the Mother weren't just monsters.

They were rot incarnate.

Hyatta's eyes followed their movements, noting the patterns— how they drifted through the underbrush with unnatural poise, not chaotic, but with purpose, direction. They were forming arcs. Dividing into waves.

He exhaled through his nose, forcing his breath steady. No time for fear. He had survived worse, hadn't he? He repeated the thought like a prayer, though some part of him wasn't so sure.

Movement below.

His eyes narrowed as figures meandered through the city streets, civilians and guards, unaware of the doom encroaching just beyond the walls. Zahadah was sleeping and the nightmare had begun.

Zahadah would fall, as Wrasas had.

He considered climbing down. Rejoining the others. Reporting what he'd seen.

But then in the distance, a flash of light appeared against the stars.

NAVI.

Saturn's drone glided across the sky, barely visible, its tiny silhouette flitting over the rooftops. If NAVI was in the air, the others already knew. Jacques would be strategizing. Lusa and U'gah would protect them.

They didn't need him for this part, but Zahadah did.

The weight of it pressed down on him. Their warband could fight, but they weren't an army. And the guards? Their patrols were sluggish, their eyes dulled by routine. They would be overwhelmed before they even understood what was happening.

And what authority did he have here?

None.

They'd see a foreigner in desert garb, ranting about ghosts and gods. They wouldn't listen.

But maybe they didn't need to.

Maybe he didn't need orders or permission.

Maybe it was time to enlighten them what kind of enemy they faced and what kind of fury could still rise to meet it.

A sharp, gut-wrenching scream shattered his thoughts.

Hyatta's blood turned to ice.

He knew that voice.

U'gah.

The cry came again—short, broken bursts like the alarm of a wounded beast, echoing off the walls Zahadah's plateau, distorted and directionless. Hyatta's muscles locked, then tensed, his grip tightening around his perch. He strained to locate the sound, but the city made it impossible. Echoes rang from every surface.

Below, guards on the parapet stirred. Moments ago, they had shuffled along with dull-eyed indifference. Now they stood still, heads snapping up, searching the gloom beyond the plateau.

That was enough to give him direction.

He vaulted from the spire, boots gliding over the steep clay shingles, then dropped soundlessly to the parapet. The guards recoiled as he landed—one clutching his spear, another startled —but Hyatta was already gone, a blur of cloak and purpose. There was no time for explanations. They would never understand anyway.

He sprinted across the alour, the city flashing by on one side, the black expanse of the forest on the other. U'gah was out there. Alone. How? It didn't matter. Not now.

If the Mother's children had caught him—

No. He wouldn't let it happen.

A narrow beam of light slashed through the darkness beyond the wall, jerking wildly in frantic bursts. Hyatta's eyes locked on it. A flashlight.

The erratic sway, the shape—it was him.

Relief surged—U'gah was alive and still moving.

Hyatta didn't hesitate.

He veered, momentum coiling through his limbs. The chain-whip slid free, iron and bone links unspooling with a hiss. He hurled himself over the outer wall, wind screaming past his ears. His cloak flared open, synthetic fibers stiffening in the rush of air. It caught like a sail, turning his dive into a glide.

The world tilted.

Below, the forest spread wide and dark, swallowing the beam of U'gah's light. Hyatta narrowed his gaze. Every twitch of his limbs, every breath, was calculated on correcting his pitch and angling his descent. A misstep meant death.

The treetops surged up like black fangs.

Hyatta twisted. He skimmed the highest branches, cloak straining, fingers spread to guide the fall. Leaves scraped past. Shadows surged around him.

And still, he tracked the light.

580

The air reeked of damp earth and decay. Crushed leaves mingled with the clawed advance of monsters, their scent churned into the soil—overlaid by a sharper stench, acrid mold. The Mother's presence clung to the forest like a veil of rot. Whether it was instinct or some ghost of her buried inside him, Hyatta could feel it. The corruption. The malice. The tightening grip that drove the Pale Ones forward like hounds unleashed.

His whip cracked out and caught a branch. His body snapped into a tight swing. Just before he would've vanished into the undergrowth, he let go. He landed soft, low, and rolling into a crouch with no more sound than a breath. His eyes locked on the trembling beam of light ahead.

U'gah.

The bergbar's flashlight bobbed wildly, casting jerking shadows across the trunks of ancient trees. Every movement threw unnatural silhouettes across the clearing, distorting scale and distance. The light wasn't helping. It was making things worse.

Hisses clicked through the canopy—wet and insectile.

Hyatta's whip coiled in his palm, the metallic links catching what little moonlight filtered through the leaves. His eyes narrowed. Shapes shifted just beyond the beam's edge, fluid and hungry.

"U'gah." The word was soft, but sharp enough to pierce the bergbar's frantic breathing.

The light jerked. U'gah turned, wide eyes meeting his for a heartbeat—relief, then fear.

The shadows surged closer, pressing into the edge of the light like a tide of teeth.

"Run," Hyatta said. "Don't look back."

U'gah didn't argue. He charged ahead, crashing through the trees with heavy, desperate strides.

He adjusted his stance, letting the whip slide long in his grip, gold and bone singing softly with tension. His mind raced. He could pull a few. Maybe more. But not all. U'gah would still be hunted. He would have to survive on his own strength.

Hyatta would just have to even the odds.

He surged, fast but loud through the brush. The motion drew them like blood. The nearest Pale Ones snapped toward him, heads cocking unnaturally, mouths yawning open in too-wide grins.

They came.

Limbs cracked and lunged, sinew folding and reforming in impossible ways. Teeth flashed. Bodies blurred. They were faster than he remembered.

Hyatta ran, his cloak snapping behind him, gait measured but tight. His muscles burned. The whip remained coiled and ready.

It was time.

With a sharp twist of his wrist, Hyatta snapped the chain-whip into motion, the links cracking through the air like pealing thunder. Metal and bone arced, slicing through undergrowth with lethal violence. Every strike was a calculated arc that cleared a path or covered his flank.

The whip cracked again and met resistance.

A spray of black ichor burst from the Pale One's chest as the links tore through flesh and shattered ribs. It let out a warped hiss, spine folding, limbs twitching as it collapsed into the brush. He pivoted mid-run, the whip wheeling overhead.

Another hiss—it was closer this time. He spun, the chain snapping out and wrapping tight around the neck of the second creature. One hard, brutal yank and the vertebrae popped. The body dropped limp, twitching in its death-spasm.

Hyatta ran on, the whip singing behind him.

The Pale Ones howled in frustration, their chittering echoing through the trees. They were closing. He felt it—heat rising in his limbs, lungs burning, but he kept his pace. He welcomed the pain.

A guttural snarl exploded to his left.

Hyatta ducked instinctively as a wendigo launched from the brush—towering, bone-thin, its arms stretched too far, claws slicing through air just inches from his skull. He rolled beneath its lunge, the attack carving wind past his cheek. He came up low, lashing the whip in a vicious arc.

The fall sliced across the creature's abdomen, followed by a wet *slurp*. Its entrails spilled onto the ground.

The abomination screamed, shrill and wounded, but the others pressed on, drawn to his blood and motion.

He couldn't hold them here. Not like this. He needed to break their rhythm.

His eyes scanned ahead.

He saw a fallen tree, thick and wide, its roots upturned in a twisted snarl of earth and stone.

Hyatta adjusted his grip, the whip coiling as he ran. He threw it high with one last crack, wrapping a high branch and vaulted. He swung over the obstacle, twisting in midair, and landed in a crouch behind the roots.

The Pale Ones faltered. Their limbs caught in vines and broken roots.

Hyatta didn't waste the moment.

He pressed against the bark, reaching into one of his belt pouches. His fingers found the soft block, small and slightly tacky. Jacques had called it "angry playdough," with that tight-lipped grin he wore before he made something that exploded.

He pressed the two buttons, arming the device, and lobbed it into the hollow of the root knot.

And then he ran like Lusa from rainmaking showers.

A heartbeat of silence.

F*woom!*

The forest lit in a sudden, searing bloom of white and heat. The blast knocked bark from trees, shredded leaves, and sent pieces of the tangled Pale Ones tumbling in shrieks of flayed agony.

With his ears ringing, he pushed off the ground and ran, hard. Into the dark. Into the trees. Into silence.

He'd bought himself seconds—maybe minutes—but they were still hunting U'gah.

***

Emerald's hands trembled as the alarm bells rang out, their relentless toll bleeding through the gardens, getting closer with every echo. What had once been a place of eerie calm—crimson stone overgrown with manicured beauty—now felt like a trap. The humid air lay heavy against her skin, thick with dread. No breath felt deep enough.

She had faced horrors before. The wreckage of the expeditionary fleet. The creeping shadows of Wrasas Station. Even Saturn's cold recitations of monstrous things. But this? This was different. U'gah's desperate flight through the guts of a dying Axis ruin. The pale things rising like a tide. And Lusa —damn him—showing up late to the party and not even with Hyatta.

Something in her had cracked.

Saturn had said the Pale Ones hadn't breached the walls yet, but they would. She knew they would. That old instinct in her gut. The kind that didn't care about logic or odds. The kind that whispered, *this is it.*

There had to be something she could do—some plan, some clever angle, some trap, or tactic. But nothing came. Just the quiet, bitter thought: *I should've updated my will.*

More bells. North. East. They were encircling.

We're going to die. The thought was steady now, rhythmic. *We are definitely going to die.*

Screw it.

She set her rifle down. The bundle of backup gear followed, clattering at her feet like armor shed before a last, desperate charge. Her heart fluttered, but her feet were already moving across the grass, through the sultry dark, straight toward the one person she had been too scared to face.

"Jacques," she said sharply, cutting through the tense whispers of Jacques's internal monologue dribbling out of his mouth.

He didn't look up. Fingers dancing across the keyboard, brow furrowed in focus. "Did Saturn find something else?"

"No." Her voice dropped, but stayed firm. "It's not that. It's important."

That got his attention.

Jacques turned, his eyes locking onto hers, tired, but alert. They scanned her face like a field report. She felt her stomach twist. Her resolve faltered for a moment. But no, she had carried this long enough.

If this was the end, she wasn't leaving with regrets.

Emerald's heart pounded so hard she could feel it in her ears. Her face burned, her lungs constricted as she struggled for words.

"We've been through a lot together," she said, her voice unsteady but unflinching. "All of us. And… you're the one who's kept us grounded. You're the one who's kept us safe."

The words trembled in the silence between them, bare and unguarded.

Jacques turned toward her. His eyes softened when they met hers. He knelt, quietly, without ceremony, closing the space between them until they were eye to eye. He raised his hands— palms open, shoulders beginning that familiar shrug of his. The one that usually came before he brushed off praise or absorbed guilt that wasn't his to carry.

Emerald could see it in his expression: the weariness, the quiet despair, the grim resolve. He believed what she did, that this might be the end. And still, somehow, he was searching for words to make her feel less alone, less scared.

It was one of a thousand reasons why she'd fallen for him.

No matter how much pain he carried, no matter how far gone the hope, Jacques Auclair still looked out for everyone else first.

She didn't let him speak.

Before his words could soften her resolve, before doubt could take root, Emerald surged forward. She cupped his face, rough with stubble, and kissed him.

It wasn't graceful. It wasn't rehearsed. But it was everything she had.

The world dropped away—no bells, no monsters, no screaming dark. Just him. His warmth under her hands, the scratch of his beard, the shock in his stillness. As the kiss deepened, his hesitation melted as he leaned in, returned it, held her there.

It wasn't a perfect moment, but it was real, and full of heat.

Her heart slammed against her ribs, breath burning in her lungs, but she didn't let go. She didn't want to.

When they finally broke apart, her hands still cradled his face. She could feel his pulse under her thumbs.

Jacques stared at her, wide-eyed, his cheeks flushed. When his voice came, it was low and hoarse. "Emerald, I—"

"Don't." She shook her head gently. Her voice was calmer now, steadier. "You don't have to say anything. I just… I couldn't go through tonight without saying something. Whatever happens… I needed you to know. I need you, Jacques Auclair."

He leaned in, pressing his forehead to hers. His hands slid up to hold hers, warm and solid.

CHAPTER THIRTY-SEVEN

Jacques stood beneath the vast canopy of stars, his gaze fixed on the endless sky above. The bells tolled through the air—a rhythmic, relentless reminder of the attack looming over Zahadah. Distant shouts from the city guard and the clatter of preparations rode the wind, merging with the noise inside his head. He folded his arms, trying to form a plan—to find something, anything, that might turn the tide. But every idea unraveled beneath scrutiny.

He needed clarity. But no matter how he tried to focus, his thoughts kept drifting back to her. Emerald. Her voice. Her eyes. The kiss. It was unexpected, like a thunderclap from clear skies, and it had broken something open inside him. Something he hadn't even known was locked away.

Her confession, the kiss—it had flipped a switch. He hadn't seen it coming, hadn't considered the possibility, but now he couldn't unsee it. He felt something for her. Stronger than he'd let himself admit. Potentially more than he knew how to carry.

He raked a hand through his hair in frustration. He'd never imagined that feelings—romantic feelings—could disrupt him so completely. And certainly not now. Not like this. Yet here he was, in a city poised on the edge of catastrophe, unable to think of anything else.

He shifted his stance, boots scraping softly against the stone. A memory surfaced: U'gah's strange behavior—his knowing laughter, Emerald's flustered reactions. The little shaman had figured it out. Jacques smiled faintly. He'd been too focused on the mission, missing what had been right in front of him.

For weeks, he'd assumed Emerald's frustration came from something he'd done. Some slip, some misstep. He'd tried to avoid making it worse by tiptoeing around her moods without realizing the truth. Now that he knew, everything made sense. The scattered pieces finally clicked into place.

And now he couldn't compartmentalize. He couldn't ignore it. Emerald wasn't just another member of the team. She wasn't just brilliant or brave. She was someone—realization ricocheting through his mind—he cared about, deeply. And the thought of her stepping into danger twisted everything inside him.

He looked out over the shadowed buildings surrounding the gardens, their rooftops haloed by electric lights. The alarms tolled on, grim and insistent. He had a responsibility—to U'gah, to Saturn, to Florence. But especially to her. And how could he lead, if his heart was caught in the line of fire?

How could he make the right decisions when every instinct screamed to shield her, to protect her, no matter the cost?

He exhaled. There was no easy answer, no clear path forward. But one thing was certain: he couldn't let his feelings paralyze him. Emerald had trusted him, confided in him, and now it was his turn to rise. He would protect her. Not out of duty, but because he wanted to. Because she deserved it.

The pressure in his chest eased, just slightly, as he admitted what had been clouding his mind. Emerald. The feelings—raw and undeniable—had been a logjam in the river of thought, choking off clarity. But now he faced them head-on. The mental fog thinned. His mind felt cleaner, less cluttered. And at the edges of that clarity, something else flared to life.

A half-formed idea tugged at him like a loose thread. He frowned, eyes narrowing as he tried to trace it. Circles—something about circles. He let the notion simmer, rifling through what he knew. The bells still tolled in the distance, but now they felt less like noise and more like rhythm. Like cadence.

Then it hit him.

Jacques's eyes widened as the memory snapped into place: the layout of Zahadah's defensive nodes. He'd skimmed it, dismissing the defenses because of more pressing matters. But now they might be the only thing that might save them.

They were layered—concentric rings, nested one within another, radiating outward from the gardens.

Defensive circles—and their activation could be staggered to maximize harm.

He straightened, pulse quickening as the strategy assembled itself.

The first wave would disrupt the front line and throw it into disarray. The second would cut off the vanguard, severing it from reinforcements. If the city's defenders were coordinated —if he could time the phalanx movements with the activations —it might be enough to fracture the swarm and drive them back into the arcs of the plasma generators ringing the perimeter.

Jacques's mind spun into motion, refining the idea. The plasma generators were powerful, but blunt and indiscriminate. Precision would be key. If he could coordinate the timing, choreograph it like a siege engine made of men and machines, it could work.

The Mother's children were relentless, but not clever. Their strength was in numbers, not cunning. And numbers could be broken by surprise and rhythmic tactics. This plan might fracture their initial charge. The city's defenders might be able to hold the line.

Because if it didn't—if the defenders are pushed past the thoroughfare bottlenecks into the gardens, it's over. The open space would become a killing field.

He turned and sprinted for the terminal. His hands braced against the console, bleeding off his momentum. The Axis software was a nightmare—redundant, arcane, buried under layers of encrypted logic—but the vision in his mind was sharp now. He could see it. A shield-and-spear strategy. Defensive pulses. Tactical kill zones. A plan, forged from antiquated stories of his youth and no small amount of desperation.

They were counting on him.

"Alright," Jacques breathed to himself. "Let's see if we can make this work." He cracked his knuckles. His fingers dropped to the digital keys, already pulling the sequence together.

The soft rhythm of keystrokes blended with the tolling of bells, the echo of shouted orders beyond the walls. The Axis system fought him, but he pressed on. The entire city, his friends and the civilians, hung on his ability to outmaneuver a machine older than half the languages he spoke.

A presence stirred behind him. That prickling awareness of someone watching was just beyond focus. He didn't turn. Not unless they planned to kill him. He couldn't afford the distraction.

Florence's voice cut in, softer than expected. Hesitant.

"What do you need us to do?"

Part of him braced for the usual follow-up: sarcasm, mockery, some quip honed to provoke. That had always been her way— relentless, needling, sharp as broken glass. And truth be told, he'd earned some of it. He'd been short with her earlier. Rude, even. Necessary, yes. But still rude.

He kept his eyes on the terminal. Don't hope. Not with Florence.

Her voice came again. Steadier now. Edged with something almost playful.

"From the way you're pounding that keyboard, you've clearly got a plan. Just tell me what to do—so long as it doesn't involve turning us all into sexual deviants."

Anger flared. Hot. Reflexive. He turned toward her, a glare already forming. Knowing now that she had seen the kiss, and believing she meant to make an issue of it.

But it died on impact.

Her face wasn't mocking. A smile was there, yes—wry, self-deprecating—but it didn't reach her eyes.

And her eyes… those stopped him cold.

No spite. No bravado. Just fear. Raw, unspoken fear—and something else beneath it. Understanding. She knew. She felt it too. The stakes.

She wasn't trying to pick a fight.

She was trying to hold herself together.

Jacques exhaled, shoulders sagging as the tension drained from him. "Florence," he said, quieter than he meant to. "This isn't a game."

Her smile wavered, then faded. She nodded. "I know," she replied, her tone stripped of any edge. "But you've got a plan. So… tell me what to do."

He studied her for a moment, trying to reconcile the woman before him. She had fear in her eyes, but remained steady and willing, regardless of being the one who had verbally sparred with him so many times. Whatever lay ahead wasn't just testing him. It was testing all of them. And Florence, flaws and all, was still here. Still fighting.

He gave a slow nod, the barest hint of a smile tugging at his mouth. "Fine," he said, his voice steady. "I'm planning on using the city's defenses—the atmospheric plasma generators. They're designed to scatter hostiles. If I can sync their pulses with the city guard's phalanxes, we can break the Pale Ones' momentum in waves. But I'll need time."

"And us?" she asked, arms crossed tight over her chest.

"Saturn will stay on NAVI. If there are surprises, I need eyes on them before they hit. Lusa needs to patrol the gardens to keep the rest of us safe. Emerald can set up a sniper's nest near the top of one of the buildings lining the plaza. High angle, clean lines."

He tapped a few keys, and a hidden compartment slid open on the terminal's side. Jacques blinked at its seamlessness, then retrieved a polished metal disc and tossed it to Florence.

"Take this. Once the generators are live, I'll route you into the PA. You'll give the city guard their instructions—formations, movement, fallback zones. With any luck, they'll think you're Frigg, or Freyja, or some goddess who has come down from Asgard to rally the defense. Keep the commands simple. Keep them moving."

Florence caught the device one-handed, her grip sure. "Got it."

Jacques turned back to the terminal, focus narrowing again. He couldn't dwell on this—on the fragile alliance forming between them. Not now. Too much was at stake. But as his fingers resumed their work, one quiet thought lingered at the back of his mind.

Maybe, just maybe, she was starting to understand that the only way out of this was together.

***

U'gah's lungs burned, every breath a brand in his chest as he tore through the darkened forest. His legs screamed with each stride, his muscles flaring from the relentless sprint, but he couldn't stop. Not with the pale things closing in. The skyfire club trembled in his grip, its beam casting wild, jittering shadows through the twisted trunks of ancient trees. It had saved him before, its light searing the flesh of those horrors bold enough to come close. When it touched their skin, they blackened and blistered, the stink of charred rot trailing behind.

But he knew its limits.

They moved smarter now—circling, herding, driving him like prey. If they swarmed from all sides, the light wouldn't save him. Panic surged in his throat, raw and rising. He clutched the small club tighter, its smooth metal slick with his sweat.

He had seen Hyatta—just a glimpse. A flash of the desert warrior tearing through the swarm, whip snapping like chain-lightning. For a heartbeat, hope had surged. But more of the children had poured from the dark. Endless. Writhing. Far too many. Hyatta was trying—U'gah knew—but they were ants drowning the lion.

He needed a way out.

A shaman's strength wasn't in club or claw. He was a guide to spirits, a walker of thresholds. The guardian spirits of his people had always protected them, their power bound to stone and soil. He had felt them before, most fiercely in the presence of the spear-toothed Earthshaker that slept within his greatclub.

But the club was gone—left behind with the others.

Still... the Earthshaker was more than carved rock. It was spirit. It was story. And spirit could be called.

He didn't need the club. He had the old ways. The elder paths. His softer senses. The ones used to speak to ancestors, to listen through the mountains and forests.

He steadied his spirit, barely. His legs didn't stop moving. The pale ones shrieked behind him, snapping branches, rattling through the underbrush. He pushed it all away—the pain, the noise, the panic—and reached inward. Beyond the flesh. Beyond what could be touched. Toward the otherworld. Toward the place where old things listened.

The forest melted away as he ran. His eyes didn't guide him now. His ears were useless. He cast his senses like a net into the deep water of the lake of spirits hoping something would rise to meet it.

"Earthshaker," he thought, or maybe whispered. His will shaped the words. "Hear me. I am your servant. I need your strength."

Silence.

Just his pounding heart. Just the thunder of feet behind him.

Then, a whisper in the dirt. A tremor, but barely there.

But he felt it.

Something vast stirred below. Ancient. Impossibly heavy. The earth spoke its name not in words but in mystical pressure in the flex of stone.

The Earthshaker had heard.

The connection slammed into him like a falling mountain. U'gah gasped, the world lurching as raw power surged into his limbs. Pain vanished. His sight sharpened. His body no longer ran, it devoured distance. And in the back of his skull, the voice came, deep as the roots of the worldtree:

"I hunger."

The voice was tectonic like broken teeth grinding.

"Speak your need. I must feed."

U'gah's voice trembled, but his stride did not falter. "The pale things," he said, glancing over his shoulder at the writhing horde. "They are the Mother's children. They trespass in your domain. I need your strength to stop them."

A low growl rumbled through his bones so deep it didn't touch his ears, only his marrow.

"I come," the Earthshaker rumbled. "I come to feed."

Sound followed.

It wasn't sound in the way wind or voice was sound. It was deeper, felt more than heard. A subsonic pressure rolled through the forest, bending trees, stirring leaves, rippling stagnant water like a great beast inhaling through the soil. The air thickened, charged, as if the land itself had opened an eye.

A bellow came from the deep, long and discordant, like a burial trumpet carved from the remains of uncountable sacrifices and blown from the roots of the world. It hit U'gah in the back, vibrating through his ribs and gut until he had difficulty taking in a breath. The forest moaned in answer. Birds fled. Even the pale things behind him faltered.

Then the footfalls began.

Slow and heavy. Each step a thunderclap. The ground shivered beneath him, leaves leaping from the carpeted forest floor with each impact. The tremors weren't noise, they were terror. A vast and sacred presence pressing down, as if the trees themselves bowed in reverence.

It was coming.

And it was hungry.

The guardian's essence surged through the earth like molten blood. U'gah felt it circle him, filling him. His fur stood on end. Every breath tasted electric. It wasn't fear that gripped him now, it was awe. Exhilaration. As if he stood at the edge of legend.

His limbs thrummed with strength that was not his own. The Earthshaker's wrath pulsed in his body like a second heart, louder than his own thoughts.

He grinned—wide and wild. Teeth bared. Not prey. Not anymore.

The Pale Ones still chased him, their hisses threading through the dark. But now he ran not to escape, but to lead them straight into the jaws of something more dangerous than the gods.

"Neco fuga ooda cha!" he roared, voice cracking the night like splitting wood. An elder's curse. Forbidden. Blasphemous. The pale ones wouldn't understand the words, but the meaning rang clear: a curse hurled at the Mother herself. A challenge.

Come, then. Come and die.

The ground lurched beneath him as the footfalls drew near. The very earth buckled under the guardian's weight. U'gah could feel the quakes through his pads now, steady and closing. From the rear, the horde's cries shifted. He heard it—a hesitation. A change in the swarm.

Something vast. Something hungry.

A predator had entered the forest.

With the spirit's power surging through him, U'gah felt unstoppable.

He turned his head, catching a glimpse of the pale forms behind him, their eerie starlit skin threading through the trees. Still they came, but not as before. No longer heedless. No longer bold.

They were hesitating.

And hesitation, in the hunt, was death.

The spirit was close now. The air had changed—thick with energy, pulsing with pressure. He could almost see it now, looming in the shadowed treeline, a vast silhouette bristling with feathers, its form cloaked in darkness like a god carved from the nightmares of monsters.

The spear-toothed Earthshaker had answered.

And the Mother's children—

They were about to learn what it meant to wake a guardian of the mountainfolk.

***

"C'était quoi, ce bordel?" Jacques muttered, voice sharp as the bone-deep rumble rolled through Zahadah. The sound hadn't even faded before Saturn chimed in urgently, more alive than Jacques had heard since the crash.

"I don't know," Saturn said, "but we've got movement, something huge out there. And Pale Ones are rushing the plateau from every side—except the east."

Jacques's gut twisted. He forced the dread down and pivoted hard into motion. His fingers flew across the terminal, punching in commands with the precision of muscle memory. *"D'accord!"* he snapped, turning toward Florence. She stood just beyond the console's glow, framed in a veil of night.

"You're up, Flo. Get on the PA. Tell the guards at the outer wall to slow the advance—thin their numbers. Whatever they can manage."

Florence blinked, as if about to argue, but Jacques cut her off with a clipped edge. "Have them fall back before the wall's breached. Inner gates stay ajar—funnel the bastards. Don't let them swarm."

Her hesitation evaporated. Florence brought the disc-shaped comms module to her lips, fingertips brushing across its polished surface. She activated the system using the brief instruction Jacques had given her. Her voice rang out across the city—measured and commanding.

"This is Angrboda," she said, crisp with authority. Jacques smirked faintly. Whatever else could be said about Florence, the woman knew how to hold a room. The guards had fallen in line the first time they'd heard her; they would again.

Jacques refocused. The city's defense grid—dormant for possibly centuries—was still intact. Reactivating it would be slow. Painfully slow. Each command required nested confirmations, layers of Axis-era bureaucracy grinding under his fingertips.

"Come on," he muttered. *"Allez, vieille conne…"*

Beads of sweat gathered on his brow as the system stalled again.

Behind him, Florence's voice rose, calm and cold as steel. The kind that left no room for argument.

"Continue the evacuation to the inner city. Prioritize women and children. All able-bodied men: arm yourselves. Defend the wall—arrows, stones, whatever you have. Fall back before the breach. Do not allow yourselves to be surrounded."

Jacques stole a glance over his shoulder. Florence stood poised with the PA, her posture sure, her voice steady. Confidence glinted faintly behind her eyes. She wasn't playing the role anymore, she was owning it. And for once, her presence didn't feel like a thorn in his side.

The console beeped.

His head snapped back to the screen. The generator status changed; the units linked to the primary system came online. With steady hands, Jacques keyed in the final sequence. The terminal's interface pulsed as the ancient defense network stirred to life. A deep hum resonated through the stone beneath his boots, a vibration like a constant thrum of thunder.

"Support generators are online," he called. "Few minutes until maximum output. If the guards hold the line, we can trap them by baiting the Pale Ones straight into the plasma field."

Florence, mid-instruction, turned sharply. "And if they don't hold the line?"

Jacques met her gaze. "Then we do."

The words hung between them, stark and unforgiving.

His jaw locked. Knuckles whitened against the console edge as the weight of it all pressed in. No backup. No fallback. Just them. And a city about to drown in monsters.

Then we do.

No contingency for that. No contingencies beyond what he'd already set in motion. But it didn't matter. They would hold. They had to. Because the alternative was annihilation.

A knot tightened in his chest.

This was his fault. All of it. The Pale Ones, the breach, the rising tide of corruption that now crawled through Zahadah's veins. It had been his hands on Yggdrasil's controls. His gamble. His failure.

Jacques exhaled sharply. No time for guilt. No room for self-pity. If he faltered now, it would all unravel. He had to make this work. He had to fix what he'd broken. Not for redemption. For the futures of all of these innocent people.

And for *her.*

His eyes lifted toward the rooftops surrounding the gardens. It took only a second to find her—Emerald. Perched on the highest building, rifle poised, silhouette crisp against the star-strewn sky. Even from this distance, her focus was unmistakable.

Since the crash, she'd been a force of will—brilliant, caustic, and relentless. And now, she was up there in the dark, guarding them against the nightmare he had unleashed.

Jacques swallowed hard.

The kiss. Her words. Her certainty.

It still didn't feel real.

But it was. He didn't know if they'd survive the night. He didn't know what would come next. But he knew this:

If the world lost Emerald, it would be poorer for it. And he couldn't let that happen.

A low hum from the terminal pulled Jacques back. Status bars inched upward. It was slow, steady progress as the generators climbed toward full power. Beneath his boots, the city vibrated with the groan of awakening machinery. Ancient defenses stirred like old gods roused from sleep. The sound was both a comfort and a warning. It was working. Not fast, not perfect, but it was working. If the guards could hold the thoroughfares…

His gaze moved once more to Emerald—her form so small against the distant glow of starlight, still holding her post, unshaken. He couldn't fail her. He wouldn't fail her.

He squared his shoulders and returned to the keys, his fingers resuming their nonstop rhythm.

The odds were grim. The enemy vast.

But as long as breath remained, there was still a chance.

And for her—for all of them—Jacques would fight to the last.

CHAPTER THIRTY-EIGHT

Hyatta ran. His breath came in sharp, measured bursts, his chain-whip lashing in lethal arcs at any Pale One that strayed too close. Every movement was necessary, his senses tuned to the chaos around him. But the sound—that monstrous, guttural roar that had torn through the night like a pressure wave—still sang in his blood. He hadn't heard it—only felt it.

If this was another of the Mother's creations, he thought grimly, *they were past saving.*

The idea chilled him. Her children were bad enough. If she had birthed something worse—something *greater*—then their odds had already collapsed.

The earth convulsed beneath him. Not a tremor, but a *pulse*—rhythmic and massive, like the beating of a thousand war drums in unison. Footfalls. Not a few, but a cadence, approaching rapidly. Louder. Closer. Each impact rolled through the forest, the spaces between them so vast it felt like some enormous thing was striding across the land. Then came the crashes. Trees fell, not one by one, but in groups. Their ancient trunks snapped like sun-bleached bone, flattened under the weight of something colossal.

Hyatta's calm began to fracture.

Whatever was coming… it was vast. Larger than anything he'd ever seen.

Ahead, through the chaos, he glimpsed U'gah's retreat, just a bobbing beam of light, jerking and tilting through the trees. The flashlight was still moving. He was still alive.

Hyatta clenched his jaw. He tightened his grip on the chain-whip, its iron links catching stray beams of starlight like broken glass. No more stragglers. No more delay.

He let the Pale Ones chase him and broke into a sprint.

U'gah was all that mattered now. They'd stand a better chance together—if he could reach him in time.

The roar came again.

Not a sound. A *shock*. It split the night, a lightning bolt through his skull. Hyatta staggered, barely keeping his footing. The world swam. It was a sound built to end things. A sound that bypassed reason and slammed straight into the animal brain.

He ran harder, his eyes scanning. He knew what came next. He *felt* it.

And then—

The forest exploded. Trees shattered. Wood splintered like chaff. And through the carnage, a head emerged—massive, scaled, hungry. A jaw wide enough to swallow a house snapped shut with a thunderclap of bone and meat. Pale Ones disappeared in sprays of ichor and pulp. The canopy bowed away in fear.

Hyatta skidded to a halt.

It wasn't just the creature's size—though that alone threatened to break a man's courage—it was the *presence*. The way it dominated the forest, tore through it like it meant nothing. This wasn't a beast.

It was nothing short of *judgment*.

Fear, an old and unwelcome companion, crept into Hyatta's mind. He had faced horrors before, had stood against overwhelming odds, but this—this was different. This was ancient. Primal. A force of nature given flesh. His mind groped for a word to name it, to make sense of it, but only one came to him. *Dragon.*

In truth, it was no dragon. Its dark red and brown feathers, sparse and ragged, clung to a hulking, muscular frame. Its body was more avian than serpentine. But Hyatta lacked the knowledge to name it anything else. To him, the gargantuan beast was every nightmare of legend come to life.

The creature's massive eye, as wide as Hyatta was tall, swiveled toward him. Its golden iris reflected the faint light of the forest, but the veins of glowing red that laced through it burned with a rage that seemed almost sentient. Hyatta barely had time to react before the beast swung its enormous head, a blow that sent trees crashing to the ground in a devastating arc.

Instinct took over. Hyatta dove to the ground, the backswing tearing past just above him as an ancient oak was ripped from the earth and hurled aside like a toy. The ground shook violently. The air filled with the sound of splintering wood and snapping branches. Hyatta rolled to his feet, his heart pounding in his ears.

The beast's head loomed closer, its maw opening slightly, revealing rows of jagged, spear-length teeth that glinted in the faint light of the broken canopy. Its breath was hot and rancid, a fetid mix of decay and raw power that made Hyatta's stomach churn. And Hyatta, for the first time in a very long time, felt the crushing weight of his own mortality.

The monster moved faster than it had any right to. It lashed out at him with terrifying speed, jaws snapping shut with a force that could have crushed him to nothing. He dodged to the side at the last possible moment, feeling the rush of air as those massive teeth clamped down mere finger-lengths from his body. His footing faltered, but he forced himself into a sprint, veering toward the beast's underbelly, hoping—*praying*—that if he vanished from its immediate field of vision, it might lose interest.

The sheer rage pouring from the creature was suffocating, a heat that burned the air itself. Hyatta had fought many things in his time—men, beasts, the horrors birthed by the Mother—but never something like this. It wasn't hunting. It wasn't even fighting. It was *killing*. It had no purpose but destruction. If he could hide from it, even for a few moments, maybe it would continue cutting through the horde of Pale Ones rather than turning its fury on him.

But the thing was not so easily fooled.

The second Hyatta disappeared beneath it, the beast *stomped*. A massive, taloned foot slammed into the earth less than an arm's length from him, the sheer impact sending tremors rippling through the ground. The depression it left in the dirt was deep enough to swallow him, and the force of the quake sent Hyatta sprawling before he could catch himself. His limbs flailed uselessly as he hit the ground hard, the breath knocked from him. His balance was thrown into chaos as the world lurched around him.

Pain flared through his side, but there was no time to think about it, because the dragon was still moving.

Even as it stomped, the massive creature pivoted into a brutal, sweeping motion, its thick tail cutting through the battlefield like a living battering ram. The motion was so fast that it blurred in Hyatta's vision, and he barely had time to register the sickening crunch of dozens of Pale Ones being obliterated as it swept through them. The sheer force sent corpses flying in every direction, their grotesque forms broken against the trees, turning into little more than shattered bone and pulped flesh.

And still, the beast didn't stop.

Its other foot—a three-toed talon the size of a warhorse—slammed down, gouging deep trenches into the earth. The soil cracked. Trees pitched. Raw power radiated from every movement. This wasn't a predator.

It was a calamity given form.

Hyatta fought to rise, but the ground bucked beneath him. Aftershocks rippled out from the creature's landing, turning roots and stone to slurry. No footing. No cover. No chance. His instincts howled—*Move. Run. Escape.* But where? There was nowhere left to go.

The thing *knew* where he was.

Its size guaranteed he couldn't outrun it, not for long. And stealth—his only real edge—was gone. Shattered by the roar, by the trees, by the monster's impossible presence.

Still shaking, Hyatta forced air into his lungs.

He wasn't deluded. This wasn't a fight. It was survival by seconds. If there was a way out, he had to find it *before* the beast stopped playing.

Before it remembered it was hungry.

***

Florence stood at the garden's edge, fingers locked white-knuckled around the PA control. Before her, Zahadah burned in silhouette—black smoke, flickering firelight, and the ragged chorus of battle. The screams of the dying rose above it all, jagged and despairing. No more alarm bells. No more commands. Just the sound of collapse.

The Battle of Zahadah was going poorly. Catastrophically.

She barely heard Saturn's dry voice in her ear, relaying tactical updates from NAVI's feed. He didn't need to describe it. She could *see* it. The civilians had fled—most of them, maybe. The guards had done their best to herd them behind the inner gates. But it hadn't been enough. Not fast enough. Too many had lagged behind.

Too many had hesitated.

Florence cut the PA feed with a flick of her wrist. Her voice wasn't needed anymore. Nothing she had to say could change what was happening.

Saturn's commentary continued in the background, emotionless. Statistical. The guards who had lingered too long on the outer walls—men who tried to hold the line when they should have retreated—were being overrun. She had ordered them to fall back. She had *begged* them, through clenched teeth and rising panic. But they had waited. Waited for a miracle, or for pride, or for nothing at all.

Now they were dying for it.

And the civilians—gods, the *civilians*.

Her fist tightened as her thoughts curdled. The ones who had burdened themselves with trinkets. Family heirlooms. Armfuls of junk they thought they could carry to safety. Let them die with it. Let them clutch their silver and silk as the Pale Ones tore them limb from limb.

But the mothers…

The ones slowed by sobbing toddlers, by empty-handed panic. Husbands nowhere in sight—off playing soldier on the ramparts, abandoning their families for a heroic death that wouldn't matter. Florence didn't know why it enraged her. Maybe because those men should've been *carrying* their children instead of brandishing spears. Maybe because it was *their* fault—the screams echoing through the avenues like the cries of dying animals.

Terrified. Alone. Betrayed.

She turned, chest rising fast, eyes stinging. Her thoughts spiraled in silence.

Not your fault. Not your fault.

She'd done everything right. Given orders. Laid it out clearly. Had they listened—had they *moved*—this could've been different.

Could've been.

She bit down on the thought, hard, and forced her gaze toward Saturn. The only silver lining: the swarm hadn't taken the main avenues. They were bleeding through side alleys and broken pathways, scattered by hunger and chaos rather than strategy. It slowed them—barely. But it bought time.

At the inner gates, the real fight had begun.

Small, brutal clashes erupted as the defenders tried to form a proper line—spear and shield against horror and claw. Not to win. Just to *slow them down.*

Florence watched from above, her knuckles still aching.

And prayed that this time, someone would listen.

Florence exhaled sharply, steeling herself.

It was only a matter of time now.

The inner city would be their last stand.

She clenched her fists, forcing calm into her spine. Zahadah was collapsing into chaos, but then again—her life always was. Time and again, they had clawed their way back from the brink. And as much as she hated to admit it, Jacques had a way of pulling them through. Scraping victory from the jaws of annihilation. Stubborn, infuriating, tactically gifted Jacques.

Even the so-called primitives had proven resourceful. Not dependable, not like Jacques—but they had survived. Endured. She'd never admit it aloud.

Saturn's dry commentary fed her more clarity than she wanted. The guards had finally formed ranks. The chaos was congealing into something that *resembled* strategy. Shields— mismatched bulwarks, round tables fitted with handles, even doors ripped from hinges—locked together into an improvised, shield wall. It looked ridiculous. But it was holding.

Behind the forward line, spearmen stood two or three deep. Guards, townsmen, anyone who could hold a weapon. They worked in a mechanical rhythm: thrust, step back, rotate. It was a metronome of death. Behind them, the archers rained down volleys—aimed low, into the knees and chests of the surging horde.

On the surface, it was obvious: kill as many as they could before the line broke. But Jacques had explained the true purpose. The shields weren't just for protection. They were to control the chaos. Slow the tide. Shape the swarm long enough for him to trigger… whatever it was he'd built. She'd stopped listening when he got technical.

Still, this part was working.

The Pale Ones pressed forward in endless waves, heedless and mindless. When one fell—, because of spear in the throat or an arrow through the gut, it was trampled underfoot. No pause. No mourning. Just the relentless churn of bodies piling into the meatgrinder.

Jacques had a plan.

And as much as Florence wanted to scoff, or to cross her arms and mutter something scathing, she couldn't. Not this time. A small, bitter part of her *hoped* he would pull it off.

Because if he didn't, none of it would matter.

Her fingers tightened around the control module as Saturn's voice cut through the air.

"It's time."

She straightened, eyes snapping back to the distant shield wall.

This was it.

The moment where everything either came together—or burned.

Her gaze swept over the defenders, their shields locked in a ragged line, shoulders braced, faces drawn tight with strain. The spearmen jabbed with mechanical precision, each thrust met with a spray of black. From above, the archers loosed another volley, their arrows hissing through the air like whispered death.

"Hold!" Florence barked into the PA, her voice firm and commanding, echoing down the narrow stone avenues. "HOLD!"

They had to. Just a little longer.

She turned toward Jacques. His focus was absolute—fingers flying across the digital keys, jaw clenched. That expression she'd come to recognize. The one he wore when the world was on fire and he intended to drag them through it anyway.

The city hummed.

It started low, barely audible like a crawl of static across her skin. Every hair on her arms stood on end. The air thickened with ozone, sharp and metallic, and the pressure shifted like the world was inhaling.

And then—

A single unbroken ring around the inner city *burned*.

From every direction came the snap-snap-SNAP of plasma, lashing through the horde in jagged arcs of lightning. The screams that followed were shrill and alien, so high-pitched they scraped the edge of hearing. Pale Ones writhed and convulsed as energy tore through them, cooking them alive in clusters.

Florence staggered back a step, her stomach lurching even as her grip on the control module tightened.

Saturn's voice seemed to crackle with the exploding energy. "Plasma generators engaged. Discharges chaining through grouped targets. Estimated eight percent neutralized on initial activation."

She didn't want to visualize it. But Saturn kept talking.

She could almost *see* the constructs through his words, towering coils like steel serpents, wound tight and crowned with glowing spheres. The charged tips flared with energy, arcing from target to target with surgical cruelty. Anything within reach was reduced to blistered meat and scorched bone. The arcs jumped again. And again. A spreading web of death.

It reminded her of something. A memory.

An old book—American history, 20th century. Backyard patios. Something called a bug zapper. A glowing blue bulb that popped and hissed as it electrocuted insects drawn to the light.

Now the Pale Ones were the insects.

Florence swallowed hard.

It was horrific. It was brilliant. And it was insanity.

She forced herself to keep watching, even as the plasma flares seared the night. Those caught inside the arcing ropes of eletricity—the scattered stragglers—were swiftly dealt with. Some were skewered on spears. Others were crushed beneath the heel of desperate defenders.

The field was holding.

The shield wall held.

The phalanx formation was working. The front line braced against the onslaught, spears thrusting in brutal unison, driving back the clawing, snapping remnants of the horde that had survived the initial plasma surge. Panic had burned away. What remained was grim resolve.

The archers had stopped firing entirely. The plasma field made arrows useless. Those loosed too late had slagged midair, superheated by atmospheric discharge, streaking into molten ribbons before vanishing in bursts of light.

This wave had been devastated.

Most of the Pale Ones had died instantly, their flesh vaporized in the moment the plasma generators flared. Others had tried to push through twitching and convulsing, heedlessly, but the moment they passed into the active range, arcs of energy caught them. They flared like dry kindling.

The air stank of ozone and burnt meat, the acrid scent layering over sweat, blood, and fear.

Saturn spoke.

"They're climbing."

Florence's stomach dropped.

She hadn't thought of that. Not once.

She'd watched them flood up the buildings lining the thoroughfare.

Bile rose in her throat.

Her head snapped toward Saturn. His goggles glowed with HUD light, casting his black eyes in pale blue as he continued, unbothered.

"They're scaling the buildings," he said, voice flat, almost bored, like reading a grocery list.

Florence turned her gaze to the rooftops.

Shapes moved—pale white against black—clawed limbs scrabbling up stone, hauling themselves up with inhuman speed. The way they climbed was wrong. Fluid. Like spiders, if spiders screamed.

They were going to bypass the shield wall.

Drop down on the spearmen.

Worse—leap straight into the gardens.

Her throat tightened.

"Saturn," she rasped, "how many?"

He didn't answer right away. His head tilted slightly, adjusting the feed.

"Enough," he said at last. Then: a pause.

And a smile.

"But, it doesn't matter."

Florence blinked. "What do you mean '*it doesn't matter*'?!"

Saturn tapped the side of his goggles, switching lenses.

"Because," he said, as if explaining something obvious to a child, "they're bursting into flames the moment they hit the rooftops."

Florence's body sagged with relief before the words had fully settled in her mind.

There were generators on the roofs.

She could see it now—through smoke and haze. Scorched corpses tumbled from the rooftops, their bodies smoldering as they slammed into the writhing swarm below. The moment they cleared the lip of the buildings, they entered the field—and died for it. Their screams echoed off stone, a rising, shrill chorus as each desperate climber was cooked alive.

She considered adding *But for how long?*—but the thought felt redundant.

Because even before Saturn spoke again, she saw them.

Coming from the south.

Their hulking silhouettes loomed against the firelit skyline, arms and legs too long, swaying in unnatural rhythm as they loped forward. Clawed limbs gleamed in the wavering light—three curved talons on each hand and foot, shaped like a hunting bird's, only thicker, and more menacing. Their skin was darker than the others—mottled shades of brown and umber, pulsing with slow, oily patterns that shifted just beneath the surface.

And their heads were blank like their lesser kin, and featureless, save for wide, gaping maws lined with needle-like teeth.

But these weren't like the rest.

They were smarter.

Florence remembered, reluctantly, her experience with them in the station. Along with the few times Jacques and Saturn had mentioned them. The Wendigo.

Bigger, yes. But not just bigger.

They thought.

They *planned*.

Her mouth went dry.

The smaller ones had thrown themselves into the slaughter—blind, frenzied, heedless of their own deaths. But the Wendigos... they watched. They studied. And when they moved, it wasn't with hunger.

It was with purpose.

Her hand rose to her mouth without thinking, the command module cold against her lips. Her fingers clenched around it, knuckles whitening.

"Begin withdrawal to the next checkpoint. Prepare for engagement."

Her voice held steady. Clear. Even confident.

She had no idea what she was doing.

Military jargon wasn't exactly in her repertoire. But she'd seen more than her share of war movies. That had to count for something.

At least, she *hoped* it did.

They're going to listen, right?

She forced herself to breathe. If she let herself dwell—on the size of those monsters, on what they could do, on how close they were—she'd lose it.

She couldn't let her mind go there.

Florence forced her focus back to the battlefield—or what remained of it. The defenders—guardsmen, townsfolk, anyone still breathing—were falling back in coordinated steps, the shield wall shifting as one. Archers repositioned to new vantage points, adjusting their angles.

Good.

They still had a chance.

But her gut screamed otherwise.

She swallowed hard, trying to override the dread crawling up her throat. The plasma fields had decimated the swarm, but would they work against the Wendigos?

They wouldn't mindlessly hurl themselves into the arcs of death.

So what *would* they do?

Her eyes locked on one of them.

It tilted its head, as if considering. The featureless face was fixed toward the humming plasma field.

Then, with cautious curiosity, it stepped sideways.

Not forward. Not back.

Along the edge.

Testing the boundary.

Florence's skin turned to ice—as the realization struck.

"They're testing the plasma range," she called out, voice rough with urgency. "They're not going to rush in—they're going to find a way through."

A beat of silence.

Then Jacques's voice: "Understood."

Florence gritted her teeth. Her pulse thundered in her ears.

She watched in stunned horror as one of them encircled writhing Pale Ones, its elongated limbs closing around them in what looked to be a wide hug. With a surge of strength, it bulldozed the small crowd into the plasma field.

A flash of lightning split the night. The pale things spasmed, flesh igniting in a burst of shrieking flame. Steam vented. Smoke billowed.

Another Wendigo followed suit, then another. each gathered their thrashing, screeching kin and shoved them forward.

Into the field.

Their bodies convulsed, blackened, and fell twitching to the ground, filling the air with the crackle of burning sinew and the gut-wrenching stench of roasted flesh.

They weren't attacking.

They were *probing*—sacrificing.

Florence's stomach lurched.

What the hell are they doing?

And then she saw it.

The corpses weren't disintegrating fast enough. The more the Wendigos shoved into the plasma field, the more the bodies *absorbed* the charge. They were stacking into a grotesque, twitching mound of scorched flesh. The generator's arcs kept lashing out, electricity snapping from node to body, but the current no longer spread outward. It grounded itself into the pile of dead.

Her knuckles went white on the PA module.

They were using their own dead as a weapon.

A fresh bolt crackled through the mass, and then—with a shove too deliberate to be anything but strategic—the Wendigos rolled the smoldering heap forward.

The charred, spasming remains lurched toward the generator.

Florence felt her gut drop. A sick, leaden weight pooled in her core.

"Saturn?" she called—though she wasn't even sure what she was asking.

Even his voice, usually flat, carried a tremor she hadn't heard before.

"One of the generators just went offline," he said. Tense. Clipped. "They overloaded it. Fried the node. First ring of the defense grid is down."

Florence went still.

The Pale Ones had just opened the first breach.

The first line of defense was gone.

Her pulse thundered in her skull, her throat, and her fingertips. Panic flared.

She spun toward Jacques, breath shallow, chest heaving.

He was still at the console. Fingers flying. Face set in stone. Cold. Focused.

She knew that look.

He'd seen this coming seconds before she had.

And he was already working on the problem.

Please, she thought, *let there still be a solution.*

But the swarm wasn't waiting.

They were moving again—reignited, relentless, surging into the breach.

The Mother's children were coming.

CHAPTER THIRTY-NINE

hy are there so many? Why won't they just die?

Emerald gritted her teeth, adjusting her aim by millimeters. The glowing reticle settled over her next target. A searing bolt of energy leapt from the barrel, striking a Wendigo dead center in its gross, featureless face. The creature convulsed, limbs jerking in thrashing spasms, collapsing into a headless heap.

She'd lost count—fourteen kills, maybe more. It didn't matter. There were always more.

From her perch atop the tallest structure bordering the gardens, Emerald had a clear view of the battlefield—but even from this height, she hadn't seen the Wendigos' strategy until it was already too late. By the time she'd turned south, the atmospheric generator was under siege.

Her stomach twisted at the sight.

A mound of charred Pale Ones, blackened and twitching involuntarily, had been shoved into the plasma node like a battering ram—absorbing the electricity, feeding it back into the core. Then came the surge: a final crackle of energy. The coil overloaded, bursting apart in a spray of sparks and molten slag.

One generator shouldn't have been enough to short the system. And yet it had. The circuit broke and with it, that layer of the defense grid.

Nausea rose in her throat, but she shoved it down. No time to panic. They had contingencies.

Trust the plan. Trust in Jacques.

Once day at a time.

She pivoted, then lined up another shot. No need to account for drop—just movement. One of the many reasons she loved the

Wrasas rifles. Zero-point energy. No recoil. No reloads. As long as she managed heat, she could fire forever.

It almost felt like cheat codes in an immersion sim.

If only this *was* a game.

She fired. The bolt punched through the chest of a Wendigo wading through the smaller white swarm. It staggered, its earthen skin sloughing away as it collapsed into the pile of bodies it had been pushing.

Two more took its place.

Emerald exhaled, steadying herself. Another shot. Then another. Each bolt found its mark, but the Wendigos just kept coming. And she wasn't even bothering with the little ones.

She couldn't stop them all.

Her eyes swept the battlefield, heart thudding. She searched for Jacques.

If the grid was failing, he'd be working on a fix.

She found him easily—right where she knew he'd be: hunched over the control terminal, eyes locked on the luminous screen. Unshaken, oblivious, the chaos spilling through the walls might as well have been miles away. As much as Emerald wished he were up here beside her, fighting shoulder to shoulder, she knew better. He needed to be there. Monitoring the defenses. Parsing Saturn's surveillance feed. Feeding tactics to Florence. He was the anchor holding this madness together.

And yet, after that tender moment between them—that fragile, stolen heartbeat in the calm before the storm—it was hard not to imagine more.

In the gaps between breath and gunfire, she caught herself drifting. Daydreams stitched together like fine embroidery: delicate, wondrous. She imagined the two of them moving as one, cutting through the horde with perfect synchronicity. No fear. No desperation. Just flow. Rifle and pistol barrels glowing with heat. The hiss of seared air. A battlefield turned ballroom. Maybe a song played in the distance—something slow, romantic, haunting. In her mind's eye, they shared smiles, jokes, even kisses between kills—it was like they were invincible. Like survival was inevitable.

All they had to do was enjoy their time together.

A sharp whir from the rifle's cooling system yanked her back. The faint tick of the temperature gauge pulsed like a warning heartbeat. She muttered a curse, swapping out the weapon for a backup beside her. The new rifle thrummed to life in her hands.

She risked a glance at the others.

Jacques was unchanged—still the most incredible man she'd ever known. Saturn sat nearby, posture neutral as he rattled off tactical updates from NAVI like he was reading shopping notes. Apocalypse or not, nothing shook him.

Florence was another story.

From up here, Emerald could see the tension in her shoulders, the iron grip she had on something in her hand. Her posture had started to waver. It wasn't panic yet—but the cracks were spreading. A dam under pressure. It wouldn't hold forever.

Lusa prowled the garden below, a pacing pillar of orange-striped muscle and barely-leashed fury. His bobbed tail flicked with irritation. He wanted to be out there—tearing through the horde, soaking his paws in blood. But he stayed. He understood his role. The final gate. If anything made it through... he'd be waiting.

And then there was Sandy.

Poor, forgotten Sandy.

The feathered sauropod had worn a ring into the grass with her nervous circling. When the Pale Ones breached the city, she'd tried to flee—her instincts screaming for escape. But there was nowhere to go. Her massive eyes rolled white as she searched for a path out. And still... she stayed. Panicked, trembling, but there was nowhere to run.

Emerald exhaled sharply. Daydreams wouldn't save them. Hope wouldn't either. Only precision, focus, and a hell of a lot of luck.

She lined up the next shot.

Time played tricks on her. It stretched and snapped, elastic and erratic—warped by stress, adrenaline, and the weight of the siege. When she focused down the scope, it dragged like syrup, every heartbeat a drawn-out throb. She tracked the Wendigos—hulking, gawky things—and picked her targets. Her job was simple: stop the big ones before they shattered the shield wall.

Each trigger pull felt like an eternity. The hum of the rifle filled her ears. Nothing else existed.

But the moment she glanced down—just a peek toward Jacques, hunched over the terminal, face lit by datafeed glow—time snapped back, fast and furious. Her pulse kicked. The world blurred forward while she remained still, suspended between moments. Two timelines: one slow and surgical, the other jagged and ruthless.

Then the city began to hum a second time.

Subtle at first—a vibration in the stone, a pressure behind her eyes—but it grew quickly. A resonance deep in her chest. The defenders had reached the second checkpoint.

Jacques's plan was in motion.

The Pale Ones didn't care. They flung themselves at the shield wall in blind frenzy, screeching and clawing, heedless of the cost. But the Wendigos paused. They sensed something. Their spindly limbs stilled. Their eyeless heads tilted upward in eerie unison, like they were listening for something no human ear could hear.

Seconds dragged.

Why hadn't the plasma fired?

Emerald's fingers tensed around the rifle. A malfunction? A delay? Her gut twisted, but she forced it down, locked into the rhythm of her breath.

The Wendigos advanced again—slow, cautious. Testing the ground. Then faster. Their confidence returned. They moved like whispers: lean, precise, monstrous.

Emerald aimed. Her finger curled against the trigger—

—and the sky cracked.

A surge of blue lightning exploded from the rooftops. Plasma arced across the air with a deafening snap, leaping from hidden coils like a storm loosed from a bottle. The atmosphere ignited. Bolts licked through those in range, coiling through the horde.

The Wendigos shrieked. Not just pain, but rage. Their limbs convulsed as arcs of searing ropes of light tore through them. Pale Ones scattered in panic, their flesh blistering, their bodies thrashing under the onslaught.

With a wicked smirk on her lips, Emerald returned to her grim, yet strangely satisfying work.

***

The dragon's jaws snapped shut on the ancient tree with terrifying force. Serrated teeth punched through dense wood, splintering the trunk in a chorus of cracks. With a violent shake, the beast wrenched it from the ground—roots tearing like snapped cords, dirt fountaining upward in a cloud of debris. It hurled the tree aside, uncaring where it landed. The creature just wanted it gone.

Hyatta crouched behind the twisted remains of another fallen trunk, his chest heaving. Each breath came shallow and sharp, his lungs clawing for air. His ears rang with a low, persistent hum—the aftershock of the angry playdough's blast and the monster's rampage. Every step the creature took turned the forest floor into a trembling drumbeat beneath him.

Strangely, the muffled quiet was almost welcome. The beast's roar, when not deadened by the damage to his hearing, was a weapon in its own right. He'd seen it drop Pale Ones mid-sprint, their bodies collapsing like puppets with cut strings. No wounds. Just death. Pure, concussive death. If his hearing hadn't already been half-broken, Hyatta doubted he'd still be breathing.

He didn't want to fight it. He wasn't trying to be noble. If he could've let it rage and moved on with its life, he would've. But fate—no, the dragon—had other plans. Its fixation was absolute. It wanted him. Specifically. Personally. And Hyatta had no intention of obliging.

So he ran.

He vaulted roots, ducked under limbs, dove through gaps in the shattered canopy. Adrenaline kept him moving, but the edges were fraying. His legs burned. His muscles screamed. Sweat stung his eyes. But he didn't stop. Couldn't. The thing behind him was rage on two legs, a living calamity. And it wanted nothing more than to erase him.

Hyatta didn't know if his goddess was listening, but he prayed anyway. His whispered pleas were drowned beneath the thunder of pursuit, but he didn't care. It seemed to be working, so far. The near misses were piling up. Each one closer. The dragon's teeth had snapped shut inches from his spine—more than once. Its tail had whipped through trees he'd just sprinted past, flattening them like stalks of wheat.

There was no time to think. No room for strategy.

If I could get on its back... The idea flared up, born of desperation. Suicidal. Ridiculous. But not without logic. On its back, he'd be out of reach—no jaws, no talons, no tail. The high ground. But how, in all the hells, was he supposed to *get* there?

The question shattered as the dragon charged.

It came like a mountain in motion, each step an earthquake. Its three-toed talons tore gouges in the forest floor, ripping through root and earth as if it were parchment. The rhythm of its steps was dirge—heavy, sure, and unstoppable.

Instinct screamed louder than thought. Hyatta twisted, his body reacting before his mind could catch up. He dove sideways, slipping between its legs, the wind of its passing slamming into him like a wall. The air was hot, reeking of turned earth and rotting breath, and thick with the coppery stench of old blood.

There was movement—a flash of white.

A Pale One.

It had been stalking him, hunched and silent, ready to strike.

It never got the chance.

The dragon's foot came down like a falling continent. There was no scream. No warning. Just a wet, bone-crunching impact, and a black smear where the Pale One had been.

Hyatta didn't smile—but something like satisfaction stirred in him. It was brief and hollow. At least *something* good had come of this nightmare.

But the moment died fast.

The tail came next—a blur of muscle and bone.

Hyatta threw himself into a dive, rolling over roots and rubble just as the tail tore through the space he'd occupied. The force of it ripped a tree from the ground, roots screaming as it toppled in a spray of dirt and loose stone—some larger than his torso.

He came up in a crouch, panting, heart pounding. Dirt and sweat streaked his skin. Blood ran into his eyes. Shallow cuts he hadn't even felt until now.

Need to get on its back.

The thought returned—louder this time. More insistent. *There has to be a way.* The beast's rage was a weapon, but also a weakness. It was reckless and unthinking. If he could time it right, use that momentum...

Hyatta's jaw clenched. *One chance. No second chances.*

The creature's fury surged, erupting into a tantrum of seismic violence. It began to leap in place—massive, full-body impacts that shook the forest floor. Trees shuddered. Ancient trunks snapped like dry bone. The ground rippled with each colossal stomp, waves of force radiating outward, flattening brush, rocks, corpses—everything.

Hyatta staggered, struggling to stay upright. His knees buckled under the concussive tremors. Debris rained down—splinters of wood, gouts of churned soil, and the mangled remains of Pale Ones crushed in the chaos. The air itself vibrated, thick with roaring breath and the howling groan of shattered earth.

But through it—he saw it.

The pattern.

Every time the creature landed, its head dipped low. A rhythm. Brief. Predictable.

A window.

Hyatta's eyes narrowed.

He sprinted—dodging falling branches, leaping over roots torn from the ground, his body screaming with exhaustion but still moving. He uncoiled his whip in one fluid motion, the iron links gleaming like wet fangs under fractured starlight. He fixed on a jagged spur of bone jutting from the dragon's lower jaw.

An anchor.

With a snap of his wrist, the whip lashed out with a crack. It caught, wrapping around the protrusion with a metallic bite.

626

The tension hit instantly. A shock through his arms, nearly wrenching the handle from his grip—and his arm from its socket.

The head rose.

Hyatta was pulled skyward, yanked from the earth in a nauseating blur of motion. Wind tore at his face. His feet flailed above the treetops. The beast's momentum carried him like a slingstone, arching toward its back.

For one impossible moment, it felt like flying. The dragon was lifting him. *Helping* him.

Then the arch turned.

Gravity snapped the tether.

The whip ripped from his hands with a sudden release and Hyatta hurtled downward, breathless.

He struck the dragon's back like a dropped stone.

The impact tore the air from his lungs, his chest spasming in a silent gasp. Pain bloomed across his body. His vision faded. But he held on, barely, clinging to jagged ridges of scale and bone as the monster raged beneath him.

Pain lanced through his ribs, sharp and searing, but there was no time to feel it. Hyatta scrambled, clawing for handholds, fingers digging into the sparse patches of dark, coarse plumage clinging to the creature's ridged hide. His heart thundered. Adrenaline surged. He anchored himself with raw desperation, refusing to be thrown.

The beast roared, a sound so close it rattled his spine, but Hyatta didn't let go.

He was on its back.

It was done.

Or so he thought.

For one breathless heartbeat, he believed he had the advantage —perched atop the dragon, ready to turn this chase into a battle of wills.

A sharp, pained yip cut through the chaos. Not loud. But unmistakable.

The beast stopped. Frozen.

Its entire frame went rigid beneath him, a sudden and unnatural stillness. The stomping ceased. The earth held its breath. Its head tilted slightly, snout raised, golden eyes narrowing, not in fury, but in recognition.

Hyatta went still. He flattened against its spine, his fingers tangled in feather and hide, every muscle tight.

Then he heard it again.

That cry—short, broken, and pained.

U'gah.

The realization struck like ice water in his veins. It wasn't just pain in the sound—it was *his* pain. Somewhere out there, in the dark, U'gah was in trouble.

And the dragon had heard it too.

The transition from stillness to motion was instant and brutal. The beast spun in place, coiling its massive body like a spring —then launched forward with breathtaking force.

The forest blurred.

Hyatta's world became nothing but speed and motion, trees and shadows whipping past in a chaotic rush. The air roared in his ears, the sheer velocity became a living thing that clawed at him, tried to tear him free. His body lifted with each step, bones jarred by every thunderous impact.

Only the swirling wind from the bristled feathers held him down—just enough suction, just enough grip, to keep him from being flung.

He tightened his hold, forearms screaming. His breath lost to the gale.

Gritting his teeth, Hyatta shifted lower—tightening his center of gravity, adjusting his posture for balance. He moved like a rider taming a cataclysm.

His heart pounded in time with the beast.

And all his thoughts narrowed to one point:

Get to U'gah.

It seemed the beast would carry him straight to the bergbar—at least that much was certain.

But certainty ended there.

Once they arrived… *then what?*

The thought struck like a cudgel, cutting clean through the adrenaline haze. His heart didn't just pound, it seized. The sheer speed of the creature beneath him was staggering. Its strides devoured the distance with terrifying ease. But it wasn't the journey that gnawed at him, it was what waited at the end.

Protect U'gah. That much was obvious. The Pale Ones—those snarling, white-skinned nightmares—were still out there. Hyatta had killed dozens, maybe more. His whip had lashed through them in spirals of steel and ichor, but it had never been enough. They always came back.

Protecting U'gah would take everything he had.

But that wasn't the real problem.

The problem was what he was riding.

He risked a glance toward the beast's head—jagged spines and coarse, matted plumage sliced through the dark like a nightmarish, battering ram. Every muscle beneath him vibrated with barely contained violence. Each thunderous stride rippling through the forest floor like a falling star.

This thing didn't just *kill.*

It *thrived* on destruction.

Its rage was not a fire to be smothered—it *was* the fire. It fed on ruin. And Hyatta? He was just a tick on its back. An afterthought. The beast didn't care about him. It didn't care about U'gah. It didn't care about anything except tearing the world to pieces.

So how do you protect someone from *that*?

His hands fisted in feathers slick with heat and sweat. He'd tried to steer it. Tried to distract it. But each near-success had been lucky, fleeting reprieves bought by proximity, noise, and chance.

If the beast wanted U'gah dead, there was no force in the world that could stop it.

Unless...

Unless he didn't *fight* the rage.

Unless he *guided* it.

Turn it. Not away, but *toward* the Pale Ones.

His thoughts shifted. They were no longer frantic, but focused.

The creature wasn't mindless. It *responded.* U'gah's cry had broken through its frenzy and diverted its wrath like a hook in its skull. The sound hadn't just caught its attention, it had *compelled* it.

What if Hyatta could do the same?

What if he could be that voice? That trigger?

What if he *aimed* the fire?

If he could hold its focus, just long enough... Keep it angry. Keep it moving. *Maybe* he could steer that fury where it belonged.

Toward the *real* enemy.

Toward the Pale Ones.

It was a reckless plan—if it could even be called that. It was the kind of gamble you only took when every other card had burned.

But it was all they had.

Hyatta drew a deep breath, the air thick with dust and the copper tang of blood. His ribs screamed. Every muscle burned, but there was no room for pain. No room for rest.

Not now.

Not with U'gah's life on the line.

CHAPTER FORTY

The sea of Pale Ones slammed again and again against the second ring of plasma generators. Blue arcs crackled and hissed like a lightning storm caught in stasis, each burst holding the line for just a little longer. For the past half hour, the defenses had miraculously held. It wasn't a victory. But it was something. A fragile breath carved out of chaos.

Emerald perched atop the tallest building overlooking the carnage, her zero-point rifle sat snug against her shoulder. The weapon hummed with every squeeze of the trigger. Another discharge—another kill. The chalk-white bodies dropped like dolls flung from rooftops. Some twitched. Most didn't.

It was too easy.

Point. Aim. Fire. Repeat.

There was no satisfaction in it. Just the rhythm of the slaughter.

Her hands moved on autopilot, but her mind—frayed and drifting—slipped elsewhere.

Jacques.

She found herself thinking of him more than she liked to admit, especially now that the fog of immediate panic had thinned. What would it be like to live the rest of her life on this cursed island—with him? Would they build something out of the wreckage? A life stitched together from hope and sheer, stubborn will?

She pictured it in fractured images. Jacques smiling across a morning fire, shadows soft on his face. The affectionate warmth of his hand on hers. Their laughter mingling with the whispers of a forest.

Simple things. Fragile things. The kind you only dreamed of when you were truly smitten.

And if—no, when—they made it off this island, would they go back to Europe?

The thought was almost absurd. Like waking from a nightmare only to find the waking world just as hostile. She could already hear her mother's voice, thin and needling beneath the polish of civility.

"Oh. You've brought someone... tall."

Emerald snorted under her breath, lined up another shot, and sent an energy bolt through the chest of a Pale One scrambling up a broken rampart.

Interracial relationships weren't forbidden in gnomish circles. Not officially. But the glances—the pauses in conversation, the smile that didn't quite touch the eyes—she'd seen it all before. She felt it settle over her like a winter shawl.

Jacques wasn't just any human.

He was Jacques. Stern. Uncomplicated. Confrontational. The kind of man who couldn't be resized to fit polite gnomish expectations.

She didn't care.

He was worth it. Worth the awkward dinners, the shallow judgments, the sideways stares across a crowded room. Because none of it mattered when he looked at her. When the armor slipped just enough to let her glimpse the man beneath the soldier, beneath the engineer, beneath the mask he wore for everyone else.

The man who had kissed her like she was the last real thing in a world unraveling.

Another Pale One crumpled below, its limbs spasming as plasma arcs licked across its body.

Emerald exhaled. Her heart was steady, even here—entrenched in chaos. Maybe that was the real difference Jacques had made.

Not in the way he fought for everyone. In the way he anchored her.

Even here, with death piling at the gates, she could imagine a future. A life.

It was strange, really—that it had taken all this: the danger, the horror, the endless, grinding war—for her to find something that felt suspiciously like peace. Not the fleeting kind born of coffee, clean socks, or a sudden discovery in the observatory. No, this was deeper. Quieter. A low hum beneath the noise.

She fired again. The movement was automatic. Her mind continued to drift, tangled in contradictions.

Maybe there was something to karma. Fate. Whatever people called it. Philosophy had never been her thing. But it made a twisted kind of sense.

Could it really be that simple?

That the universe—cold, absurd, and loud—had found some crooked way to balance the scales? To repay her losses with this improbable, fragile joy? After all the grief, the running, the survival?

And then—Jacques.

Worth the wreckage. Worth every second of fear. Worth holding on to.

She squeezed off another shot.

Maybe life wasn't about waiting for peace. Maybe it was about finding stillness in the storm. Making space for clarity where none should exist. She'd found hers. In his steady voice. In the way he looked at her, not as if she needed protecting, but like she mattered. Like she made him braver.

Maybe that was the lesson.

Choice.

And in the stripped, ruined core of this abortion of a island, she had chosen. Him. This. The life they might still build.

She lined up her next shot.

She chose him.

And for now—somehow—that was enough.

Then it hit.

Not a sound. Not a sight. A shift.

The air changed. The night—charged with ozone, stitched with distant screams—flattened. The hum of the plasma generators vanished in an instant. Gone. No warning. No sputter. Just silence. An absence so vast it hollowed her chest.

Emerald froze. Rifle steady. Her finger light on the trigger.

But her spine knew before her mind did.

Something was wrong.

A pulse of dread surged through her—primal and electric. Her skin broke into a cold sweat. She jerked east, rifle swinging with her, heart pounding out of sync with the new rhythm of the world.

And then she saw it.

A figure stood among the Pale Ones.

Cloaked in tattered robes that seemed to absorb light. It stood motionless, untouched. The creatures gave it space, their mindless frenzy dulled to a nervous orbit—less worship than wariness. Reverence, maybe. Fear, certainly.

It wasn't large. Not imposing. If anything, it looked brittle—skeletal beneath the folds of cloth, too frail to survive the wind. But that didn't matter. Emerald felt it before she truly saw it. A pressure. A warping of the world. The air around the figure shimmered subtly, as if reality itself recoiled.

And then she saw the staff.

Worse than the figure. Worse than the robes. Worse than the way her breath caught in her throat.

It was clutched in a withered hand, each finger thin as kindling. The staff didn't look crafted—it looked grown. A twisted root of something once alive and now very, very wrong. Desiccated flesh petrified into what looked like dark, gnarled wood. At its head: a blackened crown of charred bone, still smoldering. Faint embers pulsed within the cracks, like coals hidden under skin.

It radiated heat—not warmth, not fire, but suffocation. The heat of a pyre long extinguished, the kind that curled flesh without light. It wasn't just unnatural, it was offensive. Like it didn't belong in this world, or any world.

Emerald's eyes drifted to the ground.

The plasma generator was gone.

Not shattered. Not damaged.

Gone.

Only shards of blackened metal remained, scattered like scorched petals, each one curling at the edges like dead leaves. The stone beneath was cracked and blistered—deep, angry fractures spiraling outward from a scorched center.

A wound in the earth.

The hum of the generator—the backdrop of the entire defense grid—was silent. That silence pressed against her eardrums like a vacuum, so complete it made her ears ring. Her rifle felt heavier. The air colder. The light dimmer.

She tightened her grip, knuckles blanching. Her heart stumbled in her chest.

That thing had done this.

Not a Pale One. Not a Wendigo. Something worse.

This was the conductor. The mind behind the madness. Emerald was sure of it.

She trembled. She forced her sights onto the figure, centering the glowing reticle over its veiled head, her finger poised on the trigger.

Then the figure looked up. At her. Into her.

Its hood shifted. The face beneath was not a face.

Pale skin stretched too tightly over a jagged skull. Lips thin. Cheekbones sharp. And the eyes—or where eyes should have been—sealed shut with veiny, translucent flesh. Grown closed. As if the world itself had decided it was better if this thing could never look upon anything.

And yet… she felt it see her.

She felt its gaze.

Stars! The pressure of its focus—its presence.

It was like a nail driven into the center of her brain. Her lungs locked. Her finger twitched, but didn't fire. She couldn't. The weight of that stare—blind and knowing—held her still.

The figure raised its staff. Slow. Purposefully. The smoldering tip trailed ash and smoke like a dying comet.

Then it tapped the ground, once.

The sound wasn't wood on stone.

It was a rending. A splintering of—everything.

It struck the air like brittle ice crumbling from a glacier.

The echo didn't fade. It stretched, growing in intensity, carried on the wind like a scream muffled beneath a thousand tons of earth.

The Pale Ones frenzied. The creatures nearest the figure convulsed.

They spasmed violently, limbs jerking like marionettes cut from their strings, their shrieks pitching higher, wilder. Whatever thin thread of control had held them in check snapped, and what emerged was worse than insanity. Pure, feral, and unchained.

They clawed at the stone, gouging through rubble and blood with renewed violence, howling like animals that had remembered their true hunger.

Emerald's heart kicked. Her finger trembled on the trigger.

She didn't know what this thing was. But she knew this:

Her world was about to end.

That knowledge didn't creep. It didn't unfold in some poetic realization. It screamed. It tore through her, raw and immediate like a flood of fire washing through her from root to crown. And when it hit, she roared.

The sound wasn't human. It was grief. Fury. Defiance. The last howl before the sky fell.

Emerald let it fly as she squeezed the trigger.

Shot after radiant shot screamed from her rifle, streaking down like bolts of judgment. Each impact lit the cloaked figure in flashes of blue-white flame, the air hissing with heat and charged ozone.

It didn't fall.

It didn't even flinch.

Emerald's vision tunneled. Her eyes stung, but she refused the tears. Rage steadied her grip. Her jaw clenched. She kept firing. Kept screaming. Kept pushing as the line below broke— the defenders overwhelmed by the tide of white.

She didn't let herself look.

This was the thing U'gah had warned them about. The herald. The Mother's emissary. She saw it now. In the way it stood. In the silence it brought. In the way it turned its blind gaze toward Jacques.

It would take him from her.

She saw that future in its closed, hateful face. It would peel Jacques from her heart, drain every color from her world, and leave her hollow. It would smile without lips, laugh without breath, and unmake her, piece by piece.

Why won't you die?

The rifle core screamed, venting heat and smoke in choking coils. Plastic blistered. Circuits warped.

She didn't care.

She kept firing.

The herald must die.

It could not have him.

Smoke curled around her hands. The heated polymer scalded her palms. Her gloves split at the seams. The weapon choked— but still she pulled the trigger. Not thinking. Not stopping.

Just kill it.

Kill it.

KILL IT.

Only the sharp scent of melting rubber finally cut through the madness. Her weapon had fallen silent, its barrel sagged and blackened, useless in her shaking hands.

She was still squeezing the trigger. Still twitching. Still begging.

Then—an onrush of pain.

A sudden, precise stab through her thigh—white-hot and real.

It was only then, in that one pure moment of pain, that she stopped.

Her grip loosened. Her breath hitched. She blinked down in confusion, her chest heaving, vision rimmed in blur. Her leg throbbed. Her fingers trembled.

Smoke curled from her thigh.

The heat radiating from the burn was sharp and blistering, pulsing with each heartbeat. It hadn't come from an enemy. Not claws. Not a blast.

It was her own gear.

Both of her backup rifles dangled at her sides, scorched and warped beyond use. She must've slung them there mid-frenzy —swapped them out in a blind, panicked drive to keep firing at that mocking, eyeless face.

Then forgotten them.

What was I thinking?

The question rang in her skull—jagged and shattering.

The tunnel vision receded, slowly, like fog peeled away by wind. And with it came clarity.

The herald wasn't there.

It had never been there.

The space where she'd unleashed hell—where she'd seen it standing, absorbing bolt after bolt of righteous fury—was nothing but scorched stone. Pitted ground. Cracked earth. A dozen smoldering craters punched into the courtyard like burns in paper.

Far more than she remembered firing.

A chill wormed down her spine as understanding took shape.

She'd been tricked.

No. *Infected.*

The herald hadn't fought her with brute force. It had slithered into her thoughts. Wrapped itself in her grief. Her fear. Her hope. It had made her see it—made her *need* to see it—and while she poured her rage into that illusion, it had done what it came to do.

Emerald gasped.

The generator.

With her eyes wide and her chest tightening, she stared at the ruin scattered around where her target had been. Blackened metal. Still smoking fragments. Their defensive shield destroyed, by—

Her own fire.

The remnants were familiar now: the same shapes as her pattern of shots. The same warping of stone from the overheating rifle. She hadn't defended the generator.

She had destroyed it!

And in that moment, she saw it all unravel.

Her gaze snapped to the battlefield below—and her heart plummeted.

The shield walls had reengaged—and were failing.

Where once there had been order, now there was only chaos. Gaps yawned in the lines. Screaming defenders clashed with Pale Ones spilling through breaches torn by claw and needle teeth. The air was thick with blood. Bodies crumpled in twined heaps—soldiers and monsters together—limbs entangled, throats opened, eyes wide in frozen shock.

She'd let this happen. She'd done this.

Emerald stared, numb and shaking. Her burned leg pulsed with pain, but it was distant now. Secondary. Her hands trembled at her sides, stained with soot, blood, and her own recklessness.

She had given the enemy the opening.

The defenders had counted on her. Trusted her. *Needed* her.

And she'd failed them.

Whatever the herald truly was, it hadn't needed to kill her to end her. It had simply pointed and watched her burn down everything she was meant to protect.

A death warrant, signed in fire and illusion.

And now the line was breaking.

She wanted to scream. To fight. To fix it.

But she didn't know how.

All she knew was that it was her fault.

Tears welled in her eyes, warping the battlefield. She blinked them back—hard—but they came anyway, hot and relentless.

Because she was going to be responsible for the death of the man she loved.

Her gaze found Jacques—drawn to him as if her soul couldn't help itself. He stood at the terminal like a man bracing a floodgate with his bare hands, fingers dancing across controls in frantic bursts, his mouth shaping orders drowned by the battle's roar. His head jerked, sharp with emphasis, arguing with someone—Florence, probably. Every motion was clipped, the kind of panic he almost never let show.

Florence hovered nearby, her posture collapsed inward, arms wrapped around herself like she could shrink into nothing. Her lips moved, but whatever words came out were soft and defeated. Her eyes were blank.

Saturn, by contrast, looked infuriatingly calm—he sat crosslegged on the grass, as though all this carnage were background noise. That glacial detachment had always rubbed everyone the wrong way—but now? It felt like betrayal. How could he look so untouched, so unaffected, while everything was unraveling?

Movement to the north caught her attention.

Lusa.

The Mau was in motion, a streak of orange and blood and wrath, tearing through the Pale Ones with the precision of a combine harvesting a field. His paws struck like sledgehammers, his roars shaking the air. He wielded corpses like weapons—skulls caving, bones snapping. Every movement radiated fury, his body a furnace of vengeance.

But he was just one fighter.

And the tide was endless.

The northern front was crumbling. Only a few defenders still held their ground. The rest were already down, lost beneath the writhing, white mass. And that was just one side. The others weren't faring much better. East, west, south—every line bleeding, every barricade folding.

Emerald's hands trembled.

She looked down at them—bare, blistered, and useless.

Her rifles lay beside her, warped heaps of slag. Once sleek, once precise. Now melted, twisted beyond function. Frames deformed, internals fused. Nothing left to salvage.

She was weaponless.

She was useless.

And every scream below was another reminder. Another accusation. Another echo of the moment she stopped being their sniper, their overwatch, their shield from above.

Her shoulders sagged. Her vision swam. The tears returned.

She'd failed them.

She'd failed him.

She dropped her head, sobbing uncontrollably—

"Ulfrey!... Oomph!... Ulfrey!... Oomph!"

The chant cut through the noise.

Thundering. Rhythmic. Like a battle drum carving through the chaos.

Emerald didn't want to care.

Didn't feel like she could.

But her head turned anyway—slowly, numbly—drawn westward by that strange, relentless rhythm.

The tears blurred her vision, smearing the jagged cityscape into a watercolor of broken stone, firelight, and shadow. She blinked, trying to clear the fog, though it hardly mattered.

Nothing could change what she'd done.

Nothing could unspill the blood on her hands.

But then—through the haze—she saw them.

A column of men, emerging like a tide from the fractured streets of Zahadah's western thoroughfare. The vanguard's armor gleamed dully beneath layers of blood and ash. Battered shields raised. Blades drawn. Glaives, halberds, spears, axes—all slick with fresh gore. They moved with brutal precision, carving through the rear ranks of the Pale Ones like a woodchipper swallowing overripe fruit. Heads toppled. Limbs flew. The rear flank crumpled in waves.

Above them, banners whipped in the wind—red and yellow pinions marked with a black griffon, coiled in perpetual motion, its serpentine hindquarters writhing as if alive.

Behind them—civilians—the men who had stayed to defend their families, the women who had run to escape.

The city was rallying!

"Ulfrey!... Oomph!... Ulfrey!... Oomph!"

The chant rose—a thunderous cadence of rebellion, absolute and rhythmic, cutting through the death-tinged night.

Their voices were hoarse with fury.

And every step was a hammerblow.

Emerald stared, hand trembling where it clutched the lip of the building. Tears ran unchecked down her cheeks, mixing with soot and sweat. Her heart stuttered—too many emotions at once to name. Disbelief. Awe. Guilt.

Where had they come from?

The city was supposed to be lost. Everyone dead. Everyone gone. This wasn't possible.

But they were real.

A pinprick of hope flared in her chest.

Fragile. Foolish.

Already she could feel it being crushed beneath the truth.

They wouldn't reach Jacques in time.

No matter how fierce, no matter how disciplined, they were too far. The Pale Ones still surged in thick waves, clawing, biting, breaking anyone they touched. And at the heart of it all— surrounded, yet steady—Jacques stood. She could see him from her perch. Fingers moving in bursts over the terminal. Mouth tight.

Fighting with data. With decisions.

Fighting to save lives.

Emerald's sobs returned—jagged things torn from deep within her shredded heart. Her shoulders shook, her body small behind the shattered edge of the rooftop. But beneath the sorrow, something else began to rise.

Rage.

Not at the herald. Not at the monsters.

At herself.

The southern lines shattered like glass beneath a hammer. Screams filled the air—wet, frantic, and final. Snarls and gurgling cries tore through the static haze. Flesh ripped. Bones crunched. Blood misted into the air like sea spray.

Emerald's head snapped toward the breach.

But it wasn't the horror of the collapsing defenses that seized her attention—it was motion at the corner of her vision.

A single, sharp burst of movement.

Her eyes locked on it instinctively.

Jacques.

He had abandoned the console.

The terminal's glow flickered behind him like a dying lantern.

Emerald saw him drop to one knee, his silhouette sharp against the glow of street lamps and torches. His hand reached down for something small. No bigger than a fist.

A rock?

What are you doing?

Her heart was sick with dread.

The Frenchman.

My Frenchman.

The thought struck her like an arrow, clean and devastating. It cut through the suffocating fog of grief, through the rage, through the guilt. It filled her—too much, too fast—with love and terror in equal measure.

She had almost lost him once. She might lose him now.

Jacques sprinted.

Not back to the others. Not toward safety. Toward the western front—toward the nightmare. His outline softened in the smoke, streaked in blood and grit and impossible determination.

Emerald's breath came ragged, pulse fluttering as she tracked him through the cracked scope.

Why?

Why was he running?

The Ulfrey reinforcements were too far. The Pale Ones were between them. It made no sense. Florence and Saturn needed him. The command needed him. The whole defense grid was unraveling and he—

He fell.

His body hit the stones with a sickening *thud*, a spray of blood blooming beneath him as he skidded across the gore-slick street.

Emerald's heart stopped.

Then she saw it.

He was moving. Still moving. Not hurt—at least not badly. He raised the stone and hammered it into the ground. Hard. Over and over. The blows echoed faintly through her scope, rhythmic, furious. Shards of paving stone splintered outward with every strike, dust curling in thin plumes like smoke.

What are you doing?

Run, Jacques. Please—just run.

She wanted to scream it. Shout until her voice bled. But the words never left her mouth. There was no time. No power in them. Just trembling fingers gripping scorched plastic and a heart too full to beat properly.

Below, the lines broke.

A shriek of agony. A roar of collapsing resolve.

The defenders shattered under the press of Pale Ones—white limbs, black claws, fangs wet with gore. The horde surged forward in a wave of pure death, drawn to the lone figure hunched over the stone. Dozens, then hundreds.

Jacques didn't flinch.

He kept pounding.

Kept digging.

This isn't bravery, Emerald thought, numb with awe and horror.

This is madness.

But still—he stayed.

He stayed.

NO!

Emerald's body moved on instinct. She tried to raise her ruined rifle. Her finger found the trigger. Click.

Nothing.

She gritted her teeth, rage and helplessness coiling tight around her heart like barbed wire. She couldn't breathe. Couldn't scream. Could only watch.

Jacques lifted the stone high above his head, both hands locked around it. His silhouette blazed against the firelit wreckage of the city.

One more strike. No time for another.

His arms came down.

The stone slammed into the ground with everything he had left.

The paving stones shifted.

A rectangular panel dropped suddenly out of sight, like a trapdoor opening—and something rose to take its place.

A generator.

Emerald's breath caught. Her heart swelled.

The third checkpoint.

He'd done it.

A malfunction, maybe. Siege damage. It didn't matter. Jacques —*her* Jacques—had fixed it.

With a rock.

Her mind supplied it numbly: *Percussive maintenance.* It almost made her laugh. Another time. Another life.

The generator sparked, its blue glow flaring to life. Then came the hum. The charge. The detonation of arcs bursting outward in blinding waves. Plasma tore through the horde like divine lightning—flaying Pale Ones into twitching cinders. Their shrieks drowned in the storm.

The tide turned.

For one heartbeat.

Jacques's heartbeat.

Then she felt it die.

A bolt—pure white, jagged as a lightning serpent—lashed sideways from the surge. It struck him.

Jacques.

The name ripped through her mind. But her voice failed. Her scream stuck in her throat, swallowed by silence and shock.

His body jerked, spine arching in a spasm of seared nerve endings. Blue fire crawled across his chest, his flesh blackening. His mouth opened, but no sound came—only a frozen grimace, pain made silent. Then his knees buckled.

He fell.

Hard.

Twitching as the manufactured lightning cooked his meat.

Then still.

The world shattered.

He saved them—saved her—and it had cost her everything.

Emerald's body reacted before her thoughts could. She threw her head back. Her vision blurred with tears, streaking hot down her dirt-smeared cheeks.

The scream tore loose.

It wasn't just a cry—it was a detonation. Animalistic, bottomless. A sound wrenched from the core of who she was, torn free by grief too massive for flesh to hold. It cracked her open and left nothing.

And still, it kept coming.

Her body trembled with the force of it, her chest aching as if her lungs had turned to ash. It wasn't just mourning.

It was the death of a future. The death of joy.

And the moment she stopped screaming, she knew:

She would never be the same again.

If she could have willed herself to die in that moment, she would have.

She would've followed him—through fire, through shadow—all the way to the Heaven he believed in, even if she wasn't sure it existed. She would have fallen to her knees, begging his God with the last scraps of her soul to let her stay beside him.

Because how could she live in a world without Jacques?

How could she breathe, knowing he never would again?

But life is cruel.

Her scream crumbled into hoarse, racking sobs. Her body shook as she dropped to her knees, the shattered remains of her rifle clattering beside her like discarded bones. She squeezed her eyes shut, as if darkness might erase what she'd seen—what she'd lost.

When she finally opened them, she looked to the sky.

It was streaked with crimson—slashes of red cutting through the dim, early light of dawn. For one breathless second, she thought the sky was bleeding, weeping with her.

But no.

It was just the sunrise.

A bitter, broken laugh rasped from her throat. Jacques had always loved sunrises. Always found hope in their quiet arrival, in the simple promise of another day. And now, here it was—rising without him.

She didn't care if she lived.

That truth settled over her like ash after a wildfire—cold and final.

But she would endure this.

Not for herself.

For him.

She would drink in every fragile ray of light, not because she wanted to, but because it was the last gift he would ever give her.

A sunrise, born from his death.

A moment of beauty, bought with everything that mattered to her.

Thank you, she mouthed into the morning, her voice long gone.

CHAPTER FORTY-ONE

Hyatta clung to the dragon's bristled spine, its coarse feather-like ridges scraped his palms as he hauled himself toward its massive head. Each pull burned through his arms. His breath came ragged, but he didn't stop. Couldn't. Below, the beast tore through the forest with terrifying speed, its colossal frame cleaving a path of raw devastation. Trees snapped like twigs underfoot, the canopy parting in a jagged scar.

Above them, the black, star-flecked sky had begun to shift. Velvet dark gave way to bruised violet—the first hint of sunrise. Only one star remained, a lone sentinel clinging to the lightless dome. Hyatta's eyes focused to it—not for guidance, but because it was the only thing that wasn't blurring past in the headlong rush of wind and motion.

Strangely, he wasn't afraid of falling. Up here—astride a beast of fury and muscle—he felt... steady. The dragon's head soared above the trees, granting him a god's-eye view of the forest to either side. The canopy rolled like a sea of green mist, soft and endless, swaying with the rhythm of the earth. Another time, another life, it might have stilled him. Might have made him feel small in a way that soothed.

But not now.

His gut twisted. His heart thudded like a war drum inside a clenched fist.

U'gah.

The name beat through his skull, relentlessly. Not just a friend. Not just a companion. Warband. Oath-brother. A life Hyatta was bound to protect, not out of sentiment but out of sacred duty. If U'gah died... that death would be his to bear.

The guilt boiled inside him like molten steel, bitter and hot.

But then something pulled at the edge of his awareness.

The dragon was changing.

Not in form—its body still thundered with rage, its gait a hammering of muscle and weight—but something in its bearing had shifted. Its snarls grew sharper, less blind. Its pace, already brutal, quickened with a strange urgency. Each movement jittered with something more than anger.

It wasn't just rampaging.

It was reacting.

To U'gah?

Hyatta's eyes narrowed. Thoughts swirling.

It wasn't rage that drove the beast anymore.

It was fear.

Or something close to it.

Worry, maybe?

The realization struck like sun breaking through stormclouds.

It was going to him—not after him.

The dragon heard him. It remembered him.

He'd seen this beast before—not in flesh, but carved into the head of U'gah's greatclub. A symbol he'd once dismissed as stylized. Ornamental. But that design hadn't been random.

The spear-toothed Earthshaker. Shir Tetrau.

The guardian spirit bound to U'gah's weapon.

This creature wasn't some mindless terror born of chaos and aether.

It was him.

The realization hit Hyatta like a hammer to the chest. The monster he clung to—this juggernaut of muscle, feathers, and primordial wrath—was U'gah's guardian. The spear-toothed

Earthshaker, called forth into the mortal world. Not summoned by accident nor some force of nature gone rogue.

It had come for him.

For U'gah.

Maybe they weren't so different, he and the beast.

Another truth stabbed hard into Hyatta's mind: they were racing toward a battle—and he no longer had a weapon.

His chain-whip, so often his lifeline, was gone. Ripped away by the violent ascent, flung somewhere into the forest far behind. That left him with only his body. His fists. His feet. Primal tools for a primal fight. It would have to do.

He'd fought empty-handed before. The desert had taught him much. Sometimes all you had was sand and teeth. Sometimes clever positioning beat reach. But this? This was different. The enemy ahead wasn't desperate slavers or heat-maddened beasts.

These were the children of the Mother.

And they did not fall easy—or alone.

Hyatta gritted his teeth and pressed lower into the dragon's bristled back, anchoring himself against the tearing wind. The speed was punishing—wind tore the air from his lungs. His arms burned just from holding on.

I'll make do.

He flexed his fingers against the dragon's hide, willing his body to remember the rhythm of weaponless martial combat. Keep moving. Use the terrain. Find the gaps. Hit hard, evade, repeat. It wasn't elegant. It wasn't ideal.

But this was war.

And war didn't wait for weapons.

The dragon roared—a sound like the cracking of mountains— and surged faster. The sonic tremor rolled through Hyatta's body, an echo of indignation too large for flesh. Whatever bond tied this beast to U'gah, it was pulling taut now. The Earthshaker was answering the call.

It knew what lay ahead.

So did Hyatta.

They were hunting the same prey.

U'gah's cries grew louder—desperate yips that stabbed his ears like darts. Each one twisted Hyatta's heart. He crushed the fear, forced the doubt back into its cage. There would be time to feel later.

Now was for action.

The sky was now red—streaked with fire and blood. Dawn had crested the horizon, a half-sun burning orange above the jagged mountains to the east. He hadn't noticed the turn, the shift in direction, the tilt of the dragon's charge.

But now it was clear.

They were sprinting east.

Straight into the light.

Beyond the endless churn of trees, the forest broke into a small clearing.

Not wide. Just a ragged patch of tall, wild grass bowing beneath the wind—untamed, unruly, forgotten. It might've been beautiful. A breath of untouched earth spared from fire and ruin.

But not now.

Now it was a killing field.

Movement—sharp and frantic—cut through the grass.

A small form was darting low. Weaving. Dodging.

U'gah.

Hyatta's gut twisted. His eyes locked on the bergbar's silhouette—compact, frightened, desperate—surrounded. Dozens of Pale Ones churned through the clearing, their lurching white forms partially obscured in the rising mist. They swarmed like harrying wolves in loose formation, mouths agape, arms swinging wildly, their hunger dragging them forward like emaciated marionettes.

He saw the trap.

Another wave—further north, just beyond the treeline.

These didn't rush. They crept. They watched. They shifted across the meadow with malice, pincering in perfect silence. Not dumb beasts. But vicious and cruel all the same.

They were bracketing the clearing.

Once U'gah reached the center, they'd be on him from both sides.

A perfect snare. No exits.

Calculations raced through his mind—angles, speeds, timing. How far. How long. How close.

Not enough.

Even at this speed, they wouldn't reach U'gah in time.

He couldn't shout. Couldn't warn him. The wind tore every sound away.

His thoughts scrambled for options, but none came fast enough.

And then—

It wasn't words, but more like a pressure. A rhythm. The thudding ache of something sacred clawing in his chest.

Caged and wild, demanding release.

If he didn't let it out, it would tear him apart.

He opened his mouth, hoping to relieve the force swelling within.

And he sang.

> *"Oh, bright and burning light, you rise,*
> *Your flames are sharp, they pierce the skies,*
> *Harsh as the sand beneath my feet,*
> *Yet in your gaze, my heart finds heat."*

The rays of the Eye crested over the jagged eastern range, spilling golden fire across the sea of green. He felt them on his skin—a searing warmth that lingered, clinging like a brand, needling his exposed flesh—burning. The cold knot of fear unwound. Doubt unraveled. The heat didn't warm him, it stripped him bare. The morning sun burned away what weakness remained. Agony.

> *"You scorch the earth, you sear the soul,*
> *But in your fire, I find my goal.*
> *Though you bring pain, I never flee,*
> *For in your blaze, I choose to be."*

His voice rose with the gathering intensity of the light. Each line rang louder, surer—not merely a song, but a declaration. A challenge. A prayer. The fire in his throat wasn't just from effort. It burned through him, licking through his veins, stoking embers he hadn't known still lived.

> *"You rise without a word of grace,*
> *Your heat, it cracks the driest place.*
> *But in your fire, I find my way,*
> *Guided by your ruthless day."*

His skin tingled, even where the sunlight hadn't yet touched. An ache, tight and electric, stirred across his body like his flesh itself had begun to wake. The words had found a door within him and opened it wide, pouring fire inside.

> *"Each dawn you rise to claim the sky,*
> *A queen of fire, I can't deny.*

You test the strong, you break the weak,
But in your name, my soul I seek."

With one swift motion, Hyatta tore the cloak from his shoulders and cast it aside. The god-wrought armor followed, peeling from his skin and discarded like old bark. The wind kissed his bare chest, humid and alive, but the heat remained. Not just around, but within him.

"Though you take and never give,
In your blaze, I learn to live.
Your love is fire, your gift is pain,
But in your warmth, I'll rise again."

Beneath him, the dragon roared—not a sound of wrath, but of recognition. Not as a threat, but an answer. Its pace never faltered. It carried him forward like a burning arrow loosed across the dawn.

"Oh, Desert Flame, you blind my sight,
But still, I turn to face your light.
Your rays are cruel, your touch is fierce,
Yet through the pain, my love won't pierce.
I walk beneath your burning throne,
For in your heat, I feel my home."

Hyatta's voice never broke. His song carried across the wind, over the rushing trees, into the light of dawn. A hymn to the burning sky, to the relentless Eye of the Day—to the only thing that had ever truly guided him. And if he was to die today, if U'gah was to fall before he could reach him, then let it be beneath the fire of the rising sun. Let it be in the blaze of something greater than all of them.

The blissful inferno rose, swelling and consuming, until it wrapped him in a brilliant, white-hot embrace. It wasn't fire as mortals understood it. It was purer. A force that didn't just burn the flesh but purified the soul itself. His body trembled beneath its touch, muscles seizing in resistance, eyes shut tight against its unbearable radiance.

And then—it stopped.

Not just the pain.

Everything.

The wind no longer howled past his ears. The dragon's charge no longer strained his grip. Even gravity—the steady, invisible pull of the world—had vanished, like the universe itself had gone still.

For a moment, there was nothing. No motion. No sound. Just silence, profound and complete. A stillness so total it seemed to erase thought itself.

He didn't feel dead. There was no cold breath of the afterlife. No gates. No judgment. Just… stillness.

Then, a presence.

It was not seen, but felt. Not heard, but known.

It was watching him.

Hyatta's lungs seized. His fists clenched at his sides.

The white void rippled, disturbed like the surface of a still pond. A vibrant green light spilled into the space, brilliant and searing. It pulsed, converging and collapsing inward, until it became something more.

Eyes.

Two spheres, luminous and unblinking, hung in the air. No larger than a pair of watchful eyes.

Hyatta blinked.

And when his vision returned—

She was there.

A woman—

No.

Something beyond a woman.

Her green eyes burned, not with fire, but with knowing—an intensity so vast, so deep, it pierced through him. Into him. As if she already knew every thought, every doubt, every secret he'd ever buried. Her hair cascaded like flame, not fire as mortals knew it, but a living tapestry of gold, orange, and crimson, shifting with the slow, molten grace.

He had known beauty before—in the painted skies of his desert home, in the still, sacred hush that followed a night of travel.

But she— she was not beautiful.

She was beauty.

Every sunrise. Every sunset. Every whisper of light that had ever graced the world.

His body trembled from fear and recognition.

Lifting a hand, her fingers brushed his cheek, gentle and reverent. Not fire, not flame, just light. Pure. Radiant. Absolute. The warmth of her touch spread through him like summer rays through frost—not burning, but cleansing. It reached deeper than flesh. Deeper than thought. It touched the root of him.

And what it found, it freed.

The filth—the weight—he had carried, sloughed away in a breath of brilliance. The Mother's taint, her unseen fingers curled deep beneath his skin, dissolved. No agony. Only release. He hadn't known how heavy it had been until it was gone. How deeply it had sank.

She smiled, soft and knowing.

"I have always been with you."

The words didn't echo. They settled into him. Into the spaces between each beat of his heart.

He had known her.

Not in flesh. Not in name.

But in the heat that greeted him each dawn. In the way the desert sun had tested him, shaped him, guided him. In every burning moment that taught him to endure.

He had always been hers.

And now, he stood before her.

She cupped his face and tilted it upward. Her eyes, gold now instead of green, and they burned with something sacred.

"Rise, my love."

Her voice was silk woven from delicate flame. Command and comfort had been braided together, gently, yet unyielding.

Hyatta rose.

The fire that had taken root in his veins erupted. He pressed his palm to the thick, scaled armor of the dragon's back and her power poured through him.

A flood of molten gold surged from his fingertips, racing into the beast below like absolute truth. The bristled feathers, once the dull tones of dust and dried blood, shimmered and brightened beneath the sun's first light, transforming into radiant gold, crimson, and bronze.

And the dragon gathered more speed.

Hyatta's eyes—now clear, unclouded, and freed from the Mother's stain—saw everything in stark, agonizing detail.

The bergbar shaman still fought, though the Pale Ones were relentless. They tore at him in waves, claws raking across his legs, hamstringing him, dragging him into the dirt. He writhed, struck, and roared.

His friend—his little brother—was still trying. Still fighting.

Then they pounced.

A white mass engulfed him—writhing limbs, snapping jaws, hunger made flesh. Teeth tore into fur, into muscle. Blood sprayed, dark and high, silhouetted against the rose gold flare of dawn.

Hyatta saw it all.

The flailing. The last, jerking twitches. And—U'gah's face.

Tear-streaked and terrified.

He saw the exact moment the light left his brother's eyes.

Something in Hyatta shattered.

Rage flooded through him. Not hot—but searing. Not loud—but infinite. It rooted into his bones, his breath, his blood. He barely noticed the nacreous fire screaming from his skin, barely felt the dragon beneath him begin to quake. Their grief and fury—mirrored, shared.

Their pain became one.

And the world responded.

A shockwave tore outward. The trees at the meadow's edge snapped and flung wide, uprooted like dry stalks. The air itself vibrated—alive with the force of mournful wrath.

Then came the roar.

It split the sky. A cry of loss so absolute, so raw, it tore through the heavens and made the earth flinch.

Hyatta's own voice joined it, though he barely knew it. He screamed, not a battle cry. Not a challenge.

A wail of mourning.

A promise of vengeance.

Below, the Pale Ones paused. They turned and their heads lifted toward the sound with their bodies still and mouths agape. They began to shudder with a sudden, unfamiliar instinct—fear.

They tried to run.

It was too late for the damned.

Hyatta felt it in the wind—the shift. The weight of their terror. They fled not from the sun, not from fire—but from him.

He tasted their fear, and it was sweet.

CHAPTER FORTY-TWO

e couldn't be dead.

The thought looped through Florence's mind like a curse, a repetitive chant against the weight of a reality she refused to accept. Jacques couldn't be dead. It wasn't possible. It wasn't *allowed*.

He had been their strategist, their shield, their guiding light. He was the man who kept them alive when the world conspired to kill them. And now? Now he was just... gone?

Just like that?

She stood amid the gore-soaked ruins of the battlefield, a specter among the living. She barely registered the arrival of Lord Ulfrey's warriors as they flooded into the garden, forming a protective ring around the remnants of the warband. She didn't see the civilians moving among the injured, didn't hear the murmurs of triage or the soft cadence of mournful rites whispered over broken bodies.

Wise women. Hedge-doctors. Apothecaries.

Efficient. Methodical. Saving what could still be saved.

But *he* could not be saved.

Jacques was dead.

And what comfort could exist in that?

The last of the Pale Ones slunk into the shadows, chased by the harsh rays of dawn. Those too slow, too mangled to flee, were butchered where they cowered. Their shrieks rang out like brittle glass breaking under boot.

Good.

It was less than they deserved.

Florence's hands clenched, nails biting deep into her palms. If she'd believed for one second that the monsters could feel *anything*—pain, fear, regret—she would have had a dozen kept alive. Caged. Strapped down.

Not for questions—for answers made of agony.

They had taken something from her. From *them*.

Something irreplaceable.

She wanted to return the favor tenfold.

She wanted to be heartbroken for Emerald.

The girl had been so obvious. Awkward, flustered, starry-eyed —carrying a torch like it was made of fine crystal. Florence had seen it building for weeks, months maybe. And when Emerald had finally found the nerve to tell him—when she'd let herself *hope*—

He had died.

She wanted to be angry at the Frenchman. Wanted to scream at him for being a damn fool—charging into danger like men always did, as if their bones were steel and not sad, breakable things. But the fury wouldn't come.

She was too tired.

Too hollow.

Through the groans and murmurs of the wounded, she heard a sound.

A roar?

A thunderclap?

Florence couldn't tell. But whatever it was, it carried more than noise. It carried *grief*—marrow-deep grief, torn straight from the bones of the world. It wasn't a sound.

It was a wound—and it was *furious*.

There was violence laced throughout it—trembling, inevitable.

Another cry followed, closer this time. Stranger. It pierced the stunned quiet. Florence's head snapped toward it, instincts flaring. Her eyes swept the ruins—past the wounded, past the fallen, past the shattered stone and burning wreckage—

And stopped.

U'gah's greatclub.

It lay where he'd left it. Still. Untouched.

But for just a heartbeat, Florence thought she saw it *move*.

Which was impossible.

Stone didn't move on its own. Not unless there was an earthquake.

And this wasn't that.

Still, something inside her twisted. Her skin prickled. A chill that wasn't cold slid down her spine.Some presence—some force—settled over the gardens. Danger fell like a fog.

The ground bucked.

Before she could react, the greatclub exploded upward, flung into the air with such force it left a crater in the grass. The shockwave rippled outward—flattening shrubs, toppling the injured, scattering debris like brittle leaves in a gale.

Florence's eyes tracked the motion just in time to catch another blur of movement.

The scroll case.

U'gah's scroll case, that he had carried every day since they'd left Wrasas Station, had been thrown clear, tumbling end over end until it vanished into a stand of flower-choked bushes near the garden's edge.

For the briefest moment, everything was still.

Weightless. Silent.

The greatclub flew into the sky—spinning wild as it climbed, higher and higher—until it reached the apex of its flight, suspended for a breathless moment at the peak of existence.

And then—it moved.

Not fell. Not drifted. *Moved.*

It shot south like a bolt from a plasma rifle, yanked by some unseen will and hurled toward its destination with terrifying precision. The air warped in its wake, a shimmer of broken light trailing through the clouds that it cleaved apart.

Then came the sound.

A concussive *boom* ripped across the sky, shattering the morning stillness with a sonic crack so vast it seemed to split the world. The gardens trembled. Dust plumed. The wounded cried out. Florence staggered, eyes wide, breath locked in her chest.

Something had been set in motion.

Something vast. Something unknowable.

And whatever lay waiting in the south, whatever had *called* that thing...

It was about to meet all the wrath it had just summoned.

***

The deep, seething fury that coiled through Hyatta's veins felt molten and unrelenting. It filled every hollow within him, fusing with the righteous wrath already burning there, threatening to consume him entirely.

He did not resist it.

Because he was not alone in his rage.

A voice, ancient and thunderous, roared through his mind. Not his own, but now a part of him.

"Let us destroy these foul things together, Champion of Light."

The words shook the very foundation of his being.

"Call my tether and it will come. We shall devour the wicked and avenge our fallen."

Hyatta agreed.

He didn't speak. His answer was silent, furious, and absolute, reverberating through every nerve and sinew. He let the primal need consume him, sear through hesitation, fuse with bone and soul until there was no line between his will and the beast's.

He no longer rode the spear-toothed Earthshaker.

He *was* it.

And it was his.

Hyatta stood atop the creature's massive skull, steady as stone, unshaken by the breakneck speed or the seismic power surging beneath him. Movements that should have flung him to his death barely rippled through his stance. He was no longer a rider.

He was the hand wielding this weapon.

The ancient paragon-spirit bellowed—a growling chortle that vibrated through its frame as it tore through the battlefield. Every footfall crushed the Pale Ones to paste. They fled or tried to flee.

But they were vermin. Pests.

Prey—

And they had already been claimed.

A pressure built northward.

Hyatta didn't see it. He *felt* it. A presence pulsing like a second heart, an instinctual gravity that pulled at his soul. He didn't question it.

His left hand lifted.

And the sky answered.

Like a comet, the greatclub streaked across the heavens. U'gah's sacred weapon launched from a grief-struck world, called by god-magic older than time. It should have struck like a meteor, shattering him.

Instead, it slid into his palm with perfect finality.

The moment his fingers closed around the rough, scarred stone, Hyatta felt it—the weight of a life lost, of a bond unbroken.

U'gah was gone.

But his weapon still had work to do.

Hyatta channeled the light of his goddess, the incandescent radiance of the burning dawn, into the god-wrought stone.

Heat surged through him.

Power coursed down his arm, through his fingers, and into the weapon that had once belonged to the little bergbar he called brother.

And it answered.

It began to shine, bright and fierce, as if the heart of the sun had been placed in his grasp. The unyielding stone shifted, reshaping itself in response to his will. What had once been a greatclub, a crude battering instrument of brute force, lengthened and splintered into interlocked segments bound by some unseen force.

It hissed, testing the air, thirsting.

When the motion ceased, what lay coiled in his grip was no longer a club.

It was a whip.

A lash of jagged, thorned stone—still rough, still coarse, but sharp enough to cleave steel, hard enough to crack the earth.

The spear-toothed Earthshaker roared, and Hyatta answered.

He sprinted down the creature's snout, his body moving without hesitation, without fear. Fury surged behind his eyes, behind his clenched jaw, behind every burning step. And when the moment came—

He leapt.

The wind screamed past him as he plunged toward the bloody field below, his pulse beat in rhythm with the divine fire flooding his veins. He called to his goddess, not with words, but with memory: the visions she had given him, the lives he had never lived, the battles he had never fought—yet remembered as his own.

The power answered.

Fire erupted around him, cloaking his body in radiant flame. Not red. Not orange. White-hot, shifting through every color—celestial, pure. It did not burn. It did not consume.

He *became* the fire.

A living comet, falling to earth.

The Pale Ones had no time to react.

He hit like judgment.

The shockwave cracked outward, flinging creatures like dolls. The ground where he landed blackened then cracked, steaming where divine heat met blood-soaked soil. And then—

The whip struck.

A blur of razor stone and divine wrath.

It tore through them—flesh parting like wet paper, bones shattering like chalk. Trees caught in its arc exploded, trunks flayed apart by the sheer violence of the strike.

Hyatta moved without thought, without hesitation. He was no longer flesh alone. He was her vessel. Her wrath.

And they—these Pale Ones—were vermin in the path of purging flame.

For U'gah!

For every life they had taken!

For every soul they had defiled!

There would be no mercy.

***

Saturn sat cross-legged in the cool grass, methodically wiping the dust from NAVI's smooth shell. His movements were slow, precise, almost reverent. The battle had stilled.

His mind, however, had not.

It raced in slow motion, processing events in disjointed fragments, like viewing the carnage through a screen. A holo-reel. Something distant. Something curated to shock, not to wound. The screams, the ruin, the dead—none of it had struck him like it struck the others. Not really. It had felt like data. Input to be absorbed, categorized, filed.

Something to study.

Until he saw Jacques.

The charred remains of the man who had been the linchpin—their leader, their engineer, his friend.

And it hit him.

Hard.

Jacques had been right. About this, at least.

Individual lives did matter.

The truth settled into him like a corrected equation—an imbalance finally resolved. A missing variable falling into place. It didn't land with weight, but with absence. A space hollowed out inside him.

He—felt it.

Not just the intellectual confirmation of loss. Not the shifting of survival probabilities in their fragile collective. But real loss. A presence gone. A voice silenced. A gap that logic could not bridge.

Jacques had been a constant. Stubborn. Devout. Brilliant. Frustrating. Hopeful, even when he had no logical reason to be.

Now, he was a memory. A variable collapsed to zero.

But this time, it wasn't just data.

This time, it *hurt*.

And Saturn had no framework for that.

No protocol. No analysis. No next step.

So he kept cleaning NAVI's shell, long past necessity. Letting the motion carry him. Letting his mind churn. Detached analysis warred with something unfamiliar. Something far more dangerous.

Emotion.

Real emotion.

He still didn't know what to do with it.

But he wasn't the only one drowning in grief.

He saw how the others were handling Jacques's death—or rather, how poorly they were handling it.

Florence was a mess of nerves and rage, lashing out at anyone who came too close. Her fury had no direction, no focus, and it didn't need one. It was a wildfire without containment, scorching indiscriminately. She'd snarled at Saturn earlier for merely glancing her way. A wounded survivor, who was barely upright, had tried to ask her something. She'd turned on him with such venom that even Saturn, who'd never particularly feared Florence, had felt the quiver of unease.

She was going to break soon.

Lusa was—louder than usual.

The Mau had let out one long, agonized yowl when Jacques had fallen, then stalked to the far edge of the gardens after the fighting had stopped. There he curled himself into a dense, bristling knot of grief.

He wasn't crying for attention—Lusa never did that.

The yowls came in intervals, involuntary, like his body couldn't contain the grief clawing through it. His bobtail twitched erratically. His ears lay pinned to his skull. Anyone who tried to approach was met with a low, warning growl. Even now, Saturn could hear the occasional sound—mournful and broken—drifting from the shadows where Lusa lay.

And then there was Emerald.

She'd been hit the hardest.

Saturn had known she was besotted with Jacques. Everyone had, except Jacques himself. The gnome girl—bright, awkward, stubborn—had finally built up the nerve to say it. To tell him. To hope.

Now she was empty.

A flower in bloom, wilted by grief. Curling inward. Silent.

She hadn't spoken since Jacques fell.

She sat alone, arms wrapped around her knees, eyes hollow. The tears had long since dried on her cheeks, but she didn't wipe them away. She didn't move. She was trapped in that moment, reliving it again and again. Saturn didn't know how to reach her.

And the part that haunted him?

He understood.

He understood all of it now—the weight, the pain, the way it hollowed you out.

Because Saturn wasn't just observing loss anymore.

He was feeling it with them.

The day dragged on. The sun climbed higher, the heat baked the ruined city as it reached its apex.

He had long since tired of wiping dust from NAVI's plastic carapace. The repetitive motion no longer quieted his mind. Instead, he'd shifted to replacing the carbon brushes, his fingers moving with practiced precision. The task was small, almost meaningless in the grand scheme, but it gave his hands purpose. Something to do while his thoughts wandered the wreckage of his mind.

Then the ground trembled.

A deep, rhythmic shudder. One. Then another.

Saturn stopped, his screwdriver hovering mid-air. He tilted his head, listening. Something massive was moving.

The smell hit next.

Musky. Pungent. Primal.

Strong enough to send Sandy—the feathered, usually unshakable sauropod—into a panic. She honked, a strangled, wheezing sound, then folded at the knees and collapsed in a twitching heap. Saturn wasn't sure if she'd passed out from fear or if she was playing dead like some giant, scaly possum.

He leaned toward the former.

A shadow rose over the outer wall where one of the low sections, where the ancient stone had slumped with time.

The head appeared.

A gargantuan, triangular skull, jaws lined with jagged, impossibly large teeth, lifted above the stone like a god surveying its shrine. Its eyes, slitted and gold, gleamed with a sentient malice Saturn didn't like one bit. Crimson and gold feathers traced its ridged snout, giving it a kind of brutal majesty.

Saturn's stomach sank.

A Tyrannosaurus.

An absurdly oversized one.

And given how disproportionate a normal T. rex already was, this was saying something. The beast's shoulders cleared the wall as it sniffed the air, its massive frame casting a slow-moving shadow across the garden.

Saturn sighed.

He was done for the day.

He set the screwdriver beside him with care, ran a hand through his cyan hair, and exhaled slowly.

If death had chosen to come in the form of a Mesozoic apex predator, so be it.

At least it'd be spectacular.

He pulled down his goggles, tapped the magnification control, and let the HUD cycle—adjusting for sunlight, heat shimmer, and disbelief.

And there, balanced on the creature's skull, was a man—bare-chested, cradling something against his torso…

Saturn zoomed in.

Hyatta.

The desert warrior moved with eerie grace, like a figure crafted from liquid bronze and solar flares. Blood—not his—streaked his olive skin. The dinosaur shifted, craning its massive neck forward, lowering its head over the wall. With the grace of a man who had lived a hundred lifetimes and was still in his prime, Hyatta climbed down, stepping onto the ruined stone within the inner court.

The bundle in his arms never left him.

It leaked.

Dark red seeped through the cloth, soaking into his skin, dripping onto the dust-choked ground in slow drops. A trail of crimson followed where he walked.

Sable fur peeked from the folds.

Saturn's gut twisted. And for the second time in less than a day, he felt.

Loss.

Another piece of their fragile, dying world torn away.

His jaw clenched. A single tear cut down his cheek, tracing the same hollow channels the others had carved. He didn't wipe it away. He barely noticed it.

Mechanically, he rose.

One foot. Then the next. Step. Step. Step.

His body moved before his mind could offer commentary. Before he could summon something clever, something sharp-edged to dull the moment.

He pushed his goggles up, blinking against the blaze of the noon light.

And then he saw them. All of them.

Florence. Lusa. Emerald.

Tattered. Broken.

Each one moving forward—slow and unsteady—as if drawn by gravity toward the man who had returned with nothing but death in his arms.

Emerald reached him first.

Her breath seized. Her hand lifted, trembling—fingers twitching with indecision, torn between reaching for the blood-soaked bundle or holding herself together. Her eyes, red-rimmed and brimming, locked on the ruin in his arms.

She already knew.

They all did.

But knowing never softened the blow.

"Where have you been?"

Florence's voice cracked through the silence, angry and barbed —not with hatred, but grief, frustration, and helplessness.

Each word spat like venom.

Saturn barely turned. He had expected Florence to lash out. That was how she kept herself upright.

But Emerald—

Emerald, who always had words. Who filled silence with questions and theories and stray bursts of hope—

Only whispered:

"Don't."

Soft and barely audible, but steel wrapped in silk.

And, for once, Florence said no more.

Saturn exhaled slowly.

Emerald had nothing else to give. He could see it in her shoulders, in the tremble of her jaw, in the way her lips parted as if to say more—but didn't. She had nothing left.

Hyatta, unmoved by the outburst, didn't flinch.

His eyes—bloodstreaked and wild—scanned past them, beyond them, searching.

Searching for the one who should have been there.

The man who should have been waiting.

Arms crossed. Lips pressed in that dry, knowing way.

Waiting to hear what reckless stunt Hyatta had just pulled.

But he wasn't there.

"Where is Jacques?"

Hyatta's voice cracked like splintered bark—hoarse, hollow, torn raw.

Silence answered, a moment too long.

All eyes turned to Emerald—and the tears began to fall.

www.ingramcontent.com/pod-product-compliance
Lightning Source LLC
Chambersburg PA
CBHW021928110726
47901CB00003B/758